TWICE SEVEN

Fourteen Selected Stories by

ALDOUS HUXLEY

THE REPRINT SOCIETY

LONDON

THIS EDITION PUBLISHED BY THE REPRINT SOCIETY LTD.
BY ARRANGEMENT WITH CHATTO AND WINDUS
1944

PRINTED IN GREAT BRITAIN BY RICHARD CLAY AND COMPANY, LTD.
BUNGAY, SUFFOLK.

TWICE SEVEN

CONTENTS

THE GIOCONDA SMILE

I

"MISS SPENCE will be down directly, sir."

"Thank you," said Mr. Hutton, without turning round. Janet Spence's parlourmaid was so ugly—ugly on purpose, it always seemed to him, malignantly, criminally ugly—that he could not bear to look at her more than was necessary. The door closed. Left to himself, Mr. Hutton got up and began to wander round the room, looking with meditative eyes at the familiar objects it contained.

Photographs of Greek statuary, photographs of the Roman Forum, coloured prints of Italian masterpieces, all very safe and well known. Poor, dear Janet, what a prig—what an intellectual snob! Her real taste was illustrated in that water-colour by the pavement artist, the one she had paid half a crown for (and thirty-five shillings for the frame). How often he had heard her tell the story, how often expatiate on the beauties of that skilful imitation of an oleograph! "A real Artist in the streets," and you could hear the capital A in Artist as she spoke the words. She made you feel that part of his glory had entered into Janet Spence when she tendered him that half-crown for the copy of the oleograph. She was implying a compliment to her own taste and penetration. A genuine Old Master for half a crown. Poor, dear Janet!

Mr. Hutton came to a pause in front of a small oblong mirror. Stooping a little to get a full view of his face, he passed a white, well-manicured finger over his moustache. It was as curly, as freshly auburn as it had been twenty years ago. His hair still retained its colour, and there was no sign of baldness yet—only a certain elevation of the brow. "Shakespearean," thought Mr. Hutton, with a smile, as he surveyed the smooth and polished expanse of his forehead.

Others abide our question, thou art free. . . . Footsteps in

the sea . . . Majesty. . . . Shakespeare, thou shouldst be living
at this hour. No, that was Milton, wasn't it? Milton, the Lady of
Christ's. There was no lady about him. He was what the women
would call a manly man. That was why they liked him—for the
curly auburn moustache and the discreet redolence of tobacco.
Mr. Hutton smiled again; he enjoyed making fun of himself.
Lady of Christ's? No, no. He was the Christ of Ladies. Very
pretty, very pretty. The Christ of Ladies. Mr. Hutton wished
there were somebody he could tell the joke to. Poor, dear Janet
wouldn't appreciate it, alas!

He straightened himself up, patted his hair, and resumed his
peregrination. Damn the Roman Forum; he hated those dreary
photographs.

Suddenly he became aware that Janet Spence was in the room,
standing near the door. Mr. Hutton started, as though he had
been taken in some felonious act. To make these silent and spec-
tral appearances was one of Janet Spence's peculiar talents. Perhaps she had been there all the time, had seen him looking at
himself in the mirror. Impossible! But, still, it was disquieting.

"Oh, you gave me such a surprise," said Mr. Hutton, recover-
ing his smile and advancing with outstretched hand to meet her.

Miss Spence was smiling too: her Gioconda smile, he had once
called it in a moment of half-ironical flattery. Miss Spence had
taken the compliment seriously, and always tried to live up to the
Leonardo standard. She smiled on in silence while Mr. Hutton
shook hands; that was part of the Gioconda business.

"I hope you're well," said Mr. Hutton. "You look it."

What a queer face she had! That small mouth pursed forward
by the Gioconda expression into a little snout with a round hole
in the middle as though for whistling—it was like a penholder
seen from the front. Above the mouth a well-shaped nose, finely
aquiline. Eyes large, lustrous, and dark, with the largeness,
lustre, and darkness that seems to invite sties and an occasional
bloodshot suffusion. They were fine eyes, but unchangingly
grave. The penholder might do its Gioconda trick, but the eyes
never altered in their earnestness. Above them, a pair of boldly

arched, heavily pencilled black eyebrows lent a surprising air of power, as of a Roman matron, to the upper portion of the face. Her hair was dark and equally Roman; Agrippina from the brows upward.

"I thought I'd just look in on my way home," Mr. Hutton went on. "Ah, it's good to be back here"—he indicated with a wave of his hand the flowers in the vases, the sunshine and greenery beyond the windows—"it's good to be back in the country after a stuffy day of business in town."

Miss Spence, who had sat down, pointed to a chair at her side.

"No, really, I can't sit down," Mr. Hutton protested. "I must get back to see how poor Emily is. She was rather seedy this morning." He sat down, nevertheless. "It's these wretched liver chills. She's always getting them. Women——" He broke off and coughed, so as to hide the fact that he had uttered. He was about to say that women with weak digestions ought not to marry; but the remark was too cruel, and he didn't really believe it. Janet Spence, moreover, was a believer in eternal flames and spiritual attachments. "She hopes to be well enough," he added, "to see you at luncheon to-morrow. Can you come? Do!" He smiled persuasively. "It's my invitation too, you know."

She dropped her eyes, and Mr. Hutton almost thought that he detected a certain reddening of the cheek. It was a tribute; he stroked his moustache.

"I should like to come if you think Emily's really well enough to have a visitor."

"Of course. You'll do her good. You'll do us both good. In married life three is often better company than two."

"Oh, you're cynical."

Mr. Hutton always had a desire to say "Bow-wow-wow" whenever that last word was spoken. It irritated him more than any other word in the language. But instead of barking he made haste to protest.

"No, no. I'm only speaking a melancholy truth. Reality doesn't always come up to the ideal, you know. But that doesn't make me believe any the less in the ideal. Indeed, I believe in it passionately—the ideal of a matrimony between two people in perfect accord. I think it's realisable. I'm sure it is."

He paused significantly and looked at her with an arch expression. A virgin of thrity-six, but still unwithered; she had her charms. And there was something really rather enigmatic about her. Miss Spence made no reply, but continued to smile. There were times when Mr. Hutton got rather bored with the Gioconda. He stood up.

"I must really be going now. Farewell, mysterious Gioconda." The smile grew intenser, focused itself, as it were, in a narrower snout. Mr. Hutton made a Cinquecento gesture, and kissed her extended hand. It was the first time he had done such a thing; the action seemed not to be resented. "I look forward to to-morrow."

"Do you?"

For answer Mr. Hutton once more kissed her hand, then turned to go. Miss Spence accompanied him to the porch.

"Where's your car?" she asked.

"I left it at the gate of the drive."

"I'll come and see you off."

"No, no." Mr. Hutton was playful, but determined. "You must do no such thing. I simply forbid you."

"But I should like to come," Miss Spence protested, throwing a rapid Gioconda at him.

Mr. Hutton held up his hand. "No," he repeated, and then, with a gesture that was almost the blowing of a kiss, he started to run down the drive, lightly, on his toes, with long, bounding strides like a boy's. He was proud of that run; it was quite marvellously youthful. Still, he was glad the drive was no longer. At the last bend, before passing out of sight of the house, he halted and turned round. Miss Spence was still standing on the steps, smiling her smile. He waved his hand, and this time quite definitely and overtly wafted a kiss in her direction. Then, breaking once more into his magnificent canter, he rounded the last dark promontory of trees. Once out of sight of the house he let his high paces decline to a trot, and finally to a walk. He took out his handkerchief and began wiping his neck inside his collar. What fools, what fools! Had there ever been such an ass as poor, dear Janet Spence? Never, unless it was himself. Decidedly he was the more malignant fool, since he, at least, was aware of his folly and still persisted in it. Why did he persist? Ah, the problem that was himself, the problem that was other people . . .

He had reached the gate. A large, prosperous-looking motor was standing at the side of the road.

"Home, M'Nab." The chauffeur touched his cap. "And stop at the crossroads on the way, as usual," Mr. Hutton added, as he opened the door of the car. "Well?" he said, speaking into the obscurity that lurked within.

"Oh, Teddy Bear, what an age you've been!" It was a fresh and childish voice that spoke the words. There was the faintest hint of Cockney impurity about the vowel sounds.

Mr. Hutton bent his large form and darted into the car with the agility of an animal regaining its burrow.

"Have I?" he said, as he shut the door. The machine began to move. "You must have missed me a lot if you found the time so long." He sat back in the low seat; a cherishing warmth enveloped him.

"Teddy Bear . . ." and with a sigh of contentment a charming little head declined on to Mr. Hutton's shoulder. Ravished, he looked down sideways at the round, babyish face.

"Do you know, Doris, you look like the pictures of Louise de Kerouaille." He passed his fingers through a mass of curly hair.

"Who's Louise de Kera-whatever-it-is?" Doris spoke from remote distances.

"She was, alas! *Fuit*. We shall all be 'was' one of these days. Meanwhile . . ."

Mr. Hutton covered the babyish face with kisses. The car rushed smoothly along. M'Nab's back, through the front window, was stonily impassive, the back of a statue.

"Your hands," Doris whispered. "Oh, you mustn't touch me. They give me electric shocks."

Mr. Hutton adored her for the virgin imbecility of the words.

How late in one's existence one makes the discovery of one's body!

"The electricity isn't in me, it's in you." He kissed her again, whispering her name several times: Doris, Doris, Doris. The scientific appellation of the sea-mouse, he was thinking as he kissed the throat she offered him, white and extended like the throat of a victim awaiting the sacrificial knife. The sea-mouse was a sausage with iridescent fur: very peculiar. Or was Doris the sea-cucumber, which turns itself inside out in moments of alarm? He would really have to go to Naples again, just to see the aquarium. These sea creatures were fabulous, unbelievably fantastic.

"Oh, Teddy Bear!" (More zoology; but he was only a land animal. His poor little jokes!) "Teddy Bear, I'm so happy."

"So am I," said Mr. Hutton. Was it true?

"But I wish I knew if it were right. Tell me, Teddy Bear, is it right or wrong?"

"Ah, my dear, that's just what I've been wondering for the last thirty years."

"Be serious, Teddy Bear. I want to know if this is right; if it's right that I should be here with you and that we should love one another, and that it should give me electric shocks when you touch me."

"Right? Well, it's certainly good that you should have electric shocks rather than sexual repressions. Read Freud; repressions are the devil."

"Oh, you don't help me. Why aren't you ever serious? If only you knew how miserable I am sometimes, thinking it's not right. Perhaps, you know, there is a hell, and all that. I don't know what to do. Sometimes I think I ought to stop loving you."

"But could you?" asked Mr. Hutton, confident in the powers of his seduction and his moustache.

"No, Teddy Bear, you know I couldn't. But I could run away, I could hide from you, I could lock myself up and force myself not to come to you."

"Silly little thing!" He tightened his embrace.

"Oh, dear. I hope it isn't wrong. And there are times when I don't care if it is."

Mr. Hutton was touched. He had a certain protective affection for this little creature. He laid his cheek against her hair and so, interlaced, they sat in silence, while the car, swaying and pitching a little as it hastened along, seemed to draw in the white road and the dusty hedges towards it devouringly.

"Good-bye, good-bye."

The car moved on, gathered speed, vanished round a curve, and Doris was left standing by the sign-post at the cross-roads, still dizzy and weak with the languor born of those kisses and the electrical touch of those gentle hands. She had to take a deep breath, to draw herself up deliberately, before she was strong enough to start her homeward walk. She had half a mile in which to invent the necessary lies.

Alone, Mr. Hutton suddenly found himself the prey of an appalling boredom.

II

Mrs. Hutton was lying on the sofa in her boudoir, playing Patience. In spite of the warmth of the July evening a wood fire was burning on the hearth. A black Pomeranian, extenuated by the heat and the fatigues of digestion, slept before the blaze.

"Phew! Isn't it rather hot in here?" Mr. Hutton asked as he entered the room.

"You know I have to keep warm, dear." The voice seemed breaking on the verge of tears. "I get so shivery."

"I hope you're better this evening."

"Not much, I'm afraid."

The conversation stagnated. Mr. Hutton stood leaning his back against the mantelpiece. He looked down at the Pomeranian lying at his feet, and with the toe of his right boot he rolled the little dog over and rubbed its white-flecked chest and belly. The creature lay in an inert ecstasy. Mrs. Hutton continued to play Patience. Arrived at an *impasse*, she altered the position of one card, took back another, and went on playing. Her Patiences always came out.

"Dr. Libbard thinks I ought to go to Llandrindod Wells this summer."

"Well, go, my dear—go, most certainly."

Mr. Hutton was thinking of the events of the afternoon : how they had driven, Doris and he, up to the hanging wood, had left the car to wait for them under the shade of the trees, and walked together out into the windless sunshine of the chalk down.

"I'm to drink the waters for my liver, and he thinks I ought to have massage and electric treatment, too."

Hat in hand, Doris had stalked four blue butterflies that were dancing together round a scabious flower with a motion that was like the flickering of blue fire. The blue fire burst and scattered into whirling sparks; she had given chase, laughing and shouting like a child.

"I'm sure it will do you good, my dear."

"I was wondering if you'd come with me, dear."

"But you know I'm going to Scotland at the end of the month."

Mrs. Hutton looked up at him entreatingly. "It's the journey," she said. "The thought of it is such a nightmare. I don't know if I can manage it. And you know I can't sleep in hotels. And then there's the luggage and all the worries. I can't go alone."

"But you won't be alone. You'll have your maid with you." He spoke impatiently. The sick woman was usurping the place of the healthy one. He was being dragged back from the memory of the sunlit down and the quick, laughing girl, back to this unhealthy, overheated room and its complaining occupant.

"I don't think I shall be able to go."

"But you must, my dear, if the doctor tells you to. And, besides, a change will do you good."

"I don't think so."

"But Libbard thinks so, and he knows what he's talking about."

"No, I can't face it. I'm too weak. I can't go alone." Mrs. Hutton pulled a handkerchief out of her black silk bag, and put it to her eyes.

"Nonsense, my dear, you must make the effort."

"I had rather be left in peace to die here." She was crying in earnest now.

"O Lord! Now do be reasonable. Listen now, please." Mrs. Hutton only sobbed more violently. "Oh, what is one to do?" He shrugged his shoulders and walked out of the room.

Mr. Hutton was aware that he had not behaved with proper patience; but he could not help it. Very early in his manhood he had discovered that not only did he not feel sympathy for the poor, the weak, the diseased, and deformed; he actually hated them. Once, as an undergraduate, he spent three days at a mission in the East End. He had returned, filled with a profound and ineradicable disgust. Instead of pitying, he loathed the unfortunate. It was not, he knew, a very comely emotion, and he had been ashamed of it at first. In the end he had decided that it was temperamental, inevitable, and had felt no further qualms. Emily had been healthy and beautiful when he married her. He had loved her then. But now—was it his fault that she was like this?

Mr. Hutton dined alone. Food and drink left him more benevolent than he had been before dinner. To make amends for his show of exasperation he went up to his wife's room and offered to read to her. She was touched, gratefully accepted the offer, and Mr. Hutton, who was particularly proud of his accent, suggested a little light reading in French.

"French? I am so fond of French." Mrs. Hutton spoke of the language of Racine as though it were a dish of green peas.

Mr. Hutton ran down to the library and returned with a yellow volume. He began reading. The effort of pronouncing perfectly absorbed his whole attention. But how good his accent was! The fact of its goodness seemed to improve the quality of the novel he was reading.

At the end of fifteen pages an unmistakable sound aroused

him. He looked up; Mrs. Hutton had gone to sleep. He sat still for a little while, looking with a dispassionate curiosity at the sleeping face. Once it had been beautiful; once, long ago, the sight of it, the recollection of it, had moved him with an emotion profounder, perhaps, than any he had felt before or since. Now it was lined and cadaverous. The skin was stretched tightly over the cheekbones, across the bridge of the sharp, bird-like nose. The closed eyes were set in profound bone-rimmed sockets. The lamplight striking on the face from the side emphasised with light and shade its cavities and projections. It was the face of a dead Christ by Morales.

> *Le squelette était invisible*
> *Au temps heureux de l'art païen.*

He shivered a little, and tiptoed out of the room.

On the following day Mrs. Hutton came down to luncheon. She had had some unpleasant palpitations during the night, but she was feeling better now. Besides, she wanted to do honour to her guest. Miss Spence listened to her complaints about Llandrindod Wells, and was loud in sympathy, lavish with advice. Whatever she said was always said with intensity. She leaned forward, aimed, so to speak, like a gun, and fired her words. Bang! the charge in her soul was ignited, the words whizzed forth at the narrow barrel of her mouth. She was a machine-gun riddling her hostess with sympathy. Mr. Hutton had undergone similar bombardments, mostly of a literary or philosophic character—bombardments at Maeterlinck, of Mrs. Besant, of Bergson, of William James. To-day the missiles were medical. She talked about insomnia, she expatiated on the virtues of harmless drugs and beneficient specialists. Under the bombardment Mrs. Hutton opened out, like a flower in the sun.

Mr. Hutton looked on in silence. The spectacle of Janet Spence evoked in him an unfailing curiosity. He was not romantic enough to imagine that every face masked an interior physiognomy of beauty or strangeness, that every woman's small talk was like a vapour hanging over mysterious gulfs. His wife, for example, and Doris; they were nothing more than what they seemed to be. But with Janet Spence it was somehow different. Here one could be sure that there was some kind of a queer face behind the Gioconda smile and the Roman eyebrows. The only question was: What exactly was there? Mr. Hutton could never quite make out.

"But perhaps you won't have to go to Llandrindod after all," Miss Spence was saying. "If you get well quickly Dr. Libbard will let you off."

"I only hope so. Indeed, I do really feel rather better to-day."

Mr. Hutton felt ashamed. How much was it his own lack of sympathy that prevented her from feeling well every day? But he comforted himself by reflecting that it was only a case of feeling, not of being better. Sympathy does not mend a diseased liver or a weak heart.

"My dear, I wouldn't eat those red currants if I were you," he said, suddenly solicitous. "You know that Libbard has banned everything with skins and pips."

"But I am so fond of them," Mrs. Hutton protested, "and I feel so well to-day."

"Don't be a tyrant," said Miss Spence, looking first at him and then at his wife. "Let the poor invalid have what she fancies; it will do her good." She laid her hand on Mrs. Hutton's arm and patted it affectionately two or three times.

"Thank you, my dear." Mrs. Hutton helped herself to the stewed currants.

"Well, don't blame me if they make you ill again."

"Do I ever blame you, dear?"

"You have nothing to blame me for," Mr. Hutton answered playfully. "I am the perfect husband."

They sat in the garden after luncheon. From the island of shade under the old cypress tree they looked out across a flat expanse of lawn, in which the parterres of flowers shone with a metallic brilliance.

Mr. Hutton took a deep breath of the warm and fragrant air. "It's good to be alive," he said.

"Just to be alive," his wife echoed, stretching one pale, knot-jointed hand into the sunlight.

A maid brought the coffee; the silver pots and the little blue cups were set on a folding table near the group of chairs.

"Oh, my medicine!" exclaimed Mrs. Hutton. "Run in and fetch it, Clara, will you? The white bottle on the sideboard."

"I'll go," said Mr. Hutton. "I've got to go and fetch a cigar in any case."

He ran in towards the house. On the threshold he turned round for an instant. The maid was walking back across the lawn. His wife was sitting up in her deck-chair, engaged in opening her white parasol. Miss Spence was bending over the table, pouring out the coffee. He passed into the cool obscurity of the house.

"Do you like sugar in your coffee?" Miss Spence inquired.

"Yes, please. Give me rather a lot. I'll drink it after my medicine to take the taste away."

Mrs. Hutton leaned back in her chair, lowering the sunshade over her eyes, so as to shut out from her vision the burning sky.

Behind her, Miss Spence was making a delicate clinking among the coffee-cups.

"I've given you three large spoonfuls. That ought to take the taste away. And here comes the medicine."

Mr. Hutton had reappeared, carrying a wine-glass, half full of a pale liquid.

"It smells delicious," he said, as he handed it to his wife.

"That's only the flavouring." She drank it off at a gulp, shuddered, and made a grimace. "Ugh, it's so nasty. Give me my coffee."

Miss Spence gave her the cup; she sipped at it. "You've made it like syrup. But it's very nice, after that atrocious medicine."

At half-past three Mrs. Hutton complained that she did not feel as well as she had done, and went indoors to lie down. Her husband would have said something about the red currants, but checked himself; the triumph of an "I told you so" was too cheaply won. Instead, he was sympathetic, and gave her his arm to the house.

"A rest will do you good," he said. "By the way, I shan't be back till after dinner."

"But why? Where are you going?"

"I promised to go to Johnson's this evening. We have to discuss the war memorial, you know."

"Oh, I wish you weren't going." Mrs. Hutton was almost in tears. " Can't you stay? I don't like being alone in the house."

"But, my dear, I promised—weeks ago." It was a bother having to lie like this. "And now I must get back and look after Miss Spence."

He kissed her on the forehead and went out again into the garden. Miss Spence received him aimed and intense.

"Your wife is dreadfully ill," she fired off at him.

"I thought she cheered up so much when you came."

"That was purely nervous, purely nervous. I was watching her closely. With a heart in that condition and her digestion wrecked—yes, wrecked—anything might happen."

"Libbard doesn't take so gloomy a view of poor Emily's health." Mr. Hutton held open the gate that led from the garden into the drive; Miss Spence's car was standing by the front door.

"Libbard is only a country doctor. You ought to see a specialist."

He could not refrain from laughing. "You have a macabre passion for specialists."

Miss Spence held up her hand in protest. "I am serious. I think poor Emily is in a very bad state. Anything might happen —at any moment."

He handed her into the car and shut the door. The chauffeur started the engine and climbed into his place, ready to drive off.

"Shall I tell him to start?" He had no desire to continue the conversation.

Miss Spence leaned forward and shot a Gioconda in his direction. "Remember, I expect you to come and see me again soon."

Mechanically he grinned, made a polite noise, and, as the car moved forward, waved his hand. He was happy to be alone.

A few minutes afterwards Mr. Hutton himself drove away.

Doris was waiting at the cross-roads. They dined together twenty miles from home, at a roadside hotel. It was one of those bad, expensive meals which are only cooked in country hotels frequented by motorists. It revolted Mr. Hutton, but Doris enjoyed it. She always enjoyed things. Mr. Hutton ordered a not very good brand of champagne. He was wishing he had spent the evening in his library.

When they started homewards Doris was a little tipsy and extremely affectionate. It was very dark inside the car, but looking forward, past the motionless form of M'Nab, they could see a bright and narrow universe of forms and colours scooped out of the night by the electric head-lamps.

It was after eleven when Mr. Hutton reached home. Dr. Libbard met him in the hall. He was a small man with delicate hands and well-formed features that were almost feminine. His brown eyes were large and melancholy. He used to waste a great deal of time sitting at the bedside of his patients, looking sadness through those eyes and talking in a sad, low voice about nothing in particular. His person exhaled a pleasing odour, decidedly antiseptic but at the same time suave and discreetly delicious.

"Libbard?" said Mr. Hutton in surprise. "You here? Is my wife ill?"

"We tried to fetch you earlier," the soft, melancholy voice replied. "It was thought you were at Mr. Johnson's, but they had no news of you there."

"No, I was detained. I had a breakdown," Mr. Hutton answered irritably. It was tiresome to be caught out in a lie.

"Your wife wanted to see you urgently."

"Well, I can go now." Mr. Hutton moved towards the stairs.

Dr. Libbard laid a hand on his arm. "I am afraid it's too late."

"Too late?" He began fumbling with his watch; it wouldn' come out of the pocket.

"Mrs. Hutton passed away half an hour ago."

The voice remained even in its softness, the melancholy of the eyes did not deepen. Dr. Libbard spoke of death as he would speak of a local cricket match. All things were equally vain and equally deplorable.

Mr. Hutton found himself thinking of Janet Spence's words. At any moment—at any moment.   She had been extraordinarily right.

"What happened?" he asked. "What was the cause?"

Dr. Libbard explained. It was heart failure brought on by a violent attack of nausea, caused in its turn by the eating of something of an irritant nature. Red currants? Mr. Hutton suggested. Very likely. It had been too much for the heart. There was chronic valvular disease: something had collapsed under the strain. It was all over; she could not have suffered much.

III

"It's a pity they should have chosen the day of the Eton and Harrow match for the funeral," old General Grego was saying as he stood, his top hat in his hand, under the shadow of the lych gate, wiping his face with his handkerchief.

Mr. Hutton overheard the remark and with difficulty restrained a desire to inflict grievous bodily pain on the General. He would have liked to hit the old brute in the middle of his big red face. Monstrous great mulberry, spotted with meal! Was there no respect for the dead? Did nobody care? In theory he didn't much care; let the dead bury their dead. But here, at the graveside, he had found himself actually sobbing. Poor Emily, they had been pretty happy once. Now she was lying at the bottom of a seven-foot hole. And here was Grego complaining that he couldn't go to the Eton and Harrow match.

Mr. Hutton looked round at the groups of black figures that were drifting slowly out of the churchyard towards the fleet of cabs and motors assembled in the road outside. Against the brilliant background of the July grass and flowers and foliage, they had a horribly alien and unnatural appearance. It pleased him to think that all these people would soon be dead too.

That evening Mr. Hutton sat up late in his library reading the life of Milton. There was no particular reason why he should have chosen Milton; it was the book that first came to hand, that was all. It was after midnight when he had finished. He got up from his arm-chair, unbolted the french windows, and stepped out on to the little paved terrace. The night was quiet and clear. Mr. Hutton looked at the stars and at the holes between them, dropped his eyes to the dim lawns and hueless flowers of the garden, and let them wander over the farther landscape, black and grey under the moon.

He began to think with a kind of confused violence. There were the stars, there was Milton. A man can be somehow the peer of stars and night. Greatness, nobility. But is there seriously a difference between the noble and the ignoble? Milton, the stars, death, and himself—himself. The soul, the body; the higher and the lower nature. Perhaps there was something in it, after all. Milton had a god on his side and righteousness. What had he? Nothing, nothing whatever. There were only Doris's little breasts. What was the point of it all? Milton, the stars, death, and Emily in her grave, Doris and himself—always himself . . .

Oh, he was a futile and disgusting being. Everything convinced him of it. It was a solemn moment. He spoke aloud: "I will, I will." The sound of his own voice in the darkness was appalling; it seemed to him that he had sworn that infernal oath which binds even the gods: "I will, I will." There had been New Year's days and solemn anniversaries in the past, when he had felt the same contritions and recorded similar resolutions. They had all thinned away, these resolutions, like smoke, into nothingness. But this was a greater moment and he had pronounced a more fearful oath. In the future it was to be different. Yes, he would live by reason, he would be industrious, he would curb his appetites, he would devote his life to some good purpose. It was resolved and it would be so.

In practice he saw himself spending his mornings in agricultural pursuits, riding round with the bailiff, seeing that his land was farmed in the best modern way—silos and artificial manures and continuous cropping, and all that. The remainder of the day should be devoted to serious study. There was that book he had been intending to write for so long—*The Effect of Diseases on Civilisation.*

Mr. Hutton went to bed humble and contrite, but with a sense that grace had entered into him. He slept for seven and a half hours, and woke to find the sun brilliantly shining. The emotions of the evening before had been transformed by a good night's rest into his customary cheerfulness. It was not until a good many seconds after his return to conscious life that he remembered his resolution, his Stygian oath. Milton and death seemed somehow different in the sunlight. As for the stars, they were not there. But the resolutions were good; even in the day-time he could see that. He had his horse saddled after breakfast, and rode round the farm with the bailiff. After luncheon he read Thucydides on the plague at Athens. In the evening he made a few notes on malaria in Southern Italy. While he was undressing he remembered that there was a good anecdote in Skelton's jest-book about the Sweating Sickness. He would have made a note of it if only he could have found a pencil.

On the sixth morning of his new life Mr. Hutton found among his correspondence an envelope addressed in that peculiarly vulgar handwriting which he knew to be Doris's. He opened it, and began to read. She didn't know what to say; words were so inadequate. His wife dying like that, and so suddenly—it was too terrible. Mr. Hutton sighed, but his interest revived some-what as he read on:

"Death is so frightening, I never think of it when I can help it. But when something like this happens, or when I am feeling ill or depressed, then I can't help remembering it is there so close, and I think about all the wicked things I have done and about you and me, and I wonder what will happen, and I am so frightened. I am so lonely, Teddy Bear, and so unhappy, and I don't know what to do. I can't get rid of the idea of dying, I am so wretched and helpless without you. I didn't mean to write to you; I meant to wait till you were out of mourning and could come and see me again, but I was so lonely and miserable, Teddy Bear, I had to write. I couldn't help it. Forgive me, I want you so much; I have nobody in the world but you. You are so good and gentle and understanding; there is nobody like you. I shall never forget how good and kind you have been to me, and you are so clever and know so much, I can't understand how you ever came to pay any attention to me, I am so dull and stupid, much less like me and love me, because you do love me a little, don't you, Teddy Bear?"

Mr. Hutton was touched with shame and remorse. To be thanked like this, worshipped for having seduced the girl—it was too much. It had just been a piece of imbecile wantonness. Imbecile, idiotic: there was no other way to describe it. For, when all was said, he had derived very little pleasure from it. Taking all things together, he had probably been more bored than amused. Once upon a time he had believed himself to be a hedonist. But to be a hedonist implies a certain process of reasoning, a deliberate choice of known pleasures, a rejection of known pains. This had been done without reason, against it. For he knew beforehand—so well, so well—that there was no interest or pleasure to be derived from these wretched affairs. And yet each time the vague itch came upon him he succumbed, involving himself once more in the old stupidity. There had been Maggie, his wife's maid, and Edith, the girl on the farm, and Mrs. Pringle, and the waitress in London, and others—there seemed to be dozens of them. It had all been so stale and boring. He knew it would be; he always knew. And yet, and yet . . . Experience doesn't teach.

Poor little Doris! He would write to her kindly, comfortingly, but he wouldn't see her again. A servant came to tell him that his horse was saddled and waiting. He mounted and rode off. That morning the old bailiff was more irritating than usual.

Five days later Doris and Mr. Hutton were sitting together on the pier at Southend; Doris, in white muslin with pink garnishings, radiated happiness; Mr. Hutton, legs outstretched and chair tilted, had pushed the panama back from his forehead, and was trying to feel like a tripper. That night, when Doris was asleep, breathing and warm by his side, he recaptured, in this moment of darkness and physical fatigue, the rather cosmic emotion which had possessed him that evening, not a fortnight ago, when he had made his great resolution. And so his solemn oath had already gone the way of so many other resolutions. Unreason had triumphed; at the first itch of desire he had given way. He was hopeless, hopeless.

For a long time he lay with closed eyes, ruminating his humiliation. The girl stirred in her sleep. Mr. Hutton turned over and looked in her direction. Enough faint light crept in between the half-drawn curtains to show her bare arm and shoulder, her neck, and the dark tangle of hair on the pillow. She was beautiful, desirable. Why did he lie there moaning over his sins? What did it matter? If he were hopeless, then so be it; he would make the best of his hopelessness. A glorious sense of irresponsibility suddenly filled him. He was free, magnificently free. In a kind of exaltation he drew the girl towards him. She woke, bewildered, almost frightened under his rough kisses.

The storm of his desire subsided into a kind of serene merriment. The whole atmosphere seemed to be quivering with enormous silent laughter.

"Could anyone love you as much as I do, Teddy Bear?" The question came faintly from distant worlds of love.

"I think I know somebody who does," Mr. Hutton replied. The submarine laughter was swelling, rising, ready to break the surface of silence and resound.

"Who? Tell me. What do you mean?" The voice had come very close; charged with suspicion, anguish, indignation, it belonged to this immediate world.

"A—ah!"

"Who?"

"You'll never guess." Mr. Hutton kept up the joke until it began to grow tedious, and then pronounced the name: "Janet Spence."

Doris was incredulous. "Miss Spence of the Manor? That old woman?" It was too ridiculous. Mr. Hutton laughed too.

"But it's quite true," he said. "She adores me." Oh, the vast joke! He would go and see her as soon as he returned—see and conquer. "I believe she wants to marry me," he added.

"But you wouldn't . . . you don't intend . . ."

The air was fairly crepitating with humour. Mr. Hutton laughed aloud. "I intend to marry you," he said. It seemed to him the best joke he had ever made in his life.

When Mr. Hutton left Southend he was once more a married man. It was agreed that, for the time being, the fact should be kept secret. In the autumn they would go abroad together, and the world should be informed. Meanwhile he was to go back to his own house and Doris to hers.

The day after his return he walked over in the afternoon to see Miss Spence. She received him with the old Gioconda.

"I was expecting you to come."

"I couldn't keep away," Mr. Hutton gallantly replied.

They sat in the summer-house. It was a pleasant place—a little old stucco temple bowered among dense bushes of evergreen. Miss Spence had left her mark on it by hanging up over the seat a blue-and-white Della Robbia plaque.

"I am thinking of going to Italy this autumn," said Mr. Hutton. He felt like a ginger-beer bottle, ready to pop with bubbling humorous excitement.

"Italy. . . ." Miss Spence closed her eyes ecstatically. "I feel drawn there too."

"Why not let yourself be drawn?"

"I don't know. One somehow hasn't the energy and initiative to set out alone."

"Alone. . . ." Ah, sound of guitars and throaty singing! "Yes, travelling alone isn't much fun."

Miss Spence lay back in her chair without speaking. Her eyes were still closed. Mr. Hutton stroked his moustache. The silence prolonged itself for what seemed a very long time.

Pressed to stay to dinner, Mr. Hutton did not refuse. The fun had hardly started. The table was laid in the loggia. Through its arches they looked out on to the sloping garden, to the valley below and the farther hills. Light ebbed away; the heat and silence were oppressive. A huge cloud was mounting up the sky, and there were distant breathings of thunder. The thunder drew nearer, a wind began to blow, and the first drops of rain fell. The table was cleared. Miss Spence and Mr. Hutton sat on in the growing darkness.

Miss Spence broke a long silence by saying meditatively:

"I think everyone has a right to a certain amount of happiness, don't you?"

"Most certainly." But what was she leading up to? Nobody makes generalisations about life unless they mean to talk about themselves. Happiness: he looked back on his own life, and saw a cheerful, placid existence disturbed by no great griefs or discomforts or alarms. He had always had money and freedom; he had been able to do very much as he wanted. Yes, he supposed he had been happy—happier than most men. And now he was not merely happy; he had discovered in irresponsibility the secret of gaiety. He was about to say something about his happiness when Miss Spence went on speaking.

"People like you and me have a right to be happy some time in our lives."

"Me?" said Mr. Hutton, surprised.

"Poor Henry! Fate hasn't treated either of us very well."

"Oh, well, it might have treated me worse."

"You're being cheerful. That's brave of you. But don't think I can't see behind the mask."

Miss Spence spoke louder and louder as the rain came down more and more heavily. Periodically the thunder cut across her utterances. She talked on, shouting against the noise.

"I have understood you so well and for so long."

A flash revealed her, aimed and intent, leaning towards him. Her eyes were two profound and menacing gun-barrels. The darkness re-engulfed her.

"You were a lonely soul seeking a companion soul. I could sympathise with you in your solitude. Your marriage . . ."

The thunder cut short the sentence. Miss Spence's voice became audible once more with the words:

". . . could offer no companionship to a man of your stamp. You needed a soul mate."

A soul mate—he! a soul mate. It was incredibly fantastic. "Georgette Leblanc, the ex-soul mate of Maurice Maeterlinck." He had seen that in the paper a few days ago. So it was thus that Janet Spence had painted him in her imagination—as a soulmater. And for Doris he was a picture of goodness and the cleverest man in the world. And actually, really, he was what?—Who knows?

"My heart went out to you. I could understand; I was lonely, too." Miss Spence laid her hand on his knee. "You were so patient." Another flash. She was still aimed, dangerously. "You never complained. But I could guess—I could guess."

"How wonderful of you!" So he was an *âme incomprise.* "Only a woman's intuition . . ."

The thunder crashed and rumbled, died away, and only the sound of the rain was left. The thunder was his laughter, magnified, externalised. Flash and crash, there it was again, right on top of them.

"Don't you feel that you have within you something that is akin to this storm?" He could imagine her leaning forward as she uttered the words. "Passion makes one the equal of the elements."

What was his gambit now? Why, obviously, he should have said "Yes," and ventured on some unequivocal gesture. But Mr. Hutton suddenly took fright. The ginger beer in him had gone flat. The woman was serious—terribly serious. He was appalled.

Passion? "No," he desperately answered. "I am without passion."

But his remark was either unheard or unheeded, for Miss Spence went on with a growing exaltation, speaking so rapidly, however, and in such a burningly intimate whisper that Mr.

Hutton found it very difficult to distinguish what she was saying. She was telling him, as far as he could make out, the story of her life. The lightning was less frequent now, and there were long intervals of darkness. But at each flash he saw her still aiming towards him, still yearning forward with a terrifying intensity. Darkness, the rain, and then flash! her face was there, close at hand. A pale mask, greenish white; the large eyes, the narrow barrel of the mouth, the heavy eyebrows. Agrippina, or wasn't it rather—yes, wasn't it rather George Robey?

He began devising absurd plans for escaping. He might suddenly jump up, pretending he had seen a burglar—Stop thief! stop thief!—and dash off into the night in pursuit. Or should he say that he felt faint, a heart attack? or that he had seen a ghost—Emily's ghost—in the garden? Absorbed in his childish plotting, he had ceased to pay any attention to Miss Spence's words. The spasmodic clutching of her hand recalled his thoughts.

"I honoured you for that, Henry," she was saying.

Honoured him for what?

"Marriage is a sacred tie, and your respect for it, even when the marriage was, as it was in your case, an unhappy one, made me respect you and admire you, and—shall I dare say the word?——"

Oh, the burglar, the ghost in the garden! But it was too late.

". . . yes, love you, Henry, all the more. But we're free now, Henry."

Free? There was a movement in the dark, and she was kneeling on the floor by his chair.

"Oh, Henry, Henry, I have been unhappy too."

Her arms embraced him, and by the shaking of her body he could feel that she was sobbing. She might have been a suppliant crying for mercy.

"You mustn't, Janet," he protested. Those tears were terrible, terrible. "Not now, not now! You must be calm; you must go to bed." He patted her shoulder, then got up, disengaging himself from her embrace. He left her still crouching on the floor beside the chair on which he had been sitting.

Groping his way into the hall, and without waiting to look for his hat, he went out of the house, taking infinite pains to close the front door noiselessly behind him. The clouds had blown over, and the moon was shining from a clear sky. There were puddles all along the road, and a noise of running water rose from the gutters and ditches. Mr. Hutton splashed along, not caring if he got wet.

How heartrendingly she had sobbed! With the emotions of pity and remorse that the recollection evoked in him there was a certain resentment: why couldn't she have played the game that he was playing—the heartless, amusing game? Yes, but he had known all the time that she wouldn't, she couldn't, play that game; he had known and persisted.

What had she said about passion and the elements? Something absurdly stale, but true, true. There she was, a cloud black-bosomed and charged with thunder, and he, like some absurd little Benjamin Franklin, had sent up a kite into the heart of the menace. Now he was complaining that his toy had drawn the lightning.

She was probably still kneeling by that chair in the loggia, crying.

But why hadn't he been able to keep up the game? Why had his irresponsibility deserted him, leaving him suddenly sober in a cold world? There were no answers to any of his questions. One idea burned steady and luminous in his mind—the idea of flight. He must get away at once.

IV

"What are you thinking about, Teddy Bear?"

"Nothing."

There was a silence. Mr. Hutton remained motionless, his elbows on the parapet of the terrace, his chin in his hands, looking down over Florence. He had taken a villa on one of the hilltops to the south of the city. From a little raised terrace at the end of the garden one looked down a long fertile valley on to the town and beyond it to the bleak mass of Monte Morello and, eastward of it, to the peopled hill of Fiesole, dotted with white houses. Everything was clear and luminous in the September sunshine.

"Are you worried about anything?"

"No, thank you."

"Tell me, Teddy Bear."

"But, my dear, there's nothing to tell." Mr. Hutton turned round, smiled, and patted the girl's hand. "I think you'd better go in and have your siesta. It's too hot for you here."

"Very well, Teddy Bear. Are you coming too?"

"When I've finished my cigar."

"All right. But do hurry up and finish it, Teddy Bear." Slowly, reluctantly, she descended the steps of the terrace and walked towards the house.

Mr. Hutton continued his contemplation of Florence. He had need to be alone. It was good sometimes to escape from Doris and the restless solicitude of her passion. He had never known the pains of loving hopelessly, but he was experiencing now the pains of being loved. These last weeks had been a period of growing discomfort. Doris was always with him, like an obsession, like a guilty conscience. Yes, it was good to be alone.

He pulled an envelope out of his pocket and opened it, not without reluctance. He hated letters; they always contained something unpleasant—nowadays, since his second marriage. This was from his sister. He began skimming through the insulting home-truths of which it was composed. The words "indecent haste," "social suicide," "scarcely cold in her grave," "person of the lower classes," all occurred. They were inevitable now in any communication from a well-meaning and right-thinking relative. Impatient, he was about to tear the stupid letter to pieces when his eye fell on a sentence at the bottom of the third page. His heart beat with uncomfortable violence as he read it. It was too monstrous! Janet Spence was going about telling everyone that he had poisoned his wife in order to marry Doris. What damnable malice! Ordinarily a man of the suavest temper, Mr. Hutton found himself trembling with rage. He took the childish satisfaction of calling names—he cursed the woman.

Then suddenly he saw the ridiculous side of the situation. The notion that he should have murdered anyone in order to marry Doris! If they only knew how miserably bored he was. Poor, dear Janet! She had tried to be malicious; she had only succeeded in being stupid.

A sound of footsteps aroused him; he looked round. In the garden below the little terrace the servant girl of the house was picking fruit. A Neapolitan, strayed somehow as far north as Florence, she was a specimen of the classical type—a little debased. Her profile might have been taken from a Sicilian coin of a bad period. Her features, carved floridly in the grand tradition, expressed an almost perfect stupidity. Her mouth was the most beautiful thing about her; the calligraphic hand of nature had richly curved it into an expression of mulish bad temper. . . . Under her hideous black clothes, Mr. Hutton divined a powerful body, firm and massive. He had looked at her before with a vague interest and curiosity. To-day the curiosity defined and focused itself into a desire. An idyll of Theocritus. Here was the woman; he, alas, was not precisely like a goatherd on the volcanic hills. He called to her.

"Armida!"

The smile with which she answered him was so provocative, attested so easy a virtue, that Mr. Hutton took fright. He was on the brink once more—on the brink. He must draw back, oh! quickly, quickly, before it was too late. The girl continued to look up at him.

"*Ha chiamato?*" she asked at last.

Stupidity or reason? Oh, there was no choice now. It was imbecility every time.

"*Scendo*," he called back to her. Twelve steps led from the garden to the terrace. Mr. Hutton counted them. Down, down, down, down. . . . He saw a vision of himself descending from one circle of the inferno to the next—from a darkness full of wind and hail to an abyss of stinking mud.

V

For a good many days the Hutton case had a place on the front page of every newspaper. There had been no more popular murder trial since George Smith had temporarily eclipsed the European War by drowning in a warm bath his seventh bride. The public imagination was stirred by this tale of a murder brought to light months after the date of the crime. Here, it was felt, was one of those incidents in human life, so notable because they are so rare, which do definitely justify the ways of God to man. A wicked man had been moved by an illicit passion to kill his wife. For months he had lived in sin and fancied security— only to be dashed at last more horribly into the pit he had prepared for himself. Murder will out, and here was a case of it. The readers of the newspapers were in a position to follow every movement of the hand of God. There had been vague, but persistent, rumours in the neighbourhood; the police had taken action at last. Then came the exhumation order, the post-mortem examination, the inquest, the evidence of the experts, the verdict of the coroner's jury, the trial, the condemnation. For once Providence had done its duty, obviously, grossly, didactically, as in a melodrama. The newspapers were right in making of the case the staple intellectual food of a whole season.

Mr. Hutton's first emotion when he was summoned from Italy to give evidence at the inquest was one of indignation. It was a monstrous, a scandalous thing that the police should take such idle, malicious gossip seriously. When the inquest was over he would bring an action for malicious prosecution against the Chief Constable; he would sue the Spence woman for slander.

The inquest was opened; the astonishing evidence unrolled itself. The experts had examined the body, and had found traces of arsenic; they were of opinion that the late Mrs. Hutton had died of arsenic poisoning.

Arsenic poisoning. . . . Emily had died of arsenic poisoning? After that, Mr. Hutton learned with surprise that there was enough arsenicated insecticide in his greenhouses to poison an army.

It was now, quite suddenly, that he saw it: there was a case against him. Fascinated, he watched it growing, growing, like some monstrous tropical plant. It was enveloping him, surrounding him; he was lost in a tangled forest.

When was the poison administered? The experts agreed that it must have been swallowed eight or nine hours before death. About lunch-time? Yes, about lunch-time. Clara, the parlourmaid, was called. Mrs. Hutton, she remembered, had asked her to go and fetch her medicine. Mr. Hutton had volunteered to go instead; he had gone alone. Miss Spence—ah, the memory of the storm, the white aimed face! the horror of it all!—Miss Spence confirmed Clara's statement, and added that Mr. Hutton had come back with the medicine already poured out in a wineglass, not in the bottle.

Mr. Hutton's indignation evaporated. He was dismayed, frightened. It was all too fantastic to be taken seriously, and yet this nightmare was a fact—it was actually happening.

M'Nab had seen them kissing, often. He had taken them for a drive on the day of Mrs. Hutton's death. He could see them reflected in the wind-screen, sometimes out of the tail of his eye.

The inquest was adjourned. That evening Doris went to bed with a headache. When he went to her room after dinner, Mr. Hutton found her crying.

"What's the matter?" He sat down on the edge of her bed and began to stroke her hair. For a long time she did not answer, and he went on stroking her hair mechanically, almost unconsciously; sometimes, even, he bent down and kissed her bare shoulder. He had his own affairs, however, to think about. What had happened? How was it that the stupid gossip had actually come true? Emily had died of arsenic poisoning. It was absurd, impossible. The order of things had been broken, and he was at the mercy of an irresponsibility. What had happened, what was going to happen? He was interrupted in the midst of his thoughts.

"It's my fault—it's my fault!" Doris suddenly sobbed out. "I shouldn't have loved you; I oughtn't to have let you love me. Why was I ever born?"

Mr. Hutton didn't say anything, but looked down in silence at the abject figure of misery lying on the bed.

"If they do anything to you I shall kill myself."

She sat up, held him for a moment at arm's length, and looked at him with a kind of violence, as though she were never to see him again.

"I love you, I love you, I love you." She drew him, inert and passive, towards her, clasped him, pressed herself against him. "I didn't know you loved me as much as that, Teddy Bear. But why did you do it—why did you do it?"

Mr. Hutton undid her clasping arms and got up. His face became very red. "You seem to take it for granted that I murdered my wife," he said. "It's really too grotesque. What do you all take me for? A cinema hero?" He had begun to lose his temper. All the exasperation, all the fear and bewilderment of the day, was transformed into a violent anger against her. "It's all such damned stupidity. Haven't you any conception of a civilised man's mentality? Do I look the sort of man who'd go about slaughtering people? I suppose you imagined I was so insanely in love with you that I could commit any folly. When will you women understand that one isn't insanely in love? All one asks for is a quiet life, which you won't allow one to have. I don't know what the devil ever induced me to marry you. It was all a damned stupid, practical joke. And now you go about saying I'm a murderer. I won't stand it."

Mr. Hutton stamped towards the door. He had said horrible things, he knew—odious things that he ought speedily to unsay. But he wouldn't. He closed the door behind him.

"Teddy Bear!" He turned the handle; the latch clicked into place. "Teddy Bear!" The voice that came to him through the closed door was agonised. Should he go back? He ought to go back. He touched the handle, then withdrew his fingers and quickly walked away. When he was half-way down the stairs he

halted. She might try to do something silly—throw herself out
of the window or God knows what! He listened attentively;
there was no sound. But he pictured her very clearly, tiptoeing
across the room, lifting the sash as high as it would go, leaning
out into the cold night air. It was raining a little. Under the
window lay the paved terrace. How far below? Twenty-five or
thirty feet? Once, when he was walking along Piccadilly, a dog
had jumped out of a third-storey window of the Ritz. He had
seen it fall; he had heard it strike the pavement. Should he go
back? He was damned if he would; he hated her.

He sat for a long time in the library. What had happened?
What was happening? He turned the question over and over in
his mind and could find no answer. Suppose the nightmare
dreamed itself out to its horrible conclusion. Death was waiting
for him. His eyes filled with tears; he wanted so passionately to
live. "Just to be alive." Poor Emily had wished it too, he remembered: "Just to be alive." There were still so many places
in this astonishing world unvisited, so many queer delightful
people still unknown, so many lovely women never so much as
seen. The huge white oxen would still be dragging their wains
along the Tuscan roads, the cypresses would still go up, straight
as pillars, to the blue heaven; but he would not be there to see
them. And the sweet southern wines—Tear of Christ and Blood
of Judas—others would drink them, not he. Others would walk
down the obscure and narrow lanes between the bookshelves in
the London Library, sniffing the dusty perfume of good literature, peering at strange titles, discovering unknown names, ex-
ploring the fringes of vast domains of knowledge. He would be
lying in a hole in the ground. And why, why? Confusedly he
felt that some extraordinary kind of justice was being done. In
the past he had been wanton and imbecile and irresponsible.
Now Fate was playing as wantonly, as irresponsibly, with him.
It was tit for tat, and God existed after all.

He felt that he would like to pray. Forty years ago he used to
kneel by his bed every evening. The nightly formula of his
childhood came to him almost unsought from some long un-

opened chamber of the memory. "God bless Father and Mother, Tom and Cissie and the Baby, Mademoiselle and Nurse, and everyone that I love, and make me a good boy. Amen." They were all dead now—all except Cissie.

His mind seemed to soften and dissolve; a great calm descended upon his spirit. He went upstairs to ask Doris's forgiveness. He found her lying on the couch at the foot of the bed. On the floor beside her stood a blue bottle of liniment, marked "Not to be taken"; she seemed to have drunk about half of it.

"You didn't love me," was all she said when she opened her eyes to find him bending over her.

Dr. Libbard arrived in time to prevent any very serious consequences. "You mustn't do this again," he said while Mr. Hutton was out of the room.

"What's to prevent me?" she asked defiantly.

Dr. Libbard looked at her with his large, sad eyes. "There's nothing to prevent you," he said. "Only yourself and your baby. Isn't it rather bad luck on your baby, not allowing it to come into the world because you want to go out of it?"

Doris was silent for a time. "All right," she whispered. "I won't."

Mr. Hutton sat by her bedside for the rest of the night. He felt himself now to be indeed a murderer. For a time he persuaded himself that he loved this pitiable child. Dozing in his chair, he woke up, stiff and cold, to find himself drained dry, as it were, of every emotion. He had become nothing but a tired and suffering carcase. At six o'clock he undressed and went to bed for a couple of hours' sleep. In the course of the same afternoon the coroner's jury brought in a verdict of "Wilful Murder," and Mr. Hutton was committed for trial.

VI

Miss Spence was not at all well. She had found her public appearances in the witness-box very trying, and when it was all over she had something that was very nearly a breakdown. She slept badly, and suffered from nervous indigestion. Dr. Libbard used to call every other day. She talked to him a great deal— mostly about the Hutton case. . . . Her moral indignation was always on the boil. Wasn't it appalling to think that one had had a murderer in one's house? Wasn't it extraordinary that one could have been for so long mistaken about the man's character? (But she had had an inkling from the first.) And then the girl he had gone off with—so low class, so little better than a prostitute. The news that the second Mrs. Hutton was expecting a baby— the posthumous child of a condemned and executed criminal— revolted her; the thing was shocking—an obscenity. Dr. Lib-bard answered her gently and vaguely, and prescribed bromide.

One morning he interrupted her in the midst of her customary tirade. "By the way," he said in his soft, melancholy voice, "I suppose it was really you who poisoned Mrs. Hutton."

Miss Spence stared at him for two or three seconds with enormous eyes, and then quietly said, "Yes." After that she started to cry.

"In the coffee, I suppose."

She seemed to nod assent. Dr. Libbard took out his fountain-pen, and in his neat, meticulous calligraphy wrote out a pre-scription for a sleeping-draught.

UNCLE SPENCER

SOME people I know can look back over the long series of their childish holidays and see in their memory always a different landscape—chalk downs or Swiss mountains; a blue and sunny sea or the grey, ever-troubled fringe of the ocean; heathery moors under the cloud with far away a patch of sunlight on the hills, golden as happiness and, like happiness, remote, precarious, impermanent, or the untroubled waters of Como, the cypresses and the Easter roses.

I envy them the variety of their impressions. For it is good to have seen something of the world with childish eyes, disinterestedly and uncritically, observing not what is useful or beautiful and interesting, but only such things as, to a being less than four feet high and having no knowledge of life or art, seem immediately significant. It is the beggars, it is the green umbrellas under which the cabmen sit when it rains, not Brunelleschi's dome, not the extortions of the hotel-keeper, not the tombs of the Medici that impress the childish traveller. Such impressions, it is true, are of no particular value to us when we are grown up. (The famous wisdom of babes, with those childish intimations of immortality and all the rest, never really amounted to very much; and the man who studies the souls of children in the hope of finding out something about the souls of men is about as likely to discover something important as the man who thinks he can explain Beethoven by referring him to the savage origins of music or religion by referring it to the sexual instincts.) None the less, it is good to have had such childish impressions, if only for the sake of comparing (so that we may draw the philosophic moral) what we saw of a place when we were six or seven with what we see again at thirty.

My holidays had no variety. From the time when I first went to my preparatory school to the time when my parents came back for good from India—I was sixteen or seventeen then, I suppose

—they were all passed with my Uncle Spencer. For years the only places on the earth's surface of which I had any knowledge were Eastbourne, where I was at school; Dover (and that reduced itself to the harbour and station), where I embarked; Ostend, where Uncle Spencer met me; Brussels, where we changed trains; and finally Longres in Limburg, where my Uncle Spencer owned the sugar factory, which his mother, my grandmother, had inherited in her turn from her Belgian father, and had his home.

Hanging over the rail of the steamer as it moved slowly, stern foremost, through the narrow gullet of Ostend harbour, I used to strain my eyes, trying to pick out from among the crowd at the quay's edge the small, familiar figure. And always there he was, waving his coloured silk handkerchief, shouting inaudible greetings and advice, getting in the way of the porters and ticket-collectors, fidgeting with a hardly controllable impatience behind the barrier, until at last, squeezed and almost suffocated amongst the grown men and women—whom the process of disembarkation transformed as though by some malevolent Circean magic into brute beasts, reasonless and snarling—I struggled to shore, clutching in one hand my little bag and with the other holding to my head, if it was summer, a speckled straw, gaudy with the school colours; if winter, a preposterous bowler, whose eclipsing melon crammed over my ears made me look like a child in a comic paper pretending to be grown up.

"Well, here you are, here you are," my Uncle Spencer would say, snatching my bag from me. "Eleven minutes late." And we would dash for the custom-house as though our lives depended on getting there before the other trans-beasted passengers.

My Uncle Spencer was a man of about forty when first I came from my preparatory school to stay with him. Thin he was, rather short, very quick, agile, and impulsive in his movements, with small feet and small, delicate hands. His face was narrow, clear-cut, steep, and aquiline; his eyes dark and extraordinarily bright, deeply set under overhanging brows; his hair was black, and he wore it rather long, brushed back from his forehead. At the sides of his head it had already begun to go grey, and above his ears, as it were, two grey wings were folded against his head, so that, to look at him, one was reminded of Mercury in his winged cap.

"Hurry up!" he called. And I scampered after him. "Hurry up!" But of course there was no use whatever in our hurrying; for even when we had had my little hand-bag examined, there was always the registered trunk to wait for; and that, for my Uncle Spencer, was agony. For though our places in the Brussels express were reserved, though he knew that the train would not in any circumstances start without us, this intellectual certainty was not enough to appease his passionate impatience, to allay his instinctive fears.

"Terribly slow," he kept repeating. "Terribly slow." And for the hundredth time he looked at his watch. "Ditesmoi," he would say, yet once more, to the sentry at the door of the customs-house, "le grand bagage . . . ?" until in the end the fellow, exasperated by these questions which it was not his business to answer, would say something rude; upon which my Uncle Spencer, outraged, would call him *mal élevé* and a *grossier personnage*—to the fury of the sentry but correspondingly great relief of his own feelings; for after such an outburst he could wait in patience for a good five minutes, so far forgetting his anxiety about the trunk that he actually began talking to me about other subjects, asking how I had got on this term at school, what was my batting average, whether I liked Latin, and whether Old Thunderguts, which was the name we gave to the headmaster on account of his noble baritone, was still as ill-tempered as ever.

But at the end of the five minutes, unless the trunk had previously appeared, my Uncle Spencer began looking at his watch again.

"Scandalously slow," he said. And addressing himself to another official, "Ditesmoi, monsieur, le grand bagage . . . ?"

But when at last we were safely in the train and there was nothing to prevent him from deploying all the graces and ami-abilities of his character, my Uncle Spencer, all charm and kindness now, devoted himself wholeheartedly to me.

"Look!" he said; and from the pocket of his overcoat he pulled out a large and dampish parcel of whose existence my nose had long before made me aware. "Guess what's in here."

"Prawns," I said, without an instant's hesitation.

And prawns it was, a whole kilo of them. And there we sat in opposite corners of our first-class carriage, with the little folding table opened out between us and the pink prawns on the table, eating with infinite relish and throwing the rosy carapaces, the tails, and the sucked heads out of the window. And the Flemish plain moved past us; the long double files of poplars, planted along the banks of the canals, along the fringes of the high roads, moving as we moved, marched parallel with our course or presented, as we crossed them at right angles, for one significant flashing moment the entrance to Hobbema's avenue. And now the belfries of Bruges beckoned from far off across the plain; a dozen more shrimps and we were roaring through its station, all gloom and ogives in honour of Memling and the Gothic past. By the time we had eaten another hectogram of prawns, the modern quarter of Ghent was reminding us that art was only five years old and had been invented in Vienna. At Alost the factory chimneys smoked; and before we knew where we were, we were almost on the outskirts of Brussels, with two or three hundred grammes of sea-fruit still intact on the table before us.

"Hurry up!" cried my Uncle Spencer, threatened by another access of anxiety. "We must finish them before we get to Brussels."

And during the last five miles we ate furiously, shell and all; there was hardly time even to spit out the heads and tails.

"Nothing like prawns," my Uncle Spencer never failed to say, as the express drew slowly into the station at Brussels, and the last tails and whiskers with the fishy paper were thrown out of the window. "Nothing like prawns when the brain is tired. It's the phosphorus, you know. After all your end-of-term examinations you need them." And then he patted me affectionately on the shoulder.

How often since then have I repeated in all earnestness my Uncle Spencer's words. "It's the phosphorus," I assure my fagged friends, as I insist that they shall make their lunch off shellfish. The words come gushing spontaneously out of me; the opinion that prawns and oysters are good for brain-fag is very nearly one of my fundamental and, so to say, instinctive beliefs. But sometimes, as I say the words, suddenly I think of my Uncle Spencer. I see him once more sitting opposite me in a corner of the Brussels express, his eyes flashing, his thin face expressively moving as he talks, while his quick, nervous fingers pick impatiently at the pink carapaces or with a disdainful gesture drop a whiskered head into the Flemish landscape outside the open window. And remembering my Uncle Spencer, I find myself somehow believing less firmly than I did in what I have been saying. And I wonder with a certain sense of disquietude how many other relics of my Uncle Spencer's spirit I still carry, all unconsciously, about with me.

How many of our beliefs—more serious even than the belief that prawns revive the tired brain—come to us haphazardly from sources far less trustworthy than my Uncle Spencer! The most intelligent men will be found holding opinions about certain things, inculcated in them during their childhood by nurses or stable-boys. And up to the very end of our adolescence, and even after, there are for all of us certain admired beings, whose words sink irresistibly into our minds, generating there beliefs which reason does not presume to question, and which though they may be quite out of harmony with all our other opinions persist along with them without our ever becoming aware of the contradictions between the two sets of ideas. Thus an emancipated young man, whose father happens to have been a distinguished Indian civilian, is an ardent apostle of liberty and self-determination; but insists that the Indians are and for ever will be completely incapable of governing themselves. And an art critic, extremely sound on Vlaminck and Marie Laurencin, will praise as masterly and in the grand manner—and praise sincerely, for he genuinely finds them so—the works of an artist whose dim pretentious paintings of the Tuscan landscape used to delight, because they reminded her of her youth, an old lady, now dead, but whom as a very young man he greatly loved and admired.

My Uncle Spencer was for me, in my boyhood, one of these admired beings, whose opinions possess a more than earthly value for the admiring listener. For years my most passionately cherished beliefs were his. Those opinions which I formed myself, I held more diffidently, with less ardour; for they, after all, were only the fruits of my own judgment and observation, superficial rational growths; whereas the opinions I had taken from my Uncle Spencer—such as this belief in the curative properties of prawns—had nothing to do with my reason, but had been suggested directly into the subrational depths, where they seemed to attach themselves, like barnacles, to the very keel and bottom of my mind. Most of them, I hope, I have since contrived to scrape off; and a long, laborious, painful process it has been. But there are still, I dare say, a goodly number of them left, so deeply ingrained and grown in, that it is impossible for me to be aware of them. And I shall go down to my grave making certain judgments, holding certain opinions, regarding certain things and actions in a certain way—and the way, the opinions, the judgments will not be mine, but my Uncle Spencer's; and the obscure chambers of my mind will to the end be haunted by his bright, erratic, restless ghost.

There are some people whose habits of thought a boy or a young man might, with the greatest possible advantage to himself, make his own. But my Uncle Spencer was not one of them. His active mind darted hither and thither too wildly and erratically for it to be a safe guide for an inexperienced understanding. It was all too promptly logical to draw conclusions from false premises, too easily and enthusiastically accepted as true. Living as he did in solitude—in a mental solitude; for though he was no recluse and took his share in all social pleasures, the society of Longres could not offer much in the way of high intellectual companionship—he was able to give free play to the native eccentricity of his mind. Having nobody to check or direct him, he would rush headlong down intellectual roads that led nowhere or into morasses of nonsense. When, much later, I used to amuse myself by listening on Sunday afternoons to the speakers at Marble Arch, I used often to be reminded of my Uncle Spencer. For they, like Uncle Spencer, lived in solitude, apart from the main contemporary world of ideas, unaware, or so dimly aware that it hardly counted, of the very existence of organised and systematic science, not knowing even where to look for the accumulated stores of human knowledge. I have talked in the Park to Bible students who boasted that during the day they cobbled or sold cheese, while at night they sat up learning Hebrew and studying the critics of the Holy Book. And I have been ashamed of my own idleness, ashamed of the poor use I have made of my opportunities. These humble scholars heroically pursuing enlightenment are touching and noble figures—but how often, alas, pathetically ludicrous too! For the critics my Bible students used to read and meditate upon were always at least three-quarters of a century out of date—exploded Tübingen scholars or literal inspirationalists; their authorities were always books written before the invention of modern historical research; their philology was the picturesque *lucus a non lucendo*, bloody from by-our-Lady type; their geology had irrefutable proofs of the existence of Atlantis; their physiology, if they happened to be atheists, was obsoletely mechanistic, if Christians, merely providential. All their dogged industry, all their years of heroic striving, had been completely wasted—wasted, at any rate, so far as the increase of human knowledge was concerned, but not for themselves, since the labour, the disinterested ambition, had brought them happiness.

My Uncle Spencer was spiritually a cousin of these Hyde Park orators and higher critics. He had all their passion for enlightenment and profound ideas, but not content with concentrating, like them, on a single subject such as the Bible, he allowed himself to be attracted by everything under the sun. The whole field of history, of science (or rather what my Uncle Spencer thought was science), of philosophy, religion, and art was his province. He had their industry too—an industry, in his case, rather erratic, fitful, and inconstant; for he would start passionately studying one subject, to turn after a little while to another whose aspect seemed to him at the moment more attractive. And like them he displayed—though to a less pronounced degree, since his education had been rather better than theirs (not much better, however, for he had never attended any seat of learning but one of our oldest and most hopeless public schools)—he displayed a vast unawareness of contemporary thought and an uncritical faith in authorities which to a more systematically educated man would have seemed quite obviously out of date; coupled with a profound ignorance of even the methods by which one could acquire a more accurate or at any rate a more "modern" and fashionable knowledge of the universe.

My Uncle Spencer had views and information on almost every subject one cared to mention; but the information was almost invariably faulty and the judgments he based upon it fantastic. What things he used to tell me as we sat facing one another in the corners of our first-class carriage, with the prawns piled up in a little coralline mountain on the folding table between us! Fragments of his eager talk come back to me.

"There are cypresses in Lombardy that were planted by Julius Cæsar. . . ."

"The human race is descended from African pygmies. Adam was black and only four feet high. . . ."

"*Similia similibus curantur.* Have you gone far enough with your Latin to know what that means?" (My Uncle Spencer was an enthusiastic homœopathist, and the words of Hahnemann were to him as a mystic formula, a kind of *Om mani padme hum* the repetition of which gave him an immense spiritual satisfaction.)

And once, I remember, as we were passing through the fabulous new station of Ghent—that station which fifteen or sixteen years later I was to see all smashed and gutted by the departing invaders—he began, apropos of a squad of soldiers standing on the platform, to tell me how a German professor had proved, mathematically, using the theories of ballistics and probabilities, that war was now impossible, modern quick-firing rifles and machine-guns being so efficient that it was, as my Uncle Spencer put it, "sci-en-tif-ic-ally impossible" for any body of men to remain alive within a mile of a sufficient number of mitrailleuses, moving backwards and forwards through the arc of a circle and firing continuously all the time. I passed my boyhood in the serene certainty that war was now a thing of the past.

Sometimes he would talk to me earnestly across the prawns of the cosmogonies of Boehme or Swedenborg. But all this was so exceedingly obscure that I never took it in at all. In spite of my Uncle Spencer's ascendancy over my mind I was never infected by his mystical enthusiasms. These mental dissipations had been my Uncle Spencer's wild oats. Reacting from the rather stuffily orthodox respectability of his upbringing, he ran into, not vice, not atheism, but Swedenborg. He had preserved —a legacy from his prosperous nineteenth-century youth—an easy optimism, a great belief in progress and the superiority of modern over ancient times, together with a convenient ignorance of the things about which it would have been disquieting to think too much. This agreeable notion of the world I sucked in easily and copiously with my little crustaceans; my views about the universe and the destinies of man were as rosy in those days as the prawns themselves.

It was not till seven or eight o'clock in the evening that we finally got to our destination. My Uncle Spencer's carriage— victoria or brougham, according to the season and the state of the weather—would be waiting for us at the station door. In we climbed and away we rolled on our rubbered wheels in a silence that seemed almost magical, so deafeningly did common carts and the mere station cabs go rattling over the cobbles of the long and dismal Rue de la Gare. Even in the winter, when there was nothing to be seen of it but an occasional green gas-lamp, with a little universe of pavement, brick wall and shuttered window de-

pendent upon it and created by it out of the surrounding darkness, the Rue de la Gare was signally depressing, if only because
it was so straight and long. But in summer, when the dismal
brick houses by which it was flanked revealed themselves in the
evening light, when the dust and the waste-paper came puffing
along it in gusts of warm, stale-smelling wind, then the street
seemed doubly long and disagreeable. But, on the other hand,
the contrast between its sordidness and the cool, spacious Grand'
Place into which, after what seemed a carefully studied preparatory twisting and turning among the narrow streets of the old
town, it finally debouched, was all the more striking and refreshing. Like a ship floating out from between the jaws of a canyon
into a wide and sunlit lake, our carriage emerged upon the
Grand' Place. And the moment was solemn, breathlessly anticipated and theatrical, as though we were gliding in along the
suspended calling of the oboes and bassoons, and the violins
trembling with amorous anxiety all around us, rolling silently
and with not a hitch in the stage carpentry on to some vast and
limelit stage where, as soon as we had taken up our position well
forward and in the centre, something tremendous, one imagined,
would suddenly begin to happen—a huge orchestral tutti from
contrabass trombone to piccolo, from bell instrument to triangle,
and then the tenor and soprano in such a duet as had never in all
the history of opera been heard before.

But when it came to the point, our entrance was never quite so
dramatic as all that. One found, when one actually got there,
that one had mistaken one's opera; it wasn't *Parsifal* or *Rigoletto*;
it was *Pelléas* or perhaps the *Village Romeo and Juliet*. For there
was nothing grandiosely Wagnerian, nothing Italian and showy
about the Grand' Place at Longres. The last light was rosy on
its towers, the shadows of the promenaders stretched half across
the place, and in the vast square the evening had room to be cool
and quiet. The Gothic Church had a sharp steeple and the
seminary by its side a tower, and the little seventeenth-century
Hôtel de Ville, with its slender belfry, standing in the middle of
that open space as though not afraid to let itself be seen from

every side, was a miracle of gay and sober architecture; and the houses that looked out upon it had faces simple indeed, burgess and ingenuous, but not without a certain nobility, not without a kind of unassuming provincial elegance. In, then, we glided, and the suspended oboeings of our entrance, instead of leading up to some grand and gaudy burst of harmony, fruitily protracted themselves in this evening beauty, exulted quietly in the rosy light, meditated among the lengthening shadows; and the violins, ceasing to tremble with anticipation, swelled and mounted, like light and leaping towers, into the serene sky.

And if the clock happened to strike at the moment that we entered, how charmingly the notes of the mechanical carillon harmonised with this imaginary music! At the hours, the bells in the high tower of the Hôtel de Ville played a minuet and trio, tinkly and formal like the first composition of an infant Boccherini, which lasted till fully three minutes past. At the half-hours it was a patriotic air of the same length. But at the quarters the bells no more than began a tune. Three or four bars and the music broke off, leaving the listener wondering what was to have followed, and attributing to this fragmentary stump of an air some rich outflowering in the pregnant and musical silence, some subtle development which should have made the whole otherwise enchanting than the completed pieces that followed, and preceded, and whose charm, indeed, consisted precisely in their old-fashioned mediocrity, in the ancient, cracked, and quavering sweetness of the bells that played them, and the defects in the mechanism, which imparted to the rhythm that peculiar and unforeseeable irregularity which the child at the piano, tongue between teeth, eyes anxiously glancing from printed notes to fingers and back again, laboriously introduces into the flawless evenness of "The Merry Peasant."

This regular and repeated carillonage was and indeed still is— for the invaders spared the bells—an essential part of Longres, a feature like the silhouette of its three towers seen from far away between the poplars across the wide, flat land, characteristic and recognisable.

It is with a little laugh of amused delight that the stranger to Longres first hears the jigging airs and the clashes of thin, sweet harmony floating down upon him from the sky, note succeeding unmuted note, so that the vibrations mingle in the air, surrounding the clear outlines of the melody with a faint quivering halo of discord. After an hour or two the minuet and trio, the patriotic air, become all too familiar, while with every repetition the broken fragments at the quarters grow more and more enigmatic, pregnant, dubious, and irritating. The pink light fades from the three towers, the Gothic intricacies of the church sink into a flat black silhouette against the night sky; but still from high up in the topless darkness floats down, floats up and out over the house-tops, across the flat fields, the minuet and trio. The patriotic air continues still, even after sunset, to commemorate the great events of 1830; and still the fragments between, like pencillings in the notebook of a genius, suggest to the mind in the scribble of twenty notes a splendid theme and the possibility of fifteen hundred variations. At midnight the bells are still playing; at half-past one the stranger starts yet again out of his sleep; re-evoked at a quarter to four his speculations about the possible conclusions of the unfinished symphony keep him awake long enough to hear the minuet and trio at the hour and to wonder how any one in Longres manages to sleep at all. But in a day or two he answers the question himself by sleeping unbrokenly through the hints from Beethoven's notebook, and the more deliberate evocations of Boccherini's childhood and the revolution of 1830. The disease creates its own antidote, and the habit of hearing the carillon induces gradually a state of special mental deafness in which the inhabitants of Longres permanently live.

Even as a small boy, to whom insomnia was a thing unknown, I found the bells, for the first night or two after my arrival in Longres, decidedly trying. My Uncle Spencer's house looked on to the Grand' Place itself, and my window on the third floor was within fifty yards of the belfry of the Hôtel de Ville and the source of the aerial music. Three-year-old Boccherini might have been in the room with me whenever the wind came from the south, banging his minuet in my ears. But after the second night he might bang and jangle as much as he liked; there was no bell in Longres could wake me.

What did wake me, however—every Saturday morning at about half-past four or five—was the pigs coming into market. One had to have spent a month of Saturdays in Longres before one could acquire the special mental deafness that could ignore the rumbling of cart-wheels over the cobbles and the squealing and grunting of two or three thousand pigs. And when one looked out what a sight it was! All the Grand' Place was divided up by rails into a multitude of pens and pounds, and every pound was seething with pink naked pigs that looked from above like so much Bergsonian *élan vital* in a state of incessant agitation. Men came and went between the enclosures, talking, bargaining, critically poking potential bacon or ham with the point of a stick. And when the bargain was struck, the owner would step into the pen, hunt down the victim, and, catching it up by one leather ear and its thin bootlace of a tail, carry it off amid grunts that ended in the piercing, long-drawn harmonics of a squeal to a netted cart or perhaps to some other pen a little farther down the line. Brought up in England to regard the infliction of discomfort upon an animal as being, if anything, rather more reprehensible than cruelty to my fellow-humans, I remember being horrified by this spectacle. So, too, apparently was the German army of occupation. For between 1914 and 1918 no pig in the Longres market might be lifted by tail or ear, the penalty for disobedience being a fine of twenty marks for the first offence, a hundred for the second, and after that a term of forced labour on the lines of communication. Of all the oppressive measures of the invader there was hardly one which more profoundly irritated the Limburgian peasantry. Nero was unpopular with the people of Rome, not because of his crimes and vices, not because he was a tyrant and a murderer, but for having built in the middle of the city a palace so large that it blocked the entrance to several of the main roads. If the Romans hated him, it was because his golden house compelled them to make a circuit of a quarter of a mile every time they wanted to go shopping. The little customary liberties, the right to do in small things what we have always done, are more highly valued than the greater, more abstract, and less immediate freedoms. And, similarly, most people will rather run the risk of catching typhus than take a few irksome sanitary precautions to which they are not accustomed. In this particular case, moreover, there was the further question: How *is* one to carry a pig except by its tail and ears? One must either throw the creature on its back and lift it up by its four cloven feet—a process hardly feasible, since a pig's centre of gravity is so near the ground that it is all but impossible to topple him over. Or else— and this is what the people of Longres found themselves disgustedly compelled to do—one must throw one's arms round the animal and carry it clasped to one's bosom as though it were a baby, at the risk of being bitten in the ear and with the certainty of stinking like a hog for the rest of the day.

The first Saturday after the departure of the German troops was a bad morning for the pigs. To carry a pig by the tail was an outward and visible symbol of recovered liberty; and the squeals of the porkers mingled with the cheers of the population and the trills and clashing harmonies of the bells awakened by the carilloneur from their four years' silence.

By ten o'clock the market was over. The railings of the pens had been cleared away, and but for the traces on the cobbles— and those too the municipal scavengers were beginning to sweep up—I could have believed that the scene upon which I had looked from my window in the bright early light had been a scene in some agitated morning dream.

But more dream-like and fantastical was the aspect of the Grand' Place when, every year during the latter part of August, Longres indulged in its traditional kermesse. For then the whole huge square was covered with booths, with merry-go-rounds turning and twinkling in the sun, with swings and switchbacks, with temporary pinnacles rivalling in height with the permanent and secular towers of the town, and from whose summits one slid, whooping uncontrollably with horrified delight, down a polished spiral track to the ground below. There was bunting everywhere, there were sleek balloons and flags, there were gaudily painted signs. Against the grey walls of the church, against the whitewashed house-fronts, against the dark brick-work of the seminary and the soft yellow stucco of the gabled Hôtel de Ville, a sea of many colours beat tumultuously. And an immense and featureless noise that was a mingling of the music of four or five steam organs, of the voices of thousands of people, of the blowing of trumpets and whistles, the clashing of cymbals, the beating of drums, of shouting, of the howling of children, of enormous rustic laughter, filled the space between the houses from brim to brim—a noise so continuous and so amorphous that hearkening from my high window it was almost, after a time, as though there were no noise at all, but a new kind of silence, in which the tinkling of the infant Boccherini's minuet, the patriotic air, and the fragmentary symphonies had become for some obscure reason utterly inaudible.

And after sunset the white flares of acetylene and the red flares of coal-gas scooped out of the heart of the night a little private day, in which the fun went on more noisily than ever. And the gaslight striking up on to the towers mingled half-way up their shafts with the moonlight from above, so that to me at my window the belfries seemed to belong half to the earth, half to the pale silence overhead. But gradually, as the night wore on, earth abandoned its claims; the noise diminished; one after another the flares were put out, till at last the moon was left in absolute possession, with only a few dim greenish gas-lamps here and there, making no attempt to dispute her authority. The towers were hers down to the roots, the booths and the hooded roundabouts, the Russian mountains, the swings—all wore the moon's livery of silver and black; and audible once more the bells seemed in her honour to sound a sweeter, clearer, more melancholy note.

But it was not only from my window that I viewed the ker-messe. From the moment that the roundabouts began to turn,

which was as soon as the eleven o'clock Mass on the last Sunday
but one in August was over, to the moment when they finally
came to rest, which was at about ten or eleven on the night of the
following Sunday, I moved almost unceasingly among the delights of the fair. And what a fair it was! I have never seen its
like in England. Such splendour, such mechanical perfection in
the swings, switchbacks, merry-go-rounds, towers, and the like!
Such astonishing richness and variety in the side-shows! And
withal such marvellous cheapness.

When one was tired of sliding and swinging, of being whirled
and jogged, one could go and see for a penny the man who pulled
out handfuls of his skin, to pin it up with safety-pins into ornamental folds and pleats. Or one could see the woman with no
arms who opened a bottle of champagne with her toes and drank
your health, lifting her glass to her lips with the same members.
And then in another booth, over whose entry there waved—a
concrete symbol of good faith—a pair of enormous female panta-
loons, sat the Fat Woman—so fat that she could (and would, you
were told, for four sous extra), in the words of the Flemish notice
at the door, which I prefer to leave in their original dialectical
obscurity, "heur gezicht bet heur tiekes wassen."

Next to the Fat Woman's hutch was a much larger tent in
which the celebrated Monsieur Figaro, with his wife and seven
children, gave seven or eight times daily a dramatic version of
the Passion of Our Saviour, at which even the priesthood was
authorised to assist. The Figaro family was celebrated from one
end of the country to another, and had been for I do not know
how many years—forty or fifty at least. For there were several
generations of Figaros; and if seven charming and entirely
genuine children did indeed still tread the boards, it was not that
the seven original sons and daughters of old M. Figaro had remained by some miracle perpetually young; but that marrying
and becoming middle-aged they had produced little Figaros of
their own, who in their turn gave rise to more, so that the aged
and original M. Figaro could count among the seven members of
his suppositious family more than one of his great-grandchildren.

So celebrated was M. Figaro that there was even a song about him, of which unfortunately I can remember only two lines:

> "Et le voilà, et le voilà, Fi-ga-ro,
>   Le plus comique de la Belgique, Fi-ga-ro!"

But on what grounds and in what remote epoch of history he had been called "Le plus comique de la Belgique," I was never able to discover. For the only part I ever saw the venerable old gentleman play was that of Caiaphas in the *Passion of Our Saviour*, which was one of the most moving, or at any rate one of the most harrowingly realistic, performances I ever remember to have seen; so much so, that the voices of the actors were often drowned by sobs and sometimes by the piercing screams of a child who thought that they were really and genuinely driving nails into the graceful young Figaro of the third generation, who played the part of the Saviour.

Not a day of my first kermesses passed without my going at least once, and sometimes two or three times, to see the Figaros at their performance; partly, no doubt, because, between the ages of nine and thirteen, I was an extremely devout broad church-man, and partly because the rôle of the Magdalene was played by a little girl of twelve or thereabouts, with whom I fell in love, wildly, extravagantly, as one only can love when one is a child. I would have given fortunes and years of my life to have had the courage to go round to the back after the performance and talk to her. But I did not dare; and to give an intellectual justification for my cowardice, I assured myself that it would have been un-seemly on my part to intrude upon a privacy which I invested with all the sacredness of the Magdalene's public life, an act of sacrilege like going into church with one's hat on. Moreover, I comforted myself, I should have profited little by meeting my inamorata face to face, since in all likelihood she spoke nothing but Flemish, and besides my own language I only spoke at that time a little French, with enough Latin to know what my Uncle Spencer meant when he said, "*Similia similibus curantur.*" My passion for the Magdalene lasted through three kermesses, but waned, or rather suddenly came to an end, when, rushing to the first of the Figaros' performances at the fourth, I saw that the little Magdalene, who was now getting on for sixteen, had become, like so many young girls in their middle teens, plump and moony almost to the point of grossness. And my love after falling to zero in the theatre was turned to positive disgust when I saw her, a couple of mornings later before the performance began, walking about the Grand' Place in a dark blue blouse with a sailor collar, a little blue skirt down to her knees, and a pair of bright yellow boots lacing high up on her full-blown calves, which they compressed so tightly that the exuberant flesh overflowed on to the leather. The next year one of old M. Figaro's great-grandchildren, who could hardly have been more than seven or eight, took her place on the stage. My Magdalene had left it—to get married, no doubt. All the Figaros married early: it was important that there should be no failure in the supply of juvenile apostles and holy women. But by that time I had ceased to take the slightest interest either in her, her family, or their sacred performance; for it was about the time of my fifth kermesse, if I remember rightly, that my period of atheism began —an atheism, however, still combined with all my Uncle Spencer's cheerful optimism about the universe.

My Uncle Spencer, though it would have annoyed him to hear any one say so, enjoyed the kermesse almost as much as I did. In all the year, August was his best month; it contained within its thirty-one days less cause for anxiety, impatience, or irritation than any other month; so that my Uncle Spencer, left in peace by the malignant world, was free to be as high-spirited, as gay and kind-hearted as he possibly could be. And it was astonishing what a stock of these virtues he possessed. If he could have lived on one of those happy islands where nature provides bananas and cocoanuts enough for all and to spare, where the sun shines every day and a little tattooing is all the raiment one needs, where love is easy, commerce unknown, and neither sin nor progress ever heard of—if he could have lived on one of these carefree islands, how entirely happy and how uniformly a saint my Uncle Spencer would have been! But cares and worldly preoccupations too often overlaid his gaiety, stopped up the vents of his kindness; and his quick, nervous, and impulsive temperament—in the Augusts of his life a bubbling source of high spirits—boiled up in a wild impatience, in bilious fountains of irritation, whenever he found himself confronted by the passive malignity of matter, the stupidity or duplicity of man.

He was at his worst during the Christmas holidays; for the season of universal goodwill happened unfortunately to coincide with the season of sugar-making. With the first frosts the beet-roots were taken out of the ground, and every day for three or four months three hundred thousand kilograms of roots went floating down the labyrinth of little canals that led to the wash-ing-machines and the formidable slicers of my Uncle Spencer's factory. From every vent of the huge building issued a sickening smell of boiled beetroot, mingled with the more penetrating stink of the waste products of the manufacture—the vegetable fibre drained of its juice, which was converted on the upper floors of the building into cattle food and in the backyard into manure. The activity during those few months of the beetroot season was feverish, was delirious. A wild orgy of work, day and night, three shifts in the twenty-four hours. And then the factory was shut up, and for the rest of the year it stood there, alone, in the open fields beyond the fringes of the town, desolate as a ruined abbey, lifeless arfd dumb.

During the beetroot season my Uncle Spencer was almost out of his mind. Rimmed with livid circles of fatigue, his eyes glit-tered like the eyes of a madman; his thin face was no more than pale skin stretched over the starting bones. The slightest con-trariety set him cursing and stamping with impatience; it was a torture for him to sit still. One Christmas holidays, I remember, something went wrong with the machinery at the factory, and for nearly five hours the slicers, the churning washers were still. My Uncle Spencer was almost a lost man when he got back to the Grand' Place for dinner that evening. It was as though a demon had possessed him, and had only been cast out as the result of a horrible labour. If the breakdown had lasted another hour, I really believe he would have gone mad.

No, Christmas at Uncle Spencer's was never very cheerful. But by the Easter holidays he was beginning to recover. The frenzied making of sugar had given place to the calmer selling of it. My Uncle Spencer's good nature began to have a chance of reasserting itself. By August, at the end of a long, calm summer, he was perfect; and the kermesse found him at his most exquisitely mellow. But with September a certain premonitory anxiety began to show itself; the machinery had to be overhauled, the state of the labour market examined, and when, about the twentieth of the month, I left again for school, it was a frowning, melancholy, and taciturn Uncle Spencer who travelled with me from Longres to Brussels, from Brussels to Ostend, and who, preoccupied with other thoughts, waved absent-mindedly from the quay, while the steamer slowly slid out through the false calm of the harbour mouth towards a menacing and equinoctial Channel.

But at the kermesse, as I have said, my Uncle Spencer was at his richest and ripest. Enjoying it all as much as I did myself, he would spend long evenings with me, loitering among the attractions of the Grand' Place. He was sad, I think, that the dignity of his position as one of the leading citizens of Longres did not permit him to mount with me on the roundabouts, the swings, and the mountain railways. But a visit to the side-shows was not inconsistent with his gravity; we visited them all. While professing to find the exhibition of freaks and monsters a piece of deplorable bad taste, my Uncle Spencer never failed to take me to look at all of them. It was a cardinal point in his theory of education that the young should be brought as early as possible into contact with what he called the Realities of Life. And as nothing, it was obvious, could be more of a Reality than the armless woman or the man who pinned up his skin with safety-pins, it was important that I should make an early acquaintance with them, in spite of the undoubtedly defective taste of the exhibition. It was in obedience to the same educational principle that

my Uncle Spencer took me, one Easter holidays, to see the
Lunatic Asylum. But the impression made upon me by the huge
prison-like building and its queer occupants—one of whom, I
remember, gambolled playfully around me wherever I went,
patting my cheeks or affectionately pinching my legs—was so
strong and disagreeable, that for several nights I could not sleep;
or if I did, I was oppressed by hideous nightmares that woke me,
screaming and sweating in the dark. My Uncle Spencer had to
renounce his intention of taking me to see the anatomy room in
the hospital.

Scattered among the monsters, the rifle-ranges, and the games
of skill were little booths where one could buy drink and victuals.
There was one vendor, for instance, who always did a roaring
trade by selling, for two sous, as many raw mussels as any one
could eat without coughing. Torn between his belief in the
medicinal qualities of shellfish and his fear of typhoid fever, my
Uncle Spencer hesitated whether he ought to allow me to spend
my penny. In the end he gave his leave. ("It's the phosphorus,
you know.") I put down my copper, took my mussel, bit, swallowed, and violently coughed. The fish were briny as though
they had come out of the Dead Sea. The old vendor did an excellent business. Still, I have seen him sometimes looking anxious;
for not all his customers were as susceptible as I. There were
hardy young peasants who could put down half a pound of this
Dead Sea fruit without turning a hair. In the end, however, the
brine did its work on even the toughest gullet.

More satisfactory as food were the apple fritters, which were
manufactured by thousands in a large temporary wooden struc-
ture that stood under the shade of the Hôtel de Ville. The
Quality, like Uncle Spencer and myself, ate their fritters in the
partial privacy of a number of little cubicles arranged like loose-
boxes along one side of the building. My Uncle Spencer walked
resolutely to our appointed box without looking to the left hand
or to the right; and I was bidden to follow his example and not to
show the least curiosity respecting the occupants of the other
loose-boxes, whose entrances we might pass on the way to our

own. There was a danger, my Uncle Spencer explained to me, that some of the families eating apple fritters in the loose-boxes might be Blacks—Blacks, I mean, politically, not ethnically— while we were Liberals or even, positively, Freemasons. There- fore—but as a mere stranger to Longres I was never, I confess, quite able to understand the force of this conclusion—therefore, though we might talk to male Blacks in a café, have business re- lations and even be on terms of friendship with them, it was im- possible for us to be known by the female Blacks, even under a booth and over the ferial apple fritters; so that we must not look into the loose-boxes for fear that we might see there a dear old friend who would be in the embarrassing situation of not being able to introduce us to his wife and daughters. I accepted, with- out understanding, this law; and it seemed to be a perfectly good law until the day came when I found that it forbade me to make the acquaintance of even a single one of the eleven ravishing daughters of M. Moulle. It seemed to me then a stupid law.

In front of the booths where they sold sweets my Uncle Spencer never cared to linger. It was not that he was stingy; on the contrary, he was extremely generous. Nor that he thought it bad for me to eat sweets; he had a professional belief in the virtues of sugar. The fact was that the display in the booths embarrassed him. For already at the kermesse one began to see a sprinkling of those little objects in chocolate which, between the Feast of St. Nicholas and the New Year, fill the windows of every con- fectioner's shop in Belgium. My Uncle Spencer had passed a third of a lifetime at Longres, but even after all these years he was still quite unable to excuse or understand the innocent coprophily of its inhabitants. The spectacle, in a sweet-shop window, of a little *pot de chambre* made of chocolate brought the blush of em- barrassment to his cheeks. And when at the kermesse I asked him to buy me some barley-sugar or a few *bêtises de Cambrai*, he pretended not to have heard what I asked, but walked hastily on; for his quick eyes had seen, on one of the higher shelves of the confectioner's booth, a long line of little brown pots, on whose equivocal aspect it would have been an agony to him if, standing there and waiting for the barley-sugar to be weighed out, I had naïvely commented. Not that I ever should have commented upon them; for I was as thoroughly English as my Uncle Spencer himself—more thoroughly, indeed, as being a generation further away from the Flemish mother, the admixture of whose blood, however, had availed nothing against my uncle's English upbringing. Me, too, the little brown pots astonished and appalled by their lack of reticence. If my companion had been another schoolboy of my own age, I should have pointed at the nameless things and sniggered. But since I was with my Uncle Spencer, I preserved with regard to them an eloquent and pregnant silence; I pretended not to have seen them, but so guiltily, that my ignoring of them was in itself a comment that filled my poor Uncle Spencer with embarrassment. If we could have talked about them, if only we could have openly deplored them and denounced their makers, it would have been better. But obviously, somehow, we could not.

In the course of years, however, I learned, being young and still malleable, to be less astonished and appalled by the little chocolate pots and the other manifestations of the immemorial Flemish coprophily. In the end I took them almost for granted, like the natives themselves, till finally, when St. Nicholas had filled the shops with these scatological symbols, I could crunch a pot or two between meals as joyously and with as little self-consciousness as any Belgian child. But I had to eat my chocolate, when it was moulded in this particular form, out of my Uncle Spencer's sight. He, poor man, would have been horrified if he had seen me on these occasions.

On these occasions, then, I generally took refuge in the housekeeper's room—and in any case, at this Christmas season, when the sugar was being made, it was better to sit in the cheerful company of Mlle Leeauw than with my gloomy, irritable, demon-ridden Uncle Spencer. Mlle Leeauw was almost from the first one of my firmest and most trusted friends. She was a woman of, I suppose, about thirty-five when I first knew her, rather worn already by a life of active labour, but still preserving a measure

C

of that blonde, decided, and regular beauty which had been hers in girlhood. She was the daughter of a small farmer near Longres, and had received the usual village education, supplemented, however, in recent years by what she had picked up from my Uncle Spencer, who occupied himself every now and then, in his erratic and enthusiastic way, with the improvement of her mind, lent her books from his library, and delivered lectures to her on the subjects that were at the moment nearest to his heart. Mlle Leeauw, unlike most women of her antecedents, felt an insatiable curiosity with regard to all that mysterious and fantastic knowledge which the rich and leisured keep shut up in their libraries; and not only in their books, as she had seen herself (for as a girl had she not served as nursery-maid in the house of that celebrated collector, the Comte de Zuitigny?) not only in their books, but in their pictures too—some of which, Mlle Leeauw assured me, a child could have painted, so badly drawn they were, so unlike life (and yet the count had given heaven only knew how much for them), in their Chinese pots, in the patterns of the very carpets on the floor. Whatever my Uncle Spencer gave her she read with eagerness, she listened attentively to what he said; and there emerged, speck-like in the boundless blank ocean of her ignorance, a few little islands of strange knowledge. One, for example, was called homœopathy; another the Construction-of-Domes (a subject on which my Uncle Spencer was prepared to talk with a copious and perverse erudition for hours at a time; his thesis being that any mason who knew how to turn the vaulted roof of an oven could have built the cupolas of St. Peter's, St. Paul's, and Santa Maria del Fiore, and that therefore the praises lavished on Michelangelo, Wren, and Brunelleschi were entirely undeserved). A third was called Anti-Vivisection. A fourth Swendenborg. . . .

The result of my Uncle Spencer's teaching was to convince Mlle Leeauw that the knowledge of the rich was something even more fantastic than she had supposed—something unreal and utterly remote from life as it is actually lived, artificial and arbitrary, like the social activities of these same rich, who pass their time in one another's houses, eating at one another's expense, and being bored.

This conviction of the complete futility of knowledge did not make her any the less eager to learn what my Uncle Spencer, whom she regarded as a mine and walking compendium of all human learning, could offer her. And she enchanted him by her respectful attentiveness, by the quickness of her understanding— for she was a woman of very great natural intelligence—and her eagerness for every fresh enlightenment. She did not confide to him her real opinion of knowledge, which was that it was a kind of curious irrelevant joke on the margin of life, worth learning for precisely the same reasons as it is worth learning to handle the fork at table—because it is one of the secrets of the rich. Admiring my Uncle Spencer sincerely, she yet took nothing that he taught her seriously, and though, when with him, she believed in millionth-of-a-grain doses and high spiritual potencies, she continued, when she felt out of sorts or I had overeaten, to resort to the old tablespoonful of castor-oil; though with him she was a convinced Swedenborgian, in church she was entirely orthodox; though in his presence she thought vivisection monstrous, she would tell me with gusto of those happy childish days on the farm, when her father cut the pig's throat, her mother held the beast by the hind-legs, her sister danced on the body to make the blood flow, and she held the pail under the spouting artery.

If to my Uncle Spencer his housekeeper appeared as he liked to see her, and not as at ordinary times she really was, it was not that she practised with him a conscious insincerity. Hers was one of those quick, sensitive natures that adapt themselves almost automatically to the social atmosphere in which at the moment they happen to be. Thus with well-bred people she had beautiful manners; but the peasants from whose stock she had sprung found her as full of a hearty Flemish gusto, as grossly and inno- cently coarse as themselves. The core of her being remained solidly peasant; but the upper and conscious part of her mind was, so to speak, only loosely fastened to the foundation, so that it could turn freely this way and that, without strain or difficulty, according to changing circumstances. My Uncle Spencer valued her, not only as a competent, intelligent woman, which she always was in every company, but also because she was, considering her class and origins, so remarkably well-mannered and refined, which, except with him and his likes, she was not.

With me, however, Mlle Leeauw was thoroughly natural and Flemish. With her quick and, I might say, instinctive understanding of character, she saw that my abashed reaction to coprology, being of so much more recent date than that of my Uncle Spencer, was much less strong, less deeply rooted. At the same time, she perceived that I had no great natural taste for grossness, no leaning to what I may call Flemishism; so that in my presence she could be her natural Flemish self and thus correct an absurd acquired delicacy without running the risk of encouraging to any undue or distressing degree a congenital bias in the opposite direction. And I noticed that whenever Matthieu (or Tcheunke, as they called him), her cousin's boy, came into town and paid a call on her, Mlle Leeauw became almost as careful and refined as she was with my Uncle Spencer. Not that Tcheunke shared my uncle's susceptibilities. On the contrary, he took such an immoderate delight in everything that was excrementitious that she judged it best not in any way to indulge him in his taste, just as she judged it best not to indulge my national prejudice in favour of an excessive reticence about these and similar matters. She was right, I believe, in both cases.

Mlle Leeauw had an elder sister, Louise—Louiseke, in the language of Longres, where they put the symbol of the diminutive after almost every name. Louiseke, like her sister, had never married; and considering the ugliness of the woman—for she resembled Mlle Leeauw as a very mischievous caricature resembles its original, that is to say, very closely and at the same time hardly at all, the unlikeness being emphasised in this case by the fact that nature had, for the shaping of certain features, drawn on other ancestral sources, and worse ones, than those from which her sister's face had been made up—considering her ugliness, I repeat, it was not surprising. Though considering her dowry, perhaps it was. Louiseke was by no means rich; but she had the five hundred francs a year, or thereabouts, which her sister also had, after their father died and the farm was sold, together with another two hundred inherited from an old aunt of her mother's. This was a sufficient income to allow her to live without working in a leisure principally occupied by the performance of religious exercises.

On the outskirts of Longres there stands a small béguinage, long since abandoned by its Béguines, who are now all over Belgium a diminishing and nearly extinct community, and inhabited by a colony of ordinary poor folk. The little old gabled houses are built round the sides of a large grassy square, in the centre of which stands an abandoned church. Louiseke inhabited one of these houses, partly because the rent was very low, but also because she liked the religious associations of the place. There, in her peaked high house, looking out across the monastic quadrangle to the church, she could almost believe herself a genuine Béguine. Every morning she went out to hear early Mass, and on Sundays and days of festival she was assiduous in church almost to the point of supererogation.

At my Uncle Spencer's we saw a great deal of her; on her way to church, on her way home again, she never failed to drop in for a word with her sister Antonieke. Sometimes, I remember, she brought with her—hurrying on these occasions across the Grand' Place with the quick, anxious tread, the frightened, suspicious glances to left and right, of a traveller crossing a brigand-haunted moor—a large bag of green baize, full of strange treasures: the silver crown and sceptre of Our Lady, the gilded diadem of the Child, St. Joseph's halo, the jewelled silver book of I forget which Doctor of the Church, St. Dominick's lilies, and a mass of silver hearts with gilded flames coming out of them. Louiseke, whose zeal was noted and approved of by M. le Curé, had the rare privilege of being allowed to polish the jewellery belonging to the images in the church. A few days before each of the important feasts the painted plaster saints were stripped of their finery and the spoil handed over to Louiseke, who, not daring to walk with her precious burden under her arm as far as her own house in the béguinage, slipped across the Grand' Place to my Uncle Spencer's. There, on the table in Antonieke's room, the green baize bag was opened, and the treasures, horribly dirty and tarnished after their weeks or months of neglect, were spread out in the light. A kind of paste was then made out of french chalk mixed with gin, which the two sisters applied to the crowns and hearts with nail-brushes, or if the work was fine and intricate, with an old toothbrush. The silver was then wiped dry with a cloth and polished with a piece of leather.

A feeling of manly pride forbade me to partake in what I felt to be a womanish labour; but I liked to stand by with my hands in my pockets, watching the sisters at work among these regal and sacred symbols, and trying to understand, so far as my limited knowledge of Flemish and my almost equally limited knowledge of life would admit, the gossip which Louiseke poured out incessantly in a tone of monotonous and unvarying censoriousness.

I myself always found Louiseke a little forbidding. She lacked the charm and the quality, which I can only call mellowness, of her sister; to me she seemed harsh, sour-tempered, and rather malevolent. But it is very possible that I judged her unfairly; for, I confess, I could never quite get over her ugliness. It was a sharp, hooky, witch-like type of ugliness, which at that time I found particularly repulsive.

How difficult it is, even with the best will in the world, even for a grown and reasonable man, to judge his fellow-beings without reference to their external appearance! Beauty is a letter of recommendation which it is almost impossible to ignore; and we attribute too often the ugliness of the face to the character. Or, to be more precise, we make no attempt to get beyond the opaque mask of the face to the realities behind it, but run away from the ugly at sight without even trying to find out what they are really like. That feeling of instinctive dislike which ugliness inspires in a grown man, but which he has reason and strength enough of

will to suppress, or at least conceal, is uncontrollable in a child.
At three or four years old a child will run screaming from the
room at the aspect of a certain visitor whose face strikes him as
disagreeable. Why? Because the ugly visitor is "naughty," is a
"bad man." And up to a much later age, though we have succeeded in preventing ourselves from screaming when the ugly
visitor makes his appearance, we do our best—at first, at any
rate, or until his actions have strikingly proved that his face belies
his character—to keep out of his way. So that if I always disliked Louiseke, it may be that she was not to blame, and that my
own peculiar horror of ugliness made me attribute to her unpleasant characteristics which she did not in reality possess. She
seemed to me, then, harsh and sour-tempered; perhaps she wasn't;
but, in any case, I thought so. And that accounts for the fact
that I never got to know her, never tried to know her, as I knew
her sister. Even after the extraordinary event which, a year or
two after my first visit to Longres, was to alter completely the
whole aspect of her life, I still made no effort to understand
Louiseke's character. How much I regret my remissness now!
But, after all, one cannot blame a small boy for failing to have the
same standards as a man. To-day, in retrospect, I find Louiseke's
character and actions in the highest degree curious and worthy
of study. But twenty years ago, when I knew her, her ugliness
at first appalled me, and always, even after I had got over my disgust, surrounded her, for me, with a kind of unbreathable atmosphere, through which I could never summon the active interest
to penetrate. Moreover, the event which now strikes me as so
extraordinary, seemed to me then almost normal and of no particular interest. And since she died before my opinion about it
had had time to change, I can only give a child's impression of
her character and a bald recital of the facts so far as I knew them.

It was, then, at my second or third kermesse that a side-show,
novel not only for me (to whom indeed everything—fat women.
fire-swallowers, elastic men, and down to the merest dwarfs and
giants—was a novelty), but even to the oldest inhabitants of
Longres, who might have been expected to have seen, in their

time, almost everything that the world had ever parturated of marvels, rarities, monsters, and abortions, made its appearance on the Grand' Place. This was a troupe of devil dancers, self-styled Tibetan for the sake of the name's high-sounding and mysterious ring; but actually made up of two expatriated Hindus and a couple of swarthy meridional Frenchmen, who might pass at a pinch as the Aryan compatriots of these dark Dravidians. Not that it mattered much what the nationality or colour of the dancers might be; for on the stage they wore enormous masks—huge false heads, grinning, horned, and diabolic, which, it was claimed in the announcement, were those in which the ritual dances were performed before the Dalai Lama in the principal convent of Lhassa. Comparing my memories of them with such knowledge of oriental art as I now possess, I imagine that they came in reality from the shop of some theatrical property maker in Marseilles, from which place the devil dancers had originally started. But they were none the less startling and blood-curdling for that; just as the dances themselves were none the less salaciously symbolical, none the less typically and conventionally "oriental" for having been in great measure invented by the Frenchmen, who provided all the plot and dramatic substance of the ballets, while the astonished and admiring Indians contributed only a few recollections of Siva worship and the cult of the beneficent *linga*. This co-operation between East and West was what ensured the performance its success; the western substance satisfied by its perfect familiarity, while the eastern detail gave to the old situations a specious air of novelty and almost a new significance.

Charmed by the prospect of seeing what he supposed would be a few characteristic specimens of the religious rites of the mysterious East, and ambitious to improve my education by initiating me into the secrets of this Reality, my Uncle Spencer took me to see the dancers. But the dramatic pantomime of the Frenchmen represented a brand of Reality that my uncle did not at all approve of. He got up abruptly in the middle of the first dance, saying that he thought the circus would be more amusing;

which, for me, it certainly was. For I was not of an age to appreciate either the plastic beauty or the peculiar moral significance of the devil dancers' performance.

"Hinduism," said my Uncle Spencer, as we threaded our way between the booths and the whirling machines, "has sadly degenerated from its original Brahmanistic purity." And he began to expound to me, raising his voice to make itself heard through the noise of the steam organs, the principles of Brahmanism. My Uncle Spencer had a great weakness for oriental religions.

"Well," asked Mlle Leeauw, when we got back for dinner, "and how did you enjoy the dancers?"

I told her that my Uncle Spencer had thought that I should find the circus more amusing. Antonieke nodded with a significant air of understanding. "Poor man," she said, and she went on to wonder how Louiseke, who was going to see the dancers that evening, would enjoy the show.

I never knew precisely what happened; for a mystery and, as it were, a zone of silence surrounded the event, and my curiosity about everything to do with Louiseke was too feeble to carry me through it. All I know is that, two or three days later, near the end of the kermesse, young Albert Snyders, the lawyer's son, came up to me in the street and asked, with the gleeful expression of one who says something which he is sure his interlocutor will find disagreeable: "Well, and what do you think of your Louiseke and her carryings on with the black man?"

I answered truthfully that I had heard nothing about any such thing, and that in any case Louiseke wasn't our Louiseke, and that I didn't care in the least what she did or what might happen to her.

"Not heard about it?" said young Snyders incredulously. "But the black man goes to her house every evening, and she gives him gin, and they sing together, and people see their shadows dancing on the curtains. Everybody's talking about it."

I am afraid that I disappointed young Snyders. He had hoped to get a rise out of me, and he miserably failed. His errors were two: first, to have supposed that I regarded Louiseke as our

Louiseke, merely because her sister happened to be my Uncle Spencer's housekeeper; and, secondly, to have attributed to me a knowledge of the world sufficient to allow me to realise the scandalousness of Louiseke's conduct. Whereas I disliked Louiseke, took no interest in her actions, and could, moreover, see nothing out of the ordinary in what she was supposed to have done.

Confronted by my unshakable calm, young Snyders retired, rather crestfallen. But he revenged himself before he went by telling me that I must be very stupid and, what I found more insulting, a great baby not to understand.

Antonieke, to whom I repeated young Snyders's words, merely said that the boy ought to be whipped, specifying with a wealth of precise detail and a gusto that were entirely Flemish how, with what instrument, and where the punishment ought to be applied. I thought no more about the incident. But I noticed after the kermesse was over and the Grand' Place had become once more the silent and empty Grand' Place of ordinary days, I noticed loitering aimlessly about the streets a stout, coffee-coloured man, whom the children of Longres, like those three rude boys in *Struwwelpeter*, pursued at a distance, contorting themselves with mirth. That year I went back to England earlier than usual; for I had been invited to spend the last three weeks of my holidays with a school friend (alas, at Hastings, so that my knowledge of the earth's surface was not materially widened by the visit). When I returned to Longres for the Christmas holidays I found that Louiseke was no longer mere Louiseke, but the bride of a coffee-coloured husband. Madame Alphonse they called her; for nobody could bother with the devil dancer's real name: it had an Al- in it somewhere—that was all that was known. Monsieur and Madame Alphonse. But the news when I heard it did not particularly impress me.

And even if I had been curious to know more, dense silence continued to envelop the episode. Antonieke never spoke to me of it; and lacking all interest in this kind of Reality, disapproving of it even, my Uncle Spencer seemed to take it silently for granted. That the subject was copiously discussed by the gossips of Longres I do not doubt; and remembering Louiseke's own censorious anecdotage, I can imagine how. But in my hearing it was never discussed; expressly, I imagine—for I lived under the protection of Antonieke, and people were afraid of Antonieke. So it came about that the story remained for me no more remarkable than that story recorded by Edward Lear of the

> ". . . old Man of Jamaica
> Who casually married a Quaker;
> But she cried out, 'Alack,
> I have married a black!'
> Which distressed that old Man of Jamaica."

And perhaps, after all, that is the best way of regarding such incidents—unquestioningly, without inquisitiveness. For we are all much too curious about the affairs of our neighbours. Particularly about the affairs of an erotic nature. What an itch we have to know whether Mr. Smith makes love to his secretary, whether his wife consoles herself, whether a certain Cabinet Minister is really the satyr he is rumoured to be. And meanwhile the most incredible miracles are happening all round us: stones, when we lift them and let them go, fall to the ground; the sun shines; bees visit the flowers; seeds grow into plants, a cell in nine months multiplies its weight a few thousands of thousands of time, and is a child; and men think, creating the world they live in. These things leave us almost perfectly indifferent.

But concerning the ways in which different individuals satisfy the cravings of one particular instinct we have, in spite of the frightful monotony of the situation, in spite of the one well-known, inevitable consummation, an endless and ever-fresh curiosity. Some day, perhaps, we may become a little tired of books whose theme is always this particular instinct. Some day, it may be, the successful novelist will write about man's relation to God, to nature, to his own thoughts and the obscure reality on which they work, not about man's relation with woman. Meanwhile, however . . .

By what stages the old maid passed from her devoutness and

her censorious condemnation of love to her passion for the Dravidian, I can only guess. Most likely there were no stages at all, but the conversion was sudden and fulgurating, like that upon the road to Damascus—and like that, secretly and unconsciously prepared for, long before the event. It was the sheer wildness, no doubt, the triumphant bestiality and paganism of the dances that bowled her over, that irresistibly broke down the repressive barriers behind which, all too human, Louiseke's nature had so long chafed. As to Alphonse himself, there could be no question about his motives. Devil dancing, he had found, was an exhausting, precarious, and not very profitable profession. He was growing stout, his heart was not so strong as it had been, he was beginning to feel himself middle-aged. Louiseke and her little income came as a providence. What did her face matter? He did not hesitate.

Monsieur and Madame Alphonse took a little shop in the Rue Neuve. Before he left India and turned devil dancer, Alphonse had been a cobbler in Madras—and as such was capable of contaminating a Brahman at a distance of twenty-four feet; now, having become an eater of beef and an outcast, he was morally infectious at no less than sixty-four feet. But in Longres, luckily, there were no Brahmans.

He was a large, fat, snub-faced, and shiny man, constantly smiling, with a smile that reminded me of a distended accordion. Many a pair of boots I took to him to be soled—for Antonieke, though she was horrified at having what she called a negro for her brother-in-law, though she had quarrelled with her sister about her insane and monstrous folly, and would hardly be reconciled to her, Antonieke insisted that all our custom should go to the new cobbler. That, as she explained, "owed itself." The duty of another's affairs overrode, in her estimation, the mere personal quarrels that might arise between them.

My Uncle Spencer was a frequent caller at the cobbler's shop, where he would sit for hours, while M. Alphonse tapped away at his last, listening to mythological anecdotes out of the "Ramayana" or "Mahabharata," and discussing the Brahmanistic philosophy, of which, of course, he knew far more than a poor Sudra like Alphonse. My Uncle Spencer would come back from these visits in the best of humours.

"A most interesting man, your brother-in-law," he would say to Antonieke. "We had a long talk about Siva this afternoon. Most interesting!"

But Antonieke only shrugged her shoulders. "*Mais c'est un nègre*," she muttered. And my Uncle Spencer might assure her as much as he liked that Dravidians were not negroes and that Alphonse very likely had good Aryan blood in his veins. It was useless. Antonieke would not be persuaded, would not even listen. It was all very well for the rich to believe things like that, but a negro, after all, was a negro; and that was all about it.

M. Alphonse was a man of many accomplishments; for besides all the rest, he was an expert palmist and told fortunes from the hand with a gravity, a magisterial certainty, that were almost enough in themselves to make what he said come true. This magian and typically oriental accomplishment was learnt on the road between Marseilles and Longres from a charlatan in the travelling company of amusement makers with whom he had come. But he did the trick in the grand prophetic style, so that people credited his cheiromancy with all the magical authority of the mysterious East. But M. Alphonse could not be persuaded to prophesy for every comer. It was noticed that he selected his subjects almost exclusively from among his female customers, as though he were only interested in the fates of women. I could hint as much as I liked that I should like to have my fortune told, I could ask him outright to look at my hand; but in vain. On these occasions he was always too busy to look, or was not feeling in the prophetic mood. But if a young woman should now come into the shop, time immediately created itself, the prophetic mood came back. And without waiting for her to ask him, he would seize her hand, pore over it, pat and prod the palm with his thick brown fingers, every now and then turning up towards his subject those dark eyes, made the darker and more expressive by the brilliance of the bluish whites in which they were set, and expanding his accordion smile. And he would prophesy love—a great deal of it—love with superb dark men, and rows of children; benevolent dark strangers and blond villains; unexpected fortunes, long life—all, in fact, that the heart could desire. And all the time he squeezed and patted the hand—white between his dark Dravidian paws—from which he read these secrets; he rolled his eyes within their shiny blue enamel setting, and across all the breadth of his fat cheeks the accordion of his smile opened and shut.

My pride and my young sense of justice were horribly offended on these occasions. The inconsistency of a man who had no time to tell my fortune, but an infinite leisure for others, seemed to me abstractly reprehensible and personally insulting. I professed, even at that age, not to believe in palmistry; that is to say, I found the fortunes which M. Alphonse prophesied for others absurd. But my interest in my own personality and my own fate was so enormous that it seemed to me, somehow, that everything said about me must have a certain significance. And if M. Alphonse had taken my hand, looked at it, and said, "You are generous; your head is as large as your heart; you will have a severe illness at thirty-eight, but your life after that will be healthy into extreme old age; you will make a large fortune early in your career, but you must beware of fair-haired strangers with blue eyes," I should have made an exception and decided for the nonce that there must be something in it. But, alas, M. Alphonse never did take my hand; he never told me anything. I felt most cruelly offended, and I felt astonished too. For it seemed to me a most extraordinary thing that a subject which was so obviously fascinating and so important as my character and future should not interest M. Alphonse as much as it did me. That he should prefer to dabble in the dull fates and silly insignificant characters of a lot of stupid young women seemed to me incredible and outrageous.

There was another who, it seemed, shared my opinion. That was Louiseke. If ever she came into the shop from the little back sitting-room—and she was perpetually popping out through the dark doorway like a cuckoo on the stroke of noon from its clock —and found her husband telling the fortune of a female customer, her witch-like face would take on an expression more than ordinarily malevolent.

"Alphonse!" she would say significantly.

And Alphonse dropped his subject's hand, looked round towards the door, and, rolling his enamelled eyes, creasing his fat cheeks in a charming smile, flashing his ivory teeth, would say something amiable.

But Louiseke did not cease to frown. "If you must tell somebody's fortune," she said, when the customer had left the shop, "why don't you tell the little gentleman's?" pointing to me. "I'm sure he would be only too delighted."

But instead of being grateful to Louiseke, instead of saying, "Oh, of course I'd like it," and holding out my hand, I always perversely shook my head. "No, no," I said. "I don't want to worry M. Alphonse." But I longed for Alphonse to insist on telling me about my exquisite and marvellous self. In my pride, I did not like to owe my happiness to Louiseke, I did not want to feel that I was taking advantage of her irritation and Alphonse's desire to mollify her. And besides pride, I was actuated by that strange nameless perversity, which so often makes us insist on doing what we do not want to do—such as making love to a woman we do not like and whose intimacy, we know, will bring us nothing but vexation—or makes us stubbornly decline to do what we have been passionately desiring, merely because the opportunity of doing what we wanted has not presented itself in exactly the way we anticipated, or because the person who offered to fulfil our desires has not been sufficiently insistent with his offers. Alphonse, on these occasions, having no curiosity about my future and taking no pleasure in kneading my small and dirty hand, always took my refusals quite literally and finally, and began to work again with a redoubled ardour. And I would leave the shop, vexed with myself for having let slip the opportunity when it was within my grasp; furious with Louiseke for having presented it in such a way that the seizing of it would be humiliating, and with Alphonse for his obtuseness in failing to observe how much I desired that he should look at my hand, and his gross discourtesy for not insisting even in the teeth of my refusal.

Years passed; my holidays and the seasons succeeded one another with regularity. Summer and the green poplars and my Uncle Spencer's amiability gave place to the cold season of sugar-making, to scatological symbols in chocolate, to early darkness and the moral gloom of my Uncle Spencer's annual neurasthenia. And half-way between the two extremes came the Easter holidays, pale green and hopefully burgeoning, tepid with temperate warmth and a moderate amiability. There were terms, too, as well as holidays. Eastbourne knew me no more; my knowledge of the globe expanded; I became a public schoolboy.

At fifteen, I remember, I entered upon a period of priggishness which made me solemn beyond my years. There are many boys who do not know how young they are till they have come of age, and a young man is often much less on his dignity than a growing schoolboy, who is afraid of being despised for his callowness. It was during this period that I wrote from Longres a letter to one of my school friends, which he fortunately preserved, so that we were able to re-read it, years later, and to laugh and marvel at those grave, academic old gentlemen we were in our youth. He had written me a letter describing his sister's marriage, to which I replied in these terms:

"How rapidly, my dear Henry, the saffron robe and Hymen's torches give place to the nænia, the funeral urn, and the cypress! While your days have been passed among the jocundities of a marriage feast, mine have been darkened by the circumambient horrors of death. Such, indeed, is life."

And I underlined the philosophic reflection.

The horrors of death made more show in my sonorous anti-theses than they did in my life. For though the event made a certain impression upon me—for it was the first thing of the kind that had happened within my own personal orbit—I cannot pretend that I was very seriously moved when Louiseke died, too old to have attempted the experiment, in giving birth to a half-Flemish, half-Dravidian daughter, who died with her. My Uncle Spencer, anxious to introduce me to the Realities of Life, took me to see the corpse. Death had a little tempered Louiseke's ugliness. In the presence of that absolute repose I suddenly felt ashamed of having always disliked Louiseke so much. I wanted to be able to explain to her that, if only I had known she was going to die, I would have been nicer to her, I would have tried to like her more. And all at once I found myself crying.

Downstairs in the back parlour M. Alphonse was crying too, noisily, lamentably, as was his duty. Three days later, when his duty had been sufficiently done and the conventions satisfied, he became all at once exceedingly philosophic about his loss. Louiseke's little income was now his; and adding to it what he made by his cobbling, he could live in almost princely style. A week or two after the funeral the kermesse began. His old companions, who had danced several times backwards and forwards across the face of Europe since they were last in Longres, reappeared unexpectedly on the Grand' Place. Alphonse treated himself to the pleasure of playing the generous host, and every evening when their show was over the devils unhorned themselves, and over the glasses in the little back parlour behind Alphonse's shop they talked convivially of old times, and congratulated their companion, a little enviously, on his prodigious good fortune.

In the years immediately preceding the war I was not often in Longres. My parents had come back from India; my holidays were passed with them. And when holidays transformed themselves into university vacations and I was old enough to look after myself, I spent most of my leisure in travelling in France, Italy, or Germany, and it was only rarely and fleetingly—on the way to Milan, on my way back from Cologne, or after a fortnight among the Dutch picture galleries—that I now revisited the house on the Grand' Place, where I had passed so many, and on the whole such happy, days. I liked my Uncle Spencer still, but he had ceased to be an admired being, and his opinions, instead of rooting themselves and proliferating within my mind, as once they did, seemed mostly, in the light of my own knowledge and experience, too fantastic even to be worth refuting. I listened to him now with all the young man's intolerance of the opinions of the old (and my Uncle Spencer, though only fifty, seemed to me utterly fossilised and antediluvian), acquiescing in all that he said with a smile in which a more suspicious and less single-hearted man would have seen the amused contempt. My Uncle Spencer was leaning during these years more and more towards the occult sciences. He talked less of the construction of domes and more of Hahnemann's mystic high potentials, more of Swedenborg, more of Brahmanistic philosophy, in which he had by this time thoroughly indoctrinated M. Alphonse; and he was enthusiastic now about a new topic—the calculating horses of Elberfeld, which, at that time, were making a great noise in the world by their startling ability to extract cube roots in their heads. Strong in the materialistic philosophy, the careless and unreflecting scepticism which were, in those days, the orthodoxy of every young man who thought himself intelligent, I found my Uncle Spencer's mystical and religious preoccupations marvellously ludicrous. I should think them less ridiculous now, when it is the easy creed of my boyhood that has come to look rather queer. Now it is possible—it is, indeed, almost necessary—for a man of science to be also a mystic. But there were excuses then for supposing that one could only combine mysticism with the faulty knowledge and the fantastic mental eccentricity of an Uncle Spencer. One lives and learns.

With Mlle Leeauw, on these later visits, I felt, I must confess, not entirely at my ease. Antonieke saw me as essentially the same little boy who had come so regularly all those years, holiday after holiday, to Longres. Her talk with me was always of the joyous events of the past—of which she had that extraordinarily accurate and detailed memory which men and women, whose minds are not exercised by intellectual preoccupations and who do not read much, always astonish their more studious fellows by possessing. Plunged as I then was in all the newly-discovered delights of history, philosophy, and art, I was too busy to take more than a very feeble interest in my childish past. Had there been skating on the canals in 1905? Had I been bitten by a horse-fly, the summer before, so poisonously that my cheek swelled up like a balloon and I had to go to bed? Possibly, possibly; now that I was reminded of these things I did, dimly, remember. But of what earthly interest were facts such as these when I had Plato, the novels of Dostoievsky, the frescoes of Michelangelo to think of? How entirely irrelevant they were to, shall we say, David Hume! How insipid compared with the sayings of Zara-thustra, the Coriolan overture, the poetry of Arthur Rimbaud! But for poor Antonieke they were all her life. I felt all the time that I was not being as sympathetic with her as I ought to have been. But was it my fault? Could I rebecome what I had been, or make her suddenly different from what she was?

At the beginning of August 1914 I was staying at Longres on my way to the Ardennes, where I meant to settle down quietly for a month or so with two or three friends, to do a little solid reading before going south to Italy in September. Strong in the faith of the German professor who had proved, by the theories of ballistics and probabilities, that war was now out of the question, my Uncle Spencer paid no attention to the premonitory rumbles. It was just another little Agadir crisis and would lead to nothing. I too—absorbed, I remember, in the reading of William James's *Varieties of Religious Experience*—paid no attention; I did not even look at the papers. At that time, still, my Uncle Spencer's convictions about the impossibility of war were also mine; I had had no experience to make me believe them unfounded, and, besides, they fitted in very well with my hopes, my aspirations, my political creed—for at that time I was an ardent syndicalist and internationalist.

And then, suddenly, it was all on top of us.

My Uncle Spencer, however, remained perfectly optimistic.

After a week of fighting, he prophesied, the German professor would be proved right and they would have to stop. My own feeling, I remember, was one of a rather childish exhilaration; my excitement was much more powerful than my shock of horror. I felt rather as I had felt on the eve of the kermesse when, looking from my window, I gazed down at the mountebanks setting up their booths and engines in the square below. Something was really going to happen. That childish sense of excitement is, I suppose, the prevailing emotion at the beginning of a war. An intoxicating Bank Holiday air seems to blow through the streets. War is always popular, at the beginning.

I did not return immediately to England, but lingered for a few days at Longres, in the vague hope that I might "see something," or that perhaps my Uncle Spencer might really—as I still believed—be right, and that, perhaps, the whole thing would be over in a few days. My hope that I should "see something" was fulfilled. But the something was not one of those brilliant and romantic spectacles I had imagined. It consisted of a few little troops of refugees from the villages round Liége—unshaven men, and haggard women with long tear-marks on their dusty cheeks, and little boys and girls tottering along as though in their sleep, dumb and stupid with fatigue. My Uncle Spencer took a family of them into his house. "In a few days," he said, "when everything's over, they'll be able to go home again." And when indignantly Antonieke repeated to him their stories of burnings and shootings, he wouldn't believe them.

"After all," he said, "this is the twentieth century. These things don't happen nowadays. These poor people are too tired and frightened to know exactly what they are saying."

In the second week of August I went back to England. My Uncle Spencer was quite indignant when I suggested that he should come back with me. To begin with, he said, it would all be over so very soon. In the second place, this was the twentieth century—which was what the Cretans said, no doubt, when in 1500 B.C., after two thousand years of peace, prosperity, and progressive civilisation, they were threatened by the wild men from the north. In the third place, he must stay at Longres to look after his interests. I did not press him any further; it would have been useless.

"Good-bye, dear boy," he said, and there was an unaccustomed note of emotion in his voice, "good-bye."

The train slowly moved away. Looking out of the window, I could see him standing on the platform, waving his hat. His hair was white all over now, but his face was as young, his eyes as darkly bright, his small spare body as straight and agile as when I had known him first.

"Good-bye, good-bye."

I was not to see him again for nearly five years.

Louvain was burnt on the 19th of August. The Germans entered Brussels on the 20th. Longres, though farther east than Louvain, was not occupied till two or three days later—for the town lay off the direct route to Brussels and the interior. One of the first acts of the German commandant was to put my Uncle Spencer and M. Alphonse under arrest. It was not that they had done anything; it was merely to their existence that he objected. The fact that they were British subjects was in itself extremely incriminating.

"Aber wir sind," my Uncle Spencer protested in his rather rudimentary German, "im zwanzigsten jahrhunderd. Und der— or is it das?—krieg wird nicht lang . . . " he stammered, searched hopelessly for the word, "well, in any case," he concluded, relapsing into his own language and happy to be able to express his astonished protest with fluency, "it won't last a week."

"So we hope," the commandant replied in excellent English, smiling. "But meanwhile I regret . . ."

My Uncle Spencer and his fellow-Briton were locked up for the time being in the lunatic asylum. A few days later they were sent under escort to Brussels. Alphonse, my Uncle Spencer told me afterwards, bore his misfortune with exemplary and oriental patience. Mute, uncomplaining, obedient, he stayed where his captors put him, like a large brown bundle left by the traveller on the platform, while he goes to the buffet for a drink and a sandwich. And more docile than a mere bundle, mutely, obediently, he followed wherever he was led.

"I wish I could have imitated him," said my Uncle Spencer. "But I couldn't. My blood fairly boiled."

And from what I remembered of him in the sugar-making season I could imagine the depth, the fury of my Uncle Spencer's impatience and irritation.

"But this is the twentieth century," he kept repeating to the guards. "And I have nothing to do with your beastly war. And where the devil are you taking us? And how much longer are we to wait in this damned station without our lunch?" He spoke as a rich man, accustomed to being able to buy every convenience and consideration. The soldiers, who had the patience of poor men and were well used to being ordered hither and thither, to waiting indefinitely in the place where they were told to wait, could not understand this wild irritation against what they regarded as the natural order of things. My Uncle Spencer first amused them; then, as his impatience grew greater instead of less, he began to annoy them.

In the end, one of his guards lost patience too, and gave him a great kick in the breech to make him hold his tongue. My Uncle Spencer turned round and rushed at the man; but another soldier tripped him up with his rifle, and he tumbled heavily to the ground. Slowly he picked himself up; the soldiers were roaring with laughter. Alphonse, like a brown package, stood where they had put him, motionless, expressionless, his eyes shut.

In the top floor of the Ministry of the Interior the German authorities had established a sort of temporary internment camp. All suspicious persons—dubious foreigners, recalcitrant natives, any one suspected by the invaders of possessing a dangerous influence over his neighbours—were sent to Brussels and shut up in the Ministry of the Interior, to remain there until the authorities should have time to go into their case. It was into this makeshift prison that my Uncle Spencer and his Dravidian compatriot were ushered, one sweltering afternoon towards the end of August. In an ordinary year, my Uncle Spencer reflected, the kermesse at Longres would now be in full swing. The fat woman would be washing her face with her bosom, the Figaros would be re-enacting amid sobs the Passion of Our Saviour, the armless lady would be drinking healths with her toes, the vendor of raw mussels would be listening anxiously for the first hoarse sound that might be taken for a cough. Where were they all this year, all these good people? And where was he himself? Incredulously he looked about him.

In the attics of the Ministry of the Interior the company was strange and mixed. There were Belgian noblemen whom the invaders considered it unsafe to leave in their châteaux among their peasantry. There were a Russian countess and an anarchist, incarcerated on account of their nationality. There was an opera singer, who might be an international spy. There was a little golden-haired male impersonator, who had been appearing at a music-hall in Liége, and whose offence, like that of my Uncle Spencer and the Dravidian, was to have been a British subject. There were a number of miscellaneous Frenchmen and French-women, caught on the wrong side of the border. There was an organ-grinder, who had gone on playing the "Brabançonne" when told to stop, and a whole collection of other Belgians, of all classes and both sexes, from every part of the country, who had committed some crime or other, or perhaps had contrived merely to look suspicious, and who were now waiting to have their fate decided, as soon as the authorities should have time to pay attention to them.

Into this haphazardly assembled society my Uncle Spencer and the Dravidian were now casually dropped. The door closed behind them; they were left, like new arrivals in hell, to make the best of their situation.

The top floor of the Ministry of the Interior was divided up into one very large and a number of small rooms, the latter lined, for the most part, with pigeon-holes and filing cabinets in which were stored the paper products of years of bureaucratic activity.

In the smaller chambers the prisoners had placed the straw mattresses allotted to them by their gaolers; the men slept in the rooms at one end of the corridor, the women in those at the other end. The big room, which must once have housed the staff of the Ministry's registry, still contained a number of desks, tables, and chairs; it served now as the prisoners' drawing-room, dining-room, and recreation ground. There was no bathroom, and only one washing-basin and one *chalet de nécessité*, as my Uncle Spencer, with a characteristic euphemism, always called it. Life in the attics of the Ministry of the Interior was not particularly agreeable.

My Uncle Spencer noticed that those of the prisoners who were not sunk in gloom and a sickening anxiety for the future, preserved an almost too boisterous cheerfulness. You had, it seemed, either to take this sort of thing as a prodigious joke, or brood over it as the most horrible of nightmares. There seemed to be no alternative. In time, no doubt, the two extremes would level down to the same calm resignation. But confinement had still been too short for that; the situation was still too new, dream-like, and phantasmagorical, and fate too uncertain.

The cheerful ones abounded in japes, loud laughter, and practical jokes. They had created in the prison a kind of private-school atmosphere. Those whose confinement was oldest (and some had been in the Ministry for nearly a week now, almost from the day of the German entry into Brussels) assumed the inalienable right of seniors to make the new arrivals feel raw and uncomfortable. Each freshman was subjected to a searching cross-examination, like that which awaits the new boy at his first school. Sometimes, if the latest victim seemed particularly ingenuous, they would play a little practical joke on him.

The leader of the cheerful party was a middle-aged Belgian journalist—a powerful, stout man, with carroty red moustaches and a high crimson complexion, a huge roaring voice and a boundless gift for laughter and genial Rabelaisian conversation. At the appearance of the meek Dravidian he had fairly whooped with delight. So great, indeed, was his interest in Alphonse that my Uncle Spencer escaped with the most perfunctory examination and the minimum of playful "ragging." It was perhaps for the best; my Uncle Spencer was in no mood to be trifled with, even by a fellow-sufferer.

Round poor Alphonse the journalist immediately improvised a farce. Sitting like a judge at one of the desks in the large room, he had the Dravidian brought before him, giving him to understand that he was the German commissary who had to deal with his case. Under cross-examination the Dravidian was made to tell his whole history. Born, Madras; profession, cobbler—a clerk took down all his answers as he delivered them. When he spoke of devil dancing, the judge made him give a specimen of his performance there and then in front of the desk. The question of his marriage with Louiseke was gone into in the most intimate detail. Convinced that his liberty and probably his life depended on his sincerity, Alphonse answered every question as truthfully as he possibly could.

In the end, the journalist, clearing his throat, gravely summed up and gave judgment. Innocent. The prisoner would forthwith be released. On a large sheet of official paper he wrote *laissez passer*, signed it Von der Golz, and, opening a drawer of the desk, selected from among the numerous official seals it contained that with which, in happier times, certain agricultural diplomas were stamped. On the thick red wax appeared the figure of a prize shorthorn cow with, round it, the words: "Pour l'amélioration de la race bovine."

"Here," roared the journalist, handing him the sealed paper. "You may go."

Poor Alphonse took his *laissez passer* and, bowing at intervals almost to the ground, retreated backwards out of the room. Joyously he picked up his hat and his little bundle, ran to the door, knocked and called. The sentry outside opened to see what was the matter. Alphonse produced his passport.

"Aber wass ist das?" asked the sentry.

Alphonse pointed to the seal: for the amelioration of the bovine race; to the signature: Von der Golz. The sentry, thinking that it was he, not the Dravidian, who was the victim of the joke, became annoyed. He pushed Alphonse roughly back through the door; and when, protesting, propitiatively murmuring and smiling, the poor man advanced again to explain to the sentry his mistake, the soldier picked up his rifle and with the butt gave him a prod in the belly, which sent him back, doubled up and coughing, along the corridor. The door slammed to. Vainly, when he had recovered, Alphonse hammered and shouted. It did not open again. My Uncle Spencer found him standing there—knocking, listening, knocking again. The tears were streaming down his cheeks; it was a long time before my Uncle Spencer could make him understand that the whole affair had been nothing but a joke. At last, however, Alphonse permitted himself to be led off to his mattress. In silence he lay down and closed his eyes. In his right hand he still held the passport—firmly, preciously between his thick brown fingers. He would not throw it away; not yet. Perhaps if he went to sleep this incident at the door would prove, when he woke up, to have been a dream. The paper would have ceased to be a joke, and when, to-morrow, he showed it again, who knew? the sentry would present arms and he would walk downstairs; and all the soldiers in the courtyard would salute and he would walk out into the sunny streets, waving the signature, pointing to the thick red seal.

Quite still he lay there. His arm was crossed over his body. From between the fingers of his hand hung the paper. Bold, as only the signature of a conquering general could be, Von der Golz sprawled across the sheet. And in the bottom right-hand corner, stamped in the red wax, the image of the sacred cow was like a symbol of true salvation from across the separating ocean and the centuries. *Pour l'amélioration de la race bovine.* But might it not be more reasonable, in the circumstances, to begin with the human race?

My Uncle Spencer left him to go and expostulate with the journalist on the barbarity of his joke. He found the man sitting on the floor—for there were not enough chairs to go round—teaching the golden-haired male impersonator how to swear in French.

"And this," he was saying, in his loud, jolly voice, "this is

what you must say to Von der Golz if ever you see him." And
he let off a string of abusive words, which the little male impersonator carefully repeated, distorted by her drawling English
intonation, in her clear, shrill voice: "Sarl esspayss de coshaw."
The journalist roared with delighted laughter and slapped his
thighs. "What comes after that?" she asked.

"Excuse me," said my Uncle Spencer, breaking in on the
lesson. He was blushing slightly. He never liked hearing this
sort of language—and in the mouth of a young woman (a compatriot too, it seemed) it sounded doubly distressing. "Excuse
me." And he begged the journalist not to play any more jokes
on Alphonse. "He takes it too much to heart," he explained.

At his description of the Dravidian's despair, the little male
impersonator was touched almost to tears. And the journalist,
who, like all the rest of us, had a heart of gold whenever he was
reminded of its existence—and, like all the rest of us, he needed
pretty frequent reminders; for his own pleasures and interests
prevented him very often from remembering it—the journalist
was extremely sorry at what he had done, declared that he had no
idea that Alphonse would take the little farce so seriously, and
promised for the future to leave him in peace.

The days passed; the nightmare became habitual, followed a
routine. Three times a day the meagre supply of unappetising
food arrived and was consumed. Twice a day an officer with a
little squad of soldiers behind him made a tour of inspection. In
the morning one waited for one's turn to wash; but the afternoons were immense gulfs of hot time, which the prisoners tried
to fill with games, with talk, with the reading of ancient dossiers
from the files, with solitary brooding or with pacing up and
down the corridor—twenty steps each way, up and down, up
and down, till one had covered in one's imagination the distance
between one loved and familiar place and another. Up and down,
up and down. My Uncle Spencer sometimes walked along the
poplar-lined high road between Longres and Waret; sometimes
from Charing Cross along the Strand, under the railway bridge
and up the hill to St. Paul's, and from St. Paul's to the Bank, and

from the Bank tortuously to the Tower of London, the river, and the ships. Sometimes he walked with his brother from Chamonix to the Montanvert; from Grenoble over the pass to the Grande Chartreuse. Sometimes, less strenuously, he walked with his long-dead mother through the glades of Windsor Forest, where the grass is so green in early summer that it seems as though each blade were an emerald illumined from within; and here and there among the oak trees the dark-leaved rhododendrons light their innumerable rosy lamps.

In the evening the cheerful ones, with the journalist at their head, organised entertainments for the amusement of the company. The journalist himself recited poems of his own composition about the Kaiser. One of the Frenchmen did some amateur conjuring with packs of cards, handkerchiefs, and coins. The opera singer bawled out at the top of his prodigious tenor, "La donna è mobile," "O sole mio," and when something more serious was called for, César Franck's "Dieu s'avance à travers la lande"; which last, however, he sang in so richly operatic a style that my Uncle Spencer, who was very fond of this particular song, could hardly recognise it. But the most popular turn was always that of "the celebrated diva, Emmy Wendle," as the journalist called her, when he introduced her to the company. The enthusiasm was tremendous when Emmy Wendle appeared —dressed in an Eton jacket, broad starched collar, striped trousers, and a top hat, and carrying in her hand a little cane—did two or three rattling clog dances and sang a song with the chorus:

> "We are the nuts that get the girls
> Ev-ery time;
> We get the ones with the curly curls,
> We get the peaches, we get the pearls—
> Ev-ery time."

And when, at the end of the turn, she took off her top hat, and, standing rigidly at attention, like a soldier, her childish snubby little face very grave, her blue eyes fixed on visions not of this world, sang in her tuneless street-urchin's voice an astonishingly English version of the "Brabançonne," then there was something more than enthusiasm. For men would suddenly feel the tears coming into their eyes, and women wept outright; and when it was over, everybody violently stamped and clapped and waved handkerchiefs, and laughed, and shouted imprecations against the Germans, and said, "Vive la Belgique!" and ran to Emmy Wendle, and took her hand, or slapped her on the back as though she had really been a boy, or kissed her—but as though she were not a girl, and dressed in rather tight striped trousers at that—kissed her as though she were a symbol of the country, a visible and charming personification of their own patriotism and misfortunes.

When the evening's entertainment was over, the company began to disperse. Stretched on their hard mattresses along the floor, the prisoners uneasily slept or lay awake through the sultry nights, listening to the steps of the sentries in the court below and hearing every now and then through the unnatural silence of the invaded town, the heavy beat, beat, beat of a regiment marching along the deserted street, the rumble and sharp, hoofy clatter of a battery on the move towards some distant front.

The days passed. My Uncle Spencer soon grew accustomed to the strange little hell into which he had been dropped. He knew it by heart. A huge, square room, low-ceilinged and stifling under the hot leads. Men in their shirt-sleeves standing, or sitting, some on chairs, some on the corner of a desk or a table, some on the floor. Some leaned their elbows on the window-sill and looked out, satisfying their eyes with the sight of the trees in the park across the street, breathing a purer air—for the air in the room was stale, twice-breathed, and smelt of sweat, tobacco, and cabbage soup.

From the first the prisoners had divided themselves, automatically almost, into little separate groups. Equal in their misery, they still retained their social distinctions. The organ-grinder and the artisans and peasants always sat together in one corner on the floor, playing games with a greasy pack of cards, smoking and, in spite of expostulations, in spite of sincere efforts to restrain themselves, spitting on the floor all round them.

"Mine!" the organ-grinder would say triumphantly, and plank down his ace of hearts. "Mine!" And profusely, to emphasise his satisfaction, he spat. "Ah, pardon!" Remembering too late, he looked apologetically round the room. "Excuse me." And he would get up, rub the gob of spittle into the floor with his boot, and going to the window would lean out and spit again— not that he felt any need to, having spat only a moment before, but for the sake of showing that he had good manners and could spit out of the window and not on the floor when he thought of it.

Another separate group was that of the aristocracy. There was the little old count with a face like a teapot—such shiny round cheeks, such a thin, irrelevant nose; and the young count with the monocle—the one so exquisitely affable with every one and yet so remote and aloof under all his politeness; the other so arrogant in manner, but, one could see, so wistfully wishing that his social position would permit him to mingle with his spiritual equals. The old count politely laughed whenever the journalist or some other member of the cheerful party made a joke; the young count scowled, till the only smooth surface left in his corrugated face was the monocle. But he longed to be allowed to join in the horse-play and the jokes. With the two counts were associated two or three rich and important citizens, among them during the first days my Uncle Spencer. But other interests were to make him abandon their company almost completely after a while.

On the fringes of their circle hovered occasionally the Russian countess. This lady spent most of the day in her sleeping apartment, lying on her mattress and smoking cigarettes. She had decided views about the respect that was due to her rank, and expected the wash-house to be immediately evacuated whenever she expressed a desire to use it. On being told that she must wait her turn, she flew into a rage. When she was bored with being alone, she would come into the living-room to find somebody to talk to. On one occasion she took my Uncle Spencer aside and told him at great length and with a wealth of intimate detail about the ninth and greatest love affair of her life. In future, whenever my Uncle Spencer caught sight of her turning her large, dark, rather protruding eyes round the room, he took care to be absorbed in conversation with somebody else.

Her compatriot, the anarchist, was a Jewish-looking man with a black beard and a nose like the figure six. He associated himself with none of the little groups, was delighted by the war, which he gleefully prophesied would destroy so-called civilisation, and made a point of being as disagreeable as he could to every one— particularly to the countess, whom he was able to insult confidentially in Russian. It was in obedience to the same democratic principles that he possessed himself of the only arm-chair in the prison—it must have been the throne of at least a *sous chef de division*—refusing to part with it even for a lady or an invalid. He sat in it immovably all day, put it between his mattress and the wall at night, and took it with him even into the wash-house and the *chalet de nécessité*.

The cheerful party grouped itself, planet fashion, round the radiant jollity of the journalist. His favourite amusement was hunting through the files for curious dossiers which he could read out, with appropriate comments and improvised emendations to the assembled group. But the most relished of all his jokes was played ritually every morning when he went through the papers of nobility of the whole Belgic aristocracy (discovered, neatly stowed away, in a cupboard in the corridor), selecting from among the noble names a few high-sounding titles which he would carry with him to the chalet of necessity. His disciples included a number of burgesses, French and Belgian; a rather odious and spotty young English bank clerk caught on his foreign holiday; the Russian countess in certain moods; the male impersonator, on and off; and the opera singer.

With this last my Uncle Spencer, who was a great lover of music and even a moderately accomplished pianist, made frequent attempts to talk about his favourite art. But the opera singer, he found, was only interested in music in so far as it affected the tenor voice. He had consequently never heard of Bach or Beethoven. On Leoncavallo, however, on Puccini,

Saint-Saëns, and Gounod he was extremely knowledgeable. He was an imposing personage, with a large, handsome face and the gracious, condescending smile of a great man who does not object to talking even with you. With ladies, as he often gave it to be understood, he had a great success. But his fear of doing anything that might injure his voice was almost as powerful as his lasciviousness and his vanity; he passed his life, like a monk of the Thebaid, in a state of perpetual conflict. Outwardly and professedly a member of the cheerful party, the opera singer was secretly extremely concerned about his future. In private he discussed with my Uncle Spencer the horrors of the situation.

More obviously melancholy was the little grey-haired professor of Latin who spent most of the day walking up and down the corridor like a wolf in a cage, brooding and pining. Poor Alphonse, squatting with his back to the wall near the door, was another sad and solitary figure. Sometimes he looked thoughtfully about him, watching his fellow-prisoners at their various occupations with the air of an inhabitant of eternity watching the incomprehensible antics of those who live in time. Sometimes he would spend whole hours with closed eyes in a state of meditation. When some one spoke to him, he came back to the present as though from an immense distance.

But, for my Uncle Spencer, how remote, gradually, they all became! They receded, they seemed to lose light; and with their fading the figure of Emmy Wendle came closer, grew larger and brighter. From the first moment he set eyes on her, sitting there on the floor, taking her lesson in vituperation from the journalist, my Uncle Spencer had taken particular notice of her. Making his way towards the pair of them, he had been agreeably struck by the childishness and innocence of her appearance—by the little snub nose, the blue eyes, the yellow hair, so stubbornly curly that she had to wear it cut short like a boy's, for there was no oiling down or tying back a long mane of it; even in her private feminine life there was a hint—and it only made her seem the more childish—of male impersonation. And then, coming within earshot, it had been "sarl esspayss de coshaw" and a string besides of less endearing locutions proceeding from these lips. Startling, shocking. But a moment later, when he was telling them how hardly poor Alphonse had taken the joke, she said the most charming things and with such real feeling in her cockney voice, such a genuine expression of sympathy and commiseration on her face, that my Uncle Spencer wondered whether he had heard aright, or if that "sarl coshaw" and all the rest could really have been pronounced by so delicate and sensitive a creature.

The state of agitation in which my Uncle Spencer had lived ever since his arrest, the astonishing and horrible novelty of his situation, had doubtless in some measure predisposed him to falling in love. For it frequently happens that one emotion—providing that it is not so powerful as to make us unconscious of anything but itself—will stimulate us to feel another. Thus danger, if it is not acute enough to cause panic, tends to attach us to those with whom we risk it, the feelings of compassion, sympathy, and even love being stimulated and quickened by apprehension. Grief, in the same way, often brings with it a need of affection and even, though we do not like to admit it to ourselves, even obscurely a kind of desire; so that a passion of sorrow will convert itself by scarcely perceptible degrees, or sometimes suddenly, into a passion of love. My Uncle Spencer's habitual attitude towards women was one of extreme reserve. Once, as a young man, he had been in love and engaged to be married; but the object of his affections had jilted him for somebody else. Since then, partly from a fear of renewing his disappointment, partly out of a kind of romantic fidelity to the unfaithful one, he had avoided women, or at least taken pains not to fall in love any more, living always in a state of perfect celibacy, which would have done credit to the most virtuous of priests. But the agitations of the last few days had disturbed all his habits of life and thought. Apprehension of danger, an indignation that was a very different thing from the recurrent irritability of the sugar-making season, profound bewilderment, and a sense of mental disorientation had left him without his customary defences and in a state of more than ordinary susceptibility; so that when he saw, in the midst of his waking nightmare, that charming childish head, when he heard those gentle words of sympathy for the poor Dravidian, he was strangely moved; and he found himself aware of Emmy Wendle as he had not been aware of any woman since the first unfaithful one of his youth had left him.

Everything conspired to make my Uncle Spencer take an interest in Emmy Wendle—everything, not merely his own emotional state, but the place, the time, the outward circumstances. He might have gone to see her at the music-hall every night for a year; and though he might have enjoyed her turn—and as a matter of fact he would not, for he would have thought it essentially rather vulgar—though he might have found her pretty and charming, it would never have occurred to him to try to make her acquaintance or introduce himself into her history. But here, in this detestable makeshift prison, she took on a new significance, she became the personification of all that was gracious, sweet, sympathetic, of all that was not war. And at the end of her performance (still, it was true, in poorish taste, but more permissible, seeing that it was given for the comfort of the afflicted) how profoundly impressive was her singing of the "Brabançonne"! She had become great with the greatness of the moment, with the grandeur of the emotions to which she was giving utterance in that harsh guttersnipe's voice of hers—singing of exultations, agonies, and man's unconquerable mind. We attribute to the symbol something of the sacredness of the thing or idea symbolised. Two bits of wood set cross-wise are not two ordinary bits of wood, and a divinity has hedged the weakest and worst of kings. Similarly, at any crisis in our lives, the most trivial object, or a person in himself insignificant, may become, for some reason, charged with all the greatness of the moment.

Even the "sarl coshaw" incident had helped to raise my Uncle Spencer's interest in Emmy Wendle. For if she was gentle, innocent, and young, if she personified in her small, bright self all the unhappiness and all the courage of a country, of the whole afflicted world, she was also fallible, feminine, and weak; she was

subject to bad influences, she might be led astray. And the recollection of those gross phrases, candidly, innocently, and openly
uttered (as the most prudish can always utter them when they
happen to be in an unfamiliar language, round whose words
custom has not crystallised that wealth of associations which
give to the native locutions their peculiar and, from age to age,
varying significance), filled my Uncle Spencer with alarm and
with a missionary zeal to rescue so potentially beautiful and even
grand a nature from corruption.

For her part, Emmy Wendle was charmed, at any rate during
the first days of their acquaintance, with my Uncle Spencer. He
was English, to begin with, and spoke her language; he was also
—which the equally English and intelligible bank clerk was not
—a gentleman. More important for Emmy, in her present mood,
he did not attempt to flirt with her. Emmy wanted no admirers,
at the moment. In the present circumstances she felt that it would
have been wrong, uncomely, and rather disreputable to think of
flirtation. She sang the "Brabançonne" with too much religious
ardour for that; the moment was too solemn, too extraordinary.
True, the solemnity of the moment and the ardour of her patriotic
feelings might, if a suitable young man had happened to find
himself with her in the attics of the Ministry of the Interior, have
caused her to fall in love with a fervour having almost the religious quality of her other feelings. But no suitable young man,
unfortunately, presented himself. The bank clerk had spots on
his face and was not a gentleman, the journalist was middle-aged
and too stout. Both tried to flirt with her. But their advances
had, for Emmy, all the impropriety of a flirtation in a sacred
place. With my Uncle Spencer, however, she felt entirely safe.
It was not merely that he had white hair; Emmy had lived long
enough to know that that symbol was no guarantee of decorous
behaviour—on the contrary; but because he was, obviously,
such a gentleman, because of the signs of unworldliness and mild
idealism stamped all over his face.

At first, indeed, it was only to escape from the tiresome and
indecorous attentions of the bank clerk and the journalist that

she addressed herself to Uncle Spencer. But she soon came to like his company for its own sake; she began to take an interest in what he said, she listened seriously to my Uncle Spencer's invariably serious conversation—for he never talked except on profitable and intellectual themes, having no fund of ordinary small talk.

During the first days Emmy treated him with the respectful courtesy which, she felt, was due to a man of his age, position, and character. But later, when he began to follow her with his abject adoration, she became more familiar. Inevitably; for one cannot expect to be treated as old and important by some one at whom one looks with the appealing eyes of a dog. She called him Uncle Spenny and ordered him about, made him carry and fetch as though he were a trained animal. My Uncle Spencer was only too delighted, of course, to obey her. He was charmed by the familiarities she took with him. The period of her pretty teasing familiarity (intermediate between her respectfulness and her later cruelty) was the happiest, so far as my Uncle Spencer was concerned, in their brief connection. He loved and felt himself, if not loved in return, at least playfully tolerated.

Another man would have permitted himself to take liberties in return, to be sportive, gallant, and importunate. But my Uncle Spencer remained gravely and tenderly himself. His only reprisal for "Uncle Spenny" and the rest was to call her by her Christian name instead of "Miss Wendle," as he had always solemnly done before. Yes, Emmy felt herself safe with Uncle Spenny; almost too safe, perhaps.

My Uncle Spencer's conversations were always, as I have said, of a very serious cast. They were even more serious at this time than usual; for the catastrophe, and now his passion, had brought on in his mind a very severe fit of thinking. There was so much that, in the light of the happenings of the last few weeks, needed reconsidering. From the German professor's theory to the problem of good and evil; from the idea of progress (for, after all, was not this the twentieth century?) to the austere theory and the strange new fact of love; from internationalism to God—everything had to be considered afresh. And he considered them out loud with Emmy Wendle. Goodness, for example, was that no more than a relative thing, an affair of social conventions, gauged by merely local and accidental standards? Or was there something absolute, ultimate, and fundamental about the moral idea? And God—could God be absolutely good? And was there such a vast difference between the twentieth and other centuries? Could fact ever rhyme with ideal? All these disturbing questions had to be asked and answered to his own satisfaction once again.

It was characteristic of my Uncle Spencer that he answered them all—even after taking into consideration everything that had happened—on the hopeful side, just as he had done before the catastrophe; and what was more, with a deeper conviction. Before, he had accepted the cheerful idealistic view a little too easily. He had inherited it from the century in which he was born, had sucked it in from the respectable and ever-prospering elders among whom he had been brought up. Circumstances were now making that facile cheerfulness seem rather stupid. But it was precisely because he had to reconsider the objections to optimism, the arguments against hopefulness, not theoretically in the void, but practically and in the midst of personal and universal calamity (the latter very bearable if one is comfortably placed oneself, but real, but disturbing, if one is also suffering a little), that he now became convinced, more hardly but more profoundly, of the truth of what he had believed before, but lightly and, as he now saw, almost accidentally. Events were shortly to disturb this new-found conviction.

Emmy listened to him with rapture. The circumstances, the time, the place, inclined her to the serious and reflective mood. My Uncle Spencer's discourses were just what she needed at this particular moment. Naturally superstitious, she lived at all times under the protection of a small gold lucky pig and a coral cross which had once belonged to her mother. And when luck was bad, she went to church and consulted crystal gazers. That time she broke her leg and had to cancel that wonderful engagement to tour in Australia, she knew it was because she had been neglecting God in all the prosperous months before; she prayed and she promised amendment. When she got better, God sent her an offer from Cohen's Provincial Alhambras Ltd., in token that her repentance was accepted and she was forgiven. And now, though she had seemed to belong to the cheerful party in the attics of the Ministry of the Interior, her thoughts had secretly been very grave. At night, lying awake on her mattress, she wondered in the darkness what was the reason of all this— the war, her bad luck in getting caught by the Germans. Yes, what could the reason be? Why was God angry with her once again?

But of course she knew why. It was all that dreadful, dreadful business last June when she was working at Wimbledon. That young man who had waited for her at the stage door; and would she do him the honour of having supper with him? And she had said yes, though it was all against her rules. Yes: because he had such a beautiful voice, so refined, almost like a very high-class West End actor's voice. "I came to see the marionettes," he told her. "Marionettes never seem to get farther than the suburbs, do they? But I stayed for you."

They drove in a taxi all the way from Wimbledon to Piccadilly. "Some day," she said, pointing to the Pavilion, "you'll see my name there, in big electric letters: EMMY WENDLE." A hundred pounds a week and the real West End. What a dream!

He had such beautiful manners and he looked so handsome when you saw him in the light. They had champagne for supper.

In the darkness, Emmy blushed with retrospective shame. She buried her face in the pillow as though she were trying to hide from some searching glance. No wonder God was angry. In an agony she kissed the coral cross. She pulled at the blue ribbon, at the end of which, between her two small breasts, hung the golden pig; she held the mascot in her hand, tightly, as though hoping to extract from it something of that power for happiness stored mysteriously within it, as the power to attract iron filings is stored within the magnet.

A few feet away the Russian countess heavily breathed. At the stertorous sound Emmy shuddered, remembering the wickedness that slumbered so near her. For if she herself had ceased to be, technically, a good girl, she was—now that her luck had turned—ashamed of it; she knew, from God's anger, that she had done wrong. But the countess, if sleep had not over-taken her, would have gone on boasting all night about her lovers. To middle-class Emmy the countess's frankness, her freedom from the ordinary prejudices, her aristocratic contempt for public opinion, and her assumption—the assumption of almost all idle women and of such idle men as have nothing better to do or think about—that the only end of life is to make love, complicatedly, at leisure and with a great many people, seemed profoundly shocking. It didn't so much matter that she wasn't a good girl—or rather a good ripe widow. What seemed to Emmy so dreadful was that she should talk about it as though not being good were natural, to be taken for granted, and even positively meritorious. No wonder God was angry.

To Emmy my Uncle Spencer—or shall I call him now her Uncle Spenny?—came as a comforter and sustainer in her re-morseful misery. His wandering speculations were not, it was true, always particularly relevant to her own trouble; nor did she always understand what he was talking about. But there was a certain quality in all his discourses, whatever the subject, which she found uplifting and sustaining. Thus my Uncle Spencer quoting Swedenborg to prove that, in spite of all present appear-ances to the contrary, things were probably all right, was the greatest of comforts. There was something about him like a very high-class clergyman—a West End clergyman, so to say. When he talked she felt better and in some sort safer.

He inspired in her so much confidence that one day, while the journalist was playing some noisy joke that kept all the rest of the company occupied, she took him aside into the embrasure of one of the windows and told him all, or nearly all, about the episode on account of which God was now so angry. My Uncle Spencer assured her that God didn't see things in quite the way she imagined; and that if He had decided that there must be a European War, it was not, in all human probability, to provide an excuse for getting Emmy Wendle—however guilty—locked up in the attics of the Ministry of the Interior at Brussels. As for the sin itself, my Uncle Spencer tried to make her believe that it was not quite so grave as she thought. He did not know that she only thought it grave because she was in prison and, naturally, depressed.

" No, no," he said comfortingly, "you mustn't take it to heart like that."

But the knowledge that this exquisite and innocent young creature had once—and if once, why not twice, why not (my Uncle Spencer left to his own midnight thoughts feverishly speculated), why not fifty times?—fallen from virtue distressed him. He had imagined her, it was true, surrounded by bad influences, like the journalist; but between being taught to say "sarl coshaw" and an actual lapse from virtue, there was a considerable difference. It had never occurred to my Uncle Spencer that Emmy could have got beyond the "coshaw" stage. And now he had it from her own lips that she had.

Celibate like a priest, my Uncle Spencer had not enjoyed the priest's vicarious experience in the confessional. He had not read those astonishing handbooks of practical psychology, fruit of the accumulated wisdom of centuries, from which the seminarist learns to understand his penitents, to classify and gauge their sins, and, incidentally—so crude, bald, and uncompromising are the descriptions of human vice that they contain —to loathe the temptations which, when rosily and delicately painted, can seem so damnably alluring. His ignorance of human beings was enormous. In his refinement he had preferred not to know; and circumstances, so far, had wonderfully conspired to spare him knowledge.

Years afterwards, I remember, when we met again, he asked me after a silence, and speaking with an effort, as though overcoming a repugnance, what I really thought about women and all "that sort of thing." It was a subject about which at that time

I happened to feel with the bitterness and mirthful cynicism of one who has been only too amply successful in love with the many in whom he took no interest, and lamentably and persistently unsuccessful with the one being, in whose case success would have been in the least worth while.

"You really think, then," said my Uncle Spencer, when I paused for breath, "that a lot of that sort of thing actually does go on?"

I really did.

He sighed and shut his eyes, as though to conceal their expression from me. He was thinking of Emmy Wendle. How passionately he had hoped that I should prove her, necessarily and *a priori*, virtuous!

There are certain sensitive and idealistic people in whom the discovery that the world is what it is brings on a sudden and violent reaction towards cynicism. From soaring in spheres of ideal purity they rush down into the mud, rub their noses in it, eat it, bathe and wallow. They lacerate their own highest feelings and delight in the pain. They take pleasure in defiling the things which before they thought beautiful and noble; they pore with a disgusted attention over the foul entrails of the things whose smooth and lovely skin was what they had once worshipped.

Swift, surely, was one of these—the greatest of them. His type our islands still produce; and more copiously, perhaps, during the last two or three generations than ever before. For the nineteenth century specialised in that romantic, optimistic idealism which postulates that man is on the whole good and inevitably becoming better. The idealism of the men of the Middle Ages was more sensible; for it insisted, to begin with, that man was mostly and essentially bad, a sinner by instinct and heredity. Their ideals, their religion, were divine and unnatural antidotes to original sin. They saw the worst first and could be astonished by no horror—only by the occasional miracle of sweetness and light. But their descendants of the romantic, optimistic, humanitarian century, in which my Uncle Spencer was born and brought up, vented their idealism otherwise. They began by seeing the best; they insisted that men were naturally good, spiritual, and lovely. A sensitive youth brought up in this genial creed has only to come upon a characteristic specimen of original sin to be astonished, shocked, and disillusioned into despair. Circumstances and temperament had permitted my Uncle Spencer to retain his romantic optimism very much longer than most men.

The tardy recognition of the existence of original sin disturbed my Uncle Spencer's mind. But the effects of it were not immediate. At the moment, while he was in Emmy's pretty and intoxicating presence, and while she was still kind, he could not believe that she too had her share of original sin. And even when he forced himself to do so, her childish ingenuous face was in itself a complete excuse. It was later—and especially when he was separated from her—that the poison began slowly to work, embittering his whole spirit. At present Emmy's confession only served to increase his passion for her. For, to begin with, it made her seem more than ever in need of protection. And next, by painfully satisfying a little of his curiosity about her life, it quickened his desire to know all, to introduce himself completely into her history. And at the same time it provoked a retrospective jealousy, together with an intense present suspiciousness and an agonised anticipation of future dangers. His passion became like a painful disease. He pursued her with an incessant and abject devotion.

Relieved, partly by my Uncle Spencer's spiritual ministrations, partly by the medicating power of time, from her first access of remorse, depression, and self-reproach, Emmy began to recover her normal high spirits. My Uncle Spencer became less necessary to her as a comforter. His incomprehensible speculations began to bore her. Conversely, the jokes of the cheerful ones seemed more funny, while the gallantries of the journalist and the bank clerk appeared less repulsive, because—now that her mood had changed—they struck her as less incongruous and indecorous. She was no longer, spiritually speaking, in church. In church, my Uncle Spencer's undemonstrative and unimportunate devotion had seemed beautifully in place. But now that she was emerging again out of the dim religious into the brightly secular mood, she found it rather ridiculous and, since she did not return the adoration, tiresome.

"If you could just see yourself now, Uncle Spenny," she said to him, "the way you look."

And she drew down the corners of her mouth, then opened her eyes in a fishy, reverential stare. Then the grimace in which my Uncle Spencer was supposed to see his adoration truly mirrored, disintegrated in laughter; the eyes screwed themselves up, a little horizontal wrinkle appeared near the tip of the snub nose, the mouth opened, waves of mirth seemed to ripple out from it across the face, and a shrill peal of laughter mocked him into an attempted smile.

"Do I really look like that?" he asked.

"You really do," Emmy nodded. "Not a very cheerful thing to have staring at one day and night, is it?"

Sometimes—and this to my Uncle Spencer was inexpressibly painful—she would even bring in some third person to share the sport at his expense; she would associate the bank clerk, the opera singer, or the journalist in her mocking laughter. The teasing which, in the first days, had been so light and affectionate, became cruel.

Emmy would have been distressed, no doubt, if she had known how much she hurt him. But he did not complain. All she knew was that my Uncle Spencer was ridiculous. The temptation to say something smart and disagreeable about him was irresistible.

To my Uncle Spencer's company she now preferred that of the journalist, the bank clerk, and the opera singer. With the bank clerk she talked about West End actors and actresses, music-hall artists, and cinema stars. True, he was not much of a gentleman; but on this absorbing subject he was extremely knowledgeable. The singer revealed to her the gorgeous and almost unknown universe of the operatic stage—a world of art so awe-inspiringly high that it was above even the West End. The journalist told her spicy stories of the Brussels stage. My Uncle Spencer would sit at the fringes of the group, listening in silence and across a gulf of separation, while Emmy and the bank clerk agreed that Clarice Mayne was sweet, George Robey a scream, and Florence Smithson a really high-class artist. When asked for his opinion, my Uncle Spencer always had to admit that he had never seen the artist in question. Emmy and the bank clerk would set up a howl of derision; and the opera singer, with biting sarcasm, would ask my Uncle Spencer how a man who professed to be fond of music could have gone through life without even making an attempt to hear Caruso. My Uncle Spencer was too sadly depressed to try to explain.

The days passed. Sometimes a prisoner would be sent for and examined by the German authorities. The little old nobleman like a teapot was released a week after my Uncle Spencer's arrival; and a few days later the haughty and monocled one disappeared. Most of the peasants next vanished. Then the Russian anarchist was sent for, lengthily examined and sent back again, to find that his arm-chair was being occupied by the journalist.

In the fourth week of my Uncle Spencer's imprisonment Alphonse fell ill. The poor man had never recovered from the effects of the practical joke that had been played upon him on the day of his arrival. Melancholy, oppressed by fears, the more awful for being vague and without a definite object (for he could never grasp why and by whom he had been imprisoned; and as to his ultimate fate—no one could persuade him that it was to be anything but the most frightful and lingering of deaths), he sat brooding by himself in a corner. His free pardon, signed Von der Golz and sealed with the image of the Sacred Cow, he still preserved; for though he was now intellectually certain that the paper was valueless, he still hoped faintly in the depths of his being that it might turn out, one day, to be a talisman; and, in any case, the image of the Cow was very comforting. Every now and then he would take the paper out of his pocket, tenderly unfold it and gaze with large sad eyes at the sacred effigy: *Pour l'amélioration de la race bovine*—and tears would well up from under his eyelids, would hang suspended among the lashes and roll at last down his brown cheeks.

They were not so round now, those cheeks, as they had been. The skin sagged, the bright convex high-lights had lost their brilliance. Miserably he pined. My Uncle Spencer did his best to cheer him. Alphonse was grateful, but would take no comfort. He had lost all interest even in women; and when, learning from my Uncle Spencer that the Indian was something of a prophet, Emmy asked him to read her hand, he looked at her listlessly as though she had been a mere male and not a male impersonator, and shook his head.

One morning he complained that he was feeling too ill to get up. His head was hot, he coughed, breathed shortly and with difficulty, felt a pain in his right lung. My Uncle Spencer tried to think what Hahnemann would have prescribed in the circumstances, and came to the conclusion that the thousandth of a grain of aconite was the appropriate remedy. Unhappily, there was not so much as a millionth of a grain of aconite to be found in all the prison. Inquiry produced only a bottle of aspirin tablets and, from the Russian countess, a packet of cocaine snuff. It was thought best to give the Dravidian a dose of each and wait for the doctor.

At his midday visit the inspecting officer was informed of Alphonse's state, and promised to have the doctor sent at once. But it was not, in point of fact, till the next morning that the doctor came. My Uncle Spencer, meanwhile, constituted himself the Dravidian's nurse. The fact that Alphonse was the widower of his housekeeper's sister, and had lived in his city of adoption, made my Uncle Spencer feel somehow responsible for the poor Indian. Moreover, he was glad to have some definite occupation which would allow him to forget, if only partially and for an occasional moment, his unhappy passion.

From the first, Alphonse was certain that he was going to die. To my Uncle Spencer he foretold his impending extinction, not merely with equanimity, but almost with satisfaction. For by dying, he felt, he would be spiting and cheating his enemies, who desired so fiendishly to put an end to him at their own time and in their own horrible fashion. It was in vain that my Uncle Spencer assured him that he would not die, that there was nothing serious the matter with him. Alphonse stuck to his assertion.

"In eight days," he said, "I shall be dead."

And shutting his eyes, he was silent.

The doctor, when he came next day, diagnosed acute lobar pneumonia. Through the oppression of his fever, Alphonse smiled at my Uncle Spencer with a look almost of triumph. That night he was delirious and began to rave in a language my Uncle Spencer could not understand.

My Uncle Spencer listened in the darkness to the Dravidian's incomprehensible chattering; and all at once, with a shudder, with a sense of terror he felt—in the presence of this man of another race, speaking in an unknown tongue words uttered out of obscure depths for no man's hearing and which even his own soul did not hear or understand—he felt unutterably alone. He was imprisoned within himself. He was an island surrounded on every side by wide and bottomless solitudes. And while the Indian chattered away, now softly, persuasively, cajolingly, now with bursts of anger, now loudly laughing, he thought of all the millions and millions of men and women in the world—all alone, all solitary and confined. He thought of friends, incomprehensible to one another and opaque after a lifetime of companionship; he thought of lovers remote in one another's arms. And the hopelessness of his passion revealed itself to him—the hopelessness of every passion, since every passion aims at attaining to what, in the nature of things, is unattainable: the fusion and interpenetration of two lives, two separate histories, two solitary and for ever sundered individualities.

The Indian roared with laughter.

But the unattainableness of a thing was never a reason for ceasing to desire it. On the contrary, it tends to increase and even to create desire. Thus our love for those we know, and our longing to be with them, are often increased by their death. And the impossibility of ever communicating with him again will actually create out of indifference an affection, a respect and esteem for some one whose company in life seemed rather tedious than desirable. So, for the lover, the realisation that what he desires is unattainable, and that every possession will reveal yet vaster tracts of what is unpossessed and unpossessable, is not a deterrent, is not an antidote to his passion; but serves rather to exacerbate his desire, sharpening it to a kind of desperation, and at the same time making the object of his desire seem more than ever precious.

The Indian chattered on, a ghost among the ghosts of his imagination, remote as though he were speaking from another world. And Emmy—was she not as far away, as unattainable? And being remote, she was the more desirable; being mysterious, she was the more lovely. A more brutal and experienced man than my Uncle Spencer would have devoted all his energies to seducing the young woman, knowing that after a time the satisfaction of his physical desire would probably make him cease to take any interest in her soul or her history. But physical possession was the last thing my Uncle Spencer thought of, and his love had taken the form of an immense desire for the impossible union, not of bodies, but of minds and lives. True, what he had so far learned about her mind and history was not particularly encouraging. But for my Uncle Spencer her silliness, love of pleasure, and frivolity were strange and mysterious qualities— for he had known few women in his life and none, before, like Emmy Wendle—rather lovely still in their unfamiliarity, and if recognised as at all bad, excused as being the symptoms of a charming childishness and an unfortunate upbringing. Her solicitude, that first day, about poor Alphonse convinced him that she was fundamentally good-hearted; and if she had proved herself cruel since then towards himself, that was more by mistake and because of surrounding bad influences than from natural malignity. And, then, there was the way in which she sang the "Brabançonne." It was noble, it was moving. To be able to sing like that one must have a fine and beautiful character. In thinking like this, my Uncle Spencer was forgetting that no characteristic is incompatible with any other, that any deadly sin may be found in company with any cardinal virtue, even the apparently contradictory virtue. But unfortunately that is the kind of wisdom which one invariably forgets precisely at the moment when it might be of use to one. One learns it almost in the cradle; at any rate, I remember at my preparatory school reading, in Professor Oman's *Shorter History of England*, of "the heroic though profligate Duke of Ormond," and of a great English king who was none the less, "a stuttering, lolling pedant with a tongue too big for his mouth." But though one knows well enough in theory that a duke can be licentious as well as brave, that majestic wisdom may be combined with pedantry and defective speech, yet in practice one continues to believe that an attractive woman is kind because she is charming, and virtuous because she rejects your first advances; without reflecting that the grace of her manner may thinly conceal an unyielding ruth-lessness and selfishness, while the coyness in face of insistence may be a mere device for still more completely ensnaring the victim. It is only in the presence of unsympathetic persons that we remember that the most odious actions are compatible with the most genuinely noble sentiments, and that a man or woman who does one thing, while professing another, is not necessarily a conscious liar or hypocrite. If only we could steadfastly bear this knowledge in mind when we are with persons whom we find sympathetic!

Desiring Emmy as passionately as he did, my Uncle Spencer would not have had much difficulty in persuading himself—even in spite of her recent cruelty towards him—that the spirit with which he longed to unite his own was on the whole a beautiful and interesting spirit; would indeed have had no difficulty at all, had it not been for that unfortunate confession of hers. This, though it flattered him as a token of her confidence in his discre-tion and wisdom, had sadly disturbed him and was continuing to disturb him more and more. For out of all her history—the history in which it was his longing to make himself entirely at home as though he had actually lived through it with her—this episode was almost the only chapter he knew. Like a thin ray of light her confession had picked it out for him, from the surrounding obscurity. And what an episode! The more my Uncle Spencer reflected on it, the more he found it distressing.

The brutal practical man my Uncle Spencer was not would have taken this incident from the past as being of good augury for his own future prospects. But since he did not desire, consciously at any rate, the sort of success it augured, the knowledge of this incident brought him an unadulterated distress. For however much my Uncle Spencer might insist in his own mind on the guiltiness of external circumstance and of the other party, he could not entirely exonerate Emmy. Nor could he pretend that she had not in some sort, if only physically, taken part in her own lapse. And perhaps she had participated willingly. And even if she had not, the thought that she had been defiled, however reluctantly, by the obscene contact was unspeakably painful to him. And while the Indian raved, and through the long, dark silences during which there was no sound but the unnaturally quick and shallow breathing, and sometimes a moan, and sometimes a dry cough, my Uncle Spencer painfully thought and thought; and his mind oscillated between a conviction of her purity and the fear that perhaps she was utterly corrupt. He saw in his imagination, now her childish face and the rapt expression upon it while she sang the "Brabançonne," now the sweet, solicitous look while she commiserated on poor Alphonse's unhappiness, and then, a moment later, endless embracements, kisses brutal and innumerable. And always he loved her.

Next day the Dravidian's fever was still high. The doctor, when he came, announced that red hepatisation of both lungs was already setting in. It was a grave case which ought to be at the hospital; but he had no authority to have the man sent there. He ordered tepid spongings to reduce the fever.

In the face of the very defective sanitary arrangements of the prison, my Uncle Spencer did his best. He had a crowd of willing assistants; everybody was anxious to do something helpful. Nobody was more anxious than Emmy Wendle. The forced

inaction of prison life, even when it was relieved by the jokes of
the cheerful ones, by theatrical discussions and the facetious
gallantry of the bank clerk and the journalist, was disagreeable
to her. And the prospect of being able to do something, and
particularly (since it was war-time, after all) of doing something
useful and charitable, was welcomed by her with a real satisfaction. She sat by the Dravidian's mattress, talked to him, gave
him what he asked for, did the disagreeable jobs that have to be
done in the sick-room, ordered my Uncle Spencer and the others
about, and seemed completely happy.

For his part, my Uncle Spencer was delighted by what he regarded as a reversion to her true self. There could be no doubt
about it now: Emmy was good, was kind, a ministering angel,
and therefore (in spite of the professor's heroic though profligate
duke), therefore pure, therefore interesting, therefore worthy of
all the love he could give her. He forgot the confession, or at
least he ceased to attach importance to it; he was no longer
haunted by the odious images which too much brooding over it
evoked in his mind. What convinced him, perhaps, better than
everything of her essential goodness, was the fact that she was
once more kind to him. Her young energy, fully occupied in
practical work (which was not, however, sufficiently trying to
overtax the strength or set the nerves on edge), did not have to
vent itself in laughter and mockery, as it had done when she recovered from the mood of melancholy which had depressed it
during the first days of her imprisonment. They were fellow-
workers now.

The Dravidian, meanwhile, grew worse and worse, weaker
and weaker every day. The doctor was positively irritated.

"The man has no business to be so ill as he is," he grumbled.
"He's not old, he isn't an alcoholic or a syphilitic, his constitution
is sound enough. He's just letting himself die. At this rate he'll
never get past the crisis."

At this piece of news Emmy became grave. She had never
seen death at close quarters—a defect in her education which my
Uncle Spencer, if he had had the bringing up of her, would have

remedied. For death was one of those Realities of Life with which, he thought, every one ought to make the earliest possible acquaintance. Love, on the other hand, was not one of the desirable Realities. It never occurred to him to ask himself the reason for this invidious distinction. Indeed, there was no reason; it just was so.

"Tell me, Uncle Spenny," she whispered, when the doctor had gone, "what *does* really happen to people when they die?"

Charmed by this sign of Emmy's renewed interest in serious themes, my Uncle Spencer explained to her what Alphonse at any rate thought would happen to him.

At midday, over the repeated cabbage soup and the horrible boiled meat, the bank clerk, with characteristically tasteless facetiousness, asked, "How's our one little nigger boy?"

Emmy looked at him with disgust and anger. "I think you're perfectly horrible," she said. And, lowering her voice reverently, she went on, "The doctor says he's going to die."

The bank clerk was unabashed. "Oh, he's going to kick the bucket, is he? Poor old blacky!"

Emmy made no answer; there was a general silence. It was as though somebody had started to make an unseemly noise in a church.

Afterwards, in the privacy of the little room, where, among the filing cabinets and the dusty papers, the Dravidian lay contentedly dying, Emmy turned to my Uncle Spencer and said, "You know, Uncle Spenny, I think you're a wonderfully decent sort. I do, really."

My Uncle Spencer was too much overcome to say anything but "Emmy, Emmy," two or three times. He took her hand and, very gently, kissed it.

That afternoon they went on talking about all the things that might conceivably happen after one were dead. Emmy told my Uncle Spencer all that she had thought when she got the telegram—two years ago it was, and she was working in a hall at Glasgow, one of her first engagements, too—saying that her father had suddenly died. He drank too much, her father did;

and he wasn't kind to mother when he wasn't himself. But she had been very fond of him, all the same; and when that telegram came she wondered and wondered. . . .

My Uncle Spencer listened attentively, happy in having this new glimpse of her past; he forgot the other incident, which the beam of her confession had illumined for him.

Late that evening, after having lain for a long time quite still, as though he were asleep, Alphonse suddenly stirred, opened his large black eyes, and began to talk, at first in the incomprehensible language which came from him in delirium, then, when he realised that his listeners did not understand him, more slowly and in his strange pidgin-French.

"I have seen everything just now," he said—"everything."

"But what?" they asked.

"All that is going to happen. I have seen that this war will last a long time—a long time. More than fifty months." And he prophesied enormous calamities.

My Uncle Spencer, who knew for certain that the war couldn't possibly last more than three months, was incredulous. But Emmy, who had no preconceived ideas on war and a strong faith in oracles, stopped him impatiently when he wanted to bring the Dravidian to silence.

"Tell me," she said, "what's going to happen to us." She had very little interest in the fate of civilisation.

"I am going to die," Alphonse began.

My Uncle Spencer made certain deprecating little noises. "No, no," he protested.

The Indian paid no attention to him. "I am going to die," he repeated. "And you," he said to My Uncle Spencer, "you will be let go and then again be put into prison. But not here. Somewhere else. A long way off. For a long time—a very long time. You will be very unhappy." He shook his head. "I cannot help it; even though you have been so good to me. That is what I see. But the man who deceived me"—he meant the journalist—"he will very soon be set free and he will live in freedom, all the time. In such freedom as there will be here. And he who sits in the chair will at last go back to his own country. And he who sings will go free like the man who deceived me. And the small grey man will be sent to another prison in another country. And the fat woman with a red mouth will be sent to another country; but she will not be in prison. I think she will be married there— again." The portraits were recognisably those of the Russian countess and the professor of Latin. "And the man with carbuncles on his face " (this was the bank clerk, no doubt) "will be sent to another prison in another country; and there he will die. And the woman in black who is so sad . . ."

But Emmy could bear to wait no longer. "What about me?" she asked. "Tell me what you see about me."

The Dravidian closed his eyes and was silent for a moment. "You will be set free," he said. "Soon. And some day," he went on, "you will be the wife of this good man." He indicated my Uncle Spencer. "But not yet; not for a long time; till all this strife is at an end. You will have children . . . good fortune. . . ." His words grew fainter; once more he closed his eyes. He sighed as though utterly exhausted. "Beware of fair strangers," he murmured, reverting to the old familiar formula. He said no more.

Emmy and my Uncle Spencer were left looking at one another in silence.

"What do you think, Uncle Spenny?" she whispered at last. "Is it true?"

Two hours later the Indian was dead.

My Uncle Spencer slept that night, or rather did not sleep, in the living-room. The corpse lay alone among the archives. The words of the Indian continued to echo and re-echo in his mind: "Some day you will be the wife of this kind man." Perhaps, he thought, on the verge of death, the spirit already begins to try its wings in the new world. Perhaps already it has begun to know the fringes, as it were, of secrets that are to be revealed to it. To my Uncle Spencer there was nothing repugnant in the idea. There was room in his universe for what are commonly and perhaps wrongly known as miracles. Perhaps the words were a promise, a statement of future fact. Lying on his back, his eyes fixed on the dark blue starry sky beyond the open window, he meditated on that problem of fixed fate and free will, with which the devils in Milton's hell wasted their infernal leisure. And like a refrain the words repeated themselves: "Some day you will be the wife of this good man." The stars moved slowly across the opening of the window. He did not sleep.

In the morning an order came for the release of the journalist and the opera singer. Joyfully they said good-bye to their fellow-prisoners; the door closed behind them. Emmy turned to my Uncle Spencer with a look almost of terror in her eyes; the Indian's prophesies were already beginning to come true. But they said nothing to one another. Two days later the bank clerk left for an internment camp in Germany.

And then, one morning, my Uncle Spencer himself was sent for. The order came quite suddenly; they left him no time to take leave. He was examined by the competent authority, found harmless, and permitted to return to Longres, where, however, he was to live under supervision. They did not even allow him to go back to the prison and say good-bye; a soldier brought his effects from the Ministry; he was put on to the train, with orders to report to the commandant at Longres as soon as he arrived.

Antonieke received her master with tears of joy. But my Uncle Spencer took no pleasure in his recovered freedom. Emmy Wendle was still a prisoner. True, she would soon be set free; but then, he now realised to his horror, she did not know his address. He had been released at such startlingly short notice that he had had no time to arrange with her about the possibilities of future meetings; he had not even seen her on the morning of his liberation.

Two days after his return to Longres, he asked permission from the commandant, to whom he had to report himself every day, whether he might go to Brussels. He was asked why; my Uncle Spencer answered truthfully that it was to visit a friend in the prison from which he himself had just been released. Permission was at once refused.

My Uncle Spencer went to Brussels all the same. The sentry at the door of the prison arrested him as a suspicious person. He was sent back to Longres; the commandant talked to him menacingly. The next week, my Uncle Spencer tried again. It was sheer insanity, he knew; but doing something idiotic was preferable to doing nothing. He was again arrested.

This time they condemned him to internment in a camp in Germany. The Indian's prophecies were being fulfilled with a remarkable accuracy. And the war did last for more than fifty months. And the carbuncular bank clerk, whom he found again in the internment camp, did, in fact, die. . . .

What made him confide in me—me, whom he had known as a child and almost fathered—I do not know. Or perhaps I do know. Perhaps it was because he felt that I should be more competent to advise him on this sort of subject than his brother—my father—or old Mr. Bullinger, the Dante scholar, or any other of his friends. He would have felt ashamed, perhaps, to talk to them about this sort of thing. And he would have felt, too, that perhaps it wouldn't be much good talking to them, and that I, in spite of my youth, or even because of it, might actually be more experienced in these matters than they. Neither my father nor Mr. Bullinger, I imagine, knew very much about male impersonators.

At any rate, whatever the cause, it was to me that he talked about the whole affair, that spring of 1919, when he was staying with us in Sussex, recuperating after those dreary months of confinement. We used to go for long walks together, across the open downs, or between the grey pillars of the beechwoods; and painfully overcoming reluctance after reluctance, proceeding from confidence to more intimate confidence, my Uncle Spencer told me the whole story.

The story involved interminable discussions by the way. For we had to decide, first of all, whether there was any possible scientific explanation of prophecy; whether there was such a thing as an absolute future waiting to be lived through. And at much greater length, even, we had to argue about women— whether they were really "like that" (and into what depths of cynicism my poor Uncle Spencer had learned, during the long, embittered meditations of his prison days and nights, to plunge and wallow!), or whether they were like the angels he had desired them to be.

But more important than to speculate on Emmy's possible character was to discover where she now was. More urgent than to wonder if prophecy could conceivably be reliable, was to take steps to fulfil this particular prophecy. For weeks my Uncle Spencer and I played at detectives.

I have often fancied that we must have looked, when we made our inquiries together, uncommonly like the traditional pair in the stories—my Uncle Spencer, the bright-eyed, cadaverous, sharp-featured genius, the Holmes of the combination; and I, moon-faced and chubby, a very youthful Watson. But, as a matter of fact, it was I, if I may say so without fatuity, who was the real Holmes of the two. My Uncle Spencer was too innocent of the world to know how to set about looking for a vanished mistress; just as he was too innocent of science to know how or where to find out what there was to be discovered on any abstracter subject.

It was I who took him to the British Museum and made him look up all the back numbers of the theatrical papers to see when Emmy had last advertised her desire to be engaged. It was I, the apparent Watson, who thought of the theatrical agencies and the stage doors of all the suburban music-halls. Sleuth-like in aspect, innocent at heart, my Uncle Spencer followed, marvelling at my familiarity with the ways of the strange world.

But I must temper my boasting by the confession that we were always entirely unsuccessful. No agency had heard of Emmy Wendle since 1914. Her card had appeared in no paper. The porters of music-halls remembered her, but only as something antediluvian. "Emmy Wendle? Oh yes, Emmy Wendle . . ." And scratching their heads, they strove by a mental effort to pass from the mere name to the person, like palæontologists reconstructing the whole diplodocus from the singlefossil bone.

Two or three times we were even given addresses. But the

landladies of the lodging-houses where she had stayed did not even remember her; and the old aunt at Ealing, from whom we joyfully hoped so much, had washed her hands of Emmy two or three months before the war began. And the conviction she then had that Emmy was a bad girl was only intensified and confirmed by our impertinent inquiries. No, she knew nothing about Emmy Wendle, now, and didn't want to know. And she'd trouble us to leave respectable people like herself in peace. And, defeated, we climbed back into our taxi, while the inhabitants of the squalid little street peered out at us and our vehicle, as though we had been visitors from another planet, and the metropolitan hackney carriage a fairy chariot.

"Perhaps she's dead," said my Uncle Spencer softly, after a long silence.

"Perhaps," I said brutally, "she's found a husband and retired into private life."

My Uncle Spencer shut his eyes, sighed, and drew his hand across his forehead. What dreadful images filled his mind? He would almost have preferred that she should be dead.

"And yet the Indian," he murmured, " he was always right . . ."

And perhaps he may still be right in this. Who knows?

LITTLE MEXICAN

THE shopkeeper called it, affectionately, a little Mexican; and little, for a Mexican, it may have been. But in this Europe of ours, where space is limited and the scale smaller, the little Mexican was portentous, a giant among hats. It hung there, in the centre of the hatter's window, a huge black aureole, fit for a king among devils. But no devil walked that morning through the streets of Ravenna; only the mildest of literary tourists. Those were the days when very large hats seemed in my eyes very desirable, and it was on my head, all unworthy, that the aureole of darkness was destined to descend. On my head; for at the first sight of the hat, I had run into the shop, tried it on, found the size correct, and bought it, without bargaining, at a foreigner's price. I left the shop with the little Mexican on my head, and my shadow on the pavements of Ravenna was like the shadow of an umbrella pine.

The little Mexican is very old now, and moth-eaten and green. But I still preserve it. Occasionally, for old associations' sake, I even wear it. Dear Mexican! it represents for me a whole epoch of my life. It stands for emancipation and the first year at the university. It symbolises the discovery of how many new things, new ideas, new sensations!—of French literature, of alcohol, of modern painting, of Nietzsche, of love, of metaphysics, of Mallarmé, of syndicalism, and of goodness knows what else. But, above all, I prize it because it reminds me of my first discovery of Italy. It re-evokes for me, my little Mexican, all the thrills and astonishments and virgin raptures of that first Italian tour in the early autumn of 1912. Urbino, Rimini, Ravenna, Ferrara, Modena, Mantua, Verona, Vicenza, Padua, Venice—my first impressions of all these fabulous names lie, like a hatful of jewels, in the crown of the little Mexican. Shall I ever have the heart to throw it away?

And then, of course, there is Tirabassi. Without the little

Mexican I should never have made Tirabassi's acquaintance. He would never have taken me, in my small unemphatic English hat, for a painter. And I should never, in consequence, have seen the frescoes, never have talked with the old Count, never heard of the Colombella. Never. . . . When I think of that, the little Mexican seems to me more than ever precious.

It was, of course, very typical of Tirabassi to suppose, from the size of my hat, that I must be a painter. He had a neat military mind that refused to accept the vague disorder of the world. He was for ever labelling and pigeon-holing and limiting his universe; and when the classified objects broke out of their pigeon-holes and tore the labels from off their necks, Tirabassi was puzzled and annoyed. In any case, it was obvious to him from the first moment he saw me in the restaurant at Padua, that I must be a painter. All painters wear large black hats. I was wearing the little Mexican. Ergo, I was a painter. It was syllogistic, unescapable.

He sent the waiter to ask me whether I would do him the honour of taking coffee with him at his table. For the first moment, I must confess, I was a little alarmed. This dashing young lieutenant of cavalry—what on earth could he want with me? The most absurd fancies filled my mind: I had committed, all unconsciously, some frightful solecism; I had trodden on the toes of the lieutenant's honour, and he was about to challenge me to a duel. The choice of weapons, I rapidly reflected, would be mine. But what—oh, what on earth should I choose? Swords? I had never learnt to fence. Pistols? I had once fired six shots at a bottle, and missed it with every shot. Would there be time to write one or two letters, make some sort of a testament about my personal belongings? From this anguish of mind the waiter, returning a moment later with my fried octopus, delivered me. The Lieutenant Count, he explained in a whisper of confidence, had a villa on the Brenta, not far from Strà. A villa—he spread out his hands in a generous gesture—full of paintings. Full, full, full. And he was anxious that I should see them, because he felt sure that I was interested in paintings. Oh, of course—I smiled rather foolishly, for the waiter seemed to expect some sort of confirmatory interpolation from me—I *was* interested in paintings; very much. In that case, said the waiter, the Count would be delighted to take me to see them. He left me, still puzzled, but vastly relieved. At any rate, I was not being called upon to make the very embarrassing choice between swords and pistols.

Surreptitiously, whenever he was not looking in my direction, I examined the Lieutenant Count. His appearance was not typically Italian (but then what is a typical Italian?). He was not, that is to say, blue-jowled, beady-eyed, swarthy, and aquiline. On the contrary, he had pale ginger hair, grey eyes, a snub nose, and a freckled complexion. I knew plenty of young Englishmen who might have been Count Tirabassi's less vivacious brothers.

He received me, when the time came, with the most exquisite courtesy, apologising for the unceremonious way in which he had made my acquaintance. "But as I felt sure," he said, "that you were interested in art, I thought you would forgive me for the sake of what I have to show you." I couldn't help wondering why the Count felt so certain about my interest in art. It was only later, when we left the restaurant together, that I understood; for, as I put on my hat to go, he pointed with a smile at the little Mexican. "One can see," he said, "that you are a real artist." I was left at a loss, not knowing what to answer.

After we had exchanged the preliminary courtesies, the Lieutenant plunged at once, entirely for my benefit I could see, into a conversation about art. "Nowadays," he said, "we Italians don't take enough interest in art. In a modern country, you see . . ." He shrugged his shoulders, leaving the sentence unfinished. "But I don't think that's right. I adore art. Simply adore it. When I see foreigners going round with their guidebooks, standing for half an hour in front of one picture, looking first at the book, then at the picture "—and here he gave the most brilliantly finished imitation of an Anglican clergyman conscientiously "doing" the Mantegna chapel: first a glance at the imaginary guide-book held open in his two hands, then, with the movement of a chicken that drinks, a lifting of the face towards an imaginary fresco, a long stare between puckered eyelids, a falling open of the mouth, and finally a turning back of the eyes towards the inspired pages of Baedeker—"when I see them, I feel ashamed for us Italians." The Count spoke very earnestly, feeling, no doubt, that his talent for mimicry had carried him a little too far. "And if they stand for half an hour looking at the thing, I go and stand there for an hour. That's the way to understand great art. The only way." He leaned back in his chair and sipped his coffee. "Unfortunately," he added, after a moment, "one hasn't got much time."

I agreed with him. "When one can only get to Italy for a month at a stretch, like myself . . ."

"Ah, but if only I could travel about the world like you!" The Count sighed. "But here I am, cooped up in this wretched town. And when I think of the enormous capital that's hanging there on the walls of my house . . ." He checked himself, shaking his head. Then, changing his tone, he began to tell me about his house on the Brenta. It sounded altogether too good to be true. Carpioni, yes—I could believe in frescoes by Carpioni; almost any one might have those. But a hall by Veronese, but rooms by Tiepolo, all in the same house—that sounded incredible. I could not help believing that the Count's enthusiasm for art had carried him away. But, in any case, to-morrow I should be able to judge for myself; the Count had invited me to lunch with him.

We left the restaurant. Still embarrassed by the Count's references to my little Mexican, I walked by his side in silence up the arcaded street.

"I am going to introduce you to my father," said the Count. " He, too, adores the arts."

More than ever I felt myself a swindler. I had wriggled into the Count's confidence on false pretences; my hat was a lie. I felt that I ought to do something to clear up the misunderstanding. But the Count was so busy complaining to me about his father that I had no opportunity to put in my little explanation.

I didn't listen very attentively, I confess, to what he was saying. In the course of a year at Oxford, I had heard so many young men complain of their fathers. Not enough money, too much interference—the story was a stale one. And at that time, moreover, I was taking a very high philosophical line about this sort of thing. I was pretending that people didn't interest me—only books, only ideas. What a fool one can make of oneself at that age!

"*Eccoci*," said the Count. We halted in front of the Café Pedrochi. "He always comes here for his coffee."

And where else, indeed, should he come for his coffee? Who, in Padua, would go anywhere else?

We found him sitting out on the terrace at the farther end of the building. I had never, I thought, seen a jollier-looking old gentleman. The old Count had a red weather-beaten face, with white moustaches bristling gallantly upwards and a white imperial in the grand Risorgimento manner of Victor Emmanuel the Second. Under the white tufty eyebrows, and set in the midst of a webwork of fine wrinkles, the eyes were brown and bright like a robin's. His long nose looked, somehow, more practically useful than the ordinary human nose, as though made for fine judicial sniffing, for delicate burrowing and probing. Thick set and strong, he sat there solidly in his chair, his knees apart, his hands clasped over the knob of his cane, carrying his paunch with dignity, nobly I had almost said, before him. He was dressed all in white linen—for the weather was still very hot— and his wide grey hat was tilted rakishly forward over his left eye. It gave one a real satisfaction to look at him; he was so complete, so perfect in his kind.

The young Count introduced me. "This is an English gentleman. Signor . . ." He turned to me for the name.

"Oosselay," I said, having learnt by experience that that was as near as any Italian could be expected to get to it.

"Signor Oosselay," the young Count continued, "is an artist."

"Well, not exactly an artist," I was beginning; but he would not let me make an end.

"He is also very much interested in ancient art," he continued. "To-morrow I am taking him to Dolo to see the frescoes. I know he will like them."

We sat down at the old Count's table; critically he looked at me and nodded. "*Benissimo*," he said, and then added, "Let's hope you'll be able to do something to help us sell the things."

This was startling. I looked in some perplexity towards the young Count. He was frowning angrily at his father. The old gentleman had evidently said the wrong thing; he had spoken, I guessed, too soon. At any rate, he took his son's hint and glided off serenely on another tack.

"The fervid phantasy of Tiepolo," he began rotundly, "the cool, unimpassioned splendour of Veronese—at Dolo you will see them contrasted." I listened attentively, while the old gentleman thundered on in what was evidently a set speech. When it was over, the young Count got up; he had to be back at the barracks by half-past two. I too made as though to go; but the old man laid his hand on my arm. "Stay with me," he said. "I enjoy your conversation infinitely." And as he himself had hardly ceased speaking for one moment since first I set eyes on him, I could well believe it. With the gesture of a lady lifting her skirts out of the mud (and those were the days when skirts still had to be lifted) the young Count picked up his trailing sabre and swaggered off, very military, very brilliant and glittering, like a soldier on the stage, into the sunlight, out of sight.

The old man's bird-bright eyes followed him as he went. "A good boy, Fabio," he said, turning back to me at last, "a good son." He spoke affectionately; but there was a hint, I thought, in his smile, in the tone of his voice, a hint of amusement, of irony. It was as though he were adding, by implication, "But good boys, after all, are fools to be so good." I found myself, in spite of my affectation of detachment, extremely curious about this old gentleman. And he, for his part, was not the man to allow any one in his company to remain for long in splendid isolation. He insisted on my taking an interest in his affairs. He told me all about them—or at any rate all about some of them—pouring out

his confidences with an astonishing absence of reserve. Next to
the intimate and trusted friend, the perfect stranger is the best of
all possible confidants. There is no commercial traveller, of
moderately sympathetic appearance, who has not, in the course
of his days in the train, his evenings in the parlours of commercial hotels, been made the repository of a thousand intimate
secrets—even in England. And in Italy—goodness knows what
commercial travellers get told in Italy. Even I, a foreigner,
speaking the language badly, and not very skilful anyhow in
conducting a conversation with strangers, have heard queer
things in the second-class carriages of Italian trains. . . . Here,
too, on Pedrochi's terrace I was to hear queer things. A door
was to be left ajar, and through the crack I was to have a peep at
unfamiliar lives.

"What I should do without him," the old gentleman continued, "I really don't know. The way he manages the estate is
simply wonderful." And he went rambling off into long digressions about the stupidity of peasants, the incompetence and dis-
honesty of bailiffs, the badness of the weather, the spread of
phylloxera, the high price of manure. The upshot of it all was
that, since Fabio had taken over the estate, everything had gone
well; even the weather had improved. "It's such a relief," the
Count concluded, "to feel that I have some one in charge on
whom I can rely, some one I can trust, absolutely. It leaves me
free to devote my mind to more important things."

I could not help wondering what the important things were;
but it would have been impertinent, I felt, to ask. Instead, I put
a more practical question. "But what will happen," I asked,
"when your son's military duties take him away from Padua?"

The old Count gave me a wink and laid his forefinger, very
deliberately, to the side of his long nose. The gesture was rich
with significance. "They never will," he said. "It's all arranged.
A little *combinazione*, you know. I have a friend in the Ministry.
His military duties will always keep him in Padua." He winked
again and smiled.

I could not help laughing, and the old Count joined in with a joyous ha-ha that was the expression of a profound satisfaction, that was, as it were, a burst of self-applause. He was evidently proud of his little *combinazione*. But he was prouder still of the other combination, about which he now confidentially leaned across the table to tell me. It was decidedly the subtler of the two.

"And it's not merely his military duties," he said, wagging at me the thick, yellow-nailed forefinger which he had laid against his nose, "it's not merely his military duties that'll keep the boy in Padua. It's his domestic duties. He's married. I married him." He leaned back in his chair, and surveyed me, smiling. The little wrinkles round his eyes seemed to be alive. "That boy, I said to myself, must settle down. He must have a nest, or else he'll fly away. He must have roots, or else he'll run. And his poor old father will be left in the lurch. He's young, I thought, but he must marry. He *must* marry. At once." And the old gentleman made great play with his forefinger. It was a long story. His old friend, the Avvocato Monaldeschi, had twelve children—three boys and nine girls. (And here there were digressions about the Avvocato and the size of good Catholic families.) The eldest girl was just the right age for Fabio. No money, of course; but a good girl and pretty, and very well brought up and religious. Religious—that was very important, for it was essential that Fabio should have a large family—to keep him more effectually rooted, the old Count explained—and with these modern young women brought up outside the Church one could never be certain of children. Yes, her religion was most important; he had looked into that very carefully before selecting her. Well, the next thing, of course, was that Fabio should be induced to select her. It had been a matter of bringing the horse to water *and* making him drink. Oh, a most difficult and delicate business! For Fabio prided himself on his independence; and he was obstinate, like a mule. Nobody should interfere with his affairs, nobody should make him do what he didn't want to. And he was so touchy, he was so pig-headed that often he wouldn't do what he really wanted, merely because somebody else had suggested that he ought to do it. So I could imagine—

E

the old Count spread out his hands before me—just how difficult and delicate a business it had been. Only a consummate diplomat could have succeeded. He did it by throwing them together a great deal and talking, meanwhile, about the rashness of early marriages, the uselessness of poor wives, the undesirability of wives not of noble birth. It worked like a charm; within four months, Fabio was engaged; two months later he was married, and ten months after that he had a son and heir. And now he was fixed, rooted. The old gentleman chuckled, and I could fancy that I was listening to the chuckling of some old white-haired tyrant of the quattrocento, congratulating himself on the success of some peculiarly ingenious stroke of policy—a rich city induced to surrender itself by fraud, a dangerous rival lured by fair words into a cage and trapped. Poor Fabio, I thought; and also, what a waste of talent!

Yes, the old Count went on, now he would never go. He was not like his younger brother, Lucio. Lucio was a rogue, *furbo*, sly; he had no conscience. But Fabio had ideas about duty, and lived up to them. Once he had engaged himself, he would stick to his engagements, obstinately, with all the mulishness of his character. Well, now he lived on the estate, in the big painted house at Dolo. Three days a week he came into Padua for his military duties, and the rest of his time he devoted to the estate. It brought in, now, more than it had ever done before. But goodness knew, the old man complained, that was little enough. Bread and oil, and wine and milk, and chickens and beef—there was plenty of those and to spare. Fabio could have a family of fifty and they would never starve. But ready money—there wasn't much of that. "In England," the Count concluded, "you are rich. But we Italians . . ." He shook his head.

I spent the next quarter of an hour trying to persuade him that we were not all millionaires. But in vain. My statistics, based on somewhat imperfect memories of Mr. and Mrs. Sidney Webb, carried no conviction. In the end I gave it up.

The next morning Fabio appeared at the door of my hotel in a large, very old and very noisy Fiat. It was the family machine-of-all-work, bruised, scratched, and dirtied by years of service. Fabio drove it with a brilliant and easy recklessness. We rushed through the town, swerving from one side of the narrow street to the other, with a disregard for the rules of the road which, in a pedantic country like England, would have meant at the least a five-pound fine and an endorsed licence. But here the Carabiniers, walking gravely in couples under the arcades, let us pass without comment. Right or left—after all, what did it matter?

"Why do you keep the silencer out?" I shouted through the frightful clamour of the engine.

Fabio slightly shrugged his shoulders. "*È piu allegro così,*" he answered.

I said no more. From a member of this hardy race which likes noise, which enjoys discomfort, a nerve-ridden Englishman could hardly hope to get much sympathy.

We were soon out of the town. Trailing behind us a seething white wake of dust and with the engine rattling off its explosions like a battery of machine-guns, we raced along the Fusina road. On either hand extended the cultivated plain. The road was bordered by ditches, and on the banks beyond, instead of hedges, stood rows of little pollards, with grape-laden vines festooned from tree to tree. White with the dust, tendrils, fruit, and leaves hung there like so much goldsmith's work sculptured in frosted metal, hung like the swags of fruit and foliage looped round the flanks of a great silver bowl. We hurried on. Soon, on our right hand, we had the Brenta, sunk deep between the banks of its canal. And now we were at Strà. Through gateways rich with fantastic stucco, down tunnels of undeciduous shade, we looked in a series of momentary glimpses into the heart of the park. And now for an instant the statues on the roof of the villa beckoned against the sky and were passed. On we went. To right and left, on either bank of the river, I got every now and then a glimpse of some enchanting mansion, gay and brilliant even in decay. Little baroque garden houses peeped at me over walls; and through great gates, at the end of powdery cypress avenues, half humorously, it seemed, the magniloquent and frivolous façades soared up in defiance of all the rules. I should have liked to do the journey slowly, to stop here and there, to look, to savour at leisure; but Fabio disdained to travel at anything less than fifty kilometres to the hour, and I had to be content with momentary and precarious glimpses. It was in these villas, I reflected, as we bumped along at the head of our desolation of white dust, that Casanova used to come and spend the summer; seducing the chamber-maids, taking advantage of terrified marchionesses in *calèches* during thunderstorms, bamboozling soft-witted old senators of Venice with his fortune-telling and black magic. Gorgeous and happy scoundrel! In spite of my professed detachment, I envied him. And, indeed, what was that famous detachment but a disguised expression of the envy which the successes and audacities of a Casanova must necessarily arouse in every timid and diffident mind? If I lived in splendid isolation, it was because I lacked the audacity to make war—even to make entangling alliances. I was absorbed in these pleasing self-condemnatory thoughts, when the car slowed down and came to a standstill in front of a huge imposing gate. Fabio hooted impatiently on his horn; there was a scurry of footsteps, the sound of bolts being drawn, and the gate swung open. At the end of a short drive, very large and grave, very chaste and austere, stood the house. It was considerably older than most of the other villas I had seen in glimpses on our way. There was no frivolousness in its façade, no irregular grandiloquence. A great block of stuccoed brick; a central portico approached by steps and topped with a massive pediment; a row of rigid statues on the balustrade above the cornice. It was correctly, coldly even, Palladian. Fabio brought the car to a halt in front of the porch. We got out. At the top of the steps stood a young woman with a red-headed child in her arms. It was the Countess with the son and heir.

The Countess impressed me very agreeably. She was slim and tall—two or three inches taller than her husband; with dark hair, drawn back from the forehead and twisted into a knot on the nape of her neck; dark eyes, vague, lustrous, and melancholy, like the eyes of a gentle animal; a skin brown and transparent like darkened amber. Her manner was gentle and unemphatic. She rarely gesticulated; I never heard her raise her voice. She spoke, indeed, very little. The old Count had told me that his daughter-in-law was religious, and from her appearance I could easily believe it. She looked at you with the calm, remote regard of one whose life mostly goes on behind the eyes.

Fabio kissed his wife and then, bending his face towards the child, he made a frightful grimace and roared like a lion. It was all done in affection; but the poor little creature shrank away, terrified. Fabio laughed and pinched its ear.

"Don't tease him," said the Countess gently. "You'll make him cry."

Fabio turned to me. "That's what comes of leaving a boy to be looked after by women. He cries at everything. Let's come in," he added. "At present we only use two or three rooms on the ground floor, and the kitchen in the basement. All the rest is deserted. I don't know how these old fellows managed to keep up their palaces. I can't." He shrugged his shoulders. Through a door on the right of the portico we passed into the house. "This is our drawing-room and dining-room combined."

It was a fine big room, nobly proportioned—a double cube, I guessed—with doorways of sculptured marble and a magnificent fireplace flanked by a pair of nymphs on whose bowed shoulders rested a sloping overmantel carved with coats of arms and festoons of foliage. Round the walls ran a frieze, painted in grisaille; in a graceful litter of cornucopias and panoplies, goddesses sumptuously reclined, cherubs wriggled and flew. The furniture was strangely mixed. Round a sixteenth-century dining-table that was a piece of Palladian architecture in wood, were ranged eight chairs in the Viennese secession style of 1905. A large chalet-shaped cuckoo clock from Bern hung on the wall between two cabinets of walnut, pilastered and pedimented to look like little temples, and with heroic statuettes in yellow boxwood, standing in niches between the pillars. And then the pictures on the walls, the cretonnes with which the arm-chairs were covered! Tactfully, however, I admired everything, new as well as old.

"And now," said the Count, "for the frescoes."

I followed him through one of the marble-framed doorways and found myself at once in the great central hall of the villa. The Count turned round to me. "There!" he said, smiling triumphantly with the air of one who has really succeeded in producing a rabbit out of an empty hat. And, indeed, the spectacle was sufficiently astonishing.

The walls of the enormous room were completely covered with frescoes which it did not need much critical judgment or knowledge to perceive were genuine Veroneses. The authorship was obvious, palpable. Who else could have painted those harmoniously undulating groups of figures set in their splendid architectural frame? Who else but Veronese could have combined such splendour with such coolness, so much extravagant opulence with such exquisite suavity?

"*È grandioso!*" I said to the Count.

And indeed it was. Grandiose; there was no other word. A rich triumphal arcade ran all round the room, four or five arches appearing on each wall. Through the arches one looked into a garden; and there, against a background of cypresses and statues and far-away blue mountains, companies of Venetian ladies and gentlemen gravely disported themselves. Under one arch they were making music; through another, one saw them sitting round a table, drinking one another's health in glasses of red wine, while a little blackamoor in a livery of green and yellow carried round the silver jug. In the next panel they were watching a fight between a monkey and a cat. On the opposite wall a poet was reading his verses to the assembled company, and next to him Veronese himself—the self-portrait was recognisable—stood at his easel, painting the picture of an opulent blonde in rose-coloured satin. At the feet of the artist lay his dog; two parrots and a monkey were sitting on the marble balustrade in the middle distance.

I gazed with delight. "What a marvellous thing to possess!"

I exclaimed, fairly carried away by my enthusiasm. "I envy you."

The Count made a little grimace and laughed. "Shall we come and look at the Tiepolos?" he asked.

We passed through a couple of cheerful rooms by Carpioni—satyrs chasing nymphs through a romantic forest and, on the fringes of a seascape, a very eccentric rape of mermaids by centaurs—to step across a threshold into that brilliant universe, at once delicate and violently extravagant, wild and subtly orderly, which Tiepolo, in the last days of Italian painting, so masterfully and magically created. It was the story of Eros and Psyche, and the tale ran through three large rooms, spreading itself even on to the ceilings, where, in a pale sky dappled with white and golden clouds, the appropriate deities balanced themselves, diving or ascending through the empyrean with that air of being perfectly at home in their element which seems to belong, in nature, only to fishes and perhaps a few winged insects and birds.

Fabio had boasted to me that, in front of a picture, he could outstare any foreigner. But I was such a mortally long time admiring these dazzling phantasies that in the end he quite lost patience.

"I wanted to show you the farm before lunch," he said, looking at his watch. "There's only just time." I followed him reluctantly.

We looked at the cows, the horses, the prize bull, the turkeys. We looked at the tall, thin haystacks, shaped like giant cigars set on end. We looked at the sacks of wheat in the barn. For lack of any better comment I told the Count that they reminded me of the sacks of wheat in English barns; he seemed delighted.

The farm buildings were set round an immense courtyard. We had explored three sides of this piazza; now we came to the fourth, which was occupied by a long, low building pierced with round archways and, I was surprised to see, completely empty.

"What's this?" I asked, as we entered.

"It *is* nothing," the Count replied. "But it might, some day, become . . . *chi sa?*" He stood there for a moment in silence, frowning pensively, with the expression of Napoleon on St. Helena—dreaming of the future, regretting past opportunities for ever lost. His freckled face, ordinarily a lamp for brightness, became incongruously sombre. Then all at once he burst out—damning life, cursing fate, wishing to God he could get away and do something instead of wasting himself here. I listened, making every now and then a vague noise of sympathy. What could I do about it? And then, to my dismay, I found that I could do something about it, that I was expected to do something. I was being asked to help the Count to sell his frescoes. As an artist, it was obvious, I must be acquainted with rich patrons, museums, millionaires. I had seen the frescoes; I could honestly recommend them. And now there was this perfected process for transferring frescoes on to canvas. The walls could easily be peeled of their painting, the canvases rolled up and taken to Venice. And from there it would be the easiest thing in the world to smuggle them on board a ship and get away with them. As for prices—if he could get a million and a half of lire, so much the better; but he'd take a million, he'd even take three-quarters. And he'd give me ten per cent. commission. . . .

And afterwards, when he'd sold his frescoes, what would he do? To begin with—the Count smiled at me triumphantly—he'd turn this empty building in which we were now standing into an up-to-date cheese-factory. He could start the business handsomely on half a million, and then, using cheap female labour from the country round, he could be almost sure of making big profits at once. In a couple of years, he calculated, he'd be a netting eighty or a hundred thousand a year from his cheeses. And then, ah then, he'd be independent, he'd be able to get away, he'd see the world. He'd go to Brazil and the Argentine. An enterprising man with capital could always do well out there. He'd go to New York, to London, to Berlin, to Paris. There was nothing he could not do.

But meanwhile the frescoes were still on the walls—beautiful, no doubt (for, the Count reminded me, he adored art), but futile;

a huge capital frozen into the plaster, eating its head off, utterly useless. Whereas, with his cheese-factory . . .

Slowly we walked back towards the house.

I was in Venice again in the September of the following year, 1913. There were, I imagine, that autumn, more German honeymoon-couples, more parties of rucksacked Wander-Birds than there had ever been in Venice before. There were too many, in any case, for me; I packed my bag and took the train for Padua.

I had not originally intended to see young Tirabassi again. I didn't know, indeed, how pleased he would be to see me. For the frescoes, so far as I knew, at any rate, were still safely on the walls, the cheese-factory still remote in the future, in the imagination. I had written to him more than once, telling him that I was doing my best, but that at the moment, etcetera, etcetera. Not that I had ever held out much hope. I had made it clear from the first that my acquaintance among millionaires was limited, that I knew no directors of American museums, that I had nothing to do with any of the international picture dealers. But the Count's faith in me had remained, none the less, unshaken. It was the little Mexican, I believe, that inspired so much confidence. But now, after my letters, after all this lapse of time and nothing done, he might feel that I had let him down, deceived him somehow. That was why I took no steps to seek him out. But chance overruled my decision. On the third day of my stay in Padua, I ran into him in the street. Or rather he ran into me.

It was nearly six o'clock, and I had strolled down to the Piazza del Santo. At that hour, when the slanting light is full of colour and the shadows are long and profound, the great church, with its cupolas and turrets and campaniles, takes on an aspect more than ever fantastic and oriental. I had walked round the church, and now I was standing at the foot of Donatello's statue, looking up at the grim bronze man, the ponderously stepping beast, when I suddenly became aware that some one was standing very close behind me. I took a step to one side and turned round. It was Fabio. Wearing his famous expression of the sight-seeing parson, he was gazing up at the statue, his mouth open in a vacant and fish-like gape. I burst out laughing.

"Did I look like that?" I asked.

"Precisely." He laughed too. "I've been watching you for the last ten minutes, mooning round the church. You English! Really . . ." He shook his head.

Together we strolled up the Via del Santo, talking as we went.

"I'm sorry I wasn't able to do anything about the frescoes," I said. "But really . . ." I entered into explanations.

"Some day, perhaps." Fabio was still optimistic.

"And how's the Countess?"

"Oh, she's very well," said Fabio, "considering. You know she had another son three or four months after you came to see us."

"No?"

"She's expecting another now." Fabio spoke rather gloomily, I thought. More than ever I admired the old Count's sagacity. But I was sorry, for his son's sake, that he had not a wider field in which to exercise his talents.

"And your father?" I asked. "Shall we find him sitting at Pedrochi's, as usual?"

Fabio laughed. "We shall not," he said significantly. "He's flown."

"Flown?"

"Gone, vanished, disappeared."

"But where?"

"Who knows?" said Fabio. "My father is like the swallows; he comes and he goes. Every year. . . . But the migration isn't regular. Sometimes he goes away in the spring; sometimes it's the autumn, sometimes it's the summer. . . . One fine morning his man goes into his room to call him as usual, and he isn't there. Vanished. He might be dead. Oh, but he isn't." Fabio laughed. "Two or three months later, in he walks again, as though he were just coming back from a stroll in the Botanical Gardens. 'Good evening. Good evening.'" Fabio imitated the old Count's voice and manner, snuffing the air like a war-horse,

twisting the ends of an imaginary white moustache. " 'How's
your mother? How are the girls? How have the grapes done
this year?' Snuff, snuff. 'How's Lucio? And who the devil has
left all this rubbish lying about in my study?' " Fabio burst into
an indignant roar that made the loiterers in the Via Roma turn,
astonished, in our direction.

"And where does he go?" I asked.

"Nobody knows. My mother used to ask, once. But she soon
gave it up. It was no good. 'Where have you been, Ascanio?'
'My dear, I'm afraid the olive crop is going to be very poor this
year.' Snuff, snuff. And when she pressed him, he would fly into
a temper and slam the doors. . . . What do you say to an
aperitif?" Pedrochi's open doors invited. We entered, chose a
retired table, and sat down.

"But what do you suppose the old gentleman does when he's
away?"

"Ah!" And making the richly significant gesture I had so
much admired in his father, the young Count laid his finger
against his nose and slowly, solemnly winked his left eye.

"You mean . . . ?"

Fabio nodded. "There's a little widow here in Padua." With
his extended finger the young Count described in the air an
undulating line. "Nice and plump. Black eyes. I've noticed that
she generally seems to be out of town just at the time the old man
does his migrations. But it may, of course, be a mere coinci-
dence." The waiter brought us our vermouth. Pensively the
young Count sipped. The gaiety went out of his open, lamp-
like face. "And meanwhile," he went on slowly and in an altered
voice, "I stay here, looking after the estate, so that the old man
can go running round the world with his little pigeon—*la sua
colombella*." (The expression struck me as particularly choice.)
"Oh, it's funny, no doubt," the young Count went on. "But it
isn't right. If I wasn't married, I'd go clean away and try my luck
somewhere else. I'd leave him to look after everything himself.
But with a wife and two children—three children soon—how
can I take the risk? At any rate, there's plenty to eat as long as

I stay here. My only hope," he added, after a little pause, "is in the frescoes."

Which implied, I reflected, that his only hope was in me; I felt sorry for him.

In the spring of 1914 I sent two rich Americans to look at Fabio's villa. Neither of them made any offer to buy the frescoes; it would have astonished me if they had. But Fabio was greatly encouraged by their arrival. "I feel," he wrote to me, "that a beginning has now been made. These Americans will go back to their country and tell their friends. Soon there will be a procession of millionaires coming to see the frescoes. Meanwhile, life is the same as ever. Rather worse, if anything. Our little daughter, whom we have christened Emilia, was born last month. My wife had a very bad time and is still far from well, which is very troublesome." (It seemed a curious adjective to use, in the circumstances. But coming from Fabio, I understood it; he was one of those exceedingly healthy people to whom any sort of illness is mysterious, unaccountable, and above all extraordinarily tiresome and irritating.) "The day before yesterday my father disappeared again. I have not yet had time to find out if the Colombella has also vanished. My brother, Lucio, has succeeded in getting a motor-bicycle out of him, which is more than I ever managed to do. But then I was never one for creeping diplomatically round and round a thing, as he can do. . . . I have been going very carefully into the cheese-factory business lately, and I am not sure that it might not be more profitable to set up a silk-weaving establishment instead. When you next come, I will go into details with you."

But it was a very long time before I saw Padua and the Count again. . . . The War put an end to my yearly visits to Italy, and for various reasons, even when it was over, I could not go south again as soon as I should have liked. Not till the autumn of 1921 did I embark again on the Venice express.

It was in an Italy not altogether familiar that I now found myself—an Italy full of violence and bloodshed. The Fascists and the Communists were still busily fighting. Roaring at the head of their dust-storms, the motor-lorries, loaded with cargoes of singing boys, careered across the country in search of adventure and lurking Bolshevism. One stood respectfully in the gutter while they passed; and through the flying dust, through the noise of the engine, a snatch of that singing would be blown back: "*Giovinezza, giovinezza, primavera di bellezza . . .*" (Youth, youth, spring-time of beauty). Where but in Italy would they have put such words to a political song? And then the proclamations, the manifestos, the denunciations, the appeals! Every hoarding and blank wall was plastered with them. Between the station and Pedrochi's I walked through a whole library of these things. "Citizens!" they would begin. "A heroic wind is to-day reviving the almost asphyxiated soul of our unhappy Italy, overcome by the poisonous fumes of Bolshevism and wallowing in ignoble abasement at the feet of the Nations." And they finished, for the most part, with references to Dante. I read them all with infinite pleasure.

I reached Pedrochi's at last. On the terrace, sitting in the very corner where I had seen him first, years before, was the old Count. He stared at me blankly when I saluted him, not recognising me at all. I began to explain who I was; after a moment he cut me short, almost impatiently, protesting that he remembered now, perfectly well. I doubted very much whether he really did; but he was too proud to confess that he had forgotten. Meanwhile, he invited me to sit at his table.

At a first glance, from a distance, I fancied that the old Count had not aged a day since last I saw him. But I was wrong. From the street, I had only seen the rakish tilt of his hat, the bristling of his white moustache and imperial, the parted knees, the noble protrusion of the paunch. But now that I could look at him closely and at leisure, I saw that he was in fact a very different man. Under the tilted hat his face was unhealthily purple; the flesh sagged into pouches. In the whites of his eyes, discoloured and as though tarnished with age, the little broken veins showed red. And, lustreless, the eyes themselves seemed to look without interest at what they saw. His shoulders were bent as though under a weight, and when he lifted his cup to his lips his hand trembled so much that a drop of coffee splashed on to the table. He was an old man now, old and tired.

"How's Fabio?" I asked; since 1916 I had had no news of him.

"Oh, Fabio's well," the old Count answered, "Fabio's very well. He has six children now, you know." And the old gentleman nodded and smiled at me without a trace of malice. He seemed quite to have forgotten the reasons for which he had been at so much pains to select a good Catholic for a daughter-in-law. "Six," he repeated. "And then, you know, he did very well in the war. We Tirabassi have always been warriors." Full of pride, he went on to tell me of Fabio's exploits and sufferings. Twice wounded, special promotion on the field of battle, splendid decorations. He was a major now.

"And do his military duties still keep him in Padua?"

The old gentleman nodded, and suddenly there appeared on his face something like the old smile. "A little *combinazione* of mine," he said, and chuckled.

"And the estate?" I asked.

Oh, that was doing all right, everything considered. It had got rather out of hand during the war, while Fabio was at the front. And then, afterwards, there had been a lot of trouble with the peasants; but Fabio and his Fascists were putting all that to rights. "With Fabio on the spot," said the old gentleman, "I have no anxieties." And then he began to tell me, all over again, about Fabio's exploits in the war.

The next day I took the tram to Strà, and after an hour agreeably spent in the villa and the park, I walked on at my leisure towards Dolo. It took me a long time to get there, for on this occasion I was able to stop and look for as long as I liked at all the charming things on the way. Casanova seemed, now, a good deal less enviable, I noticed, looking inwards on myself, than he had when last I passed this way. I was nine years older.

The gates were open; I walked in. There stood the house, as grave and ponderous as ever, but shabbier than when I saw it last. The shutters needed painting, and here and there the stucco was peeling off in scabs. I approached. From within the house came a cheerful noise of children's laughter and shouting. The family, I supposed, was playing hide-and-seek, or trains, or perhaps some topical game of Fascists and Communists. As I climbed the steps of the porch, I could hear the sound of small feet racing over the tiled floors; in the empty rooms footsteps and shouting strangely echoed. And then suddenly, from the sitting-room on the right, came the sound of Fabio's voice, furiously shouting, "Oh, for God's sake," it yelled, "keep those wretched children quiet." And then, petulantly, it complained, "How do you expect me to do accounts with this sort of thing going on?" There was at once a profound and as it were unnatural silence; then the sound of small feet tiptoeing away, some whispering, a little nervous laugh. I rang the bell.

It was the Countess who opened the door. She stood for a moment hesitatingly, wondering who I was; then remembered, smiled, held out her hand. She had grown, I noticed, very thin, and with the wasting of her face, her eyes seemed to have become larger. Their expression was as gentle and serene as ever; she seemed to be looking at me from a distance.

"Fabio will be delighted to see you," she said, and she took me through the door on the right of the porch straight into the sitting-room. Fabio was sitting at the Palladian table in front of a heap of papers, biting the end of his pencil.

Even in his grey-green service uniform the young Count looked wonderfully brilliant, like a soldier on the stage. His face was still boyishly freckled, but the skin was deeply lined; he looked very much older than when I had seen him last—older than he really was. The open cheerfulness, the shining, lamp-like brightness were gone. On his snubby-featured face he wore a ludicrously incongruous expression of chronic melancholy. He brightened, it is true, for a moment when I appeared; I think he was genuinely glad to see me.

"*Caspita!*" he kept repeating. "*Caspita!*" (It was his favourite expression of astonishment, an odd, old-fashioned word.) "Who would have thought it? After all this time!"

"And all the eternity of the war as well," I said.

But when the first ebullition of surprise and pleasure subsided, the look of melancholy came back.

"It gives me the spleen," he said, "to see you again; still travelling about; free to go where you like. If you knew what life was like here . . ."

"Well, in any case," I said, feeling that I ought, for the Countess's sake, to make some sort of protest, "in any case the war's over, and you have escaped a real revolution. That's something."

"Oh, you're as bad as Laura," said the Count impatiently. He looked towards his wife, as though hoping that she would say something. But the Countess went on with her sewing without even looking up. The Count took my arm. "Come along," he said, and his tone was almost one of anger. "Let's take a turn outside." His wife's religious resignation, her patience, her serenity angered him, I could see, like a reprimand—tacit, indeed, and unintentionally given, but none the less galling.

Along the weed-grown paths of what had once, in the ancient days of splendour, been the garden, slowly we walked towards the farm. A few ragged box-trees grew along the fringes of the paths; once there had been neat hedges. Poised over a dry basin a Triton blew his waterless conch. At the end of the vista a pair of rapes—Pluto and Proserpine, Apollo and Daphne—writhed desperately against the sky.

"I saw your father yesterday," I said. "He looks aged."

"And so he ought," said Fabio murderously. "He's sixty-nine."

I felt uncomfortably that the subject had become too serious for light conversation. I had wanted to ask after the Colombella; in the circumstances, I decided that it would be wiser to say nothing about her. I repressed my curiosity. We were walking now under the lea of the farm buildings.

"The cows look very healthy," I said politely, looking through an open doorway. In the twilight within, six grey rumps plastered with dry dung presented themselves in file; six long leather tails swished impatiently from side to side. Fabio made no comment; he only grunted.

"In any case," he went on slowly, after another silence, "he can't live much longer. I shall sell my share and clear off to South America, family or no family." It was a threat against his own destiny, a threat of which he must have known the vanity. He was deceiving himself to keep up his spirits.

"But I say," I exclaimed, taking another and better opportunity to change the conversation, "I see you have started a factory here after all." We had walked round to the farther side of the square. Through the windows of the long low building which, at my last visit, had stood untenanted, I saw the complicated shapes of machines, rows of them in a double line down the whole length of the building. "Looms? Then you decided against cheese? And the frescoes?" I turned questioningly towards the Count. I had a horrible fear that, when we got back to the house, I should find the great hall peeled of its Veroneses and a blank of plaster where once had been the history of Eros and Psyche.

"Oh, the frescoes are still there, what's left of them." And in spite of Fabio's long face, I was delighted at the news. "I persuaded my father to sell some of his house property in Padua, and we started this weaving business here two years ago. Just in time," Fabio added, "for the Communist revolution."

Poor Fabio, he had no luck. The peasants had seized his factory and had tried to possess themselves of his land. For three weeks he had lived at the villa in a state of siege, defending the place, with twenty Fascists to help him, against all the peasants of the countryside. The danger was over now; but the machines were broken, and in any case it was out of the question to start them again; feeling was still too high. And what, for Fabio, made it worse was the fact that his brother Lucio, who had also got a little capital out of the old man, had gone off to Bulgaria and invested it in a bootlace factory. It was the only bootlace factory in the country, and Lucio was making money hand over fist. Free as air he was, well off, with a lovely Turkish girl for a mistress. For Fabio, the Turkish girl was evidently the last straw. "*Una Turca, una vera Turca*," he repeated, shaking his head. The female infidel symbolised in his eyes all that was exotic, irregular, undomestic; all that was not the family; all that was remote from Padua and the estate.

"And they were such beautiful machines," said Fabio, pausing for a moment to look in at the last of the long line of windows. "Whether to sell them, whether to wait till all this has blown over and have them put right and try to start again—I don't know." He shrugged his shoulders hopelessly. "Or just let things slide till the old man dies." We turned the corner of the square and began to walk back towards the house. "Sometimes," he added, after a silence, "I don't believe he ever will die."

The children were playing in the great hall of the Veroneses. The majestic double doors which gave on to the portico were ajar; through the opening we watched them for a moment without being seen. The family was formed up in order of battle. A red-headed boy of ten or eleven led the van, a brown boy followed. Then came three little girls, diminishing regularly in size, like graded pearls; and finally a little toddling creature in blue linen crawlers. All six of them carried shouldered bamboos, and they were singing in ragged unison to a kind of trumpet call of three notes: "*All' armi i Fascisti; a morte i Comunisti; a basso i Socialisti*"—over and over again. And as they sang they marched, round and round, earnestly, indefatigably. The huge empty room echoed like a swimming-bath. Remote under their triumphal arches, in their serene world of fantastic beauty, the silken ladies and gentlemen played their music, drank their wine; the poet declaimed, the painter poised his brush before the canvas; the monkeys clambered among the Roman ruins, the parrots dozed on the balustrades. "*All' armi i Fascisti, a morte i Comunisti . . .*" I should have liked to stand there in silence, merely to see how long the children would continue their patriotic march. But Fabio had none of my scientific curiosity; or if he ever had, it had certainly been exhausted long before the last of his children was born. After indulging me for a moment with the spectacle, he pushed open the door and walked in. The children looked round and were immediately silent. What with his bad temper and his theory of education by teasing, they seemed to be thoroughly frightened of their father.

"Go on," he said, "go on." But they wouldn't; they obviously couldn't, in his terrifying presence. Unobtrusively they slipped away.

Fabio led me round the painted room. "Look here," he said, "and look here." In one of the walls of the great hall there were half a dozen bullet holes. A chip had been taken off one of the painted cornices; one lady was horribly wounded in the face; there were two or three holes in the landscape, and a monkey's tail was severed. "That's our friends, the peasants," Fabio explained.

In the Carpioni rooms all was still well; the satyrs still pursued their nymphs, and in the room of the centaurs and the mermaids, the men who were half horses still galloped as tumultuously as ever into the sea, to ravish the women who were half fish. But the tale of Eros and Psyche had suffered dreadfully. The exquisite panel in which Tiepolo had painted Psyche holding up the lamp to look at her mysterious lover was no more than a faint, mildewy smudge. And where once the indignant young god had flown upwards to rejoin his Olympian relatives (who still, fortunately, swam about intact among the clouds on the ceiling) there was nothing but the palest ghost of an ascending Cupid, while Psyche weeping on the earth below was now quite invisible.

"That's our friends the French," said Fabio. "They were quartered here in 1918, and they didn't trouble to shut the windows when it rained."

Poor Fabio! Everything was against him. I had no consolation to offer. That autumn I sent him an art critic and three more Americans. But nothing came of their visits. The fact was that he had too much to offer. A picture—that might easily have been disposed of. But what could one do with a whole houseful of paintings like this?

The months passed. About Easter time of the next year I had another letter from Fabio. The olive crop had been poor. The Countess was expecting another baby and was far from well. The two eldest children were down with measles, and the last but one had what the Italians call an "asinine cough." He expected all the children to catch both diseases in due course. He was very doubtful now if it would ever be worth while to restart his looms; the position of the silk trade was not so sound as it had been at the end of 1919. If only he had stuck to cheese, as he first intended! Lucio had just made fifty thousand lire by a lucky stroke of speculation. But the female infidel had run off with a Rumanian. The old Count was ageing rapidly; when Fabio saw him last, he had told the same anecdote three times in the space of ten minutes. With these two pieces of good news—they were for him, I imagine, the only bright spots in the surrounding gloom—Fabio closed his letter. I was left wondering why he troubled to write to me at all. It may be that he got a certain lacerating satisfaction by thus enumerating his troubles.

That August there was a musical festival in Salzburg. I had never been in Austria; the occasion seemed to me a good one. I went, and I enjoyed myself prodigiously. Salzburg at the moment is all in the movement. There are baroque churches in abundance; there are Italianate fountains; there are gardens and palaces that mimic in their extravagantly ponderous Teutonic way the gardens and palaces of Rome. And, choicest treasure of all, there is a tunnel, forty feet high, bored through a precipitous crag—a tunnel such as only a Prince Bishop of the seventeenth century could have dreamed of, having at either end an arch of triumph, with pilasters, broken pediments, statues, scutcheons, all carved out of the living rock—a masterpiece among tunnels, and in a town where everything, without being really good, is exquisitely "amusing," the most amusing feature of all. Ah, decidedly, Salzburg is in the movement.

One afternoon I took the funicular up to the castle. There is a beer-terrace under the walls of the fortress from which you get a view that is starred in Baedeker. Below you on one side lies the town, spread out in the curving valley, with a river running through it, like a small and German version of Florence. From the other side of the terrace you look out over a panorama that makes no pretence to Italianism; it is as sweetly and romantically German as an air out of Weber's *Freischütz*. There are mountains on the horizon, spiky and blue like mountains in a picture book; and in the foreground, extending to the very foot of the extremely improbable crag on which the castle and the beer-garden are perched, stretches a flat green plain—miles upon miles of juicy meadows dotted with minusculous cows, with here and there a neat toy farm, or, more rarely, a cluster of dolls' houses, with a spire going up glittering from the midst of them.

I was sitting with my blond beer in front of this delicious and slightly comical landscape, thinking comfortably of nothing in particular, when I heard behind me a rapturous voice exclaiming, "Bello, bello!" I looked round curiously—for it seemed to me somehow rather surprising to hear Italian spoken here—and saw one of those fine sumptuous women they admire so much in the South. She was a *bella grassa*, plump to the verge of overripeness and perilously near middle age; but still in her way exceedingly handsome. Her face had the proportions of an iceberg—one-fifth above water, four-fifths below. Ample and florid from the eyes downwards, it was almost foreheadless; the hair began immediately above the brows. The eyes themselves were dark, large, and, for my taste, at least, somewhat excessively tender in expression. I took her in in a moment and was about to look away again when her companion, who had been looking at the view on the other side, turned round. It was the old Count.

I was far more embarrassed, I believe, than he. I felt myself blushing, as our eyes met, as though it were I who had been travelling about the world with a Colombella and he who had caught me in the act. I did not know what to do—whether to smile and speak to him, or to turn away as though I had not recognised him, or to nod from a distance and then, discreetly, to disappear. But the old Count put an end to my irresolution by calling out my name in astonishment, by running up to me and seizing my hand. What a delight to see an old friend! Here of all places! In this God-forsaken country—though it was cheap enough, didn't I find? He would introduce me to a charming compatriot of his own, an Italian lady he had met yesterday in the train from Vienna.

I was made known to the Colombella, and we all sat down at my table. Speaking resolutely in Italian, the Count ordered two more beers. We talked. Or rather the Count talked; for the conversation was a monologue. He told us anecdotes of the Italy of fifty years ago; he gave us imitations of the queer characters he had known; he even, at one moment, imitated the braying of an ass—I forget in what context; but the braying remains vividly in my memory. Snuffing the air between every sentence, he gave us his views on women. The Colombella screamed indignant protests, dissolved herself in laughter. The old Count twisted his moustaches, twinkling at her through the network of his wrinkles. Every now and then he turned in my direction and gave me a little wink.

I listened in astonishment. Was this the man who had told the same anecdote three times in ten minutes? I looked at the old Count. He was leaning towards the Colombella whispering something in her ear which made her laugh so much that she had to wipe the tears from her eyes. Turning away from her, he caught my eye; smiling, he shrugged his shoulders as though to say, "These women! What imbeciles, but how delicious, how indispensable!" Was this the tired old man I had seen a year ago sitting on Pedrochi's terrace? It seemed incredible.

"Well, good-bye, *a rivederci*." They had to get down into the town again. The funicular was waiting.

"I'm delighted to have seen you," said the old Count, shaking me affectionately by the hand.

"And so am I," I protested. "Particularly delighted to see you so well."

"Yes, I'm wonderfully well now," he said, blowing out his chest.

And young," I went on. "Younger than I am! How have you done it?"

"Aha!" The old Count cocked his head on one side mysteriously.

More in joke than in earnest, "I believe you've been seeing Steinach in Vienna," I said. "Having a rejuvenating operation."

For all reply, the old Count raised the forefinger of his right hand, laying it first to his lips, then along the side of his nose, and as he did so he winked. Then clenching his fist, and with his thumb sticking rigidly up, he made a complicated gesture which would, I am sure, for an Italian, have been full of a profound and vital significance. To me, however, unfamiliar with the language of signs, the exact meaning was not entirely clear. But the Count offered no verbal explanation. Still without uttering a word, he raised his hat; then laying his finger once more to his lips, he turned and ran with an astonishing agility down the steep path towards the little carriage of the funicular, in which the Colombella had already taken her seat.

HUBERT AND MINNIE

FOR Hubert Lapell this first love-affair was extremely important. "Important" was the word he had used himself when he was writing about it in his diary. It was an event in his life, a real event for a change. It marked, he felt, a genuine turning-point in his spiritual development.

"Voltaire," he wrote in his diary—and he wrote it a second time in one of his letters to Minnie—"Voltaire said that one died twice: once with the death of the whole body and once before, with the death of one's capacity to love. And in the same way one is born twice, the second time being on the occasion when one first falls in love. One is born, then, into a new world—a world of intenser feelings, heightened values, more penetrating insights." And so on.

In point of actual fact Hubert found this new world a little disappointing. The intenser feelings proved to be rather mild; not by any means up to literary standards.

> "I tell thee I am mad
> In Cressid's love. Thou answer'st: she is fair;
> Pour'st in the open ulcer of my heart
> Her eyes, her hair, her cheek, her gait, her voice. . . ."

No, it certainly wasn't quite that. In his diary, in his letters to Minnie, he painted, it is true, a series of brilliant and romantic landscapes of the new world. But they were composite imaginary landscapes in the manner of Salvator Rosa—richer, wilder, more picturesquely clear-obscure than the real thing. Hubert would seize with avidity on the least velleity of an unhappiness, a physical desire, a spiritual yearning, to work it up in his letters and journals into something substantially romantic. There were times, generally very late at night, when he succeeded in persuading himself that he was indeed the wildest, unhappiest, most passionate of lovers. But in the daytime he went about his business nourishing something like a grievance against love. The

148

thing was a bit of a fraud; yes, really, he decided, rather a fraud. All the same, he supposed it was important.

For Minnie, however, love was no fraud at all. Almost from the first moment she had adored him. A common friend had brought him to one of her Wednesday evenings. "This is Mr. Lapell; but he's too young to be called anything but Hubert." That was how he had been introduced. And, laughing, she had taken his hand and called him Hubert at once. He too had laughed, rather nervously. "My name's Minnie," she said. But he had been too shy to call her anything at all that evening. His brown hair was tufty and untidy, like a little boy's, and he had shy grey eyes that never looked at you for more than a glimpse at a time, but turned away almost at once, as though they were afraid. Quickly he glanced at you, eagerly—then away again; and his musical voice, with its sudden emphases, its quick modulations from high to low, seemed always to address itself to a ghost floating low down and a little to one side of the person to whom he was talking. Above the brows was a forehead beautifully domed, with a pensive wrinkle running up from between the eyes. In repose his full-lipped mouth pouted a little, as though he were expressing some chronic discontent with the world. And, of course, thought Minnie, the world wasn't beautiful enough for his idealism.

"But after all," he had said earnestly that first evening, "one has the world of thought to live in. That, at any rate, is simple and clear and beautiful. One can always live apart from the brutal scramble."

And from the depths of the arm-chair in which, fragile, tired, and in these rather "artistic" surroundings almost incongruously elegant, she was sitting, Helen Glamber laughed her clear little laugh. "I think, on the contrary," she said (Minnie remembered every incident of that first evening), "I think one ought to rush about and know thousands of people, and eat and drink enormously, and make love incessantly, and shout and laugh and knock people over the head." And having vented these Rabelaisian sentiments, Mrs. Glamber dropped back with a sigh of fatigue, covering her eyes with a thin white hand; for she had a splitting headache, and the light hurt her.

"Really!" Minnie protested, laughing. She would have felt rather shocked if any one else had said that; but Helen Glamber was allowed to say anything.

Hubert reaffirmed his quietism. Elegant, weary, infinitely fragile, Mrs. Glamber lay back in her arm-chair, listening. Or perhaps, under her covering hand, she was trying to go to sleep.

She had adored him at first sight. Now that she looked back she could see that it had been at first sight. Adored him protectively, maternally—for he was only twenty and very young, in spite of the wrinkle between his brows, and the long words, and the undergraduate's newly discovered knowledge; only twenty, and she was nearly twenty-nine. And she had fallen in love with his beauty, too. Ah, passionately.

Hubert, perceiving it later, was surprised and exceedingly flattered. This had never happened to him before. He enjoyed being worshipped, and since Minnie had fallen so violently in love with him, it seemed the most natural thing in the world for him to be in love with Minnie. True, if she had not started by adoring him, it would never have occurred to Hubert to fall in love with her. At their first meeting he had found her certainly very nice, but not particularly exciting. Afterwards, the manifest expression of her adoration had made him find her more interesting, and in the end he had fallen in love himself. But perhaps it was not to be wondered at if he found the process a little disappointing.

But still, he reflected on those secret occasions when he had to admit to himself that something was wrong with this passion, love without possession could never, surely, in the nature of things, be quite the genuine article. In his diary he recorded aptly those two quatrains of John Donne:

"So must pure lovers' souls descend
    To affections and to faculties,
Which sense may reach and apprehend,
    Else a great prince in prison lies.

> To our bodies turn we then, that so
>   Weak men on love revealed my look;
> Love's mysteries in souls do grow,
>   But yet the body is his book."

At their next meeting he recited them to Minnie. The conversation which followed, compounded as it was of philosophy and personal confidences, was exquisite. It really, Hubert felt, came up to literary standards.

The next morning Minnie rang up her friend Helen Glamber and asked if she might come to tea that afternoon. She had several things to talk to her about. Mrs. Glamber sighed as she hung up the receiver. "Minnie's coming to tea," she called, turning towards the open door.

From across the passage her husband's voice came back to her. "Good Lord!" it said in a tone of far-away horror, of absent-minded resignation; for John Glamber was deep in his work and there was only a little of him left, so to speak, above the surface to react to the bad news.

Helen Glamber sighed again, and propping herself more comfortably against her pillows she reached for her book. She knew that far-away voice and what it meant. It meant that he wouldn't answer if she went on with the conversation; only say "h'm" or "m'yes." And if she persisted after that, it meant that he'd say, plaintively, heart-breakingly, "Darling, you *must* let me get on with my work." And at that moment she would so much have liked to talk a little. Instead, she went on reading at the point where she had broken off to answer Minnie's telephone call.

"By this time the flames had enveloped the gynecæum. Nineteen times did the heroic Patriarch of Alexandria venture into the blazing fabric, from which he succeeded in rescuing all but two of its lovely occupants, twenty-seven in number, all of whom he caused to be transported at once to his own private apartments. . . ."

It was one of those instructive books John liked her to read. History, mystery, lesson, and law. But at the moment she didn't feel much like history. She felt like talking. And that was out of the question; absolutely out of it.

She put down her book and began to file her nails and think of poor Minnie. Yes, poor Minnie. Why was it that one couldn't help saying Good Lord! heartfeltly, when one heard she was coming to tea? And why did one never have the heart to refuse to let her come to tea? She was pathetic, but pathetic in such a boring way. There are some people you like being kind to, people you want to help and befriend. People that look at you with the eyes of sick monkeys. Your heart breaks when you see them. But poor Minnie had none of the charms of a sick monkey. She was just a great big healthy young woman of twenty-eight who ought to have been married and the mother of children, and who wasn't. She would have made such a good wife, such an admirably solicitous and careful mother. But it just happened that none of the men she knew had ever wanted to marry her. And why should they want to? When she came into a room, the light seemed to grow perceptibly dimmer, the electric tension slackened off. She brought no life with her; she absorbed what there was, she was like so much blotting-paper. No wonder nobody wanted to marry her. And yet, of course, it was the only thing. Particularly as she was always falling in love herself. The only thing.

"John!" Mrs. Glamber suddenly called. "Is it really true about ferrets?"

"Ferrets?" the voice from across the passage repeated with a remote irritation. "Is what true about ferrets?"

"That the females die if they're not mated."

"How on earth should I know?"

"But you generally know everything."

"But, my darling, really . . ." The voice was plaintive, full of reproach.

Mrs. Glamber clapped her hand over her mouth and only took it off again to blow a kiss. "All right," she said very quickly. "All right. Really. I'm sorry. I won't do it again. Really." She blew another kiss towards the door.

"But ferrets . . ." repeated the voice.

"Sh—sh, sh—sh."

"Why ferrets?"

"Darling," said Mrs. Glamber almost sternly, "you really must go on with your work."

Minnie came to tea. She put the case—hypothetically at first, as though it were the case of a third person; then, gaining courage, she put it personally. It was her own case. Out of the depths of her untroubled, pagan innocence, Helen Glamber brutally advised her. "If you want to go to bed with the young man," she said, "go to bed with him. The thing has no importance in itself. At least not much. It's only important because it makes possible more secret confidences, because it strengthens affection, makes the man in a way dependent on you. And then, of course, it's the natural thing. I'm all for nature except when it comes to painting one's face. They say that ferrets . . ." But Minnie noticed that she never finished the sentence. Appalled and fascinated, shocked and yet convinced, she listened.

"My darling," said Mrs. Glamber that evening when her husband came home—for he hadn't been able to face Minnie; he had gone to the Club for tea—"who was it that invented religion, and sin, and all that? And why?"

John laughed. "It was invented by Adam," he said, "for various little transcendental reasons which you would probably find it difficult to appreciate. But also for the very practical purpose of keeping Eve in order."

"Well, if you call complicating people's lives keeping them in order, then I dare say you're right." Mrs. Glamber shook her head. "I find it all too obscure. At sixteen, yes. But one really ought to have grown out of that sort of thing by twenty. And at thirty—the woman's nearly thirty, you know—well, really . . ."

In the end, Minnie wrote to Hubert telling him that she had made up her mind. Hubert was staying in Hertfordshire with his friend Watchett. It was a big house, the food was good, one was very comfortable; and old Mr. Watchett, moreover, had a very sound library. In the impenetrable shade of the Wellingtonias Hubert and Ted Watchett played croquet and discussed the best methods of cultivating the Me. You could do a good deal, they decided, with art—books, you know, and pictures and music. "Listen to Stravinsky's *Sacre*," said Ted Watchett, "and you're for ever excused from going to Tibet or the Gold Coast or any of those awful places. And then there's Dostoievsky instead of murder, and D. H. Lawrence as a substitute for sex."

"All the same," said Hubert, "one must have a *certain* amount of actual non-imaginative experience." He spoke earnestly, abstractedly; but Minnie's letter was in his pocket. "*Gnosce teipsum*. You can't really know yourself without coming into collision with events, can you?"

Next day, Ted's cousin, Phœbe, arrived. She had red hair and a milky skin, and was more or less on the musical comedy stage. "One foot on and one foot off," she explained. "The splits." And there and then she did them, the splits, on the drawing-room carpet. "It's quite easy," she said, laughing, and jumped up again with an easy grace that fairly took one's breath away. Ted didn't like her. "Tiresome girl," he said. "So silly, too. Consciously silly, silly on purpose, which makes it worse." And, it was true, she did like boasting about the amount of champagne she could put away without getting buffy, and the number of times she had exceeded the generous allowance and been "blind to the world." She liked talking about her admirers in terms which might make you suppose that they were all her accepted lovers. But then she had the justification of her vitality and her shining red hair.

"Vitality," Hubert wrote in his diary (he contemplated a distant date, after, or preferably before, his death, when these confessions and aphorisms would be published), "vitality can make claims on the world almost as imperiously as can beauty. Sometimes beauty and vitality meet in one person."

It was Hubert who arranged that they should stay at the mill. One of his friends had once been there with a reading party, and found the place comfortable, secluded, and admirably quiet.

Quiet, that is to say, with the special quietness peculiar to mills.
For the silence there was not the silence of night on a mountain;
it was a silence made of continuous thunder. At nine o'clock
every morning the mill-wheel began to turn, and its roaring
never stopped all day. For the first moments the noise was terrifying, was almost unbearable. Then, after a little, one grew
accustomed to it. The thunder became, by reason of its very un-
intermittence, a perfect silence, wonderfully rich and profound.

At the back of the mill was a little garden hemmed in on three
sides by the house, the outhouses, and a high brick wall, and
open on the fourth towards the water. Looking over the parapet,
Minnie watched it sliding past. It was like a brown snake with
arrowy markings on its back; and it crawled, it glided, it slid
along for ever. She sat there, waiting: her train, from London,
had brought her here soon after lunch; Hubert, coming across
country from the Watchetts, would hardly arrive before six.
The water flowed beneath her eyes like time, like destiny,
smoothly towards some new and violent event.

The immense noise that in this garden was silence enveloped
her. Inured, her mind moved in it as though in its native
element. From beyond the parapet came the coolness and the
weedy smell of water. But if she turned back towards the garden,
she breathed at once the hot perfume of sunlight beating on
flowers and ripening fruit. In the afternoon sunlight all the
world was ripe. The old red house lay there, ripe, like a dropped
plum; the walls were riper than the fruits of the nectarine trees
so tenderly and neatly crucified on their warm bricks. And that
richer silence of unremitting thunder seemed, as it were, the
powdery bloom on a day that had come to exquisite maturity
and was hanging, round as a peach and juicy with life and happiness, waiting in the sunshine for the bite of eager teeth.

At the heart of this fruit-ripe world Minnie waited. The water
flowed towards the wheel; smoothly, smoothly—then it fell, it
broke itself to pieces on the turning wheel. And time was sliding
onwards, quietly towards an event that would shatter all the
smoothness of her life.

"If you really want to go to bed with the young man, go to bed with him." She could hear Helen's clear, shrill voice saying impossible, brutal things. If any one else had said them, she would have run out of the room. But in Helen's mouth they seemed, somehow, so simple, so innocuous, and so true. And yet all that other people had said or implied—at home, at school, among the people she was used to meeting—seemed equally true.

But then, of course, there was love. Hubert had written a Shakespearean sonnet which began:

"Love hallows all whereon 'tis truly placed,
    Turns dross to gold with one touch of his dart,
Makes matter mind, extremest passion chaste,
    And builds a temple in the lustful heart."

She thought that very beautiful. And very true. It seemed to throw a bridge between Helen and the other people. Love, true love, made all the difference. It justified. Love—how much, how much she loved!

Time passed and the light grew richer as the sun declined out of the height of the sky. The day grew more and more deliciously ripe, swelling with unheard-of sweetness. Over its sun-flushed cheeks the thundery silence of the mill-wheel spread the softest, peachiest of blooms. Minnie sat on the parapet, waiting. Sometimes she looked down at the sliding water, sometimes she turned her eyes towards the garden. Time flowed, but she was now no more afraid of that shattering event that thundered there, in the future. The ripe sweetness of the afternoon seemed to enter into her spirit, filling it to the brim. There was no more room for doubts, or fearful anticipations, or regrets. She was happy. Tenderly, with a tenderness she could not have expressed in words, only with the gentlest of light kisses, with fingers caressingly drawn through the ruffled hair, she thought of Hubert, her Hubert.

Hubert, Hubert. . . . And suddenly, startlingly, he was standing there at her side.

"Oh," she said, and for a moment she stared at him with round brown eyes, in which there was nothing but astonishment. Then the expression changed. "Hubert," she said softly.

Hubert took her hand and dropped it again; looked at her for an instant, then turned away. Leaning on the parapet, he stared down into the sliding water; his face was unsmiling. For a long time both were silent. Minnie remained where she was, sitting quite still, her eyes fixed on the young man's averted face. She was happy, happy, happy. The long day ripened and ripened, perfection after perfection.

"Minnie," said the young man suddenly, and with a loud abruptness, as though he had been a long time deciding himself to speak and had at last succeeded in bringing out the prepared and pent-up words, "I feel I've behaved very badly towards you. I never ought to have asked you to come here. It was wrong. I'm sorry."

"But I came because I wanted to," Minnie exclaimed.

Hubert glanced at her, then turned away his eyes and went on addressing a ghost that floated, it seemed, just above the face of the sliding water. "It was too much to ask. I shouldn't have done it. For a man it's different. But for a woman . . ."

"But, I tell you, I wanted to."

"It's too much."

"It's nothing," said Minnie, "because I love you." And leaning forward, she ran her fingers through his hair. Ah, tenderness that no words could express! "You silly boy," she whispered. "Did you think I didn't love you enough for that?"

Hubert did not look up. The water slid and slid away before his eyes; Minnie's fingers played in his hair, ran caressingly over the nape of his neck. He felt suddenly a positive hatred for this woman. Idiot! Why couldn't she take a hint? He didn't want her. And why on earth had he ever imagined that he did? All the way in the train he had been asking himself that question. Why? Why? And the question had asked itself still more urgently just now as, standing at the garden door, he had looked out between the apple tree and watched her, unobserved, through

F

a long minute—watched her sitting there on the parapet, turning her vague brown eyes now at the water, now towards the garden, and smiling to herself with an expression that had seemed to him so dim and vacuous that he could almost have fancied her an imbecile.

And with Phœbe yesterday he had stood on the crest of the bare chalk down. Like a sea at their feet stretched the plain, and above the dim horizon towered heroic clouds. Fingers of the wind lifted the red locks of her hair. She stood as though poised, ready to leap off into the boisterous air. "How I should like to fly!" she said. "There's something particularly attractive about airmen, I always think." And she had gone running down the hill.

But Minnie, with her dull hair, her apple-red cheeks, and big, slow body, was like a peasant girl. How had he ever persuaded himself that he wanted her? And what made it much worse, of course, was that she adored him, embarrassingly, tiresomely, like a too affectionate spaniel that insists on tumbling about at your feet and licking your hand just when you want to sit quietly and concentrate on serious things.

Hubert moved away, out of reach of her caressing hand. He lifted towards her for a moment a pair of eyes that had become, as it were, opaque with a cold anger; then dropped them again.

"The sacrifice is too great," he said in a voice that sounded to him like somebody else's voice. He found it very difficult to say this sort of thing convincingly. "I can't ask it of you," the actor pursued. "I won't."

"But it isn't a sacrifice," Minnie protested. "It's a joy, it's happiness. Oh, can't you understand?"

Hubert did not answer. Motionless, his elbows on the parapet, he stared down into the water. Minnie looked at him, perplexed only, at first; but all at once she was seized with a nameless agonising doubt that grew and grew within her, as the silence prolonged itself, like some dreadful cancer of the spirit, until it had eaten away all her happiness, until there was nothing left in her mind but doubt and apprehension.

"What is it?" she said at last. "Why are you so strange? What is it, Hubert? What is it?"

Leaning forward, she laid her two hands on either side of his averted face and turned it towards her. Blank and opaque with anger were the eyes. "What is it?" she repeated. "Hubert, what is it?"

Hubert disengaged himself. "It's no good," he said in a smothered voice. "No good at all. It was a mistake. I'm sorry. I think I'd better go away. The trap's still at the door."

And without waiting for her to say anything, without explaining himself any further, he turned and walked quickly away, almost ran, towards the house. Well, thank goodness, he said to himself, he was out of that. He hadn't done it very well, or handsomely, or courageously; but, at any rate, he was out of it. Poor Minnie! He felt sorry for her; but after all, what could he do about it? Poor Minnie! Still, it rather flattered his vanity to think that she would be mourning over him. And in any case, he reassured his conscience, she couldn't really mind very much. But on the other hand, his vanity reminded him, she did adore him. Oh, she absolutely worshipped . . .

The door closed behind him. Minnie was alone again in the garden. Ripe, ripe it lay there in the late sunshine. Half of it was in shadow now; but the rest of it, in the coloured evening light, seemed to have come to the final and absolute perfection of maturity. Bloomy with thundery silence, the choicest fruit of all time hung there, deliciously sweet, sweet to the core; hung flushed and beautiful on the brink of darkness.

Minnie sat there quite still, wondering what had happened. Had he gone, had he really gone? The door closed behind him with a bang, and almost as though the sound were a signal prearranged, a man walked out from the mill on to the dam and closed the sluice. And all at once the wheel was still. Apocalyptically there was silence; the silence of soundlessness took the place of that other silence that was uninterrupted sound. Gulfs opened endlessly out around her; she was alone. Across the void of soundlessness a belated bee trailed its thin buzzing; the sparrows chirped, and from across the water came the sound of voices and far-away laughter. And as though woken from a sleep, Minnie looked up and listened, fearfully, turning her head from side to side.

FARD

THEY had been quarrelling now for nearly three-quarters of an hour. Muted and inarticulate, the voices floated down the corridor, from the other end of the flat. Stooping over her sewing, Sophie wondered, without much curiosity, what it was all about this time. It was Madame's voice that she heard most often. Shrill with anger and indignant with tears, it burst out in gusts, in gushes. Monsieur was more self-controlled, and his deeper voice was too softly pitched to penetrate easily the closed doors and to carry along the passage. To Sophie, in her cold little room, the quarrel sounded, most of the time, like a series of monologues by Madame, interrupted by strange and ominous silences. But every now and then Monsieur seemed to lose his temper outright, and then there was no silence between the gusts, but a harsh, deep, angry shout. Madame kept up her loud shrillness continuously and without flagging; her voice had, even in anger, a curious, level monotony. But Monsieur spoke now loudly, now softly, with emphases and modulations and sudden outbursts, so that his contributions to the squabble, when they were audible, sounded like a series of separate explosions. Bow, wow, wow-wow-wow, wow—a dog barking rather slowly.

After a time Sophie paid no more heed to the noise of quarrelling. She was mending one of Madame's camisoles, and the work required all her attention. She felt very tired; her body ached all over. It had been a hard day; so had yesterday, so had the day before. Every day was a hard day, and she wasn't so young as she had been. Two years more and she'd be fifty. Every day had been a hard day ever since she could remember. She thought of the sacks of potatoes she used to carry when she was a little girl in the country. Slowly, slowly she was walking along the dusty road with the sack over her shoulder. Ten steps more; she could manage that. Only it never was the end; one always had to begin again.

161

She looked up from her sewing, moved her head from side to side, blinked. She had begun to see lights and spots of colour dancing before her eyes; it often happened to her now. A sort of yellowish bright worm was wriggling up towards the right-hand corner of her field of vision; and though it was always moving upwards, upwards, it was always there in the same place. And there were stars of red and green that snapped and brightened and faded all round the worm. They moved between her and her sewing; they were there when she shut her eyes. After a moment she went on with her work; Madame wanted her camisole most particularly to-morrow morning. But it was difficult to see round the worm.

There was suddenly a great increase of noise from the other end of the corridor. A door had opened; words articulated themselves.

". . . bien tort, mon ami, si tu crois que je suis ton esclave. Je ferai ce que je voudrai."

"Moi aussi." Monsieur uttered a harsh, dangerous laugh. There was the sound of heavy footsteps in the passage, a rattling in the umbrella stand; then the front door banged.

Sophie looked down again at her work. Oh, the worm, the coloured stars, the aching fatigue in all her limbs! If one could only spend a whole day in bed—in a huge bed, feathery, warm and soft, all the day long . . .

The ringing of the bell startled her. It always made her jump, that furious wasp-like buzzer. She got up, put her work down on the table, smoothed her apron, set straight her cap, and stepped out into the corridor. Once more the bell buzzed furiously. Madame was impatient.

"At last, Sophie. I thought you were never coming."

Sophie said nothing; there was nothing to say. Madame was standing in front of the open wardrobe. A bundle of dresses hung over her arm, and there were more of them lying in a heap on the bed.

"Une beauté à la Rubens," her husband used to call her when he was in an amorous mood. He liked these massive, splendid,

great women. None of your flexible drain-pipes for him.
"Hélène Fourmont" was his pet name for her.

"Some day," Madame used to tell her friends, "some day I
really must go to the Louvre and see my portrait. By Rubens,
you know. It's extraordinary that one should have lived all one's
life in Paris and never have seen the Louvre. Don't you think
so?"

She was superb to-night. Her cheeks were flushed; her blue
eyes shone with an unusual brilliance between their long lashes;
her short, red-brown hair had broken wildly loose.

"To-morrow, Sophie," she said dramatically, "we start for
Rome. To-morrow morning." She unhooked another dress
from the wardrobe as she spoke, and threw it on to the bed.
With the movement her dressing-gown flew open, and there
was a vision of ornate underclothing and white exuberant flesh.
"We must pack at once."

"For how long, Madame?"

"A fortnight, three months—how should I know?"

"It makes a difference, Madame."

"The important thing is to get away. I shall not return to
this house, after what has been said to me to-night, till I am
humbly asked to."

"We had better take the large trunk, then, Madame; I will go
and fetch it."

The air in the box-room was sickly with the smell of dust and
leather. The big trunk was jammed in a far corner. She had to
bend and strain at it in order to pull it out. The worm and the
coloured stars flickered before her eyes; she felt dizzy when she
straightened herself up. "I'll help you to pack, Sophie," said
Madame, when the servant returned, dragging the heavy trunk
after her. What a death's-head the old woman looked nowadays!
She hated having old, ugly people near her. But Sophie was so
efficient; it would be madness to get rid of her.

"Madame need not trouble." There would be no end to it,
Sophie knew, if Madame started opening drawers and throwing
things about. "Madame had much better go to bed. It's late."

No, no. She wouldn't be able to sleep. She was to such a degree enervated. These men . . . What an embeastment! One was not their slave. One would not be treated in this way.

Sophie was packing. A whole day in bed, in a huge, soft bed, like Madame's. One would doze, one would wake up for a moment, one would doze again.

"His latest game," Madame was saying indignantly, "is to tell me he hasn't got any money. I'm not to buy any clothes, he says. Too grotesque. I can't go about naked, can I?" She threw out her hands. "And as for saying he can't afford, that's simply nonsense. He can, perfectly well. Only he's mean, mean, horribly mean. And if he'd only do a little honest work, for a change, instead of writing silly verses and publishing them at his own expense, he'd have plenty and to spare." She walked up and down the room. "Besides," she went on, "there's his old father. What's he for, I should like to know? 'You must be proud of having a poet for a husband,' he says." She made her voice quaver like an old man's. "It's all I can do not to laugh in his face. 'And what beautiful verses Hégésippe writes about you! What passion, what fire!'" Thinking of the old man, she grimaced, wobbled her head, shook her finger, doddered on her legs. "And when one reflects that poor Hégésippe is bald, and dyes the few hairs he has left." She laughed. "As for the passion he talks so much about in his beastly verses," she laughed— "that's all pure invention. But, my good Sophie, what are you thinking of? Why are you packing that hideous old green dress?"

Sophie pulled out the dress without saying anything. Why did the woman choose this night to look so terribly ill? She had a yellow face and blue teeth. Madame shuddered; it was too horrible. She ought to send her to bed. But, after all, the work had to be done. What could one do about it? She felt more than ever aggrieved.

"Life is terrible." Sighing, she sat down heavily on the edge of the bed. The buoyant springs rocked her gently once or twice before they settled to rest. "To be married to a man like this. I shall soon be getting old and fat. And never once unfaithful. But look how he treats me." She got up again and began to wander aimlessly about the room. "I won't stand it, though," she burst out. She had halted in front of the long mirror, and was admiring her own splendid tragic figure. No one would believe, to look at her, that she was over thirty. Behind the beautiful tragedian she could see in the glass a thin, miserable, old creature, with a yellow face and blue teeth, crouching over the trunk. Really, it was too disagreeable. Sophie looked like one of those beggar women one sees on a cold morning, standing in the gutter. Does one hurry past, trying not to look at them? Or does one stop, open one's purse, and give them one's copper and nickel—even as much as a two-franc note, if one has no change? But whatever one did, one always felt uncomfortable, one always felt apologetic for one's furs. That was what came of walking. If one had a car—but that was another of Hégésippe's meannesses—one wouldn't, rolling along behind closed windows, have to be conscious of them at all. She turned away from the glass.

"I won't stand it," she said, trying not to think of the beggar women, of blue teeth in a yellow face; "I won't stand it." She dropped into a chair.

But think of a lover with a yellow face and blue, uneven teeth! She closed her eyes, shuddered at the thought. It would be enough to make one sick. She felt impelled to take another look: Sophie's eyes were the colour of greenish lead, quite without life. What was one to do about it? The woman's face was a reproach, an accusation. And besides, the sight of it was making her feel positively ill. She had never been so profoundly enervated.

Sophie rose slowly and with difficulty from her knees; an expression of pain crossed her face. Slowly she walked to the chest of drawers, slowly counted out six pairs of silk stockings. She turned back towards the trunk. The woman was a walking corpse!

"Life is terrible," Madame repeated with conviction, "terrible, terrible, terrible."

She ought to send the woman to bed. But she would never be able to get her packing done by herself. And it was so important to get off to-morrow morning. She had told Hégésippe she would go, and he had simply laughed; he hadn't believed it. She must give him a lesson this time. In Rome she would see Luigino. Such a charming boy, and a marquis, too. Perhaps . . . But she could think of nothing but Sophie's face; the leaden eyes, the bluish teeth, the yellow, wrinkled skin.

"Sophie," she said suddenly; it was with difficulty that she prevented herself screaming, "look on my dressing-table. You'll see a box of rouge, the Dorin number twenty-four. Put a little on your cheeks. And there's a stick of lip salve in the right-hand drawer."

She kept her eyes resolutely shut while Sophie got up—with what a horrible creaking of the joints!—walked over to the dressing-table, and stood there, rustling faintly, through what seemed an eternity. What a life, my God, what a life! Slow footsteps trailed back again. She opened her eyes. Oh, that was far better, far better.

"Thank you, Sophie. You look much less tired now." She got up briskly. "And now we must hurry." Full of energy, she ran to the wardrobe. "Goodness me," she exclaimed, throwing up her hands, "you've forgotten to put in my blue evening dress. How could you be so stupid, Sophie?"

THE PORTRAIT

"PICTURES," said Mr. Bigger; "you want to see some pictures? Well, we have a very interesting mixed exhibition of modern stuff in our galleries at the moment. French and English, you know."

The customer held up his hand, shook his head. "No, no. Nothing modern for me," he declared, in his pleasant northern English. "I want real pictures, old pictures. Rembrandt and Sir Joshua Reynolds and that sort of thing."

"Perfectly." Mr. Bigger nodded. "Old Masters. Oh, of course we deal in the old as well as the modern."

"The fact is," said the other, "that I've just bought a rather large house—a Manor House," he added, in impressive tones.

Mr. Bigger smiled; there was an ingenuousness about this simple-minded fellow which was most engaging. He wondered how the man had made his money. "A Manor House." The way he had said it was really charming. Here was a man who had worked his way up from serfdom to the lordship of a manor, from the broad base of the feudal pyramid to the narrow summit. His own history and all the history of classes had been implicit in that awed proud emphasis on the "Manor." But the stranger was running on; Mr. Bigger could not allow his thoughts to wander farther. "In a house of this style," he was saying, "and with a position like mine to keep up, one must have a few pictures. Old Masters, you know; Rembrandts and What's-his-names."

"Of course," said Mr. Bigger, "an Old Master is a symbol of social superiority."

"That's just it," cried the other, beaming; "you've said just what I wanted to say."

Mr. Bigger bowed and smiled. It was delightful to find some one who took one's little ironies as sober seriousness.

"Of course, we should only need Old Masters downstairs, in

the reception-room. It would be too much of a good thing to have them in the bedrooms too."

"Altogether too much of a good thing," Mr. Bigger assented.

"As a matter of fact," the Lord of the Manor went on, "my daughter—she does a bit of sketching. And very pretty it is. I'm having some of her things framed to hang in the bedrooms. It's useful having an artist in the family. Saves you buying pictures. But, of course, we must have something old downstairs."

"I think I have exactly what you want." Mr. Bigger got up and rang the bell. "My daughter does a little sketching"—he pictured a large, blonde, barmaidish personage, thirty-one and not yet married, running a bit to seed. His secretary appeared at the door. "Bring me the Venetian portrait, Miss Pratt, the one in the back room. You know which I mean."

"You're very snug in here," said the Lord of the Manor. "Business good, I hope."

Mr. Bigger sighed. "The slump," he said. "We art dealers feel it worse than any one."

"Ah, the slump." The Lord of the Manor chuckled. "I foresaw it all the time. Some people seemed to think the good times were going to last for ever. What fools! I sold out of everything at the crest of the wave. That's why I can buy pictures now."

Mr. Bigger laughed too. This was the right sort of customer. "Wish I'd had anything to sell out during the boom," he said.

The Lord of the Manor laughed till the tears rolled down his cheeks. He was still laughing when Miss Pratt re-entered the room. She carried a picture, shieldwise, in her two hands, before her.

"Put it on the easel, Miss Pratt," said Mr. Bigger. "Now," he turned to the Lord of the Manor, "what do you think of that?"

The picture that stood on the easel before them was a half-length portrait. Plump-faced, white-skinned, high-bosomed in her deeply scalloped dress of blue silk, the subject of the picture seemed a typical Italian lady of the middle eighteenth century. A little complacent smile curved the pouting lips, and in one

hand she held a black mask, as though she had just taken it off
after a day of carnival.

"Very nice," said the Lord of the Manor; but he added doubtfully, "It isn't very like Rembrandt, is it?" It's all so clear and
bright. Generally in Old Masters you can never see anything at
all, they're so dark and foggy."

"Very true," said Mr. Bigger. "But not all Old Masters are
like Rembrandt."

"I suppose not." The Lord of the Manor seemed hardly to be
convinced.

"This is eighteenth-century Venetian. Their colour was
always luminous. Giangolini was the painter. He died young,
you know. Not more than half a dozen of his pictures are known.
And this is one."

The Lord of the Manor nodded. He could appreciate the
value of rarity.

"One notices at a first glance the influence of Longhi," Mr.
Bigger went on airily. "And there is something of the morbi-
dezza of Rosalba in the painting of the face."

The Lord of the Manor was looking uncomfortably from Mr.
Bigger to the picture and from the picture to Mr. Bigger. There
is nothing so embarrassing as to be talked at by some one possessing more knowledge than you do. Mr. Bigger pressed his
advantage.

"Curious," he went on, "that one sees nothing of Tiepolo's
manner in this. Don't you think so?"

The Lord of the Manor nodded. His face wore a gloomy expression. The corners of his baby's mouth drooped. One
almost expected him to burst into tears.

"It's pleasant," said Mr. Bigger, relenting at last, "to talk to
somebody who really knows about painting. So few people do."

"Well, I can't say I've ever gone into the subject very deeply,"
said the Lord of the Manor modestly. "But I know what I like
when I see it." His face brightened again, as he felt himself on
safer ground.

"A natural instinct," said Mr. Bigger. "That's a very precious gift. I could see by your face that you had it; I could see that the moment you came into the gallery."

The Lord of the Manor was delighted. "Really, now," he said. He felt himself growing larger, more important. "Really." He cocked his head critically on one side. "Yes. I must say I think that's a very fine bit of painting. Very fine. But the fact is, I should rather have liked a more historical piece, if you know what I mean. Something more ancestor-like, you know. A portrait of somebody with a story—like Anne Boleyn, or Nell Gwynn, or the Duke of Wellington, or some one like that."

"But, my dear sir, I was just going to tell you. This picture has a story." Mr. Bigger leaned forward and tapped the Lord of the Manor on the knee. His eyes twinkled with benevolent and amused brightness under his bushy eyebrows. There was a knowing kindliness in his smile. "A most remarkable story is connected with the painting of that picture."

"You don't say so?" The Lord of the Manor raised his eyebrows.

Mr. Bigger leaned back in his chair. "The lady you see there," he said, indicating the portrait with a wave of the hand, "was the wife of the fourth Earl Hurtmore. The family is now extinct. The ninth Earl died only last year. I got this picture when the house was sold up. It's sad to see the passing of these old ancestral homes." Mr. Bigger sighed. The Lord of the Manor looked solemn, as though he were in church. There was a moment's silence; then Mr. Bigger went on in a changed tone. "From his portraits, which I have seen, the fourth Earl seems to have been a long-faced, gloomy, grey-looking fellow. One can never imagine him young; he was the sort of man who looks permanently fifty. His chief interests in life were music and Roman antiquities. There's one portrait of him holding an ivory flute in one hand and resting the other on a fragment of Roman carving. He spent at least half his life travelling in Italy, looking for antiques and listening to music. When he was about fifty-five, he suddenly decided that it was about time to get married. This was the lady of his choice." Mr. Bigger pointed to the picture. "His money and his title must have made up for many deficiencies. One can't imagine, from her appearance, that Lady Hurtmore took a great deal of interest in Roman antiquities. Nor, I should think, did she care much for the science and history of music. She liked clothes, she liked society, she liked gambling, she liked flirting, she liked enjoying herself. It doesn't seem that the newly-wedded couple got on too well. But still, they avoided an open breach. A year after the marriage Lord Hurtmore decided to pay another visit to Italy. They reached Venice in the early autumn. For Lord Hurtmore, Venice meant unlimited music. It meant Galuppi's daily concerts at the orphanage of the Misericordia. It meant Piccini at Santa Maria. It meant new operas at the San Moise; it meant delicious cantatas at a hundred churches. It meant private concerts of amateurs; it meant Porpora and the finest singers in Europe; it meant Tartini and the greatest violinists. For Lady Hurtmore, Venice meant something rather different. It meant gambling at the Ridotto, masked balls, gay supper-parties—all the delights of the most amusing city in the world. Living their separate lives, both might have been happy here in Venice almost indefinitely. But one day Lord Hurtmore had the disastrous idea of having his wife's portrait painted. Young Giangolini was recommended to him as the promising, the coming painter. Lady Hurtmore began her sittings. Giangolini was handsome and dashing, Giangolini was young. He had an amorous technique as perfect as his artistic technique. Lady Hurtmore would have been more than human if she had been able to resist him. She was not more than human."

"None of us are, eh?" The Lord of the Manor dug his finger into Mr. Bigger's ribs and laughed.

Politely, Mr. Bigger joined in his mirth; when it had subsided, he went on. "In the end they decided to run away together across the border. They would live at Vienna—live on the Hurtmore family jewels, which the lady would be careful to pack in her suit-case. They were worth upwards of twenty thousand, the Hurtmore jewels; and in Vienna, under Maria-Theresa, one could live handsomely on the interest of twenty thousand.

"The arrangements were easily made. Giangolini had a friend who did everything for them—got them passports under an assumed name, hired horses to be in waiting on the mainland, placed his gondola at their disposal. They decided to flee on the day of the last sitting. The day came. Lord Hurtmore, according to his usual custom, brought his wife to Giangolini's studio in a gondola, left her there, perched on the high-backed model's throne, and went off again to listen to Galuppi's concert at the Misericordia. It was the time of full carnival. Even in broad daylight people went about in masks. Lady Hurtmore wore one of black silk—you see her holding it, there, in the portrait. Her husband, though he was no reveller and disapproved of carnival junketings, preferred to conform to the grotesque fashion of his neighbours rather than attract attention to himself by not conforming.

"The long black cloak, the huge three-cornered black hat, the long-nosed mask of white paper were the ordinary attire of every Venetian gentleman in these carnival weeks. Lord Hurtmore did not care to be conspicuous; he wore the same. There must have been something richly absurd and incongruous in the spectacle of this grave and solemn-faced English milord dressed in the clown's uniform of a gay Venetian masker. 'Pantaloon in the clothes of Pulcinella,' was how the lovers described him to one another; the old dotard of the eternal comedy dressed up as the clown. Well, this morning, as I have said, Lord Hurtmore came as usual in his hired gondola, bringing his lady with him. And she in her turn was bringing, under the folds of her capacious cloak, a little leather box wherein, snug on their silken bed, reposed the Hurtmore jewels. Seated in the dark little cabin of the gondola they watched the churches, the richly fretted palazzi, the high mean houses gliding past them. From under his Punch's mask Lord Hurtmore's voice spoke gravely, slowly, imperturbably.

" 'The learned Father Martini,' he said, 'has promised to do me the honour of coming to dine with us to-morrow. I doubt if any man knows more of musical history than he. I will ask you to be at pains to do him special honour.'

" 'You may be sure I will, my lord.' She could hardly contain the laughing excitement that bubbled up within her. To-morrow at dinner-time she would be far away—over the frontier, beyond Gorizia, galloping along the Vienna road. Poor old Pantaloon! But no, she wasn't in the least sorry for him. After all, he had his music, he had his odds and ends of broken marble. Under her cloak she clutched the jewel-case more tightly. How intoxicatingly amusing her secret was!"

Mr. Bigger clasped his hands and pressed them dramatically over his heart. He was enjoying himself. He turned his long, foxy nose towards the Lord of the Manor, and smiled benevolently. The Lord of the Manor for his part was all attention.

"Well?" he inquired.

Mr. Bigger unclasped his hands, and let them fall on to his knees.

"Well," he said, "the gondola draws up at Giangolini's door, Lord Hurtmore helps his wife out, leads her up to the painter's great room on the first floor, commits her into his charge with his usual polite formula, and then goes off to hear Galuppi's morning concert at the Misericordia. The lovers have a good two hours to make their final preparations.

"Old Pantaloon safely out of sight, up pops the painter's useful friend, masked and cloaked like every one else in the streets and on the canals of this carnival Venice. There follow embracements and handshakings and laughter all round; everything has been so marvellously successful, not a suspicion roused. From under Lady Hurtmore's cloak comes the jewel-case. She opens it, and there are loud Italian exclamations of astonishment and admiration. The brilliants, the pearls, the great Hurtmore emeralds, the ruby clasps, the diamond ear-rings—all these bright, glittering things are lovingly examined, knowingly handled. Fifty thousand sequins at the least is the estimate of the useful friend. The two lovers throw themselves ecstatically into one another's arms.

"The useful friend interrupts them; there are still a few last things to be done. They must go and sign for their passports at the Ministry of Police. Oh, a mere formality; but still it has to be done. He will go out at the same time and sell one of the lady's diamonds to provide the necessary funds for the journey."

Mr. Bigger paused to light a cigarette. He blew a cloud of smoke, and went on.

"So they set out, all in their masks and capes, the useful friend in one direction, the painter and his mistress in another. Ah, love in Venice!" Mr. Bigger turned up his eyes in ecstasy. "Have you ever been in Venice and in love, sir?" he inquired of the Lord of the Manor.

"Never farther than Dieppe," said the Lord of the Manor, shaking his head.

"Ah, then you've missed one of life's great experiences. You can never fully and completely understand what must have been the sensations of little Lady Hurtmore and the artist as they glided down the long canals, gazing at one another through the eyeholes of their masks. Sometimes, perhaps, they kissed— though it would have been difficult to do that without unmask- ing, and there was always the danger that some one might have recognised their naked faces through the windows of their little cabin. No, on the whole," Mr. Bigger concluded reflectively, "I expect they confined themselves to looking at one another. But in Venice, drowsing along the canals, one can almost be satisfied with looking—just looking."

He caressed the air with his hand and let his voice droop away into silence. He took two or three puffs at his cigarette without saying anything. When he went on, his voice was very quiet and even.

"About half an hour after they had gone, a gondola drew up at Giangolini's door and a man in a paper mask, wrapped in a black cloak and wearing on his head the inevitable three-cornered hat, got out and went upstairs to the painter's room. It was empty. The portrait smiled sweetly and a little fatuously from the easel. But no painter stood before it and the model's throne was untenanted. The long-nosed mask looked about the room with an expressionless curiosity. The wandering glance came to rest at last on the jewel-case that stood where the lovers had carelessly left it, open on the table. Deep-set and darkly shadowed behind the grotesque mask, the eyes dwelt long and fixedly on this object. Long-nosed Pulcinella seemed to be wrapped in meditation.

"A few minutes later there was the sound of footsteps on the stairs, of two voices laughing together. The masker turned away to look out of the window. Behind him the door opened noisily; drunk with excitement, with gay, laughable irresponsibility, the lovers burst in.

" 'Aha, *caro amico*! Back already. What luck with the diamond?'

"The cloaked figure at the window did not stir; Giangolini rattled gaily on. There had been no trouble whatever about the signatures, no questions asked; he had the passports in his pocket. They could start at once.

"Lady Hurtmore suddenly began to laugh uncontrollably; she couldn't stop.

" 'What's the matter?' asked Giangolini, laughing too.

" 'I was thinking,' she gasped between the paroxysms of her mirth, 'I was thinking of old Pantalone sitting at the Misericordia, solemn as an owl, listening'—she almost choked, and the words came out shrill and forced as though she were speaking through tears—'listening to old Galuppi's boring old cantatas.'

"The man at the window turned round. 'Unfortunately, madam,' he said, 'the learned maestro was indisposed this morning. There was no concert.' He took off his mask. 'And so I took the liberty of returning earlier than usual.' The long, grey, unsmiling face of Lord Hurtmore confronted them.

"The lovers stared at him for a moment speechlessly. Lady Hurtmore put her hand to her heart; it had given a fearful jump, and she felt a horrible sensation in the pit of her stomach. Poor Giangolini had gone as white as his paper mask. Even in these days of *cicisbei*, of official gentlemen friends, there were cases on record of outraged and jealous husbands resorting to homicide.

He was unarmed, but goodness only knew what weapons of destruction were concealed under that enigmatic black cloak. But Lord Hurtmore did nothing brutal or undignified. Gravely and calmly, as he did everything, he walked over to the table, picked up the jewel-case, closed it with the greatest care, and saying, 'My box, I think,' put it in his pocket and walked out of the room. The lovers were left looking questioningly at one another."

There was a silence.

"What happened then?" asked the Lord of the Manor.

"The anti-climax," Mr. Bigger replied, shaking his head mournfully. "Giangolini had bargained to elope with fifty thousand sequins. Lady Hurtmore didn't, on reflection, much relish the idea of love in a cottage. Woman's place, she decided at last, is in the home—with the family jewels. But would Lord Hurtmore see the matter in precisely the same light? That was the question, the alarming, disquieting question. She decided to go and see for herself.

"She got back just in time for dinner. 'His Illustrissimous Excellency is waiting in the dining-room,' said the major-domo. The tall doors were flung open before her; she swam in majestically, chin held high—but with what a terror in her soul! Her husband was standing by the fireplace. He advanced to meet her.

" 'I was expecting you, madam,' he said, and led her to her place.

"That was the only reference he ever made to the incident. In the afternoon he sent a servant to fetch the portrait from the painter's studio. It formed part of their baggage when, a month later, they set out for England. The story has been passed down with the picture from one generation to the next. I had it from an old friend of the family when I bought the portrait last year."

Mr. Bigger threw his cigarette end into the grate. He flattered himself that he had told that tale very well.

"Very interesting," said the Lord of the Manor, "very interesting indeed. Quite historical, isn't it? One could hardly do better with Nell Gwynn or Anne Boleyn, could one?"

Mr. Bigger smiled vaguely, distantly. He was thinking of Venice—the Russian countess staying in his pension, the tufted tree in the courtyard outside his bedroom, that strong, hot scent she used (it made you catch your breath when you first smelt it), and there was the bathing on the Lido, and the gondola, and the dome of the Salute against the hazy sky, looking just as it looked when Guardi painted it. How enormously long ago and far away it all seemed now! He was hardly more than a boy then; it had been his first great adventure. He woke up with a start from his reverie.

The Lord of the Manor was speaking. "How much, now, would you want for that picture?" he asked. His tone was detached, off-hand; he was a rare one for bargaining.

"Well," said Mr. Bigger, quitting with reluctance the Russian countess, the paradisaical Venice of five-and-twenty years ago, "I've asked as much as a thousand for less important works than this. But I don't mind letting this go to you for seven-fifty."

The Lord of the Manor whistled. "Seven-fifty?" he repeated. "It's too much."

"But, my dear sir," Mr. Bigger protested, "think what you'd have to pay for a Rembrandt of this size and quality—twenty thousand at least. Seven hundred and fifty isn't at all too much. On the contrary, it's very little considering the importance of the picture you're getting. You have a good enough judgment to see that this is a very fine work of art."

"Oh, I'm not denying that," said the Lord of the Manor. "All I say is that seven-fifty's a lot of money. Whe-ew! I'm glad my daughter does sketching. Think if I'd had to furnish the bedrooms with pictures at seven-fifty a time!" He laughed.

Mr. Bigger smiled. "You must also remember," he said, "that you're making a very good investment. Late Venetians are going up. If I had any capital to spare——" The door opened and Miss Pratt's blonde and frizzy head popped in.

"Mr. Crowley wants to know if he can see you, Mr. Bigger."

Mr. Bigger frowned. "Tell him to wait," he said irritably. He coughed and turned back to the Lord of the Manor. "If I had any capital to spare, I'd put it all into late Venetians. Every penny."

He wondered, as he said the words, how often he had told people that he'd put all his capital, if he had any, into primitives, cubism, nigger sculpture, Japanese prints. . . .

In the end the Lord of the Manor wrote him a cheque for six hundred and eighty.

"You might let me have a typewritten copy of the story," he said, as he put on his hat. "It would be a good tale to tell one's guests at dinner, don't you think? I'd like to have the details quite correct."

"Oh, of course, of course," said Mr. Bigger, "the details are most important."

He ushered the little round man to the door. "Good morning. Good morning." He was gone.

A tall, pale youth with side whiskers appeared in the doorway. His eyes were dark and melancholy; his expression, his general appearance, were romantic and at the same time a little pitiable. It was young Crowley, the painter.

"Sorry to have kept you waiting," said Mr. Bigger. "What did you want to see me for?"

Mr. Crowley looked embarrassed, he hesitated. How he hated having to do this sort of thing ! "The fact is," he said at last, "I'm horribly short of money. I wondered if perhaps you wouldn't mind—if it would be convenient to you—to pay me for that thing I did for you the other day. I'm awfully sorry to bother you like this."

"Not at all, my dear fellow." Mr. Bigger felt sorry for this wretched creature who didn't know how to look after himself. Poor young Crowley was as helpless as a baby. "How much did we settle it was to be?"

"Twenty pounds, I think it was," said Mr. Crowley timidly.

Mr. Bigger took out his pocket-book. "We'll make it twenty-five," he said.

"Oh no, really, I couldn't. Thanks very much." Mr. Crowley blushed like a girl. "I suppose you wouldn't like to have a show of some of my landscapes, would you?" he asked, emboldened by Mr. Bigger's air of benevolence.

"No, no. Nothing of your own." Mr. Bigger shook his head inexorably.

"There's no money in modern stuff. But I'll take any number of those sham Old Masters of yours." He drummed with his fingers on Lady Hurtmore's sleekly painted shoulder. "Try another Venetian," he added. "This one was a great success."

YOUNG ARCHIMEDES

IT was the view which finally made us take the place. True, the house had its disadvantages. It was a long way out of town and had no telephone. The rent was unduly high, the drainage system poor. On windy nights, when the ill-fitting panes were rattling so furiously in the window-frames that you could fancy yourself in an hotel omnibus, the electric light, for some mysterious reason, used invariably to go out and leave you in the noisy dark. There was a splendid bathroom; but the electric pump, which was supposed to send up water from the rain-water tanks in the terrace, did not work. Punctually every autumn the drinking well ran dry. And our landlady was a liar and a cheat.

But these are the little disadvantages of every hired house, all over the world. For Italy they were not really at all serious. I have seen plenty of houses which had them all and a hundred others, without possessing the compensating advantages of ours —the southward facing garden and terrace for the winter and spring, the large cool rooms against the midsummer heat, the hilltop air and freedom from mosquitoes, and finally the view.

And what a view it was! Or rather, what a succession of views. For it was different every day; and without stirring from the house one had the impression of an incessant change of scene: all the delights of travel without its fatigues. There were autumn days when all the valleys were filled with mist and the crests of the Apennines rose darkly out of a flat white lake. There were days when the mist invaded even our hilltop and we were enveloped in a soft vapour in which the mist-coloured olive trees, that sloped away below our windows towards the valley, disappeared as though into their own spiritual essence; and the only firm and definite things in the small, dim world within which we found ourselves confined were the two tall black cypresses growing on a little projecting terrace a hundred feet down the hill.

Black, sharp, and solid, they stood there, twin pillars of Hercules at the extremity of the known universe; and beyond them there was only pale cloud and round them only the cloudy olive trees.

These were the wintry days; but there were days of spring and autumn, days unchangingly cloudless, or—more lovely still— made various by the huge floating shapes of vapour that, snowy above the far-away snow-capped mountains, gradually unfolded, against the pale bright blue, enormous heroic gestures. And in the height of the sky the bellying draperies, the swans, the aerial marbles, hewed and left unfinished by gods grown tired of creation almost before they had begun, drifted sleeping along the wind, changing form as they moved. And the sun would come and go behind them; and now the town in the valley would fade and almost vanish in the shadow, and now, like an immense fretted jewel between the hills, it would glow as though by its own light. And looking across the nearer tributary valley that wound from below our crest down towards the Arno, looking over the low dark shoulder of hill on whose extreme promontory stood the towered church of San Miniato, one saw the huge dome airily hanging on its ribs of masonry, the square campanile, the sharp spire of Santa Croce, and the canopied tower of the Signoria, rising above the intricate maze of houses, distinct and brilliant, like small treasures carved out of precious stones. For a moment only, and then their light would fade away once more, and the travelling beam would pick out, among the indigo hills beyond, a single golden crest.

There were days when the air was wet with passed or with approaching rain, and all the distances seemed miraculously near and clear. The olive trees detached themselves one from another on the distant slopes; the far-away villages were lovely and pathetic like the most exquisite small toys. There were days in summer-time, days of impending thunder when, bright and sunlit against huge bellying masses of black and purple, the hills and the white houses shone as it were precariously, in a dying splendour, on the brink of some fearful calamity.

How the hills changed and varied! Every day and every hour

of the day, almost, they were different. There would be moments when, looking across the plain of Florence, one would see only a dark blue silhouette against the sky. The scene had no depth; there was only a hanging curtain painted flatly with the symbols of mountains. And then, suddenly almost, with the passing of a cloud, or when the sun had declined to a certain level in the sky, the flat scene transformed itself; and where there had been only a painted curtain, now there were ranges behind ranges of hills, graduated tone after tone from brown, or grey, or a green gold to far-away blue. Shapes that a moment before had been fused together indiscriminately into a single mass, now came apart into their constituents. Fiesole, which had seemed only a spur of Monte Morello, now revealed itself as the jutting headland of another system of hills, divided from the nearest bastions of its greater neighbour by a deep and shadowy valley.

At noon, during the heats of summer, the landscape became dim, powdery, vague, and almost colourless under the midday sun; the hills disappeared into the trembling fringes of the sky. But as the afternoon wore on the landscape emerged again, it dropped its anonymity, it climbed back out of nothingness into form and life. And its life, as the sun sank and slowly sank through the long afternoon, grew richer, grew more intense with every moment. The level light, with its attendant long, dark shadows, laid bare, so to speak, the anatomy of the land; the hills—each western escarpment shining, and each slope averted from the sunlight profoundly shadowed—became massive, jutty, and solid. Little folds and dimples in the seemingly even ground revealed themselves. Eastward from our hill-top, across the plain of the Ema, a great bluff cast its ever-increasing shadow; in the surrounding brightness of the valley a whole town lay eclipsed within it. And as the sun expired on the horizon, the farther hills flushed in its warm light, till their illumined flanks were the colour of tawny roses; but the valleys were already filled with the blue mist of evening. And it mounted, mounted; the fire went out of the western windows of the populous slopes; only the crests were still alight, and at last

they too were all extinct. The mountains faded and fused together again into a flat painting of mountains against the pale
evening sky. In a little while it was night; and if the moon were
full, a ghost of the dead scene still haunted the horizons.

Changeful in its beauty, this wide landscape always preserved
a quality of humanness and domestication which made it, to my
mind at any rate, the best of all landscapes to live with. Day by
day one travelled through its different beauties; but the journey,
like our ancestors' Grand Tour, was always a journey through
civilisation. For all its mountains, its steep slopes and deep
valleys, the Tuscan scene is dominated by its inhabitants. They
have cultivated every rood of ground that can be cultivated;
their houses are thickly scattered even over the hills, and the
valleys are populous. Solitary on the hilltop, one is not alone in
a wilderness. Man's traces are across the country, and already—
one feels it with satisfaction as one looks out across it—for
centuries, for thousands of years, it has been his, submissive,
tamed, and humanised. The wide, blank moorlands, the sands,
the forests of innumerable trees—these are places for occasional
visitation, healthful to the spirit which submits itself to them for
not too long. But fiendish influences as well as divine haunt
these total solitudes. The vegetative life of plants and things is
alien and hostile to the human. Men cannot live at ease except
where they have mastered their surroundings and where their
accumulated lives outnumber and outweigh the vegetative lives
about them. Stripped of its dark woods, planted, terraced, and
tilled almost to the mountains' tops, the Tuscan landscape is
humanised and safe. Sometimes upon those who live in the
midst of it there comes a longing for some place that is solitary,
inhuman, lifeless, or peopled only with alien life. But the longing
is soon satisfied, and one is glad to return to the civilised and
submissive scene.

I found that house on the hilltop the ideal dwelling-place. For
there, safe in the midst of a humanised landscape, one was yet
alone; one could be as solitary as one liked. Neighbours whom one
never sees at close quarters are the ideal and perfect neighbours.

Our nearest neighbours, in terms of physical proximity, lived very near. We had two sets of them, as a matter of fact, almost in the same house with us. One was the peasant family, who lived in a long, low building, part dwelling-house, part stables, storerooms and cowsheds, adjoining the villa. Our other neighbours —intermittent neighbours, however, for they only ventured out of town every now and then, during the most flawless weather— were the owners of the villa, who had reserved for themselves the smaller wing of the huge L-shaped house—a mere dozen rooms or so—leaving the remaining eighteen or twenty to us.

They were a curious couple, our proprietors. An old husband, grey, listless, tottering, seventy at least; and a signora of about forty, short, very plump, with tiny fat hands and feet and a pair of very large, very dark black eyes, which she used with all the skill of a born comedian. Her vitality, if you could have harnessed it and made it do some useful work, would have supplied a whole town with electric light. The physicists talk of deriving energy from the atom; they would be more profitably employed nearer home—in discovering some way of tapping those enormous stores of vital energy which accumulate in unemployed women of sanguine temperament and which, in the present imperfect state of social and scientific organisation, vent themselves in ways that are generally so deplorable: in interfering with other people's affairs, in working up emotional scenes, in thinking about love and making it, and in bothering men till they cannot get on with their work.

Signora Bondi got rid of her superfluous energy, among other ways, by "doing in" her tenants. The old gentleman, who was a retired merchant with a reputation for the most perfect rectitude, was allowed to have no dealings with us. When we came to see the house, it was the wife who showed us round. It was she who, with a lavish display of charm, with irresistible rollings of the eyes, expatiated on the merits of the place, sang the praises of the electric pump, glorified the bathroom (considering which, she insisted, the rent was remarkably moderate), and when we suggested calling in a surveyor to look over the house, earnestly begged us, as though our well-being were her only consideration, not to waste our money unnecessarily in doing anything so super- fluous. "After all," she said, "we are honest people. I wouldn't dream of letting you the house except in perfect condition. Have confidence." And she looked at me with an appealing, pained expression in her magnificent eyes, as though begging me not to insult her by my coarse suspiciousness. And leaving us no time to pursue the subject of surveyors any further, she began assuring us that our little boy was the most beautiful angel she had ever seen. By the time our interview with Signora Bondi was at an end, we had definitely decided to take the house.

"Charming woman," I said, as we left the house. But I think that Elizabeth was not quite so certain of it as I.

Then the pump episode began.

On the evening of our arrival in the house we switched on the electricity. The pump made a very professional whirring noise; but no water came out of the taps in the bathroom. We looked at one another doubtfully.

"Charming woman?" Elizabeth raised her eyebrows.

We asked for interviews; but somehow the old gentleman could never see us, and the Signora was invariably out or indis- posed. We left notes; they were never answered. In the end, we found that the only method of communicating with our land- lords, who were living in the same house with us, was to go down into Florence and send a registered express letter to them. For this they had to sign two separate receipts and even, if we chose to pay forty centimes more, a third incriminating docu- ment, which was then returned to us. There could be no pre- tending, as there always was with ordinary letters or notes, that the communication had never been received. We began at last to get answers to our complaints. The Signora, who wrote all the letters, started by telling us that, naturally, the pump didn't work, as the cisterns were empty, owing to the long drought. I had to walk three miles to the post office in order to register my letter reminding her that there had been a violent thunderstorm only last Wednesday, and that the tanks were consequently more than half full. The answer came back: bath water had not been guaranteed in the contract; and if I wanted it, why hadn't I had the pump looked at before I took the house? Another walk into town to ask the Signora next door whether she remembered her adjurations to us to have confidence in her, and to inform her that the existence in a house of a bathroom was in itself an implicit guarantee of bath water. The reply to that was that the Signora couldn't continue to have communications with people who wrote so rudely to her. After that I put the matter into the hands of a lawyer. Two months later the pump was actually replaced. But we had to serve a writ on the lady before she gave in. And the costs were considerable.

One day, towards the end of the episode, I met the old gentleman in the road, taking his big maremman dog for a walk—or being taken, rather, for a walk by the dog. For where the dog pulled the old gentleman had perforce to follow. And when it stopped to smell, or scratch the ground, or leave against a gatepost its visiting-card or an offensive challenge, patiently, at his end of the leash, the old man had to wait. I passed him standing at the side of the road, a few hundred yards below our house. The dog was sniffing at the roots of one of the twin cypresses which grew one on either side of the entry to a farm; I heard the beast growling indignantly to itself, as though it scented an intolerable insult. Old Signor Bondi, leashed to his dog, was waiting. The knees inside the tubular grey trousers were slightly bent. Leaning on his cane, he stood gazing mournfully and vacantly at the view. The whites of his old eyes were discoloured, like ancient billiard balls. In the grey, deeply wrinkled face, his nose was dyspeptically red. His white moustache, ragged and yellowing at the fringes, drooped in a melancholy curve. In his black tie he wore a very large diamond; perhaps that was what Signora Bondi had found so attractive about him.

I took off my hat as I approached. The old man stared at me absently, and it was only when I was already almost past him that he recollected who I was.

"Wait," he called after me, "wait!" And he hastened down

the road in pursuit. Taken utterly by surprise and at a dis-
advantage—for it was engaged in retorting to the affront im-
printed on the cypress roots—the dog permitted itself to be
jerked after him. Too much astonished to be anything but
obedient, it followed its master. "Wait!"

I waited.

"My dear sir," said the old gentleman, catching me by the
lapel of my coat and blowing most disagreeably in my face, "I
want to apologise." He looked around him, as though afraid
that even here he might be overheard. "I want to apologise," he
went on, "about that wretched pump business. I assure you
that, if it had been only my affair, I'd have put the thing right as
soon as you asked. You were quite right: a bathroom is an implicit guarantee of bath water. I saw from the first that we should
have no chance if it came to court. And besides, I think one
ought to treat one's tenants as handsomely as one can afford to.
But my wife "—he lowered his voice—"the fact is that she likes
this sort of thing, even when she knows that she's in the wrong
and must lose. And besides, she hoped, I dare say, that you'd get
tired of asking and have the job done yourself. I told her from
the first that we ought to give in; but she wouldn't listen. You
see, she enjoys it. Still, now she sees that it must be done. In
the course of the next two or three days you'll be having your bath
water. But I thought I'd just like to tell you how . . ." But the
Maremmano, which had recovered by this time from its surprise
of a moment since, suddenly bounded, growling, up the road.
The old gentleman tried to hold the beast, strained at the leash,
tottered unsteadily, then gave way and allowed himself to be
dragged off. ". . . how sorry I am," he went on, as he receded
from me, "that this little misunderstanding . . ." But it was no
use. "Good-bye." He smiled politely, made a little deprecating
gesture, as though he had suddenly remembered a pressing engagement, and had no time to explain what it was. "Good-bye."
He took off his hat and abandoned himself completely to the
dog.

A week later the water really did begin to flow, and the day after our first bath Signora Bondi, dressed in dove-grey satin and wearing all her pearls, came to call.

"Is it peace now?" she asked, with a charming frankness, as she shook hands.

We assured her that, so far as we were concerned, it certainly was.

"But why *did* you write me such dreadfully rude letters?" she said, turning on me a reproachful glance that ought to have moved the most ruthless malefactor to contrition. "And then that writ. How *could* you? To a lady . . ."

I mumbled something about the pump and our wanting baths.

"But how could you expect me to listen to you while you were in that mood? Why didn't you set about it differently—politely, charmingly?" She smiled at me and dropped her fluttering eyelids.

I thought it best to change the conversation. It is disagreeable, when one is in the right, to be made to appear in the wrong.

A few weeks later we had a letter—duly registered and by express messenger—in which the Signora asked us whether we proposed to renew our lease (which was only for six months), and notifying us that, if we did, the rent would be raised 25 per cent., in consideration of the improvements which had been carried out. We thought ourselves lucky, at the end of much bargaining, to get the lease renewed for a whole year with an increase in the rent of only 15 per cent.

It was chiefly for the sake of the view that we put up with these intolerable extortions. But we had found other reasons, after a few days' residence, for liking the house. Of these the most cogent was that, in the peasant's youngest child, we had discovered what seemed the perfect playfellow for our own small boy. Between little Guido—for that was his name—and the youngest of his brothers and sisters there was a gap of six or seven years. His two elder brothers worked with their father in the fields; since the time of the mother's death, two or three years before we knew them, the eldest sister had ruled the house, and the younger, who had just left school, helped her and in between-whiles kept an eye on Guido, who by this time, however, needed very little looking after; for he was between six and seven years old and as precocious, self-assured, and responsible as the children of the poor, left as they are to themselves almost from the time they can walk, generally are.

Though fully two and a half years older than little Robin—and at that age thirty months are crammed with half a lifetime's experience—Guido took no undue advantage of his superior intelligence and strength. I have never seen a child more patient, tolerant, and untyrannical. He never laughed at Robin for his clumsy efforts to imitate his own prodigious feats; he did not tease or bully, but helped his small companion when he was in difficulties and explained when he could not understand. In return, Robin adored him, regarded him as the model and perfect Big Boy, and slavishly imitated him in every way he could.

These attempts of Robin's to imitate his companion were often exceedingly ludicrous. For by an obscure psychological law, words and actions in themselves quite serious become comic as soon as they are copied; and the more accurately, if the imitation is a deliberate parody, the funnier—for an overloaded imitation of some one we know does not make us laugh so much as one that is almost indistinguishably like the original. The bad imitation is only ludicrous when it is a piece of sincere and earnest flattery which does not quite come off. Robin's imitations were mostly of this kind. His heroic and unsuccessful attempts to perform the feats of strength and skill, which Guido could do with ease, were exquisitely comic. And his careful, long-drawn imitations of Guido's habits and mannerisms were no less amusing. Most ludicrous of all, because most earnestly undertaken and most incongruous in the imitator, were Robin's impersonations of Guido in the pensive mood. Guido was a thoughtful child, given to brooding and sudden abstractions. One would find him sitting in a corner by himself, chin in hand, elbow on knee, plunged, to all appearances, in the profoundest meditation. And sometimes, even in the midst of his play, he

G

would suddenly break off, to stand, his hands behind his back, frowning and staring at the ground. When this happened, Robin became overawed and a little disquieted. In a puzzled silence he looked at his companion. "Guido," he would say softly, "Guido." But Guido was generally too much pre-occupied to answer; and Robin, not venturing to insist, would creep near him, and throwing himself as nearly as possible into Guido's attitude—standing Napoleonically, his hands clasped behind him, or sitting in the posture of Michelangelo's Lorenzo the Magnificent—would try to meditate too. Every few seconds he would turn his bright blue eyes towards the elder child to see whether he was doing it quite right. But at the end of a minute he began to grow impatient; meditation wasn't his strong point. "Guido," he called again and, louder, "Guido!" And he would take him by the hand and try to pull him away. Sometimes Guido roused himself from his reverie and went back to the interrupted game. Sometimes he paid no attention. Melancholy, perplexed, Robin had to take himself off to play by himself. And Guido would go on sitting or standing there, quite still; and his eyes, if one looked into them, were beautiful in their grave and pensive calm.

They were large eyes, set far apart and, what was strange in a dark-haired Italian child, of a luminous pale blue-grey colour. They were not always grave and calm, as in these pensive moments. When he was playing, when he talked or laughed, they lit up; and the surface of those clear, pale lakes of thought seemed, as it were, to be shaken into brilliant sunflashing ripples. Above those eyes was a beautiful forehead, high and steep and domed in a curve that was like the subtle curve of a rose petal. The nose was straight, the chin small and rather pointed, the mouth drooped a little sadly at the corners.

I have a snapshot of the two children sitting together on the parapet of the terrace. Guido sits almost facing the camera, but looking a little to one side and downwards; his hands are crossed in his lap and his expression, his attitude are thoughtful, grave, and meditative. It is Guido in one of those moods of abstraction

into which he would pass even at the height of laughter and play
—quite suddenly and completely, as though he had all at once
taken it into his head to go away and had left the silent and beautiful body behind, like an empty house, to wait for his return.
And by his side sits little Robin, turning to look up at him, his
face half averted from the camera, but the curve of his cheek
showing that he is laughing; one little raised hand is caught at
the top of a gesture, the other clutches at Guido's sleeve, as
though he were urging him to come away and play. And the legs
dangling from the parapet have been seen by the blinking instrument in the midst of an impatient wriggle; he is on the point of
slipping down and running off to play hide-and-seek in the
garden. All the essential characteristics of both the children are
in that little snapshot.

"If Robin were not Robin," Elizabeth used to say, "I could
almost wish he were Guido."

And even at that time, when I took no particular interest in
the child, I agreed with her. Guido seemed to me one of the
most charming little boys I had ever seen.

We were not alone in admiring him. Signora Bondi when, in
those cordial intervals between our quarrels, she came to call,
was constantly speaking of him. "Such a beautiful, beautiful
child!" she would exclaim with enthusiasm. "It's really a waste
that he should belong to peasants who can't afford to dress him
properly. If he were mine, I should put him into black velvet;
or little white knickers and a white knitted silk jersey with a red
line at the collar and cuffs; or perhaps a white sailor suit would be
pretty. And in winter a little fur coat, with a squirrel skin cap,
and possibly Russian boots . . ." Her imagination was running
away with her. "And I'd let his hair grow, like a page's, and
have it just curled up a little at the tips. And a straight fringe
across his forehead. Every one would turn round and stare
after us if I took him out with me in Via Tornabuoni."

What you want, I should have liked to tell her, is not a child;
it's a clockwork doll or a performing monkey. But I did not say
so—partly because I could not think of the Italian for a clock-

work doll and partly because I did not want to risk having the rent raised another 15 per cent.

"Ah, if only I had a little boy like that!" She sighed and modestly dropped her eyelids. "I adore children. I sometimes think of adopting one—that is, if my husband would allow it."

I thought of the poor old gentleman being dragged along at the heels of his big white dog and inwardly smiled.

"But I don't know if he would," the Signora was continuing, "I don't know if he would." She was silent for a moment, as though considering a new idea.

A few days later, when we were sitting in the garden after luncheon, drinking our coffee, Guido's father, instead of passing with a nod and the usual cheerful good-day, halted in front of us and began to talk. He was a fine handsome man, not very tall, but well proportioned, quick and elastic in his movements, and full of life. He had a thin brown face, featured like a Roman's and lit by a pair of the most intelligent-looking grey eyes I ever saw. They exhibited almost too much intelligence when, as not infrequently happened, he was trying, with an assumption of perfect frankness and a childlike innocence, to take one in or get something out of one. Delighting in itself, the intelligence shone there mischievously. The face might be ingenuous, impassive, almost imbecile in its expression; but the eyes on these occasions gave him completely away. One knew, when they glittered like that, that one would have to be careful.

To-day, however, there was no dangerous light in them. He wanted nothing out of us, nothing of any value—only advice, which is a commodity, he knew, that most people are only too happy to part with. But he wanted advice on what was, for us, rather a delicate subject: on Signora Bondi. Carlo had often complained to us about her. The old man is good, he told us, very good and kind indeed. Which meant, I dare say, among other things, that he could easily be swindled. But his wife . . . Well, the woman was a beast. And he would tell us stories of her insatiable rapacity: she was always claiming more than the half of the produce which, by the laws of the metayage system, was the proprietor's due. He complained of her suspiciousness: she was for ever accusing him of sharp practices, of downright stealing—him, he struck his breast, the soul of honesty. He complained of her shortsighted avarice: she wouldn't spend enough on manure, wouldn't buy him another cow, wouldn't have electric light installed in the stables. And we had sympathised, but cautiously, without expressing too strong an opinion on the subject. The Italians are wonderfully non-committal in their speech; they will give nothing away to an interested person until they are quite certain that it is right and necessary and, above all, safe to do so. We had lived long enough among them to imitate their caution. What we said to Carlo would be sure, sooner or later, to get back to Signora Bondi. There was nothing to be gained by unnecessarily embittering our relations with the lady —only another 15 per cent., very likely, to be lost.

To-day he wasn't so much complaining as feeling perplexed. The Signora had sent for him, it seemed, and asked him how he would like it if she were to make an offer—it was all very hypothetical in the cautious Italian style—to adopt little Guido. Carlo's first instinct had been to say that he wouldn't like it at all. But an answer like that would have been too coarsely committal. He had preferred to say that he would think about it. And now he was asking for our advice.

Do what you think best, was what in effect we replied. But we gave it distantly but distinctly to be understood that we didn't think that Signora Bondi would make a very good foster-mother for the child. And Carlo was inclined to agree. Besides, he was very fond of the boy.

"But the thing is," he concluded rather gloomily, "that if she has really set her heart on getting hold of the child, there's nothing she won't do to get him—nothing."

He too, I could see, would have liked the physicists to start on unemployed childless women of sanguine temperament before they tried to tackle the atom. Still, I reflected, as I watched him striding away along the terrace, singing powerfully from a brazen gullet as he went, there was force there, there was life enough in those elastic limbs, behind those bright grey eyes, to put up a good fight even against the accumulated vital energies of Signora Bondi.

It was a few days after this that my gramophone and two or three boxes of records arrived from England. They were a great comfort to us on the hilltop, providing as they did the only thing in which that spiritually fertile solitude—otherwise a perfect Swiss Family Robinson's island—was lacking: music. There is not much music to be heard nowadays in Florence. The times when Dr. Burney could tour through Italy, listening to an un-ending succession of new operas, symphonies, quartets, cantatas, are gone. Gone are the days when a learned musician, inferior only to the Reverend Father Martini of Bologna, could admire what the peasants sang and the strolling players thrummed and scraped on their instruments. I have travelled for weeks through the peninsula and hardly heard a note that was not "Salome" or the Fascists' song. Rich in nothing else that makes life agreeable or even supportable, the northern metropolises are rich in music. That is perhaps the only inducement that a reasonable man can find for living there. The other attractions—organised gaiety, people, miscellaneous conversation, the social pleasures—what are those, after all, but an expense of spirit that buys nothing in return? And then the cold, the darkness, the mouldering dirt, the damp and squalor. . . . No, where there is no necessity that retains, music can be the only inducement. And that, thanks to the ingenious Edison, can now be taken about in a box and un-packed in whatever solitude one chooses to visit. One can live at Benin, or Nuneaton, or Tozeur in the Sahara, and still hear Mozart quartets, and selections from the Well-Tempered Clavi-chord, and the Fifth Symphony, and the Brahms clarinet quintet, and motets by Palestrina.

Carlo, who had gone down to the station with his mule and cart to fetch the packing-case, was vastly interested in the machine.

"One will hear some music again," he said, as he watched me

unpacking the gramophone and the disks. "It is difficult to do much oneself.'"

Still, I reflected, he managed to do a good deal. On warm nights we used to hear him, where he sat at the door of his house, playing his guitar and softly singing; the eldest boy shrilled out the melody on the mandoline, and sometimes the whole family would join in, and the darkness would be filled with their passionate, throaty singing. Piedigrotta songs they mostly sang; and the voices drooped slurringly from note to note, lazily climbed or jerked themselves with sudden sobbing emphases from one tone to another. At a distance and under the stars the effect was not unpleasing.

"Before the war," he went on, "in normal times" (and Carlo had a hope, even a belief, that the normal times were coming back and that life would soon be as cheap and easy as it had been in the days before the flood), "I used to go and listen to the operas at the Politeama. Ah, they were magnificent. But it costs five lire now to get in."

"Too much," I agreed.

"Have you got *Trovatore*?" he asked.

I shook my head.

"*Rigoletto?*"

"I'm afraid not."

"*Bohème? Fanciulla del West? Pagliacci?*"

I had to go on disappointing him.

"Not even *Norma?* Or the *Barbiere?*"

I put on Battistini in "La ci darem" out of *Don Giovanni*. He agreed that the singing was good; but I could see that he didn't much like the music. Why not? He found it difficult to explain.

"It's not like *Pagliacci*," he said at last.

"Not palpitating?" I suggested, using a word with which I was sure he would be familiar; for it occurs in every Italian political speech and patriotic leading article.

"Not palpitating," he agreed.

And I reflected that it is precisely by the difference between *Pagliacci* and *Don Giovanni*, between the palpitating and the non-palpitating, that modern musical taste is separated from the old. The corruption of the best, I thought, is the worst. Beethoven taught music to palpitate with his intellectual and spiritual passion. It has gone on palpitating ever since, but with the passion of inferior men. Indirectly, I thought, Beethoven is responsible for *Parsifal*, *Pagliacci*, and the *Poem of Fire*; still more indirectly for *Samson and Delilah* and "Ivy, cling to me." Mozart's melodies may be brilliant, memorable, infectious; but they don't palpitate, don't catch you between wind and water, don't send the listener off into erotic ecstasies.

Carlo and his elder children found my gramophone, I am afraid, rather a disappointment. They were too polite, however, to say so openly; they merely ceased, after the first day or two, to take any interest in the machine and the music it played. They preferred the guitar and their own singing.

Guido, on the other hand, was immensely interested. And he liked, not the cheerful dance tunes, to whose sharp rhythms our little Robin loved to go stamping round and round the room, pretending that he was a whole regiment of soldiers, but the genuine stuff. The first record he heard, I remember, was that of the slow movement of Bach's Concerto in D Minor for two violins. That was the disk I put on the turnable as soon as Carlo had left me. It seemed to me, so to speak, the most musical piece of music with which I could refresh my long-parched mind—the coolest and clearest of all draughts. The movement had just got under way and was beginning to unfold its pure and melancholy beauties in accordance with the laws of the most exacting intellectual logic, when the two children, Guido in front and little Robin breathlessly following, came clattering into the room from the loggia.

Guido came to a halt in front of the gramophone and stood there, motionless, listening. His pale blue-grey eyes opened themselves wide; making a little nervous gesture that I had often noticed in him before, he plucked at his lower lip with his thumb and forefinger. He must have taken a deep breath; for I noticed that, after listening for a few seconds, he sharply expired and drew in a fresh gulp of air. For an instant he looked at me—a questioning, astonished, rapturous look—gave a little laugh that ended in a kind of nervous shudder, and turned back towards the source of the incredible sounds. Slavishly imitating his elder comrade, Robin had also taken up his stand in front of the gramophone, and in exactly the same position, glancing at Guido from time to time to make sure that he was doing everything, down to plucking at his lip, in the correct way. But after a minute or so he became bored.

"Soldiers," he said, turning to me; "I want soldiers. Like in London." He remembered the rag-time and the jolly marches round and round the room.

I put my fingers to my lips. "Afterwards," I whispered.

Robin managed to remain silent and still for perhaps another twenty seconds. Then he seized Guido by the arm, shouting, "Vieni, Guido! Soldiers. Soldati. Vieni giuocare soldati."

It was then, for the first time, that I saw Guido impatient. "Vai!" he whispered angrily, slapped at Robin's clutching hand and pushed him roughly away. And he leaned a little closer to the instrument, as though to make up by yet intenser listening for what the interruption had caused him to miss.

Robin looked at him, astonished. Such a thing had never happened before. Then he burst out crying and came to me for consolation.

When the quarrel was made up—and Guido was sincerely repentant, was as nice as he knew how to be when the music had stopped and his mind was free to think of Robin once more—I asked him how he liked the music. He said he thought it was beautiful. But *bello* in Italian is too vague a word, too easily and frequently uttered, to mean very much.

"What did you like best?" I insisted. For he had seemed to enjoy it so much that I was curious to find out what had really impressed him.

He was silent for a moment, pensively frowning. "Well," he said at last, "I liked the bit that went like this." And he hummed a long phrase. "And then there's the other thing singing at the same time—but what are those things," he interrupted himself, "that sing like that?"

"They're called violins," I said.

"Violins." He nodded. "Well, the other violin goes like this." He hummed again. "Why can't one sing both at once? And what is in that box? What makes it make that noise?" The child poured out his questions.

I answered him as best I could, showing him the little spirals on the disk, the needle, the diaphragm. I told him to remember how the string of the guitar trembled when one plucked it; sound is a shaking in the air, I told him, and I tried to explain how those shakings get printed on the black disk. Guido listened to me very gravely, nodding from time to time. I had the impression that he understood perfectly well everything I was saying.

By this time, however, poor Robin was so dreadfully bored that in pity for him I had to send the two children out into the garden to play. Guido went obediently; but I could see that he would have preferred to stay indoors and listen to more music. A little while later, when I looked out, he was hiding in the dark recesses of the big bay tree, roaring like a lion, and Robin, laughing, but a little nervously, as though he were afraid that the horrible noise might possibly turn out, after all, to be the roaring of a real lion, was beating the bush with a stick, and shouting, "Come out, come out! I want to shoot you."

After lunch, when Robin had gone upstairs for his afternoon sleep, he reappeared. "May I listen to the music now?" he asked. And for an hour he sat there in front of the instrument, his head cocked slightly on one side, listening while I put on one disk after another.

Thenceforward he came every afternoon. Very soon he knew all my library of records, had his preferences and dislikes, and could ask for what he wanted by humming the principal theme.

"I don't like that one," he said of Strauss's "Till Eulen Spiegel." "It's like what we sing in our house. Not really like, you know. But somehow rather like, all the same. You understand?" He looked at us perplexedly and appealingly, as though begging us to understand what he meant and so save him from going on explaining. We nodded. Guido went on. "And then," he said, "the end doesn't seem to come properly out of the beginning. It's not like the one you played the first time." He hummed a bar or two from the slow movement of Bach's D Minor Concerto.

"It isn't," I suggested, "like saying: All little boys like playing. Guido is a little boy. Therefore Guido likes playing."

He frowned. "Yes, perhaps that's it," he said at last. "The one you played first is more like that. But, you know," he added, with an excessive regard for truth, "I don't like playing as much as Robin does."

Wagner was among his dislikes; so was Debussy. When I played the record of one of Debussy's Arabesques, he said, "Why does he say the same thing over and over again? He ought to say something new, or go on, or make the thing grow. Can't he think of anything different?" But he was less censorious about the "Après-Midi d'un Faune." "The things have beautiful voices," he said.

Mozart overwhelmed him with delight. The duet from *Don Giovanni*, which his father had found insufficiently palpitating, enchanted Guido. But he preferred the quartets and the orchestral pieces.

"I like music," he said, "better than singing."

Most people, I reflected, like singing better than music; are more interested in the executant than in what he executes, and find the impersonal orchestra less moving than the soloist. The touch of the pianist is the human touch, and the soprano's high C is the personal note. It is for the sake of this touch, that note, that audiences fill the concert halls.

Guido, however, preferred music. True, he liked "La ci darem"; he liked "Deh vieni alla finestra"; he thought "Che soave zefiretto" so lovely that almost all our concerts had to begin with it. But he preferred the other things. The *Figaro* overture was one of his favourites. There is a passage not far from the beginning of the piece, where the first violins suddenly go rocketing up into the heights of loveliness; as the music approached that point, I used always to see a smile developing and gradually brightening on Guido's face, and when, punctually, the thing happened, he clapped his hands and laughed aloud with pleasure.

On the other side of the same disk, it happened, was recorded Beethoven's *Egmont* overture. He liked that almost better than *Figaro*.

"It has more voices," he explained. And I was delighted by the acuteness of the criticism; for it is precisely in the richness of its orchestration that *Egmont* goes beyond *Figaro*.

But what stirred him almost more than anything was the *Coriolan* overture. The third movement of the Fifth Symphony, the second movement of the Seventh, the slow movement of the Emperor Concerto—all these things ran it pretty close. But none excited him so much as *Coriolan*. One day he made me play it three or four times in succession; then he put it away.

"I don't think I want to hear that any more," he said.

"Why not?"

"It's too . . . too . . ." he hesitated, "too big," he said at last. "I don't really understand it. Play me the one that goes like this." He hummed the phrase from the D Minor Concerto.

"Do you like that one better?" I asked.

He shook his head. "No, it's not that exactly. But it's easier."

"Easier?" It seemed to me rather a queer word to apply to Bach.

"I understand it better."

One afternoon, while we were in the middle of our concert, Signora Bondi was ushered in. She began at once to be overwhelmingly affectionate towards the child; kissed him, patted his head, paid him the most outrageous compliments on his appearance. Guido edged away from her.

"And do you like music?" she asked.

The child nodded.

"I think he has a gift," I said. "At any rate, he has a wonderful ear and a power of listening and criticising such as I've never met with in a child of that age. We're thinking of hiring a piano for him to learn on."

A moment later I was cursing myself for my undue frankness in praising the boy. For Signora Bondi began immediately to protest that, if she could have the upbringing of the child, she would give him the best masters, bring out his talent, make an accomplished maestro of him—and, on the way, an infant prodigy. And at that moment, I am sure, she saw herself sitting maternally, in pearls and black satin, in the lea of the huge Steinway, while an angelic Guido, dressed like little Lord Fauntleroy, rattled out Liszt and Chopin, to the loud delight of a thronged auditorium. She saw the bouquets and all the elaborate floral tributes, heard the clapping and the few well-chosen words with which the veteran maestri, touched almost to tears, would hail the coming of the little genius. It became more than ever important for her to acquire the child.

"You've sent her away fairly ravening," said Elizabeth, when Signora Bondi had gone. "Better tell her next time that you made a mistake, and that the boy's got no musical talent whatever."

In due course, the piano arrived. After giving him the minimum of preliminary instruction, I let Guido loose on it. He began by picking out for himself the melodies he had heard, reconstructing the harmonies in which they were embedded. After a few lessons, he understood the rudiments of musical notation and could read a simple passage at sight, albeit very slowly. The whole process of reading was still strange to him; he had picked up his letters somehow, but nobody had yet taught him to read whole words and sentences.

I took occasion, next time I saw Signora Bondi, to assure her that Guido had disappointed me. There was nothing in his musical talent, really. She professed to be very sorry to hear it; but I could see that she didn't for a moment believe me. Probably she thought that we were after the child too, and wanted to bag the infant prodigy for ourselves, before she could get in her claim, thus depriving her of what she regarded almost as her feudal right. For, after all, weren't they her peasants? If any one was to profit by adopting the child it ought to be herself.

Tactfully, diplomatically, she renewed her negotiations with Carlo. The boy, she put it to him, had genius. It was the foreign gentleman who had told her so, and he was the sort of man, clearly, who knew about such things. If Carlo would let her adopt the child, she'd have him trained. He'd become a great maestro and get engagements in the Argentine and the United States, in Paris and London. He'd earn millions and millions. Think of Caruso, for example. Part of the millions, she explained, would of course come to Carlo. But before they began to roll in, those millions, the boy would have to be trained. But training was very expensive. In his own interest, as well as in that of his son, he ought to let her take charge of the child. Carlo said he would think it over, and again applied to us for advice. We suggested that it would be best in any case to wait a little and see what progress the boy made.

He made, in spite of my assertions to Signora Bondi, excellent progress. Every afternoon, while Robin was asleep, he came for his concert and his lesson. He was getting along famously with his reading; his small fingers were acquiring strength and agility. But what to me was more interesting was that he had begun to make up little pieces on his own account. A few of them I took down as he played them and I have them still. Most of them, strangely enough, as I thought then, are canons. He had a passion for canons. When I explained to him the principles of the form he was enchanted.

"It is beautiful," he said, with admiration. "Beautiful, beautiful. And so easy!"

Again the word surprised me. The canon is not, after all, so conspicuously simple. Thenceforward he spent most of his time at the piano in working out little canons for his own amusement. They were often remarkably ingenious. But in the invention of other kinds of music he did not show himself so fertile as I had hoped. He composed and harmonised one or two solemn little airs like hymn tunes, with a few sprightlier pieces in the spirit of the military march. They were extraordinary, of course, as being the inventions of a child. But a great many children can do extraordinary things; we are all geniuses up to the age of ten. But I had hoped that Guido was a child who was going to be a genius at forty; in which case what was extraordinary for an ordinary child was not extraordinary enough for him. "He's hardly a Mozart," we agreed, as we played his little pieces over. I felt, it must be confessed, almost aggrieved. Anything less than a Mozart, it seemed to me, was hardly worth thinking about.

He was not a Mozart. No. But he was somebody, as I was to find out, quite as extraordinary. It was one morning in the early summer that I made the discovery. I was sitting in the warm shade of our westward-facing balcony, working. Guido and Robin were playing in the little enclosed garden below. Absorbed in my work, it was only, I suppose, after the silence had prolonged itself a considerable time that I became aware that the children were making remarkably little noise. There was no shouting, no running about; only a quiet talking. Knowing by experience that when children are quiet it generally means that they are absorbed in some delicious mischief, I got up from my chair and looked over the balustrade to see what they were doing. I expected to catch them dabbling in water, making a bonfire, covering themselves with tar. But what I actually saw was Guido, with a burnt stick in his hand, demonstrating on the smooth paving-stones of the path, that the square on the hypotenuse of a right-angled triangle is equal to the sum of the squares on the other two sides.

Kneeling on the floor, he was drawing with the point of his blackened stick on the flagstones. And Robin, kneeling imitatively beside him, was growing, I could see, rather impatient with this very slow game.

"Guido," he said. But Guido paid no attention. Pensively frowning, he went on with his diagram. "Guido!" The younger child bent down and then craned round his neck so as to look up into Guido's face. "Why don't you draw a train?"

"Afterwards," said Guido. "But I just want to show you this first. It's *so* beautiful," he added cajolingly.

"But I want a train," Robin persisted.

"In a moment. Do just wait a moment." The tone was almost imploring. Robin armed himself with renewed patience. A minute later Guido had finished both his diagrams.

"There!" he said triumphantly, and straightened himself up to look at them. "Now I'll explain."

And he proceeded to prove the theorem of Pythagoras—not in Euclid's way, but by the simpler and more satisfying method which was, in all probability, employed by Pythagoras himself. He had drawn a square and dissected it, by a pair of crossed perpendiculars, into two squares and two equal rectangles. The equal rectangles he divided up by their diagonals into four equal right-angled triangles. The two squares are then seen to be the squares on the two sides of any one of these triangles other than the hypotenuse. So much for the first diagram. In the next he took the four right-angled triangles into which the rectangles had been divided and rearranged them round the original square so that their right angles filled the corners of the square, the hypotenuses looked inwards, and the greater and less sides of the triangles were in continuation along the sides of the square (which are each equal to the sum of these sides). In this way the original square is redissected into four right-angled triangles and the square on the hypotenuse. The four triangles are equal to the two rectangles of the original dissection. Therefore the square on the hypotenuse is equal to the sum of the two squares—the squares on the other two sides—into which, with the rectangles, the original square was first dissected.

In very untechnical language, but clearly and with a relentless logic, Guido expounded his proof. Robin listened, with an expression on his bright, freckled face of perfect incomprehension.

"Treno," he repeated from time to time. "Treno. Make a train."

"In a moment," Guido implored. "Wait a moment. But do

just look at this. *Do.*" He coaxed and cajoled. "It's so beautiful. It's so easy."

So easy. . . . The theorem of Pythagoras seemed to explain for me Guido's musical predilections. It was not an infant Mozart we had been cherishing; it was a little Archimedes with, like most of his kind, an incidental musical twist.

"Treno, treno!" shouted Robin, growing more and more restless as the exposition went on. And when Guido insisted on going on with his proof, he lost his temper. "Cattivo Guido," he shouted, and began to hit out at him with his fists.

"All right," said Guido resignedly. "I'll make a train." And with his stick of charcoal he began to scribble on the stones.

I looked on for a moment in silence. It was not a very good train. Guido might be able to invent for himself and prove the theorem of Pythagoras; but he was not much of a draughtsman.

"Guido!" I called. The two children turned and looked up. "Who taught you to draw those squares?" It was conceivable, of course, that somebody might have taught him.

"Nobody." He shook his head. Then, rather anxiously, as though he were afraid there might be something wrong about drawing squares, he went on to apologise and explain. "You see," he said, "it seemed to me so beautiful. Because those squares"—he pointed at the two small squares in the first figure —"are just as big as this one." And, indicating the square on the hypotenuse in the second diagram, he looked up at me with a deprecating smile.

I nodded. "Yes, it's very beautiful," I said—"it's very beautiful indeed."

An expression of delighted relief appeared on his face; he laughed with pleasure. "You see, it's like this," he went on, eager to initiate me into the glorious secret he had discovered. "You cut these two long squares"—he meant the rectangles— "into two slices. And then there are four slices, all just the same, because, because—oh, I ought to have said that before—because these long squares are the same, because those lines, you see . . ."

"But I want a train," protested Robin.

Leaning on the rail of the balcony, I watched the children below. I thought of the extraordinary thing I had just seen and of what it meant.

I thought of the vast differences between human beings. We classify men by the colour of their eyes and hair, the shape of their skulls. Would it not be more sensible to divide them up into intellectual species? There would be even wider gulfs between the extreme mental types than between a Bushman and a Scandinavian. This child, I thought, when he grows up, will be to me, intellectually, what a man is to a dog. And there are other men and women who are, perhaps, almost as dogs to me.

Perhaps the men of genius are the only true men. In all the history of the race there have been only a few thousand real men. And the rest of us—what are we? Teachable animals. Without the help of the real men, we should have found out almost nothing at all. Almost all the ideas with which we are familiar could never have occurred to minds like ours. Plant the seeds there and they will grow; but our minds could never spontaneously have generated them.

There have been whole nations of dogs, I thought; whole epochs in which no Man was born. From the dull Egyptians the Greeks took crude experience and rules of thumb and made sciences. More than a thousand years passed before Archimedes had a comparable successor. There has been only one Buddha, one Jesus, only one Bach that we know of, one Michelangelo.

Is it by a mere chance, I wondered, that a Man is born from time to time? What causes a whole constellation of them to come contemporaneously into being and from out of a single people? Taine thought that Leonardo, Michelangelo, and Raphael were born when they were because the time was ripe for great painters and the Italian scene congenial. In the mouth of a rationalising nineteenth-century Frenchman the doctrine is strangely mystical; it may be none the less true for that. But what of those born out of time? Blake, for example, What of those?

This child, I thought, has had the fortune to be born at a time when he will be able to make good use of his capacities. He will find the most elaborate analytical methods lying ready to his hand; he will have a prodigious experience behind him. Suppose him born while Stone Henge was building; he might have spent a lifetime discovering the rudiments, guessing darkly where now he might have had a chance of proving. Born at the time of the Norman Conquest, he would have had to wrestle with all the preliminary difficulties created by an inadequate symbolism; it would have taken him long years, for example, to learn the art of dividing MMMCCCCLXXXVIII by MCMXIX. In five years, nowadays, he will learn what it took generations of Men to discover.

And I thought of the fate of all the Men born so hopelessly out of time that they could achieve little or nothing of value. Beethoven born in Greece, I thought, would have had to be content to play thin melodies on the flute or lyre; in those intellectual surroundings it would hardly have been possible for him to imagine the nature of harmony.

From drawing trains, the children in the garden below had gone on to playing trains. They were trotting round and round; with blown round cheeks and pouting mouth, like the cherubic symbol of a wind, Robin puff-puffed, and Guido, holding the skirt of his smock, shuffled behind him, tooting. They ran forward, backed, stopped at imaginary stations, shunted, roared over bridges, crashed through tunnels, met with occasional collisions and derailments. The young Archimedes seemed to be just as happy as the little tow-headed barbarian. A few minutes ago he had been busy with the theorem of Pythagoras. Now, tooting indefatigably along imaginary rails, he was perfectly content to shuffle backwards and forwards among the flower-beds, between the pillars of the loggia, in and out of the dark tunnels of the laurel tree. The fact that one is going to be Archimedes does not prevent one from being an ordinary cheerful child meanwhile. I thought of this strange talent distinct and separate from the rest of the mind, independent, almost, of experience. The typical child-prodigies are musical and mathematical; the other talents ripen slowly under the influence of emotional experience and growth. Till he was thirty Balzac gave proof of nothing but ineptitude; but at four the young Mozart was already a musician, and some of Pascal's most brilliant work was done before he was out of his teens.

In the weeks that followed, I alternated the daily piano lessons with lessons in mathematics. Hints rather than lessons they were; for I only made suggestions, indicated methods, and left the child himself to work out the ideas in detail. Thus I introduced him to algebra by showing him another proof of the theorem of Pythagoras. In this proof one drops a perpendicular from the right angle on to the hypotenuse, and arguing from the fact that the two triangles thus created are similar to one another and to the original triangle, and that the proportions which their corresponding sides bear to one another are therefore equal, one can show in algebraical form that $c^2 + d^2$ (the squares on the other two sides) are equal to $a^2 + b^2$ (the squares on the two segments of the hypotenuse) $+2ab$; which last, it is easy to show geometrically, is equal to $(a+b)^2$, or the square on the hypotenuse. Guido was as much enchanted by the rudiments of algebra as he would have been if I had given him an engine worked by steam, with a methylated spirit lamp to heat the boiler; more enchanted, perhaps—for the engine would have got broken, and, remaining always itself, would in any case have lost its charm, while the rudiments of algebra continued to grow and blossom in his mind with an unfailing luxuriance. Every day he made the discovery of something which seemed to him exquisitely beautiful; the new toy was inexhaustible in its potentialities.

In the intervals of applying algebra to the second book of Euclid, we experimented with circles; we stuck bamboos into the parched earth, measured their shadows at different hours of the day, and drew exciting conclusions from our observations. Sometimes, for fun, we cut and folded sheets of paper so as to make cubes and pyramids. One afternoon Guido arrived carrying carefully between his small and rather grubby hands a flimsy dodecahedron.

"È tanto bello!" he said, as he showed us his paper crystal; and when I asked him how he had managed to make it, he merely smiled and said it had been so easy. I looked at Elizabeth and laughed. But it would have been more symbolically to the point, I felt, if I had gone down on all fours, wagged the spiritual outgrowth of my os coccyx, and barked my astonished admiration.

It was an uncommonly hot summer. By the beginning of July our little Robin, unaccustomed to these high temperatures, began to look pale and tired; he was listless, had lost his appetite and energy. The doctor advised mountain air. We decided to spend the next ten or twelve weeks in Switzerland. My parting gift to Guido was the first six books of Euclid in Italian. He turned over the pages, looking ecstatically at the figures.

"If only I knew how to read properly," he said. "I'm so stupid. But now I shall really try to learn."

From our hotel near Grindelwald we sent the child, in Robin's name, various post cards of cows, Alp-horns, Swiss chalets, edelweiss, and the like. We received no answers to these cards; but then we did not expect answers. Guido could not write, and there was no reason why his father or his sisters should take the trouble to write for him. No news, we took it, was good news. And then one day, early in September, there arrived at the hotel a strange letter. The manager had it stuck up on the glass-fronted notice-board in the hall, so that all the guests might see it, and whoever conscientiously thought that it belonged to him might claim it. Passing the board on the way into lunch, Elizabeth stopped to look at it.

"But it must be from Guido," she said.

I came and looked at the envelope over her shoulder. It was unstamped and black with postmarks. Traced out in pencil, the big uncertain capital letters sprawled across its face. In the first line was written: AL BABBO DI ROBIN, and there followed a travestied version of the name of the hotel and the place. Round the address bewildered postal officials had scrawled suggested emendations. The letter had wandered for a fortnight at least, back and forth across the face of Europe.

"Al Babbo di Robin. To Robin's father." I laughed. "Pretty smart of the postmen to have got it here at all." I went to the manager's office, set forth the justice of my claim to the letter and, having paid the fifty-centime surcharge for the missing stamp, had the case unlocked and the letter given me. We went in to lunch.

"The writing's magnificent," we agreed, laughing, as we examined the address at close quarters. "Thanks to Euclid," I added. "That's what comes of pandering to the ruling passion."

But when I opened the envelope and looked at its contents I no longer laughed. The letter was brief and almost telegraphical in style. "SONO DALLA PADRONA," it ran, "NON MI PIACE HA RUBATO IL MIO LIBRO NON VOGLIO SUONARE PIU VOGLIO TORNARE A CASA VENGA SUBITO GUIDO."

"What is it?"

I handed Elizabeth the letter. "That blasted woman's got hold of him," I said.

Busts of men in Homburg hats, angels bathed in marble tears extinguishing torches, statues of little girls, cherubs, veiled figures, allegories and ruthless realisms—the strangest and most diverse idols beckoned and gesticulated as we passed. Printed indelibly on tin and embedded in the living rock, the brown photographs looked out, under glass, from the humbler crosses, headstones, and broken pillars. Dead ladies in the cubistic geometrical fashions of thirty years ago—two cones of black satin meeting point to point at the waist, and the arms: a sphere to the elbow, a polished cylinder below—smiled mournfully out of their marble frames; the smiling faces, the white hands, were the only recognisably human things that emerged from the solid geometry of their clothes. Men with black moustaches, men with white beards, young clean-shaven men, stared or averted their gaze to show a Roman profile. Children in their stiff best opened wide their eyes, smiled hopefully in anticipation of the little bird that was to issue from the camera's muzzle, smiled sceptically in the knowledge that it wouldn't, smiled laboriously and obediently because they had been told to. In spiky Gothic cottages of marble the richer dead privately reposed; through grilled doors one caught a glimpse of pale Inconsolables weeping, of distraught

Geniuses guarding the secret of the tomb. The less prosperous sections of the majority slept in communities, close-crowded but elegantly housed under smooth continuous marble floors, whose every flagstone was the mouth of a separate grave.

These continental cemeteries, I thought, as Carlo and I made our way among the dead, are more frightful than ours, because these people pay more attention to their dead than we do. That primordial cult of corpses, that tender solicitude for their material well-being, which led the ancients to house their dead in stone, while they themselves lived between wattles and under thatch, still lingers here; persists, I thought, more vigorously than with us. There are a hundred gesticulating statues here for every one in an English graveyard. There are more family vaults, more "luxuriously appointed" (as they say of liners and hotels) than one would find at home. And embedded in every tombstone there are photographs to remind the powdered bones within what form they will have to resume on the Day of Judgment; beside each are little hanging lamps to burn optimistically on All Souls' Day. To the Man who built the Pyramids they are nearer, I thought, than we.

"If I had known," Carlo kept repeating, "if only I had known." His voice came to me through my reflections as though from a distance. "At the time he didn't mind at all. How should I have known that he would take it so much to heart afterwards? And she deceived me, she lied to me."

I assured him yet once more that it wasn't his fault. Though, of course, it was, in part. It was mine too, in part; I ought to have thought of the possibility and somehow guarded against it. And he shouldn't have let the child go, even temporarily and on trial, even though the woman was bringing pressure to bear on him. And the pressure had been considerable. They had worked on the same holding for more than a hundred years, the men of Carlo's family; and now she had made the old man threaten to turn him out. It would be a dreadful thing to leave the place; and besides, another place wasn't so easy to find. It was made quite plain, however, that he could stay if he let her have the child. Only for a little to begin with; just to see how he got on. There would be no compulsion whatever on him to stay if he didn't like it. And it would be all to Guido's advantage; and to his father's, too, in the end. All that the Englishman had said about his not being such a good musician as he had thought at first was obviously untrue—mere jealousy and little-mindedness: the man wanted to take credit for Guido himself, that was all. And the boy, it was obvious, would learn nothing from him. What he needed was a real good professional master.

All the energy that, if the physicists had known their business, would have been driving dynamos, went into this campaign. It began the moment we were out of the house, intensively. She would have more chance of success, the Signora doubtless thought, if we weren't there. And besides, it was essential to take the opportunity when it offered itself and get hold of the child before we could make our bid—for it was obvious to her that we wanted Guido just as much as she did.

Day after day she renewed the assault. At the end of a week she sent her husband to complain about the state of the vines: they were in a shocking condition; he had decided, or very nearly decided, to give Carlo notice. Meekly, shamefacedly, in obedience to higher orders, the old gentleman uttered his threats. Next day Signora Bondi returned to the attack. The padrone, she declared, had been in a towering passion; but she'd do her best, her very best, to mollify him. And after a significant pause she went on to talk about Guido.

In the end Carlo gave in. The woman was too persistent and she held too many trump cards. The child could go and stay with her for a month or two on trial. After that, if he really expressed a desire to remain with her, she could formally adopt him.

At the idea of going for a holiday to the seaside—and it was to the seaside, Signora Bondi told him, that they were going—Guido was pleased and excited. He had heard a lot about the sea from Robin. "Tanta acqua!" It had sounded almost too good to be true. And now he was actually to go and see this marvel. It was very cheerfully that he parted from his family.

But after the holiday by the sea was over, and Signora Bondi had brought him back to her town house in Florence, he began to be homesick. The Signora, it was true, treated him exceedingly kindly, bought him new clothes, took him out to tea in the Via Tornabuoni and filled him up with cakes, iced strawberry-ade, whipped cream, and chocolates. But she made him practise the piano more than he liked, and what was worse, she took away his Euclid, on the score that he wasted too much time with it. And when he said that he wanted to go home, she put him off with promises and excuses and downright lies. She told him that she couldn't take him at once, but that next week, if he were good and worked hard at his piano meanwhile, next week . . . And when the time came she told him that his father didn't want him back. And she redoubled her petting, gave him expensive presents, and stuffed him with yet unhealthier foods. To no purpose. Guido didn't like his new life, didn't want to practise scales, pined for his book, and longed to be back with his brothers and sisters. Signora Bondi, meanwhile, continued to hope that time and chocolates would eventually make the child hers; and to keep his family at a distance, she wrote to Carlo every few days letters which still purported to come from the seaside (she took the trouble to send them to a friend, who posted them back again to Florence), and in which she painted the most charming picture of Guido's happiness.

It was then that Guido wrote his letter to me. Abandoned, as he supposed, by his family—for that they shouldn't take the trouble to come to see him when they were so near was only to be explained on the hypothesis that they really had given him up—he must have looked to me as his last and only hope. And the letter, with its fantastic address, had been nearly a fortnight on its way. A fortnight—it must have seemed hundreds of years; and as the centuries succeeded one another, gradually, no doubt, the poor child became convinced that I too had abandoned him. There was no hope left.

"Here we are," said Carlo.

I looked up and found myself confronted by an enormous

monument. In a kind of grotto hollowed in the flanks of a monolith of grey sandstone, Sacred Love, in bronze, was embracing a funerary urn. And in bronze letters riveted into the stone was a long legend to the effect that the inconsolable Ernesto Bondi had raised this monument to the memory of his beloved wife, Annunziata, as a token of his undying love for one whom, snatched from him by a premature death, he hoped very soon to join beneath this stone. The first Signora Bondi had died in 1912. I thought of the old man leashed to his white dog; he must always, I reflected, have been a most uxorious husband.

"They buried him here."

We stood there for a long time in silence. I felt the tears coming into my eyes as I thought of the poor child lying there underground. I thought of those luminous grave eyes, and the curve of that beautiful forehead, the droop of the melancholy mouth, of the expression of delight which illumined his face when he learned of some new idea that pleased him, when he heard a piece of music that he liked. And this beautiful small being was dead; and the spirit that inhabited this form, the amazing spirit, that too had been destroyed almost before it had begun to exist.

And the unhappiness that must have preceded the final act, the child's despair, the conviction of his utter abandonment—those were terrible to think of, terrible.

"I think we had better come away now," I said at last, and touched Carlo on the arm. He was standing there like a blind man, his eyes shut, his face slightly lifted towards the light; from between his closed eyelids the tears welled out, hung for a moment, and trickled down his cheeks. His lips trembled and I could see that he was making an effort to keep them still. "Come away," I repeated.

The face which had been still in its sorrow, was suddenly convulsed; he opened his eyes, and through the tears they were bright with a violent anger. "I shall kill her," he said, "I shall kill her. When I think of him throwing himself out, falling through the air . . ." With his two hands he made a violent gesture, bringing them down from over his head and arresting them with a sudden jerk when they were on a level with his breast. "And then crash." He shuddered. "She's as much responsible as though she had pushed him down herself. I shall kill her." He clenched his teeth.

To be angry is easier than to be sad, less painful. It is comforting to think of revenge. "Don't talk like that," I said. "It's no good. It's stupid. And what would be the point?" He had had those fits before, when grief became too painful and he had tried to escape from it. Anger had been the easiest way of escape. I had had, before this, to persuade him back into the harder path of grief. "It's stupid to talk like that," I repeated, and I led him away through the ghastly labyrinth of tombs, where death seemed more terrible even than it is.

By the time we had left the cemetery, and were walking down from San Miniato towards the Piazzale Michelangelo below, he had become calmer. His anger had subsided again into the sorrow from which it had derived all its strength and its bitterness. In the Piazzale we halted for a moment to look down at the city in the valley below us. It was a day of floating clouds—great shapes, white, golden, and grey; and between them patches of a thin, transparent blue. Its lantern level, almost, with our eyes, the dome of the cathedral revealed itself in all its grandiose lightness, its vastness and aerial strength. On the innumerable brown and rosy roofs of the city the afternoon sunlight lay softly, sumptuously, and the towers were as though varnished and enamelled with an old gold. I thought of all the Men who had lived here and left the visible traces of their spirit and conceived extraordinary things. I thought of the dead child.

TWO OR THREE GRACES

THE word "bore" is of doubtful etymology. Some authorities derive it from the verb meaning to pierce. A bore is a person who drills a hole in your spirit, who tunnels relentlessly through your patience, through all the crusts of voluntary deafness, inattention, rudeness, which you vainly interpose—through and through till he pierces to the very quick of your being. But there are other authorities, as good or even better, who would derive the word from the French *bourrer*, to stuff, to satiate. If this etymology be correct, a bore is one who stuffs you with his thick and suffocating discourse, who rams his suety personality, like a dumpling, down your throat. He stuffs you; and you, to use an apposite modern metaphor, are "fed up with him." I like to think, impossibly, that both these derivations of the word are correct; for bores are both piercers and stuffers. They are like dentists' drills, and they are also like stale buns. But they are characterised by a further quality, which drills and dough-nuts do not possess; they cling. That is why (though no philologist) I venture to suggest a third derivation, from "burr." Burr, *bourrer*, bore—all the sticking, stuffing, piercing qualities of boredom are implicit in those three possible etymologies. Each of the three of them deserves to be correct.

Herbert Comfrey was above all a sticking bore. He attached himself to any one who had the misfortune to come in contact with him; attached himself and could not be shaken off. A burr-bore, vegetable and passive; not actively penetrating. For Herbert, providentially, was not particularly talkative; he was too lazy and lymphatic for that. He was just exceedingly sociable, like a large sentimental dog that cannot bear to be left alone. Like a dog, he followed people about; he lay, metaphorically speaking, at their feet in front of the fire. And like a dog, he did not talk. It was just your company that made him happy; he was quite content if he might trot at your side or doze under our chair. He did not demand that you should pay much attention to him; all that he asked was to be permitted to enjoy the sight of your countenance and bask in the warmth of your presence. If once a week he got the equivalent of a pat on the head and a "Good dog, Herbert," he wagged his spirit's tail and was perfectly happy.

To some of my friends—the quick, the impatient, the highly strung—poor vegetable Herbert was exasperating to the point of madness. His very virtues—that good nature of his, that placidity, that unshakable fidelity—infuriated them. Even his appearance drove them wild. The sight of his broad smiling face, of his big, lazy, lubberly body and limbs was alone sufficient to set their nerves twittering and jumping like a frightened aviary. I have known people who, after living in the same house with Herbert for three days, have secretly packed their trunks, caught the first convenient train, and, leaving no address, have travelled hundreds of miles in order to escape from him.

To me, poor Herbert was boring indeed, but not exasperatingly or intolerably so. Mine is a patient temper; my nerves are not easily set twittering. I even liked him in a way; he was such a good, faithful, kind old dog. And I soon acquired, in his dumb presence, a knack of quite ignoring him, of regarding him simply as a piece of furniture—so much so, that I sometimes caught myself on the point of carelessly setting down my emptied coffee-cup on his head as he sat on the floor beside me (he always sat on the floor whenever it was possible), or of flicking my cigarette ash into the inviting cranny between his neck and his coat collar.

As boys, Herbert and I had been at the same public school. But as we were in different houses and he was two years older than I (two years, at that age, is an enormous seniority), we had hardly ever spoken to one another. But none the less, it was on the strength of our old school that Herbert reintroduced himself into my life. His return was doubly disastrous. A bore entered my existence and, in the entering, drove out, temporarily at least, a being who, whatever his other qualities, was the very antithesis of boredom.

It was in a café of the Passage du Panorama in Paris that the thing happened. We had been sitting there for an hour, Kingham and I, talking and drinking vermouth. It was characteristic of Kingham that he did most of both—drinking as well as talking. Characteristic, too, that he should have been abusing me among many other things, for wasting my time and spirit in precisely these two occupations.

"You sit about," he said, "letting every thought in your head trickle out uselessly in talk. Not that there are many thoughts of course, because you daren't think. You do anything not to think. You create futile business, you rush about seeing people you don't like and don't take the slightest interest in, you drift from bar to bar, you swill till you're stupefied—all because you daren't think and can't bring yourself to make the effort to do something serious and decent. It's the result partly of laziness, partly of lack of faith—faith in anything. *Garçon!*" He ordered another vermouth. "It's the great modern vice," he went on, "the great temptation of every young man or woman who's intelligent and acutely conscious. Everything that's easy and momentarily diverting and anæsthetic tempts—people, chatter, drink, fornication. Everything that's difficult and big, everything that needs thought and effort, repels. It's the war that did it. Not to mention the peace. But it would have come gradually in any case. Modern life was making it inevitable. Look at the young people who had nothing to do with the war—were only children when it happened—they're the worst of all. It's time to stop, it's time to do something. Can't you see that you can't go on like this? Can't you see?"

He leaned across the table at me, angrily. He hated these vices which he had attributed to me, hated them with a special fury because they happened really to be his. He was confessing the weakness he hated in himself—hated and could not eradicate.

Kingham looked handsome in anger. He had dark eyes, beautiful and very bright; his hair was dark brown, fine and plentiful; a close-cut beard, redder than his hair, disguised the lower part of his face, with whose pale, young smoothness it

seemed curiously incongruous. There was a brilliancy, a vividness about him. If I were less slow to kindle, I should have
burned responsively with his every ardour. Being what I am, I
could always remain cool, critical, and cautious, however
passionately he might burn. My uninflammableness, I believe,
had somehow fascinated him. I exasperated him, but he continued
to frequent my company—chiefly to abuse me, to tell me
passionately how hopeless I was. I winced under these dissec-
tions; for though he often talked, as far as I was concerned, wildly
at random (accusing me, as he had done on this particular
occasion, of the weakness which he felt and resented in himself)
his analysis was often painfully exact and penetrating. I winced,
but all the same I delighted in his company. We irritated one
another profoundly; but we were friends.

I suppose I must have smiled at Kingham's question. Goodness knows, I am no teetotaller, I am not averse to wasting my
time over agreeable futilities. But compared with Kingham—
particularly the Kingham of 1920—I am a monument of industry,
dutiful steadiness, sobriety. I take no credit to myself for it; I
happen to be one of nature's burgesses, that is all. I am as little
capable of leading a perfectly disorderly life as I am of, shall we
say, writing a good book. Kingham was born with both talents.
Hence the absurdity, so far as I was concerned, of his hortatory
question. I did not mean to smile; but some trace of my amusement must have appeared on my face, for Kingham suddenly
became most passionately angry.

"You think it's a joke?" he cried, and thumped the marble
table. "I tell you, it's the sin against the Holy Ghost. It's
unforgivable. It's burying your talent. Damn this blasted
Bible," he added with parenthetic fury. "Why is it that one
can never talk about anything serious without getting mixed
up in it?"

"It happens to be quite a serious book," I suggested.

"A lot you understand about it," said Kingham. "I tell you,"
he went on impressively. . . . But at this moment Herbert
made his second entry into my life.

I felt a hand laid on my shoulder, looked up, and saw a stranger.

"Hullo, Wilkes," said the stranger. "You don't remember me."

I looked more attentively, and had to admit that I didn't.

"I am Comfrey," he explained, "Herbert Comfrey. I was at Dunhill's, don't you remember? You were at Struthers', weren't you? Or was it Lane's?"

At the names of these pedagogues, who had figured so largely in my boyhood, recesses in my mind, long closed, suddenly burst open, as though before a magical word. Visions of inky schoolrooms, football fields, cricket fields, fives courts, the school chapel, rose up confusedly; and from the midst of this educational chaos there disengaged itself the loutish figure of Comfrey of Dunhill's.

"Of course," I said, and took him by the hand. Through the corner of my eye, I saw Kingham angrily frowning. "How did you remember me?"

"Oh, I remember every one," he answered. It was no vain boast, as I afterwards discovered; he *did* remember. He remembered every one he had ever met, and all the trivial incidents of his past life. He had the enormous memory of royal personages and family retainers—the memory of those who never read, or reason, or reflect, and whose minds are therefore wholly free to indulge in retrospect. "I never forget a face," he added, and without being invited, sat down at our table.

Indignantly, Kingham threw himself back in his chair. He kicked me under the table. I looked at him and made a little grimace, signifying my helplessness.

I mumbled a perfunctory introduction. Kingham said nothing, only frowned more blackly, as he shook hands with Herbert. And for his part, Herbert was hardly more cordial. True, he smiled his amiable dim smile; but he said nothing, he hardly even looked at Kingham. He was in too much of a hurry to turn back to me and talk about the dear old school. The dear old school— it was the only subject that ever made Herbert really loquacious.

It metamorphosed him from a merely vegetable burr-bore into an active, piercing dentist's drill of tediousness. He had a passion for the school, and thought that all ex-members of it ought to be in constant and friendly communication with one another. I have noticed that, as a general rule, people of decided individuality very rarely continue their schoolboy acquaintanceships into later life. It is only to be expected. The chances that they will have found in the tiny microcosm of school the sort of friends they will like when they are grown up—grown out of recognition— are obviously very small. Coteries whose bond of union consists in the fact that their component members happened to be at the same school at the same time are generally the dreariest of assemblages. It could scarcely be otherwise; men who have no better reasons for associating with one another must be colourless indeed, and insipid. Poor Herbert, who regarded the accident of our having worn similarly striped caps and blazers at a certain period of our boyhood as being a sufficient reason for our entering into a bosom friendship, was only an extreme specimen of the type.

I put on my chilliest and most repellant manner. But in vain. Herbert talked and talked. Did I remember the exciting match against Winchester in 1910? And how poor old Mr. Cutler had been ragged? And that memorable occasion when Pye had climbed on to the roof of the school chapel, at night, and hung a chamber-pot on one of the Gothic pinnacles? Anxiously, I looked towards Kingham. He had exchanged his expression of anger for one of contempt, and was leaning back, his eyes shut, tilting his chair.

Kingham had never been to a public school. He had not had the luck (or the misfortune) to be born a hereditary, professional gentleman. He was proud of the fact, he sometimes even boasted of it. But that did not prevent him from being morbidly sensitive to anything that might be interpreted as a reference to his origin. He was always on the look-out for insults from "gentlemen." Veiled insults, insults offered unconsciously even, unintentionally, in perfect ignorance—any sort of insult was enough to set

H

him quivering with pain and fury. More than once I had seen him take violent offence at words that were entirely well-intentioned. Would he regard Herbert's dreary recollections of the dear old school as an insult? He was quite capable of it. I looked forward nervously to an outburst and a violent exit. But the scene, this time, was not to be acted in public. After listening for a few minutes to Herbert's anecdotage, Kingham got up, excused himself with ironical politeness, and bade us good evening. I laid my hand on his arm.

"Do stay."

"A thousand regrets"; he laid his hand on his heart, smiled, bowed, and was gone, leaving me (I may add parenthetically that it was his habit) to pay for his drinks.

We public school men were left to ourselves.

The next morning I lay late in bed. At about eleven o'clock Kingham burst into my room. The scene which I had been spared the night before was enacted for me now with redoubled passion. Another man would have slept on the supposed insult and, waking, have found it negligible. Not so Kingham. He had brooded over his wrongs, till what was originally small had grown enormous. The truth was that Kingham liked scenes. He loved to flounder in emotion—his own and other people's. He was exhilarated by these baths of passion; he felt that he really lived, that he was more than a man, while he splashed about in them. And the intoxication was so delicious that he indulged in it without considering the consequences—or perhaps it would be truer to say that he considered the consequences (for intellectually no man could be clearer-sighted than Kingham) but deliberately ignored them.

When I say that he had a great facility for making scenes, I do not mean to imply that he ever simulated an emotion. He felt genuinely about things—genuinely and strongly, but too easily. And he took pleasure in cultivating and working up his emotions. For instance, what in other men would have been a passing irritation, held in check by self-control, to be modified very likely by subsequent impressions, was converted by Kingham, almost deliberately, into a wild fury which no second thoughts were allowed to assuage. Often these passions were the result of mere mistakes on the part of those who had provoked them. But once emotionally committed, Kingham would never admit a mistake—unless, of course, his passion for self-humiliation happened at the moment to be stronger than his passion for self-assertion. Often, too, he would take up unchanging emotional attitudes towards people. A single powerful impression would be allowed to dominate all other impressions. His intellect was put into blinkers, the most manifest facts were ignored; and until further orders the individual in question produced in Kingham only one particular set of reactions.

As he approached my bed, I could see from the expression on his white face that I was in for a bad quarter of an hour.

"Well?" I said, with an affectation of careless cordiality.

"I always knew you were an intellectual snob," Kingham began in a low, intense voice, drawing up a chair to my bedside as he spoke. "But really, I thought you were above being an ordinary, suburban, lower-middle-class social snob."

I made the grimace which in French novels is represented by the sign "——?"

"I know that my father was a plumber," he went on, "and that I was educated at the expense of the State and by scholarships for the encouragement of clever paupers. I know I speak Cockney, and not Eton and Oxford. I know that my manners are bad and that I eat dirtily, and that I don't wash my teeth enough." (None of these things were true; but it suited Kingham, at the moment, to believe that they were. He wanted to feel abased, in order that he might react with greater violence. He insulted himself in order that he might attribute the insults, under which he genuinely winced, to me, and so have an excuse for being angry with me.) "I know I'm a cad and a little bounder." He spoke the words with an extraordinary gusto, as though he enjoyed the pain he was inflicting on himself. "I know I'm an outsider, only tolerated for my cleverness. A sort of buffoon or tame monkey for the amusement of cultured gentlemen. I know all this, and I know you knew it. But I really thought you didn't mind, that we met as human beings, not as specimens of upper and lower classes. I was fool enough to imagine that you liked me in spite of it all. I thought you even preferred me to the people in your own herd. It only shows what an innocent I am. No sooner does a gentleman come along, an old school chum, what?" (derisively he assumed the public school accent as rendered on the music-hall stage) "than you fling your arms round his neck and leave the dirty little outsider very definitely outside." He laughed ferociously.

"My good Kingham," I began, "why will you make a bloody fool of yourself?"

But Kingham, who doubtless knew as well as I did that he was making a fool of himself, only went on with the process more vehemently. He was committed to making a fool of himself, and he liked it. Shifting his ground a little, he began telling me home truths—real home truths this time. In the end, I too began to get angry.

"I'll trouble you to get out," I said.

"Oh, I've not finished yet."

"And stay out till you've got over your fit of hysterics. You're behaving like a girl who needs a husband."

"As I was saying," Kingham went on in a voice that had become softer, more sinisterly quiet, more poisonously honied in proportion as mine had grown louder and harsher, "your great defect is spiritual impotence. Your morality, your art—they're just impotence organised into systems. Your whole view of life—impotence again. Your very strength, such as it is— your horrible passive resistance—that's based in impotence too."

"Which won't prevent me from throwing you downstairs if you don't clear out at once." It is one thing to know the truth about oneself; it is quite another thing to have it told one by somebody else. I knew myself a natural bourgeois; but when Kingham told me so—and in his words—it seemed to me that I was learning a new and horribly unpleasant truth.

"Wait," Kingham drawled out with exasperating calm, "wait one moment. One more word before I go."

"Get out," I said. "Get out at once."

There was a knock at the door. It opened. The large, ruddy face of Herbert Comfrey looked round it into the room.

"I hope I don't disturb," said Herbert, grinning at us.

"Oh, not a bit, not a bit," cried Kingham. He jumped up, and with an excessive politeness proffered his vacant chair. "I was just going. Do sit down. Wilkes was impatiently expecting you. Sit down, do sit down." He propelled Herbert towards the chair.

"Really," Herbert began, politely protesting.

But Kingham cut him short. "And now I leave you two old friends together," he said. "Good-bye. Good-bye. I'm only sorry I shan't have an opportunity for saying that last word I wanted to say."

Cumbrously, Herbert made as though to get up. "I'll go," he said. "I had no idea. . . . I'm so sorry."

But Kingham put his hands on his shoulders and forced him back into the chair. "No, no," he insisted. "Stay where you are. I'm off."

And picking up his hat, he ran out of the room.

"Queer fellow," said Herbert. "Who is he?"

"Oh, a friend of mine," I answered. My anger had dropped, and I wondered, sadly, whether in calling him a friend I was telling the truth. And to think that, if he were no longer my friend, it was because of this lumpish imbecile sitting by my bed! I looked at Herbert pensively. He smiled at me—a smile that was all good nature. One could not bear a grudge against such a man.

The breach was complete, at any rate for the time; it was more than two years before Kingham and I met again. But if I had lost Kingham, I had acquired Herbert Comfrey—only too completely. From that moment, my life in Paris was no longer my own; I had to share it with Herbert. Being at that moment quite unattached, a dog without a master, he fastened himself to me, taking it ingenuously for granted that I would be just as happy in his company as he was in mine. He established himself in my hotel, and for the rest of my stay in Paris I was almost never alone. I ought, I know, to have been firm with Herbert; I ought to have been rude, told him to go to the devil, kicked him downstairs. But I lacked the heart. I was too kind. (Another symptom of my spiritual impotence! My morality—impotence systematised. I know, I know.) Herbert preyed on me, and, like the Brahman who permits himself, unresistingly, to be devoured by every passing blood-sucker, from mosquitoes to tigers, I suffered him to prey on me. The most I did was occasionally to run away from him. Herbert was, fortunately, a sluggard. The Last Trump would hardly have got him out of bed before ten. When I wanted a day's freedom, I ordered an eight-o'clock breakfast and left the hotel while Herbert was still asleep. Returning at night from these holidays, I would find him waiting, dog-like, in my room. I always had the impression that he had been waiting there the whole day—from dawn (or what for him was dawn —about noon) to midnight. And he was always so genuinely pleased to see me back that I was almost made to feel ashamed, as though I had committed an act of perfidy. I would begin to apologise and explain. I had had to go out early to see a man about something; and then I had met another man, who had asked me to have lunch with him; and then I had had to go to my dear old friend, Madame Dubois, for tea; after which I had dropped in on Langlois, and we had dined and gone to a concert. In fine, as he could see, I could not have got back a minute earlier.

It was in answer to the reproaches of my own conscience that I made these apologies. Poor Herbert never complained; he was only too happy to see me back. I could not help feeling that his clinging fidelity had established some sort of claim on me, that I was somehow a little responsible for him. It was absurd, of course, unreasonable and preposterous. For why should I, the victim, feel pity for my persecutor? Preposterous; and yet the fact remained that I did feel pity for him. I have always been too tender-hearted, insufficiently ruthless.

The time came for me to return to London. Herbert, who had just enough money to make it unnecessary for him to do anything or to be anywhere at any particular time, packed his bags and got into the same train. It was a very disagreeable journey; the train was crowded, the sea just choppy enough to make me sick. Coming on deck as we drew into Dover harbour, I found Herbert looking exasperatingly well. If I had not been feeling so ill, I should have found an excuse for quarrelling with him. But I had not the requisite energy. Meanwhile, it must be admitted, Herbert made himself very useful about the luggage.

Experience was shortly to teach me that, instead of feeling exasperated with poor Herbert, I ought to have been thankful that he was not far worse. For Herbert, after all, was only a burr-bore, a passive vegetable clinger. I might have been fastened on by one who was actively and piercingly as well as just clingingly boring. Herbert might, for example, have been like his brother-in-law, John Peddley; and then there would have been only three alternatives left me: murder, suicide, exile. I was feeling annoyed with Herbert as we slid slowly across Dover harbour. A few hours later, I had realised that I ought to have been feeling thankful that he was no worse than he was. On Dover quay we met John Peddley.

Peddley was an active bore, the most active, I think, that I ever met; an indefatigable piercer, a relentless stuffer and crammer. He talked incessantly, and his knowledge of uninteresting subjects was really enormous. All that I know of the Swiss banking system, of artificial manures, of the law relating to insurance companies, of pig-breeding, of the ex-sultan of Turkey, of sugar rationing during the war, and a hundred other similar subjects, is due to Peddley. He was appalling, really appalling; there is no other word. I know no human being with whom I would less willingly pass an hour.

And yet the man was extremely amiable and full of good qualities. He had a kind heart. He was energetic and efficient. He was even intelligent. One could not listen to his account of insurance companies or artificial manures without realising that he had completely mastered his subject. Moreover, a successful solicitor, like Peddley, cannot be a fool; at least, that is what those of us who are not solicitors like to believe. What made the man so afflicting was his genius for dullness; his self-assertive pedantry; his voice; his highly developed social instinct; and finally his insensitiveness. His genius for dullness caused him unfailingly to take an interest in the things which interested nobody else; and even when, by some mistake, he embarked on some more promising theme than the Swiss banking system, he had the power of rendering the most intrinsically fascinating of subjects profoundly dull. By a process of inverse alchemy he transmuted the purest gold to lead. His self-assertiveness and a certain pedagogic instinct made him ambitious to be the instructor of his fellows; he loved the sound of his own lecturing voice. And what a voice! Not unmusical, but loud, booming, persistent. It set up strange, nay, positively dangerous vibrations in one's head. I could never listen to it for more than a few minutes without feeling confused and dizzy. If I had had to live with that voice, I believe I should have begun, one day, to turn and turn like those Japanese waltzing mice—for ever. Peddley's voice affected the semi-circular canals. And then there was his sociability. It was a passion, a vice; he could not live without the company of his fellow-beings. It was an agony for him to be alone. He hunted company ferociously, as wild beasts pursue their prey. But the odd thing was that he never seemed to crave for friendship or intimacy. So far as I know, he had no friends, in the ordinarily accepted sense of the term. He desired only acquaintances and auditors; and acquaintances and reluctant auditors were all that he had. In the first period of my acquaintance with Peddley I used to wonder what he did when he felt the need of confiding his intimate and private feelings. Later on I came to doubt whether, at ordinary times, he had any private life that needed talking about. Only very rarely and when something catastrophic had explosively shattered the crust of his public existence, did he ever develop a private life. When things were running smoothly in their regular daily grooves, he lived only on the public surface, at the office, at the club, at his own dinner-table, perfectly content so long as there was somebody present to listen to his talk. It mattered not that his auditors might be listening with manifest and extreme reluctance. Like Herbert—and indeed like most bores—John Peddley was more than half unaware of the people upon whom he inflicted himself. He realised that they were there, physically there; that was all. To their feelings and thoughts he was utterly insensitive. It was this insensitiveness, coupled with his passionate sociability, that gave him his power. He could hunt down his victims and torture them without remorse. The wolf, if he were really sensitive to the feelings of the lamb, might end by turning vegetarian. But he is not sensitive. He is aware only of his own hunger and the deliciousness of mutton. It was the same with John Peddley. Ignorant of the terror which he inspired, of the mental agonies which he inflicted, he could pursue his course relentlessly and with a perfect equanimity.

My first impressions of John Peddley were not unfavourable. True, the halloo with which he greeted Herbert from the quay-side, as we were waiting our turn in the shoving crowd of human sheep to pass down the gangway on to dry land, sounded to me, in my present condition, rather distressingly hearty. And his appearance, when Herbert pointed him out to me, offended me by its robustious healthiness. Nor, when Herbert had introduced us, did I much appreciate the vehemence of his handshake and the loud volubility of his expressions of sympathy. But, on the other hand, he was very kind and efficient. He produced a silver flask from his pocket and made me take a swig of excellent old brandy. Noticing that I was chilled and green with cold, he insisted on my putting on his fur coat. He darted to the custom-house and returned, in an incredibly short space of time, with the official hieroglyph duly chalked upon our suit-cases. A minute later we were sitting in his car, rolling briskly out of Dover along the Canterbury road.

I was feeling, at the time, too ill to think; and it hardly occurred to me that the situation was, after all, rather odd. Peddley had been waiting on the quay—but not for us; for we were un-expected. Waiting, then, for whom? The question did propound itself to me at the time, but uninsistently. There was no room in my mind for anything but the consciousness of sea-sickness. I forgot to wonder, and took my seat in the car, as though it were the most natural thing in the world that we should have been met at the quay by somebody who did not know that we were crossing. And the apparent naturalness of the situation was confirmed for me by the behaviour of my companions. For Peddley had taken it for granted from the first that we should come and stay with him at his country house. And Herbert, for whom one place was always just as good as another, had accepted the invitation at once. I began by protesting; but feebly, and more out of politeness than in earnest. For it was not essential for me to get back to London that evening; and the prospect of that dismal journey from Dover, of the cab drive in the chill of the night across London, of a home-coming to fireless and deserted rooms, was very dreadful to me. If I accepted Peddley's invitation, I should find myself in less than half an hour in a warm, comfortable room, at rest and without responsibilities. The temptation to a sea-sick traveller was great; I succumbed.

"Well," said Peddley heartily, in his loud, trombone-like voice, "well, this *is* luck." He brought down his hand with a tremendous clap on to my knee, as though he were patting a horse. "The greatest luck! Think of running into you and Herbert at the gangway! And carrying you off like this! Too delightful, too delightful!"

I was warmed by his gladness; it seemed so genuine. And genuine it was—the genuine gladness of an ogre who has found a chubby infant straying alone in the woods.

"Extraordinary," Peddley went on, "how many acquaintances one meets at Dover quay. I come every day, you know, when I'm staying in the country; every day, to meet the afternoon boat. It's a great resource when one's feeling dull. All the advantages of a London club in the country. And there's always time for a good chat before the train starts. That's what makes me like this district of Kent so much. I'm trying to persuade my landlord to sell me the house. I've nearly coaxed him, I think."

"And then," said Herbert, who had a way of occasionally breaking his habitual silence with one of those simple and devastatingly judicious reflections which render children so dangerous in polite, adult society, "and then you'll find that every one will be travelling by aeroplane. You'll have to sell the house and move to Croydon, near the aerodrome."

But Peddley was not the man to be put out by even the most terrible of terrible infants. Wrapped in his insensitiveness, he was not so much as aware of the infant's terribleness.

"Pooh!" he retorted. "I don't believe in aeroplanes. They'll never be safe or cheap or comfortable enough to compete with the steamers. Not in our day." And he embarked on a long discourse about helicopters and gyroscopes, air pockets and the cost of petrol.

Meanwhile, I had begun to wonder, in some alarm, what manner of man this kind, efficient, hospitable host of mine could be. A man who, on his own confession, drove into Dover every afternoon to meet the packet; who waylaid sea-sick acquaintances and had good chats with them while they waited for the train; and who so much loved his afternoon diversions at the quay-side that he felt moved to refute in serious, technical argument the prophet of aerial travel. . . . Decidedly, a strange, a dangerous man. And his voice, meanwhile, boomed and boomed in my ears till I felt dizzy with the sound of it. Too late, it occurred to me that it might have been better if I had faced that dreary journey, that chilly drive, that icy and inhospitable homecoming to empty rooms. Too late.

I discovered afterwards that Peddley's holidays were always spent at railway junctions, frontier towns and places of international resort, where he was likely to find a good supply of victims. For week-ends, Whitsun and Easter, he had his country house near Dover. At Christmas time he always took a week or ten days on the French Riviera. And during the summer he simultaneously satisfied his social passions and his passion for mountain scenery by taking up some strategic position on the Franco-Swiss, Italo-French, or Swiss-Italian frontier, where he could go for walks in the hills and, in the intervals, meet the trans-continental trains. One year he would take his family to Pontarlier; another to Valorbes; another to Modane; another to Brigue; another to Chiasso. In the course of a few years he had visited all the principal frontier towns in the mountainous parts of central and southern Europe. He knew the best seasons for each. Valorbes, for example, had to be visited early in the season. It was in July and at the beginning of August that the greatest number of English people passed through on their way to Switzerland. When he had seen them on their homeward way at the end of August, Peddley would move on for a fortnight's stay to one of the Italian frontier towns, so as to catch the September tourists on their way to Florence or Venice. His favourite haunt at this season was Modane. There are lots of good walks round Modane; and the principal trains wait there for two and a half hours. Rosy with healthful exercise, Peddley would come striding down at the appointed hour to meet the express. The victim was marked down, caught, and led away to the station buffet. For the next two hours Peddley indulged in what he called "a *really* good chat."

Peddley's circle of acquaintanceship was enormous. There was his legal practice, to begin with; that brought him into pro-fessional contact with a great variety of people. Then there were his clubs; he was a member of three or four, which he frequented assiduously. And, finally, there was his own constantly hospit-able dinner-table; it is astonishing what even the richest men will put up with for the sake of a good free meal. He was on talking terms with hundreds, almost thousands, of his fellows. It was not to be wondered at if he often spied familiar faces in the Modane custom-house. But there were many days, of course, when nobody of his acquaintance happened to be going South. On these occasions Peddley would seek out some particularly harassed-looking stranger and offer his assistance. The kindness, so far as Peddley was concerned, was entirely whole-hearted; he was not conscious of the wolf concealed beneath his sheep's clothing. He just felt a desire to be friendly and helpful and, incidentally, chatty. And helpful he certainly was. But in the buffet, when the ordeal of the custom-house was over, the stranger would gradually come to the conclusion, as he listened to Peddley's masterly exposition of the financial policy of Sweden, that he would have preferred, on the whole, to face the rapacious porters and the insolent douaniers alone and unassisted.

John Peddley had not yet enumerated all his reasons for supposing that aeroplanes would never cut out the cross-channel steamers, when we reached our destination.

"Ah, here we are," he said, and opened the door for me to get out. "But as I was saying," he added, turning back to Herbert, "the great defect of gyroscopes is their weight and the excessive rigidity they give to the machine. Now I grant you, my dear boy . . ."

But I forget what he granted. All I remember is that he was still granting it when we entered the drawing-room, where Mrs. Peddley was sitting with her children.

From the first, I found Grace Peddley charming. Positively and actively charming. And yet she was Herbert's own sister and in many respects very like him. Which only shows (what, after all, is sufficiently obvious) that we are prepared to tolerate and even admire in persons of the opposite sex qualities which infuriate us when we meet with them in persons of our own. I found Herbert a bore because he was mentally blank and vague, because he was without initiative, because he attached himself and clung. But Grace, whose character was really very similar to Herbert's, charmed me, in spite, or perhaps even because, of these qualities which made me rank her brother among the minor calamities of my existence.

But it is not only the moral and mental qualities of our fellow-beings that inspire our love or hate. I should not, I am sure, have found Herbert so deplorable if he had been smaller and less cumbrous, less clumsy of body. He was altogether too much the lubber fiend for my taste. Physically, Grace displayed little resemblance to her brother. She was tall, it is true, but slim and light of movement. Herbert was thick, shambling and leaden-footed. In a heavy, large-featured way, Herbert was not unhandsome. He had a profile; his nose and chin were Roman and positively noble. At a distance you might mistake him for some formidable Cæsarean man of action. But when you came close enough to see his eyes and read the expression on that large pretentious face, you perceived that, if Roman, he was the dullest and blankest Roman of them all.

Grace was not in the least imposing or classical. You could never, at however great a distance, have mistaken her for the mother of the Gracchi. Her features were small and seemed, somehow, still indefinite, like the features of a child. A lot of dark red-brown hair which, at that epoch, when fashion still permitted women to have hair, she wore looped up in a couple of spirally coiled plaits over either ear, emphasised the pallor of that childish face. A pair of very round, wide-open grey eyes looked out from under the hair with an expression of slightly perplexed ingenuousness. Her face was the face of a rather ugly but very nice little girl. And when she smiled, she was suddenly almost beautiful. Herbert smiled in the same way—a sudden smile, full of kindness and good nature. It was that smile of his that made it impossible, for me at any rate, to treat him with proper ruthlessness. In both of them, brother and sister, it was a singularly dim and helpless goodness that expressed itself in that smile—a gentle, inefficient kindliness that was tinged, in Herbert's case, with a sort of loutish rusticity. He was a bumpkin even in his goodness. Grace's smile was dim, but expressive at the same time of a native refinement which Herbert did not possess. They were brother and sister; but hers was a soul of better, more aristocratic birth.

It was in her relations with her children that the inefficiency of Grace's benevolence revealed itself most clearly in practice. She loved them, but she didn't know what to do with them or how to treat them. It was lucky for her—and for the children too—that she could afford to keep nurses and governesses. She could never have brought her children up by herself. They would either have died in infancy, or, if they had survived the first two years of unpunctual and hopelessly unhygienic feeding, would have grown up into little savages. As it was, they had been well brought up by professional child-tamers, were healthy and, except towards their mother, beautifully behaved. Their mother, however, they regarded as a being of another species—a lovely and eminently adorable being, but not serious, like nurse or Miss Phillips, not really grown up; more than half a child, and what wasn't child, mostly fairy. Their mother was the elfin being who permitted or even herself suggested the most fantastic breaches of all the ordinary rules. It was she, for example, who had invented the sport of bathing, in summer-time, under the revolving sprinkler which watered the lawn. It was she who had first suggested that excellent game, so strenuously disapproved of by Miss Phillips, nurse and father, of biting your slice of bread, at dinner-time, into the shape of a flower or a heart, a little bridge, a letter of the alphabet, a triangle, a railway engine. They adored her, but they would not take her seriously, as a person in authority; it never even occurred to them to obey her.

"You're a little girl," I once heard her four-year-old daughter explaining to her. "You're a little girl, mummy. Miss Phillips is an old lady."

Grace turned her wide, perplexed eyes in my direction. "You see," she said despairingly, yet with a kind of triumph, as though she were conclusively proving a disputed point, "you see! What *can* I do with them?"

She couldn't do anything. When she was alone with them, the children became like little wild beasts.

"But, children," she would protest, "children! You really mustn't." But she knew that she might as well have expostulated with a litter of grizzly bears.

Sometimes, when the protest was more than ordinarily loud and despairing, the children would look up from their absorbing mischief and reassuringly smile to her. "It's all right, mummy," they would say. "It's quite all right, you know."

And then, helplessly, their mother would give it up.

In Herbert I found this helpless inefficiency intolerable. But the ineptitude of his sister had a certain style; even her clumsiness was somehow graceful. For clumsy she was. When it came to sewing, for example, her fingers were all thumbs. She had quite given up trying to sew when I first knew her. But she still regarded it as part of her maternal duty to knit warm mufflers—she never attempted anything more complicated than a muffler—for the children. She knitted very slowly, painfully concentrating her whole attention on the work in hand until, after a few minutes, exhausted by the mental strain, she was forced, with a great sigh, to give up and take a little rest. A muffler took months to finish. And when it was finished, what an extraordinary object it was! A sort of woollen fishing-net.

"Not *quite* right, I'm afraid," Grace would say, holding it out at arm's length. "Still," she added, cocking her head on one side and half closing her eyes, as though she were looking at a *pointilliste* picture, "it isn't bad, considering."

Secretly, she was very proud of these mufflers, proud with the pride of a child who has written its first letter or embroidered on canvas its first kettle-holder, with practically no help at all from nurse. It still seemed to her extraordinary that she could do things all by herself, unassisted.

This graceful ineptitude of hers amused and charmed me. True, if I had had to marry it, I might not have found it quite so enchanting, if only for the reason that I should never have been able to afford a sufficiency of servants and child-tamers to counteract its effects on domestic, daily life. Nor, I am afraid, would the absurd charm of her intellectual vagueness have survived a long intimacy. For how vague, how bottomlessly vague she was! For example, she was quite incapable—and no experience could teach her—of realising the value of money. At one moment she was lavishly extravagant, would spend pounds as though they were pence. The next, overvaluing her money as wildly as she had undervalued it, she would grudge every penny spent on the first necessities of life. Poor Peddley would sometimes come home from his office to find that there was nothing for dinner but lentils. Another man would have been violently and explosively annoyed; but Peddley, whose pedagogic passions were more powerful than his anger, only made a reasoned expostulation in the shape of a discourse on the meaning of money and the true nature of wealth, followed by a brief lecture on dietetics and the theory of calories. Grace listened attentively and with humility. But try as she would, she could never remember a word of what he had said; or rather she remembered, partially, but remembered all wrong. The phrases which Peddley had built up into a rational discourse, Grace rearranged in her mind so as to make complete nonsense. It was the same with what she read. The arguments got turned upside down. The non-essential facts were vividly remembered, the essential forgotten. Dates were utterly meaningless to her. Poor Grace! she was painfully conscious of her inefficiency of mind; she longed above everything to be learned, authoritative, capable. But though she read a great number of serious books—and read them with genuine pleasure, as well as on principle—she could never contrive to be well read. Inside her head everything got muddled. It was as though her mind were inhabited by some mischievous imp which delighted in taking to pieces the beautifully composed mosaics of learning and genius, and resetting the tesseræ (after throwing a good many of them away) in the most fantastic and ludicrous disorder.

The consciousness of these defects made her particularly admire those who were distinguished by the opposite and positive qualities. It was this admiration, I am sure, which made her Peddley's wife. She was very young when he fell in love with her and asked her to marry him—eighteen to his thirty-four or thereabouts—very young and (being fresh from school, with its accompaniment of examination failures and pedagogic reproaches) more than ordinarily sensitive to her own shortcomings and to the merits of those unlike herself. Peddley made his entry into her life. The well-documented accuracy of his knowledge of artificial manures and the Swiss banking system astonished her. True, she did not feel a passionate interest in these subjects; but for that she blamed herself, not him. He seemed to her the personification of learning and wisdom—omniscient, an encyclopædia on legs.

It is not uncommon for schoolgirls to fall in love with their aged professors. It is the tribute paid by youth—by flighty, high-spirited, but passionately earnest youth—to venerable mind. Grace was not lucky. The most venerable mind with which, at eighteen, she had yet come into contact was Peddley's. Peddley's! She admired, she was awed by what seemed to her the towering, Newtonian intellect of the man. And when the Newtonian intellect laid itself at her feet, she felt at first astonished—was it possible that he, Peddley, the omniscient, should abase himself before one who had failed three times, ignominiously, in the Cambridge Locals?—then flattered and profoundly grateful. Moreover, Peddley, unlike the proverbial professor, was neither grey-bearded nor decrepit. He was in the prime of life, extremely active, healthy, and energetic; good-looking, too, in the ruddy, large-chinned style of those Keen Business Men one sees portrayed in advertisements and the illustrations of magazine stories. Quite inexperienced in these matters, she easily persuaded herself that her gratitude and her schoolgirl's excitement were the genuine passion of the novels. She imagined that she was in love with him. And it would have mattered little, in all probability, if she had not. Peddley's tireless courtship would have ended infallibly by forcing her to surrender. There was no strength in Grace; she could be bullied into anything. In this case, however, only a very little bullying was necessary. At his second proposal, she accepted him. And so, in 1914, a month or two before the outbreak of war, they were married.

A marriage which began with the war might have been expected to be a strange, unusual, catastrophic marriage. But for the Peddleys, as a matter of fact, the war had next to no significance; it did not touch their life. For the first year John Peddley made Business as Usual his motto. Later, after being rejected for active service on account of his short sight, he enrolled himself as a temporary bureaucrat; was highly efficient in a number of jobs; had managed, when the medical boards became stricter, to make himself indispensable, as a sugar rationer; and ended up with an O.B.E. Grace, meanwhile, lived quietly at home and gave birth, in three successive years, to three children. They kept her occupied; the war, for her, was an irrelevance. She witnessed neither its tragedies, nor its feverish and sordid farces. She knew as little of apprehension, suspense, grief, as she knew of the reckless extravagances, the intoxications, the too facile pleasures, the ferocious debaucheries which ran parallel with the agonies, which mingled and alternated with them. Ineffectually, Grace nursed her babies; she might have been living in the eighteenth century.

At the time I knew her first Grace had been married about six years. Her eldest child was five years old, her youngest about two. Peddley, I judged, was still in love with her—in his own way, that is. The wild passion which had hurried him into a not very reasonable marriage, a passion mainly physical, had subsided. He was no longer mad about Grace; but he continued to find her eminently desirable. Habit, moreover, had endeared her to him, had made her indispensable; it had become difficult for him to imagine an existence without her. But for all that, there was no intimacy between them. Possessing, as I have said, no private life of his own, Peddley did not understand the meaning of intimacy. He could give no confidences and therefore asked for none. He did not know what to do with them when they came to him unasked. I do not know if Grace ever tried to confide in him; if so, she must soon have given it up as a bad job. One might as well have tried to confide into a gramophone; one might whisper the most secret and sacred thoughts into the trumpet of the machine, but there came back only a loud booming voice that expounded the financial policy of Sweden, food control, or the law relating to insurance companies—it depended which particular record out of the large, but still limited repertory, happened at the moment to be on the turn-table. In the spiritual home of the Peddleys there was only a bedroom and a lecture-room—no sentimental boudoir for confidences, no quiet study pleasantly violated from time to time by feminine intrusion. Nothing between the physical intimacies of the bed-room and the impersonal relations of pupil and sonorously braying professor in the reverberant lecture-hall. And then, what lectures!

Grace, who still believed in the intellectual eminence of her husband, continued to blame herself for finding them tedious. But tedious they were to her; that was a fact she could not deny. Long practice had taught her to cultivate a kind of mental deafness. Peddley's discourses no longer got on her nerves, because she no longer heard them. I have often seen her sitting, her wide eyes turned on Peddley with an expression, apparently, of rapt attention, seeming to drink in every word he uttered. It was so she must have sat in those first months of her marriage, when she really did listen, when she still tried her hardest to be interested and to remember correctly. Only in those days, I fancy, there can never have been quite so perfect a serenity on her face. There must have been little frowns of concentration and agonisingly suppressed yawns. Now there was only an unruffled calm, the calm of complete and absolute abstraction.

I found her out on the very first evening of our acquaintance. John Peddley, who must have been told (I suppose by Herbert) that I was interested, more or less professionally, in music, began, in my honour, a long description of the mechanism of pianolas. I was rather touched by this manifest effort to make me feel spiritually at home, and, though I was dizzied by the sound of his voice, made a great show of being interested in what he was saying. In a pause, while Peddley was helping himself to the vegetables (what a blessing it was to have a moment's respite from that maddening voice!), I turned to Grace and asked her politely, as a new guest should, whether she were as much inter-ested in pianolas as her husband. She started, as though I had woken her out of sleep, turned on me a pair of blank, rather frightened eyes, blushed scarlet.

"As much interested as John in *what?*" she asked.

"Pianolas."

"Oh, pianolas." And she uttered the word in a puzzled, be-wildered tone which made it quite clear that she had no idea that pianolas had been the subject of conversation for at least the last ten minutes. "Pianolas?" she repeated almost incredulously. And she had seemed so deeply attentive.

I admired her for this power of absenting herself, for being, spiritually, not there. I admired, but I also pitied. To have to live in surroundings from which it was necessary, in mere self-preservation, to absent oneself—that was pitiable indeed.

Next morning, assuming an invalid's privilege, I had breakfast in bed. By the time I came down from my room, Peddley and Herbert had set out for a hearty walk. I found Grace alone, arranging flowers. We exchanged good-mornings. By the expression of her face, I could see that she found my presence rather formidable. A stranger, a high-brow, a musical critic—what to say to him? Courageously doing her duty, she began to talk to me about Bach. Did I like Bach? Didn't I think he was the greatest musician? I did my best to reply; but somehow, at that hour of the morning, there seemed to be very little to say about Bach. The conversation began to droop.

"And the *Well-Tempered Clavichord*," she went on desperately. "What lovely things in that!"

"And so useful for torturing children who learn the piano," I replied, as desperately. Facetiousness, the last resort.

But my words had touched a chord in Grace's mind. "Torture," she said. "That's the word. I remember when I was at school . . ."

And there we were, happily launched at last upon an interesting, because a personal, subject.

Grace was as fond of her dear old school as Herbert was of his. But, with the rest of her sex, she had a better excuse for her fondness. For many women, the years spent in that uncomplicated, companionable, exciting, purely feminine world, which is the world of school, are the happiest of their lives. Grace was one of them. She adored her school; she looked back on her schooldays as on a golden age. True, there had been Cambridge Locals and censorious mistresses; but on the other hand, there had been no Peddley, no annual child-bearing, no domestic responsibilities, no social duties, no money to be too lavish or too stingy with, no servants. She talked with enthusiasm, and I listened with pleasure.

An hour and a half later, when the bores came back, red-faced and ravenous, from their walk, we were sorry to be interrupted. I had learned a great many facts about Grace's girlhood. I knew that she had had an unhappy passion for the younger of the visiting music mistresses; that one of her friends had received a love-letter from a boy of fifteen, beginning: "I saw a photograph of you in the *Sketch*, walking in the Park with your mother. Can I ever forget it?" I knew that she had had mumps for five weeks, that she had climbed on the roof by moonlight in pyjamas, that she was no good at hockey.

From time to time most of us feel a need, often urgent and imperious, to talk about ourselves. We desire to assert our personalities, to insist on a fact which the world about us seems in danger of forgetting—the fact that we exist, that we are we. In some people the desire is so chronic and so strong, that they can never stop talking about themselves. Rather than be silent, they will pour out the most humiliating and discreditable confidences. Grace was afflicted by no such perverse and extravagant longings; there was nothing of the exhibitionist in her. But she did like, every now and then, to have a good talk about her soul, her past history, her future. She liked to talk, and she too rarely had an opportunity. In me she found a sympathetic listener and commentator. By the end of the morning she was regarding me as an old friend. And I, for my part, had found her charming. So charming, indeed, that for Grace's sake I was prepared to put up even with John Peddley's exposition of the law regarding insurance companies.

Within a few weeks of our first introduction we were finding it the most natural thing in the world that we should be constantly meeting. We talked a great deal, on these occasions, about ourselves, about Life and about Love—subjects which can be discussed with the fullest pleasure and profit only between persons of opposite sexes. On none of these three topics, it must be admitted, did Grace have very much of significance to say. She had lived very little and loved not at all; it was impossible, therefore, that she should know herself. But it was precisely this ignorance and her ingenuous, confident expression of it that charmed me.

"I feel I'm already old," she complained to me. "Old and finished. Like those funny straw hats and leg-of-mutton sleeves in the bound volumes of the *Illustrated London News*," she added, trying to make her meaning clearer for me.

I laughed at her. "You're absurdly young," I said, "and you haven't begun."

She shook her head and sighed.

When we talked about love, she professed a sad, middle-aged scepticism.

"People make a most ridiculous fuss about it."

"Rightly."

"But it's not worth making a fuss about," she insisted. "Not in reality. Not outside of books."

"Isn't it?" I said. "You'll think differently," I told her, "when you've waited two or three hours for somebody who hasn't turned up, when you can't sleep for wondering where somebody's been and with whom, and you want to cry—yes, you do cry—and you feel as though you were just going to have influenza."

"Ah, but that isn't love," Grace retorted sententiously, in the tone of one who has some private and certain source of information.

"What is it, then?"

"It's . . ." Grace hesitated and suddenly blushed, "it's . . . well, it's physical."

I could not help laughing, uproariously.

Grace was vexed. "Well, isn't it true?" she insisted obstinately.

"Perfectly," I had to admit. "But why isn't that love?" I added, hoping to elicit Grace's views on the subject.

She let me have them. They were positively Dantesque. I can

only suppose that Peddley's ardours had left her cold, disgusted even.

But Life and Love were not our only topics. Grace's ignorance and my own native reticence made it impossible for us to discuss these themes with any profit for very long at a stretch. In the intervals, like John Peddley, I played the pedagogic part. Through casual remarks of mine, Grace suddenly became aware of things whose very existence had previously been unknown to her—things like contemporary painting and literature, young music, new theories of art. It was a revelation. All her efforts, it seemed to her, all her strivings towards culture had been wasted. She had been laboriously trying to scale the wrong mountain, to force her way into the wrong sanctuary. At the top, if she had ever reached it, within the holy of holies, she would have found—what? a grotesque and moth-eaten collection of those funny little straw hats and leg-of-mutton sleeves from the bound volumes of the *Illustrated London News*. It was dreadful, it was humiliating. But now she had caught a glimpse of another sanctuary, upholstered by Martine, enriched by the offerings of the Poirets and Lanvins of the spirit; a modish, modern sanctuary; a fashionable Olympus. She was eager to climb, to enter.

Acting the part of those decayed gentle-women who, for a consideration, introduce *parvenus* into good society, I made Grace acquainted with all that was smartest and latest in the world of the spirit. I gave her lessons in intellectual etiquette, warned her against æsthetic *gaffes*. She listened attentively, and was soon tolerably at home in the unfamiliar world—knew what to say when confronted by a Dada poem, a picture by Picasso, a Schoenberg quartet, an Archipenko sculpture.

I was working, at that period, as a musical critic, and two or three times a week I used to take Grace with me to my concerts. It did not take me long to discover that she had very little feeling for music and no analytical understanding of it. But she professed, hypocritically, to adore it. And as it bored me most excruciatingly to have to go by myself to listen to second-rate pianists playing the same old morsels of Liszt and Chopin, second-rate contraltos fruitily hooting Schubert and Brahms, second-rate fiddlers scraping away at Tartini and Wieniawski, I pretended to believe in Grace's enthusiasm for the musical art and took her with me to all the most painful recitals. If the hall were empty—which, to the eternal credit of the music-loving public, it generally was—one could get a seat at the back, far away from the other sparsely sprinkled auditors, and talk very pleasantly through the whole performance.

At first, Grace was terribly shocked when, after listening judicially to the first three bars of *Du bist wie eine Blume* or the *Trillo del Diavolo*, I opened a conversation. She herself had a very perfect concert-goer's technique, and listened with the same expression of melancholy devotion, as though she were in church, to every item on the programme. My whispered chatter seemed to her sacrilegious. It was only when I assured her, professionally and *ex cathedra*, that the stuff wasn't worth listening to, that she would consent, albeit with considerable misgivings in the early days of our concert-going, to take her part in the conversation. In a little while, however, she grew accustomed to the outrage; so much so, that when the music or the performance happened to be good (a little detail which Grace was not sufficiently musical to notice) it was I who had to play the verger's part and hush her sacrilegious chatter in a place suddenly made holy. She learned in the end to take her cue from me—to look devout when I looked devout, to chatter when I chattered.

Once, rather maliciously, I put on my raptest expression while some maudlin incompetent was pounding out Rachmaninoff. After a quick glance at me through the tail of her eye, Grace also passed into ecstasy, gazing at the pianist as St. Theresa might have gazed at the uplifted Host. When the ordeal was over, she turned on me a pair of bright, shining eyes.

"Wasn't that splendid?" she said. And such is the power of self-suggestion, that she had genuinely enjoyed it.

"I thought it the most revolting performance I ever listened to," was my answer.

Poor Grace turned fiery red, the tears came into her eyes; to hide them from me, she averted her face. "I thought it very good," she insisted, heroically. "But of course I'm no judge."
. "Oh, of course it wasn't as bad as all that," I made haste to assure her. "One exaggerates, you know." The sight of her unhappy face had made me feel profoundly penitent. I had meant only to make mild fun of her, and I had managed somehow to hurt her, cruelly. I wished to goodness that I had never played the stupid trick. It was a long time before she completely forgave me.

Later, when I knew her better, I came to understand why it was that she had taken my little clownery so hardly. Rudely and suddenly, my joke had shattered one of those delightful pictures of herself which Grace was for ever fancifully creating and trying to live up to. What had been a joke for me had been, for her, a kind of murder.

Grace was a born visualiser. I discovered, for example, that she had what Galton calls a "number form." When she had to do any sort of arithmetical calculation, she saw the figures arranged in space before her eyes. Each number had its own peculiar colour and its own position in the form. After a hundred the figures became dim; that was why she always found it so difficult to work in large numbers. The difference between three thousand, thirty thousand, and three hundred thousand was never immediately apparent to her, because in the case of these large numbers she could *see* nothing; they floated indistinctly on the blurred fringes of her number form. A million, however, she saw quite clearly; its place was high up, to the left, above her head, and it consisted of a huge pile of those envelopes they have at banks for putting money in—thousands and thousands of them, each marked with the word MILLION in large black letters. All her mental processes were a succession of visual images; and these mental pictures were so vivid as to rival in brightness and definition the images she received through her eyes. What she could not visualise, she could not think about.

I am myself a very poor visualiser. I should find it very diffi-

cult, for example, to describe from memory the furniture in my
room. I know that there are so many chairs, so many tables,
doors, bookshelves, and so on; but I have no clear mental vision
of them. When I do mental arithmetic, I see no coloured
numbers. The word Africa does not call up in my mind, as
Grace assured me once that it always did in hers, a vision of sand
with palm trees and lions. When I make plans for the future, I
do not see myself, as though on the stage, playing a part in
imaginary dramas. I think without pictures, abstractly and in
the void. That is why I cannot pretend to write with complete
understanding of the workings of Grace's mind. The con-
genitally deaf are not the best judges of music. I can only guess,
only imaginatively reconstruct.

From what I gathered in conversation with her, I imagine that
Grace was in the habit of vividly "seeing herself" in every kind
of situation. Some of these situations had no relation to her
actual life, were the purely fantastic and hypothetical situations
of daydreams. Others were real, or at any rate potentially real,
situations. Living her life, she saw herself living it, acting in the
scenes of the flat quotidian drama a very decided and definite
part. Thus, when she went for a walk in the country, she saw
herself walking—a female mountaineer for tireless strength and
energy. When she accompanied Peddley on his annual expedi-
tions to the Riviera, she saw herself as she climbed into the
wagon lit, or swam along the Promenade des Anglais, as an
immensely rich and haughty milady, envied by the *canaille*, remote and star-like above them. On certain socially important
occasions at home, a similar character made its appearance. I
saw the milady once or twice during the first months of our
acquaintanceship. Later on the milady turned into a very
Parisian, very twentieth-cum-eighteenth-century *grande dame*.
But of that in its place.

Grace was much assisted in these visualisations of herself by
her clothes. In the costume which she donned for a two-mile
walk in Kent she might have crossed the Andes. And in all her
garments, for every occasion, one noticed the same dramatic

appropriateness. It was a pity that she did not know how to change her features with her clothes. Her face, whether she lolled along the sea-fronts of the Riviera or addressed herself, in brogues, short skirts, and sweaters to the ascent of some Kentish hillock, was always the same—the face of a rather ugly but very nice little girl; a face that opened on to the world through large, perplexed eyes, and that became, from time to time, suddenly and briefly beautiful with a dim benevolence when she smiled.

Grace's visions of herself were not merely momentary and occasional. There was generally one predominating character in which she saw herself over considerable periods of time. During the first four years of her marriage, for example, she had seen herself predominantly as the housewife and mother. But her manifest incapacity to act either of these parts successfully had gradually chilled her enthusiasm for them. She wanted to run the house, she saw herself tinkling about with keys, giving orders to the maids; but, in practice, whenever she interfered with the rule of her masterful old cook, everything went wrong. She loved her children, she pictured them growing up, healthy and good, under her influence; but they were always sick when she fed them, they behaved like beasts when she tried to make them obey. To one who tried to see herself as the complete, the almost German matron, it was not encouraging. By the time her last child was born, she had practically abandoned the attempt. From the first, the baby had been handed over, body and soul, to the nurses. And except when she was seized with a financial panic and forbade the ordering of anything but lentils, she let the old cook have her way.

When I first met her, Grace was not seeing herself continuously in any one predominating rôle. Punctured by sharp experience, the matron had flattened out and collapsed; and the matron had had, so far, no successor. Left without an imaginary character to live up to, Grace had relapsed into that dim characterlessness which in her, as in Herbert, seemed to be the natural state. She still saw herself vividly enough in the separate, occasional incidents of her life—as the mountain climber, as the

rich and haughty milady. But she saw no central and permanent
figure in whose life these incidents of mountaineering and opu-
lently visiting the Riviera occurred. She was a succession of
points, so to speak; not a line.

Her friendship with me was responsible for the emergence
into her consciousness of a new permanent image of herself. She
discovered in my company a new rôle, not so important, indeed,
not so rich in potentialities as that of the matron, but still a leading lady's part. She had been so long without a character that she
eagerly embraced the opportunity of acquiring one, however
incongruous. And incongruous it was, this new character; odd
and eminently unsuitable. Grace had come to see herself as a
musical critic.

It was our concert-going—our professional concert-going—
that had done it. If I had happened not to be a journalist, if we
had paid for admission instead of coming in free on my complimentary tickets, it would never have occurred to her to see herself as a critic. Simple mortals, accustomed to pay for their
pleasures, are always impressed by the sight of a free ticket.
The critic's *jus primæ noctis* seems to them an enviable thing.
Sharing the marvellous privilege, Grace came to feel that she
must also share the judicial duties of a critic. She saw herself
distributing praise and blame—a rapturous listener when the
performance was worth listening to, a contemptuous chatterer
when it wasn't. Identifying herself with me—not the real but an
ideal exalted me—she pictured herself as the final arbiter of
musical reputations. My malicious little practical joke had
thrown down this delightful image of herself. The critic had
suddenly been murdered.

At the time I did not understand why poor Grace should have
been so deeply hurt. It was only in the light of my later knowledge that I realised what must have been her feelings. It was
only later, too, that I came to understand the significance of that
curious little pantomime which she used regularly to perform as
we entered a concert hall. That languid gait with which she
strolled across the vestibule, dragging her feet with a kind of

reluctance, as though she were on boring business; that sigh, that drooping of the eyelids as she stood, patiently, while the attendant looked at my tickets; that air, when we were in the concertroom, of being perfectly at home, of owning the place (she used, I remember, to put her feet up on the seat in front); and that smile of overacted contempt, that wearily amused smile with which she used (once she had got over the idea that she was committing a sacrilege) to respond, during a bad performance, to my whispered chatter—these were the gait, the bored patience, the possessive at-homeness, the contempt of a hardened critic.

And what a quantity of music she bought at this time and never played! How many volumes of musical criticism and biography she took out of the library! And the grave pronouncements she used to make across the dinner-table! "Beethoven was the greatest of them all"; and so on in the same style. I understood it all afterwards. And the better I understood, the more I regretted my cruel little joke. As the critic, she had been so happy. My joke destroyed that happiness. She became diffident and self-conscious, got actor's fright; and though I never repeated the jest, though I always encouraged her, after that, to believe in her musicianship, she could never whole-heartedly see herself in the part again.

But what a poor part, at the best of times, the critic's was! It was too dry, too intellectual and impersonal to be really satisfying. That it lay within my power to provide her with a much better rôle—the guilty wife's—I do not and did not at the time much doubt. True, when I knew her first Grace was a perfectly virtuous young woman. But her virtue was founded on no solid principle—on a profound love for her husband, for example; or on strong religious prejudices. It was not a virtue that in any way involved her intimate being. If she happened to be virtuous, it was more by accident than on principle or from psychological necessity. She had not yet had any occasion for not being virtuous, that was all. She could have been bullied or cajoled into infidelity as she had been bullied and cajoled by Peddley into marriage. Grace floated vaguely on the surface of life without compass or destination; one had only to persuade her that adultery was Eldorado, and she would have shaped her course forthwith towards that magical shore. It was just a question of putting the case sufficiently speciously. She still retained, at this time, the prejudices of her excellent upper middle-class upbringing; but they were not very deeply rooted. Nothing in Grace was so deeply rooted that it could not quite easily be eradicated.

I realised these facts at the time. But I did not try to take advantage of them. The truth is that, though I liked Grace very much, I was never urgently in love with her. True, one can very agreeably and effectively act the part of the "lover," in the restricted and technical sense of that term, without being wildly in love. And if both parties could always guarantee to keep their emotions in a state of equilibrium, these little sentimental sensualities would doubtless be most exquisitely diverting. But the equilibrium can never be guaranteed. The balanced hearts begin sooner or later, almost inevitably, to tilt towards love or hatred. In the end, one of the sentimental sensualities turns into a passion —whether of longing or disgust it matters not—and then, farewell to all hope of tranquillity. I should be chary of saying so in Kingham's presence; but the fact remains that I like tranquillity. For me, the love-game, without love, is not worth the candle. Even as a mere hedonist I should have refrained. And I had other scruples—scruples which an overmastering passion might have overridden, but which were sufficient to keep a mere mild sensuality in check. I was never Grace's lover; neither genuinely, by right of passion, nor technically by the accident of physical possession. Never her lover. An ironic fate had reserved for me a less glorious part—the part, not of the lover, but of the introducer of lovers. All unintentionally, I was to play benevolent Uncle Pandarus to Grace's Cressida. And there were two Troiluses.

The first of them was no less—or shouldn't I rather say "no more"? for how absurdly his reputation was exaggerated!—than Clegg, *the* Clegg, Rodney Clegg, the painter. I have known Clegg for years and liked him, in a way—liked him rather as one likes Grock, or Little Tich, or the Fratellini: as a comic spectacle. This is not the best way of liking people, I know. But with Rodney it was the only way. You had either to like him as a purveyor of amusement, or dislike him as a human being. That, at any rate, was always my experience. I have tried hard to get to know and like him intimately—off the stage, so to speak. But it was never any good. In the end, I gave up the attempt once and for all, took to regarding him quite frankly as a music-hall comedian, and was able, in consequence, thoroughly to enjoy his company. Whenever I feel like a tired business man, I go to see Rodney Clegg.

Perhaps, as a lover, Rodney was somehow different from his ordinary self. Perhaps he dropped his vanity and his worldliness. Perhaps he became unexpectedly humble and unselfish, forgot his snobbery, craved no longer for cheap successes and, for love, thought the world well lost. Perhaps. Or more probably, I am afraid, he remained very much as he always was, and only in Grace's eyes seemed different from the Rodney whose chatter and little antics diverted the tired business man in me. Was hers the correct vision of him, or was mine? Neither, I take it.

It must have been in the spring of 1921 that I first took Grace to Rodney's studio. For her, the visit was an event; she was about to see, for the first time in her life, a famous man. Particularly famous at the moment, it happened; for Rodney was very much in the papers that season. There had been a fuss about his latest exhibition. The critics, with a fine contemptuous inaccuracy, had branded his pictures as post-impressionistic, cubistic, futuristic; they threw any brick-bat that came to hand. And the pictures had been found improper as well as disturbingly "modern." Professional moralists had been sent by the Sunday papers to look at them; they came back boiling with professional indignation. Rodney was delighted, of course. This was fame—and a fame, moreover, that was perfectly compatible with prosperity. The outcry of the professional moralists did not interfere with his sales. He was doing a very good business.

Rodney's conversion to "modern art," instead of ruining him, had been the source of increased profit and an enhanced notoriety. With his unfailing, intuitive knowledge of what the public wanted, he had devised a formula which combined modernity with the more appealing graces of literature and pornography. Nothing, for example, could have been less academic than his nudes. They were monstrously elongated; the paint was laid on quite flatly; there was no modelling, no realistic light and shade; the human form was reduced to a paper silhouette. The eyes were round black boot-buttons, the nipples magenta berries, the lips vermilion hearts; the hair was represented by a collection of crinkly black lines. The exasperated critics of the older school protested that a child of ten could have painted them. But the child of ten who could have painted such pictures must have been an exceedingly perverse child. In comparison, Freud's Little Hans would have been an angel of purity. For Rodney's nudes, however unrealistic, were luscious and voluptuous, were even positively indecent. What had distressed the public in the work of the French post-impressionists was not so much the distortion and the absence of realism as the repellant austerity, the intellectual asceticism, which rejected the appeal both of sex and of the anecdote. Rodney had supplied the deficiencies. For these engagingly luscious nudities of his were never represented in the void, so to speak, but in all sorts of curious and amusing situations—taking tickets at railway stations, or riding bicycles, or sitting at cafés with negro jazz-bands in the background, drinking *crème de menthe*. All the people who felt that they ought to be in the movement, that it was a disgrace not to like modern art, discovered in Rodney Clegg, to their enormous delight, a modern artist whom they could really and honestly admire. His pictures sold like hot cakes.

The conversion to modernism marked the real beginning of Rodney's success. Not that he had been unknown or painfully poor before his conversion. A man with Rodney's social talents, with Rodney's instinct for popularity, could never have known real obscurity or poverty. But all things are relative; before his conversion, Rodney had been obscurer and poorer than he

I

deserved to be. He knew no duchesses, no millionairesses, then; he had no deposit at the bank—only a current account that swelled and ebbed capriciously, like a mountain stream. His conversion changed all that.

When Grace and I paid our first visit, he was already on the upward path.

"I hope he isn't very formidable," Grace said to me, as we were making our way to Hampstead to see him. She was always rather frightened by the prospect of meeting new people.

I laughed. "It depends what you're afraid of," I said. "Of being treated with high-brow haughtiness, or losing your virtue. I never heard of any woman who found him formidable in the first respect."

"Oh, that's all right, then," said Grace, looking relieved.

Certainly, there was nothing very formidable in Rodney's appearance. At the age of thirty-five he had preserved (and he also cultivated with artful care) the appearance of a good-looking boy. He was small and neatly made, slim, and very agile in his movements. Under a mass of curly brown hair, which was always in a state of picturesque and studied untidiness, his face was like the face of a lively and impertinent cherub. Smooth, rounded, almost unlined, it still preserved its boyish contours. (There were always pots and pots of beauty cream on his dressing-table.) His eyes were blue, bright, and expressive. He had good teeth, and when he smiled two dimples appeared in his cheeks.

He opened the studio door himself. Dressed in his butcher's blue overalls, he looked charming. One's instinct was to pat the curly head and say: "Isn't he too sweet! Dressed up like that, pretending to be a workman!" Even I felt moved to make some such gesture. To a woman, a potential mother of chubby children, the temptation must have been almost irresistible.

Rodney was very cordial. "Dear old Dick!" he said, and patted me on the shoulder. I had not seen him for some months; he had spent the winter abroad. "What a delight to see you!" I believe he genuinely liked me.

I introduced him to Grace. He kissed her hand. "Too charming of you to have come. And what an enchanting ring!" he added, looking down again at her hand, which he still held in his own. "Do, please, let me look at it."

Grace smiled and blushed with pleasure as she gave it him. "I got it in Florence," she said. "I'm so glad you like it."

It was certainly a charming piece of old Italian jewellery. Sadly I reflected that I had known Grace intimately for more than six months and never so much as noticed the ring, far less made any comment on it. No wonder that I had been generally unlucky in love.

We found the studio littered with specimens of Rodney's latest artistic invention. Naked ladies in brown boots leading borzoi dogs; tenderly embracing one another in the middle of a still-life of bottles, guitars, and newspapers (the old familiar modern still-life rendered acceptable to the great public and richly saleable by the introduction of the equivocal nudes); more naked ladies riding on bicycles (Rodney's favourite subject, his patent, so to say); playing the concertina; catching yellow butterflies in large green nets. Rodney brought them out one by one. From her arm-chair in front of the easel, Grace looked at them; her face wore that rapt religious expression which I had so often noticed in the concert-room.

"Lovely," she murmured, as canvas succeeded canvas, "too lovely."

Looking at the pictures, I reflected with some amusement that, a year before, Rodney had been painting melodramatic crucifixions in the style of Tiepolo. At that time he had been an ardent Christian.

"Art can't live without religion," he used to say then. "We must get back to religion."

And with his customary facility Rodney had got back to it. Oh, those pictures! They were really shocking in their accomplished insincerity. So emotional, so dramatic, and yet so utterly false and empty. The subjects, you felt, had been apprehended as a cinema producer might apprehend them, in terms of "effectiveness." There were always great darknesses and tender serene lights, touches of vivid colour and portentous silhouettes. Very "stark," was what Rodney's admirers used to call those pictures, I remember. They were too stark by half for my taste.

Rodney set up another canvas on the easel.

"I call this 'The Bicycle made for Two,' " he said.

It represented a negress and a blonde with a Chinese white skin, riding on a tandem bicycle against a background of gigantic pink and yellow roses. In the foreground, on the right, stood a plate of fruit, tilted forward towards the spectator, in the characteristic "modern" style. A greyhound trotted along beside the bicycle.

"Really too . . ." began Grace ecstatically. But finding no synonym for "lovely," the epithet which she had applied to all the other pictures, she got no further, but made one of those noncommittal laudatory noises, which are so much more satisfactory than articulate speech, when you don't know what to say to an artist about his works. She looked up at me. "Isn't it really . . . ?" she asked.

"Yes, absolutely . . ." I nodded my affirmation. Then, rather maliciously, "Tell me, Rodney," I said, "do you still paint religious pictures? I remember a most grandiose Descent from the Cross you were busy on not so long ago."

But my malice was disappointed. Rodney was not in the least embarrassed by this reminder of the skeleton in his cupboard. He laughed.

"Oh, *that*," he said. "I painted it over. Nobody would buy. One cannot serve God and Mammon." And he laughed again, heartily, at his own witticism.

It went into his repertory at once, that little joke. He took to introducing the subject of his religious paintings himself, in order to have an opportunity of bringing out the phrase, with a comical parody of clerical unction, at the end of his story. In the course of the next few weeks I heard him repeat it, in different assemblages, three or four times.

"God and Mammon," he chuckled again. "Can't be combined."

"Only goddesses and Mammon," I suggested, nodding in the direction of his picture.

Later, I had the honour of hearing my words incorporated into Rodney's performance. He had a wonderfully retentive memory.

"Precisely," he said. "Goddesses, I'm happy to say, of a more popular religion. Are you a believer, Mrs. Peddley?" He smiled at her, raising his eyebrows. "I am—fervently. I'm *croyant* and" (he emphasised the "and" with arch significance) *"pratiquant."*

Grace laughed rather nervously, not knowing what to answer. "Well, I suppose we all are," she said. She was not accustomed to this sort of gallantry.

Rodney smiled at her more impertinently than ever. "How happy I should be," he said, "if I could make a convert of you!"

Grace repeated her nervous laugh and, to change the subject, began to talk about the pictures.

We sat there for some time, talking, drinking tea, smoking cigarettes. I looked at my watch; it was half-past six. I knew that Grace had a dinner-party that evening.

"We shall have to go," I said to her. "You'll be late for your dinner."

"Good heavens!" cried Grace, when she heard what the time was. She jumped up. "I must fly. Old Lady Wackerbath—imagine if I kept her waiting!" She laughed, but breathlessly; and she had gone quite pale with anticipatory fright.

"Stay, do stay," implored Rodney. "Keep her waiting."

"I daren't."

"But, my dear lady, you're young," he insisted; "you have the right—I'd say the duty, if the word weren't so coarse and masculine—to be unpunctual. At your age you must do what you like. You see, I'm assuming that you like being here," he added parenthetically.

She returned his smile. "Of course."

"Well then, stay; do what you like; follow your caprices. After all, that's what you're there for." Rodney was very strong on the Eternal Feminine.

Grace shook her head. "Good-bye. I've loved it so much."

Rodney sighed, looked sad and slowly shook his head. "If you'd loved it as much as all that," he said, "as much as I've loved it, you wouldn't be saying good-bye. But if you must. . . ." He smiled seductively; the teeth flashed, the dimples punctually appeared. He took her hand, bent over it and tenderly kissed it. "You must come again," he added. "Soon. And," turning to me with a laugh, and patting my shoulder, "without old Dick."

"He's frightfully amusing, isn't he?" Grace said to me a minute later when we had left the studio.

"Frightfully," I agreed, laying a certain emphasis on the adverb.

"And really," she continued, "most awfully nice, I thought." I made no comment.

"And a wonderful painter," she added.

All at once I felt that I detested Rodney Clegg. I thought of my own sterling qualities of mind and heart, and it seemed to me outrageous, it seemed to me scandalous and intolerable that people, that is to say women in general, and Grace in particular, should be impressed and taken in and charmed by this little middle-aged charlatan with the pretty boy's face and the horribly knowing, smart, impertinent manner. It seemed to me a disgrace. I was on the point of giving vent to my indignation; but it occurred to me, luckily, just in time that I should only be quite superfluously making a fool of myself if I did. Nothing is more ridiculous than a scene of jealousy, particularly when the scene is made by somebody who has no right to make it and on no grounds whatever. I held my tongue. My indignation against Rodney died down; I was able to laugh at myself. But driving southward through the slums of Camden Town, I looked attentively at Grace and found her more than ordinarily charming, desirable even. I would have liked to tell her so and, telling, kiss her. But I lacked the necessary impudence; I felt diffident of my

capacity to carry the amorous undertaking through to a successful issue. I said nothing, risked no gesture. But I decided, when
the time should come for us to part, that I would kiss her hand.
It was a thing I had never done before. At the last moment, however, it occurred to me that she might imagine that, in kissing her
hand, I was only stupidly imitating Rodney Clegg. I was afraid
she might think that his example had emboldened me. We parted
on the customary handshake.

Four or five weeks after our visit to Rodney's studio, I went
abroad for a six months' stay in France and Germany. In the
interval, Grace and Rodney had met twice, the first time in my
flat, for tea, the second at her house, where she had asked us both
to lunch. Rodney was brilliant on both occasions. A little too
brilliant indeed—like a smile of false teeth, I thought. But Grace
was dazzled. She had never met any one like this before. Her
admiration delighted Rodney.

"Intelligent woman," was his comment, as we left her house
together after lunch.

A few days later I set out for Paris.

"You must promise to write," said Grace in a voice full of
sentiment when I came to say good-bye.

I promised, and made her promise too. I did not know exactly
why we should write to one another or what we should write
about; but it seemed, none the less, important that we should
write. Letter-writing has acquired a curious sentimental prestige
which exalts it, in the realm of friendship, above mere conversation; perhaps because we are less shy at long range than face to
face, because we dare to say more in written than in spoken words.

It was Grace who first kept her promise.

"MY DEAR DICK," she wrote. "Do you remember what you
said about Mozart? That his music seems so gay on the surface—
so gay and careless; but underneath it is sad and melancholy,
almost despairing. I think life is like that, really. Everything
goes with such a bustle; but what's it all for? And how sad, how
sad it is! Now you mustn't flatter yourself by imagining that I
feel like this just because you happen to have gone away—though

as a matter of fact I *am* sorry you aren't here to talk about music and people and life and so forth. No, don't flatter yourself; because I've really felt like this for years, almost for ever. It's, so to speak, the bass of my music, this feeling; it throbs along all the time, regardless of what may be happening in the treble. Jigs, minuets, mazurkas, Blue Danube waltzes; but the bass remains the same. This isn't very good counterpoint, I know; but you see what I mean? The children have just left me, yelling. Phyllis has just smashed that hideous Copenhagen rabbit Aunt Eleanor gave me for Christmas. I'm delighted, of course; but I mayn't say so. And in any case, why must they always act such knockabouts? Sad, sad. And Lecky's *History of European Morals*, that's sadder still. It's a book I can never find my place in. Page 100 seems exactly the same as page 200. No clue. So that—you know how conscientious I am—I always have to begin again at the beginning. It's very discouraging. I haven't the spirit to begin again, yet again, this evening. I write to you instead. But in a moment I must go and dress for dinner. John's partner is coming; surely no man has a right to be so bald. And Sir Walter Magellan, who is something at the Board of Trade and makes jokes; with Lady M——, who's *so* affectionate. She has a way of kissing me, suddenly and intently, like a snake striking. And she spits when she talks. Then there's Molly Bone, who's so nice; but why can't she get married? And the Robsons, about whom there's nothing to say. Nothing whatever. Nothing, nothing, nothing. That's how I feel about it all. I shall put on my old black frock and wear no jewels. Good-bye. GRACE."

Reading this letter, I regretted more than ever my lack of impudence and enterprise in the taxi, that day we had driven down from Rodney's studio. It seemed to me, now, that the impudence would not have been resented.

I returned a letter of consolation; wrote again a week later; again ten days after that; and again, furiously, after another fortnight. A letter at last came back. It smelt of sandalwood and the stationery was pale yellow. In the past, Grace's correspondence had always been odourless and white. I looked and sniffed with a certain suspicion; then unfolded and read.

"I am surprised, my good Dick," the letter began, "that you don't know us better. Haven't you yet learned that we women don't like the sound of the words Must and Ought? We can't abide to have our sense of duty appealed to. That was why I never answered any of your impertinent letters. They were too full of 'you must write,' and 'you promised.' What do I care what I promised? That was long ago. I am a different being now. I have been thousands of different beings since then—re-born with each caprice. Now, at last, I choose, out of pure grace and kindness, to relent. Here's a letter. But beware of trying to bully me again; don't ever attempt to blackmail my conscience. I may be crueller next time. This is a warning.

"Were you trying, with your descriptions of diversions and entertainments, to make me envious of your Paris? If so, you haven't succeeded. We have our pleasures here too—even in London. For example, the most exquisite masked ball a few days since. Like Longhi's Venice or Watteau's Cythera—and at moments, let me add, towards the end of the evening, almost like Casanova's Venice, almost like the gallant, *grivois* Arcadia of Boucher. But hush! It was in Chelsea; I'll tell you no more. You might come bursting in on the next dance, pulling a long face because the band wasn't playing Bach and the dancers weren't talking about the 'Critique of Pure Reason.' For the fact is, my poor Dick, you're too solemn and serious in your pleasures. I shall really have to take you in hand, when you come back. You must be taught to be a little lighter and more fantastic. For the truth about you is that you're absurdly Victorian. You're still at the Life-is-real-life-is-earnest, Low-living-and-high-thinking stage. You lack the courage of your instincts. I want to see you more frivolous and sociable, yes, and more gluttonous and lecherous, my good Dick. If I were as free as you are, oh, what an Epicurean I'd be! Repent of your ways, Dick, before it's too late and you're irrecoverably middle-aged. No more. I am being called away on urgent pleasure. GRACE."

I read through this extraordinary epistle several times. If the untidy, illegible writing had not been so certainly Grace's, I should have doubted her authorship of the letter. That sham *dix-huitième* language, those neorococo sentiments—these were not hers. I had never heard her use the words "caprice" or "pleasure"; she had never generalised in that dreadfully facile way about "we women." What, then, had come over the woman since last she wrote? I put the two letters together. What could have happened? Mystery. Then, suddenly, I thought of Rodney Clegg, and where there had been darkness I saw light.

The light, I must confess, was extremely disagreeable to me, at any rate in its first dawning. I experienced a much more violent return of that jealousy which had overtaken me when I heard Grace expressing her admiration of Rodney's character and talents. And with the jealousy a proportionately violent renewal of my desires. An object hitherto indifferent may suddenly be invested in our eyes with an inestimable value by the mere fact that it has passed irrevocably out of our power into the possession of some one else. The moment that I suspected Grace of having become Rodney's mistress I began to imagine myself passionately in love with her. I tortured myself with distressing thoughts of their felicity; I cursed myself for having neglected opportunities that would never return. At one moment I even thought of rushing back to London, in the hope of snatching my now suddenly precious treasure out of Rodney's clutches. But the journey would have been expensive; I was luckily short of money. In the end I decided to stay where I was. Time passed and my good sense returned. I realised that my passion was entirely imaginary, home-made, and self-suggested. I pictured to myself what would have happened if I had returned to London under its influence. Burning with artificial flames, I should have burst dramatically into Grace's presence, only to discover, when I was actually with her, that I was not in love with her at all. Imaginary love can only flourish at a distance from its object; reality confines the fancy and puts it in its place. I had imagined myself unhappy because Grace had given herself to Rodney; but the situation, I perceived, would have been infinitely more distressing if I had returned, had succeeded in capturing her for myself, and then discovered that, much as I liked and charming as I found her, I did not love her.

It was deplorable, no doubt, that she should have been taken in by a charlatan like Rodney; it was a proof of bad taste on her part that she had not preferred to worship me, hopelessly, with an unrequited passion. Still, it was her business and in no way mine. If she felt that she could be happy with Rodney, well then, poor idiot! let her be happy. And so on. It was with reflections such as these that I solaced myself back into the indifference of a mere spectator. When Herbert turned up a few days later at my hotel, I was able to ask him, quite without agitation, for news of Grace.

"Oh, she's just the same as usual," said Herbert.

Crass fool! I pressed him. "Doesn't she go out more than she used to?" I asked. "To dances and that sort of thing? I had heard rumours that she was becoming so social."

"She may be," said Herbert. "I hadn't noticed anything in particular."

It was hopeless. I saw that if I wanted to know anything, I should have to use my own eyes and my own judgment. Meanwhile, I wrote to tell her how glad I was to know that she was happy and amusing herself. She replied with a long and very affected essay about "pleasures." After that, the correspondence flagged.

A few months later—I had just returned to London—there was a party at Rodney's studio, at which I was present. Rodney's latest masterpiece looked down from an easel set up at the end of the long room. It was an amusingly indecent pastiche of the Douanier Rousseau. "Wedding," the composition was called; and it represented a nuptial party, the bride and bridegroom at the centre, the relatives standing or sitting round them, grouped as though before the camera of a provincial photographer. In the background a draped column, palpably cardboard; a rustic bridge; fir-trees with snow and, in the sky, a large pink dirigible.

The only eccentric feature of the picture was that, while the bridegroom and the other gentlemen of the party were duly clothed in black Sunday best, the ladies, except for boots and hats, were naked. The best critics were of opinion that "Wedding" represented the highest flight, up to date, of Rodney's genius. He was asking four hundred and fifty pounds for it; a few days later, I was told, he actually got them.

Under the stonily fixed regard of the nuptial group Rodney's guests were diverting themselves. The usual people sat, or stood, or sprawled about, drinking white wine or whisky. Two of the young ladies had come dressed identically in the shirts and black velvet trousers of Gavarni's *débardeurs*. Another was smoking a small briar pipe. As I came into the room I heard a young man saying in a loud, truculent voice: "We're absolutely modern, we are. Anybody can have my wife, so far as I'm concerned. I don't care. She's free. And I'm free. That's what I call modern."

I could not help wondering why he should call it modern. To me it rather seemed primeval—almost pre-human. Love, after all, is the new invention; promiscuous lust geologically old-fashioned. The really modern people, I reflected, are the Brownings.

I shook hands with Rodney.

"Don't be too contemptuous of our simple London pleasures," he said.

I smiled; it amused me to hear on his lips the word with which Grace's letters had made me so familiar.

"As good as the pleasures of Paris, any day," I answered, looking round the room. Through the crowd, I caught sight of Grace.

With an air of being spiritually and physically at home, she was moving from group to group. In Rodney's rooms, I could see, she was regarded as the hostess. The mistress of the house, in the left-handed sense of the word. (A pity, I reflected, that I could not share that little joke with Rodney; he would have enjoyed it so much, about any one else.) In the intervals of conversation I curiously observed her; I compared the Grace before my eyes with the remembered image of Grace as I first knew her.

That trick of swaying as she walked—rather as a serpent sways to the piping of the charmer—that was new. So, too, was the carriage of the hands—the left on the hip, the right held breast-high, palm upwards, with a cigarette between the fingers. And when she put the cigarette to her lips, she had a novel way of turning up her face and blowing the smoke almost perpendicularly into the air, which was indescribably dashing and Bohemian. Haughty milady had vanished to be replaced by a new kind of aristocrat—the gay, terrible, beyond-good-and-evil variety.

From time to time snatches of her talk came to my ears. Gossip, invariably scandalous; criticisms of the latest exhibitions of pictures; recollections or anticipations of "perfect parties"— these seemed to be the principal topics, all of them, in Grace's mouth, quite unfamiliar to me. But the face, the vague-featured face of the nice but ugly little girl, the bewildered eyes, the occasional smile, so full of sweetness and a dim benevolence—these were still the same. And when I overheard her airily saying to one of her new friends of I know not what common acquaintance, "She's almost too hospitable—positively keeps open bed, you know," I could have burst out laughing, so absurdly incongruous with the face, the eyes, the smile, so palpably borrowed and not her own did the smart words seem.

Meanwhile, at the table, Rodney was doing one of his famous "non-stop" drawings—a figure, a whole scene rendered in a single line, without lifting the pencil from the paper. He was the centre of an admiring group.

"Isn't it too enchanting?"

"Exquisite!"

"Ravishing!"

The words exploded laughingly all around him.

"There," said Rodney, straightening himself up.

The paper was handed round for general inspection. Incredibly ingenious it was, that drawing, in a single sinuous line, of a fight between a bull and three naked female toreros. Every one applauded, called for more.

"What shall I do next?" asked Rodney.

"Trick cyclists," somebody suggested.

"Stale, stale," he objected.

"Self portrait."

Rodney shook his head. "Too vain."

"Adam and Eve."

"Or why not Salmon and Gluckstein?" suggested some one else.

"Or the twelve Apostles."

"I have it," shouted Rodney, waving his pencil. "King George and Queen Mary."

He bent over his scribbling block, and in a couple of minutes had produced a one-line portrait of their Britannic Majesties. There was a roar of laughter.

It was Grace who brought me the paper. "Isn't he wonderful?" she said, looking at me with a kind of eager anxiety, as though she were anxious to have my commendation of her choice, my sacerdotal benediction.

I had only seen her once, for a brief unintimate moment, since my return. We had not mentioned Rodney's name. But this evening, I saw, she was taking me into her confidence; she was begging me, without words, but none the less eloquently, to tell her that she had done well. I don't exactly know why she should have desired my blessing. She seemed to regard me as a sort of old, grey-haired, avuncular Polonius. (Not a very flattering opinion, considering that I was several years younger than Rodney himself.) To her, my approval was the approval of embodied wisdom.

"Isn't he wonderful?" she repeated. "Do you know of any other man now living, except perhaps Picasso, who could improvise a thing like that? For fun—as a game."

I handed the paper back to her. The day before, as it happened, finding myself in the neighbourhood, I had dropped in on Rodney at his studio. He was drawing when I entered, but, seeing me, had closed his book and come to meet me. While we were talking, the plumber called and Rodney had left the studio to give some instructions on the spot, in the bathroom. I got up and strolled about the room, looking at the latest canvases. Perhaps too inquisitively, I opened the note-book in which he had been drawing when I entered. The book was blank but for the first three or four pages. These were covered with "non-stop" drawings. I counted seven distinct versions of the bull with the female toreros, and five, a little corrected and improved each time, of King George and Queen Mary. I wondered at the time why he should be practising this peculiar kind of art; but feeling no urgent curiosity about the subject, I forgot, when he came back, to ask him. Now I understood.

"Extraordinary," I said to Grace, as I returned her the paper. "Really extraordinary!"

Her smile of gratitude and pleasure was so beautiful that I felt quite ashamed of myself for knowing Rodney's little secret.

Grace and I both lived in Kensington; it was I who drove her home when the party was over.

"Well, that was great fun," I said, as we settled into the taxi.

We had driven past a dozen lamp-posts before she spoke.

"You know, Dick," she said, "I'm so happy."

She laid her hand on my knee; and for lack of any possible verbal comment, I gently patted it. There was another long silence.

"But why do you despise us all?" she asked, turning on me suddenly.

"But when did I ever say I despised you?" I protested.

"Oh, one needn't say such things. They proclaim themselves."

I laughed, but more out of embarrassment than because I was amused. "A woman's intuition, what?" I said facetiously. "But you've really got too much of it, my dear Grace. You intuit things that aren't there at all."

"But you despise us all the same."

"I don't. Why should I?"

"Exactly. Why should you?"

"Why?" I repeated.

"For the sake of what?" she went on quickly. "And in com-

parison with what do you find our ways so despicable? I'll tell
you. For the sake of something impossible and inhuman. And
in comparison with something that doesn't exist. It's stupid,
when there's real life with all its pleasures." That word again—
Rodney's word! It seemed to me that she had a special, almost
unctuous tone when she pronounced it. "So delightful. So rich
and varied. But you turn up your nose and find it all vapid and
empty. Isn't it true?" she insisted.

"No," I answered. I could have told her that life doesn't
necessarily mean parties with white wine and whisky, social
stunts, fornication and chatter. I might have told her; but however studiously I might have generalised, it was obvious that my
remarks would be interpreted (quite correctly, indeed) as a set of
disparaging personalities. And I didn't want to quarrel with
Grace or offend her. And besides, when all was said, I did go to
Rodney's parties. I was an accomplice. The knockabout amused
me; I found it hard to deny myself the entertainment. My objection was only theoretical; I did what I denounced. I had no right
to strike pontifical attitudes and condemn. "No, of course it isn't
true," I repeated.

Grace sighed. "Of course, I can't really expect you to admit
it," she said. "But bless you," she added with a forced and unnatural gaiety, "I don't mind being despised. When one is rich,
one can afford the luxury of being disapproved of. And I am
rich, you know. Happiness, pleasures—I've got everything.
And after all," she went on, with a certain argumentative trucu-
lence in her voice, "I'm a woman. What do I care for your
ridiculous masculine standards. I do what I like, what amuses
me." The quotation from Rodney rang a little false, I thought.
There was a silence.

I wondered what John Peddley thought about it all, or
whether any suspicion of what was happening had yet pene-
trated the horny carapace of his insensitiveness.

And as though she were answering my unspoken question,
Grace began again with a new seriousness. "And there's my
other life, parallel. It doesn't make any difference to that, you

know. Doesn't touch it. I like John just as much as I did. And the children, of course."

There was another long silence. All at once, I hardly know why, I felt profoundly sad. Listening to this young woman talking about her lover, I wished that I too were in love. Even the "pleasures" glittered before my fancy with a new and tempting brilliance. My life seemed empty. I found myself thinking of the melody of the Countess's song in *Figaro: Dove sono i bei momenti di dolcezza e di piacer?*

That Grace's adventure made little or no difference to her other life, I had an opportunity of judging for myself in the course of a subsequent week-end with the Peddleys in Kent. John was there—"in great form," as he put it himself; and Grace, and the children, and Grace's father and mother. Nothing could have been more domestic and less like Rodney's party, less "modern." Indeed, I should be justified in writing that last word without its inverted commas. For there was something extraordinarily remote and uncontemporary about the whole household. The children were geologically remote in their childishness—only a little beyond the pithecanthropus stage. And Peddley was like a star, separated from the world by the unbridgeable gulfs of his egoism and unawareness. The subjects of his discourse might be contemporary; but spiritually, none the less, he was timeless, an inhabitant of blank and distant space. As for Grace's parents, they were only a generation away; but, goodness knows, that was far enough. They had opinions about socialism and sexual morality, and gentlemen, and what ought or ought not to be done by the best people—fixed, unalterable, habit-ingrained and by now almost instinctive opinions that made it impossible for them to understand or forgive the contemporary world.

This was especially true of Grace's mother. She was a big, handsome woman of about fifty-five, with the clear ringing voice of one who has been accustomed all her life to give orders. She busied herself in doing good works and generally keeping the poor in their places. Unlike her husband, who had a touch of

Peddley's star-like remoteness, she was very conscious of contemporaneity and, consequently, very loud and frequent in her denunciations of it.

Grace's father, who had inherited money, filled his leisure by farming a small estate unprofitably, sitting on committees, and reading Persian, an acquirement of which, in his quiet way, he was very proud. It was a strangely disinterested hobby. He had never been to Persia and had not the slightest intention of ever going. He was quite uninterested in Persian literature or history, and was just as happy reading a Persian cookery book as the works of Hafiz or Rumi. What he liked was the language itself. He enjoyed the process of reading the unfamiliar letters, of looking up the words in the dictionary. For him, Persian was a kind of endlessly complicated jigsaw puzzle. He studied it solely for the sake of killing time and in order not to think. A dim, hopeless sort of man was Mr. Comfrey. And he had an irritating way of looking at you over the top of his spectacles with a puzzled expression, as though he had not understood what you meant; which, indeed, was generally the case. For Mr. Comfrey was very slow of mind and made up for his knowledge of Persian by the most extraordinary ignorance of almost all other subjects under the sun.

"Say that again," he would say, when his incomprehension was too complete.

How strange, how utterly fantastic it seemed, that week-end. I felt as though I had been suddenly lifted out of the contemporary world and plunged into a kind of limbo.

John Peddley's latest subject was the Einstein theory.

"It's so simple," he assured us the first evening, between the soup and the fish. "I don't pretend to be a mathematician or anything like one; but I understand it perfectly. All that it needs is a little common sense." And for the next half-hour the common sense came braying out, as though from the mouth of a trombone.

Grace's father looked at him dubiously over the top of his spectacles.

"Say that again, will you?" he said, after every second sentence.

And John Peddley was only too delighted to oblige.

At the other end of the table, Grace and her mother were discussing the children, their clothes, characters, education, diseases. I longed to join in their conversation. But the simple domesticities were not for me. I was a man; John Peddley and the intellect were my portion. Reluctantly, I turned back towards my host.

"What I'd like you to explain," Grace's father was saying, "is just exactly how time can be at right angles to length, breadth, and thickness. Where precisely does it come in?" With two forks and a knife he indicated the three spatial dimensions. "Where do you find room for another right angle?"

And John Peddley set himself to explain. It was terrible.

Meanwhile, at my other ear, Grace's mother had begun to talk about the undesirable neighbours who had taken the house next to theirs on Campden Hill. A man and a woman, living together, unmarried. And the garden behind the houses was the common property of all the householders. What a situation! Leaving Peddley and the old gentleman to find room for the fourth right angle, I turned definitely to the ladies. For my benefit, Grace's mother began the horrid story again from the beginning. I was duly sympathetic.

Once, for a moment, I caught Grace's eye. She smiled at me, she almost imperceptibly raised her eyebrows. That little grimace was deeply significant. In the first months of our friendship, I had often seen her in the company of her father and mother, and her bearing, on these occasions, had always impressed me. I had never met a young woman of the generation which had come to maturity during the war who was so perfectly at ease with her elders, so unconstrainedly at home in their moral and mental atmosphere as was Grace. She had taken her father and mother entirely for granted, had regarded their views of life as the obvious, natural views of every sane human being. That embarrassment which—in these days, more perhaps than at any other period—afflicts young people when in the presence of their elders had never, so far as I had observed, touched Grace. This smile of apologetic and slightly contemptuous indulgence, this raising of the eyebrows, were symptomatic of a change. Grace had become contemporary, even (in inverted commas) "modern."

Outwardly, however, there was no change. The two worlds were parallel; they did not meet. They did not meet, even when Rodney came to dine *en famille*, even when John accompanied his wife to one of Rodney's less aggressively "artistic" (which in inverted commas means very much the same as "modern") evening parties. Or perhaps it would be truer to say that Rodney's world met John's, but John's did not meet Rodney's. Only if Rodney had been a Zulu and his friends Chinese would John have noticed that they were at all different from the people he was used to meeting. The merely spiritual differences which distinguished them were too small for his notice. He moved through life surrounded by his own atmosphere; only the most glaring lights could penetrate that half opaque and intensely refractive medium. For John, Rodney and his friends were just people, like everybody else; people who could be button-holed and talked to about the Swiss banking system and Einstein's theory, and the rationing of sugar. Sometimes, it was true, they seemed to him rather frivolous; their manners, sometimes, struck him as rather unduly brusque; and John had even remarked that they were sometimes rather coarse-spoken in the presence of ladies—or, if they happened to be ladies themselves, in the presence of gentlemen.

"Curious, these young people," he said to me, after an evening at Rodney's studio. "Curious." He shook his head. "I don't know that I quite understand them."

Through a rift in his atmosphere he had caught a glimpse of the alien world beyond; he had seen something, not refracted, but as it really was. But John was quite incurious; careless of its significance, he shut out the unfamiliar vision.

"I don't know what your opinion about modern art may be,"

he went on, disappointing me of his comments on modern people. "But what I always say is this."

And he said it, copiously.

Modern art became another gramophone record added to his repertory. That was the net result of his meeting with Rodney and Rodney's friends.

For the next few months I saw very little either of Grace or of Rodney. I had met Catherine, and was too busy falling in love to do or think of anything else. We were married towards the close of 1921, and life became for me, gradually, once more normal.

From the first Catherine and Grace were friends. Grace admired Catherine for her coolness, her quiet efficiency, her reliableness; admired and liked her. Catherine's affection for Grace was protective and elder-sisterly; and at the same time, she found Grace slightly comic. Affections are not impaired by being tempered with a touch of benevolent laughter. Indeed, I would almost be prepared to risk a generalisation and say that all true affections are tempered with laughter. For affection implies intimacy; and one cannot be intimate with another human being without discovering something to laugh at in his or her character. Almost all the truly virtuous characters in fiction are also slightly ridiculous; perhaps that is because their creators were so fond of them. Catherine saw the joke—the rather pathetic joke—of Grace. But she liked her none the less; perhaps, even, the more. For the joke was appealing; it was a certain childishness that raised the laugh.

At the time of my marriage, Grace was acting the eternally feminine part more fervently than ever. She had begun to dress very smartly and rather eccentrically, and was generally unpunctual; not very unpunctual (she was by nature too courteous for that), but just enough to be able to say that she was horribly late, but that she couldn't help it; it was in her nature—her woman's nature. She blamed Catherine for dressing too sensibly.

"You must be gayer in your clothes," she insisted, "more fantastic and capricious. It'll make you *feel* more fantastic. You think too masculinely."

And to encourage her in thinking femininely, she gave her six pairs of white kid gloves, marvellously piped with coloured leather and with fringed and intricately scalloped gauntlets. But perhaps the most feminine and fantastic thing about them was the fact that they were several sizes too small for Catherine's hand.

Grace had become a good deal more loquacious of late and her style of conversation had changed. Like her clothes, it was more fantastic than in the past. The principle on which she made conversation was simple: she said whatever came into her head. And into that vague, irresponsible head of hers the oddest things would come. A phantasmagoria of images, changing with every fresh impression or as the words of her interlocutor called up new associations, was for ever dancing across her field of mental vision. She put into words whatever she happened to see at any given moment. For instance, I might mention the musician Palestrina.

"Yes, yes," Grace would say, "what a marvellous composer!" Then, reacting to the Italian reference, she would add in the same breath: "And the way they positively *drink* the macaroni. Like those labels that come out of the mouth of caricatures. You know."

Sometimes I did know. I skipped over the enormous ellipses in this allusive thinking and caught the reference. Sometimes, when the association of her ideas was too exclusively private, I was left uncomprehending. The new technique was rather disconcerting, but it was always amusing, in a way. The unexpectedness of her remarks, the very nonsensicality of them, surprised one into finding them witty.

As a child, Grace had been snubbed when she talked in this random, fantastic fashion. "Talk sense," her governesses had said severely, when she told them during the geography lesson that she didn't like South America because it looked like a boiled leg of mutton. "Don't be silly." Grace was taught to be ashamed of her erratic fancy. She tried to talk sense—sense as governesses understand it—found it very difficult, and relapsed into silence. Peddley was even more sensible, in the same style, than the governesses themselves; devastatingly sensible. He was incapable of understanding fancy. If Grace had ever told Peddley why she didn't like South America, he would have been puzzled, he would have asked her to explain herself. And learning that it was the mutton-like shape of the continent on the map that prejudiced Grace against it, he would have given her statistics of South America's real dimensions, would have pointed out that it extended from the tropics almost into the antarctic circle, that it contained the largest river and some of the highest mountains in the world, that Brazil produced coffee and the Argentine beef, and that consequently, in actual fact, it was not in the very least like a boiled leg of mutton. With Peddley, Grace's only resources were laboriously talked sense or complete silence.

In Rodney's circle, however, she found that her gift of nonsense was appreciated and applauded. An enthusiast for the "fantastic" and the "feminine," Rodney encouraged her to talk at random, as the spirit of associative fancy might move her. Diffidently at first, Grace let herself go; her conversation achieved an immediate success. Her unstitched, fragmentary utterances were regarded as the last word in modern wit. People repeated her *bons mots*. A little bewildered by what had happened, Grace suddenly found herself in the movement, marching at the very head of the forces of contemporaneity. In the eighteenth century, when logic and science were the fashion, women tried to talk like the men. The twentieth century has reversed the process. Rodney did Grace the honour of appropriating to himself the happiest of her extravagances.

Success made Grace self-confident; and confident, she went forward triumphantly to further successes. It was a new and intoxicating experience for her. She lived in a state of chronic spiritual tipsiness.

"How stupid people are not to be happy!" she would say, whenever we discussed these eternal themes.

To Catherine, who had taken my place as a confidant—my

place and a much more intimate, more confidential place as well —she talked about love and Rodney.

"I can't think why people manage to make themselves unhappy about love," she said. "Why can't everybody love gaily and freely, like us? Other people's love seems to be all black and clotted, like Devonshire cream made of ink. Ours is like champagne. That's what love ought to be like: champagne. Don't you think so?"

"I think I should prefer it to be like clear water," said Catherine. To me, later on, she expressed her doubts. "All this champagne and gaiety," she said; "one can see that Rodney is a young man with a most wholesome fear of emotional entanglements."

"We all knew that," I said. "You didn't imagine, I suppose, that he was in love with her?"

"I hoped," said Catherine.

"Because you didn't know Rodney. Now you do. Champagne—you have the formula. The problem is Grace."

Was she really in love with him? Catherine and I discussed the question. I was of opinion that she was.

"When Rodney flutters off," I said, "she'll be left there, broken."

Catherine shook her head. "She only imagines she's in love," she insisted. "It's the huge excitement of it all that makes her happy; that, and the novelty of it, and her sense of importance, and her success. Not any deep passion for Rodney. She may think it's a passion—a champagnish passion, if you like. But it isn't really. There's no passion; only champagne. It was his prestige and her boredom that made her fall to him originally. And now it's her success and the fun of it that make her stick to him."

Events were to show that Catherine was right, or at least more nearly right than I. But before I describe these events, I must tell how it was that Kingham re-entered my world.

It was I who took the first step to end our ridiculous quarrel. I should have made the attempt earlier, if it had not been for

Kingham's absence from Europe. A little while after our squabble he left, with a commission to write articles as he went, first for North Africa and thence for the farther East. I heard of him once or twice from people who had seen him at Tunis, at Colombo, at Canton. And I read the articles, the admirably original articles, as they appeared at intervals in the paper which had commissioned them. But direct communication with him I had none. I did not write; for I was uncertain, to begin with, if my letter would ever reach him. And in any case, even if we had made up our quarrel by letter, what good would that have been? Reconciliations across eight thousand miles of space are never very satisfactory. I waited till I heard of his return and then wrote him a long letter. Three days later he was sitting at our dinner-table.

"This is good," he said, "this is very good." He looked this way and that, quickly, taking in everything—the furniture, the books, Catherine, me—with his bright, quick eyes. "Definitely settled."

"Oh, not so definitely as all that, let us hope." I laughed in Catherine's direction.

"I envy you," he went on. "To have got hold of something fixed, something solid and absolute—that's wonderful. Domestic love, marriage—after all, it's the nearest thing to an absolute that we can achieve, practically. And it takes on more value, when you've been rambling round the world for a bit, as I have. The world proves to you that nothing has any meaning except in relation to something else. Good, evil, justice, civilisation, cruelty, beauty. You think you know what these words mean. And perhaps you do know, in Kensington. But go to India or China. You don't know anything there. It's uncomfortable at first; but then, how exciting! And how much more copiously and multifariously you begin to live! But precisely for that reason you feel the need for some sort of fixity and definition, some kind of absolute, not merely of the imagination, but in actual life. That's where love comes in, and domesticity. Not to mention God and Death and the Immortality of the Soul and all the rest. When you live narrowly and snugly, those things seem absurd and superfluous. You don't even appreciate your snugness. But multiply yourself with travelling, knock the bottom out of all your old certainties and prejudices and habits of thought; then you begin to see the real significance of domestic snugness, you appreciate the reality and importance of the other fixities."

He spoke with all his old passionate eagerness. His eyes had the same feverish, almost unearthly brightness. His face, which had been smooth and pale when I saw it last, was burnt by the sun and lined. He looked more mature, tougher and stronger than in the past.

"Yes, I envy you," he repeated.

"Then why don't you get married yourself?" asked Catherine.

Kingham laughed. "Why not, indeed? You'd better ask Dick. He knows me well enough to answer, I should think."

"No, tell us yourself," I said.

Kingham shook his head. "It would be a case of cruelty to animals," he said enigmatically, and began to talk about something else.

"I envy you," he said again, later that same evening, when Catherine had gone to bed and we were alone together. "I envy you. But you don't deserve what you've got. You haven't earned your right to a fixed domestic absolute, as I have. I've realised, intimately and personally realised, the flux and the interdependence and the relativity of things; consequently I know and appreciate the meaning and value of fixity. But you—you're domestic just as you're moral; you're moral and domestic by nature, unconsciously, instinctively, without having known the opposites which give these attitudes their significance—like a worker bee, in fact; like a damned cabbage that just grows because it can't help it."

I laughed. "I like the way you talk about flux and relativity," I said, "when you yourself are the fixed, unchanging antithesis of these things. The same old Kingham! Why, you're a walking ixity; you're the Absolute in flesh and blood. How well I know those dear old home truths, for example!"

"But that doesn't prevent their being true," he insisted, laughing, but at the same time rather annoyed by what I had said. 'And besides, I *have* changed. My views about everything are quite different. A sensitive man can't go round the world and come back with the same philosophy of life as the one he started with."

"But he can come back with the same temperament, the same habits of feeling, the same instinctive reactions."

Kingham ran his fingers through his hair and repeated his petulant laughter. "Well, I suppose he can," he admitted reluctantly.

I was only too well justified in what I had said. A few days of renewed intimacy were enough to convince me that Kingham preserved all his old love of a scene, that he enjoyed as much as ever the luxury of a hot emotional bath. He burst in on me one morning, distracted with fury, to tell me about a violent quarrel he had had the previous evening with some insignificant young undergraduate—rather tipsy at that—who had told him (with considerable insight, I must admit, in spite of his tipsiness) that he, Kingham, was either insincere or hysterical.

"And the awful thing is that he may be right," he added, when he had finished his story. "Perhaps I *am* insincere." Restlessly, he walked about the room. From time to time he withdrew a hand from the pocket into which it was deeply plunged and made a gesture, or ran the fingers through his hair. "Perhaps I'm just a little comedian," he went on, "just a mouther of words, a ranter." The self-laceration hurt him, but he enjoyed the pain. "Do I really feel things deeply?" he went on speculating. "Or do I just deceive myself into believing that I care? Is it all a mere lie?" The operation continued interminably.

The tipsy undergraduate had diagnosed insincerity or hysteria. It was in my power to relieve Kingham of his haunting fear of insincerity by assuring him that the second of these alternatives was the more correct. But I doubted the efficacy of the consolation; and besides I had no desire for a quarrel. I held my tongue.

I did not make Kingham known to Grace; for knowing that he had a passionate and rooted dislike of Rodney, I was afraid that, in spite of my preliminary warnings (or even precisely because of them, for the sake of creating an intolerably unpleasant situation) he might burst out, in Grace's presence, into some violent denunciation of her lover. It was a risk that was not worth running. And besides, I did not imagine that they would get on well together. We were intimate with both; but we kept them, so to speak, in separate water-tight compartments of our intimacy.

One day, when I came home to dinner, I was greeted by Catherine with a piece of news.

"Rodney's being unfaithful," she said. "Poor little Grace was here for tea to-day. She pretends not to mind—to be very modern and hard and gay about it. But I could see that she was dreadfully upset."

"And who's the lucky lady?" I asked.

"Mrs. Melilla."

"A step up in the world." I thought of the emeralds and the enormous pearls, which added lustre to the already dazzling Jewish beauty of Mrs. Melilla. "He'll be in the baronetcy and peerage soon."

"What a pig!" said Catherine indignantly. "I'm so dreadfully sorry for poor Grace."

"But according to your theory, she isn't really in love with him."

"No, she isn't," said Catherine. "Not *really*. But she thinks she is. And she'll think so much more, of course, now that he's leaving her. And besides, she has put so many of her eggs into his basket; this smashes them all. She'd committed herself body and soul to Rodney and Rodneyism. This affair with Rodney gave sense to her whole existence. Can't you see that?"

"Perfectly." I remembered the days when Grace had seen herself as a musical critic and how cruelly I had murdered this comforting vision of herself by my little practical joke about the player of Rachmaninoff. A much more significant, much more intimately cherished dream was being murdered now.

She did her best, as Catherine had said, to be very "modern" about it. I saw her a few days later at one of Rodney's parties; she was smoking a great many cigarettes, drinking glass after glass of white wine and talking more wildly than ever. Her dress was a close-fitting sheath of silver tissue, designed so as to make the wearer look almost naked. Fatigued with sleeplessness, her eyes were circled with dark, bruise-coloured rings; seen in conjunction with the bright, unnatural red of her rouged cheeks and lips, these dark circles looked as though they had been painted on with a fard, to heighten the brilliance of the eyes, to hint provocatively at voluptuous fatigues and amorous vigils. She was having a great success and her admirers had never been more numerous. She flirted outrageously with all of them. Even when she was talking with me, she seemed to find it necessary to shoot languorous sidelong glances; to lean towards me, as though offering her whole person to my desires. But looking at her, I could see, under the fard, only the face of the nice but rather ugly little girl; it seemed, I thought, more than usually pathetic.

Rodney sat down at the table to do his usual non-stop drawing. "What shall it be?" he asked.

"Draw Jupiter and *all* his mistresses," cried Grace, who was beginning to be rather tipsy. "Europa and Leda and Semele and Danae," she clapped her hands at each name, "and Io and . . . and Clio and Dio and Scio and Fi-fio and O-my-Eyeo. . . ."

The jest was not a very good one. But as most of Rodney's guests had drunk a good deal of wine and all were more or less intoxicated by the convivial atmosphere of a successful party, there was a general laugh. Grace began to laugh too, almost hysterically. It was a long time before she could control herself.

Rodney, who had made no preparations for improvising a picture of Jove's mistresses, found an excuse for rejecting the suggestion. He ended by drawing Mrs. Eddy pursued by a satyr.

Deserted by Rodney, Grace tried to pretend that it was she

who was the deserter. The rôle of the capricious wanton seemed to her more in harmony with the Rodneyan conception of the eternal feminine as well as less humiliating than that of the victim. Provocatively, promiscuously, she flirted. In those first days of her despair she would, I believe, have accepted the advances of almost any tolerably presentable man. Masterman, for example, or Gane the journalist, or Levitski—it was one of those three, I surmised, judging by what I saw at the party, who would succeed to Rodney's felicity, and that very soon.

The day after the party, Grace paid another visit to Catherine. She brought a small powder-puff as a present. In return, she asked, though not in so many words, for comfort, advice, and above all for approval. In a crisis, on the spur of the moment, Grace could be rashly and unreflectingly impulsive; but when there was time to think, when it was a question of deliberately planning she was timorous, she hated to stand alone and take responsibilities. She liked to know that the part in which she saw herself was approved of by some trustworthy judge. The powder-puff was a bribe and an argument; an argument in favour of the eternal feminine, with all that that connoted, a bribe for the judge, an appeal to her affection, that she might approve of Grace's sentiments and conduct.

Grace put her case. "The mistake people make," she said, "is getting involved, like the man on the music-halls who does that turn with the fly-paper. I refuse to be involved; that's my principle. I think one ought to be heartless and just amuse one-self, that's all. Not worry about anything else."

"But do you think one can really be amused if one doesn't worry and takes things heartlessly?" asked Catherine. "*Really* amused, I mean. Happy, if you'll permit me to use an old-fashioned word. Can one be happy?" She thought of Levitski, of Gane and Masterman.

Grace was silent; perhaps she too was thinking of them. Then, making an effort, "Yes, yes," she said with a kind of obstinate, determined gaiety, "one can; of course one can."

I was at the Queen's Hall that afternoon. Coming out, when

the concert was over, I caught sight of Kingham in the issuing crowd.

"Come home for a late cup of tea and stay to dinner."

"All right," he said.

We climbed on to a bus and rode westward. The sun had just set. Low down in the sky in front of us there were streaks of black and orange cloud, and above them a pale, watery-green expanse, limpid and calm up to the zenith. We rode for some time in silence, watching the lovely death of yet another of our days.

"It's all very well," said Kingham at last, indicating these western serenities with a gesture of his fine, expressive hand, "it's all very well, no doubt, for tired business men. Gives them comfort, I dare say; makes them feel agreeably repentant for the swindles they've committed during the day, and all that. Oh, it's full of uplift, I've no doubt. But I don't happen to be a tired business man. It just makes me sick."

"Come, come," I protested.

He wouldn't listen to me. "I won't have Gray's 'Elegy' rammed down my throat," he said. "What I feel like is *The Marriage of Heaven and Hell*, or *Zarathustra*, or the *Chants de Maldoror*."

"Well, all that I can suggest" (I suggested it mildly) "is that you should travel inside the bus and not look at the sunset."

"Ass!" he said contemptuously.

We came in, to find Grace still sitting there, over the tea-cups, with Catherine. I was annoyed; still, there was nothing to be done about it. I introduced Kingham. All unconsciously, I was playing Pandarus for the second time.

My sources for the history of Grace's second love affair are tolerably copious. To begin with, I had opportunities of personally observing it, during a considerable part of its duration. I heard much, too, from Kingham himself. For Kingham was not at all a discreet lover. He was as little capable of being secretive about this class of experiences as about any other. He simply had to talk. Talking renewed and multiplied the emotions which he described. Talk even created new emotions—emotions which he had not felt at the time but which it occurred to him, when he was describing the scene, to think that he ought to have felt. He had no scruples about projecting these *sentiments d'escalier* backwards, anachronistically, into his past experience, falsifying history for the sake of future drama. To his memories of a scene with Grace he would add emotional complications, so that the next scene might be livelier. It was in the heat of talk that his finest emendations of history occurred to him. The genuine, or at any rate the on the whole more genuine, story came to me through Catherine from Grace. It was to Catherine that, in moments of crisis (and this particular love affair was almost uninterruptedly a crisis) Grace came for solace and counsel.

The affair began with a misunderstanding. No sooner had Kingham entered the room than Grace, who had been talking quite simply and naturally with Catherine, put on her brazen "modern" manner of the party and began with a kind of desperate recklessness to demand the attention and provoke the desires of the newcomer. She knew Kingham's name, of course, and all about him. In Rodney's circle it was admitted, albeit with some reluctance, that the man had talent; but he was deplored as a barbarian.

"He's one of those tiresome people," I once heard Rodney complain, "who will talk about their soul—and your soul, which is almost worse. Terribly Salvation Army. One wouldn't be surprised to see him on Sundays in Hyde Park telling people what they ought to do to be saved."

At the sight of him, Grace had felt, no doubt, that it would be amusing to bring this curious wild animal to heel and make it do tricks. (It did not occur to her that it might be she who would be doing the tricks.) Kingham was a quarry worthy of any huntswoman. Still, I believe that she would have flirted as outrageously with almost any stranger. This provocative attitude of hers—an attitude which might be described as one of chronic and universal unfaithfulness—was her retort to unkind fate and unfaithful Rodney. She wanted to capture a new lover—several lovers, even—in order to prove to Rodney, to the world at large and above all, surely, to herself, that she was modern, knew how to take love lightly and gaily, as the most exquisite of entertainments, and that, in a word, she didn't care a pin. In another woman, this promiscuous flirtatiousness might have been distasteful, detestable even. But there was, in Grace, a certain fundamental innocence that rendered what ought, by all the rules, to have been the most reprehensible of actions entirely harmless. Text-book moralists would have called her bad, when in fact she was merely pathetic and a trifle comic. The text-books assign to every action its place in the moral hierarchy; the text-book moralists judge men exclusively by their actions. The method is crude and unscientific. For in reality certain characters have power to sterilize a dirty action; certain others infect and gangrene actions which, according to the book, should be regarded as clean. The harshest judges are those who have been so deeply hypnotised by the spell of the text-book words, that they have become quite insensitive to reality. They can think only of words—"purity," "vice," "depravity," "duty"; the existence of men and women escapes their notice.

Grace, as I have said, possessed an innocence which made nonsense of all the words which might have been used to describe her actions. To any one but a text-book theorist it was obvious that the actions hardly mattered; her innocence remained intact. It was this same innocence which enabled her to give utterance—with perfect unconcern and a complete absence of daring affectation—to those scabrous sentiments, those more than scientific expressions which were almost *de rigueur* in the conversation of Rodney's circle. In a foreign language one can talk of subjects, one can unconcernedly use words, the uttering, the mention of which in one's native idiom would horribly embarrass. For Grace, all these words, the most genuinely Old English, all these themes, however intimately connected by gossip with the names of known men and women, were foreign and remote. Even the universal language of coquettish gestures was foreign to her; she acted its provocations and innuendoes with a frankness which

K

would have been shameless, if she had really known what they meant. Kingham entered the room; she turned on him at once all her batteries of looks and smiles—a bombardment of provocations. I knew Grace so well that, in my eyes, the performance seemed merely absurd. These smiles, these sidelong glances and flutteringly dropped eyelids, this teasing mockery by which she irritated Kingham into paying attention to her, struck me as wholly uncharacteristic of Grace and therefore ridiculous—above all, unconvincing. Yes, unconvincing. I could not believe that any one could fail to see what Grace was really like. Was it possible that Kingham didn't realise just as well as I did that she was, in spirit, as in features, just a nice little girl, pretending without much success—particularly in this rôle—to be grown up?

It seemed to me incredible. But Kingham was certainly taken in. He accepted her at her face value of this particular moment—as an aristocratically reckless hedonist in wanton search of amusement, pleasure, excitement, and power. To the dangerous siren he took her to be, Kingham reacted with a mixed emotion that was half angry contempt, half amorous curiosity. On principle, Kingham violently disapproved of professional *femmes fatales*, sirens, vampires—all women, in fact, who make love and the subjugation of lovers the principal occupation of their lives. He thought it outrageous that self-respecting and useful men should suddenly find themselves at the mercy of these dangerous and irresponsible beings. What perhaps increased his moral indignation was the fact that he himself was constantly falling a victim to them. Youth, vitality, strong personality, frank and unbridled vice had irresistible attractions for him. He was drawn sometimes to the vulgarest possessors of these characteristics. He felt it an indignity, a humiliation (and yet, who knows? perhaps with Kingham this sense of humiliation was only another attraction); but he was none the less unfailingly drawn. He resisted, but never quite firmly enough (that, after all, would have spoiled all the fun). He resisted, succumbed and was subjected. But it must be admitted that his love, however abject it might be in the first moment of his surrender, was generally a vengeance in itself. Kingham might suffer; but he contrived in most cases to inflict as much suffering as he received. And while he, with a part of his spirit at any rate, actually enjoyed pain, however acutely and genuinely felt, the tormentors whom he in his turn tormented were mostly quite normal young women with no taste for the pleasures of suffering. He got the best of it; but he regarded himself, none the less, as the victim, and was consequently in a chronic state of moral indignation.

This first meeting convinced Kingham that Grace was the sort of woman she wanted to persuade him (not to mention herself) that she was—a vampire. Like many persons of weak character and lacking in self-reliance, Grace was often extraordinarily reckless. Passive generally and acquiescent, she sometimes committed herself wildly to the most extravagant courses of action— not from any principle of decision, but because, precisely, she did not know what decision was, because she lacked the sense of responsibility, and was incapable of realising the irrevocable nature of an act. She imagined that she could do things irresponsibly and without committing herself; and feeling no inward sense of commitment, she would embark on courses of action which—externalised and become a part of the great machine of the world—dragged her, sometimes reluctant, sometimes willing, but always ingenuously surprised, into situations the most bewilderingly unexpected. It was this irresponsible impulsiveness of a character lacking the power of making deliberate decisions (this coupled with her fatal capacity for seeing herself in any rôle that seemed, at the moment, attractive) that had made her at one moment a socialist canvasser at the municipal elections; at another, an occasional opium smoker in that sordid and dangerous den near the Commercial Docks which Tim Masterman used to frequent; at another, though she was terrified of horses, a rider to hounds; and at yet another—to her infinite distress; but having light-heartedly insisted that she didn't know what modesty was, she couldn't draw back—the model for one of Levitski's nudes. And if she now threw herself at Kingham's head (just as, a few nights before, she had thrown herself at

Masterman's, at Gane's, at Levitski's), it was irresponsibly, without considering what might be the results of her action, without even fully realising that there would be any results at all. True, she saw herself as a "modern" young woman; and her abandonment by Rodney had made her anxious, for the mere saving of her face, to capture a new lover, quickly. And yet it would be wrong to say that she had decided to employ coquettish provocations in order to get what she wanted. She had not decided anything; for decision is deliberate and the fruit of calculation. She was just wildly indulging in action, in precisely the same way as she indulged in random speech, without thinking of what the deeds or the words committed her to. But whereas logical inconsistencies matter extremely little and false intellectual positions can easily be abandoned, the effects of action or of words leading to action are not so negligible. For action commits what is much more important than the intellect—the body. To get the bodily self out of a false position is a difficult and often painful business. Grace, the indecisive, the all too easily and lightly moved to action, had often found it so to her cost. But that did not prevent her from repeating her mistake. Experience never does.

Kingham, as I have said, took her for what she irresponsibly wanted him to believe she was. He was duly provoked by what had been meant to be provocative. To this sort of amorous teasing he was extraordinarily susceptible. So much so, indeed, that his interest in Grace was no great tribute to her style. It was enough that a woman should exhibit a certain lively, vampirish interest in him; Kingham was almost certain to succumb to the attack. I remember one occasion in Paris when he was positively swept off his feet by the shrill, metallic sallies of an American chorus-girl from the Folies Bergères.

This first impression of Grace—as a "modern," dangerously provocative, actively wanton vampire—persisted in Kingham's mind and no evidence to the contrary could obliterate it. In the course of their first meeting, he had taken up his emotional attitude towards her; and the attitude once taken, he would not shift his ground, however palpable the proofs that he was wrong.

Whether he ceased to be able to use his intelligence and became incapable of recognising the facts that would have upset his prejudices, or whether he deliberately shut his eyes to what he did not wish to see, I do not exactly know. A powerful emotion had the double effect, I surmise, of rendering him at one and the same time stupid and most ingeniously perverse.

"I think there's something really devilish about the women of this generation," he said to me, in his intense, emphatic way, some two or three days later. "Something devilish," he repeated, "really devilish." It was a trick of his, in writing as well as in speech, to get hold of a word and, if he liked the sound of it, work it to death.

I laughed. "Oh, come," I protested. "Do you find Catherine, for example, so specially diabolic?"

"She isn't of this generation," Kingham answered. "Spiritually, she doesn't belong to it."

I laughed again; it was always difficult arguing with Kingham. You might think you had him cornered; you raised your logical cudgel to smash him. But while you were bringing it down, he darted out from beneath the stroke through some little trap door of his own discovery, clean out of the argument. It was impossible to prove him in the wrong, for the simple reason that he never remained long enough in any one intellectual position to be proved anything.

"No, not Catherine," he went on, after a little pause. "I was thinking of that Peddley woman."

"Grace?" I asked in some astonishment. "Grace devilish?"

He nodded. "Devilish," he repeated with conviction. The word, I could see, had acquired an enormous significance for him. It was the core round which, at the moment, all his thoughts and feelings were crystallising. All his universe was arranging itself in patterns round the word "devilish," round the idea of devilishness in general, and Grace's devilishness in particular.

I protested. "Of all the un-devilish people I've ever known," I said, "Grace seems to me the most superlatively so."

"You don't know her," he retorted.

"But I've known her for years."

"Not really known," insisted Kingham, diving through another of his little trap doors out of the argument. "You've never inspired her with one of her devilish concupiscences." (I thought of Grace and could not help smiling; the smile exasperated Kingham.) "Grin away," he said. "Imagine you're omniscient, if it gives you any pleasure. All I say is this: she's never tried to hunt you down."

"I suppose you mean that she was rather stupidly flirtatious the other evening," I said.

Kingham nodded. "It was devilish," he said softly, more for himself than for me. "Devilish concupiscence."

"But I assure you," I went on, "that business the other night was all mere silliness. She's childish, not devilish. She still sees herself in terms of Rodney Clegg, that's all. And she wants to pretend, now that he's deserted her, that she doesn't care. I'm not sure, indeed, that she doesn't want to make us believe that it was she who deserted him. That's why she wants to get hold of another lover quickly—for the sake of her prestige. But as for devilishness—why, the idea's simply absurd. She isn't definite enough to be a devil. She's just what circumstances and her imagination and other people happen to make her. A child, that's all."

"You may think you know her," Kingham persisted obstinately, "but you don't. How can you, if you've never been hunted by her?"

"Bosh!" I said impatiently.

"I tell you she's devilish," he insisted.

"Then why on earth did you accept her invitation to lunch with such alacrity?"

"There are things that are unescapable," he answered oracularly.

"I give you up," I said, shrugging my shoulders. The man exasperated me. "The best thing you can do," I added, "is to go to your devil and be damned as quickly as possible."

"That's exactly where I am going," he said. And as though I

had reminded him of an appointment, Kingham looked at his watch. "And by God," he added, in a different voice, "I shall, have to take a taxi, if I'm to get there in time."

Kingham looked deeply put out; for he hated parting with money unnecessarily. He was tolerably well off now; but he still preserved the habits of prudence, almost of avarice, which he had acquired, painfully, in the days of his lower middle class boyhood and his poverty-stricken literary novitiate. He had asked Grace to dine with him in Soho; that had already cost him an effort. And now he was going to be compelled to take a taxi, so as to be in time to pay for the dinner. The thought of it made him suffer. And suffering for her sake, suffering a mean, unavowable pain for which he could not hope to get any sympathy, even his own, he found the ultimate cause of it, Grace, all the more devilish.

"Unescapable," he repeated, still frowning, as he put on his hat to go. There was an expression positively of ferocity on his face. "Unescapable." He turned and left me.

"Poor Grace!" I was thinking, as I closed the front door and walked back to my study. It was just as unescapable for her as for Kingham. And I knew Kingham; my sympathies were all with Grace.

I was quite right, as it turned out, in according my sympathies as I did. For if any one ever needed, ever deserved sympathy, it was poor Grace, during those deplorable months of 1922. She fell in love with Kingham—fell in love, though it was the third time she had given herself, for the first, the very first time in her life, painfully, desperately, insanely. She had proposed to herself a repetition of her affair with Rodney. It was to be all charmingly perverse dalliances, with champagne and sandwiches and lightly tender conversation in the intervals; and exquisite little letters in the *dix-huitième* manner; and evening parties; and amusing escapades. That was what it had been with Rodney. He made this kind of love, it must be admitted, with real style; it was charming. Grace imagined that she would make it in just the same way with Rodney's successor. And so she might have, more or less, if the successor had been Levitski, or Masterman, or Gane. But the successor was Kingham. The choice was fatal; but the worst results of it might have been avoided if she had not loved him. Unloving, she might simply have left him when he made things too insupportable. But she did love him and, in love, she was utterly at his mercy.

Kingham had said that the thing was unescapable; and if for him it was so, that was due to the need he perversely felt of giving himself over periodically to strong emotions, the need of being humiliated and humiliating, of suffering and making other people suffer. What he had always loved was the passion itself, not the women who were the cause or excuse of it. These occasional orgies of passion were necessary to him, just as the periodical drinking bout is necessary to the dipsomaniac. After a certain amount of indulgence, the need was satisfied and he felt quite free to detach himself from the lover who had been dear to him only as the stimulator of his emotions, not for her own sake. Kingham could satisfy his craving; it was an appetite that could be quenched by indulgence. But Grace's desire was one of those desperate, hopeless desires that can only be assuaged by a kind of miracle. What she desired was nothing less than to unite herself wholly with another being, to know him through and through and to be made free of all his secrets. Only the all but miraculous meeting of two equal loves, two equally confiding temperaments can bring fulfilment to that longing. There was no such meeting here.

Kingham made a habit of telling all his acquaintances, sooner or later, what he thought of them—which was invariably disagreeable. He called this process a "clearing of the atmosphere." But in point of fact, it never cleared anything; it obscured and made turbid, it created thunder in clear skies. Kingham might not admit the fact; but this was, none the less, precisely what he intended should happen. Clear skies bored him; he enjoyed storms. But always, when he had succeeded in provoking a storm, he expressed a genuine astonishment at the inability of the world at large to tolerate frankness, however sincere, however manifestly for its own good. Hurt by his brutally plain speaking, his old friends were reproached for being hurt. Few of Kingham's loves or friendships had long survived the effects of his frankness. The affair with Grace was one of the exceptions.

From the very beginning, Kingham had found it necessary to "clear the atmosphere." Even at their first meeting, in our house, he was rather rude. Later on, he developed into a kind of Timon of Athens. Her frivolity, her voluptuary's philosophy of life, her heartlessness, her "devilish concupiscence"—these were the characteristics about which he told her, with all the concentrated passion of which he was capable, what he indignantly thought.

I met him again, at the Queen's Hall, on the day after his dinner in Soho.

"I told her what I thought of her," he let me know.

"And what did she think about what you thought?" I asked.

Kingham frowned. "She seemed to be rather pleased than otherwise," he answered. "That's the devilish strength of these women. They simply glory in the things they ought to be ashamed of. It makes them impervious to anything decent. Impervious, and therefore utterly ruthless and unscrupulous."

"How incorrigibly romantic you are!" I mocked at him.

Told—and very mildly, after all—what I thought of him, Kingham winced like a stung horse. Other people's frankness hurt him just as much as his hurt other people; perhaps more. The only difference was that he enjoyed being hurt.

"What nonsense!" he began indignantly.

His retort lasted as long as the interval and was only drowned by the first blaring chords of the *Meistersinger* overture. Bottled up within compulsory silence, what were his emotions? It amused me to speculate. Various, emphatic, tirelessly unflagging and working themselves up into ever more and more clotted complications—were they not the spiritual counterpart of this music to which we were now listening? When the Wagnerian tumult was over, Kingham continued his interrupted protest.

"She seemed to be rather pleased." That, according to Kingham, had been Grace's reaction to his home truths. I felt sure, on reflection, that he had observed her rightly. For Grace still saw herself in terms of Rodneyism—as "modern" and "eighteenth-century" (curious how these terms have come to be largely interchangeable) and what Rodney imagined to be "eternally feminine." Of course she would be pleased at finding that Kingham had accepted her at her own valuation—and not only accepted her valuation but even voluntarily outbidden it by adding devilishness to the modernity, eighteenth-centuriness, and eternal femininity which she had modestly—too modestly, as she now perceived—attributed to herself. She took Kingham's denunciations as compliments and smiled with unaffected pleasure when he talked to her of her vampire's ruthlessness, when he reproached her with her devilish concupiscence for the shuddering souls as well as the less reluctant flesh of her victims. In Rodney's circle a temperament was as much *de rigueur* as a train and ostrich feathers at Court. Grace saw herself as a prodigy of temperament; but she liked to have this vision of herself confirmed by outside testimony. Kingham's home truths convinced her that she had seen herself correctly. The more abusive Kingham became, the better pleased she was and the more she liked him. She felt that he was really taking her seriously as a frivolous woman, that he was appreciating her as she deserved. His appreciation heightened her confidence and, under the rain of his anathemas, she played her part with an easier grace, a more stylish perfection. The spectacle of Grace impertinently blossoming under what had been meant to blast exasperated Kingham. He abused her more violently; and the greater his violence, the more serenely airy her eternal, modern, eighteenth-century femininity.

Underneath, meanwhile, and almost unconsciously, Grace was falling in love with him.

I have seen Kingham in his relations with many men and women. To none of them was he merely indifferent. Either they detested him—and I have never known a man who had more and bitterer enemies—or else they loved him. (Many of the lovers, I may add, turned subsequently into haters.) When I analyse my own feelings towards him, I am forced to the conclusion that I myself was in some manner in love with him. For why should I, who knew him so well and how insufferable he could be and, indeed, generally was, why should I have put up with him, in spite of everything? And why should I always have made such efforts to patch up all our incessant quarrels? Why shouldn't I have allowed him to go to the devil, so far as I was concerned, a dozen times? or at least thankfully accepted the estrangement which followed our most violent squabble—the squabble over poor loutish Herbert—and allowed the separation to lengthen into permanency? The only explanation is that, like all those who did not loathe him, I was somehow in love with Kingham. He was in some way important for me, deeply significant and necessary. In his presence I felt that my being expanded. There was suddenly, so to speak, a high tide within me; along dry, sand-silted, desolate channels of my being life strongly, sparklingly flowed. And Kingham was the moon that drew it up across the desert.

All those whom we find sympathetic exercise, in a greater or less degree, this moon-like influence upon us, drawing up the tides of life till they cover what had been, in an antipathetic environment, parched and dead. But there are certain individuals who, by their proximity, raise a higher tide, and in a vastly greater number of souls, than the ordinary man or woman. Kingham was one of these exceptional beings. To those who found him sympathetic he was more sympathetic than other and much more obviously amiable acquaintances. There was a glow, a vividness, a brilliance about the man. He could charm you even when he was saying things with which you disagreed, or doing things which you disapproved. Even his enemies admitted the existence and the power of this brilliant charm. Catherine, who was not exactly an enemy, but who profoundly disliked his way of life and habits of mind, had to confess that, whenever he wanted and took the trouble to do so, he could silence, for the moment at any rate, all her prejudices and compel her, so long as he was actually there, in the room with her, to like him. Grace started with no prejudices against him—no prejudices, beyond the opinion, inherited from Rodney, that the man was a savage; and savages, after all, are more attractive than repellant. She was suggestible and easily swayed by stronger and more definite personalities than her own. It was not surprising that she should succumb to his charm to the extent of first liking the man and soon wildly loving him.

It was some little time, however, before Grace discovered that she loved him. In the first days of their intimacy, she was too busy playing the modern part to realise that she felt so un-Rodneyan an emotion. Love, the real insane thing, was out of harmony with the character she had assumed. It needed a sudden, startling shock to make her understand what she felt for him, to make her, in the same moment, forget to be "modern" and "feminine" in Rodney's sense of the terms, and become—what? I had meant to say "herself." But after all, can one be said to be "oneself" when one is being transfigured or dolorously distorted by love? In love, nobody is himself; or if you prefer, romantic-ally, to put it the other way round, nobody is really himself when he is not in love. It comes to very much the same thing. The difference between Grace in love and Grace out of it seemed all the wider, because it was the difference between a Rodneyan eternal female and a woman, and a Kinghamised woman at that. For even in love, Grace saw herself in the part and saw herself, inevitably, in terms of her lover. Her Rodneyisms disappeared and were replaced by Kinghamisms. She saw herself no longer as a modern young aristocrat, but as the primevally "passional" incarnation ("passional" was one of Kingham's too favourite words) of her new lover's feminine ideal.

Their intimacy had lasted more than a month before Grace discovered the true nature of her feelings. Kingham's courtship had been unremitting. Denunciations of her devilishness had alternated with appeals to her to become his mistress. Grace took the denunciations as compliments and laughingly replied to them at random with any nonsense that came into her head.

These airy irrelevant retorts of hers, which Rodney would have applauded as the height of modern wit, seemed to Kingham the very height of diabolism.

"She's like Nero," he said to me one day, "fiddling over Rome."

He was Rome—the centre of the universe—in flames. Grace, having kindled, watched him burn and, in the face of his destruction, talked nonsense.

What was more, she would not quench his conflagration. In spite of the "devilish concupiscence," which Kingham had attributed to her, she refused, during the first five or six weeks of their acquaintance, to become his mistress. She had captivated Kingham; that was sufficient to restore her self-confidence and that fantastic image of herself, as a successful, modern siren, which Rodney's desertion had temporarily shattered. To have tumbled into his arms at once might, perhaps, have been in the *dix-huitième* part; but a certain native modesty prevented Grace from being perfectly consistent.

Kingham regarded her refusal to capitulate immediately as yet another piece of devilishness; according to his theory, she was exercising an unnatural self-control merely in order to torment him. A perverse taste for cruelty was added to his list of accusations. Grace was charmed by this soft impeachment.

Kingham's attacks had seemed to her, so far, more amusing than painful, more complimentary than insulting. She was still protected by the armour of her indifference. The realisation that she loved him was soon to strip her of that armour, and with every increase of that love, her naked spirit was to grow more tremulously sensitive to Kingham's assaults upon it.

The critical, the apocalyptic event took place in Kingham's rooms. It was a damp, hot afternoon of early summer. The sky was overcast when Grace arrived, and there was thunder in the air. She was wearing—the fact came out in her account to Catherine of the afternoon's events—she was wearing, for the first time, a brand new frock from Paris; mouse-coloured, with two subtly harmonious, almost discordant, tones of red about the collar, and a repetition of the same colours at the cuffs and in a panel let into the skirt. Poiret, I think, was the inventor; and it was very modern and rather eccentrically elegant. In a word, it was a dress created for Rodney's mistress.

Grace, who was very much aware of herself in her clothes, had felt the incongruity most painfully, afterwards. The more so, since, when she came in, she was feeling so happy about her dress. She was thinking what a success it was and how elegant, how original the people who saw her in the street must find her. And she was wondering what effect the dress would have on Kingham. She hoped, she thought that he would like it.

In his way, Kingham was nearly as observant in the matter of clothes as Rodney. True, he had not Rodney's almost professional eye for style and cut and smartness. Rodney was a great couturier *manqué*. The fashionable dressmaker was visible in every picture he painted; he had mistaken his profession. Kingham's way of looking at clothes was different. His was the moralist's eye, not the couturier's. For him, clothes were symbols, the visible expressions of states of soul. Thus, Grace's slightly eccentric, very dashing elegance seemed to him the expressive symbol of her devilishness. He regarded her clothes as an efflorescence of her spirit. They were part of her, and she was directly wholly responsible for them. It never seemed to strike him that tailors, dressmakers and advisory friends might share the responsibility. He took in Grace's frock at a glance.

"You've got a new dress on," he said accusingly.

"Do you like it?" she asked.

"No," said Kingham.

"Why not?"

"Why not?" he repeated. "Well, I suppose it's because the thing's so expressive of you, because it suits you so devilishly well."

"I should have thought that would be a reason for liking it."

"Oh, it would be, no doubt," said Kingham, "it would be, if I could just regard you as a spectacle, as something indifferent, to be looked at—that's all—like a picture. But you're not indifferent to me, and you know it and you deliberately torture me. How can I be expected to like what makes you seem more devilishly desirable and so increases my torture?"

He glared at her ferociously. It was with an effort that Grace kept her own gaze steady before those bright, dark, expressive eyes. He advanced towards her and laid his two hands on her shoulders.

"To-day," he said, "you're going to be my lover."

Grace shook her head, smiling a capricious, eternally feminine smile.

"Yes, you are." His grip on her shoulders tightened.

"No, I'm not," Grace answered. She drew in her breath rather sharply; he was hurting her.

"I tell you, you are."

They looked at one another, face close to face, enemies. Grace's heart violently beat.

"At one moment, I thought he was going to throttle me," she told Catherine.

But she braved it out, and conquered.

Kingham withdrew his hands from her shoulders and turned away. He walked across to the other side of the room and, leaning against the wall in the embrasure of the window, looked out in silence at the grey sky.

Greatly relieved, Grace sat down on the divan. With a saucy and defiant movement that was, unfortunately, quite lost on Kingham's stubbornly presented back, she tucked up her feet under her. Opening her handbag, she took out her cigarette case, opened that in its turn, extracted a cigarette and lighted it—all very nonchalantly and deliberately. She was steadying her nerves to resist another attack—steadying her nerves and perhaps, at the same time, preparing to annoy him, when he should turn round, by the spectacle of her unconcernedness.

She had expected a repetition of the violences of a moment since, of the familiar denunciations of all the other days. She was not prepared to resist the new kind of attack which he now launched against her emotions. When at last—and she had more than half finished her cigarette before the long silence was broken —Kingham turned round and came towards her, she saw that he was weeping.

Kingham, as I have said, was no comedian. All that he professed to feel he felt, I am sure, genuinely. But he felt too easily and he was too fond of feeling. In situations where others would have exercised a restraint upon themselves, Kingham gave free rein to his emotions, or even actually roused and goaded them into a more violent and more prolonged activity. He needed no dervish tricks to work himself up, no dancing, no howling and drumming, no self-laceration. He could do the thing inwardly, by intense concentration on the object of his desire or hatred, on the cause of his pain or pleasure. He brooded over his loves or his grievances, making them seem more significant than they really were; he brooded, conjuring up in his imagination appropriate visions—of unpermitted raptures, when he was suffering from the pangs of desire; of scenes of insult, humiliation, rage, when he was angry with any one; of his own miserable self, when he desired to feel self-pity—himself, pictured as unloved, in solitude, utterly deserted, even dying. . . .

Long practice had made him an adept in the art of working up his emotions, of keeping himself uninterruptedly on the boil, so to speak, over a long period of time. In the course of these few brief weeks of his courtship, he had managed to convince himself that the interest he took in Grace was the most violent of passions and that he was suffering excruciatingly from her refusal—her devilish, her sadistic refusal—to be his mistress. Painfully and profoundly, he was enjoying it. The zest was still in the orgy; he felt no sense of satiety.

These tears were the result of a sudden and overwhelming feeling of self-pity, which had succeeded his mood of violence. He had perceived, all at once, that his violence was futile; it was absurd to suppose that he could shake or beat or throttle her into accepting him. He turned away in despair. He was alone, an outcast; nobody cared for him; he was expending his spirit in a waste of shame—his precious, beautiful spirit—and there was no saving himself, the madness was too strong. He was done for, absolutely done for.

Standing there, in the embrasure of the window, he had brooded over his miseries, until his sense of them became all of a sudden intolerable. The tears came into his eyes. He felt like a child, like a tired child who abandons himself, hopelessly, to misery.

All the animation went out of his face; it became like the face of a dead man, frozen into a mask of quiet misery. Pale, ruddy-bearded, delicately featured, it was like the face of a dead or dying Christ in some agonising Flemish picture.

It was this dead Christ's face that now turned back towards Grace Peddley. This dead Christ's face—and it had been the face of Lucifer, burning with life and passion, menacingly, dangerously beautiful, that had turned away from her. The eyes, which had shone so brightly then, were almost shut, giving the face an appearance of blindness; and between the half-closed lids there was a slow welling out of tears.

The first sight of this suffering face startled her into a kind of terror. But the terror was succeeded almost at once by a great pity. That face, at once lifeless and suffering! And those tears! She had never seen a man shed tears before. She was over-whelmed by pity—by pity and, at the thought that it was all her fault, by a passion of repentance and self-abasement, by a desire to make amends. And at the same time she felt another and greater emotion, an emotion in which the pity and the repentance were included and from which they derived their strange intensity. It was the feeling that, for her, Kingham was the only person in the world who in any way mattered. It was love.

In silence he crossed the room, dropped down on his knees before the divan where Grace, her cigarette still smoking between her fingers, half sat, half reclined, frozen by astonishment into a statue of lolling modernity, and laying his head in her lap, silently sobbed.

The spell of Grace's immobility was broken. She bent forward over him, she caressed his hair. The gesture recalled to her atten-

tion the half-smoked cigarette; she threw it into the fire-place
Her fingers touched his scalp, the nape of his neck, his ears, hi
averted cheek.

"My darling," she whispered, "my darling. You mustn't cry
It's terrible when you cry."

And she herself began to cry. For a long time they remained i
the same position, Kingham kneeling, his face pressed against he
knees, Grace bending over him, stroking his hair, both weeping

Our thoughts and feelings are interdependent. It is only i
language, not in fact, that they are separate and sharply differ
entiated. Some men are better mathematicians when they are i
love than when they are out of it; some are worse. But in eithe
case the emotion of love conditions the working of the intellect
Still more powerfully does it affect the other emotions, such a
pity, courage, shame, fear of ridicule, which it enhances o
diminishes as the case may be. It may be laid down as a genera
rule that the feeling of one strong emotion predisposes us auto
matically to the feeling of other emotions, however apparentl
incongruous with the first. Thus joy may predispose to pity an
shame to anger. Anger and grief may both dispose to sensua
desire. Violent disputes often end in love-making; and there ar
sometimes strange orgies over new-made graves, orgies, to th
eye of the indifferent spectator, most unseemly, but which, a
often as not, should be attributed less to a cynical lack of feelin
than to its abundant presence. Grief creates a sense of loneliness
a desire in those who feel it to be comforted. At the same tim
by throwing the whole personality into commotion, it render
the soul of the sufferer peculiary susceptible to voluptuou
influences and peculiarly unapt, in its state of disorganisation, t
exercise the customary self-restraints; so that when the desire
comforter appears, it sometimes happens (conditions of sex an
age being propitious) that sympathy is transformed, not merel
into love, but into desires demanding immediate satisfactior
Some such transformation took place now. Tears gave place t
kisses less and less tearful, to caresses and embraces. Ther
were languors and ecstatic silences.

"I love you, I love you," Grace repeated, and was almost frightened by the vehemence of the new emotions, the intensity of the new and piercing sensations which she expressed in these old, blunted words. "I love you."

And Kingham kissed her and permitted himself, for the moment, to be happy without reserve or inward comment, without a touch of that anticipated afterthought which turns the present into history, even as it unrolls itself, and—criticising, appraising, judging and condemning—takes all the zest out of immediacy. He was simply happy.

The time came for them to part.

"I must go," said Grace, sighing.

But the Grace who went was a different woman from the Grace who had come, two hours before. It was a worshipping, adoring Grace, a Grace made humble by love, a Grace for whom being modern and a *grande dame* and eighteenth-century and intellectually fashionable had suddenly ceased to have the slightest importance. Adjusting her hair before the glass, she was struck by the incongruity, the garish out-of-placeness of her new frock. Her love for Kingham, she felt, was something vast and significant, something positively holy; in the presence of that love, the new dress seemed a clown's livery worn in a church. Next day she wore an old, pre-Rodney dress—white muslin with black dots; not at all showy, fashionable, or eccentric. Her soul had dressed itself, so to speak, to match.

But Kingham, who had had time in the intervening hours to poison the memory of yesterday's joy with every kind of venomous afterthought, to discover subtle and horrible explanations for actions that were obviously innocent and simple, received her as though she had changed neither her dress nor her spirit and were indeed the woman whose part she had been playing all these weeks.

"Well," he said, as he opened the door to her, "I see you've come for more."

Grace, who had expected to be received with the gentle and beautiful tenderness which he had displayed on the previous day, was cruelly surprised by the brutality of his tone, the coldness and bitterness of his expression.

"More what?" she asked; and from brightly exultant her eyes became apprehensive in their expression, the smile with which she had so eagerly entered the room faded, as she halted in front of him. Anxiously she looked into his face. "More what?"

Kingham laughed a loud, unpleasant, mirthless laugh, and pointed to the divan. Grace's devilish concupiscence—that was what he had been chiefly dwelling on since last he saw her.

For the first second Grace did not understand what he meant. This particular aspect of their love was so far from her mind, that it did not occur to her to imagine that it could be in Kingham's. Then all at once his meaning dawned upon her. The blood ran up into her cheeks.

"Kingham!" she protested. (Kingham was one of those men whom everybody, even his closest intimates, called by his surname. For the rest, he had only a pair of initials—J. G. I never knew what they stood for. John George, I should think. But it was quite irrelevant; he was always "Kingham," pure and simple.) "Kingham! How can you say such things?"

"How can I?" he repeated mockingly. "Why, by not keeping a fig-leaf over my mouth, which is where the truly respectable, who never talk about their vices, always keep it. Do what you like, but don't talk about it; that's respectability. But dear me," he bantered on, "I thought you were as much beyond respectability as you are beyond good and evil—or below, whichever the case may be."

Grace, who had come in expecting a kiss and gentle words, walked slowly away from him across the room, sat down on the divan and began to cry.

A moment later Kingham was holding her in his arms and kissing away her tears. He spoke no word; the kisses became more passionate. At first, she averted her face from them. But in the end she abandoned herself. For a time she was happy. She forgot Kingham's cruel words, or if she remembered them, she remembered them as words spoken in a nightmare—by mistake, so to say, not on purpose, not seriously.

She had begun to feel almost perfectly reassured, when Kingham disengaged himself suddenly and roughly from her embrace, jumped up and began restlessly walking up and down the room, ruffling his hair as he went.

"What a horrible thing it is to have a vice!" he began. "Something you carry about with you, but that isn't yourself. Something that's stronger than you are, that you want to resist and conquer, but can't. A vice, a vice." He was enchanted by the word; it became, for the moment, the core of his universe. "It's horrible. We're possessed by devils, that's what's wrong with us. We carry our private devils about with us, our vices, and they're too strong for us. They throw us down and horribly triumph." He shuddered disgustedly. "It's horrible to feel yourself being murdered by your vice. The devil spiritually murdering you, suffocating your soul with warm soft flesh. My devil uses you as his instrument of murder; your devil uses me. Our vices conspire; it's a conspiracy, a murder plot."

By this time Grace was unhappier than she had ever been in her life before. (And yet, if Rodney had said the same thing, expressed a little differently—in terms of compliments on her "temperament"—she would have been delighted, two months ago.)

"But you know I love you, you *know*," was all that she could say. "What makes you say these things, when you know?"

Kingham laughed. "Oh, I know," he answered, "I know, only too well. I know what women like you mean by 'love.' "

"But I'm not a woman like . . ." Grace hesitated; "like me" didn't sound quite sensible, somehow. ". . . like that."

"Not like yourself?" Kingham asked derisively.

"Not like what you think," Grace insisted through the tangled confusion of words. "Not silly, I mean; not frivolous and all that. Not really." All those months with Rodney seemed a dream; and yet she had really lived through them. And there had really been champagne and sandwiches, and more than scientific conversations. . . . "Not now, at any rate," she added. "Now I know you. It's different; can't you understand? Utterly different. Because I love you, love you, love you, love you."

Any one else would have allowed himself to be convinced, at any rate for the moment; would have begged pardon, kissed and made friends. But, for Kingham, that would have been too easy, too emotionally flat. He stuck to his position.

"I know you do," he answered, averting his gaze, as he spoke, from that pathetic, suffering face, from those wide-open grey eyes, perplexed and agonised, that looked up at him so appealingly, so abjectly even. "So do I. Your devil loves me. My devil loves you."

"But no," Grace brokenly protested. "But why? . . ."

"Loves violently," he went on in a loud voice, almost shouting, "irresistibly." And as he spoke the words he swung round and precipitated himself upon her with a kind of fury. "Do you know what it is," he went on, as he held her, struggling a little and reluctant in his arms, "do you know what it is to love, not a person, not even their whole body, but just some part of it—insanely? Do you know what it is when the vice-devil concentrates its whole desire on one point, focuses it inexorably until nothing else exists but the nape of a neck, or a pectoral muscle, a foot, a knee, a hand? This hand, for example." He took her hand and lifted it towards his face. "And not even a whole hand," he continued. "Just the ball of a thumb, just that little cushion of flesh that's marked off from the rest of the palm by the line of life; just that soft, resilient, strong little cushion of flesh."

He began to kiss the spot on Grace's hand.

"Don't, don't. You mustn't." She tried to pull her hand away.

But Kingham held it fast. He went on kissing that soft, rounded swell of muscle at the base of her palm, insistently, again and again; kissing and kissing. And sometimes he would take the flesh between his teeth and would bite, gently at first, then with a gradually increasing force, until the pain became almost unbearable and Grace cried out, when he would fall to kissing again, softly and tenderly, as though he were asking forgiveness, were trying to kiss the pain away. Grace ceased to struggle and abandoned her hand to him, to do with what he liked. And little by little this insanely limited devil's love-making seemed to evoke a special voluptuous sensibility in that particular square inch of skin upon which it was concentrated. Her whole capacity for feeling pleasure seemed to focus itself at the base of her left hand. Even the gradually increasing pain, as his teeth closed more and more tightly on her flesh, was pleasurable. She abandoned herself; but, at the same time, she felt that there was something shameful and even horrible about this pleasure. What might have been simple and beautiful and joyous had been turned into something painful, complicated, ugly, and obscure. Kingham might congratulate himself on having produced a situation full of the most promising emotional possibilities.

I have reconstructed these scenes at some length because they were characteristic and typical of the whole affair. In his search for intense and painful emotions, Kingham displayed a perverse ingenuity; he was never at a loss for a pretext to complicate the simple and distort the natural. His great resource was always Grace's devilishness. Blind, as only Kingham could be blind, to all evidence to the contrary, he persisted in regarding Grace as a frivolous vampire, a monster of heartless vice. Her vampirishness and her vice were the qualities which attracted him to her; if he could have been convinced that she was really simple, innocent and childish, that her "devilish concupiscence" was in actual fact an abject, unhappy adoration, he would have ceased to take any interest in her. Pleading meant as little to him as evidence. If Grace protested too vigorously, Kingham would bring up the affair with Rodney. What was that but vice, plain and unvarnished? Had not she herself admitted that she didn't love the man? Miserably, despairingly, Grace would confess in answer that she had certainly been silly and frivolous and feather-headed, but that now all that was done with. Everything was different, she was different, now. Because she loved him. To which Kingham would retort by expatiating with fiery eloquence about the horrors of vice, until at last Grace began to cry.

Grace's devilishness formed the staple and chronic pretext for scenes. But Kingham was inventive and there were plenty of other excuses. Observant—for he was acutely observant, wherever he chose not to be blind—Kingham had early realised the entirely vague and accidental nature of all Grace's ideas, convictions, principles, and opinions. He perceived that what she thought about music, for example, was only a distorted and fragmentary version of what I thought; that her opinions on art were Rodney's, muddled; that her philosophic and literary convictions were like a parboiled lobster—"the fading sable and the coming gules"—half Rodney's and half, already, his own. And perceiving these things, he mocked her for her intellectual hypocrisy and snobbery. He found plenty of opportunities for hurting and humiliating her.

On other occasions, he would reproach her with untruthfulness and mean dissimulation, because she did not frankly tell John Peddley of her infidelity to him.

"I don't want to make him unnecessarily miserable," Grace protested.

Kingham laughed derisively. "A lot you care about anybody's happiness," he said, "particularly his! The truth is that you want to make the best of both worlds—be respectable and vicious at the same time. At all costs, no frankness! It's a case of the misplaced fig-leaf, as usual."

And then there was a terrible scene, a whole series of terrible scenes, because Grace did not want to have a child by him.

"Our only excuse," he raged at her, "the only thing that might justify us—and you won't hear of it. It's to be vice for vice's sake, is it? The uncontaminated æsthetic doctrine."

At other times, becoming strangely solicitous for the welfare of Grace's children, he reproached her with being a bad, neglectful mother.

"And you know, it's true," she said to Catherine, with remorseful conviction. "It's quite true. I *do* neglect them."

She invited Catherine to accompany her and the two youngest to the Zoo, the very next afternoon. Over the heads of little Pat and Mittie, among the elephants and apes, the bears and the screaming parrots, she talked to Grace about her love and her unhappiness. And every now and then Pat or Mittie would interrupt with a question.

"Mummy, why do fish swim?"

Or: "How do you make tortoises?"

"You know, you're a great comfort," said Grace to Catherine, as they parted. "I don't know what I should do without you."

The next time she came, she brought Catherine a present; not a powder-puff this time, not gloves or ribbons, but a copy of Dostoievsky's *Letters from the Underworld*.

"You must read it," she insisted. "You absolutely must. It's so damnably *true*."

Grace's life during this period was one of almost uninterrupted misery. I say "almost uninterrupted"; for there were occasions when Kingham seemed to grow tired of violent emotions, of suffering, and the infliction of suffering; moments when he was all tenderness and an irresistible charm. For these brief spells of happiness, Grace was only too pathetically grateful. Her love, which an absolutely consistent ill-treatment might finally perhaps have crushed and eradicated, was revived by these occasional kindnesses into fresh outflowerings of a passionate adoration. Each time she hoped, she almost believed, that the happiness was going to be permanent. Bringing with her a few select aphorisms of Nietzsche, a pocket Leopardi, or the reproduction of one of Goya's *Desastres de la Guerra*, she would come and tell Catherine how happy she was, how radiantly, miraculously happy. Almost she believed that, this time, her happiness was going to last for ever. Almost; but never quite. There was always a doubt, an unexpressed, secret, and agonising fear. And always the doubt was duly justified, the fear was proved to be but too well founded. After two or three days' holiday from his emotional orgy—two or three days of calm and kindness—Kingham would appear before her, scowling, his face dark, his eyes angry and accusing. Grace looked at him and her heart would begin to beat with a painful irregularity and violence; she felt suddenly almost sick with anxious anticipation. Sometimes he burst out at once. Sometimes—and that was much worse—he kept her in a state of miserable suspense, that might be prolonged for hours, even for days, sulking in a gloomy silence and refusing, when Grace asked him, to tell her what was the matter. If she ventured to approach him in one of these moods with a kiss or a soothing caress, he pushed her angrily away.

The excuses which he found for these renewals of tempest after calm were of the most various nature. One of the periods of happiness ended by his reproaching her with having been too tenderly amorous (too devilishly concupiscent) when he made love to her. On another occasion it was her crime to have remarked, two days before he chose actually to reproach her for it, that she liked the critical essays of Dryden. ("Such an intolerable piece of humbug and affectation," he complained. "Just because it's the fashion to admire these stupid, boring classical writers. Mere hypocrisy, that's what it is." And so on.) Another time he was furious because she had insisted on taking a taxi all the way to Hampton Court. True, she had proposed from the first to pay for it. None the less, when the time came for paying, he had felt constrained in mere masculine decency to pull out his pocketbook. For one painful moment he had actually thought that she was going to accept his offer. He avenged himself for that moment of discomfort by accusing her of stupid and heartless extravagance.

"There's something extraordinarily coarse," he told her, "something horribly thick-skinned and unfeeling about people who have been born and brought up with money. The idea of spending a couple of pounds on a mere senseless caprice, when there are hundreds of thousands of people with no work, living precariously, or just not dying, on state charity! The idea!"

Grace, who had proposed the excursion because she thought that Hampton Court was the most romantic place in the world, and because it would be so wonderful to be two and lovers by the side of the Long Water, in the deep embrasures of the windows, before the old grey mirrors, before the triumphing Mantegnas—Grace was appalled that reality should have turned out so cruelly different from her anticipatory dreams. And meanwhile yet another moment of happiness had irrevocably passed.

It was not surprising that Grace should have come to look tired and rather ill. She was paler than in the past and perceptibly thinner. Rimmed with dark circles of fatigue, her eyes seemed to have grown larger and of a paler grey. Her face was still the face of a nice but rather ugly little girl—but of a little girl most horribly ill-treated, hopelessly and resignedly miserable.

Confronted by this perfect resignation to unhappiness, Catherine became impatient.

"Nobody's got any business to be so resigned," she said. "Not nowadays, at any rate. We've got beyond the Patient Griselda stage."

But the trouble was that Grace hadn't got beyond it. She loved abjectly. When Catherine urged and implored her to break with Kingham, she only shook her head.

"But you're unhappy," Catherine insisted.

"There's no need for you to tell me that," said Grace, and the tears came into her eyes. "Do you suppose I don't know it?"

"Then why don't you leave him?" asked Catherine. "Why on earth don't you?"

"Because I can't." And after she had cried a little, she went on in a voice that was still unsteady and broken by an occasional sob: "It's as though there were a kind of devil in me, driving me on against my will. A kind of dark devil." She had begun to think in terms of Kingham even about herself. The case seemed hopeless.

We went abroad that summer, to the seaside, in Italy. In the lee of that great limestone mountain which rises suddenly, like the mountain of Paradise, out of the Pomptine marshes and the blue plains of the Mediterranean, we bathed and basked and were filled with the virtue of the life-giving sun. It was here, on the flanks of this mountain, that the enchantress Circe had her palace. Circeus Mons, Monte Circeo—the magic of her name has lingered, through Roman days, to the present. In coves at the mountain's foot stand the ruins of imperial villas, and walking under its western precipices you come upon the ghost of a Roman seaport, with the fishponds of Lucullus close at hand, like bright eyes looking upwards out of the plain. At dawn, before the sun has filled all space with the quivering gauzes of heat and the colourless brightness of excessive light, at dawn and again at evening, when the air once more grows limpid and colour and distant form are re-born, a mountain shape appears, far off, across the blue gulf of Terracina, a mountain shape and a plume of white unwavering smoke: Vesuvius. And once, climbing before sunrise to the crest of our Circean hill, we saw them both—Vesuvius to the southward, across the pale sea and northwards, beyond the green marshes, beyond the brown and ilex-dark Alban hills, the great symbolical dome of the world, St. Peter's, glittering above the mists of the horizon.

We stayed at Monte Circeo for upwards of two months, time enough to become brown as Indians and to have forgotten, or at least to have become utterly careless of, the world outside. We saw no newspapers; discouraged all correspondents by never answering their letters, which we hardly even took the trouble to read; lived, in a word, the life of savages in the sun, at the edge of a tepid sea. All our friends and relations might have died, England been overwhelmed by war, pestilence and famine, all books, pictures, music destroyed irretrievably out of the world—at Monte Circeo we should not have cared a pin.

But the time came at last when it was necessary to return to London and make a little money. We loaded our bodies with unaccustomed garments, crammed our feet—our feet that had for so long enjoyed the liberty of sandals—into their imprisoning shoes, took the omnibus to Terracina and climbed into the train.

"Well," I said, when we had managed at last to squeeze ourselves into the two vacant places which the extraordinary exuberance of a party of Neapolitans had painfully restricted, "we're going back to civilisation."

Catherine sighed and looked out of the window at the enchantress's mountain beckoning across the plain. "One might be excused," she said, "for making a little mistake and thinking it was hell we were going back to."

It was a dreadful journey. The compartment was crowded and the Neapolitans fabulously large, the weather hot, the tunnels frequent, and the smoke peculiarly black and poisonous. And with the physical there came a host of mental discomforts. How much money would there be in the bank when we got home? What bills would be awaiting us? Should I be able to get my book on Mozart finished by Christmas, as I had promised? In what state should I find my invalid sister? Would it be necessary to pay a visit to the dentist? What should we do to placate all the people to whom we had never written? Wedged between the Neapolitans, I wondered. And looking at Catherine, I could see by the expression on her face that she was similarly preoccupied. We were like Adam and Eve when the gates of the garden closed behind them.

At Genoa the Neapolitans got out and were replaced by passengers of more ordinary volume. The pressure in the compartment was somewhat relaxed. We were able to secure a couple of contiguous places. Conversation became possible.

"I've been so much wondering," said Catherine, when at last we were able to talk, "what's been happening all this time to poor little Grace. You know, I really *ought* to have written to her." And she looked at me with an expression in which consciousness of guilt was mingled with reproach.

"After all," I said, responding to her expression rather than to her words, "it wasn't my fault if you were too lazy to write. Was it?"

"Yes, it was," Catherine answered. "Just as much yours as mine. You ought to have reminded me to write, you ought to have insisted. Instead of which you set the example and encouraged my laziness."

I shrugged my shoulders. "One can't argue with women."

"Because they're almost always in the right," said Catherine
"But that isn't the point. Poor Grace is the point. What's hap
pened to her, do you suppose? And that dreadful Kingham—
what has he been up to? I wish I'd written."

At Monte Circeo, it is true, we had often spoken of Grace an
Kingham. But there, in the annihilating sunshine, among th
enormous and, for northern eyes, the almost unreal beauties c
that mythological landscape, they had seemed as remote and a
unimportant as everything and everybody else in our other life
Grace suffered. We knew it, no doubt, theoretically; but not, s
to speak, practically—not personally, not with sympatheti
realisation. In the sun it had been hardly possible to realise any
thing beyond our own well-being. Expose a northern body t
the sun and the soul within it seems to evaporate. The inrus
from the source of physical life drives out the life of the spirit
The body must become inured to light and life before the sou
can condense again into active existence. When we had talke
of Grace at Monte Circeo, we had been a pair of almost soulles
bodies in the sun. Our clothes, our shoes, the hideous discom
fort of the train gave us back our souls. We talked of Grace nov
with rediscovered sympathy, speculating rather anxiously on he
fate.

"I feel that in some way we're almost responsible for her,"
said Catherine. "Oh, I wish I'd written to her! And why
didn't she write to me?"

I propounded a comforting theory. "She probably hasn'
been with Kingham at all," I suggested. "She's gone abroac
as usual with Peddley and the children. We shall probably finc
that the whole thing has died down by the time we get home.'

"I wonder," said Catherine.

We were destined to discover the truth, or at least som
portion of it, sooner than we had expected. The first person
saw as I stepped out of the train at Modane was John Peddley.

He was standing on the platform some ten or fifteen yard
away, scanning, with eyes that sharply turned this way and that

the faces of the passengers descending from the express. His
glances were searching, quick, decisive. He might have been a
detective posted there on the frontier to intercept the escape of a
criminal. No crook, you felt, no gentleman cracksman, however
astute, could hope to sneak or swagger past those all-seeing
hunter's eyes. It was that thought, the realisation that the thing
was hopeless, that made me check my first impulse, which was
to flee—out of the station, anywhere—to hide—in the luggage-
van, the lavatory, under a seat. No, the game was obviously up.
There was no possible escape. Sooner or later, whatever I might
do now, I should have to present myself at the custom-house; he
would catch me there, infallibly. And the train was scheduled to
wait for two and a half hours.

"We're in for it," I whispered to Catherine, as I helped her
down on to the platform. She followed the direction of my
glance and saw our waiting danger.

"Heaven help us," she ejaculated with an unaccustomed piety;
then added in another tone: "But perhaps that means that Grace
is here. I shall go and ask him."

"Better not," I implored, still cherishing a foolish hope that
we might somehow slip past him unobserved. "Better not."

But in that instant, Peddley turned round and saw us. His
large, brown, handsome face beamed with sudden pleasure; he
positively ran to meet us.

Those two and a half hours in John Peddley's company at
Modane confirmed for me a rather curious fact, of which,
hitherto, I had been only vaguely and inarticulately aware: the
fact that one may be deeply and sympathetically interested in the
feelings of individuals whose thoughts and opinions—all the
products, in a word, of their intellects—are utterly indifferent,
even wearisome and repulsive. We read the Autobiography of
Alfieri, the Journals of Benjamin Robert Haydon, and read them
with a passionate interest. But Alfieri's tragedies, but Haydon's
historical pictures, all the things which, for the men themselves,
constituted their claim on the world's attention, have simply
ceased to exist, so far as we are concerned. Intellectually and

artistically, these men were more than half dead. But emotionally
they lived.

Mutatis mutandis, it was the same with John Peddley. I had
known him, till now, only as a relater of facts, an expounder of
theories—as an intellect, in short; one of the most appallingly
uninteresting intellects ever created. I had known him only in
his public capacity, so to speak, as the tireless lecturer of club
smoking-rooms and dinner-tables. I had never had a glimpse of
him in private life. It was not to be wondered at; for, as I have
said before, at ordinary times and when things were running
smoothly, Peddley had no private life more complicated than the
private life of his body. His feelings towards the majority of his
fellow-beings were the simple emotions of the huntsman:
pleasure when he had caught his victim and could talk him to
death; pain and a certain slight resentment when the prey escaped
him. Towards his wife he felt the desires of a healthy man in
early middle life, coupled with a real but rather unimaginative,
habit-born affection. It was an affection which took itself and its
object, Grace, altogether too much for granted. In his own way,
Peddley loved his wife, and it never occurred to him to doubt
that she felt in the same way towards him; it seemed to him the
natural inevitable thing, like having children and being fond of
them, having a house and servants and coming home in the evening from the office to find dinner awaiting one. So inevitable,
that it was quite unnecessary to talk or even to think about it;
natural to the point of being taken publicly for granted, like the
possession of a bank balance.

I had thought it impossible that Peddley should ever develop
a private life; but I had been wrong. I had not foreseen the possibility of his receiving a shock violent enough to shake him out
of complacency into self-questioning, a shock of sufficient
strength to shiver the comfortable edifice of his daily, taken-for-
granted life. That shock he had now received. It was a new and
unfamiliar Peddley who now came running towards us.

"I'm so glad, I'm so particularly glad to see you," he said, as
he approached us. "Quite extraordinarily glad, you know."

I have never had my hand so warmly shaken as it was then. Nor had Catherine, as I could see by the way she winced, as she abandoned her fingers to his crushing cordiality.

"You're the very man I particularly wanted to see," he went on, turning back to me. He stooped and picked up a couple of our suit-cases. "Let's make a dash for the douane," he said. "And then, when we've got those wretched formalities well over, we can have a bit of a talk."

We followed him. Looking at Catherine, I made a grimace. The prospect of that bit of a talk appalled me. Catherine gave me an answering look, then quickened her pace so as to come up with the energetically hurrying Peddley.

"Is Grace with you here?" she asked.

Peddley halted, a suit-case in each hand. "Well," he said, slowly and hesitatingly, as though it were possible to have metaphysical doubts about the correct answer to this question, "well, as a matter of fact, she isn't. Not really." He might have been discussing the problem of the Real Presence.

As if reluctant to speak about the matter any further, he turned away and hurried on towards the custom-house, leaving Catherine's next question—"Shall we find her in London when we get back?"—without an answer.

The bit of a talk, when it came, was very different from what I had gloomily anticipated.

"Do you think your wife would mind," Peddley whispered to me, when the douanier had done with us and we were making our way towards the station restaurant, "if I had a few words with you alone?"

I answered that I was sure she wouldn't, and said a word to Catherine, who replied, to me by a quick significant look, and to both of us together by a laughing dismissal.

"Go away and talk your stupid business if you want to," she said. "I shall begin my lunch."

We walked out on to the platform. It had begun to rain, violently, as it only rains among the mountains. The water beat on the vaulted glass roof of the station, filling all the space beneath with a dull, continuous roar; we walked as though within an enormous drum, touched by the innumerable fingers of the rain. Through the open arches at either end of the station the shapes of mountains were dimly visible through veils of white, wind-driven water.

We walked up and down for a minute or two without saying a word. Never, in my presence at any rate, had Peddley preserved so long a silence. Divining what embarrassments kept him in this unnatural state of speechlessness, I felt sorry for the man. In the end, after a couple of turns up and down the platform, he made an effort, cleared his throat, and diffidently began in a small voice that was quite unlike that loud, self-assured, trombone-like voice in which he told one about the Swiss banking system.

"What I wanted to talk to you about," he said, "was Grace."

The face he turned towards me as he spoke was full of a puzzled misery. That commonplacely handsome mask was strangely puckered and lined. Under lifted eyebrows, his eyes regarded me, questioningly, helplessly, unhappily.

I nodded and said nothing; it seemed the best way of encouraging him to proceed.

"The fact is," he went on, turning away from me and looking at the ground, "the fact is . . ." But it was a long time before he could make up his mind to tell me what the fact was.

Knowing so very well what the fact was, I could have laughed aloud, if pity had not been stronger in me than mockery, when he wound up with the pathetically euphemistic under-statement: "The fact is that Grace . . . well, I believe she doesn't love me. Not in the way she did. In fact I know it."

"How do you know it?" I asked, after a little pause, hoping that he might have heard of the affair only through idle gossip, which I could proceed to deny.

"She told me," he answered, and my hope disappeared.

"Ah."

So Kingham had had his way, I reflected. He had bullied her

into telling Peddley the quite unnecessary truth, just for the sake of making the situation a little more difficult and painful than it need have been.

"I'd noticed for some time," Peddley went on, after a silence, "that she'd been different."

Even Peddley could be perspicacious after the event. And besides, the signs of her waning love had been sufficiently obvious and decisive. Peddley might have no sympathetic imagination; but at any rate he had desires and knew when they were satisfied and when they weren't. He hinted at explanatory details.

"But I never imagined," he concluded—"how could I imagine?—that it was because there was somebody else. How could I?" he repeated in a tone of ingenuous despair. You saw very clearly that it was, indeed, quite impossible for him to have imagined such a thing.

"Quite," I said, affirming comfortingly I do not know exactly what proposition. "Quite."

"Well then, one day," he pursued, "one day just before we had arranged to come out here into the mountains, as usual, she suddenly came and blurted it all out—quite suddenly, you know, without warning. It was dreadful. Dreadful."

There was another pause.

"That fellow called Kingham," he went on, breaking the silence, "you know him? he's a friend of yours, isn't he?"

I nodded.

"Very able man, of course," said Peddley, trying to be impartial and give the devil his due. "But, I must say, the only times I met him I found him rather unsympathetic." (I pictured the scene: Peddley embarking on the law relating to insurance companies or, thoughtfully remembering that the chap was literary, on pianolas or modern art or the Einstein theory. And for his part, Kingham firmly and in all likelihood very rudely refusing to be made a victim of.) "A bit too eccentric for my taste."

"Queer," I confirmed, "certainly. Perhaps a little mad sometimes."

Peddley nodded. "Well," he said slowly, "it was Kingham."

I said nothing. Perhaps I ought to have "registered amazement," as they say in the world of the cinema; amazement, horror, indignation—above all amazement. But I am a poor comedian. I made no grimaces, uttered no cries. In silence we walked slowly along the platform. The rain drummed on the roof overhead; through the archway at the end of the station the all but invisible ghosts of mountains loomed up behind white veils. We walked from Italy towards France and back again from France towards Italy.

"Who could have imagined it?" said Peddley at last.

"Anybody," I might, of course, have answered. "Anybody who had a little imagination and who knew Grace; above all, who knew you." But I held my tongue. For though there is something peculiarly ludicrous about the spectacle of a self-satisfaction suddenly punctured, it is shallow and unimaginative only to laugh at it. For the puncturing of self-satisfaction gives rise to a pain that can be quite as acute as that which is due to the nobler tragedies. Hurt vanity and exploded complacency may be comic as a spectacle, from the outside; but to those who feel the pain of them, who regard them from within, they are very far from ludicrous. The feelings and opinions of the actor, even in the morally lowest dramas, deserve as much consideration as the spectator's. Peddley's astonishment that his wife could have preferred another man to himself was doubtless, from my point of view, a laughable exhibition. But the humiliating realisation had genuinely hurt him; the astonishment had been mixed with a real pain. Merely to have mocked would have been a denial, in favour of the spectator, of the actor's rights. Moreover, the pain which Peddley felt was not exclusively the product of an injured complacency. With the low and ludicrous were mingled other, more reputable emotions. His next words deprived me of whatever desire I might have had to laugh.

"What am I to do?" Peddley went on, after another long pause, and looked at me again more miserably and bewilderedly than ever. "What *am* I to do?"

"Well," I said cautiously, not knowing what to advise him, "it surely depends how you feel about it all—about Grace in particular."

"How I feel about her?" he repeated. "Well," he hesitated, embarrassed, "I'm fond of her, of course. Very fond of her." He paused; then, with a great effort, throwing down barriers which years of complacent silence, years of insensitive taking for granted had built up round the subject, he went on: "I love her."

The utterance of that decisive word seemed to make things easier for Peddley. It was as though an obstruction had been removed; the stream of confidences began to flow more easily and copiously.

"You know," he went on, "I don't think I had quite realised how much I did love her till now. That's what makes it all so specially dreadful—the thought that I ought to have loved her more, or at least more consciously when I had the opportunity, when she loved me; the thought that if I had, I shouldn't, probably, be here now all alone, without her." He averted his face and was silent, while we walked half the length of the platform. "I think of her all the time, you know," he continued. "I think how happy we used to be together and I wonder if we shall ever be happy again, as we were, or if it's all over, all finished." There was another pause. "And then," he said, "I think of her there in England, with that man, being happy with him, happier perhaps than she ever was with me; perhaps she never really did love me, not like that." He shook his head. "Oh, it's dreadful, you know, it's dreadful. I try to get these thoughts out of my head, but I can't. I walk in the hills till I'm dead-beat; I try to distract myself by talking to people who come through on the trains. But it's no good. I can't keep these thoughts away."

I might have assured him, of course, that Grace was without doubt infinitely less happy with Kingham than she had ever been with him. But I doubted whether the consolation would really be very efficacious.

"Perhaps it isn't really serious," I suggested, feebly. "Perhaps it won't last. She'll come to her senses one of these days."

Peddley sighed. "That's what I always hope, of course. I was angry at first, when she told me that she wasn't coming abroad and that she meant to stay with that man in England. I told her that she could go to the devil, so far as I was concerned. I told her that she'd only hear from me through my solicitor. But what was the good of that? I don't want her to go to the devil; I want her to be with me. I'm not angry any more, only miserable. I've even swallowed my pride. What's the good of being proud and not going back on your decisions, if it makes you unhappy? I've written and told her that I want her to come back, that I'll be happy and grateful if she does."

"And what has she answered?" I asked.

"Nothing," said Peddley.

I imagined Peddley's poor conventional letter, full of those worn phrases that make their appearance with such a mournful regularity in all the letters that are read in the divorce courts, or before coroners' juries, when people have thrown themselves under trains for unrequited love. Miserable, cold, inadequate words! A solicitor, he had often dictated them, no doubt, to clients who desired to have their plea for the restitution of conjugal rights succinctly and decorously set down in black and white, for the benefit of the judge who was, in due course, to give it legal force. Old, blunted phrases, into which only the sympathy of the reader has power to instil a certain temporary life—he had had to write them unprofessionally this time, for himself.

Grace, I guessed, would have shown the letter to Kingham. I imagined the derisive ferocity of his comments. A judicious analysis of its style can reduce almost any love-letter to emptiness and absurdity. Kingham would have made that analysis with gusto and with a devilish skill. By his mockery he had doubtless shamed Grace out of her first spontaneous feelings; she had left the letter unanswered. But the feelings, I did not doubt, still lingered beneath the surface of her mind; pity for John Peddley and remorse for what she had done. And Kingham, I felt sure, would find some ingenious method for first encouraging, then deriding these emotions. That would agreeably complicate their relations, would render her love for him a source of even greater pain to her than ever.

Peddley broke the rain-loud silence and the train of my speculations by saying: "And if it is serious, if she goes on refusing to answer when I write—what then?"

"Ah, but that won't happen," I said, speaking with a conviction born of my knowledge of Kingham's character. Sooner or later he would do something that would make it impossible for even the most abject of lovers to put up with him. "You can be sure it won't."

"I only wish I could," said Peddley dubiously: he did not know Kingham, only Grace—and very imperfectly at that. "I can't guess what she means to do. It was all so unexpected—from Grace. I never imagined . . ." For the first time he had begun to realise his ignorance of the woman to whom he was married. The consciousness of this ignorance was one of the elements of his distress. "But if it is serious," he went on, after a pause, obstinately insisting on contemplating the worst of possibilities, "what am I to do? Let her go, like that, without a struggle? Set her free to go and be permanently and respectably happy with that man?" (At the vision he thus conjured up of a domesticated Kingham, I inwardly smiled.) "That would be fairest to her, I suppose. But why should I be unfair to myself?"

Under the fingers of the drumming rain, in the presence of the ghostly, rain-blurred mountains, we prolonged the vain discussion. In the end I persuaded him to do nothing for the time being. To wait and see what the next days or weeks or months would bring. It was the only possible policy.

When we returned to the station restaurant, Peddley was considerably more cheerful than when we had left it. I had offered no very effectual consolation, invented no magical solution of his problems; but the mere fact that he had been able to talk and that I had been ordinarily sympathetic had been a relief and a comfort to him. He was positively rubbing his hands as he sat down beside Catherine.

"Well, Mrs. Wilkes," he said in that professionally hearty tone which clergymen, doctors, lawyers, and all those whose business it is to talk frequently and copiously with people they do not know, so easily acquire, "well, Mrs. Wilkes, I'm afraid we've shamefully neglected you. I'm afraid you'll never forgive me for having carried off your husband in this disgraceful way." And so on.

After a little, he abandoned this vein of graceful courtesy for more serious conversation.

"I met a most interesting man at this station a few days ago," he began. "A Greek. Theotocopulos was his name. A very remarkable man. He told me a number of most illuminating things about King Constantine and the present economic situation in Greece. He assured me, for one thing, that . . ." And the information about King Constantine and the economic situation in Hellas came pouring out. In Mr. Theotocopulos, it was evident, John Peddley had found a kindred soul. When Greek meets Greek then comes, in this case, an exchange of anecdotes about the deposed sovereigns of eastern Europe—in a word, the tug of bores. From private, Peddley had returned to public life. We were thankful when it was time to continue our journey.

Kingham lived on the second floor of a once handsome and genteel eighteenth-century house, which presented its façade of blackened brick to a decayed residential street, leading north-ward from Theobald's Road towards the easternmost of the Bloomsbury Squares. It was a slummy street in which, since the war, a colony of poor but "artistic" people from another class had settled. In the windows, curtains of dirty muslin alternated with orange curtains, scarlet curtains, curtains in large bright-coloured checks. It was not hard to know where respectable slumminess ended and gay Bohemianism began.

The front door of number twenty-three was permanently open. I entered and addressed myself to the stairs. Reaching the second landing, I was surprised to find the door of Kingham's rooms ajar. I pushed it open and walked in.

"Kingham," I called, "Kingham!"

There was no answer. I stepped across the dark little vestibule and tapped at the door of the main sitting-room.

"Kingham!" I called again more loudly.

I did not want to intrude indiscreetly upon some scene of domestic happiness or, more probably, considering the relations existing between Grace and Kingham, of domestic strife.

"Kingham!"

The silence remained unbroken. I walked in. The room was empty. Still calling discreetly as I went, I looked into the second sitting-room, the kitchen, the bedroom. A pair of suit-cases were standing, ready packed, just inside the bedroom door. Where could they be going? I wondered, hoped I should see them before they went. Meanwhile, I visited even the bathroom and the larder; the little flat was quite empty of life. They must have gone out, leaving the front door open behind them as they went. If preoccupation and absence of mind be signs of love, why then, I reflected, things must be going fairly well.

It was twenty to six on my watch. I decided to wait for their return. If they were not back within the hour, I would leave a note, asking them to come to see us, and go.

The two small and monstrously lofty sitting-rooms in Kingham's flat had once been a single room of nobly classical proportions. A lath-and-plaster partition separated one room from the other, dividing into two unsymmetrical parts the gracefully moulded design which had adorned the ceiling of the original room. A single tall sash window, having no proportionable relation to the wall in which it found itself accidentally placed, illuminated either room—the larger inadequately, the smaller almost to excess. It was in the smaller and lighter of the two sitting-rooms that Kingham kept his books and his writing-table. I entered it, looked round the shelves, and having selected two or three miscellaneous volumes, drew a chair up to the window and settled down to read.

"I have no patience," I read (and it was a volume of Kingham's own writings that I had opened), "I have no patience with those silly prophets and Utopia-mongers who offer us prospects of uninterrupted happiness. I have no patience with them. Are they too stupid even to realise their own stupidity? Can't they see that if happiness were uninterrupted and well-being universal, these things would cease to be happiness and well-being and become merely boredom and daily bread, daily business, *Daily Mail*? Can't they understand that, if everything in the world were pea-green, we shouldn't know what pea-green was? 'Asses, apes and dogs!' (Milton too, thank God for Milton! didn't suffer fools gladly. Satan—portrait of the artist.) Asses, apes, and dogs. Are they too stupid to see that, in order to know happiness and virtue, men must also know misery and sin? The Utopia I offer is a world where happiness and unhappiness are more intense, where they more rapidly and violently alternate than here, with us. A world where men and women endowed with more than our modern sensitiveness, more than our acute and multifarious modern consciousness, shall know the unbridled pleasures, the cruelties and dangers of the ancient world, with all the scruples and remorses of Christianity, all its ecstasies, all its appalling fears. That is the Utopia I offer you—not a sterilised nursing home, with Swedish drill before breakfast, vegetarian cookery, classical music on the radio, chaste mixed sun-baths, and rational free love between aseptic sheets. Asses, apes and dogs!"

One thing at least, I reflected, as I turned the pages of the book in search of other attractive paragraphs, one thing at least could be said in Kingham's favour; he was no mere academic theorist. Kingham practised what he preached. He had defined Utopia, he was doing his best to realise it—in Grace's company.

"Vows of chastity," the words caught my eye and I read on, "vows of chastity are ordinarily taken in that cold season, full of disgusts and remorses, which follows after excess. The taker of the oath believes the vow to be an unbreakable chain about his flesh. But he is wrong; the vow is no chain, only a hempen strand. When the blood is cold, it holds fast. But when, with the natural rebirth of appetite, the blood turns to flame, that fire burns through the hemp—the tindery hemp which the binder had thought to be a rope of steel—burns it, and the flesh breaks loose. With renewed satiety come coldness, disgust, remorse, more acute this time than before, and with them a repetition of the Stygian vows. And so on, round and round, like the days of the week, like summer and winter. Futile, you say, no doubt; weak-minded. But I don't agree with you. Nothing that intensifies and quickens life is futile. These vows, these remorses and the deep-rooted feeling from which they spring—the feeling that the pleasure of the senses is somehow evil—sharpen this pleasure to the finest of points, multiply the emotions to which it gives rise by creating, parallel with the body's delight, an anguish and tragedy of the mind."

I had read them before, these abbreviated essays or expanded maxims (I do not know how to name them ; Kingham himself had labelled them merely as "Notions"); had read them more than once and always enjoyed their violence, their queerness, their rather terrifying sincerity. But this time, it seemed to me, I read them with greater understanding than in the past. My knowledge of Kingham's relations with Grace illuminated them for me; and they, in their turn, threw light on Kingham and his relations with Grace. For instance, there was that sentence about love: "All love is in the nature of a vengeance; the man revenges himself on the woman who has caught and humiliated him; the woman revenges herself on the man who has broken down her reserves and reluctances, who has dared to convert her from an individual into a mere member and mother of the species." It seemed particularly significant to me, now. I remember noticing, too, certain words about the sin against the Holy Ghost. "Only those who know the Holy Ghost are tempted to sin against him —indeed, can sin against him. One cannot waste a talent unless one first possesses it. One cannot do what is wrong, or stupid, or futile, unless one first knows what is right, what is reasonable, what is worth doing. Temptation begins with knowledge and grows as knowledge grows. A man knows that he has a soul to save and that it is a precious soul; it is for that very reason that he passes his time in such a way that it must infallibly be damned. You, reader," the paragraph characteristically concluded, "you who have no soul to save, will probably fail to understand what I am talking about."

I was considering these words in the light of the recent increases of my knowledge of Kingham, when I was suddenly interrupted in the midst of my meditations by the voice of Kingham himself.

"It's no good," it was saying. "Can't you understand?" The voice sounded all at once much louder, as the door of the larger sitting-room opened to admit the speaker and his companion. Their footsteps resounded on the uncarpeted boards. "Why will you go on like this?" He spoke wearily, like one who is tired of being importuned and desires only to be left in peace. "Why will you?"

"Because I love you." Grace's voice was low and dulled. It seemed to express a kind of obstinate misery.

"Oh, I know, I know," said Kingham with an impatience that was muted by fatigue. He sighed noisily. "If you only knew how sick I was of all this unnecessary higgling and arguing!" The tone was almost pathetic; it seemed to demand that one should condole with the speaker, that one should do one's best to spare him pain. One might have imagined, from the tone of his voice, that Kingham was the persecuted victim of a relentless Grace. And it was thus indeed that he now saw himself, if, as I guessed, he had reached that inevitable closing phase of all his passions—the phase of emotional satiety. He had drunk his fill of strong feeling; the bout was over, for this time, the zest had gone out of the orgy. He wanted only to live quietly, soberly. And here was Grace, importuning him to continue the orgy. An orgy in cold blood—ugh! For a man sobered by complete satiety, the idea was disgustful, a thought to shudder at. No wonder he spoke thus plaintively. "I tell you," he went on, "it's settled. Definitely. Once and for all."

"You mean it? You mean definitely that you're going?"

"Definitely," said Kingham.

"Then I mean what I've said," the miserable, dully obstinate voice replied. "Definitely. I shall kill myself if you go."

My first impulse, when I heard Kingham's voice, had been—goodness knows why—to hide myself. A sudden sense of guilt, a schoolboy's terror of being caught, entirely possessed me. My heart beating, I jumped up and looked about me for some place of concealment. Then, after a second or two, my reason reasserted itself. I remembered that I was not a schoolboy in danger of being caught and caned; that, after all, I had been waiting here in order to ask Kingham and Grace to dinner; and that, so far from hiding myself, I ought immediately to make my presence known to them. Meanwhile, sentence had succeeded sentence in their muffled altercation. I realised that they were involved in some terrible, mortal quarrel; and realising, I hesitated to interrupt them. One feels shy of breaking in on an exhibition of strong and intimate emotion. To intrude oneself, clothed and armoured in one's daily indifference, upon naked and quivering souls is an insult, almost, one feels, an indecency. This was evidently no vulgar squabble, which could be allayed by a little tact, a beaming face and a tepid douche of platitude. Perhaps it was even so serious, so agonising that it ought to be put an end to at all costs. I wondered. Ought I to intervene? Knowing Kingham, I was afraid that my intervention might only make things worse. So far from shaming him into peace, it would in all probability have the effect of rousing all his latent violences. To continue an intimately emotional scene in the presence of a third party is a kind of indecency. Kingham, I reflected, would probably be only too glad to enhance and complicate the painfulness of the scene by introducing into it this element of spiritual outrage. I stood hesitating, wondering what I ought to do. Go in to them and run the risk of making things worse? Or stay where I was, at the alternative risk of being discovered, half an hour hence, and having to explain my most inexplicable presence? I was still hesitating when, from the other room, the muffled, obstinate voice of Grace pronounced those words:

"I shall kill myself if you go."

"No, you won't," said Kingham. "I assure you, you won't." The weariness of his tone was tinged with a certain ironic mockery.

I imagined the excruciations which might result if I gave Kingham an audience to such a drama, and decided not to intervene—not yet, at any rate. I tiptoed across the room and sat down where it would be impossible for me to be seen through the open door.

"I've played that little farce myself," Kingham went on. "Oh, dozens of times. Yes, and really persuaded myself at the moment that it was the genuinely tragic article." Even without my intervention, his mockery was becoming brutal enough.

"I shall kill myself," Grace repeated, softly and stubbornly.

"But as you see," Kingham pursued, "I'm still alive." A new vivacity had come into his weary voice. "Still alive and perfectly intact. The cyanide of potassium always turned out to be almond icing: and however carefully I aimed at my cerebellum, I never managed to score anything but a miss." He laughed at his own jest.

"Why will you talk in that way?" Grace asked, with a weary patience. "That stupid, cruel way?"

"I may talk," said Kingham, "but it's you who act. You've destroyed me, you've poisoned me: you're a poison in my blood. And you complain because I talk!"

He paused, as if expecting an answer: but Grace said nothing. She had said all that there was for her to say so often, she had said "I love you," and had had the words so constantly and malevolently misunderstood, that it seemed to her, no doubt, a waste of breath to answer him.

"I suppose it's distressing to lose a victim," Kingham went on in the same ironic tone. "But you can't really expect me to believe that it's so distressing that you've got to kill yourself. Come, come, my dear Grace. That's a bit thick."

"I don't expect you to believe anything," Grace replied. "I just say what I mean and leave it at that. I'm tired." I could hear by the creaking of the springs that she had thrown herself down on the divan. There was a silence.

"So am I," said Kingham, breaking it at last. "Mortally tired." All the energy had gone out of his voice; it was once more blank and lifeless. There was another creaking of springs; he had evidently sat down beside her on the divan. "Look here," he said, "for God's sake let's be reasonable." From Kingham, the appeal was particularly cogent; I could not help smiling. "I'm sorry I spoke like that just now. It was silly; it was bad-tempered. And you know the way one word begets another; one's carried away. I didn't mean to hurt you. Let's talk calmly. What's the point of making an unnecessary fuss? The thing's inevitable, fatal. A bad business, perhaps; but let's try to make the best of it, not the worst."

I listened in astonishment, while Kingham wearily unwound a string of such platitudes. Wearily, wearily; he seemed to be boring himself to death with his own words. Oh, to have done with it, to get away, to be free, never again to set eyes on her! I imagined his thoughts, his desires.

There are moments in every amorous intimacy, when such thoughts occur to one or other of the lovers, when love has turned to weariness and disgust, and the only desire is a desire for solitude. Most lovers overcome this temporary weariness by simply not permitting their minds to dwell on it. Feelings and desires to which no attention is paid soon die of inanition; for the attention of the conscious mind is their food and fuel. In due course love reasserts itself and the moment of weariness is forgotten. To Kingham, however, Kingham who gave his whole attention to every emotion or wish that brushed against his consciousness, the slightest velleity of weariness became profoundly significant. Nor was there, in his case, any real enduring love for the object of his thoughtfully fostered disgust, any strong and steady affection capable of overcoming what should have been only a temporary weariness. He loved because he felt the need of violent emotion. Grace was a means to an end, not an end in herself. The end—satisfaction of his craving for emotional excitement—had been attained; the means had therefore ceased to possess the slightest value for him. Grace would have been merely indifferent to him, if she had shown herself in this crisis as emotionally cold as he felt himself. But their feelings did not synchronise. Grace was not weary; she loved him, on the contrary, more passionately than ever. Her importunate warmth had conspired with his own habit of introspection to turn weariness and emotional neutrality into positive disgust and even hatred. He was making an effort, however, not to show these violent feelings; moreover he was tired—too tired to want to give them their adequate expression. He would have liked to slip away quietly, without any fuss. Wearily, wearily, he uttered his sedative phrases. He might have been a curate giving Grace a heart-to-heart chat about Life.

"We must be sensible," he said. And: "There are other things besides love." He even talked about self-control and the consolations of work. It lasted a long time.

Suddenly Grace interrupted him. "Stop!" she cried in a startlingly loud voice. "For heaven's sake stop! How can you be so dishonest and stupid?"

"I'm not," Kingham answered, sullenly. "I was simply saying . . ."

"You were simply saying that you're sick of me," said Grace, taking up his words. "Simply saying it in a slimy, stupid, dishonest way. That you're sick to death of me and that you wish to goodness I'd go away and leave you in peace. Oh, I will, I will. You needn't worry." She uttered a kind of laugh.

There was a long silence.

"Why don't you go?" said Grace at last. Her voice was muffled, as though she were lying with her face buried in a cushion.

"Well," said Kingham awkwardly. "Perhaps it might be best." He must have been feeling the beginnings of a sense of enormous relief, a joy which it would have been indecent to display, but which was bubbling only just beneath the surface. "Good-bye, then, Grace," he said, in a tone that was almost cheerful. "Let's part friends."

Grace's laughter was muffled by the cushion. Then she must

have sat up; for her voice, when she spoke a second later, was clear and unmuted.

"Kiss me," she said peremptorily. "I want you to kiss me, just once more."

There was a silence.

"Not like that," Grace's voice came almost angrily. "Kiss me really, really, as though you still loved me."

Kingham must have tried to obey her; anything for a quiet life and a prompt release. There was another silence.

"No, no." The anger in Grace's voice had turned to despair. "Go away, go, go. Do I disgust you so that you can't even kiss me?"

"But, my dear Grace . . ." he protested.

"Go, go, go."

"Very well, then," said Kingham in a dignified and slightly offended tone. But inwardly, what joy! Liberty, liberty! The key had turned in the lock, the prison door was opening. "If you want me to, I will." I heard him getting up from the divan. "I'll write to you when I get to Munich," he said.

I heard him walking to the door, along the passage to the bed-room, where, I suppose, he picked up his suit-cases, back along the passage to the outer door of the apartment. The latch clicked, the door squeaked on its hinges as it swung open, squeaked as it closed; there was an echoing bang.

I got up from my chair and cautiously peeped round the edge of the doorway into the other room. Grace was lying on the divan in precisely the position I had imagined, quite still, her face buried in a cushion. I stood there watching her for perhaps half a minute, wondering what I should say to her. Everything would sound inadequate, I reflected. Therefore, perhaps, the most in-adequate of all possible words, the most perfectly banal, trivial, and commonplace, would be the best in the circumstances.

I was pondering thus when suddenly that death-still body stirred into action. Grace lifted her face from the pillow, listened for a second, intently, then with a series of swift motions, she turned on her side, raised herself to a sitting position, dropped her feet to the ground and, springing up, hastened across the room towards the door. Instinctively, I withdrew into concealment. I heard her cross the passage, heard the click and squeak of the front door as it opened. Then her voice, a strange, inhuman, strangled voice, called "Kingham!" and again, after a listening silence that seemed portentously long, "Kingham!" There was no answer.

After another silence, the door closed. Grace's footsteps approached once more, crossed the room, came to a halt. I peeped out from my ambush. She was standing by the window, her forehead pressed against the glass, looking out—no, looking down, rather. Two storeys, three, if you counted the area that opened like a deep grave at the foot of the wall beneath the window—was she calculating the height? What were her thoughts?

All at once, she straightened herself up, stretched out her hands and began to raise the sash. I walked into the room towards her.

At the sound of my footsteps, she turned and looked at me— but looked with the disquietingly blank, unrecognising eyes and expressionless face of one who is blind. It seemed as though her mind were too completely preoccupied with its huge and dreadful idea to be able to focus itself at once on the trivialities of life.

"Dear Grace," I said, "I've been looking for you. Catherine sent me to ask you to come and have dinner with us."

She continued to look at me blankly. After a second or two, the significance of my words seemed to reach her; it was as though she were far away, listening to sounds that laboured slowly across the intervening gulfs of space. When at last she had heard my words—heard them with her distant mind—she shook her head and her lips made the movement of saying "No."

I took her arm and led her away from the window. "But you must," I said.

My voice seemed to come to her more quickly this time. It was only a moment after I had finished speaking that she again shook her head.

"You must," I repeated. "I heard everything, you know. I shall make you come with me."

"You heard?" she repeated, staring at me.

I nodded, but did not speak. Picking up her small, close-fitting, casque-shaped hat from where it was lying on the floor, near the divan, I handed it to her. She turned with an automatic movement towards the dim, grey-glassed Venetian mirror that hung above the fireplace and adjusted it to her head: a wisp of hair straggled over her temple; tidily, she tucked it away.

"Now, let's go," I said, and led her away, out of the flat, down the dark stairs, into the street.

Walking towards Holborn in search of a taxi, I made futile conversation. I talked, I remember, about the merits of omnibuses as opposed to undergrounds, about second-hand book-shops, and about cats. Grace said nothing. She walked at my side, as though she were walking in her sleep.

Looking at that frozen, unhappy face—the face of a child who has suffered more than can be borne—I was filled with a pity that was almost remorse. I felt that it was somehow my fault; that it was heartless and insensitive of me not to be as unhappy as she was. I felt, as I have often felt in the presence of the sick, the miserably and hopelessly poor, that I owed her an apology. I felt that I ought to beg her pardon for being happily married, healthy, tolerably prosperous, content with my life. Has one a right to be happy in the presence of the unfortunate, to exult in life before those who desire to die? Has one a right?

"The population of cats in London," I said, "must be very nearly as large as the population of human beings."

"I should think so," Grace whispered, after a sufficient time had elapsed for her to hear, across the gulfs that separated her mind from mine, what I had said. She spoke with a great effort; her voice was scarcely audible.

"Literally millions," I pursued.

And then, fortunately, I caught sight of a taxi. Driving home to Kensington, I talked to her of our Italian holiday. I did not think it necessary, however, to tell her of our meeting with Peddley at Modane.

Arrived, I told Catherine in two words what had happened and, handing Grace over to her care, took refuge in my workroom. I felt, I must confess, profoundly and selfishly thankful to be back there, alone, with my books and my piano. It was the kind of thankfulness one feels, motoring out of town for the week-end, to escape from dark and sordid slums to a comfortable, cool-gardened country house, where one can forget that there exist other human beings beside oneself and one's amusing, cultivated friends, and that ninety-nine out of every hundred of them are doomed to misery. I sat down at the piano and began to play the Arietta of Beethoven's Op. 111.

I played it very badly, for more than half my mind was preoccupied with something other than the music. I was wondering what would become of Grace now. Without Rodney, without Kingham, what would she do? What would she be? The question propounded itself insistently.

And then, all at once, the page of printed music before my eyes gave me the oracular reply. *Da capo*. The hieroglyph sent me back to the beginning of my passage. *Da capo*. After all, it was obvious. *Da capo*. John Peddley, the children, the house, the blank existence of one who does not know how to live unassisted. Then another musical critic, a second me—introduction to the second theme. Then the second theme, *scherzando*; another Rodney. Or *molto agitato*, the equivalent of Kingham. And then, inevitably, when the agitation had agitated itself to the climax of silence, *da capo* again to Peddley, the house, the children, the blankness of her unassisted life.

The miracle of the Arietta floated out from under my fingers. Ah, if only the music of our destinies could be like this!

CHAWDRON

FROM behind the outspread *Times* I broke a silence. "Your friend Chawdron's dead, I see."

"Dead?" repeated Tilney, half incredulously. "Chawdron dead?"

" 'Suddenly, of heart failure,' " I went on, reading from the obituary, " 'at his residence in St. James's Square.' "

"Yes, his heart . . ." He spoke meditatively. "How old was he? Sixty?"

"Fifty-nine. I didn't realise the ruffian had been rich for so long. '. . . the extraordinary business instinct, coupled with a truly Scottish doggedness and determination, which raised him, before he was thirty-five, from obscurity and comparative poverty to the height of opulence.' Don't you wish you could write like that? My father lost a quarter of a century's savings in one of his companies."

"Served him right for saving!" said Tilney with a sudden savagery. Surprised, I looked at him over the top of my paper. On his gnarled and ruddy face was an expression of angry gloom. The news had evidently depressed him. Besides, he was always ill-tempered at breakfast. My poor father was paying. "What sort of jam is that by you?" he asked fiercely.

"Strawberry."

"Then I'll have some marmalade."

I passed him the marmalade and, ignoring his bad temper, "When the Old Man," I continued, "and along with him, of course, most of the other shareholders, had sold out at about eighty per cent. dead loss, Chawdron did a little quiet conjuring and the price whizzed up again. But by that time he was the owner of practically all the stock."

"I'm always on the side of the ruffians," said Tilney. "On principle."

"Oh, so am I. All the same, I do regret those twelve thousand pounds."

Tilney said nothing. I returned to the obituary.

"What do they say about the New Guinea Oil Company scandal?" he asked after a silence.

"Very little; and the touch is beautifully light. 'The findings of the Royal Commission were on the whole favourable, though it was generally considered at the time that Mr. Chawdron had acted somewhat inconsiderately.'"

Tilney laughed. "'Inconsiderately' is good. I wish I made fourteen hundred thousand pounds each time I was inconsiderate."

"Was that what he made out of the New Guinea Oil business?"

"So he told me, and I don't think he exaggerated. He never lied for pleasure. Out of business hours he was remarkably honest."

"You must have known him very well."

"Intimately," said Tilney, and, pushing away his plate, he began to fill his pipe.

"I envy you. What a specimen for one's collection! But didn't you get rather bored with living inside the museum, so to speak, behind the menagerie bars? Being intimate with a specimen—it must be trying."

"Not if the specimen's immensely rich," Tilney answered. "You see, I'm partial to Napoleon brandy and Corona Coronas; parasitism has its rewards. And if you're skilful, it needn't have too many penalties. It's possible to be a high-souled louse, an independent tapeworm. But Napoleon brandy and Coronas weren't the only attractions Chawdron possessed for me. I have a disinterested, scientific curiosity about the enormously wealthy. A man with an income of more than fifty thousand a year is such a fantastic and improbable being. Chawdron was specially interesting because he'd *made* all his money—mainly dishonestly; that was the fascinating thing. He was a large-scale, Napoleonic crook. And, by God, he looked it! Did you know him by sight?"

I shook my head.

"Like an illustration to Lombroso. A criminal type. But intelligently criminal, not brutally. He wasn't brutal."

"I thought he was supposed to look like a chimpanzee," I put in.

"He did," said Tilney. "But, after all, a chimpanzee isn't brutal-looking. What you're struck by in a chimpanzee is its all-but-human appearance. So very intelligent, so nearly a man. Chawdron's face had just that look. But with a difference. The chimpanzee looks gentle and virtuous and quite without humour. Whereas Chawdron's intelligent all-but-humanity was sly and, underneath the twinkling jocularity, quite ruthless. Oh, a strange, interesting creature! I got a lot of fun out of my study of him. But in the end, of course, he did bore me. Bored me to death. He was so drearily uneducated. Didn't know the most obvious things, couldn't understand a generalisation. And then quite disgustingly without taste, without æsthetic sense or understanding. Metaphysically and artistically a cretin."

"The obituarist doesn't seem to be of your opinion." I turned again to the *Times*. "Where is it now? Ah! 'A remarkable writer was lost when Chawdron took up finance. Not entirely lost, however; for the brilliant *Autobiography*, published in 1921, remains as a lasting memorial to his talents as a stylist and narrator.' What do you say to that?" I asked, looking up at Tilney.

He smiled enigmatically. "It's quite true."

"I never read the book, I confess. Is it any good?"

"It's damned good." His smile mocked, incomprehensibly.

"Are you pulling my leg?"

"No, it was really and genuinely good."

"Then he can hardly have been such an artistic cretin as you make out."

"Can't he?" Tilney echoed and, after a little pause, suddenly laughed aloud. "But he *was* a cretin," he continued on a little gush of confidingness that seemed to sweep away the barriers of his willed discretion, "and the book *was* good. For the excellent reason that he didn't write it. I wrote it."

"You?" I looked at him, wondering if he were joking. But his face, after the quick illumination of laughter, had gone serious, almost gloomy. A curious face, I reflected. Handsome in its way, intelligent, aware, yet with something rather sinister about it, almost repulsive. The superficial charm and good humour of the man seemed to overlie a fundamental hardness, an uncaringness, a hostility even. Too much good living, moreover, had left its marks on that face. It was patchily red and lumpy. The fine features had become rather gross. There was a coarseness mingled with the native refinement. Did I like Tilney or did I not? I never rightly knew. And perhaps the question was irrelevant. Perhaps Tilney was one of those men who are not meant to be liked or disliked as men—only as performers. I liked his conversation, I was amused, interested, instructed by what he said. To ask myself if I also liked what he *was*—this was, no doubt, beside the point.

Tilney got up from the table and began to walk up and down the room, his pipe between his teeth, smoking. "Poor Chawdron's dead now, so there's no reason . . ." He left the sentence unfinished, and for a few seconds was silent. Standing by the window, he looked out through the rain-blurred glass on to the greens and wet greys of the Kentish landscape. "England looks like the vegetables at a Bloomsbury boarding-house dinner," he said slowly. "Horrible! Why do we live in this horrible country? Ugh!" He shuddered and turned away. There was another silence. The door opened and the maid came in to clear the breakfast table. I say "the maid"; but the brief impersonal term is inaccurate. Inaccurate, because wholly inadequate to describe Hawtrey. What came in, when the door opened, was personified efficiency, was a dragon, was stony ugliness, was a pillar of society, was the Ten Commandments on legs. Tilney, who did not know her, did not share my terror of the domestic monster. Unaware of the intense disapproval which I could feel her silently radiating (it was after ten; Tilney's slug-a-bed habits had thrown out of gear the whole of her morning's routine) he continued to walk up and down, while Hawtrey busied herself round the table. Suddenly he laughed. "Chawdron's *Auto-biography* was the only one of my books I ever made any money out of," he said. I listened apprehensively, lest he should say anything which might shock or offend the dragon. "He turned over all the royalties to me," Tilney went on. "I made the best part of three thousand pounds out of his *Autobiography*. Not to mention the five hundred he gave me for writing it." (Was it quite delicate, I wondered, to talk of such large sums of money in front of one so incomparably more virtuous than ourselves and so much poorer? Fortunately, Tilney changed the subject.) "You ought to read it," he said. "I'm really quite offended that you haven't. All that lower middle-class childhood in Peebles—it's really masterly." ("Lower middle-class"—I shuddered. Hawtrey's father had owned a shop; but he had had misfortunes.) "It's *Clayhanger* and *L'Education Sentimentale* and *David Copperfield* all rolled into one. Really superb. And the first adventurings into the world of finance were pure Balzac—magnificent." He laughed again, this time without bitterness, amusedly; he was warming to his subject. "I even put in a Rastignac soliloquy from the top of the dome of St. Paul's, made him shake his fist at the City. Poor old Chawdron! he was thrilled. 'If only I'd known what an interesting life I'd had,' he used to say to me. 'Known while the life was going on.'" (I looked at Hawtrey to see if she was resenting the references to an interesting life. But her face was closed; she worked as though she were deaf.) "'You wouldn't have lived it,' I told him. 'You must leave the discovery of the excitingness to the artists.'" He was silent again. Hawtrey laid the last spoon on the tray and moved towards the door. Thank heaven! "Yes, the artists," Tilney went on in a tone that had gone melancholy again. "I really was one, you know." (The departing Hawtrey must have heard that damning confession. But then, I reflected, she always did know that I and my friends were a bad lot.) "Really *am* one," he insisted. "*Qualis artifex!* But *pereo, pereo*. Somehow, I've never done anything but perish all my life. Perish, perish, perish. Out of laziness and because there always seemed so much time. But I'm going to be forty-eight next June. Forty-eight! There isn't any time. And the laziness is such a habit. So's the talking. It's so easy to talk. And so amusing. At any rate for oneself."

"For other people too," I said; and the compliment was sincere. I might be uncertain whether or no I liked Tilney. But I genuinely liked his performance as a talker. Sometimes, perhaps, that performance was a little too professional. But, after all, an artist must be a professional.

"It's what comes of being mostly Irish," Tilney went on. "Talking's the national vice. Like opium-smoking with the Chinese!" (Hawtrey re-entered silently to sweep up the crumbs and fold the table-cloth.) "If you only knew the number of masterpieces I've allowed to evaporate at dinner tables, over the cigars and the whisky!" (Two things of which, I knew, the Pillar of Society virtuously disapproved.) "A whole library. I might have been—what? Well, I suppose I might have been a frightful old bore," he answered himself with a forced self-mockery. " 'The Complete Works of Edmund Tilney, in Thirty-Eight Volumes, post octavo.' I dare say the world ought to be grateful to me for sparing it *that*. All the same, I get a bit depressed when I look over the back numbers of the *Thursday Review* and read those measly little weekly articles of mine. *Parturiunt montes . . .*"

"But they're good articles," I protested. If I had been more truthful, I would have said that they were sometimes good—when he took the trouble to make them good. Sometimes, on the contrary . . .

"*Merci, cher maître!*" he answered ironically. "But hardly more perennial than brass, you must admit. Monuments of wood pulp. It's depressing being a failure. Particularly if it's your fault, if you might have been something else."

I mumbled something. But what was there to say? Except as a professional talker, Tilney *had* been a failure. He had great talents and he was a literary journalist who sometimes wrote a good article. He had reason to feel depressed.

"And the absurd, ironical thing," he continued, "is that the

one really good piece of work I ever did is another man's autobiography. I could never prove my authorship even if I wanted
to. Old Chawdron was very careful to destroy all the evidences
of the crime. The business arrangements were all verbal. No
documents of any kind. And the manuscript, *my* manuscript—
he bought it off me. It's burnt."

I laughed. "He took no risks with you." Thank heaven! The
dragon was preparing to leave the room for good.

"None whatever," said Tilney. "He was going to be quite
sure of wearing his laurel wreath. There was to be no other
claimant. And at the time, of course, I didn't care two pins. I
took the high line about reputation. Good art—and Chawdron's
Autobiography was good art, a really first-rate novel—good art
is its own reward." (Hawtrey's comment on this was almost to
slam the door as she departed.) "You know the style of thing?
And in this case it was more than its own reward. There was
money in it. Five hundred down and all the royalties. And I was
horribly short of money at the moment. If I hadn't been, I'd
never have written the book. Perhaps that's been one of my disadvantages—a small independent income and not very extravagant tastes. I happened to be in love with a very expensive young
woman at the time when Chawdron made his offer. You can't
go dancing and drinking champagne on five hundred a year.
Chawdron's cheque was timely. And there I was, committed to
writing his memoirs for him. A bore, of course. But luckily the
young woman jilted me soon afterwards; so I had time to waste.
And Chawdron was a ruthless taskmaster. And besides, I really
enjoyed it once I got started. It really was its own reward. But
now—now that the book's written and the money's spent and
I'm soon going to be fifty, instead of forty as it was then—now,
I must say, I'd rather like to have at least one good book to my
credit. I'd like to be known as the author of that admirable
novel, *The Autobiography of Benjamin Chawdron*, but, alas, I
shan't be." He sighed. "It's Benjamin Chawdron, not Edmund
Tilney, who'll have his little niche in the literary histories. Not
that I care much for literary history. But I do rather care, I must

confess, for the present anticipations of the niche. The drawing-room reputation, the mentions in the newspapers, the deference of the young, the sympathetic curiosity of the women. All the by-products of successful authorship. But there, I sold them to Chawdron. For a good price. I can't complain. Still, I *do* complain. Have you got any pipe tobacco? I've run out of mine."

I gave him my pouch. "If I had the energy," he went on, as he refilled his pipe, "or if I were desperately hard up, which, thank heaven and at the same time alas! I'm not at the moment, I could make another book out of Chawdron. Another and a better one. Better," he began explaining, and then interrupted himself to suck at the flame of the match he had lighted, "because . . . so much more . . . malicious." He threw the match away. "You can't write a good book without being malicious. In the *Autobiography* I made a hero of Chawdron. I was paid to; besides, it was Chawdron himself who provided me with my documents. In this other book he'd be the villain. Or in other words, he'd be himself as others saw him, not as he saw himself. Which is, incidentally, the only valid difference between the virtuous and the wicked that *I*'ve ever been able to detect. When you yourself indulge in any of the deadly sins, you're always justified—they're never deadly. But when any one else indulges, you're very properly indignant. Old Rousseau had the courage to say that he was the most virtuous man in the world. The rest of us only silently believe it. But to return to Chawdron. What I'd like to do now is to write his biography, not his autobiography. And the biography of a rather different aspect of the man. Not about the man of action, the captain of industry, the Napoleon of finance and so forth. But about the domestic, the private, the sentimental Chawdron."

"The *Times* had its word about that," said I; and picking up the paper once more, I read: " 'Under a disconcertingly brusque and even harsh manner Mr. Chawdron concealed the kindliest of natures. A stranger meeting him for the first time was often repelled by a certain superficial roughness. It was only to his intimates that he revealed'—guess what!—'the heart of gold beneath.' "

"Heart of gold!" Tilney took his pipe out of his mouth to laugh.

"And he also, I see, had 'a deep religious sense.' " I laid the paper down.

"Deep? It was bottomless."

"Extraordinary," I reflected aloud, "the way they *all* have hearts of gold and religious senses. Every single one, from the rough old man of science to the tough old business man and the gruff old statesman."

"Hearts of Gold!" Tilney repeated. "But gold's much too hard. Hearts of putty, hearts of vaseline, hearts of hog-wash. That's more like it. Hearts of hog-wash. The tougher and bluffer and gruffer they are outside, the softer they are within. It's a law of nature. I've never come across an exception. Chawdron was the rule incarnate. Which is precisely what I want to show in this other, potential book of mine—the ruthless Napoleon of finance paying for his ruthlessness and his Napoleonism by dissolving internally into hog-wash. For that's what happened to him: he dissolved into hog-wash. Like the Strange Case of Mr. Valdemar in Edgar Allan Poe. I saw it with my own eyes. It's a terrifying spectacle. And the more terrifying when you realise that, but for the grace of God, there goes yourself—and still more so when you begin to doubt of the grace of God, when you see that there in fact you *do* go. Yes, you and I, my boy. For it isn't only the tough old business men who have the hearts of hog-wash. It's also, as you yourself remarked just now, the gruff old scientists, the rough old scholars, the bluff old admirals and bishops and all the other pillars of Christian society. It's everybody, in a word, who has made himself too hard in the head or the carapace; everybody who aspires to be non-human—whether angel or machine it doesn't matter. Super-humanity is as bad as sub-humanity, is the same thing finally. Which shows how careful one should be if one's an intellectual. Even the mildest sort of intellectual. Like me, for example. I'm not one of your genuine ascetic scholars. God forbid! But I'm decidedly high-brow, and I'm literary; I'm even what the newspapers call a 'thinker.' I suffer from a passion for ideas. Always have, from boyhood onwards. With what results? That I've never been attracted by any woman who wasn't a bitch."

I laughed. But Tilney held up his hand in a gesture of protest. "It's a serious matter," he said. "It's disastrous, even. Nothing but bitches. Imagine!"

"I'm imagining," I said. "But where do the books and the ideas come in? *Post* isn't necessarily *propter*."

"It's *propter* in this case all right. Thanks to the books and the ideas, I never learnt how to deal with real situations, with solid people and things. Personal relationships—I've never been able to manage them effectively. Only ideas. With ideas I'm at home. With the *idea* of personal relationships, for example. People think I'm an excellent psychologist. And I suppose I am. Spectatorially. But I'm a bad experiencer. I've lived most of my life posthumously, if you see what I mean; in reflections and conversations after the fact. As though my existence were a novel or a text-book of psychology or a biography, like any of the others on the library shelves. An awful situation. That was why I've always liked the bitches so much, always been so grateful to them—because they were the only women I ever contrived to have a non-posthumous, contemporary, concrete relation with. The only ones." He smoked for a moment in silence.

"But why the only ones?" I asked.

"Why?" repeated Tilney. "But isn't it rather obvious? For the shy man, that is to say the man who doesn't know how to deal with real situations and people, bitches are the only possible lovers, because they're the only women who are prepared to come to meet him, the only ones who'll make the advances he doesn't know how to make."

I nodded. "Shy men have cause to be drawn to bitches: I see that. But why should the bitches be drawn to the shy men? What's their inducement to make those convenient advances? That's what I don't see."

"Oh, of course they don't make them unless the shy man's attractive," Tilney answered. "But in my case the bitches always were attracted. Always. And, quite frankly, they were right. I was tolerably picturesque, I had that professional Irish charm, I could talk, I was several hundred times more intelligent than any of the young men they were likely to know. And then, I fancy, my very shyness was an asset. You see, it didn't really look like shyness. It exteriorised itself as a kind of god-like impersonality and remoteness—most exciting for such women. I had the charm in their eyes of Mount Everest or the North Pole —something difficult and unconquered that aroused the record-breaking instincts in them. And at the same time my shy remoteness made me seem somehow superior; and, as you know, few pleasures can be compared with the sport of dragging down superiority and proving that it's no better than oneself. My air of disinterested remoteness has always had a *succès fou* with the bitches. They all adore me because I'm so 'different.' 'But you're different, Edmund, you're different,' " he fluted in falsetto. "The bitches! Under their sentimentalities, their one desire, of course, was to reduce me as quickly as possible to the most ignoble un-difference. . . ."

"And were they successful?" I asked.

"Oh, always. Naturally. It's not because a man's shy and bookish that he isn't a *porco di prim' ordine*. Indeed, the more shyly bookish, the more likely he is to be secretly porkish. Or if not a *porco*, at least an *asino*, an *oca*, a *vitello*. It's the rule, as I said just now; the law of nature. There's no escaping."

I laughed. "I wonder which of the animals I am?"

Tilney shook his head. "I'm not a zoologist. At least," he added, "not when I'm talking to the specimen under discussion. Ask your own conscience."

"And Chawdron?" I wanted to hear more about Chawdron. "Did Chawdron grunt, or bray, or moo?"

"A little of each. And if earwigs made a noise . . . No, not earwigs. Worse than that. Chawdron was an extreme case, and the extreme cases are right outside the animal kingdom."

"What are they, then? Vegetables?"

"No, no. Worse than vegetables. They're spiritual. Angels, that's what they are: putrefied angels. It's only in the earlier stages of the degeneration that they bleat and bray. After that they twang the harp and flap their wings. Pigs' wings, of course. They're Angels in pigs' clothing. Hearts of hog-wash. Did I ever tell you about Chawdron and Charlotte Salmon?"

"The 'cellist?"

He nodded. "What a woman!"

"And her playing! So clotted, so sagging, so greasy . . ." I fumbled for the apt description.

"So terribly Jewish, in a word," said Tilney. "That retching emotionalism, that sea-sickish spirituality—purely Hebraic. If only there were a few more Aryans in the world of music! The tears come into my eyes whenever I see a blonde beast at the piano. But that's by the way. I was going to tell you about Charlotte. You know her, of course?"

"Do I not!"

"Well, it was Charlotte who first revealed to me poor Chawdron's heart of hog-wash. Mine too, indirectly. It was one evening at old Cryle's. Chawdron was there, and Charlotte, and myself, and I forget who else. People from all the worlds, anyhow. Cryle, as you know, has a foot in each. He thinks it's his mission to bring them together. He's the match-maker between God and Mammon. In this case he must have imagined that he'd really brought off the marriage. Chawdron was Mammon all right; and though you and I would be chary of labelling Charlotte as God, old Cryle, I'm sure, had no doubts. After all, she plays the 'cello; she's an Artist. What more can you want?"

"What indeed!"

"I must say, I admired Charlotte that evening," he went on. "She knew so exactly the line to take with Chawdron; which was the more surprising as with me she's never quite pulled it off. She tries the siren on me, very dashing and at the same time extremely mysterious. Her line is to answer my most ordinary remarks with something absolutely incomprehensible, but obviously very significant. If I ask her, for example: 'Are you going to the Derby this year?' she'll smile a really Etruscan smile and answer: 'No, I'm too busy watching the boat-race in my own heart.' Well, then, obviously it's my cue to be terribly intrigued. 'Fascinating Sphinx,' I ought to say, 'tell me more about your visceral boat-race,' or words to that effect. Whereupon it would almost certainly turn out that I was rowing stroke in the winning boat. But I'm afraid I can't bring myself to do what's expected of me. I just say: 'What a pity! I was making up a party to go to Epsom'—and hastily walk away. No doubt, if she was less blackly Semitic I'd be passionately interested in her boat-race. But as it is, her manœuvre doesn't come off. She hasn't yet been able to think of a better one. With Chawdron, however, she discovered the correct strategy from the first moment. No siren, no mystery for him. His heart was too golden and hog-washy for that. Besides, he was fifty. It's the age when clergymen first begin to be preoccupied with the underclothing of little schoolgirls in trains, the age when eminent archæologists start taking a really passionate interest in the Scout movement. Under Chawdron's criminal mask Charlotte detected the pig-like angel, the sentimental Pickwickian child-lover with a taste for the *détournement de mineurs*. Charlotte's a practical woman: a child was needed, she immediately became the child. And what a child! I've never seen anything like it. Such prattling! Such innocent big eyes! Such merry, merry laughter! Such a wonderfully ingenuous way of saying extremely *risqué* things without knowing (sweet innocent) what they meant! I looked on and listened—staggered. Horrified too. The performance was really frightful. Suffer little children . . . But when the little child's twenty-eight and tough for her age—ah, no; of such is the kingdom of hell. For me, at any rate. But Chawdron was enchanted. Really did seem to imagine he'd got hold of something below the age of consent. I looked at him in amazement. Was it possible he should be taken in? The acting was so bad, so incredibly unconvincing. Sarah Bernhardt at seventy playing L'Aiglon looked more

M

genuinely like a child than our tough little Charlotte. But Chawdron didn't see it. This man who had lived by his wits, and not merely lived, but made a gigantic fortune by them:— was it possible that the most brilliant financier of the age should be so fabulously stupid? 'Youth's infectious,' he said to me after dinner, when the women had gone out. And then—you should have seen the smile on his face: beatific, lubrically tender— 'She's like a jolly little kitten, don't you think?' But what I thought of was the New Guinea Oil Company. How was it possible? And then suddenly I perceived that it wasn't merely possible; it was absolutely necessary. Just because he'd made fourteen hundred thousand pounds out of the New Guinea Oil scandal, it was inevitable that he should mistake a jolly little tarantula like Charlotte for a jolly little kitten. Inevitable. Just as it was inevitable that I should be bowled over by every bitch that came my way. Chawdron had spent his life thinking of oil and stock markets and flotations. I'd spent mine reading the Best that has been Thought or Said. Neither of us had had the time or energy to live—completely and intensely live, as a human being ought to, on every plane of existence. So he was taken in by the pseudo-kitten, while I succumbed to the only too genuine bitch. Succumbed, what was worse, with full knowledge. For I was never really taken in. I always knew that the bitches were bitches and not milk-white hinds. And now I also know why I was captivated by them. But that, of course, didn't prevent me from continuing to be captivated by them. *Experientia* doesn't, in spite of Mrs. Micawber's Papa. Nor does knowledge." He paused to relight his pipe.

"What does, then?" I asked.

Tilney shrugged his shoulders. "Nothing does, once you've gone off the normal instinctive rails."

"I wonder if they really exist, those rails?"

"So do I, sometimes," he confessed. "But I piously believe."

"Rousseau and Shelley piously believed too. But has anybody ever seen a Natural Man? Those Noble Savages . . . Read Malinowsky about them; read Frazer; read . . ."

"Oh, I have, I have. And of course the savage isn't noble. Primitives are horrible. I know. But then the Natural Man isn't Primitive Man. He isn't the raw material of humanity; he's the finished product. The Natural Man is a manufactured article— no, not manufactured; rather, a work of art. What's wrong with people like Chawdron is that they're such bad works of art. Unnatural because inartistic. Ary Scheffer instead of Manet. But with this difference. An Ary Scheffer is statically bad; it doesn't get worse with the passage of time. Whereas an inartistic human being degenerates, dynamically. Once he's started badly, he becomes more and more inartistic. It needs a moral earthquake to arrest the process. Mere flea-bites, like experience or knowledge, are quite unavailing. *Experientia* doesn't. If it did, I should never have succumbed as I did, never have got into financial straits, and therefore never have written Chawdron's autiobiography, never have had an opportunity for collecting the intimate and discreditable materials for the biography that, alas, I shall never write. No, no; experience didn't save me from falling a victim yet once more. And to such a ruinously expensive specimen. Not that she was mercenary," he put in parenthetically. "She was too well off to need to be. So well off, however, that the mere cost of feeding and amusing her in the style she was accustomed to being fed and amused in was utterly beyond my means. Of course she never realised it. People who are born with more than five thousand a year can't be expected to realise. She'd have been terribly upset if she had; for she had a heart of gold—like all the rest of us." He laughed mournfully. "Poor Sybil! I expect you remember her."

The name evoked for me a pale-eyed, pale-haired ghost. What an astonishingly lovely creature she was!"

"Was, was," he echoed. "*Fuit*. Lovely and fatal. The agonies she made me suffer! But she was as fatal to herself as to other people. Poor Sybil! I could cry when I think of that inevitable course of hers, that predestined trajectory." With a stretched forefinger he traced in the air a curve that rose and fell away again. "She had just passed the crest when I knew her.

The descending branch of the curve was horribly steep. Wha
depths awaited her! That horrible little East-Side Jew she eve
went to the trouble of marrying! And after the Jew, the Mexica
Indian. And meanwhile a little champagne had become rather
lot of champagne, rather a lot of brandy; and the occasiona
Good Times came to be incessant, a necessity, but so boring
such a dismal routine, so terribly exhausting. I didn't see her fo
four years after our final quarrel; and then (you've no idea ho
painful it was) I suddenly found myself shaking hands with
Memento Mori. So worn and ill and tired, so terribly old. Ol
at thirty-four. And the last time I'd seen her, she'd been radiant
Eighteen months later she was dead; but not before the India
had given place to a Chinaman and the brandy to cocaine. It wa
all inevitable, of course, all perfectly foreseeable. Nemesis ha
functioned with exemplary regularity. Which only made i
worse. Nemesis is all right for strangers and casual acquaint
ances. But for oneself, for the people one likes—ah, no! W
ought to be allowed to sow without reaping. But we mayn't.
sowed books and reaped Sybil. Sybil sowed me (not to mentio
the others) and reaped Mexicans, cocaine, death. Inevitable, bu
an outrage, an insulting denial of one's uniqueness and difference
Whereas when people like Chawdron sow New Guinea Oil an
reap kittenish Charlottes, one's delighted; the punctuality of fat
seems admirable."

"I never knew that Charlotte had been reaped by Chawdron,
I put in. "The harvesting must have been done with extra
ordinary discretion. Charlotte's usually so fond of publicity
even in these matters. I should never have expected her . . ."

"But the reaping was very brief and partial," Tilney explainec

That surprised me even more. "Charlotte who's always s
determined and clinging! And with Chawdron's millions t
cling to. . . ."

"Oh, it wasn't her fault that it went no further. She had ever
intention of being reaped and permanently garnered. But sh
had arranged to go to America for two months on a concert tou
It would have been troublesome to break the contract; Chawdro

seemed thoroughly infatuated; two months are soon passed. So she went. Full of confidence. But when she came back, Chawdron was otherwise occupied."

"Another kitten?"

"A kitten? Poor Charlotte was a grey-whiskered old tigress by comparison. She even came to me in her despair. No enigmatic subtleties this time; she'd forgotten she was the Sphinx. 'I think you ought to warn Mr. Chawdron against that woman,' she told me. 'He ought to be made to realise that she's exploiting him. It's outrageous.' She was full of righteous indignation. Not unnaturally. Even got angry with me because I wouldn't do anything. 'But he wants to be exploited,' I told her. 'It's his only joy in life.' Which was perfectly true. But I couldn't resist being a little malicious. 'What makes you want to spoil his fun?' I asked. She got quite red in the face. 'Because I think it's disgusting.'" Tilney made his voice indignantly shrill. "'It really shocks me to see a man like Mr. Chawdron being made a fool of in that way.' Poor Charlotte! Her feelings did her credit. But they were quite unavailing. Chawdron went on being made a fool of, in spite of her moral indignation. Charlotte had to retreat. The enemy was impregnably entrenched."

"But who was she—the enemy?"

"The unlikeliest *femme fatale* you ever saw. Little; rather ugly; sickly—yes, genuinely sickly, I think, though she did a good deal of pathetic malingering too; altogether too much the lady—refained; you know the type. A governess; not the modern breezy, athletic sort of governess—the genteel, Jane Eyre, daughter-of-clergyman kind. Her only visible merit was that she was young. About twenty-five, I suppose."

"But how on earth did they meet? Millionaires and governesses . . ."

"A pure miracle," said Tilney. "Chawdron himself detected the hand of Providence. That was the deep religious sense coming in. 'If it hadn't been for *both* my secretaries falling ill on the same day,' he said to me solemnly (and you've no idea how ridiculous he looked when he was being solemn—the saintly forger, the burglar in the pulpit), 'if it hadn't been for that—and after all, how unlikely it is that both one's secretaries should fall ill at the same moment; what a *fateful* thing to happen!—I should never have got to know my little Fairy.' And you must imagine the last words pronounced with a reverent and beautiful smile—indescribably incongruous on that crook's mug of his. 'My little Fairy' (her real name, incidentally, was Maggie Spindell), 'my little Fairy!' " Tilney seraphically smiled and rolled up his eyes. "You can't imagine the expression. St. Charles Borromeo in the act of breaking into the till."

"Painted by Carlo Dolci," I suggested.

"With the assistance of Rowlandson. Do you begin to get it?"

I nodded. "But the secretaries?" I was anxious to hear the story.

"They had orders to deal summarily with all begging letters, all communications from madmen, inventors, misunderstood geniuses, and, finally, women. The job was a heavy one, I can tell you. You've no idea what a rich man's post-bag is like. Fantastic. Well, as I say, Providence had given both private secretaries the 'flu. Chawdron happened to have nothing better to do that morning (Providence again); so he started opening his own correspondence. The third letter he opened was from the Fairy. It bowled him over."

"What was in it?"

Tilney shrugged his shoulders. "He never showed it me. But from what I gathered, she wrote about God and the Universe in general and her soul in particular, not to mention *his* soul. Having no taste, and being wholly without education, Chawdron was tremendously impressed by her philosophical rigmarole. It appealed to that deep religious sense! Indeed, he was so much impressed that he immediately wrote giving her an appointment. She came, saw, and conquered. 'Providential, my dear boy, providential.' And of course he was right. Only I'd have de-christened the power and called it Nemesis. Miss Spindell was the instrument of Nemesis; she was Atè in the fancy dress that

Chawdron's way of life had caused him to find irresistible. She was the finally ripened fruit of sowings in New Guinea Oil and the like."

"But if your account's correct," I put in, "delicious fruit—that is, for *his* taste. Being exploited by kittens was his only joy; you said it yourself. Nemesis was rewarding him for his offences, not punishing."

Tilney paused in his striding up and down the room, meditatively knitted his brows and, taking his pipe out of his mouth, rubbed the side of his nose with the hot bowl. "Yes," he said slowly, "that's an important point. I've had it vaguely in my head before now; but now you've put it clearly. From the point of view of the offender, the punishments of Nemesis may actually look like rewards. Yes, it's quite true."

"In which case your Nemesis isn't much use as a police-woman."

He held up his hand. "But Nemesis isn't a policewoman. Nemesis isn't moral. At least she's only incidentally moral, more or less by accident. Nemesis is something like gravitation, indifferent. All that she does is to guarantee that you shall reap what you sow. And if you sow self-stultification, as Chawdron did with his excessive interest in money, you reap grotesque humiliation. But as you're already reduced by your offences to a sub-human condition, you won't notice that the grotesque humiliation is a humiliation. There's your explanation why Nemesis sometimes seems to reward. What she brings is a humiliation only in the absolute sense—for the ideal and complete human being; or at any rate, in practice, for the nearly complete, the approaching-the-ideal human being. For the sub-human specimen it may seem a triumph, a consummation, a fulfilment of the heart's desire. But then, you must remember, the desiring heart is a heart of hog-wash. . . ."

"Moral," I concluded: "Live sub-humanly and Nemesis may bring you happiness."

"Precisely. But *what* happiness!"

I shrugged my shoulders.

"But after all, for the relativist, one sort of happiness is as good as another. You're taking the God's-eye view."

"The Greek's-eye view," he corrected.

"As you like. But anyhow, from the Chawdron's-eye view the happiness is perfect. Therefore we ought to make ourselves like Chawdron."

Tilney nodded. "Yes," he said, "you need to be a bit of a platonist to see that the punishments *are* punishments. And of course if there *were* another life . . . Or better still, metempsychosis: there are some unbelievably disgusting insects. . . But even from the merely utilitarian point of view Chawdronism is dangerous. Socially dangerous. A society constructed by and for men can't work if all its components are emotionally submen. When the majority of hearts have turned to hog-wash something catastrophic must happen. So that Nemesis turns out to be a policewoman after all. I hope you're satisfied."

"Perfectly."

"You always did have a very discreditable respect for law and order and morality," he complained.

"They must exist . . ."

"I don't know why," he interrupted me.

"In order that you and I may be immoral in comfort," I explained. "Law and order exist to make the world safe for lawless and disorderly individualists."

"Not to mention ruffians like Chawdron. From whom, by the way, we seem to have wandered. Where was I?"

"You'd just got to his providential introduction to the Fairy."

"Yes, yes. Well, as I said, she came, saw, conquered. Three days later she was installed in the house. He made her his librarian."

"*And* his mistress, I suppose."

Tilney raised his shoulders and threw out his hands in a questioning gesture. "Ah," he said, "that's the question. There you're touching the heart of the mystery."

"But you don't mean to tell me . . ."

"I don't mean to tell you anything, for the good reason that I don't know. I only guess."

"And what do you guess?"

"Sometimes one thing and sometimes another. The Fairy was genuinely enigmatic. None of poor Charlotte's fabricated sphinxishness; a real mystery. With the Fairy anything was possible."

"But not with Chawdron surely. In these matters, wasn't he . . . well, all too human?"

"No, only sub-human. Which is rather different. The Fairy roused in him all his sub-human spirituality and religiosity. Whereas with Charlotte it was the no less sub-human passion for the *détournement de mineurs* that came to the surface."

I objected. "That's too crude and schematic to be good psychology. Emotional states aren't so definite and clear-cut as that. There isn't one compartment for spirituality and another, water-tight, for the *détournement de mineurs*. There's an over-lapping, a fusion, a mixture."

"You're probably right," said Tilney. "And, indeed, one of my conjectures was precisely of such a fusion. You know the the sort of thing: discourses insensibly giving place to amorous action—though 'action' seems too strong a word to describe what I have in mind. Something ever so softly senile and girlish. Positively spiritual contacts. The loves of the angels—so angelic that, when it was all over, one wouldn't be quite sure whether there had been any interruption in the mystical conversation or not. Which would justify the Fairy in her righteous indignation when she heard of any one's venturing to suppose that she was anything more than Chawdron's librarian. She could almost honestly believe she wasn't. 'I think people are too horrid,' she used to say to me on these occasions. 'I think they're simply disgusting. Can't they even believe in the possibility of purity?' Angry she was, outraged, hurt. And the emotion seemed abso-lutely real. Which was such a rare occurrence in the Fairy's life —at any rate, so it seemed to me—that I was forced to believe it had a genuine cause."

"Aren't we all genuinely angry when we hear that our acquaintances say the same sort of things about us as we say about them?"

"Of course; and the truer the gossip, the angrier we are. But the Fairy was angry because the gossip was untrue. She insisted on that—and insisted so genuinely (this is the point I was trying to make) that I couldn't help believing she had some justification. Either nothing had happened, or else something so softly and slimily angelic that it slipped past the attention, escaped notice, counted for nothing."

"But after all," I protested, "it's not because one looks truthful that one's telling the truth."

"No. But then you didn't know the Fairy. She hardly ever looked or sounded truthful. There was hardly anything she said that didn't strike me as being in one way or another a manifest lie. So that when she did seem to be telling the truth (and it was incredible how rarely that happened), I was always impressed. I couldn't help thinking there must be a reason. That's why I attach such importance to the really heart-felt way she got angry when doubts were cast on the purity of her relations with Chawdron. I believe that they really were pure, or else, more probably, that the impurity was such a little one, so to speak, that she could honestly regard it as non-existent. You'd have had the same impression too, if you'd heard her. The genuineness of the anger, the outraged protest, was obvious. And then suddenly she remembered that she was a Christian, practically a saint; she'd start forgiving her enemies. 'One's sorry for them,' she'd say, 'because they don't know any better. Poor people! ignorant of all the finer feelings, all the more beautiful relationships.' I can't tell you how awful the word 'beautiful' was in her mouth! Really blood-curdling. Be-yütiful. Very long-drawn-out, with the oo sound thinned and refined into German u-modified. Be-yütiful. Ugh!" He shuddered. "It made one want to kill her. But then the whole tone of these Christian sentiments made one want to kill her. When she forgave the poor misguided people who couldn't see the be-yüty of her relations with Chawdron you were horrified, you felt sick, you went cold all over. For the whole thing was such a lie, so utterly and bottomlessly false. After the genuine anger against the scandalmongers, the falseness rang even falser than usual. Obvious, unmistakable, painful— like an untuned piano, like a cuckoo in June. Chawdron was deaf to it, of course; just didn't hear the falseness. If you have a deep religious sense, I suppose you don't notice those things. 'I think she has the most beautiful character I've ever met with in a human being,' he used to tell me. ('Beautiful' again, you notice. Chawdron caught the trick from her. But in his mouth it was merely funny, not gruesome.) 'The most beautiful character'—and then his beatific smile. Grotesque! It was just the same as with Charlotte; he swallowed her whole. Charlotte played the jolly kitten and he accepted her as the jolly kitten. The Fairy's ambition was to be regarded as a sanctified Christian kitten; and duly, as a Christian kitten, a confirmed, communicant, Catholic, canonised Kitten, he did regard her. Incredible; but, there! if you spend all your wits and energies knowing about oil, you can't be expected to know much about anything else. You can't be expected to know the difference between tarantulas and kittens, for example; nor the difference between St. Catherine of Siena and a little liar like Maggie Spindell."

"But did she know she was lying?" I asked. "Was she consciously a hypocrite?"

Tilney repeated his gesture of uncertainty. "*Chi lo sa?*" he said. "That's the finally unanswerable question. It takes us back to where we were just now with Chawdron—to the borderland between biography and autobiography. Which is more real: you as you see yourself, or you as others see you? you in your intentions and motives, or you in the product of your intentions? you in your actions, or you in the results of your actions? And anyhow, what *are* your intentions and motives? And who is the 'you' who has intentions? So that when you ask if the Fairy was a conscious liar and hypocrite, I just have to say that I don't know. Nobody knows. Not even the Fairy herself. For, after all, there were several Fairies. There was one that wanted to be fed and looked after and given money and perhaps married one day, if Chawdron's wife happened to die."

"I didn't know he had a wife," I interrupted in some astonishment.

"Mad," Tilney telegraphically explained. "Been in an asylum for the last twenty-five years. I'd have gone mad too, if I'd been married to Chawdron. But that didn't prevent the Fairy from aspiring to be the second Mrs. C. Money is always money. Well, there was *that* Fairy—the adventuress, the Darwinian specimen struggling for existence. But there was also a Fairy that genuinely wanted to be Christian and saintly. A spiritual Fairy. And if the spirituality happened to pay with tired business men like Chawdron—well, obviously, *tant mieux*."

"But the falseness you spoke of, the lying, the hypocrisy?"

"Mere inefficiency," Tilney answered. "Just bad acting. For, when all's said and done, what is hypocrisy but bad acting? It differs from saintliness as a performance by Lucien Guitry differed from a performance by his son. One's artistically good and the other isn't."

I laughed. "You forget I'm a moralist; at least, you said I was. These æsthetic heresies . . ."

"Not heresies; just obvious statements of the facts. For what is the practice of morality? It's just pretending to be somebody that by nature you aren't. It's acting the part of a saint, or a hero, or a respectable citizen. What's the highest ethical ideal in Christianity? It's expressed in A Kempis's formula—'The Imitation of Christ.' So that the organised Churches turn out to be nothing but vast and elaborate Academies of Dramatic Art. And every school's a school of acting. Every family's a family of Crummleses. Every human being is brought up as a mummer. All education, aside from merely intellectual education, is just a series of rehearsals for the part of Jesus or Podsnap or Alexander the Great, or whoever the local favourite may be. A virtuous man is one who's learned his part thoroughly and acts it competently and convincingly. The saint and the hero are great actors; they're Kembles and Siddonses—people with a genius for representing heroic characters not their own; or people with the luck to be born so like the heroic ideal that they can just step straight into the part without rehearsal. The wicked are those who either can't or won't learn to act. Imagine a scene-shifter, slightly drunk, dressed in his overalls and smoking a pipe; he comes reeling on to the stage in the middle of the trial scene in the *Merchant of Venice*, shouts down Portia, gives Antonio a kick in the stern, knocks over a few Magnificos and pulls off Shylock's false beard. That's a criminal. As for a hypocrite— he's either a criminal interrupter disguised, temporarily and for his own purposes, as an actor (that's Tartuffe); or else (and I think this is the commoner type) he's just a bad actor. By nature, like all the rest of us, he's a criminal interrupter; but he accepts the teaching of the local Academies of Dramatic Art and admits that man's highest duty is to act star parts to applauding houses. But he is wholly without talent. When he's thinking of his noble part, he mouths and rants and gesticulates, till you feel really ashamed as you watch him—ashamed for yourself, for him, for the human species. 'Methinks the lady, or gentleman, doth protest too much,' is what you say. And these protestations seem even more excessive when, a few moments later, you observe that the protester has forgotten altogether that he's playing a part and is behaving like the interrupting criminal that it's his nature to be. But he himself is so little the mummer, so utterly without a talent for convincing representation, that he simply doesn't notice his own interruptions; or if he notice them, does so only slightly and with the conviction that nobody else will notice them. In other words, most hypocrites are more or less unconscious hypocrites. The Fairy, I'm sure, was one of them. She was simply not aware of being an adventuress with an eye on Chawdron's millions. What she was conscious of was her rôle—the rôle of St. Catherine of Siena. She believed in her acting; she was ambitious to be a high-class West-End artiste. But, unfortunately, she was without talent. She played her part so unnaturally, with such grotesque exaggerations, that a normally sensitive person could only shudder at the shameful spectacle. It was a performance that only the spiritually deaf and blind could be convinced by. And, thanks to his preoccupations with New Guinea Oil, Chawdron *was* spiritually deaf and blind. His deep religious sense was the deep religious sense of a sub-man. When she paraded the canonised kitten, I felt sea-sick; but Chawdron thought she had the most be-yütiful character he'd ever met with in a human being. And not only did he think she had the most beautiful character; he also, which was almost funnier, thought she had the finest mind. It was her metaphysical conversation that impressed him. She'd read a few snippets from Spinoza and Plato and some little book on the Christian mystics and a fair amount of that flabby theosophical literature that's so popular in Garden Suburbs and among retired colonels and ladies of a certain age; so she could talk about the cosmos very profoundly. And, by God, she was profound! I used to lose my temper sometimes, it was such drivel, so dreadfully illiterate. But Chawdron listened reverently, fairly goggling with rapture and faith and admiration. He believed every word. When you're totally uneducated and have amassed an enormous fortune by legal swindling, you can afford to believe in the illusoriness of matter, the non-existence of evil, the oneness of all diversity and the spirituality of everything. All his life he'd kept up his childhood's Presbyterianism—most piously. And now he grafted the Fairy's rigmarole on to the Catechism, or whatever it is that Presbyterians learn in infancy. He didn't see that there was any contradiction between the two metaphysics, just as he'd never seen that there was any incongruity in his being both a good Presbyterian and a consummate swindler. He had acted the Presbyterian part only on Sundays and when he was ill, never in business hours. Religion had never been permitted to invade the sanctities of private life. But with the advance of middle age his mind grew flabbier; the effects of a misspent life began to make themselves felt. And at the same time his retirement from business removed almost all the external distractions. His deep religious sense had more chance to express itself. He could wallow in sentimentality and silliness undisturbed. The Fairy made her providential appearance and showed him which were the softest emotional and intellectual muck-heaps to wallow on. He was grateful—loyally, but a little ludicrously. I shall never forget, for example, the time he talked about the Fairy's genius. We'd been dining at his house, he and I and the Fairy. A terrible dinner, with the Fairy, as a mixture between St. Catherine of Siena and Mahatma Gandhi, explaining why she was a vegetarian and an ascetic. She had that awful genteel middle-class food complex which makes table manners at Lyons' Corner Houses so appallingly good—that haunting fear of being low or vulgar which causes people to eat as though they weren't eating. They never take a large mouthful, and only masticate with their front teeth, like rabbits. And they never touch anything with their fingers. I've actually seen a woman eating cherries with a knife and fork at one of those places. Most extraordinary and most repulsive. Well, the Fairy had that complex—it's a matter of class—but it was rationalised, with her, in terms of *ahimsa* and ascetic Christianity. Well, she'd been chattering the whole evening about the spirit of love and its incompatibility with a meat diet, and the necessity of mortifying the body for the sake of the soul, and about Buddha and St. Francis and mystical ecstasies and, above all, herself. Drove me almost crazy with irritation, not to mention the fact that she really began putting me off my food with her rhapsodies of pious horror and disgust. I was thankful when at last she left us in peace to our brandy and cigars. But Chawdron leaned across the table towards me, spiritually beaming from every inch of that forger's face of his. 'Isn't she wonderful?' he said. 'Isn't she simply *wonderful*?' 'Wonderful,' I agreed. And then, very solemnly, wagging his finger at me, 'I've known three great intellects in my time,' he said, 'three minds of genius—Lord Northcliffe, Mr. John Morley, and this little girl. Those three.' And he leant back in his chair and nodded at me almost fiercely, as though challenging me to deny it."

"And did you accept the challenge?" I asked, laughing.

Tilney shook his head. "I just helped myself to another nip

of his 1820 brandy; it was the only retort a rational man could make."

"And did the Fairy share Chawdron's opinion about her mind?"

"Oh, I think so," said Tilney, "I think so. She had a great conceit of herself. Like all these spiritual people. An inordinate conceit. She played the superior rôle very badly and inconsistently. But all the same she was convinced of her superiority. Inevitably; for, you see, she had an enormous capacity for autosuggestion. What she told herself three times became true. For example, I used at first to think there was some hocus-pocus about her asceticism. She ate so absurdly little in public and at meals that I fancied she must do a little tucking-in privately in between whiles. But later I came to the conclusion that I'd maligned her. By dint of constantly telling herself and other people that eating was unspiritual and gross, not to mention impolite and lower-class, she'd genuinely succeeded, I believe, in making food disgust her. She'd got to a point where she really couldn't eat more than a very little. Which was one of the causes of her sickliness. She was just under-nourished. But undernourishment was only *one* of the causes. She was also diplomatically sick. She threatened to die as statesmen threaten to mobilise, in order to get what she wanted. Blackmail, in fact. Not for money; she was curiously disinterested in many ways. What she wanted was his interest, was power over him, was self-assertion. She had headaches for the same reason as a baby howls. If you give in to the baby and do what it wants, it'll howl again, it'll make a habit of howling. Chawdron was one of the weak-minded sort of parents. When the Fairy had one of her famous headaches, he was terribly disturbed. The way he fluttered round the sick-room with ice and hot-water bottles and eau-de-Cologne! The *Times* obituarist would have wept to see him; such a touching exhibition of the heart of gold! The result was that the Fairy used to have a headache every three or four days. It was absolutely intolerable."

"But were they purely imaginary, these headaches?"

Tilney shrugged his shoulders. "Yes and no. There was certainly a physiological basis. The woman did have pains in her head from time to time. It was only to be expected; she was run down, through not eating enough; she didn't take sufficient exercise, so she had chronic constipation; chronic constipation probably set up a slight chronic inflammation of the ovaries; and she certainly suffered from eye-strain—you could tell that from the beautifully vague, spiritual look in her eyes, the look that comes from uncorrected myopia. There were, as you see, plenty of physiological reasons for her headaches. Her body made her a present, so to speak, of the pain. Her mind then proceeded to work up this raw material. Into what remarkable forms! Touched by her imagination, the headaches became mystic, transcendental. It was infinity in a grain of sand and eternity in an intestinal stasis. Regularly every Tuesday and Friday she died—died with a beautiful Christian resignation, a martyr's fortitude. Chawdron used to come down from the sick-room with tears in his eyes. He'd never seen such patience, such courage, such grit. There were few men she wouldn't put to shame. She was a wonderful example. And so on. And I dare say it was all quite true. She started by malingering a little, by pretending that the headaches were worse than they were. But her imagination was too lively for her; it got beyond her control. Her pretendings gradually came true and she really did suffer martyrdom each time; she really did very nearly die. And then she got into the habit of being a martyr, and the attacks came on regularly; imagination stimulated the normal activities of inflamed ovaries and poisoned intestines; the pain made its appearance and at once became the raw material of a mystic, spiritual martyrdom taking place on a higher plane. Anyhow, it was all very complicated and obscure. And, obviously, if the Fairy herself had given you an account of her existence at this time, it would have sounded like St. Lawrence's reminiscences of life on the grill. Or rather it would have sounded like the insincere fabrication of such reminiscences. For the Fairy, as I've said before, was without talent, and sincerity and saintliness are matters of talent. Hypocrisy and insincerity are the products of native incompetence. Those who are guilty of them are people without skill in the arts of behaviour and self-expression. The Fairy's talk would have sounded utterly false to you. But for her it was all genuine. She really suffered, really died, really was good and resigned and courageous. Just as the paranoiac is really Napoleon Bonaparte and the young man with *dementia præcox* is really being spied on and persecuted by a gang of fiendishly ingenious enemies. If *I* were to tell the story from *her* point of view, it would sound really beautiful—not be-yütiful, mind you; but truly and genuinely beautiful; for the good reason that *I* have a gift of expression, which the poor Fairy hadn't. So that, for all but emotional cretins like Chawdron, she was obviously a hypocrite and a liar. Also a bit of a pathological case. For that capacity for auto-suggestion really was rather pathological. She could make things come *too* true. Not merely diseases and martyrdoms and saintliness, but also historical facts, or rather historical not-facts. She authenticated the not-facts by simply repeating that they had happened. For example, she wanted people to believe—she wanted to believe herself—that she had been intimate with Chawdron for years and years, from childhood, from the time of her birth. The fact that he had known her since she was 'so high' would explain and justify her present relationship with him. The scandalmongers would have no excuse for talking. So she proceeded bit by bit to fabricate a lifelong intimacy, even a bit of an actual kinship, with her Uncle Benny. I told you that that was what she called him, didn't I? That nickname had its significance; it planted him at once in the table of consanguinity and so disinfected their relations, so to speak, automatically made them innocent."

"Or incestuous," I added.

"Or incestuous. Quite. But she didn't consider the D'Annunzioesque refinements. When she gave him that name, she promoted Chawdron to the rank of a dear old kinsman, or at least a dear old family friend. Sometimes she even called him 'Nunky Benny,' so as to show that she had known him from the cradle—had lisped of nunkies, for the nunkies came. But that wasn't enough. The evidence had to be fuller, more circumstantial. So she invented it—romps with Nunky in the hay, visits to the pantomime with him, a whole outfit of childish memories."

"But what about Chawdron?" I asked. "Did he share the invented memories?"

Tilney nodded. "But for him, of course, they *were* invented. Other people, however, accepted them as facts. Her reminiscences were so detailed and circumstantial that, unless you *knew* she was a liar, you simply had to accept them. With Chawdron himself she couldn't, of course, pretend that she'd known him, literally and historically, all those years. Not at first, in any case. The lifelong intimacy started by being figurative and spiritual. I feel as though I'd known my Uncle Benny ever since I was a tiny baby,' she said to me in his presence, quite soon after she'd first got to know him; and as always, on such occasions, she made her voice even more whiningly babyish than usual. Dreadful that voice was—so whiny-piny, so falsely sweet. 'Ever since I was a teeny, tiny baby. Don't you feel like that, Uncle Benny?' And Chawdron heartily agreed; of course he felt like that. From that time forward she began to expatiate on the incidents which ought to have occurred in that far-off childhood with darling Nunky. They were the same incidents, of course, as those which she actually remembered when she was talking to strangers and he wasn't there. She made him give her old photographs of himself—visions of him in high collars and frock-coats, in queer-looking Norfolk jackets, in a top-hat sitting in a victoria. They helped her to make her fancies real. With their aid and the aid of his reminiscences she constructed a whole life in common with him. 'Do you remember, Uncle Benny, the time we went to Cowes on your yacht and I fell into the sea?' she'd ask. And Chawdron, who thoroughly entered into the game, would answer: 'Of course I remember. And when we'd fished you out, we had to wrap you in hot blankets and give you warm rum and milk. And you got quite drunk.' 'Was I funny when I was

drunk, Uncle Benny?' And Chawdron would rather lamely and
ponderously invent a few quaintnesses which were then incorporated in the history. So that on a future occasion the Fairy
could begin: 'Nunky Benny, do you remember those ridiculou
things I said when you made me drunk with rum and hot mill
that time I fell into the sea at Cowes?' And so on. Chawdroi
loved the game, thought it simply too sweet and whimsical and
touching—positively like something out of Barrie or A. A
Milne—and was never tired of playing it. As for the Fairy—fo
her it wasn't a game at all. The not-facts had been repeated til
they became facts. 'But, come, Miss Spindell,' I said to her once
when she'd been telling me—me!—about some adventure she'
had with Uncle Benny when she was a toddler, 'come, come
Miss Spindell' (I always called her that, though she longed to b
my Fairy as well as Chawdron's, and would have called m
Uncle Ted if I'd given her the smallest encouragement; but I too.
a firm line; she was always Miss Spindell for me), 'come,' I said
'you seem to forget that it's only just over a year since you sav
Mr. Chawdron for the first time.' She looked at me quite blankl
for a moment without saying anything. 'You can't seriousl
expect me to forget too,' I added. Poor Fairy! The blanknes
suddenly gave place to a painful, blushing embarrassment. 'Ol
of course,' she began, and laughed nervously. 'It's as thoug
I'd known him for ever. My imagination . . .' She tailed o
into silence, and a minute later made an excuse to leave me.
could see she was upset, physically upset, as though she'd bee
woken up too suddenly out of a sound sleep, jolted out of on
world into another moving in a different direction. But when
saw her the next day, she seemed to be quite herself again. Sh
had suggested herself back into the dream world; from the othe
end of the table, at lunch, I heard her talking to an America
business acquaintance of Chawdron's about the fun she an
Uncle Benny used to have on his grouse moor in Scotland. Bu
from that time forth, I noticed, she never talked to me about he
apocryphal childhood again. A curious incident; it made me loo
at her hypocrisy in another light. It was then I began to reali

that the lie in her soul was mainly an unconscious lie, the product of pathology and a lack of talent. Mainly; but sometimes, on the contrary, the lie was only too conscious and deliberate. The most extraordinary of them was the lie at the bottom of the great Affair of the Stigmata."

"The stigmata?" I echoed. "A pious lie, then."

"Pious." He nodded. "That was how she justified it to herself. Though, of course, in her eyes, all her lies were pious lies. Pious, because they served *her* purposes and she was a saint; her cause was sacred. And afterwards, of course, when she'd treated the lies to her process of imaginative disinfection, they ceased to be lies and fluttered away as snow-white pious truths. But to start with they were undoubtedly pious lies, even for her. The Affair of the Stigmata made that quite clear. I caught her in the act. It all began with a boil that developed on Chawdron's foot."

"Curious place to have a boil."

"Not common," he agreed. "I once had one there myself, when I was a boy. Most unpleasant, I can assure you. Well, the same thing happened to Chawdron. He and I were down at his country place, playing golf and in the intervals concocting the *Autobiography*. We'd settle down with brandy and cigars and I'd gently question him. Left to himself, he was apt to wander and become incoherent and unchronological. I had to canalise his narrative, so to speak. Remarkably frank he was. I learned some curious things about the business world, I can tell you. Needless to say, they're not in the *Autobiography*. I'm reserving them for the *Life*. Which means, alas, that nobody will ever know them. Well, as I say, we were down there in the country for a long week-end, Friday to Tuesday. The Fairy had stayed in London. Periodically she took her librarianship very seriously and protested that she simply had to get on with the catalogue. 'I have my duties,' she said when Chawdron suggested that she should come down to the country with us. 'You must let me get on with my duties. I don't think one ought to be just frivolous; do you, Uncle Benny? Besides, I really love my work.' God, how she enraged me with that whiney-piney talk! But Chawdron, of course, was touched and enchanted. 'What an extraordinary little person she is!' he said to me as we left the house together. Even more extraordinary than you suppose, I thought. He went on rhapsodising as far as Watford. But in a way, I could see, when we arrived, in a way he was quite pleased she hadn't come. It was a relief to him to be having a little masculine holiday. She had the wit to see that he needed these refreshments from time to time. Well, we duly played our golf, with the result that by Sunday morning poor Chawdron's boil, which had been a negligible little spot on the Friday, had swollen up with the chafing and the exercise into a massive red hemisphere that made walking an agony. Unpleasant, no doubt; but nothing, for any ordinary person, to get seriously upset about. Chawdron, however, wasn't an ordinary person where boils were concerned. He had a carbuncle-complex, a boilophobia. Excusably, perhaps; for it seems that his brother had died of some awful kind of gangrene that had started, to all appearances harmlessly, in a spot on his cheek. Chawdron couldn't develop a pimple without imagining that he'd caught his brother's disease. This affair on his foot scared him out of his wits. He saw the bone infected, the whole leg rotting away, amputations, death. I offered what comfort and encouragement I could and sent for the local doctor. He came at once and turned out to be a young man, very determined and efficient and confidence-inspiring. The boil was anæsthetised, lanced, cleaned out, tied up. Chawdron was promised there'd be no complications. And there weren't. The thing healed up quite normally. Chawdron decided to go back to town on the Tuesday, as he'd arranged. 'I wouldn't like to disappoint Fairy,' he explained. 'She'd be so sad if I didn't come back when I'd promised. Besides, she might be nervous. You've no idea what an intuition that little girl has—almost uncanny, like second sight. She'd guess something was wrong and be upset; and you know how bad it is for her to be upset.' I did indeed; those mystic headaches of hers were the bane of my life. No, no, I agreed. She mustn't be upset. So it was decided that the Fairy should be kept in blissful ignorance of the boil until Chawdron had actually arrived. But the question then arose: how should he arrive? We had gone down into the country in Chawdron's Bugatti. He had a weakness for speed. But it wasn't the car for an invalid. It was arranged that the chauffeur should drive the Bugatti up to town and come back with the Rolls. In the unlikely event of his seeing Miss Spindell, he was not to tell her why he had been sent to town. Those were his orders. The man went and duly returned with the Rolls. Chawdron was installed, almost as though he were in an ambulance, and we rolled majestically up to London. What a home-coming! In anticipation of the sympathy he would get from the Fairy, Chawdron began to have a slight relapse as we approached the house. 'I feel it throbbing,' he assured me; and when he got out of the car, what a limp! As though he'd lost a leg at Gallipoli. Really heroic. The butler had to support him up to the drawing-room. He was lowered on to the sofa. 'Is Miss Spindell in her room?' The butler thought so. 'Then ask her to come down here at once.' The man went out; Chawdron closed his eyes—wearily, like a very sick man. He was preparing to get all the sympathy he could and, I could see, luxuriously relishing it in advance. 'Still throbbing?' I asked, rather irreverently. He nodded, without opening his eyes. 'Still throbbing.' The manner was grave and sepulchral. I had to make an effort not to laugh. There was a silence; we waited. And then the door opened. The Fairy appeared. But a maimed Fairy. One foot in a high-heeled shoe, the other in a slipper. Such a limp! 'Another leg lost at Gallipoli,' thought I. When he heard the door open, Chawdron shut his eyes tighter than ever and turned his face to the wall, or at any rate the back of the sofa. I could see that this rather embarrassed the Fairy. Her entrance had been dramatic; she had meant him to see her disablement at once; hadn't counted on finding a death-bed scene. She had hastily to improvise another piece of stage business, a new set of lines; the scene she had prepared wouldn't do. Which was the more embarrassing for her as I was there, looking on—a very cool spectator, as she knew; not in the least a Maggie Spindell fan. She hesitated a second near the door,

hoping Chawdron would look round; but he kept his eyes resolutely shut and his face averted. He'd evidently decided to play
the moribund part for all it was worth. So, after one rather
nervous glance at me, she limped across the room to the sofa.
'Uncle Benny!' He gave a great start, as though he hadn't known
she was there. 'Is that you, Fairy?' This was *pianissimo, con
espressione*. Then, *molto agitato* from the Fairy: 'What is it,
Nunky Benny? What is it? Oh, tell me.' She was close enough
now to lay a hand on his shoulder. 'Tell me.' He turned his face
towards her—the tenderly transfigured burglar. His heart overflowed—'Fairy!'—a slop of hog-wash. 'But what's the matter,
Nunky Benny?' 'Nothing, Fairy.' The tone implied that it was
a heroic under-statement in the manner of Sir Philip Sidney.
'Only my foot.' 'Your foot!' The fairy registered such astonishment that we both fairly jumped. 'Something wrong with your
foot?' 'Yes, why not?' Chawdron was rather annoyed; he wasn't
getting the kind of sympathy he'd looked forward to. She
turned to me. 'But when did it happen, Mr. Tilney?' I was
breezy. 'A nasty boil,' I explained. 'Walking round the course
did it no good. It had to be lanced on Sunday.' 'At about half-
past eleven on Sunday morning?' 'Yes, I suppose it was about
half-past eleven,' I said, thinking the question was an odd one.
'It was just half-past eleven when *this* happened,' she said
dramatically, pointing to her slippered foot. 'What's "this"?'
asked Chawdron crossly. He was thoroughly annoyed at being
swindled out of sympathy. I took pity on the Fairy; things
seemed to be going so badly for her. I could see that she had
prepared a coup and that it hadn't come off. 'Miss Spindell also
seems to have hurt her foot,' I explained. 'You didn't see how
she limped.' 'How did you hurt it?' asked Chawdron. He was
still very grumpy. 'I was sitting quietly in the library, working
at the catalogue,' she began: and I guessed, by the way the
phrases came rolling out, that she was at last being able to make
use of the material she had prepared, 'when suddenly, almost
exactly at half-past eleven (I remember looking at the clock), I
felt a terrible pain in my foot. As though some one were driving

a sharp, sharp knife into it. It was so intense that I nearly fainted.' She paused for a moment, expecting appropriate comment. But Chawdron wouldn't make it. So I put in a polite 'Dear me, most extraordinary!' with which she had to be content. 'When I got up,' she continued, 'I could hardly stand, my foot hurt me so; and I've been limping ever since. And the most extraordinary thing is that there's a red mark on my foot, like a scar.' Another expectant pause. But still no word from Chawdron. He sat there with his mouth tight shut, and the lines that divided his cheeks from that wide simian upper lip of his were as though engraved in stone. The Fairy looked at him and saw that she had taken hopelessly the wrong line. Was it too late to remedy the mistake? She put the new plan of campaign into immediate execution. 'But you poor Nunky Benny!' she began, in the sort of tone in which you'd talk to a sick dog. 'How selfish of me to talk about my ailments, when you're lying there with your poor foot bandaged up!' The dog began to wag his tail at once. The beatific look returned to his face. He took her hand. I couldn't stand it. 'I think I'd better be going,' I said; and I went."

"But the foot?" I asked. "The stabbing pain at exactly half-past eleven?"

"You may well ask. As Chawdron himself remarked, when next I saw him, 'There are more things in heaven and earth, Horatio, than are dreamt of in your philosophy.'" Tilney laughed. "The Fairy had triumphed. After he'd had his dose of mother love and Christian charity and kittenish sympathy, he'd been ready, I suppose, to listen to *her* story. The stabbing pain at eleven-thirty, the red scar. Strange, mysterious, unaccountable. He discussed it all with me, very gravely and judiciously. We talked of spiritualism and telepathy. We distinguished carefully between the miraculous and the super-normal. 'As you know,' he told me, 'I've been a good Presbyterian all my life, and as such have been inclined to dismiss as mere fabrications all the stories of the Romish saints. I never believed in the story of St. Francis's stigmata, for example. But now I accept it!' Solemn and tremendous pause. 'Now I *know* it's true.' I just bowed my head in silence. But the next time I saw M'Crae, the chauffeur, I asked a few questions. Yes, he *had* seen Miss Spindell that day he drove the Bugatti up to London and came back with the Rolls. He'd gone into the secretaries' office to see if there were any letters to take down for Mr. Chawdron, and Miss Spindell had run into him as he came out. She'd asked him what he was doing in London and he hadn't been able to think of anything to answer, in spite of Mr. Chawdron's orders, except the truth. It had been on his conscience ever since; he hoped it hadn't done any harm. 'On the contrary,' I assured him, and that I certainly wouldn't tell Mr. Chawdron. Which I never did. I thought . . . But good heavens!" he interrupted himself; "what's this?" It was Hawtrey, who had come in to lay the table for lunch. She ignored us, actively. It was not only as though we didn't exist; it was as though we also had no right to exist. Tilney took out his watch. "Twenty past one. God almighty! Do you mean to say I've been talking here the whole morning since breakfast?"

"So it appears," I answered.

He groaned. "You see," he said, "you see what it is to have gift of the gab. A whole precious morning utterly wasted."

"Not for me," I said.

He shrugged his shoulders. "Perhaps not. But then for you the story was new and curious. Whereas for me it's known, it's stale."

"But for Shakespeare so was the story of Othello, even before he started to write it."

"Yes, but he *wrote*, he didn't talk. There was something to show for the time he'd spent. His Othello didn't just disappear into thin air, like my poor Chawdron." He sighed and was silent. Stone-faced and grim, Hawtrey went rustling starchily round the table; there was a clinking of steel and silver as she laid the places. I waited till she had left the room before I spoke again. When one's servants are more respectable than one is oneself (and nowadays they generally are), one cannot be too careful.

"And how did it end?" I asked.

"How did it end?" he repeated in a voice that had suddenly gone flat and dull; he was bored with his story, wanted to think of something else. "It ended, so far as I was concerned, with my finishing the *Autobiography* and getting tired of its subject. I gradually faded out of Chawdron's existence. Like the Cheshire Cat."

"And the Fairy?"

"Faded out of life about a year after the Affair of the Stigmata. She retired to her mystic death-bed once too often. Her pretending came true at last; it was always the risk with her. She really did die."

The door opened; Hawtrey re-entered the room, carrying a dish.

"And Chawdron, I suppose, was inconsolable?" Inconsolability is, happily, a respectable subject.

Tilney nodded. "Took to spiritualism, of course. Nemesis again."

Hawtrey raised the lid of the dish; a smell of fried soles escaped into the air. "Luncheon is served," she said, with what seemed to me an ill-concealed contempt and disapproval.

"Luncheon is served," Tilney echoed, moving towards his place. He sat down and opened his napkin. "One meal after another, punctually, day after day, day after day. Such is life. Which would be tolerable enough if something ever got done between meals. But in my case nothing does. Meal after meal, and between meals a vacuum, a kind of . . ." Hawtrey, who had been offering him the *sauce tartare* for the past several seconds, here gave him the discreetest nudge. Tilney turned his head. "Ah, thank you," he said, and helped himself.

THE REST CURE

SHE was a tiny woman, dark-haired and with grey-blue eyes, very large and arresting in a small pale face. A little girl's face, with small, delicate features, but worn—prematurely; for Mrs. Tarwin was only twenty-eight; and the big, wide-open eyes were restless and unquietly bright. "Moira's got nerves," her husband would explain when people enquired why she wasn't with him. Nerves that couldn't stand the strain of London or New York. She had to take things quietly in Florence. A sort of rest cure. "Poor darling!" he would add in a voice that had suddenly become furry with sentiment; and he would illuminate his ordinarily rather blankly intelligent face with one of those lightning smiles of his—so wistful and tender and charming. Almost too charming, one felt uncomfortably. He turned on the charm and the wistfulness like electricity. Click! his face was briefly illumined. And then, click! the light went out again and he was once more the blankly intelligent research student. Cancer was his subject.

Poor Moira! Those nerves of hers! She was full of caprices and obsessions. For example, when she leased the villa on the slopes of Bellosguardo, she wanted to be allowed to cut down the cypresses at the end of the garden. "So terribly like a cemetery," she kept repeating to old Signor Bargioni. Old Bargioni was charming, but firm. He had no intention of sacrificing his cypresses. They gave the finishing touch of perfection to the loveliest view in all Florence; from the best bedroom window you saw the dome and Giotto's tower framed between their dark columns. Inexhaustibly loquacious, he tried to persuade her that cypresses weren't really at all funereal. For the Etruscans, on the contrary (he invented this little piece of archæology on the spur of the moment), the cypress was a symbol of joy; the feasts of the vernal equinox concluded with dances round the sacred tree. Boecklin, it was true, had planted cypresses on his Island of the

Dead. But then Boecklin, after all . . . And if she really found
the trees depressing, she could plant nasturtiums to climb up
them. Or roses. Roses, which the Greeks . . .

"All right, all right," said Moira Tarwin hastily. "Let's leave
the cypresses."

That voice, that endless flow of culture and foreign English!
Old Bargioni was really terrible. She would have screamed if
she had had to listen a moment longer. She yielded in mere self-
defence.

"*E la Tarwinnè?*" questioned Signora Bargioni when her
husband came home.

He shrugged his shoulders. "*Una donnina piuttosto sciocca,*"
was his verdict.

Rather silly. Old Bargioni was not the only man who had
thought so. But he was one of the not so many who regarded
her silliness as a fault. Most of the men who knew her were
charmed by it; they adored while they smiled. In conjunction
with that tiny stature, those eyes, that delicate childish face, her
silliness inspired avuncular devotions and protective loves. She
had a faculty for making men feel, by contrast, agreeably large,
superior, and intelligent. And as luck, or perhaps as ill-luck,
would have it, Moira had passed her life among men who were
really intelligent and what is called superior. Old Sir Watney
Croker, her grandfather, with whom she had lived ever since she
was five (for her father and mother had both died young), was
one of the most eminent physicians of his day. His early mono-
graph on duodenal ulcers remains even now the classical work
on the subject. Between one duodenal ulcer and another Sir
Watney found leisure to adore and indulge and spoil his little
granddaughter. Along with fly-fishing and metaphysics she was
his hobby. Time passed; Moira grew up, chronologically; but
Sir Watney went on treating her as a spoilt child, went on being
enchanted by her birdy chirrupings and ingenuousnesses and
impertinent *enfant-terrible-isms*. He encouraged, he almost compelled her to preserve her childishness. Keeping her a baby in
spite of her age amused him. He loved her babyish and could

only love her so. All those duodenal ulcers—perhaps they had
done something to his sensibility, warped it a little, kept it somehow stunted and un-adult, like Moira herself. In the depths of
his unspecialised, unprofessional being Sir Watney was a bit of
a baby himself. Too much preoccupation with the duodenum
had prevented this neglected instinctive part of him from fully
growing up. Like gravitates to like; old baby Watney loved the
baby in Moira and wanted to keep the young woman permanently childish. Most of his friends shared Sir Watney's tastes.
Doctors, judges, professors, civil servants—every member of
Sir Watney's circle was professionally eminent, a veteran
specialist. To be asked to one of his dinner parties was a privilege. On these august occasions Moira had always, from the age
of seventeen, been present, the only woman at the table. Not
really a woman, Sir Watney explained; a child. The veteran
specialists were all her indulgent uncles. The more childish she
was, the better they liked her. Moira gave them pet names. Professor Stagg, for example, the neo-Hegelian, was Uncle Bonzo;
Mr. Justice Gidley was Giddy Goat. And so on. When they
teased, she answered back impertinently. How they laughed!
When they started to discuss the Absolute or Britain's Industrial
Future, she interjected some deliciously irrelevant remark that
made them laugh even more heartily. Exquisite! And the next
day the story would be told to colleagues in the law-courts or the
hospital, to cronies at the Athenæum. In learned and professional circles Moira enjoyed a real celebrity. In the end she
had ceased not only to be a woman; she had almost ceased to be
a child. She was hardly more than their mascot.

At half-past nine she left the dining-room, and the talk would
come back to ulcers and Reality and Emergent Evolution.

"One would like to keep her as a pet," John Tarwin had said
as the door closed behind her on that first occasion he dined at
Sir Watney's.

Professor Broadwater agreed. There was a little silence. It
was Tarwin who broke it.

"What's your feeling," he asked, leaning forward with that

expression of blank intelligence on his eager, sharp-featured face, "what's *your* feeling about the validity of experiments with artificially grafted tumours as opposed to natural tumours?"

Tarwin was only thirty-three and looked even younger among Sir Watney's veterans. He had already done good work, Sir Watney explained to his assembled guests before the young man's arrival, and might be expected to do much more. An interesting fellow too. Had been all over the place—tropical Africa, India, North and South America. Well off. Not tied to an academic job to earn his living. Had worked here in London, in Germany, at the Rockefeller Institute in New York, in Japan. Enviable opportunities. A great deal to be said for a private income. "Ah, here you are, Tarwin. Good evening. No, not at all late. This is Mr. Justice Gidley, Professor Broadwater, Professor Stagg and—bless me! I hadn't noticed you, Moira; you're really too ultra-microscopic—my granddaughter." Tarwin smiled down at her. She was really ravishing.

Well, now they had been married five years, Moira was thinking, as she powdered her face in front of the looking-glass. Tonino was coming to tea; she had been changing her frock. Through the window behind the mirror one looked down between the cypress trees on to Florence—a jumble of brown roofs, and above them, in the midst, the marble tower and the huge, up-leaping, airy dome. Five years. It was John's photograph in the leather travelling-frame that made her think of their marriage. Why did she keep it there on the dressing-table? Force of habit, she supposed. It wasn't as though the photograph reminded her of days that had been particularly happy. On the contrary. There was something, she now felt, slightly dishonest about keeping it there. Prretending to love him when she didn't. . . . She looked at it again. The profile was sharp and eager. The keen young research student intently focused on a tumour. She really liked him better as a research student than when he was having a soul, or being a poet or a lover. It seemed a dreadful thing to say—but there it was: the research student was of better quality than the human being.

She had always known it—or, rather, not known, felt it. The human being had always made her rather uncomfortable. The more human, the more uncomfortable. She oughtn't ever to have married him, of course. But he asked so persistently; and then he had so much vitality; everybody spoke so well of him; she rather liked his looks; and he seemed to lead such a jolly life, travelling about the world; and she was tired of being a mascot for her grandfather's veterans. There were any number of such little reasons. Added together, she had fancied they would be the equivalent of the one big, cogent reason. But they weren't; she had made a mistake.

Yes, the more human, the more uncomfortable. The disturbing way he turned on the beautiful illumination of his smile! Turned it on suddenly, only to switch it off again with as little warning when something really serious, like cancer or philosophy, had to be discussed. And then his voice, when he was talking about Nature, or Love, or God, or something of that sort—furry with feeling! The quite unnecessarily moved and tremulous way he said Good-bye! "Like a Landseer dog," she told him once, before they were married, laughing and giving a ludicrous imitation of his too heart-felt "Good-bye, Moira." The mockery hurt him. John prided himself as much on his soul and his feelings as upon his intellect; as much on his appreciation of Nature and his poetical love-longings as upon his knowledge of tumours. Goethe was his favourite literary and historical character. Poet and man of science, deep thinker and ardent lover, artist in thought and in life—John saw himself in the rich part. He made her read *Faust* and *Wilhelm Meister*. Moira did her best to feign the enthusiasm she did not feel. Privately she thought Goethe a humbug.

"I oughtn't to have married him," she said to her image in the glass, and shook her head.

John was the pet-fancier as well as the loving educator. There were times when Moira's childishnesses delighted him as much as they had delighted Sir Watney and his veterans, when he laughed at every naïveté or impertinence she uttered, as though it were a piece of the most exquisite wit; and not only laughed, but drew public attention to it, led her on into fresh infantilities and repeated the stories of her exploits to any one who was prepared to listen to them. He was less enthusiastic, however, when Moira had been childish at his expense, when her silliness had in any way compromised *his* dignity or interests. On these occasions he lost his temper, called her a fool, told her she ought to be ashamed of herself. After which, controlling himself, he would become grave, paternal, pedagogic. Moira would be made to feel, miserably, that she wasn't worthy of him. And finally he switched on the smile and made it all up with caresses that left her like a stone.

"And to think," she reflected, putting away her powder-puff, "to think of my spending all that time and energy trying to keep up with him."

All those scientific papers she had read, those outlines of medicine and physiology, those text-books of something or other (she couldn't even remember the name of the science), to say nothing of all that dreary stuff by Goethe! And then all the going out when she had a headache or was tired! All the meeting of people who bored her, but who were really, according to John, so interesting and important! All the travelling, the terribly strenuous sight-seeing, the calling on distinguished foreigners and their generally less distinguished wives! It was difficult for her to keep up even physically—her legs were so short and John was always in such a hurry. Mentally, in spite of all her efforts, she was always a hundred miles behind.

"Awful!" she said aloud.

Her whole marriage had really been awful. From that awful honeymoon at Capri, when he had made her walk too far, too fast, uphill, only to read her extracts from Wordsworth when they reached the *Aussichtspunkt*; when he had talked to her about love and made it, much too frequently, and told her the Latin names of the plants and butterflies—from that awful honeymoon to the time when, four months ago, her nerves had gone all to pieces and the doctor had said that she must take things quietly,

N

apart from John. Awful! The life had nearly killed her. And it wasn't (she had come at last to realise), it wasn't really a life at all. It was just a galvanic activity, like the twitching of a dead frog's leg when you touch the nerve with an electrified wire. Not life, just galvanised death.

She remembered the last of their quarrels, just before the doctor had told her to go away. John had been sitting at her feet, with his head against her knee. And his head was beginning to go bald! She could hardly bear to look at those long hairs plastered across the scalp. And because he was tired with all that microscope work, tired and at the same time (not having made love to her, thank goodness! for more than a fortnight) amorous, as she could tell by the look in his eyes, he was being very sentimental and talking in his furriest voice about Love and Beauty and the necessity for being like Goethe. Talking till she felt like screaming aloud. And at last she could bear it no longer.

"For goodness' sake, John," she said in a voice that was on the shrill verge of being out of control, "be quiet!"

"What *is* the matter?" He looked up at her questioningly, pained.

"Talking like that!" She was indignant. "But you've never loved anybody, outside yourself. Nor felt the beauty of anything. Any more than that old humbug Goethe. You know what you *ought* to feel when there's a woman about, or a landscape; you know what the best people feel. And you deliberately set yourself to feel the same, out of your head."

John was wounded to the quick of his vanity. "How can you say that?"

"Because it's true, it's true. You only live out of your head. And it's a bald head too," she added, and began to laugh, uncontrollably.

What a scene there had been! She went on laughing all the time he raged at her; she couldn't stop.

"You're hysterical," he said at last; and then he calmed down. The poor child was ill. With an effort he switched on the expression of paternal tenderness and went to fetch the sal volatile.

One last dab at her lips, and there! she was ready. She went downstairs to the drawing-room, to find that Tonino had already arrived—he was always early—and was waiting. He rose as she entered, bowed over her outstretched hand and kissed it. Moira was always charmed by his florid, rather excessive Southern good manners. John was always too busy being the keen research student or the furry-voiced poet to have good manners. He didn't think politeness particularly important. It was the same with clothes. He was chronically ill-dressed. Tonino, on the other hand, was a model of dapper elegance. That pale grey suit, that lavender-coloured tie, those piebald shoes of white kid and patent leather—marvellous!

One of the pleasures or dangers of foreign travel is that you lose your class-consciousness. At home you can never, with the best will in the world, forget it. Habit has rendered your own people as immediately legible as your own language. A word, a gesture are sufficient; your man is placed. But in foreign parts your fellows are unreadable. The less obvious products of upbringing—all the subtler refinements, the finer shades of vulgarity—escape your notice. The accent, the inflexion of voice, the vocabulary, the gestures tell you nothing. Between the duke and the insurance clerk, the profiteer and the country gentleman, your inexperienced eye and ear detect no difference. For Moira, Tonino seemed the characteristic flower of Italian gentility. She knew, of course, that he wasn't well off; but then, plenty of the nicest people are poor. She saw in him the equivalent of one of those younger sons of impoverished English squires—the sort of young man who advertises for work in the Agony Column of the *Times*. "Public School education, sporting tastes; would accept any well-paid position of trust and confidence." She would have been pained, indignant, and surprised to hear old Bargioni describing him, after their first meeting, as "*il tipo del varrucchiere napoletano*"—the typical Neapolitan barber. Signora Bargioni shook her head over the approaching scandal and was secretly delighted.

As a matter of actual fact Tonino was not a barber. He was

the son of a capitalist—on a rather small scale, no doubt; but still a genuine capitalist. Vasari senior owned a restaurant at Pozzuoli and was ambitious to start a hotel. Tonino had been sent to study the tourist industry with a family friend who was the manager of one of the best establishments in Florence. When he had learnt all the secrets, he was to return to Pozzuoli and be the managing director of the rejuvenated boarding-house which his father was modestly proposing to rechristen the Grand Hotel Ritz-Carlton. Meanwhile, he was an underworked lounger in Florence. He had made Mrs. Tarwin's acquaintance romantically, on the highway. Driving, as was her custom, alone, Moira had run over a nail. A puncture. Nothing is easier than changing wheels—nothing, that is to say, if you have sufficient muscular strength to undo the nuts which hold the punctured wheel to its axle. Moira had not. When Tonino came upon her, ten minutes after the mishap, she was sitting on the running-board of the car, flushed and dishevelled with her efforts, and in tears.

"*Una signora forestiera.*" At the café that evening Tonino recounted his adventure with a certain rather fatuous self-satisfaction. In the small bourgeoisie in which he had been brought up, a Foreign Lady was an almost fabulous creature, a being of legendary wealth, eccentricity, independence. "*Inglese,*" he specified. "*Giovane,*" and "*bella, bellissima.*" His auditors were incredulous; beauty, for some reason, is not common among the specimens of English womanhood seen in foreign parts. "*Ricca,*" he added. That sounded less intrinsically improbable; foreign ladies were all rich, almost by definition. Juicily, and with unction, Tonino described the car she drove, the luxurious villa she inhabited.

Acquaintance had ripened quickly into friendship. This was the fourth or fifth time in a fortnight that he had come to the house.

"A few poor flowers," said the young man in a tone of soft, ingratiating apology; and he brought forward his left hand, which he had been hiding behind his back. It held a bouquet of white roses.

"But how kind of you!" she cried in her bad Italian. "How lovely!" John never brought flowers to any one; he regarded that sort of thing as rather nonsensical. She smiled at Tonino over the blossoms. "Thank you a thousand times."

Making a deprecating gesture, he returned her smile. His teeth flashed pearly and even. His large eyes were bright, dark, liquid, and rather expressionless, like a gazelle's. He was exceedingly good-looking. "White roses for the white rose," he said.

Moira laughed. The compliment was ridiculous; but it pleased her all the same.

Paying compliments was not the only thing Tonino could do. He knew how to be useful. When, a few days later, Moira decided to have the rather dingy hall and dining-room redistempered, he was invaluable. It was he who haggled with the decorator, he who made scenes when there were delays, he who interpreted Moira's rather special notions about colours to the workmen, he who superintended their activities.

"If it hadn't been for you," said Moira gratefully, when the work was finished, "I'd have been hopelessly swindled and they wouldn't have done anything properly."

It was such a comfort, she reflected, having a man about the place who didn't always have something more important to do and think about; a man who could spend his time being useful and a help. Such a comfort! And such a change! When she was with John, it was she who had to do all the tiresome, practical things. John always had his work, and his work took precedence of everything, including her convenience. Tonino was just an ordinary man, with nothing in the least superhuman about either himself or his functions. It was a great relief.

Little by little Moira came to rely on him for everything. He made himself universally useful. The fuses blew out; it was Tonino who replaced them. The hornets nested in the drawing-room chimney; heroically Tonino stank them out with sulphur. But his speciality was domestic economy. Brought up in a restaurant, he knew everything there was to be known about food and drink and prices. When the meat was unsatisfactory, he went to the butcher and threw the tough beefsteak in his teeth, almost literally. He beat down the extortionate charges of the green-grocer. With a man at the fish market he made a friendly arrangement whereby Moira was to have the pick of the soles and the red mullet. He bought her wine for her, her oil— wholesale, in huge glass demijohns; and Moira, who since Sir Watney's death could have afforded to drink nothing cheaper than Pol Roger 1911 and do her cooking in imported yak's butter, exulted with him in long domestic conversations over economies of a farthing a quart or a shilling or two on a hundred-weight. For Tonino the price and the quality of victuals and drink were matters of gravest importance. To secure a flask of Chianti for five lire ninety instead of six lire was, in his eyes, a real victory; and the victory became a triumph if it could be proved that the Chianti was fully three years old and had an alcohol content of more than fourteen per cent. By nature Moira was neither greedy nor avaricious. Her upbringing had confirmed her in her natural tendencies. She had the disinterested-ness of those who have never known a shortage of cash; and her abstemious indifference to the pleasures of the table had never been tempered by the housewife's pre-occupation with other people's appetites and digestions. Never; for Sir Watney had kept a professional housekeeper, and with John Tarwin, who anyhow hardly noticed what he ate, and thought that women ought to spend their time doing more important and intellectual things than presiding over kitchens, she had lived for the greater part of their married life in hotels or service flats, or else in furnished rooms and in a chronic state of picnic. Tonino re-vealed to her the world of markets and the kitchen. Still accus-tomed to thinking, with John, that ordinary domestic life wasn't good enough, she laughed at first at his earnest preoccupation with meat and halfpence. But after a little she began to be in-fected by his almost religious enthusiasm for housekeeping; she began to discover that meat and halfpence were interesting after all, that they were real and important—much more real and im-

portant, for example, than reading Goethe when one found him
a bore and a humbug. Tenderly brooded over by the most competent of solicitors and brokers, the late Sir Watney's fortune
was bringing in a steady five per cent. free of tax. But in Tonino's
company Moira could forget her bank balance. Descending
from the financial Sinai on which she had been lifted so high
above the common earth, she discovered, with him, the preoccupations of poverty. They were curiously interesting and
exciting.

"The prices they ask for fish in Florence!" said Tonino, after
a silence, when he had exhausted the subject of white roses.
"When I think how little we pay for octopus at Naples! It's
scandalous."

"Scandalous!" echoed Moira with an indignation as genuine
as his own. They talked, interminably.

Next day the sky was no longer blue, but opaquely white.
There was no sunshine, only a diffused glare that threw no
shadows. The landscape lay utterly lifeless under the dead and
fishy stare of heaven. It was very hot, there was no wind, the air
was hardly breathable and as though woolly. Moira woke up
with a headache, and her nerves seemed to have an uneasy life of
their own, apart from hers. Like caged birds they were, fluttering
and starting and twittering at every alarm; and her aching, tired
body was their aviary. Quite against her own wish and intention
she found herself in a temper with the maid and saying the un-
kindest things. She had to give her a pair of stockings to make
up for it. When she was dressed, she wanted to write some
letters; but her fountain-pen made a stain on her fingers and she
was so furious that she threw the beastly thing out of the window.
It broke to pieces on the flagstones below. She had nothing to
write with; it was too exasperating. She washed the ink off her
hands and took out her embroidery frame. But her fingers were
all thumbs. And then she pricked herself with the needle. Oh,
so painfully! The tears came into her eyes; she began to cry.
And having begun, she couldn't stop. Assunta came in five
minutes later and found her sobbing. "But what is it, signora?"

she asked, made most affectionately solicitous by the gift of the stockings. Moira shook her head. "Go away," she said brokenly. The girl was insistent. "Go away," Moira repeated. How could she explain what was the matter when the only thing that had happened was that she had pricked her finger? Nothing was the matter. And yet everything was the matter, everything.

The everything that was the matter resolved itself finally into the weather. Even in the best of health Moira had always been painfully conscious of the approach of thunder. Her jangled nerves were more than ordinarily sensitive. The tears and furies and despairs of this horrible day had a purely meteorological cause. But they were none the less violent and agonising for that. The hours passed dismally. Thickened by huge black clouds, the twilight came on in a sultry and expectant silence, and it was prematurely night. The reflection of distant lightnings, flashing far away below the horizon, illuminated the eastern sky. The peaks and ridges of the Apennines stood out black against the momentary pale expanses of silvered vapour and disappeared again in silence; the attentive hush was still unbroken. With a kind of sinking apprehension—for she was terrified of storms—Moira sat at her window, watching the black hills leap out against the silver and die again, leap out and die. The flashes brightened; and then, for the first time, she heard the approaching thunder, far off and faint like the whisper of the sea in a shell. Moira shuddered. The clock in the hall struck nine, and, as though the sound were a signal prearranged, a gust of wind suddenly shook the magnolia tree that stood at the crossing of the paths in the garden below. Its long stiff leaves rattled together like scales of horn. There was another flash. In the brief white glare she could see the two funereal cypresses writhing and tossing as though in the desperate agitation of pain. And then all at once the storm burst catastrophically, it seemed directly overhead. At the savage violence of that icy downpour Moira shrank back and shut the window. A streak of white fire zigzagged fearfully just behind the cypresses. The immediate thunder was like the splitting and fall of a solid vault. Moira

rushed away from the window and threw herself on the bed.
She covered her face with her hands. Through the continuous
roaring of the rain the thunder crashed and reverberated, crashed
again and sent the fragments of sound rolling unevenly in all
directions through the night. The whole house trembled. In the
window-frames the shaken glasses rattled like the panes of an old
omnibus rolling across the cobbles.

"Oh God, oh God," Moira kept repeating. In the enormous
tumult her voice was small and, as it were, naked, utterly
abject.

"But it's too stupid to be frightened." She remembered John's
voice, his brightly encouraging, superior manner. "The chances
are thousands to one against your being struck. And anyhow,
hiding your head won't prevent the lightning from . . ."

How she hated him for being so reasonable and right! "Oh
God!" There was another. "God, God, God. . . ."

And then suddenly a terrible thing happened; the light went
out. Through her closed eyelids she saw no longer the red of
translucent blood, but utter blackness. Uncovering her face, she
opened her eyes and anxiously looked round—on blackness
again. She fumbled for the switch by her bed, found it, turned
and turned; the darkness remained impenetrable.

"Assunta!" she called.

And all at once the square of the window was a suddenly un-
covered picture of the garden, seen against a background of
mauve-white sky and shining, down-pouring rain.

"Assunta!" Her voice was drowned in a crash that seemed to
have exploded in the very roof. "Assunta, Assunta!" In a panic
she stumbled across the grave-dark room to the door. Another
flash revealed the handle. She opened. "Assunta!"

Her voice was hollow above the black gulf of the stairs. The
thunder exploded again above her. With a crash and a tinkle of
broken glass one of the windows in her room burst open. A
blast of cold wind lifted her hair. A flight of papers rose from her
writing-table and whirled with crackling wings through the
darkness. One touched her cheek like a living thing and was

gone. She screamed aloud. The door slammed behind her. She ran down the stairs in terror, as though the fiend were at her heels. In the hall she met Assunta and the cook coming towards her, lighting matches as they came.

"Assunta, the lights!" She clutched the girl's arm.

Only the thunder answered. When the noise subsided, Assunta explained that the fuses had all blown out and that there wasn't a candle in the house. Not a single candle, and only one more box of matches.

"But then we shall be left in the dark," said Moira hysterically.

Through the three blackly reflecting windows of the hall three separate pictures of the streaming garden revealed themselves and vanished. The old Venetian mirrors on the walls blinked for an instant into life, like dead eyes briefly opened.

"In the dark," she repeated with an almost mad insistence.

"Aie!" cried Assunta, and dropped the match that had begun to burn her fingers. The thunder fell on them out of a darkness made denser and more hopeless by the loss of light.

When the telephone bell rang, Tonino was sitting in the managerial room of his hotel, playing cards with the proprietor's two sons and another friend. "Some one to speak to you, Signor Tonino," said the under-porter, looking in. "A lady." He grinned significantly.

Tonino put on a dignified air and left the room. When he returned a few minutes later, he held his hat in one hand and was buttoning up his rain-coat with the other.

"Sorry," he said. "I've got to go out."

"Go out?" exclaimed the others incredulously. Beyond the shuttered windows the storm roared like a cataract and savagely exploded. "But where?" they asked. "Why? Are you mad?"

Tonino shrugged his shoulders, as though it were nothing to go out into a tornado, as though he were used to it. The *signora forestiera*, he explained, hating them for their inquisitiveness; the Tarwin—she had asked him to go up to Bellosguardo at once. The fuses . . . not a candle in the house . . . utterly in the dark . . . very agitated . . . nerves. . . .

"But on a night like this. . . . But you're not the electrician."
The two sons of the proprietor spoke in chorus. They felt, indignantly, that Tonino was letting himself be exploited.

But the third young man leaned back in his chair and laughed.
"*Vai, caro, vai,*" he said, and then, shaking his finger at Tonino
knowingly, "*Ma fatti pagare per il tuo lavoro,*" he added. "Get
yourself paid for your trouble." Berto was notoriously the lady-
killer, the tried specialist in amorous strategy, the acknowledged
expert. "Take the opportunity." The others joined in his rather
unpleasant laughter. Tonino also grinned and nodded.

The taxi rushed splashing through the wet deserted streets
like a travelling fountain. Tonino sat in the darkness of the cab
ruminating Berto's advice. She was pretty, certainly. But somehow—why was it?—it had hardly occurred to him to think of
her as a possible mistress. He had been politely gallant with her
—on principle almost, and by force of habit—but without really
wanting to succeed; and when she had shown herself unrespon-
sive, he hadn't cared. But perhaps he ought to have cared,
perhaps he ought to have tried harder. In Berto's world it was a
sporting duty to do one's best to seduce every woman one could.
The most admirable man was the man with the greatest number
of women to his credit. Really lovely, Tonino went on to himself, trying to work up an enthusiasm for the sport. It would be
a triumph to be proud of. The more so as she was a foreigner.
And very rich. He thought with inward satisfaction of that big
car, of the house, the servants, the silver. "*Certo,*" he said to
himself complacently, "*mi vuol bene.*" She liked him; there was
no doubt of it. Meditatively he stroked his smooth face; the
muscles stirred a little under his fingers. He was smiling to himself in the darkness; naïvely, an ingenuous prostitute's smile.
"*Moira,*" he said aloud. "*Moira. Strano, quel nome. Piuttosto
ridicolo.*"

It was Moira who opened the door for him. She had been
standing at the window, looking out, waiting and waiting.

"Tonino!" She held out both her hands to him; she had never
felt so glad to see any one.

The sky went momentarily whitish-mauve behind him as he stood there in the open doorway. The skirts of his rain-coat fluttered in the wind; a wet gust blew past him, chilling her face. The sky went black again. He slammed the door behind him. They were in utter darkness.

"Tonino, it was too sweet of you to have come. Really too . . ."

The thunder that interrupted her was like the end of the world. Moira shuddered. "Oh God!" she whimpered; and then suddenly she was pressing her face against his waistcoat and crying, and Tonino was holding her and stroking her hair. The next flash showed him the position of the sofa. In the ensuing darkness he carried her across the room, sat down and began to kiss her tear-wet face. She lay quite still in his arms, relaxed, like a frightened child that has at last found comfort. Tonino held her, kissing her softly again and again. "*Ti amo, Moira*," he whispered. And it was true. Holding her, touching her in the dark, he did love her. "*Ti amo.*" How profoundly, "*Ti voglio un bene immenso*," he went on, with a passion, a deep warm tenderness born almost suddenly of darkness and soft blind contact. Heavy and warm with life, she lay pressed against him. Her body curved and was solid under his hands, her cheeks were rounded and cool, her eyelids rounded and tremulous and tear-wet, her mouth so soft, so soft under his touching lips. "*Ti amo, ti amo.*" He was breathless with love, and it was as though there were a hollowness at the centre of his being, a void of desiring tenderness that longed to be filled, that could only be filled by her, an emptiness that drew her towards him, into him, that drank her as an empty vessel eagerly drinks the water. Still, with closed eyes, quite still she lay there in his arms, suffering herself to be drunk up by his tenderness, to be drawn into the yearning vacancy of his heart, happy in being passive, in yielding herself to his soft insistent passion.

"*Fatti pagare, fatti pagare.*" The memory of Berto's words transformed him suddenly from a lover into an amorous sportsman with a reputation to keep up and records to break. "*Fatti pagare.*" He risked a more intimate caress. But Moira winced so shudderingly at the touch that he desisted, ashamed of himself.

"*Ebbene,*" asked Berto when, an hour later, he returned, "did you mend the fuses?"

"Yes, I mended the fuses."

"And did you get yourself paid?"

Tonino smiled an amorous sportsman's smile. "A little on account," he answered, and at once disliked himself for having spoken the words, disliked the others for laughing at them. Why did he go out of his way to spoil something which had been so beautiful? Pretexting a headache, he went upstairs to his bedroom. The storm had passed on, the moon was shining now out of a clear sky. He opened the window and looked out. A river of ink and quicksilver, the Arno flowed whispering past. In the street below the puddles shone like living eyes. The ghost of Caruso was singing from a gramophone, far away on the other side of the water. "*Stretti, stretti, nell' estasì d'amor. . . .*" Tonino was profoundly moved.

The sky was blue next morning, the sunlight glittered on the shiny leaves of the magnolia tree, the air was demurely windless. Sitting at her dressing-table, Moira looked out and wondered incredulously if such things as storms were possible. But the plants were broken and prostrate in their beds; the paths were strewn with scattered leaves and petals. In spite of the soft air and the sunlight, last night's horrors had been more than a bad dream. Moira sighed and began to brush her hair. Set in its leather frame, John Tarwin's profile confronted her, brightly focused on imaginary tumours. Her eyes fixed on it, Moira went on mechanically brushing her hair. Then, suddenly, interrupting the rhythm of her movements, she got up, took the leather frame and, walking across the room, threw it up, out of sight, on to the top of the high wardrobe. There! She returned to her seat and, filled with a kind of frightened elation, went on with her interrupted brushing.

When she was dressed, she drove down to the town and spent

an hour at Settepassi's, the jewellers. When she left, she was bowed out on to the Lungarno like a princess.

"No, don't smoke those," she said to Tonino that afternoon as he reached for a cigarette in the silver box that stood on the drawing-room mantelpiece. "I've got a few of those Egyptian ones you like. Got them specially for you." And, smiling, she handed him a little parcel.

Tonino thanked her profusely—too profusely, as was his custom. But when he had stripped away the paper and saw the polished gold of a large cigarette-case, he could only look at her in an embarrassed and enquiring amazement.

"Don't you think it's rather pretty?" she asked.

"Marvellous! But is it . . ." He hesitated. "Is it for me?"

Moira laughed with pleasure at his embarrassment. She had never seen him embarrassed before. He was always the self-possessed young man of the world, secure and impregnable within his armour of Southern good manners. She admired that elegant carapace. But it amused her for once to take him without it, to see him at a loss, blushing and stammering like a little boy. It amused and it pleased her; she liked him all the more for being the little boy as well as the polished and socially competent young man.

"For me?" she mimicked, laughing. "Do you like it?" Her tone changed; she became grave. "I wanted you to have something to remind you of last night." Tonino took her hands and silently kissed them. She had received him with such off-handed gaiety, so nonchalantly, as though nothing had happened, that the tender references to last night's happenings (so carefully prepared as he walked up the hill) had remained unspoken. He had been afraid of saying the wrong thing and offending her. But now the spell was broken—and by Moira herself. "One oughtn't to forget one's good actions," Moira went on, abandoning him her hands. "Each time you take a cigarette out of this case, will you remember how kind and good you were to a silly ridiculous little fool?"

Tonino had had time to recover his manners. "I shall re-

member the most adorable, the most beautiful . . ." Still holding her hands, he looked at her for a moment in silence, eloquently. Moira smiled back at him. "Moira!" And she was in
his arms. She shut her eyes and was passive in the strong circle
of his arms, soft and passive against his firm body. "I love you,
Moira." The breath of his whispering was warm on her cheek.
"*Ti amo.*" And suddenly his lips were on hers again, violently,
impatiently kissing. Between the kisses his whispered words
came passionate to her ears. "*Ti amo pazzamente . . . piccina
. . . tesoro . . . amore . . . cuore . . .*" Uttered in Italian, his love
seemed somehow specially strong and deep. Things described
in a strange language themselves take on a certain strangeness.
"*Amami, Moira, amami. Mi ami un po?*" He was insistent. "A
little, Moira—do you love me a little?"

She opened her eyes and looked at him. Then, with a quick
movement, she took his face between her two hands, drew it
down and kissed him on the mouth. "Yes," she whispered, "I
love you." And then, gently, she pushed him away. Tonino
wanted to kiss her again. But Moira shook her head and slipped
away from him. "No, no," she said with a kind of peremptory
entreaty. "Don't spoil it all now."

The days passed, hot and golden. Summer approached. The
nightingales sang unseen in the cool of the evening.

"*L'usignuolo,*" Moira whispered softly to herself as she listened
to the singing. "*L'usignuolo.*" Even the nightingales were subtly
better in Italian. The sun had set. They were sitting in the little
summer-house at the end of the garden, looking out over the
darkening landscape. The white-walled farms and villas on the
slope below stood out almost startlingly clear against the twilight
of the olive trees, as though charged with some strange and novel
significance. Moira sighed. "I'm so happy," she said; Tonino
took her hand. "Ridiculously happy." For, after all, she was
thinking, it *was* rather ridiculous to be so happy for no valid
reason. John Tarwin had taught her to imagine that one could
only be happy when one was doing something "interesting" (as
he put it), or associating with people who were "worth while."

Tonino was nobody in particular, thank goodness! And going for picnics wasn't exactly "interesting" in John's sense of the word; nor was talking about the respective merits of different brands of car; nor teaching him to drive; nor going shopping; nor discussing the problem of new curtains for the drawing-room; nor, for that matter, sitting in the summer-house and saying nothing. In spite of which, or because of which, she was happy with an unprecedented happiness. "Ridiculously happy," she repeated.

Tonino kissed her hand. "So am I," he said. And he was not merely being polite. In his own way he was genuinely happy with her. People envied him sitting in that magnificent yellow car at her side. She was so pretty and elegant, so foreign too; he was proud to be seen about with her. And then the cigarette-case, the gold-mounted, agate-handled cane she had given him for his birthday. . . . Besides, he was really very fond of her, really, in an obscure way, in love with her. It was not for nothing that he had held and caressed her in the darkness of that night of thunder. Something of that deep and passionate tenderness, born suddenly of the night and their warm sightless contact, still remained in him—still remained even after the physical longings she then inspired had been vicariously satisfied. (And under Berto's knowing guidance they *had* been satisfied, frequently.) If it hadn't been for Berto's satirical comments on the still platonic nature of his attachment, he would have been perfectly content.

"*Alle donne*," Berto sententiously generalised, "*piace sempre la violenza*. They long to be raped. You don't know how to make love, my poor boy." And he would hold up his own achievements as examples to be followed. For Berto, love was a kind of salacious vengeance on women for the crime of their purity.

Spurred on by his friend's mockeries, Tonino made another attempt to exact full payment for his mending of the fuses on the night of the storm. But his face was so soundly slapped, and the tone in which Moira threatened never to see him again unless he behaved himself was so convincingly stern, that he did not renew his attack. He contented himself with looking sad and complaining of her cruelty. But in spite of his occasionally long face, he was happy with her. Happy like a fireside cat. The car, the house, her elegant foreign prettiness, the marvellous presents she gave him, kept him happily purring.

The days passed and the weeks. Moira would have liked life to flow on like this for ever, a gay bright stream with occasional reaches of calm sentimentality but never dangerously deep or turbulent, without fall or whirl or rapid. She wanted her existence to remain for ever what it was at this moment—a kind of game with a pleasant and emotionally exciting companion, a playing at living and loving. If only this happy play-time could last for ever!

It was John Tarwin who decreed that it should not. "ATTENDING CYTOLOGICAL CONGRESS ROME WILL STOP FEW DAYS ON WAY ARRIVING THURSDAY LOVE JOHN." That was the text of the telegram Moira found awaiting her on her return to the villa one evening. She read it and felt suddenly depressed and apprehensive. Why did he want to come? He would spoil everything. The bright evening went dead before her eyes; the happiness with which she had been brimming when she returned with Tonino from that marvellous drive among the Apennines was drained out of her. Her gloom retrospectively darkened the blue and golden beauty of the mountains, put out the bright flowers, dimmed the day's laughter and talk. "Why does he want to come?" Miserably and resentfully, she wondered. "And what's going to happen, what's going to happen?" She felt cold and rather breathless and almost sick with the questioning apprehension.

John's face, when he saw her standing there at the station, lit up instantaneously with all its hundred-candle-power tenderness and charm.

"My darling!" His voice was furry and tremulous. He leaned towards her; stiffening, Moira suffered herself to be kissed. His nails, she noticed disgustedly, were dirty.

The prospect of a meal alone with John had appalled her; she

had asked Tonino to dinner. Besides, she wanted John to meet
him. To have kept Tonino's existence a secret from John would
have been to admit that there was something wrong in her relations with him. And there wasn't. She wanted John to meet him
just like that, naturally, as a matter of course. Whether he'd like
Tonino when he'd met him was another question. Moira had her
doubts. They were justified by the event. John had begun by
protesting when he heard that she had invited a guest. Their first
evening—how could she? The voice trembled—fur in a breeze.
She had to listen to outpourings of sentiment. But finally, when
dinner-time arrived, he switched off the pathos and became once
more the research student. Brightly enquiring, blankly intelligent, John cross-questioned his guest about all the interesting
and important things that were happening in Italy. What was
the real political situation? How did the new educational system
work? What did people think of the reformed penal code? On
all these matters Tonino was, of course, far less well-informed
than his interrogator. The Italy he knew was the Italy of his
friends and his family, of shops and cafés and girls and the daily
fight for money. All that historical, impersonal Italy, of which
John so intelligently read in the high-class reviews, was utterly
unknown to him. His answers to John's questions were child-
ishly silly. Moira sat listening, dumb with misery.

"What *do* you find in that fellow?" her husband asked, when
Tonino had taken his leave. "He struck me as quite particularly
uninteresting."

Moira did not answer. There was a silence. John suddenly
switched on his tenderly, protectively, yearningly marital smile.
"Time to go to bed, my sweetheart," he said. Moira looked up
at him and saw in his eyes that expression she knew so well and
dreaded. "My sweetheart," he repeated, and the Landseer dog
was also amorous. He put his arms round her and bent to kiss
her face. Moira shuddered—but helplessly, dumbly, not knowing how to escape. He led her away.

When John had left her, she lay awake far into the night, remembering his ardours and his sentimentalities with a horror

that the passage of time seemed actually to increase. Sleep came at last to deliver her.

Being an archæologist, old Signor Bargioni was decidedly "interesting."

"But he bores me to death," said Moira when, next day, her husband suggested that they should go and see him. "That voice! And the way he goes on and on! And that beard! And his wife!"

John flushed with anger. "Don't be childish," he snapped out, forgetting how much he enjoyed her childishness when it didn't interfere with his amusements or his business. "After all," he insisted, "there's probably no man living who knows more about Tuscany in the Dark Ages."

Nevertheless, in spite of darkest Tuscany, John had to pay his call without her. He spent a most improving hour, chatting about Romanesque architecture and the Lombard kings. But just before he left, the conversation somehow took another turn; casually, as though by chance, Tonino's name was mentioned. It was the signora who had insisted that it should be mentioned. Ignorance, her husband protested, is bliss. But Signora Bargioni loved scandal, and being middle-aged, ugly, envious, and malicious, was full of righteous indignation against the young wife and of hypocritical sympathy for the possibly injured husband. Poor Tarwin, she insisted—he ought to be warned. And so, tactfully, without seeming to say anything in particular, the old man dropped his hints.

Walking back to Bellosguardo, John was uneasily pensive. It was not that he imagined that Moira had been, or was likely to prove, unfaithful. Such things really didn't happen to oneself. Moira obviously liked the uninteresting young man; but, after all, and in spite of her childishness, Moira was a civilised human being. She had been too well brought up to do anything stupid. Besides, he reflected, remembering the previous evening, remembering all the years of their marriage, she had no temperament; she didn't know what passion was, she was utterly without sensuality. Her native childishness would reinforce her principles. Infants may be relied on to be pure; but not (and this was what troubled John Tarwin) worldly-wise. Moira wouldn't allow herself to be made love to ; but she might easily let herself be swindled. Old Bargioni had been very discreet and non-committal; but it was obvious that he regarded this young fellow as an adventurer, out for what he could get. John frowned as he walked, and bit his lip.

He came home to find Moira and Tonino superintending the fitting of the new cretonne covers for the drawing-room chairs.

"Carefully, carefully," Moira was saying to the upholsterer as he came in. She turned at the sound of his footsteps. A cloud seemed to obscure the brightness of her face when she saw him; but she made an effort to keep up her gaiety. "Come and look, John," she called. "It's like getting a very fat old lady into a very tight dress. Too ridiculous!"

But John did not smile with her; his face was a mask of stony gravity. He stalked up to the chair, nodded curtly to Tonino, curtly to the upholsterer, and stood there watching the work as though he were a stranger, a hostile stranger at that. The sight of Moira and Tonino laughing and talking together had roused in him a sudden and violent fury. "Disgusting little adventurer," he said to himself ferociously behind his mask.

"It's a pretty stuff, don't you think?" said Moira. He only grunted.

"Very modern too," added Tonino. "The shops are very modern here," he went on, speaking with all the rather touchy insistence on up-to-dateness which characterises the inhabitants of an under-bathroomed and over-monumented country.

"Indeed?" said John sarcastically.

Moira frowned. "You've no idea how helpful Tonino has been," she said with a certain warmth.

Effusively Tonino began to deny that she had any obligation towards him. John Tarwin interrupted him. "Oh, I've no doubt he was helpful," he said in the same sarcastic tone and with a little smile of contempt.

There was an uncomfortable silence. Then Tonino took his

leave. The moment he was gone, Moira turned on her husband. Her face was pale, her lips trembled. "How dare you speak to one of my friends like that?" she asked in a voice unsteady with anger.

John flared up. "Because I wanted to get rid of the fellow," he answered; and the mask was off, his face was nakedly furious. "It's disgusting to see a man like that hanging round the house. An adventurer. Exploiting your silliness. Sponging on you."

"Tonino doesn't sponge on me. And anyhow, what do you know about it?"

He shrugged his shoulders. "One hears things."

"Oh, it's those old beasts, is it?" She hated the Bargionis, *hated* them. "Instead of being grateful to Tonino for helping me! Which is more than you've ever done, John. You, with your beastly tumours and your rotten old *Faust!*" The contempt in her voice was blasting. "Just leaving me to sink or swim. And when somebody comes along and is just humanly decent to me, you insult him. And you fly into a rage of jealousy because I'm normally grateful to him."

John had had time to readjust his mask. "I don't fly into any sort of rage," he said, bottling his anger and speaking slowly and coldly. "I just don't want you to be preyed upon by handsome, black-haired young pimps from the slums of Naples."

"John!"

"Even if the preying *is* done platonically," he went on. "Which I'm sure it is. But I don't want to have even a platonic pimp about." He spoke coldly, slowly, with the deliberate intention of hurting her as much as he could. "How much has he got out of you so far?"

Moira did not answer, but turned and hurried from the room.

Tonino had just got to the bottom of the hill, when a loud insistent hooting made him turn round. A big yellow car was close at his heels.

"Moira!" he called in astonishment. The car came to a halt beside him.

"Get in," she commanded almost fiercely, as though she were angry with him. He did as he was told.

"But where did you think of going?" he asked.

"I don't know. Anywhere. Let's take the Bologna road, into the mountains."

"But you've got no hat," he objected, "no coat."

She only laughed and, throwing the car into gear, drove off at full speed. John spent his evening in solitude. He began by reproaching himself. "I oughtn't to have spoken so brutally," he thought, when he heard of Moira's precipitate departure. What tender, charming things he would say, when she came back, to make up for his hard words! And then, when she'd made peace, he would talk to her gently, paternally about the dangers of having bad friends. Even the anticipation of what he would say to her caused his face to light up with a beautiful smile. But when, three-quarters of an hour after dinner-time, he sat down to a lonely and overcooked meal, his mood had changed. "If she wants to sulk," he said to himself, "why, let her sulk." And as the hours passed, his heart grew harder. Midnight struck. His anger began to be tempered by a certain apprehension. Could anything have happened to her? He was anxious. But all the same he went to bed, on principle, firmly. Twenty minutes later he heard Moira's step on the stairs and then the closing of her door. She was back; nothing had happened; perversely, he felt all the more exasperated with her for being safe. Would she come and say good-night? He waited.

Absently, meanwhile, mechanically, Moira had undressed. She was thinking of all that had happened in the eternity since she had left the house. That marvellous sunset in the mountains! Every westward slope was rosily gilded; below them lay a gulf of blue shadow. They had stood in silence, gazing. "Kiss me, Tonino," she had suddenly whispered, and the touch of his lips had sent a kind of delicious apprehension fluttering under her skin. She pressed herself against him; his body was firm and solid within her clasp. She could feel the throb of his heart against her cheek, like something separately alive. Beat, beat,

beat—and the throbbing life was not the life of the Tonino she
knew, the Tonino who laughed and paid compliments and
brought flowers; it was the life of some mysterious and separate
power. A power with which the familiar individual Tonino happened to be connected, but almost irrelevantly. She shuddered a
little. Mysterious and terrifying. But the terror was somehow
attractive, like a dark precipice that allures. "Kiss me, Tonino,
kiss me." The light faded; the hills died away into featureless
flat shapes against the sky. "I'm cold," she said at last, shivering.
"Let's go." They dined at a little inn, high up between the two
passes. When they drove away, it was night. He put his arm
round her and kissed her neck, at the nape, where the cropped
hair was harsh against his mouth. "You'll make me drive into
the ditch," she laughed. But there was no laughter for Tonino.
"Moira, Moira," he repeated; and there was something like agony
in his voice. "Moira." And finally, at his suffering entreaty, she
stopped the car. They got out. Under the chestnut trees, what
utter darkness!

Moira slipped off her last garment and, naked before the mirror,
looked at her image. It seemed the same as ever, her pale body; but
in reality it was different, it was new, it had only just been born.

John still waited, but his wife did not come. "All right, then,"
he said to himself, with a spiteful little anger that disguised itself
as a god-like and impersonal serenity of justice; "let her sulk if
she wants to. She only punishes herself." He turned out the
light and composed himself to sleep. Next morning he left for
Rome and the Cytological Congress without saying good-bye;
that would teach her. But "thank goodness!" was Moira's first
reflection when she heard that he had gone. And then, suddenly,
she felt rather sorry for him. Poor John! Like a dead frog,
galvanised; twitching, but never alive. He was pathetic really.
She was so rich in happiness, that she could afford to be sorry
for him. And in a way she was even grateful to him. If he hadn't
come, if he hadn't behaved so unforgivably, nothing would have
happened between Tonino and herself. Poor John! But all the
same he was hopeless.

Day followed bright serene day. But Moira's life no longer flowed like the clear and shallow stream it had been before John's coming. It was turbulent now, there were depths and darknesses. And love was no longer a game with a pleasant companion; it was violent, all-absorbing, even rather terrible. Tonino became for her a kind of obsession. She was haunted by him—by his face, by his white teeth and his dark hair, by his hands and limbs and body. She wanted to be with him, to feel his nearness, to touch him. She would spend whole hours stroking his hair, ruffling it up, rearranging it fantastically, on end, like a golliwog's, or with hanging fringes, or with the locks twisted up into horns. And when she had contrived some specially ludicrous effect, she clapped her hands and laughed, laughed, till the tears ran down her cheeks. "If you could see yourself now!" she cried. Offended by her laughter, "You play with me as though I were a doll," Tonino would protest with a rather ludicrous expression of angry dignity. The laughter would go out of Moira's face and, with a seriousness that was fierce, almost cruel, she would lean forward and kiss him, silently, violently, again and again.

Absent, he was still unescapably with her, like a guilty conscience. Her solitudes were endless meditations on the theme of him. Sometimes the longing for his tangible presence was too achingly painful to be borne. Disobeying all his injunctions, breaking all her promises, she would telephone for him to come to her, she would drive off in search of him. Once, at about midnight, Tonino was called down from his room at the hotel by a message that a lady wanted to speak to him. He found her sitting in the car. "But I couldn't help it, I simply couldn't help it," she cried, to excuse herself and mollify his anger. Tonino refused to be propitiated. Coming like this in the middle of the night! It was madness, it was scandalous! She sat there, listening, pale and with trembling lips and the tears in her eyes. He was silent at last. "But if you knew, Tonino," she whispered, "if you only knew . . ." She took his hand and kissed it, humbly.

Berto, when he heard the good news (for Tonino proudly told

him at once), was curious to know whether the *signora forestiera* was as cold as Northern ladies were proverbially supposed to be.

"*Macchè!*" Tonino protested vigorously. On the contrary. For a long time the two young sportsmen discussed the question of amorous temperatures, discussed it technically, professionally.

Tonino's raptures were not so extravagant as Moira's. So far as he was concerned, this sort of thing had happened before. Passion with Moira was not diminished by satisfaction, but rather, since the satisfaction was for her so novel, so intrinsically apocalyptic, increased. But that which caused her passion to increase produced in his a waning. He had got what he wanted; his night-begotten, touch-born longing for her (dulled in the interval and diminished by all the sporting love-hunts undertaken with Berto) had been fulfilled. She was no longer the desired and unobtainable, but the possessed, the known. By her surrender she had lowered herself to the level of all the other women he had ever made love to; she was just another item in the sportsman's grand total.

His attitude towards her underwent a change. Familiarity began to blunt his courtesy; his manner became offhandedly marital. When he saw her after an absence, "*Ebbene, tesoro,*" he would say in a genially unromantic tone, and pat her once or twice on the back or shoulder, as one might pat a horse. He permitted her to run her own errands and even his. Moira was happy to be his servant. Her love for him was, in one at least of its aspects, almost abject. She was dog-like in her devotion. Tonino found her adoration very agreeable so long as it expressed itself in fetching and carrying, in falling in with his suggestions, and in making him presents. "But you mustn't, my darling, you shouldn't," he protested each time she gave him something. Nevertheless, he accepted a pearl tie-pin, a pair of diamond and enamel links, a half-hunter on a gold and platinum chain. But Moira's devotion expressed itself also in other ways. Love demands as much as it gives. She wanted so much—his heart, his physical presence, his caresses, his confidences, his time, his fidelity. She was tyrannous in her adoring abjection. She pestered him with devotion. Tonino was bored and irritated by her excessive love. The omniscient Berto, to whom he carried his troubles, advised him to take a strong line. Women, he pronounced, must be kept in their places, firmly. They love one all the better if they are a little maltreated.

Tonino followed his advice and, pretexting work and social engagements, reduced the number of his visits. What a relief to be free of her importunity! Disquieted, Moira presented him with an amber cigar-holder. He protested, accepted it, but gave her no more of his company in return. A set of diamond studs produced no better effect. He talked vaguely and magniloquently about his career and the necessity for unremitting labour; that was his excuse for not coming more often to see her. It was on the tip of her tongue, one afternoon, to say that *she* would be his career, would give him anything he wanted, if only . . . But the memory of John's hateful words made her check herself. She was terrified lest he might make no difficulties about accepting her offer. "Stay with me this evening," she begged, throwing her arms round his neck. He suffered himself to be kissed.

"I wish I could stay," he said hypocritically. "But I have some important business this evening." The important business was playing billiards with Berto.

Moira looked at him for a moment in silence; then, dropping her hands from his shoulders, turned away. She had seen in his eyes a weariness that was almost a horror.

Summer drew on; but in Moira's soul there was no inward brightness to match the sunshine. She passed her days in a misery that was alternately restless and apathetic. Her nerves began once more to lead their own irresponsible life apart from hers. For no sufficient cause and against her will, she would find herself uncontrollably in a fury, or crying, or laughing. When Tonino came to see her, she was almost always, in spite of all her resolutions, bitterly angry or hysterically tearful. "But why do I behave like this?" she would ask herself despairingly. "Why do I say such things? I'm making him hate me." But the next time he came, she would act in precisely the same way. It was as though she were possessed by a devil. And it was not her mind only that was sick. When she ran too quickly upstairs, her heart seemed to stop beating for a moment and there was a whirling darkness before her eyes. She had an almost daily headache, lost appetite, could not digest what she ate. In her thin sallow face her eyes became enormous. Looking into the glass, she found herself hideous, old, repulsive. "No wonder he hates me," she thought, and she would brood, brood for hours over the idea that she had become physically disgusting to him, disgusting to look at, to touch, tainting the air with her breath. The idea became an obsession, indescribably painful and humiliating.

"*Questa donna!*" Tonino would complain with a sigh, when he came back from seeing her. Why didn't he leave her, then? Berto was all for strong measures. Tonino protested that he hadn't the courage; the poor woman would be too unhappy. But he also enjoyed a good dinner and going for drives in an expensive car and receiving sumptuous additions to his wardrobe. He contented himself with complaining and being a Christian martyr. One evening his old friend Carlo Menardi introduced him to his sister. After that he bore his martyrdom with even less patience than before. Luisa Menardi was only seventeen, fresh, healthy, provocatively pretty, with rolling black eyes that said all sorts of things and an impertinent tongue. Tonino's business appointments became more numerous than ever. Moira was left to brood in solitude on the dreadful theme of her own repulsiveness.

Then, quite suddenly, Tonino's manner towards her underwent another change. He became once more assiduously tender, thoughtful, affectionate. Instead of hardening himself with a shrug of indifference against her tears, instead of returning anger for hysterical anger, he was patient with her, was lovingly and cheerfully gentle. Gradually, by a kind of spiritual infection, she too became loving and gentle. Almost reluctantly—for the devil in her was the enemy of life and happiness—she came up again into the light.

"My dear son," Vasari senior had written in his eloquent and disquieting letter, "I am not one to complain feebly of Destiny; my whole life has been one long act of Faith and unshatterable Will. But there are blows under which even the strongest man must stagger—blows which . . ." The letter rumbled on for pages in the same style. The hard unpleasant fact that emerged from under the eloquence was that Tonino's father had been speculating on the Naples stock exchange, speculating unsuccessfully. On the first of the next month he would be required to pay out some fifty thousand francs more than he could lay his hands on. The Grand Hotel Ritz-Carlton was doomed; he might even have to sell the restaurant. Was there anything Tonino could do?

"Is it possible?" said Moira with a sigh of happiness. "It seems too good to be true." She leaned against him; Tonino kissed her eyes and spoke caressing words. There was no moon; the dark-blue sky was thickly constellated; and, like another starry universe gone deliriously mad, the fire-flies darted, alternately eclipsed and shining, among the olive trees. "Darling," he said aloud, and wondered if this would be a propitious moment to speak. "*Piccina mia.*" In the end he decided to postpone matters for another day or two. In another day or two, he calculated, she wouldn't be able to refuse him anything.

Tonino's calculations were correct. She let him have the money, not only without hesitation, but eagerly, joyfully. The reluctance was all on his side, in the receiving. He was almost in tears as he took the cheque, and the tears were tears of genuine emotion. "You're an angel," he said, and his voice trembled. "You've saved us all." Moira cried outright as she kissed him. How could John have said those things? She cried and was happy. A pair of silver-backed hair-brushes accompanied the cheque—just to show that the money had made no difference to their relationship. Tonino recognised the delicacy of her intention and was touched. "You're too good to me," he insisted, "too good." He felt rather ashamed.

"Let's go for a long drive to-morrow," she suggested.

Tonino had arranged to go with Luisa and her brother to Prato. But so strong was his emotion, that he was on the point of accepting Moira's invitation and sacrificing Luisa.

"All right," he began, and then suddenly thought better of it. After all, he could go out with Moira any day. It was seldom that he had a chance of jaunting with Luisa. He struck his forehead, he made a despairing face. "But what am I thinking of!" he cried. "To-morrow's the day we're expecting the manager of the hotel company from Milan."

"But must you be there to see him?"

"Alas!"

It was too sad. Just how sad Moira only fully realised the next day. She had never felt so lonely, never longed so ardently for his presence and affection. Unsatisfied, her longings were an unbearable restlessness. Hoping to escape from the loneliness and ennui with which she had filled the house, the garden, the landscape, she took out the car and drove away at random, not knowing whither. An hour later she found herself at Pistoia, and Pistoia was as hateful as every other place; she headed the car homewards. At Prato there was a fair. The road was crowded; the air was rich with a haze of dust and the noise of brazen music. In a field near the entrance to the town, the merry-go-rounds revolved with a glitter in the sunlight. A plunging horse held up the traffic. Moira stopped the car and looked about her at the crowd, at the swings, at the whirling roundabouts, looked with a cold hostility and distaste. Hateful! And suddenly there was Tonino sitting on a swan in the nearest merry-go-round, with a girl in pink muslin sitting in front of him between the white wings and the arching neck. Rising and falling as it went, the swan turned away out of sight. The music played on. *But poor poppa, poor poppa, he's got nothin' at all.* The swan reappeared. The girl in pink was looking back over her shoulder, smiling. She was very young, vulgarly pretty, shining and plumped with health. Tonino's lips moved; behind the wall of noise what was he saying? All that Moira knew was that the girl laughed; her laughter was like an explosion of sensual young life. Tonino

raised his hand and took hold of her bare brown arm. Like an
undulating planet, the swan once more wheeled away out of
sight. Meanwhile, the plunging horse had been quieted, the
traffic had begun to move forward. Behind her a horn hooted
insistently. But Moira did not stir. Something in her soul desired
that the agony should be repeated and prolonged. Hoot, hoot,
hoot! She paid no attention. Rising and falling, the swan
emerged once more from eclipse. This time Tonino saw her.
Their eyes met; the laughter suddenly went out of his face.
"*Porco madonna!*" shouted the infuriated motorist behind her,
"can't you move on?" Moira threw the car into gear and shot
forward along the dusty road.

The cheque was in the post; there was still time, Tonino
reflected, to stop the payment of it.

"You're very silent," said Luisa teasingly, as they drove back
towards Florence. Her brother was sitting in front, at the wheel;
he had no eyes at the back of his head. But Tonino sat beside
her like a dummy. "Why are you so silent?"

He looked at her, and his face was grave and stonily unre-
sponsive to her bright and dimpling provocations. He sighed;
then, making an effort, he smiled, rather wanly. Her hand was
lying on her knee, palm upward, with a pathetic look of being
unemployed. Dutifully doing what was expected of him,
Tonino reached out and took it.

At half-past six he was leaning his borrowed motor-cycle
against the wall of Moira's villa. Feeling like a man who is about
to undergo a dangerous operation, he rang the bell.

Moira was lying on her bed, had lain there ever since she came
in; she was still wearing her dust-coat, she had not even taken off
her shoes. Affecting an easy cheerfulness, as though nothing
unusual had happened, Tonino entered almost jauntily.

"Lying down?" he said in a tone of surprised solicitude.
"You haven't got a headache, have you?" His words fell, trivial
and ridiculous, into abysses of significant silence. With a sinking
of the heart, he sat down on the edge of the bed, he laid a hand
on her knee. Moira did not stir, but lay with averted face, remote

and unmoving. "What is it, my darling?" He patted her sooth-
ingly. "You're not upset because I went to Prato, are you?" he
went on, in the incredulous voice of a man who is certain of a
negative answer to his question. Still she said nothing. This
silence was almost worse than the outcry he had anticipated.
Desperately, knowing it was no good, he went on to talk about
his old friend, Carlo Menardi, who had come round in his car to
call for him; and as the director of the hotel company had left
immediately after lunch—most unexpectedly—and as he'd
thought Moira was certain to be out, he had finally yielded and
gone along with Carlo and his party. Of course, if he'd realised
that Moira hadn't gone out, he'd have asked her to join them.
For his own sake her company would have made all the difference.

His voice was sweet, ingratiating, apologetic. "A black-haired
pimp from the slums of Naples." John's words reverberated in
her memory. And so Tonino had never cared for her at all, only
for her money. That other woman . . . She saw again that pink
dress, lighter in tone than the sleek, sunburnt skin; Tonino's
hand on the bare brown arm; that flash of eyes and laughing
teeth. And meanwhile he was talking on and on, ingratiatingly;
his very voice was a lie.

"Go away," she said at last, without looking at him.

"But, my darling . . ." Bending over her, he tried to kiss her
averted cheek. She turned and, with all her might, struck him in
the face.

"You little devil!" he cried, made furious by the pain of the
blow. He pulled out his handkerchief and held it to his bleeding
lip. "Very well, then." His voice trembled with anger. "If you
want me to go, I'll go. With pleasure." He walked heavily
away. The door slammed behind him.

But perhaps, thought Moira, as she listened to the sound of
his footsteps receding on the stairs, perhaps it hadn't really been
so bad as it looked; perhaps she had misjudged him. She sat up;
on the yellow counterpane was a little circular red stain—a drop
of his blood. And it was she who had struck him.

"Tonino!" she called; but the house was silent. "Tonino!" Still calling, she hurried downstairs, through the hall, out on to the porch. She was just in time to see him riding off through the gate on his motor-cycle. He was steering with one hand; the other still pressed a handkerchief to his mouth.

"Tonino, Tonino!" But either he didn't, or else he wouldn't hear her. The motor-cycle disappeared from view. And because he had gone, because he was angry, because of his bleeding lip, Moira was suddenly convinced that she had been accusing him falsely, that the wrong was all on her side. In a state of painful, uncontrollable agitation she ran to the garage. It was essential that she should catch him, speak to him, beg his pardon, implore him to come back. She started the car and drove out.

"One of these days," John had warned her, "you'll go over the edge of the bank, if you're not careful. It's a horrible turning."

Coming out of the garage door, she pulled the wheel hard over as usual. But too impatient to be with Tonino, she pressed the accelerator at the same time. John's prophecy was fulfilled. The car came too close to the edge of the bank; the dry earth crumbled and slid under its outer wheels. It tilted horribly, tottered for a long instant on the balancing point, and went over. But for the ilex tree, it would have gone crashing down the slope. As it was, the machine fell only a foot or so and came to rest, leaning drunkenly sideways with its flank against the bole of the tree. Shaken, but quite unhurt, Moira climbed over the edge of the car and dropped to the ground. "Assunta! Giovanni!" The maids, the gardener came running. When they saw what had happened, there was a small babel of exclamations, questions, comments.

"But can't you get it on to the drive again?" Moira insisted to the gardener; because it was necessary, absolutely necessary, that she should see Tonino at once.

Giovanni shook his head. It would take at least four men with levers and a pair of horses. . . .

"Telephone for a taxi, then," she ordered Assunta and hurried into the house. If she remained any longer with those chattering people, she'd begin to scream. Her nerves had come to separate life again; clenching her fists, she tried to fight them down.

Going up to her room, she sat down before the mirror and began, methodically and with deliberation (it was her will imposing itself on her nerves) to make up her face. She rubbed a little red on to her pale cheeks, painted her lips, dabbed on the powder. "I must look presentable," she thought, and put on her smartest hat. But would the taxi never come? She struggled with her impatience. "My purse," she said to herself. "I shall need some money for the cab." She was pleased with herself for being so full of foresight, so coolly practical in spite of her nerves. "Yes, of course; my purse."

But where was the purse? She remembered so clearly having thrown it on to the bed, when she came in from her drive. It was not there. She looked under the pillow, lifted the counterpane. Or perhaps it had fallen on the floor. She looked under the bed; the purse wasn't there. Was it possible that she hadn't put it on the bed at all? But it wasn't on her dressing-table, nor on the mantelpiece, nor on any of the shelves, nor in any of the drawers of her wardrobe. Where, where, where? And suddenly a terrible thought occurred to her. Tonino . . . Was it possible? The seconds passed. The possibility became a dreadful certainty. A thief as well as . . . John's words echoed in her head. "Black-haired pimp from the slums of Naples, black-haired pimp from the slums . . ." And a thief as well. The bag was made of gold chain-work; there were more than four thousand lire in it. A thief, a thief . . . She stood quite still, strained, rigid, her eyes staring. Then something broke, something seemed to collapse within her. She cried aloud as though under a sudden intolerable pain.

The sound of the shot brought them running upstairs. They found her lying face downwards across the bed, still faintly breathing. But she was dead before the doctor could come up from the town. On a bed standing, as hers stood, in an alcove, it was difficult to lay out the body. When they moved it out of

o

its recess, there was the sound of a hard, rather metallic fall. Assunta bent down to see what had dropped.

"It's her purse," she said. "It must have got stuck between the bed and the wall."

FARCICAL HISTORY OF
RICHARD GREENOW

I

THE most sumptuous present that Millicent received on her
seventh birthday was a doll's house. "With love to darling
little Mill from Aunty Loo." Aunt Loo was immensely rich,
and the doll's house was almost as grandiose and massive as
herself.

It was divided into four rooms, each papered in a different
colour and each furnished as was fitting: beds and washstands
and wardrobes in the upstair rooms, arm-chairs and artificial
plants below. "Replete with every modern convenience; sumptuous appointments." There was even a cold collation ready
spread on the dining-room table—two scarlet lobsters on a dish,
and a ham that had been sliced into just enough to reveal an
internal complexion of the loveliest pink and white. One might
go on talking about the doll's house for ever, it was so beautiful.
Such, at any rate, was the opinion of Millicent's brother Dick.
He would spend hours opening and shutting the front door,
peeping through the windows, arranging and rearranging the
furniture. As for Millicent, the gorgeous present left her cold.
She had been hoping—and, what is more, praying, fervently,
every night for a month—that Aunty Loo would give her a toy
sewing-machine (one of the kind that works, though) for her
birthday.

She was bitterly disappointed when the doll's house came
instead. But she bore it all stoically and managed to be wonderfully polite to Aunty Loo about the whole affair. She never
looked at the doll's house: it simply didn't interest her.

Dick had already been at a preparatory school for a couple of
terms. Mr. Killigrew, the headmaster, thought him a promising
boy. "Has quite a remarkable aptitude for mathematics," he

wrote in his report. "He has started Algebra this term and shows a"—"quite remarkable" scratched out (the language of reports is apt to be somewhat limited)—"a very unusual grasp of the subject." Mr. Killigrew didn't know that his pupil also took an interest in dolls: if he had, he would have gibed at Dick as unmercifully and in nearly the same terms as Dick's fellow-school-boys—for shepherds grow to resemble their sheep and pedagogues their childish charges. But of course Dick would never have dreamt of telling any one at school about it. He was chary of letting even the people at home divine his weakness, and when any one came into the room where the doll's house was, he would put his hands in his pockets and stroll out, whistling the tune of, "There is a Happy Land far, far away, where they have Ham and Eggs seven times a day," as though he had merely stepped in to have a look at the beastly thing—just to give it a kick.

When he wasn't playing with the doll's house, Dick spent his holiday time in reading, largely, devouringly. No length or incomprehensibility could put him off; he had swallowed down *Robert Elsmere* in the three-volume edition at the age of eight. When he wasn't reading he used to sit and think about Things in General and Nothing in Particular; in fact, as Millicent reproachfully put it, he just mooned about. Millicent, on the other hand, was always busily doing something: weeding in the garden, or hoeing, or fruit-picking (she could be trusted not to eat more than the recognised tariff—one in twenty raspberries or one in forty plums); helping Kate in the kitchen; knitting mufflers for those beings known vaguely as The Cripples, while her mother read aloud in the evenings before bedtime. She disapproved of Dick's mooning, but Dick mooned all the same.

When Dick was twelve and a half he knew enough about mathematics and history and the dead languages to realise that his dear parents were profoundly ignorant and uncultured. But, what was more pleasing to the dear parents, he knew enough to win a scholarship at Æsop College, which is one of our Greatest Public Schools.

If this were a Public School story, I should record the fact that, while at Æsop, Dick swore, lied, blasphemed, repeated dirty stories, read the articles in *John Bull* about brothels disguised as nursing-homes and satyrs disguised as curates; that he regarded his masters, with very few exceptions, as fools, not even always well-meaning. And so on. All which would be quite true, but beside the point. For this is not one of the conventional studies of those clever young men who discover Atheism and Art at School, Socialism at the University, and, passing through the inevitable stage of Sex and Syphilis after taking their B.A., turn into maturely brilliant novelists at the age of twenty-five. I prefer, therefore, to pass over the minor incidents of a difficult pubescence, touching only on those points which seem to throw a light on the future career of our hero.

It is possible for those who desire it—incredible as the thing may appear—to learn something at Æsop College. Dick even learnt a great deal. From the beginning he was the young Benjamin of his mathematical tutor, Mr. Skewbauld, a man of great abilities in his own art, and who, though wholly incapable of keeping a form in order, could make his private tuition a source of much profit to a mathematically minded boy. Mr. Skewbauld's house was the worst in Æsop: Dick described it as a mixture between a ghetto and a home for the mentally deficient, and when he read in Sir Thomas Browne that it was a Vulgar Error to suppose that Jews stink, he wrote a letter to the *School Magazine* exploding that famous doctor as a quack and a charlatan, whose statements ran counter to the manifest facts of everyday life in Mr. Skewbauld's house. It may seem surprising that Dick should have read Sir Thomas Browne at all. But he was more than a mere mathematician. He filled the ample leisure, which is Æsop's most precious gift to those of its Alumni who know how to use it, with much and varied reading in history, in literature, in physical science, and in more than one foreign language. Dick was something of a prodigy.

"Greenow's an intellectual," was Mr. Copthorne-Slazenger's contemptuous verdict. "I have the misfortune to have two or three intellectuals in my house. They're all of them friends of his. I think he's a Bad Influence in the School." Copthorne-Slazenger regarded himself as the perfect example of *mens sana in corpore sano*, the soul of an English gentleman in the body of a Greek god. Unfortunately his legs were rather too short and his lower lip was underhung like a salmon's.

Dick had, indeed, collected about him a band of kindred spirits. There was Partington, who specialised in history; Gay, who had read all the classical writings of the golden age and was engaged in the study of mediæval Latin; Fletton, who was fantastically clever and had brought the art of being idle to a pitch never previously reached in the annals of Æsop. These were his chief friends, and a queer-looking group they made—Dick, small and dark and nervous; Partington, all roundness, and whose spectacles were two moons in a moonface; Gay, with the stiff walk of a little old man; and Fletton, who looked like nobody so much as Mr. Jingle, tall and thin with a twisted, comical face.

"An ugly skulking crew," Copthorne-Slazenger, conscious of his own Olympian splendour, would say as he saw them pass.

With these faithful friends Dick should have been—and indeed for the most part was—very happy. Between them they mustered up a great stock of knowledge; they could discuss every subject under the sun. They were a liberal education and an amusement to one another. There were times, however, when Dick was filled with a vague, but acute, discontent. He wanted something which his friends could not give him; but what, but what? The discontent rankled under the surface, like a suppressed measles. It was Lord Francis Quarles who brought it out and made the symptoms manifest.

Francis Quarles was a superb creature, with the curly forehead of a bull and the face and limbs of a Græco-Roman statue. It was a sight worth seeing when he looked down through half-shut eyelids, in his usual attitude of sleepy arrogance, on the world about him. He was in effect what Mr. Copthorne-Slazenger imagined himself to be, and he shared that gentleman's dislike for Dick and his friends. "Yellow little atheists," he called them. He always stood up for God and the Church of England; they were essential adjuncts to the aristocracy. God, indeed, was almost a member of the Family; lack of belief in Him amounted to a personal insult to the name of Quarles.

It was half-way through the summer term, when Dick was sixteen, on one of those days of brilliant sunshine and cloudless blue, when the sight of beautiful and ancient buildings is peculiarly poignant. Their age and quiet stand out in melancholy contrast against the radiant life of the summer; and at Æsop the boys go laughing under their antique shadow; "Little victims"—you feel how right Gray was. Dick was idly strolling across the quadrangle, engaged in merely observing the beauty about him —the golden-grey chapel, with its deep geometrical shadows between the buttresses, the comely rose-coloured shapes of the brick-built Tudor buildings, the weather-cocks glittering in the sun, the wheeling flurries of pigeons. His old discontent had seized on him again, and to-day in the presence of all this beauty it had become almost unbearable. All at once, out of the mouth of one of the dark little tunnelled doors pierced in the flanks of the sleeping building, a figure emerged into the light. It was Francis Quarles, clad in white flannels and the radiance of the sunshine. He appeared like a revelation, bright, beautiful, and sudden, before Dick's eyes. A violent emotion seized him; his heart leapt, his bowels were moved within him; he felt a little sick and faint—he had fallen in love.

Francis passed by without deigning to notice him. His head was high, his eyes drowsy under their drooping lids. He was gone, and for Dick all the light was out, the beloved quadrangle was a prison-yard, the pigeons a loathsome flock of carrion eaters. Gay and Partington came up behind him with shouts of invitation. Dick walked rudely away. God! how he hated them and their wretched, silly talk and their yellow, ugly faces.

The weeks that followed were full of strangeness. For the first time in his life Dick took to writing poetry. There was one sonnet which began:

Is it a vision or a waking dream?
Or is it truly Apollo that I see,
Come from his sylvan haunts in Arcady
To { laugh and loiter
     { sing and saunter by an English stream. . . .

He kept on repeating the words to himself, "Sylvan haunts in Arcady," "laugh and loiter" (after much thought he had adopted that as more liquidly melodious than "sing and saunter"). How beautiful they sounded!—as beautiful as Keats—more beautiful, for they were his own.

He avoided the company of Gay and Fletton and Partington; they had become odious to him, and their conversation, when he could bring himself to listen to it, was, somehow, almost incomprehensible. He would sit for hours alone in his study; not working—for he could not understand the mathematical problems on which he had been engaged before the fateful day in the quadrangle—but reading novels and the poetry of Mrs. Browning, and at intervals writing something rather ecstatic of his own. After a long preparatory screwing up of his courage, he dared at last to send a fag with a note to Francis, asking him to tea; and when Francis rather frigidly refused, he actually burst into tears. He had not cried like that since he was a child.

He became suddenly very religious. He would spend an hour on his knees every night, praying, praying with frenzy. He mortified the flesh with fasting and watching. He even went so far as to flagellate himself—or at least tried to; for it is very difficult to flagellate yourself adequately with a cane in a room so small that any violent gesture imperils the bric-à-brac. He would pass half the night stark naked, in absurd postures, trying to hurt himself. And then, after the dolorously pleasant process of self-maceration was over, he used to lean out of the window and listen to the murmurs of the night and fill his spirit with the warm velvet darkness of midsummer. Copthorne-Slazenger, coming back by the late train from town one night, happened to see his moon-pale face hanging out of window and was delighted to be able to give him two hundred Greek lines to remind him that even a member of the Sixth Form requires sleep sometimes.

The fit lasted three weeks. "I can't think what's the matter with you, Greenow," complained Mr. Skewbauld snufflingly. "You seem incapable or unwilling to do anything at all. I suspect the cause is constipation. If only every one would take a little paraffin every night before going to bed! . . ." Mr. Skewbauld's self-imposed mission in life was the propagation of the paraffin habit. It was the universal panacea—the cure for every ill.

His friends of before the crisis shook their heads and could only suppose him mad. And then the fit ended as suddenly as it had begun.

It happened at a dinner-party given by the Cravisters. Dr. Cravister was the Headmaster of Æsop—a good, gentle, learned old man, with snow-white hair and a saintly face which the spirit of comic irony had embellished with a nose that might, so red and bulbous it was, have been borrowed from the properties of a music-hall funny man. And then there was Mrs. Cravister, large and stately as a galleon with all sails set. Those who met her for the first time might be awed by the dignity of what an Elizabethan would have called her "swelling port." But those who knew her well went in terror of the fantastic spirit which lurked behind the outward majesty. They were afraid of what that richly modulated voice of hers might utter. It was not merely that she was malicious—and she had a gift of ever-ready irony; no, what was alarming in all her conversation was the element of the unexpected. With most people one feels comfortably secure that they will always say the obvious and ordinary things; with Mrs. Cravister, never. The best one could do was to be on guard and to try and look, when she made a more than usually characteristic remark, less of a bewildered fool than one felt.

Mrs. Cravister received her guests—they were all of them boys —with stately courtesy. They found it pleasant to be taken so seriously, to be treated as perfectly grown men; but at the same time, they always had with Mrs. Cravister a faint uncomfortable suspicion that all her politeness was an irony so exquisite as to be practically undistinguishable from ingenuousness.

"Good evening, Mr. Gay," she said, holding out her hand and shutting her eyes; it was one of her disconcerting habits, this shutting of the eyes. "What a pleasure it will be to hear you talking to us again about eschatology."

Gay, who had never talked about eschatology and did not know the meaning of the word, smiled a little dimly and made a protesting noise.

"Eschatology? What a charming subject!" The fluty voice belonged to Henry Cravister, the Headmaster's son, a man of about forty who worked in the British Museum. He was almost too cultured, too erudite.

"But I don't know anything about it," said Gay desperately.

"Spare us your modesty," Henry Cravister protested.

His mother shook hands with the other guests, putting some at their ease with a charming phrase and embarrassing others by saying something baffling and unexpected that would have dismayed even the hardiest diner-out, much more a schoolboy tremblingly on his good behaviour. At the tail end of the group of boys stood Dick and Francis Quarles. Mrs. Cravister slowly raised her heavy waxen eyelids and regarded them a moment in silence.

"The Græco-Roman and the Gothic side by side!" she exclaimed. "Lord Francis is something in the Vatican, a rather late piece of work; and Mr. Greenow is a little gargoyle from the roof of Notre Dame de Paris. Two epochs of art—how clearly one sees the difference. And my husband, I always think, is purely Malayan in design—purely Malayan," she repeated as she shook hands with the two boys.

Dick blushed to the roots of his hair, but Francis' impassive arrogance remained unmoved. Dick stole a glance in his direction, and at the sight of his calm face he felt a new wave of adoring admiration sweeping through him.

The company was assembled and complete. Mrs. Cravister looked round the room and remarking, "We won't wait for Mr.

Copthorne-Slazenger," sailed majestically in the direction of the door. She particularly disliked this member of her husband's staff, and lost no opportunity of being rude to him. Thus, where an ordinary hostess might have said, "Shall we come in to dinner?" Mrs. Cravister employed the formula, "We won't wait for Mr. Copthorne-Slazenger"; and a guest unacquainted with Mrs. Cravister's habits would be surprised on entering the dining-room to find that all the seats at the table were filled, and that the meal proceeded smoothly without a single further reference to the missing Copthorne, who never turned up at all, for the good reason that he had never been invited.

Dinner began a little nervously and uncomfortably. At one end of the table the Headmaster was telling anecdotes of Æsop in the 'sixties, at which the boys in his neighbourhood laughed with a violent nervous insincerity. Henry Cravister, still talking about eschatology, was quoting from Sidonius Apollinarius and Commodianus of Gaza. Mrs. Cravister, who had been engaged in a long colloquy with the butler, suddenly turned on Dick with the remark, "And so you have a deep, passionate fondness for cats," as though they had been intimately discussing the subject for the last hour. Dick had enough presence of mind to say that, yes, he did like cats—all except those Manx ones that had no tails.

"No tails," Mrs. Cravister repeated—"no tails. Like men. How symbolical everything is!"

Francis Quarles was sitting opposite him, so that Dick had ample opportunity to look at his idol. How perfectly he did everything, down to eating his soup! The first lines of a new poem began to buzz in Dick's head:

> "All, all I lay at thy proud marble feet—
> My heart, my love and all my future days.
> Upon thy brow for ever let me gaze,
> For ever touch thy hair: oh (something) sweet . . ."

Would he be able to find enough rhymes to make it into a sonnet? Mrs. Cravister, who had been leaning back in her chair for the last few minutes in a state of exhausted abstraction, opened her eyes and said to nobody in particular:

"Ah, how I envy the calm of those Chinese dynasties!"

"Which Chinese dynasties?" a well-meaning youth inquired.

"Any Chinese dynasty, the more remote the better. Henry, tell us the names of some Chinese dynasties."

In obedience to his mother, Henry delivered a brief disquisition on the history of politics, art, and letters in the Far East.

The Headmaster continued his reminiscences.

An angel of silence passed. The boys, whose shyness had begun to wear off, became suddenly and painfully conscious of hearing themselves eating. Mrs. Cravister saved the situation.

"Lord Francis knows all about birds," she said in her most thrilling voice. "Perhaps he can tell us why it is the unhappy fate of the carrion crow to mate for life."

Conversation again became general. Dick was still thinking about his sonnet. Oh, these rhymes!—praise, bays, roundelays, amaze: greet, bleat, defeat, beat, paraclete. . . .

> ". . . to sing the praise
> In anthems high and solemn roundelays
> Of Holy Father, Son and Paraclete."

That was good—damned good; but it hardly seemed to fit in with the first quatrain. It would do for one of his religious poems, though. He had written a lot of sacred verse lately.

Then suddenly, cutting across his ecstatic thoughts, came the sound of Henry Cravister's reedy voice.

"But I always find Pater's style so *coarse*," it said.

Something explosive took place in Dick's head. It often happens when one blows one's nose that some passage in the labyrinth connecting ears and nose and throat is momentarily blocked, and one becomes deaf and strangely dizzy. Then, suddenly, the mucous bubble bursts, sound rushes back to the brain, the head feels clear and stable once more. It was something like this, but transposed into terms of the spirit, that seemed now to have happened to Dick.

It was as though some mysterious obstruction in his brain, which had dammed up and diverted his faculties from their normal course during the past three weeks, had been on a sudden overthrown. His life seemed to be flowing once more along familiar channels.

He was himself again.

"But I always find Pater's style so *coarse*."

These few words of solemn foolery were the spell which had somehow performed the miracle. It was just the sort of remark he might have made three weeks ago, before the crisis. For a moment, indeed, he almost thought it was he himself who had spoken; his own authentic voice, carried across the separating gulf of days, had woken him again to life!

He looked at Francis Quarles. Why, the fellow was nothing but a great prize ox, a monstrous animal. "There was a Lady loved a Swine. Honey, said she . . ." It was ignoble, it was ridiculous. He could have hidden his face in his hands for pure shame; shame tingled through his body. Goodness, how grotesquely he had behaved!

He leaned across and began talking to Henry Cravister about Pater and style and books in general. Cravister was amazed at the maturity of the boy's mind; for he possessed to a remarkable degree that critical faculty which in the vast majority of boys is —and from their lack of experience must be—wholly lacking.

"You must come and see me some time when you're in London," Henry Cravister said to him when the time came for the boys to get back to their houses. Dick was flattered; he had not said that to any of the others. He walked home with Gay, laughing and talking quite in his old fashion. Gay marvelled at the change in his companion; strange, inexplicable fellow! but it was pleasant to have him back again, to repossess the lost friend. Arrived in his room, Dick sat down to attack the last set of mathematical problems that had been set him. Three hours ago they had appeared utterly incomprehensible; now he understood them perfectly. His mind was like a giant refreshed, delighting in its strength.

Next day Mr. Skewbauld congratulated him on his answers.

"You seem quite to have recovered your old form, Greenow," he said. "Did you take my advice? Paraffin regularly . . ."

Looking back on the events of the last weeks, Dick was disquieted. Mr. Skewbauld might be wrong in recommending paraffin, but he was surely right in supposing that something was the matter and required a remedy. What could it be? He felt so well; but that, of course, proved nothing. He began doing Müller's exercises, and he bought a jar of malt extract and a bottle of hypophosphites. After much consultation of medical handbooks and the encyclopædia, he came to the conclusion that he was suffering from anæmia of the brain; and for some time one fixed idea haunted him: Suppose the blood completely ceased to flow to his brain, suppose he were to fall down suddenly dead or, worse, become utterly and hopelessly paralysed. . . . Happily the distractions of Æsop in the summer term were sufficiently numerous and delightful to divert his mind from this gloomy brooding, and he felt so well and in such high spirits that it was impossible to go on seriously believing that he was at death's door. Still, whenever he thought of the events of those strange weeks he was troubled. He did not like being confronted by problems which he could not solve. During the rest of his stay at school he was troubled by no more than the merest velleities of a relapse. A fit of moon-gazing and incapacity to understand the higher mathematics had threatened him one time when he was working rather too strenuously for a scholarship. But a couple of days' complete rest had staved off the peril. There had been rather a painful scene, too, at Dick's last School Concert. Oh, those Æsop concerts! Musically speaking, of course, they are deplorable; but how rich from all other points of view than the merely æsthetic! The supreme moment arrives at the very end when three of the most eminent and popular of those about to leave mount the platform together and sing the famous "Æsop, Farewell." Greatest of school songs! The words are not much, but the tune, which goes swooning along in three-four time, is perhaps the masterpiece of the late organist, Dr. Pilch.

Dick was leaving, but he was not a sufficiently heroic figure to have been asked to sing, "Æsop, Farewell." He was simply a member of the audience, and one, moreover, who had come to the concert in a critical and mocking spirit. For, as he had an ear for music, it was impossible for him to take the concert very seriously. The choir had clamorously re-crucified the Messiah; the soloists had all done their worst; and now it was time for "Æsop, Farewell." The heroes climbed on to the stage. They were three demi-gods, but Francis Quarles was the most splendid of the group as he stood there with head thrown back, eyes almost closed, calm and apparently unconscious of the crowd that seethed, actually and metaphorically, beneath him. He was wearing an enormous pink orchid in the buttonhole of his evening coat; his shirt-front twinkled with diamond studs; the buttons of his waistcoat were of fine gold. At the sight of him, Dick felt his heart beating violently; he was not, he painfully realised, master of himself.

The music struck up—Dum, dum, dumdidi, dumdidi; dum, dum, dum, and so on. So like the *Merry Widow*. In two days' time he would have left Æsop for ever. The prospect had never affected him very intensely. He had enjoyed himself at school, but he had never, like so many Æsopians, fallen in love with the place. It remained for him an institution; for others it was almost an adored person. But to-night his spirit, rocked on a treacly ocean of dominant sevenths, succumbed utterly to the sweet sorrow of parting. And there on the platform stood Francis. Oh, how radiantly beautiful! And when he began, in his rich tenor, the first verse of the Valedictory:

> Farewell, Mother Æsop,
>   Our childhood's home!
> Our spirit is with thee,
>   Though far we roam . . ."

he found himself hysterically sobbing.

II

Canteloup College is perhaps the most frightful building in Oxford—and to those who know their Oxford well this will mean not a little. Up till the middle of last century Canteloup possessed two quadrangles of fifteenth-century buildings, unimpressive and petty, like so much of College architecture, but at least quiet, unassuming, decent. After the accession of Victoria the College began to grow in numbers, wealth, and pride. The old buildings were too small and unpretentious for what had now become a Great College. In the summer of 1867 a great madness fell upon the Master and Fellows. They hired a most distinguished architect, bred up in the school of Ruskin, who incontinently razed all the existing buildings to the ground and erected in their stead a vast pile in the approved Mauro-Venetian Gothic of the period. The New Buildings contained a great number of rooms, each served by a separate and almost perpendicular staircase; and if nearly half of them were so dark as to make it necessary to light them artificially for all but three hours out of the twenty-four, this slight defect was wholly outweighed by the striking beauty, from outside, of the Neo-Byzantine loopholes by which they were, euphemistically, "lighted."

Prospects in Canteloup may not please; but man, on the other hand, tends to be less vile there than in many other places. There is an equal profusion at Canteloup of Firsts and Blues; there are Union orators of every shade of opinion and young men so languidly well bred as to take no interest in politics of any kind; there are drinkers of cocoa and drinkers of champagne. Canteloup is a microcosm, a whole world in miniature; and whatever your temperament and habits may be, whether you wish to drink, or row, or work, or hunt, Canteloup will provide you with congenial companions and a spiritual home.

Lack of athletic distinction had prevented Dick from being, at Æsop, a hero or anything like one. At Canteloup, in a less barbarically ordered state of society, things were different. His rooms in the Venetian gazebo over the North Gate became the meeting-place of all that was most intellectually distinguished in Canteloup and the University at large. He had had his sitting-room austerely upholstered and papered in grey. A large white Chinese figure of the best period stood pedestalled in one corner, and on the walls there hung a few uncompromisingly good drawings and lithographs by modern artists. Fletton, who had accompanied Dick from Æsop to Canteloup, called it the "cerebral chamber"; and with its prevailing tone of brain-coloured grey and the rather dry intellectual taste of its decorations it deserved the name.

To-night the cerebral chamber had been crammed. The Canteloup branch of the Fabian Society, under Dick's presidency, had been holding a meeting. "Art in the Socialist State" was what they had been discussing. And now the meeting had broken up, leaving nothing but three empty jugs that had once contained mulled claret and a general air of untidiness to testify to its having taken place at all. Dick stood leaning an elbow on the mantelpiece and absent-mindedly kicking, to the great detriment of his pumps, at the expiring red embers in the grate. From the depths of a huge and cavernous arm-chair, Fletton, pipe in mouth, fumed like a sleepy volcano.

"I liked the way, Dick," he said, with a laugh—"the way you went for the Arty-Crafties. You utterly destroyed them."

"I merely pointed out, what is sufficiently obvious, that crafts are not art, nor anything like it, that's all." Dick snapped out the words. He was nervous and excited, and his body felt as though it were full of compressed springs ready to jump at the most imponderable touch. He was always like that after making a speech.

"You did it very effectively," said Fletton. There was a silence between the two young men.

A noise like the throaty yelling of savages in rut came wafting up from the quadrangle on which the windows of the cerebral chamber opened. Dick started; all the springs within him had gone off at once—a thousand simultaneous Jack-in-the-boxes.

"It's only Francis Quarles' dinner-party becoming vocal,"

Fletton explained. "Blind mouths, as Milton would call them."

Dick began restlessly pacing up and down the room. When Fletton spoke to him, he did not reply or, at best, gave utterance to a monosyllable or a grunt.

"My dear Dick," said the other at last, "you're not very good company to-night," and heaving himself up from the arm-chair, Fletton went shuffling in his loose, heelless slippers towards the door. "I'm going to bed."

Dick paused in his lion-like prowling to listen to the receding sound of feet on the stairs. All was silent now: Gott sei dank. He went into his bedroom. It was there that he kept his piano, for it was a piece of furniture too smugly black and polished to have a place in the cerebral chamber. He had been thirsting after his piano all the time Fletton was sitting there, damn him! He drew up a chair and began to play over and over a certain series of chords. With his left hand he struck an octave G in the bass, while his right dwelt lovingly on F, B, and E. A luscious chord, beloved by Mendelssohn—a chord in which the native richness of the dominant seventh is made more rich, more piercing sweet by the addition of a divine discord. G, F, B, and E—he let the notes hang tremulously on the silence, savoured to the full their angelic overtones; then, when the sound of the chord had almost died away, he let it droop reluctantly through D to the simple, triumphal beauty of C natural—the diapason closing full in what was for Dick a wholly ineffable emotion.

He repeated that dying fall again and again, perhaps twenty times. Then, when he was satiated with its deliciousness, he rose from the piano and opening the lowest drawer of the wardrobe pulled out from under his evening clothes a large portfolio. He undid the strings; it was full of photogravure reproductions from various Old Masters. There was an almost complete set of Greuze's works, several of the most striking Ary Scheffers, some Alma Tadema, some Leighton, photographs of sculpture by Torwaldsen and Canova, Boecklin's "Island of the Dead," religious pieces by Holman Hunt, and a large packet of miscellaneous pictures from the Paris Salons of the last forty years. He took them into the cerebral chamber where the light was better, and began to study them, lovingly, one by one. The Cézanne lithograph, the three admirable etchings by Van Gogh, the little Picasso looked on, unmoved, from the walls.

It was three o'clock before Dick got to bed. He was stiff and cold, but full of the satisfaction of having accomplished something. And, indeed, he had cause to be satisfied; for he had written the first four thousand words of a novel, a chapter and a half of *Heartsease Fitzroy: the Story of a Young Girl.*

Next morning Dick looked at what he had written overnight, and was alarmed. He had never produced anything quite like this since the days of the Quarles incident at Æsop. A relapse? He wondered. Not a serious one in any case; for this morning he felt himself in full possession of all his ordinary faculties. He must have got overtired speaking to the Fabians in the evening. He looked at his manuscript again, and read: " 'Daddy, do the little girl angels in heaven have toys and kittens and teddy-bears?'

" 'I don't know,' said Sir Christopher gently. 'Why does my little one ask?'

" 'Because, daddy,' said the child—'because I think that soon I too may be a little angel, and I should so like to have my teddy-bear with me in heaven.'

"Sir Christopher clasped her to his breast. How frail she was, how ethereal, how nearly an angel already! Would she have her teddy-bear in heaven? The childish question rang in his ears. Great, strong man though he was, he was weeping. His tears fell in a rain upon her auburn curls.

" 'Tell me, daddy,' she insisted, 'will dearest God allow me my teddy-bear?'

" 'My child,' he sobbed, 'my child . . .' "

The blushes mounted hot to his cheeks; he turned away his head in horror. He would really have to look after himself for a bit, go to bed early, take exercise, not do much work. This sort of thing couldn't be allowed to go on.

He went to bed at half-past nine that night, and woke up the following morning to find that he had added a dozen or more closely written pages to his original manuscript during the night. He supposed he must have written them in his sleep. It was all very disquieting. The days passed by; every morning a fresh instalment was added to the rapidly growing bulk of *Heartsease Fitzroy*. It was as though some goblin, some Lob-lie-by-the-Fire, came each night to perform the appointed task, vanishing before the morning. In a little while Dick's alarm wore off; during the day he was perfectly well; his mind functioned with marvellous efficiency. It really didn't seem to matter what he did in his sleep provided he was all right in his waking hours. He almost forgot about *Heartsease*, and was only reminded of her existence when by chance he opened the drawer in which the steadily growing pile of manuscript reposed.

In five weeks *Heartsease Fitzroy* was finished. Dick made a parcel of the manuscript and sent it to a literary agent. He had no hopes of any publisher taking the thing; but he was in sore straits for money at the moment, and it seemed worth trying, on the off-chance. A fortnight later Dick received a letter beginning: "DEAR MADAM,—Permit me to hail in you a new authoress of real talent. *Heartsease Fitzroy* is GREAT,"—and signed "EBOR W. SIMS, Editor, *Hildebrand's Home Weekly*."

Details of the circulation of *Hildebrand's Home Weekly* were printed at the head of the paper; its average net sale was said to exceed three and a quarter millions. The terms offered by Mr. Sims seemed to Dick positively fabulous. And there would be the royalties on the thing in book form after the serial had run its course.

The letter arrived at breakfast; Dick cancelled all engagements for the day and set out immediately for a long and solitary walk. It was necessary to be alone, to think. He made his way along the Seven Bridges Road, up Cumnor Hill, through the village, and down the footpath to Bablock Hithe, thence to pursue the course of the "stripling Thames"—haunted at every step by the Scholar Gipsy, damn him! He drank beer and ate some bread and cheese in a little inn by a bridge, farther up the river; and it was there, in the inn parlour, surrounded by engravings of the late Queen, and breathing the slightly mouldy preserved air bottled some three centuries ago into that hermetically sealed chamber—it was there that he solved the problem, perceived the strange truth about himself.

He was a hermaphrodite.

A hermaphrodite, not in the gross obvious sense, of course, but spiritually. Two persons in one, male and female. Dr. Jekyll and Mr. Hyde: or rather a new William Sharp and Fiona Mac-Leod—a more intelligent William, a vulgarer Fiona. Everything was explained; the deplorable Quarles incident was simple and obvious now. A sentimental young lady of literary tastes writing sonnets to her Ouida guardsman. And what an unerring flair Mr. Sims had shown by addressing him so roundly and unhesitatingly as "madam"!

Dick was elated at this discovery. He had an orderly mind that disliked mysteries. He had been a puzzle to himself for a long time; now he was solved. He was not in the least distressed to discover this abnormality in his character. As long as the two parts of him kept well apart, as long as his male self could understand mathematics, and as long as his lady novelist's self kept up her regular habit of writing at night and retiring from business during the day, the arrangement would be admirable. The more he thought about it, the more it seemed an ideal state of affairs. His life would arrange itself so easily and well. He would devote the day to the disinterested pursuit of knowledge, to philosophy and mathematics, with perhaps an occasional excursion into politics. After midnight he would write novels with a feminine pen, earning the money that would make his unproductive male labours possible. A kind of spiritual *souteneur*. But the fear of poverty need haunt him no more; no need to become a wage-slave, to sacrifice his intelligence to the needs of his belly. Like a gentleman of the East, he would sit still and smoke his philosophic pipe while the womenfolk did the dirty work. Could anything be more satisfactory?

He paid for his bread and beer, and walked home, whistling as he went.

III

Two months later the first instalment of *Heartsease Fitzroy: the Story of a Young Girl*, by Pearl Bellairs, appeared in the pages of *Hildebrand's Home Weekly*. Three and a quarter millions read and approved. When the story appeared in book form, two hundred thousand copies were sold in six weeks; and in the course of the next two years no less than sixteen thousand female infants in London alone were christened Heartsease. With her fourth novel and her two hundred and fiftieth Sunday paper article, Pearl Bellairs was well on her way to becoming a household word.

Meanwhile Dick was in receipt of an income far beyond the wildest dreams of his avarice. He was able to realise the two great ambitions of his life—to wear silk underclothing and to smoke good (but really good) cigars.

IV

Dick went down from Canteloup in a blaze of glory. The most brilliant man of his generation, exceptional mind, prospects, career. But his head was not turned. When people congratulated him on his academic successes, he thanked them politely and then invited them to come and see his Memento Mori. His Memento Mori was called Mr. Glottenham and could be found at any hour of the day in the premises of the Union, or if it was evening, in the Senior Common Room at Canteloup. He was an old member of the College, and the dons in pity for his age and loneliness had made him, some years before, a member of their Common Room. This act of charity was as bitterly regretted as any generous impulse in the history of the world. Mr. Glottenham made the life of the Canteloup fellows a burden to them; he dined in Hall with fiendish regularity, never missing a night, and he was always the last to leave the Common Room. Mr. Glottenham did not prepossess at a first glance; the furrows of his face were covered with a short grey sordid stubble; his clothes were disgusting with the spilth of many years of dirty feeding; he had the shoulders and long hanging arms of an ape— an ape with a horribly human look about it. When he spoke, it was like the sound of a man breaking coke; he spoke incessantly and on every subject. His knowledge was enormous; but he possessed the secret of a strange inverted alchemy—he knew how to turn the richest gold to lead, could make the most interesting topic so intolerably tedious that it was impossible, when he talked, not to loathe it.

This was the death's-head to which Dick, like an ancient philosopher at a banquet, would direct the attention of his heartiest congratulators. Mr. Glottenham had had the most dazzling academic career of his generation. His tutors had prophesied for him a future far more brilliant than that of any of his contemporaries. They were now Ministers of State, poets, philosophers, judges, millionaires. Mr. Glottenham frequented the Union and the Canteloup Senior Common Room, and was—well, he was just Mr. Glottenham. Which was why Dick did not think too highly of his own laurels.

V

"What shall I do? What ought I to do?" Dick walked up and down the room smoking, furiously and without at all savouring its richness, one of his opulent cigars.

"My dear," said Cravister—for it was in Cravister's high-ceilinged Bloomsbury room that Dick was thus unveiling his distress of spirit—"my dear, this isn't a revival meeting. You speak as though there were an urgent need for your soul to be saved from hell fire. It's not as bad as that, you know."

"But it *is* a revival meeting," Dick shouted in exasperation— "it is. I'm a revivalist. You don't know what it's like to have a feeling about your soul. I'm terrifyingly earnest; you don't seem to understand that. I have all the feelings of Bunyan without his religion. I regard the salvation of my soul as important. How simple everything would be if one could go out with those creatures in bonnets and sing hymns like, 'Hip, hip for the blood of the Lamb, hurrah!' or that exquisite one:

> " 'The bells of Hell ring tingalingaling
>   For you, but not for me.
> For me the angels singalingaling;
>   They've got the goods for me.'

Unhappily it's impossible."

"Your ideas," said Cravister in his flutiest voice, "are somewhat Gothic. I think I can understand them, though of course I don't sympathise or approve. My advice to people in doubt about what course of action they ought to pursue is always the same: do what you want to."

"Cravister, you're hopeless," said Dick, laughing. "I suppose I am rather Gothic, but I do feel sometimes that the question of ought as well as of want does arise."

Dick had come to his old friend for advice about Life. What ought he to do? The indefatigable pen of Pearl Bellairs solved for him the financial problem. There remained only the moral problem: how could he best expend his energies and his time? Should he devote himself to knowing or doing, philosophy or politics? He felt in himself the desire to search for truth and the ability—who knows?—to find it. On the other hand, the horrors of the world about him seemed to call on him to put forth all his strength in an effort to ameliorate what was so patently and repulsively bad. Actually, what had to be decided was this: Should he devote himself to the researches necessary to carry out the plan, long ripening in his brain, of a new system of scientific philosophy; or should he devote his powers and Pearl Bellairs' money in propaganda that should put life into the English revolutionary movement? Great moral principles were in the balance. And Cravister's advice was, do what you want to!

After a month of painful indecision, Dick, who was a real Englishman, arrived at a satisfactory compromise. He started work on his new Synthetic Philosophy, and at the same time joined the staff of the *Weekly International*, to which he contributed both money and articles. The weeks slipped pleasantly and profitably along. The secret of happiness lies in congenial work, and no one could have worked harder than Dick, unless it was the indefatigable Pearl Bellairs, whose nightly output of five thousand words sufficed to support not only Dick but the *Weekly International* as well. These months were perhaps the happiest period of Dick's life. He had friends, money, liberty; he knew himself to be working well; and it was an extra, a super-erogatory happiness that he began at this time to get on much better with his sister Millicent than he had ever done before. Millicent had come up to Oxford as a student at St. Mungo Hall in Dick's third year. She had grown into a very efficient and very intelligent young woman. A particularly handsome young woman as well. She was boyishly slender, and a natural grace kept on breaking through the somewhat rigid deportment, which she always tried to impose upon herself, in little beautiful gestures and movements that made the onlooker catch his breath with astonished pleasure.

> "Wincing she was as is a jolly colt,
> Straight as a mast and upright as a bolt:"

Chaucer had as good an eye for youthful grace as for mormals and bristly nostrils and thick red jovial villainousness.

Millicent lost no time in making her presence at St. Mungo's felt. Second- and third-year heroines might snort at the forwardness of a mere fresh-girl, might resent the complete absence of veneration for their glory exhibited by this youthful bejauna; Millicent pursued her course unmoved. She founded new societies and put fresh life into the institutions which already existed at St. Mungo's to take cocoa and discuss the problems of the universe. She played hockey like a tornado, and she worked alarmingly hard. Decidedly, Millicent was a Force, very soon the biggest Force in the St. Mungo world. In her fifth term she organised the famous St. Mungo general strike, which compelled the authorities to relax a few of the more intolerably tyrannical and anachronistic rules restricting the liberty of the students. It was she who went, on behalf of the strikers, to interview the redoubtable Miss Prosser, Principal of St. Mungo's. The redoubtable Miss Prosser looked grim and invited her to sit down. Millicent sat down and, without quailing, delivered a short but pointed speech attacking the fundamental principles of the St. Mungo system of discipline.

"Your whole point of view," she assured Miss Prosser, "is radically wrong. It's an insult to the female sex; it's positively obscene. Your root assumption is simply this: that we're all in a chronic state of sexual excitement; leave us alone for a moment and we'll immediately put our desires into practice. It's disgusting. It makes me blush. After all, Miss Prosser, we are a college of intelligent women, not an asylum of nymphomaniacs."

For the first time in her career, Miss Prosser had to admit herself beaten. The authorities gave in—reluctantly and on only a few points; but the principle had been shaken, and that, as Millicent pointed out, was what really mattered.

Dick used to see a good deal of his sister while he was still in residence at Canteloup, and after he had gone down he used to come regularly once a fortnight during term to visit her. That horrible mutual reserve, which poisons the social life of most families and which had effectively made of their brotherly and sisterly relation a prolonged discomfort in the past, began to disappear. They became the best of friends.

"I like you, Dick, a great deal better than I did," said Millicent one day as they were parting at the gate of St. Mungo's after a long walk together.

Dick took off his hat and bowed. "My dear, I reciprocate the sentiment. And, what's more, I esteem and admire you. So there."

Millicent curtsied, and they laughed. They both felt very happy.

VI

"What a life!" said Dick, with a sigh of weariness as the train moved out of Euston.

Not a bad life, Millicent thought.

"But horribly fatiguing. I am quite outreined by it."

"Outreined" was Dick's translation of *éreinté*. He liked using words of his own manufacture; one had to learn his idiom before one could properly appreciate his intimate conversation.

Dick had every justification for being outreined. The spring and summer had passed for him in a whirl of incessant activity. He had written three long chapters of the *New Synthetic Philosophy*, and had the material for two more ready in the form of notes. He had helped to organise and bring to its successful conclusion the great carpenters' strike of May and June. He had written four pamphlets and a small army of political articles. And this comprised only half his labour; for nightly, from twelve till two, Pearl Bellairs emerged to compose the masterpieces which supplied Dick with his bread and butter. *Apes in Purple* had been published in May. Since then she had finished *La Belle Dame sans Morality*, and had embarked on the first chapters of *Daisy's Voyage to Cythera*. Her weekly articles, "For the Girls of Britain," had become, during this period, a regular and favourite feature in the pages of *Hildebrand's Sabbath*, that prince of Sunday papers. At the beginning of July, Dick considered that he had earned a holiday, and now they were off, he and Millicent, for the North.

Dick had taken a cottage on the shore of one of those long salt-water lochs that give to the west coast of Scotland such a dissipated appearance on the map. For miles around there was not a living soul who did not bear the name of Campbell—two families only excepted, one of whom was called Murray-Drummond and the other Drummond-Murray. However, it was not for the people that Dick and Millicent had come, so much as for the landscape, which made up in variety for anything that the inhabitants might lack. Behind the cottage, in the midst of a narrow strip of bog lying between the loch and the foot of the mountains, stood one of the numerous tombs of Ossian, a great barrow of ancient stones. And a couple of miles away the remains of Deirdre's Scottish refuge bore witness to the Celtic past. The countryside was dotted with the black skeletons of mediæval castles. Astonishing country, convulsed into fantastic mountain shapes, cut and indented by winding fiords. On summer days the whole of this improbable landscape became blue and remote and aerially transparent. Its beauty lacked all verisimilitude. It was for that reason that Dick chose the neighbourhood for his holidays. After the insistent actuality of London this frankly unreal coast was particularly refreshing to a jaded spirit.

"Nous sommes ici en plein romantisme," said Dick on the day of their arrival, making a comprehensive gesture towards the dream-like scenery, and for the rest of his holiday he acted the part of a young romantic of the palmy period. He sat at the foot of Ossian's tomb and read Lamartine; he declaimed Byron from the summit of the mountains and Shelley as he rowed along the loch. In the evening he read George Sand's *Indiana*; he agonised with the pure, but passionate, heroine, while his admiration for Sir Brown, her English lover, the impassive giant who never speaks and is always clothed in faultless hunting costume, knew no bounds. He saturated himself in the verses of Victor Hugo, and at last almost came to persuade himself that the words, *Dieu, infinité, eternité*, with which the works of that deplorable genius are so profusely sprinkled, actually possessed some meaning, though what that meaning was he could not, even in his most romantic transports, discover. Pearl Bellairs, of course, understood quite clearly their significance, and though she was a very poor French scholar she used sometimes to be moved almost to tears by the books she found lying about when she came into existence after midnight. She even copied out extracts into her notebooks with a view to using them in her next novel.

> "Les plus désespérés sont les chants les plus beaux,
> Et j'en sais d'immortels qui sont de purs sanglots,"

was a couplet which struck her as sublime.

Millicent, meanwhile, did the house-keeping with extraordinary efficiency, took a great deal of exercise, and read long, serious books; she humoured her brother in his holiday romanticism, but refused to take part in the game.

The declaration of war took them completely by surprise. It is true that a *Scotsman* found its way into the cottage by about lunch-time every day, but it was never read, and served only to light fires and wrap up fish and things of that sort. No letters were being forwarded, for they had left no address; they were isolated from the world. On the fatal morning Dick had, indeed, glanced at the paper, without however noticing anything out of the ordinary. It was only later when, alarmed by the rumours floating round the village shop, he came to examine his *Scotsman* more closely, that he found about half-way down the third column of one of the middle pages an admirable account of all that had been so tragically happening in the last twenty-four hours; he learnt with horror that Europe was at war and that his country too had entered the arena. Even in the midst of his anguish of spirit he could not help admiring the *Scotsman's* splendid impassivity—no headlines, no ruffling of the traditional aristocratic dignity. Like Sir Rodolphe Brown in *Indiana*, he thought, with a sickly smile.

Dick determined to start for London at once. He felt that he must act, or at least create the illusion of action; he could not stay quietly where he was. It was arranged that he should set out that afternoon, while Millicent should follow a day or two later with the bulk of the luggage. The train which took him to Glasgow was slower than he thought it possible for any train to be. He tried to read, he tried to sleep; it was no good. His nervous agitation was pitiable; he made little involuntary movements with his limbs, and every now and then the muscles of his face began twitching in a spasmodic and uncontrollable tic. There were three hours to wait in Glasgow; he spent them in wandering about the streets. In the interminable summer twilight the inhabitants of Glasgow came forth into the open to amuse themselves; the sight almost made him sick. Was it possible that there should be human beings so numerous and so uniformly hideous? Small, deformed, sallow, they seemed malignantly ugly, as if on purpose. The words they spoke were in-comprehensible. He shuddered; it was an alien place—it was hell.

The London train was crammed. Three gröss Italians got into Dick's carriage, and after they had drunk and eaten with loud, unpleasant gusto, they prepared themselves for sleep by taking off their boots. Their feet smelt strongly ammoniac, like a cage of mice long uncleaned. Acutely awake, while the other occupants of the compartment enjoyed a happy unconscious-ness, he looked at the huddled carcasses that surrounded him. The warmth and the smell of them was suffocating, and there came to his mind, with the nightmarish insistence of a fixed idea, the thought that every breath they exhaled was saturated with disease. To be condemned to sit in a hot bath of consumption and syphilis—it was too horrible! The moment came at last when he could bear it no longer; he got up and went into the corridor. Standing there, or sitting sometimes for a few dreary minutes in the lavatory, he passed the rest of the night. The train roared along without a stop. The roaring became articu-late: in the days of his childhood trains used to run to the tune of "Lancashire to Lancashire, to fetch a pocket-handkercher; to Lancashire, to Lancashire . . ." But to-night the wheels were shouting insistently, a million times over, two words only— "the War, the War; the War, the War." He tried desperately to make them say something else, but they refused to recite Milton; they refused to go to Lancashire; they went on with their endless Tibetan litany—the War, the War, the War.

By the time he reached London, Dick was in a wretched state. His nerves were twittering and jumping within him; he felt like a walking aviary. The tic in his face had become more violent and persistent. As he stood in the station, waiting for a cab, he overheard a small child saying to its mother, "What's the matter with that man's face, mother?"

"Sh—sh, darling," was the reply. "It's rude."

Dick turned and saw the child's big round eyes fixed with fascinated curiosity upon him, as though he were a kind of monster. He put his hand to his forehead and tried to stop the twitching of the muscles beneath the skin. It pained him to think that he had become a scarecrow for children.

Arrived at his flat, Dick drank a glass of brandy and lay down for a rest. He felt exhausted—ill. At half-past one he got up, drank some more brandy, and crept down into the street. It was intensely hot; the pavements reverberated the sunlight in a glare which hurt his eyes; they seemed to be in a state of grey incandescence. A nauseating smell of wetted dust rose from the roadway, along which a water-cart was slowly piddling its way. He realised suddenly that he ought not to have drunk all that brandy on an empty stomach; he was definitely rather tipsy. He had arrived at that state of drunkenness when the senses perceive things clearly, but do not transmit their knowledge to the understanding. He was painfully conscious of this division, and it needed all the power of his will to establish contact between his parted faculties. It was as though he were, by a great and prolonged effort, keeping his brain pressed against the back of his eyes; as soon as he relaxed the pressure, the understanding part slipped back, the contact was broken, and he relapsed into a state bordering on imbecility. The actions which ordinarily one does by habit and without thinking, he had to perform consciously and voluntarily. He had to reason out the problem of walking—first the left foot forward, then the right. How ingeniously he worked his ankles and knees and hips! How delicately the thighs slid past one another!

He found a restaurant and sat there drinking coffee and trying to eat an omelette until he felt quite sober. Then he drove to the offices of the *Weekly International* to have a talk with Hyman, the editor. Hyman was sitting in his shirt-sleeves, writing.

He lifted his head as Dick came in. "Greenow," he shouted delightedly, "we were all wondering what had become of you. We thought you'd joined the Army."

Dick shook his head, but did not speak; the hot stuffy smell of printer's ink and machinery combined with the atrocious reek of Hyman's Virginian cigarettes to make him feel rather faint.

He sat down on the window-ledge, so as to be able to breathe an uncontaminated air.

"Well," he said at last, "what about it?"

"It's going to be hell."

"Did you suppose I thought it was going to be paradise?" Dick replied irritably. "Internationalism looks rather funny now, doesn't it?"

"I believe in it more than ever I did," cried Hyman. His face lit up with the fervour of his enthusiasm. It was a fine face, gaunt, furrowed, and angular, for all that he was barely thirty, looking as though it had been boldly chiselled from some hard stone. "The rest of the world may go mad; we'll try and keep our sanity. The time will come when they'll see we were right."

Hyman talked on. His passionate sincerity and singleness of purpose were an inspiration to Dick. He had always admired Hyman—with the reservations, of course, that the man was rather a fanatic and not so well-educated as he might have been—but to-day he admired him more than ever. He was even moved by that perhaps too facile eloquence which of old had been used to leave him cold. After promising to do a series of articles on international relations for the paper, Dick went home, feeling better than he had done all day.

He decided that he would begin writing his articles at once. He collected pens, paper, and ink and sat down in a business-like way at his bureau. He remembered distinctly biting the tip of his penholder; it tasted rather bitter.

And then he realised he was standing in Regent Street, looking in at one of the windows of Liberty's.

For a long time he stood there quite still, absorbed to all appearance in the contemplation of a piece of peacock-blue fabric. But all his attention was concentrated within himself, not on anything outside. He was wondering—wondering how it came about that he was sitting at his writing-table at one moment, and standing, at the next, in Regent Street. He hadn't—the thought flashed upon him—he hadn't been drinking any more of that brandy, had he? No, he felt himself to be perfectly sober. He moved slowly away and continued to speculate as he walked.

At Oxford Circus he bought an evening paper. He almost screamed aloud when he saw that the date printed at the head of the page was August 12th. It was on August 7th that he had sat down at his writing-table to compose those articles. Five days ago, and he had not the faintest recollection of what had happened in those five days.

He made all haste back to the flat. Everything was in perfect order. He had evidently had a picnic lunch that morning—sardines, bread and jam, and raisins; the remains of it still covered the table. He opened the sideboard and took out the brandy bottle. Better make quite sure. He held it up to the light; it was more than three-quarters full. Not a drop had gone since the day of his return. If brandy wasn't the cause, then what was?

As he sat there thinking, he began in an absent-minded way to look at his evening paper. He read the news on the front page, then turned to the inner sheets. His eye fell on these words printed at the head of the column next the leading article:

"To the Women of the Empire. Thoughts in War-Time. By Pearl Bellairs." Underneath in brackets: "The first of a series of inspiring patriotic articles by Miss Bellairs, the well-known novelist."

Dick groaned in agony. He saw in a flash what had happened to his five missing days. Pearl had got hold of them somehow, had trespassed upon his life out of her own reserved nocturnal existence. She had taken advantage of his agitated mental state to have a little fun in her own horrible way.

He picked up the paper once more and began to read Pearl's article. "Inspiring and patriotic": those were feeble words in which to describe Pearl's shrilly raucous chauvinism. And the style! Christ! to think that he was responsible, at least in part, for this. Responsible, for had not the words been written by his own hand and composed in some horrible bluebeard's chamber of his own brain? They had, there was no denying it. Pearl's literary atrocities had never much distressed him; he had long

P

given up reading a word she wrote. Her bank balance was the only thing about her that interested him. But now she was invading the sanctities of his private life. She was trampling on his dearest convictions, denying his faith. She was a public danger. It was all too frightful.

He passed the afternoon in misery. Suicide or brandy seemed the only cures. Not very satisfactory ones, though. Towards evening an illuminating idea occurred to him. He would go and see Rogers. Rogers knew all about psychology—from books, at any rate: Freud, Jung, Morton Prince, and people like that. He used to try hypnotic experiments on his friends and even dabbled in amateur psychotherapy. Rogers might help him to lay the ghost of Pearl. He ate a hasty dinner and went to see Rogers in his Kensington rooms.

Rogers was sitting at a table with a great book open in front of him. The reading-lamp, which was the only light in the room, brightly illumined one side of the pallid, puffy, spectacled face, leaving the other in complete darkness, save for a little cedilla of golden light caught on the fold of flesh at the corner of his mouth. His huge shadow crossed the floor, began to climb the wall, and from the shoulders upwards mingled itself with the general darkness of the room.

"Good evening, Rogers," said Dick wearily. "I wish you wouldn't try and look like Rembrandt's 'Christ at Emmaus' with these spectacular chiaroscuro effects."

Rogers gave vent to his usual nervous giggling laugh. "This is very nice of you to come and see me, Greenow."

"How's the Board of Trade?" Rogers was a Civil Servant by profession.

"Oh, business as usual, as the *Daily Mail* would say." Rogers laughed again as though he had made a joke.

After a little talk of things indifferent, Dick brought the conversation round to himself.

"I believe I'm getting a bit neurasthenic," he said. "Fits of depression, nervous pains, lassitude, anæmia of the will. I've come to you for professional advice. I want you to nose out my suppressed complexes, analyse me, dissect me. Will you do that for me?"

Rogers was evidently delighted. "I'll do my best," he said, with assumed modesty. "But I'm no good at the thing, so you mustn't expect much."

"I'm at your disposal," said Dick.

Rogers placed his guest in a large arm-chair. "Relax your muscles and think of nothing at all." Dick sat there flabby and abstracted while Rogers made his preparations. His apparatus consisted chiefly in a notebook and a stop-watch. He seated himself at the table.

"Now," he said solemnly, "I want you to listen to me. I propose to read out a list of words; after each of the words you must say the first word that comes into your head. The very first, mind, however foolish it may seem. And say it as soon as it crosses your mind; don't wait to think. I shall write down your answers and take the time between each question and reply."

Rogers cleared his throat and started.

"Mother," he said in a loud, clear voice. He always began his analyses with the family. For since the majority of kinks and complexes date from childhood, it is instructive to investigate the relations between the patient and those who surrounded him at an early age. "Mother."

"Dead," replied Dick immediately. He had scarcely known his mother.

"Father."

"Dull." One and a fifth seconds' interval.

"Sister." Rogers pricked his ears for the reply: his favourite incest-theory depended on it.

"Fabian Society," said Dick, after two seconds' interval. Rogers was a little disappointed. He was agreeably thrilled and excited by the answer he received to his next word: "Aunt."

The seconds passed, bringing nothing with them; and then at last there floated into Dick's mind the image of himself as a child, dressed in green velvet and lace, a perfect Bubbles boy, kneeling on Auntie Loo's lap and arranging a troop of lead soldiers on the horizontal projection of her corsage.

"Bosom," he said.

Rogers wrote down the word and underlined it. Six and three-fifths seconds: very significant. He turned now to the chapter of possible accidents productive of nervous shocks.

"Fire."

"Coal."

"Sea."

"Sick."

"Train."

"Smell."

And so on. Dull answers all the time. Evidently, nothing very catastrophic had ever happened to him. Now for a frontal attack on the fortress of sex itself.

"Women." There was rather a long pause, four seconds, and then Dick replied, "Novelist." Rogers was puzzled.

"Breast."

"Chicken." That was disappointing. Rogers could find no trace of those sinister moral censors, expurgators of impulse, suppressors of happiness. Perhaps the trouble lay in religion.

"Christ," he said.

Dick replied, "Amen," with the promptitude of a parish clerk.

"God."

Dick's mind remained a perfect blank. The word seemed to convey to him nothing at all. God, God. After a long time there appeared before his inward eye the face of a boy he had known at school and at Oxford, one Godfrey Wilkinson, called God for short.

"Wilkinson." Ten seconds and a fifth.

A few more miscellaneous questions, and the list was exhausted. Almost suddenly, Dick fell into a kind of hypnotic sleep. Rogers sat pensive in front of his notes; sometimes he consulted a text-book. At the end of half an hour he awakened Dick to tell him that he had had, as a child, consciously or unconsciously, a great Freudian passion for his aunt; that later on he had had another passion, almost religious in its fervour and intensity, for somebody called Wilkinson; and that the cause of all his present troubles lay in one or other of these episodes. If he liked, he (Rogers) would investigate the matter further with a view to establishing a cure.

Dick thanked him very much, thought it wasn't worth taking any more trouble, and went home.

VII

Millicent was organising a hospital supply dépôt, organising indefatigably, from morning till night. It was October; Dick had not seen his sister since those first hours of the war in Scotland; he had had too much to think about these last months to pay attention to any one but himself. To-day, at last, he decided that he would go and pay her a visit. Millicent had commandeered a large house in Kensington from a family of Jews, who were anxious to live down a deplorable name by a display of patriotism. Dick found her sitting there in her office—young, formidable, beautiful, severe—at a big desk covered with papers.

"Well," said Dick, "you're winning the war, I see."

"You, I gather, are not," Millicent replied.

"I believe in the things I always believed in."

"So do I."

"But in a different way, my dear—in a different way," said Dick sadly. There was a silence.

"Had we better quarrel?" Millicent asked meditatively.

"I think we can manage with nothing worse than a coolness—for the duration."

"Very well, a coolness."

"A smouldering coolness."

"Good," said Millicent briskly. "Let it start smouldering at once. I must get on with my work. Good-bye, Dick. God bless you. Let me know sometimes how you get on."

"No need to ask how you get on," said Dick with a smile, as

he shook her hand. "I know by experience that you always get on, only too well, ruthlessly well."

He went out. Millicent returned to her letters with concentrated ardour; a frown puckered the skin between her eyebrows.

Probably, Dick reflected as he made his way down the stairs, he wouldn't see her again for a year or so. He couldn't honestly say that it affected him much. Other people became daily more and more like ghosts, unreal, thin, vaporous; while every hour the consciousness of himself grew more intense and all-absorbing. The only person who was more than a shadow to him now was Hyman of the *Weekly International*. In those first horrible months of the war, when he was wrestling with Pearl Bellairs and failing to cast her out, it was Hyman who kept him from melancholy and suicide. Hyman made him write a long article every week, dragged him into the office to do sub-editorial work, kept him so busy that there were long hours when he had no time to brood over his own insoluble problems. And his enthusiasm was so passionate and sincere that sometimes even Dick was infected by it; he could believe that life was worth living and the cause worth fighting for. But not for long; for the devil would return, insistent and untiring. Pearl Bellairs was greedy for life; she was not content with her short midnight hours; she wanted the freedom of whole days. And whenever Dick was overtired, or ill or nervous, she leapt upon him and stamped him out of existence, till enough strength came back for him to reassert his personality. And the articles she wrote! The short stories! The recruiting songs! Dick dared not read them; they were terrible, terrible.

VIII

The months passed by. The longer the war lasted, the longer it seemed likely to last. Dick supported life somehow. Then came the menace of conscription. The *Weekly International* organised a great anti-conscription campaign, in which Hyman and Dick were the leading spirits. Dick was almost happy. This kind of active work was new to him and he enjoyed it, finding it exciting and at the same time sedative. For a self-absorbed and brooding mind, pain itself is an anodyne. He enjoyed his incessant journeys, his speechmaking to queer audiences in obscure halls and chapels; he liked talking with earnest members of impossible Christian sects, pacifists who took not the faintest interest in the welfare of humanity at large, but were wholly absorbed in the salvation of their own souls and in keeping their consciences clear from the faintest trace of blood-guiltiness. He enjoyed the sense of power which came to him, when he roused the passion of the crowd to enthusiastic assent, or breasted the storm of antagonism. He enjoyed everything—even getting a bloody nose from a patriot hired and intoxicated by a great evening paper to break up one of his meetings. It all seemed tremendously exciting and important at the time. And yet when, in quiet moments, he came to look back on his days of activity, they seemed utterly empty and futile. What was left of them? Nothing, nothing at all. The momentary intoxication had died away, the stirred ants'-nest had gone back to normal life. Futility of action! There was nothing permanent, or decent, or worth while, except thought. And of that he was almost incapable now. His mind, when it was not occupied by the immediate and actual, turned inward morbidly upon itself. He looked at the manuscript of his book and wondered whether he would ever be able to go on with it. It seemed doubtful. Was he, then, condemned to pass the rest of his existence enslaved to the beastliness and futility of mere quotidian action? And even in action his powers were limited; if he exerted himself too much—and the limits of fatigue were soon reached—Pearl Bellairs, watching perpetually like a hungry tigress for her opportunity, leapt upon him and took possession of his conscious faculties. And then, it might be for a matter of hours or of days, he was lost, blotted off the register of living souls, while she performed, with intense and hideous industry, her self-appointed task. More than once his anti-conscription campaigns had been cut short and he himself had suddenly disappeared from public life, to return with the vaguest stories of illness or private affairs—

stories that made his friends shake their heads and wonder which it was among the noble army of vices that poor Dick Greenow was so mysteriously addicted to. Some said drink, some said women, some said opium, and some hinted at things infinitely darker and more horrid. Hyman asked him point-blank what it was, one morning when he had returned to the office after three days' unaccountable absence.

Dick blushed painfully. "It isn't anything you think," he said.

"What is it, then?" Hyman insisted.

"I can't tell you," Dick replied desperately and in torture, "but I swear it's nothing discreditable. I beg you won't ask me any more."

Hyman had to pretend to be satisfied with that.

IX

A tactical move in the anti-conscription campaign was the foundation of a club, a place where people with pacific or generally advanced ideas could congregate.

"A club like this would soon be the intellectual centre of London," said Hyman, ever sanguine.

Dick shrugged his shoulders. He had a wide experience of pacifists.

"If you bring people together," Hyman went on, "they encourage one another to be bold—strengthen one another's faith."

"Yes," said Dick dyspeptically. "When they're in a herd, they can believe that they're much more numerous and important than they really are."

"But, man, they are numerous, they are important!" Hyman shouted and gesticulated.

Dick allowed himself to be persuaded into an optimism which he knew to be ill-founded. The consolations of religion do not console the less efficaciously for being illusory.

It was a long time before they could think of a suitable name for their club. Dick suggested that it should be called the Sclopis Club. "Such a lovely name," he explained. "Sclopis—Sclopis; it tastes precious in the mouth." But the rest of the committee would not hear of it ; they wanted a name that meant something. One lady suggested that it should be called the Everyman Club; Dick objected with passion. "It makes one shudder," he said. The lady thought it was a beautiful and uplifting name, but as Mr. Greenow was so strongly opposed, she wouldn't press the claims of Everyman. Hyman wanted to call it the Pacifist Club, but that was judged too provocative. Finally, they agreed to call it the Novembrist Club, because it was November and they could think of no better title.

The inaugural dinner of the Novembrist Club was held at Piccolomini's Restaurant. Piccolomini is in, but not exactly of, Soho, for it is a cross between a Soho restaurant and a Corner House, a hybrid which combines the worst qualities of both parents—the dirt and inefficiency of Soho, the size and vulgarity of Lyons. There is a large upper chamber reserved for agapes. Here, one wet and dismal winter's evening, the Novembrists assembled.

Dick arrived early, and from his place near the door he watched his fellow-members come in. He didn't much like the look of them. "Middle class" was what he found himself thinking; and he had to admit, when his conscience reproached him for it, that he did not like the middle classes, the lower middle classes, the lower classes. He was, there was no denying it, a bloodsucker at heart—cultured and intelligent, perhaps, but a bloodsucker none the less.

The meal began. Everything about it was profoundly suspect. The spoons were made of some pale pinchbeck metal, very light and flimsy; one expected them to melt in the soup, or one would have done, if the soup had been even tepid. The food was thick and greasy. Dick wondered what it really looked like under the concealing sauces. The wine left an indescribable taste that lingered on the palate, like the savour of brass or of charcoal fumes.

From childhood upwards Dick had suffered from the intensity of his visceral reactions to emotion. Fear and shyness
were apt to make him feel very sick, and disgust produced in him
a sensation of intolerable queasiness. Disgust had seized upon
his mind to-night. He grew paler with the arrival of every dish,
and the wine, instead of cheering him, made him feel much
worse. His neighbours to right and left ate with revolting hearti-
ness. On one side sat Miss Gibbs, garishly dressed in ill-assorted
colours that might be called futuristic; on the other was Mr.
Something in pince-nez, rather ambrosial about the hair. Mr.
Something was a poet, or so the man who introduced them had
said. Miss Gibbs was just an ordinary member of the Intelli-
gentsia, like the rest of us.

The Lower Classes, the Lower Classes . . .

"Are you interested in the Modern Theatre?" asked Mr.
Something in his mellow voice. Too mellow—oh, much too
mellow!

"Passably," said Dick.

"So am I," said Mr. Thingummy. "I am a vice-president of
the Craftsmen's League of Joy, which perhaps you may have
heard of."

Dick shook his head; this was going to be terrible.

"The objects of the Craftsmen's League of Joy," Mr. Thingummy continued, "or rather, one of the objects—for it has
many—is to establish Little Theatres in every town and village
in England, where simple, uplifting, beautiful plays might be
acted. The people have no joy."

"They have the cinema and the music hall," said Dick. He
was filled with a sudden senseless irritation. "They get all the
joy they want out of the jokes of the comics and the legs of the
women."

"Ah, but that is an impure joy," Mr. What's-his-name protested.

"Impure purple, Herbert Spenser's favourite colour," flashed
irrelevantly through Dick's brain.

"Well, speaking for myself," he said aloud, "I know I get

more joy out of a good pair of legs than out of any number of uplifting plays of the kind they'd be sure to act in your little theatres. The people ask for sex and you give them a stone."

How was it, he wondered, that the right opinions in the mouths of these people sounded so horribly cheap and wrong? They degraded what was noble; beauty became fly-blown at their touch. Their intellectual tradition was all wrong. Lower classes, it always came back to that. When they talked about war and the International, Dick felt a hot geyser of chauvinism bubbling up in his breast. In order to say nothing stupid, he refrained from speaking at all. Miss Gibbs switched the conversation on to art. She admired all the right people. Dick told her that he thought Sir Luke Fildes to be the best modern artist. But his irritation knew no bounds when he found out a little later that Mr. Something had read the poems of Fulke Greville, Lord Brooke. He felt inclined to say, "You may have read them, but of course you can't understand or appreciate them."

Lower Classes . . .

How clear and splendid were the ideas of right and justice! If only one could filter away the contaminating human element. . . . Reason compelled him to believe in democracy, in internationalism, in revolution; morality demanded justice for the oppressed. But neither morality nor reason would ever bring him to take pleasure in the company of democrats or revolutionaries, or make him find the oppressed, individually, any less antipathetic.

At the end of this nauseating meal, Dick was called on to make a speech. Rising to his feet, he began stammering and hesitating; he felt like an imbecile. Then suddenly inspiration came. The great religious ideas of Justice and Democracy swept like a rushing wind through his mind, purging it of all insignificant human and personal preferences or dislikes. He was filled with pentecostal fire. He spoke in a white heat of intellectual passion, dominating his hearers, infecting them with his own high enthusiasm. He sat down amid cheers. Miss Gibbs and Mr. Thingummy leaned towards him with flushed, shining faces.

"That was wonderful, Mr. Greenow. I've never heard anything like it," exclaimed Miss Gibbs, with genuine, unflattering enthusiasm.

Mr. Thing said something poetical about a trumpet-call. Dick looked from one to the other with blank and fishy eyes. So it was for these creatures he had been speaking!

Good God! . . .

X

Dick's life was now a monotonous nightmare. The same impossible situation was repeated again and again. If it were not for the fact that he knew Pearl Bellairs to be entirely devoid of humour, Dick might have suspected that she was having a little quiet fun with him, so grotesque were the anomalies of his double life. Grotesque, but dreary, intolerably dreary. Situations which seem, in contemplation, romantic and adventurous have a habit of proving, when actually experienced, as dull and daily as a bank clerk's routine. When you read about it, a Jekyll and Hyde existence sounds delightfully amusing; but when you live through it, as Dick found to his cost, it is merely a boring horror.

In due course Dick was called up by the Military Authorities. He pleaded conscientious objection. The date of his appearance before the Tribunal was fixed. Dick did not much relish the prospect of being a Christian martyr; it seemed an anachronism. However, it would have to be done. He would be an absolutist; there would be a little buffeting, spitting, and scourging, followed by an indefinite term of hard labour. It was all very unpleasant. But nothing could be much more unpleasant than life as he was now living it. He didn't even mind very much if they killed him. Being or not being—the alternatives left him equally cold.

The days that preceded his appearance before the Tribunal were busy days, spent in consulting solicitors, preparing speeches, collecting witnesses.

"We'll give you a good run for your money," said Hyman. "I hope they'll be feeling a little uncomfortable by the time they have done with you, Greenow."

"Not nearly so uncomfortable as I shall be feeling," Dick replied, with a slightly melancholy smile.

The South Marylebone Tribunal sat in a gloomy and fetid chamber in a police station. Dick, who was extremely sensitive to his surroundings, felt his fatigue and nervousness perceptibly increase as he entered the room. Five or six pitiable creatures with paralytic mothers or one-man businesses were briskly disposed of, and then it was Dick's turn to present himself before his judges. He looked round the court, nodded to Hyman, smiled at Millicent, who had so far thawed their wartime coolness as to come and see him condemned, caught other friendly eyes. It was as though he were about to be electrocuted. The preliminaries passed off; he found himself answering questions in a loud, clear voice. Then the Military Representative began to loom horribly large. The Military Representative was a solicitor's clerk disguised as a lieutenant in the Army Service Corps. He spoke in an accent that was more than genteel; it was rich, noble, aristocratic. Dick tried to remember where he had heard a man speaking like that before. He had it now. Once when he had been at Oxford after term was over. He had gone to see the Varieties, which come twice nightly and with cheap seats to the theatre after the undergraduates have departed. One of the turns had been a Nut, a descendant of the bloods and Champagne Charlies of earlier days. A young man in an alpaca evening suit and a monocle. He had danced, sung a song, spoken some patter. Sitting in the front row of the stalls, Dick had been able to see the large, swollen, tuberculous glands in his neck. They wobbled when he danced or sang. Fascinatingly horrible, those glands; and the young man, how terribly, painfully pathetic. . . . When the Military Representative spoke, he could hear again that wretched Nut's rendering of the Eton and Oxford voice. It unnerved him.

"What is your religion, Mr. Greenow?" the Military Representative asked.

Fascinated, Dick looked to see whether he too had tuberculous glands. The Lieutenant had to repeat his question sharply.

When he was irritated, his voice went back to its more natural nasal twang. Dick recovered his presence of mind.

"I have no religion," he answered.

"But, surely, sir, you must have some kind of religion."

"Well, if I must, if it's in the Army Regulations, you had better put me down as an Albigensian, or a Bogomile, or, better still, as a Manichean. One can't find oneself in this court without possessing a profound sense of the reality and active existence of a power of evil equal to, if not greater than, the power of good."

"This is rather irrelevant, Mr. Greenow," said the Chairman.

"I apologise." Dick bowed to the court.

"But if," the Military Representative continued—"if your objection is not religious, may I ask what it is?"

"It is based on a belief that all war is wrong, and that the solidarity of the human race can only be achieved in practice by protesting against war, wherever it appears and in whatever form."

"Do you disbelieve in force, Mr. Greenow?"

"You might as well ask me if I disbelieve in gravitation. Or course, I believe in force: it is a fact."

"What would you do if you saw a German violating your sister?" said the Military Representative, putting his deadliest question.

"Perhaps I had better ask my sister first," Dick replied. "She is sitting just behind you in the court."

The Military Representative was covered with confusion. He coughed and blew his nose. The case dragged on. Dick made a speech; the Military Representative made a speech; the Chairman made a speech. The atmosphere of the court-room grew fouler and fouler. Dick sickened and suffocated in the second-hand air. An immense lassitude took possession of him; he did not care about anything—about the cause, about himself, about Hyman or Millicent or Pearl Bellairs. He was just tired. Voices buzzed and drawled in his ears—sometimes his own voice, sometimes other people's. He did not listen to what they said. He was tired—tired of all this idiotic talk, tired of the heat and smell. . . .

Tired of picking up very thistly wheat sheaves and propping them up in stooks on the yellow stubble. For that was what, suddenly, he found himself doing. Overhead the sky expanded in endless steppes of blue-hot cobalt. The pungent prickly dust of the dried sheaves plucked at his nose with imminent sneezes, made his eyes smart and water. In the distance a reaping-machine whirred and hummed. Dick looked blankly about him, wondering where he was. He was thankful, at any rate, not to be in that sweltering court-room; and it was a mercy, too, to have escaped from the odious gentility of the Military Representative's accent. And, after all, there were worse occupations than harvesting.

Gradually, and bit by bit, Dick pieced together his history. He had, it seemed, done a cowardly and treacherous thing: deserted in the face of the enemy, betrayed his cause. He had a bitter letter from Hyman. "Why couldn't you have stuck it out? I thought it was in you. You've urged others to go to prison for their beliefs, but you get out of it yourself by sneaking off to a soft alternative service job on a friend's estate. You've brought discredit on the whole movement." It was very painful, but what could he answer? The truth was so ridiculous that nobody could be expected to swallow it. And yet the fact was that he had been as much startled to find himself working at Crome as any one. It was all Pearl's doing.

He had found in his room a piece of paper covered with the large, flamboyant feminine writing which he knew to be Pearl's. It was evidently the rough copy of an article on the delights of being a land-girl: dewy dawns, rosy children's faces, quaint cottages, mossy thatch, milkmaids, healthy exercise. Pearl was being a land-girl; but he could hardly explain the fact to Hyman. Better not attempt to answer him.

Dick hated the manual labour of the farm. It was hard, monotonous, dirty, and depressing. It inhibited almost completely the functions of his brain. He was unable to think about anything at all; there was no opportunity to do anything but feel uncomfortable. God had not made him a Caliban to scatter ordure over fields, to pick up ordure from cattle-yards. His rôle was Prospero.

"Ban, Ban, Caliban"—it was to that derisive measure that he pumped water, sawed wood, mowed grass; it was a march for his slow, clotted feet as he followed the dung-carts up the winding lanes. "Ban, Ban, Caliban—Ban, Ban, Ban . . ."

"Oh, that bloody old fool Tolstoy," was his profoundest reflection on a general subject in three months of manual labour and communion with mother earth.

He hated the work, and his fellow-workers hated him. They mistrusted him because they could not understand him, taking the silence of his overpowering shyness for arrogance and the contempt of one class for another. Dick longed to become friendly with them. His chief trouble was that he did not know what to say. At meal-times he would spend long minutes in cudgelling his brains for some suitable remark to make. And even if he thought of something good, like—"It looks as though it were going to be a good year for roots," he somehow hesitated to speak, feeling that such a remark, uttered in his exquisitely modulated tones, would be, somehow, a little ridiculous. It was the sort of thing that ought to be said rustically, with plenty of Z's and long vowels, in the manner of William Barnes. In the end, for lack of courage to act the yokel's part, he generally remained silent. While the others were eating their bread and cheese with laughter and talk, he sat like the skeleton at the feast —a skeleton that longed to join in the revelry, but had not the power to move its stony jaws. On the rare occasions that he actually succeeded in uttering something, the labourers looked at one another in surprise and alarm, as though it were indeed a skeleton that had spoken.

He was not much more popular with the other inhabitants of the village. Often, in the evenings, as he was returning from work, the children would pursue him, yelling. With the unerringly cruel instinct of the young they had recognised in him a fit object for abuse and lapidation. An outcast member of another class, from whom that class in casting him out had with-drawn its protection, an alien in speech and habit, a criminal, as their zealous schoolmaster lost no opportunity of reminding them, guilty of the blackest treason against God and man—he was the obviously predestined victim of childish persecution. When stones began to fly, and dung and precocious obscenity, he bowed his head and pretended not to notice that anything unusual was happening. It was difficult, however, to look quite dignified.

There were occasional short alleviations to the dreariness of his existence. One day, when he was engaged in his usual occu-pation of manuring, a familiar figure suddenly appeared along the footpath through the field. It was Mrs. Cravister. She was evidently staying at the big house; one of the Manorial dach-shunds preceded her. He took off his cap.

"Mr. Greenow!" she exclaimed, coming to a halt. "Ah, what a pleasure to see you again! Working on the land: so Tolstoyan. But I trust it doesn't affect your æsthetic ideas in the same way as it did his. Fifty peasants singing together is music; but Bach's chromatic fantasia is mere gibbering incomprehensibility."

"I don't do this for pleasure," Dick explained. "It's hard labour, meted out to the Conscientious Objector."

"Of course, of course," said Mrs. Cravister, raising her hand to arrest any further explanation. "I had forgotten. A con-scientious objector, a Bible student. I remember how passion-ately devoted you were, even at school, to the Bible."

She closed her eyes and nodded her head several times.

"On the contrary——" Dick began; but it was no good. Mrs. Cravister had determined that he should be a Bible student and it was no use gainsaying her. She cut him short.

"Dear me, the Bible. . . . What a style! That alone would prove it to have been directly inspired. You remember how Mahomet appealed to the beauty of his style as a sign of his divine mission. Why has nobody done the same for the Bible? It remains for you, Mr. Greenow, to do so. You will write a book about it. How I envy you!"

"The style is very fine," Dick ventured, "but don't you think the matter occasionally leaves something to be desired?"

"The matter is nothing," cried Mrs. Cravister, making a gesture that seemed to send all meaning flying like a pinch of salt along the wind—"nothing at all. It's the style that counts. Think of Madame Bovary."

"I certainly will," said Dick.

Mrs. Cravister held out her hand. "Good-bye. Yes, I certainly envy you. I envy you your innocent labour and your incessant study of that most wonderful of books. If I were asked, Mr. Greenow, what book I should take with me to a desert island, what single solitary book, I should certainly say the Bible, though, indeed, there are moments when I think I should choose *Tristram Shandy*. Good-bye."

Mrs. Cravister sailed slowly away. The little brown basset trotted ahead, straining his leash. One had the impression of a great ship being towed into harbour by a diminutive tug.

Dick was cheered by this glimpse of civilisation and humanity. The unexpected arrival, one Saturday afternoon, of Millicent was not quite such an unmixed pleasure. "I've come to see how you're getting on," she announced, "and to put your cottage straight and make you comfortable."

"Very kind of you," said Dick. He didn't want his cottage put straight.

Millicent was in the Ministry of Munitions now, controlling three thousand female clerks with unsurpassed efficiency. Dick looked at her curiously, as she talked that evening of her doings. "To think I should have a sister like that," he said to himself. She was terrifying.

"You do enjoy bullying other people!" he exclaimed at last. "You've found your true vocation. One sees now how the new world will be arranged after the war. The women will continue to do all the bureaucratic jobs, all that entails routine and neatness and interfering with other people's affairs. And man, it is to be hoped, will be left free for the important statesman's business, free for creation and thought. He will stay at home and give proper education to the children, too. He is fit to do these things, because his mind is disinterested and detached. It's an arrangement which will liberate all man's best energies for their proper uses. The only flaw I can see in the system is that you women will be so fiendishly and ruthlessly tyrannical in your administration."

"You can't seriously expect me to argue with you," said Millicent.

"No, please don't. I am not strong enough. My dung-carrying has taken the edge off all my reasoning powers."

Millicent spent the next morning in completely rearranging Dick's furniture. By lunch-time every article in the cottage was occupying a new position.

"That's much nicer," said Millicent, surveying her work and seeing that it was good.

There was a knock at the door. Dick opened it and was astonished to find Hyman.

"I just ran down to see how you were getting on," he explained.

"I'm getting on very well since my sister rearranged my furniture," said Dick. He found it pleasing to have an opportunity of exercising his long unused powers of malicious irony. This was very mild, but with practice he would soon come on to something more spiteful and amusing.

Hyman shook hands with Millicent, scowling as he did so. He was irritated that she was there; he wanted to talk with Dick alone. He turned his back on her and began addressing Dick.

"Well," he said, "I haven't seen you since the fatal day. How is the turnip-hoeing?"

"Pretty beastly," said Dick.

"Better than doing hard labour in a gaol, I suppose?"

Dick nodded his head wearily, foreseeing what must inevitably come.

"You've escaped that all right," Hyman went on.

"Yes; you ought to be thankful," Millicent chimed in.

"I still can't understand why you did it, Greenow. It was a

blow to me. I didn't expect it of you." Hyman spoke with feeling. "It was desertion; it was treason."

"I agree," said Millicent judicially. "He ought to have stuck to his principles."

"He ought to have stuck to what was right, oughtn't he, Miss Greenow?" Hyman turned towards Millicent, pleased at finding some one who shared his views.

"Of course," she replied—"of course. I totally disagree with you about what is right. But if he believed it right not to fight, he certainly ought to have gone to prison for his belief."

Dick lit a pipe with an air of nonchalance. He tried to disguise the fact that he was feeling extremely uncomfortable under these two pairs of merciless, accusing eyes.

"To my mind, at any rate," said Millicent, "your position seems quite illogical and untenable, Dick."

It was a relief to be talked to and not about.

"I'm sorry about that," said Dick rather huskily—not a very intelligent remark, but what was there to say?

"Of course, it's illogical and untenable. Your sister is quite right." Hyman banged the table.

"I can't understand what induced you to take it up——"

"After you'd said you were going to be one of the absolutes," cried Hyman, interrupting and continuing Millicent's words.

"Why?" said Millicent.

"Why, why, why?" Hyman echoed.

Dick, who had been blowing out smoke at a great rate, put down his pipe. The taste of the tobacco was making him feel rather sick. "I wish you would stop," he said wearily. "If I gave you the real reasons, you wouldn't believe me. And I can't invent any others that would be in the least convincing."

"I believe the real reason is that you were afraid of prison."

Dick leaned back in his chair and shut his eyes. He did not mind being insulted now; it made no difference. Hyman and Millicent were still talking about him, but what they said did not interest him; he scarcely listened.

They went back to London together in the evening.

"Very intelligent woman, your sister," said Hyman just before they were starting. "Pity she's not on the right side about the war and so forth."

Four weeks later Dick received a letter in which Hyman announced that he and Millicent had decided to get married.

"I am happy to think," Dick wrote in his congratulatory reply, "that it was I who brought you together."

He smiled as he read through the sentence; that was what the Christian martyr might say to the two lions who had scraped acquaintance over his bones in the amphitheatre.

One warm afternoon in the summer of 1918, Mr. Hobart, Clerk to the Wibley Town Council, was disturbed in the midst of his duties by the sudden entry into his office of a small dark man, dressed in corduroys and gaiters, but not having the air of a genuine agricultural labourer.

"What may I do for you?" inquired Mr. Hobart.

"I have come to inquire about my vote," said the stranger.

"Aren't you already registered?"

"Not yet. You see, it isn't long since the Act was passed giving us the vote."

Mr. Hobart stared.

"I don't quite follow," he said.

"I may not look it," said the stranger, putting his head on one side and looking arch—"I may not look it, but I will confess to you, Mr.—er—Mr.—er——"

"Hobart."

"Mr. Hobart, that I am a woman of over thirty."

Mr. Hobart grew visibly paler. Then, assuming a forced smile and speaking as one speaks to a child or a spoiled animal, he said:

"I see—I see. Over thirty, dear me."

He looked at the bell, which was over by the fireplace at the other side of the room, and wondered how he should ring it without rousing the maniac's suspicions.

"Over thirty," the stranger went on. "You know my woman's

secret. I am Miss Pearl Bellairs, the novelist. Perhaps you have read some of my books. Or are you too busy?"

"Oh no, I've read several," Mr. Hobart replied, smiling more and more brightly and speaking in even more coaxing and indulgent tones.

"Then we're friends already, Mr. Hobart. Any one who knows my books, knows me. My whole heart is in them. Now, you must tell me all about my poor little vote. I shall be very patriotic with it when the time comes to use it."

Mr. Hobart saw his opportunity.

"Certainly, Miss Bellairs," he said. "I will ring for my clerk and we'll—er—we'll take down the details."

He got up, crossed the room, and rang the bell with violence.

"I'll just go and see that he brings the right books," he added, and darted to the door. Once outside in the passage, he mopped his face and heaved a sigh of relief. That had been a narrow shave, by Jove. A loony in the office—dangerous-looking brute, too.

On the following day Dick woke up and found himself in a bare whitewashed room, sparsely furnished with a little iron bed, a washstand, a chair, and table. He looked round him in surprise. Where had he got to this time? He went to the door and tried to open it; it was locked. An idea entered his mind: he was in barracks somewhere; the Military Authorities must have got hold of him somehow in spite of his exemption certificate. Or perhaps Pearl had gone and enlisted. . . . He turned next to the window, which was barred. Outside, he could see a courtyard, filled, not with soldiers, as he had expected, but a curious motley crew of individuals, some men and some women, wandering hither and thither with an air of complete aimlessness. Very odd, he thought—very odd. Beyond the courtyard, on the farther side of a phenomenally high wall, ran a railway line and beyond it a village, roofed with tile and thatch, and a tall church spire in the midst. Dick looked carefully at the spire. Didn't he know it? Surely—yes, those imbricated copper plates with which it was covered, that gilded ship that served as wind vane, the little gargoyles at the corner of the tower—there could be no doubt; it was Belbury church. Belbury—that was where the . . . No, no; he wouldn't believe it. But looking down again into that high-walled courtyard, full of those queer, aimless folk, he was forced to admit it. The County Asylum stands at Belbury. He had often noticed it from the train, a huge, gaunt building of sausage-coloured brick, standing close to the railway, on the opposite side of the line to Belbury village and church. He remembered how, the last time he had passed in the train, he had wondered what they did in the asylum. He had regarded it then as one of those mysterious, unapproachable places, like Lhassa or a Ladies' Lavatory, into which he would never penetrate. And now, here he was, looking out through the bars, like any other madman. It was all Pearl's doing, as usual. If there had been no bars, he would have thrown himself out of the window.

He sat down on his bed and began to think about what he should do. He would have to be very sane and show them by his behaviour and speech that he was no more mad than the commonalty of mankind. He would be extremely dignified about it all. If a warder or a doctor or somebody came in to see him, he would rise to his feet and say in the calmest and severest tones: "May I ask, pray, why I am detained here and upon whose authority?" That ought to stagger them. He practised that sentence, and the noble attitude with which he would accompany it, for the best part of an hour. Then, suddenly, there was the sound of a key in the lock. He hastily sat down again on the bed. A brisk little man of about forty, clean shaven and with pince-nez, stepped into the room, followed by a nurse and a warder in uniform. The doctor! Dick's heart was beating with absurd violence; he felt like an amateur actor at the first performance of an imperfectly rehearsed play. He rose, rather unsteadily, to his feet, and in a voice that quavered a little with an emotion he could not suppress, began:

"Pray I ask, may . . ."

Then, realising that something had gone wrong, he hesitated, stammered, and came to a pause.

The doctor turned to the nurse.

"Did you hear that?" he asked. "He called me May. He seems to think everybody's a woman, not only himself."

Turning to Dick with a cheerful smile, he went on:

"Sit down, Miss Bellairs, please sit down."

It was too much. Dick burst into tears, flung himself upon the bed, and buried his face in the pillow. The doctor looked at him as he lay there sobbing, his whole body shaken and convulsed.

"A bad case, I fear."

And the nurse nodded.

For the next three days Dick refused to eat. It was certainly unreasonable, but it seemed the only way of making a protest. On the fourth day the doctor signed a certificate to the effect that forcible feeding had become necessary. Accompanied by two warders and a nurse, he entered Dick's room.

"Now, Miss Bellairs," he said, making a last persuasive appeal, "do have a little of this nice soup. We have come to have lunch with you."

"I refuse to eat," said Dick icily, "as a protest against my unlawful detention in this place. I am as sane as any of you here."

"Yes, yes." The doctor's voice was soothing. He made a sign to the warders. One was very large and stout, the other wiry, thin, sinister, like the second murderer in a play. They closed in on Dick.

"I won't eat and I won't be made to eat!" Dick cried. "Let me go!" he shouted at the fat warder, who had laid a hand on his shoulder. His temper was beginning to rise.

"Now, do behave yourself," said the fat warder. "It ain't a bit of use kicking up a row. Now, do take a little of this lovely soup," he added wheedlingly.

"Let me go!" Dick screamed again, all his self-control gone. "I will not let myself be bullied."

He began to struggle violently. The fat warder put an arm round his shoulders, as though he were an immense mother comforting an irritable child. Dick felt himself helpless; the struggle had quite exhausted him; he was weaker than he had any idea of. He began kicking the fat man's shins; it was the only way he could still show fight.

"Temper, temper," remonstrated the warder, more motherly than ever. The thin warder stooped down, slipped a strap round the kicking legs, and drew it tight. Dick could move no more. His fury found vent in words—vain, abusive, filthy words, such as he had not used since he was a schoolboy.

"Let me go," he screamed—"let me go, you devils! You beasts, you swine! beasts and swine!" he howled again and again.

They soon had him securely strapped in a chair, his head held back ready for the doctor and his horrible-looking tubes. They were pushing the horrors up his nostrils. He coughed and choked, spat, shouted inarticulately, retched. It was like having a spoon put on your tongue and being told to say A-a-h, but worse; it was like jumping into the river and getting water up your nose—how he had always hated that!—only much worse. It was like almost everything unpleasant, only much, much worse than all. He exhausted himself struggling against his utterly immovable bonds. They had to carry him to his bed, he was so weak.

He lay there, unmoving—for he was unable to move—staring at the ceiling. He felt as though he were floating on air, unsupported, solid no longer; the sensation was not unpleasant. For that reason he refused to let his mind dwell upon it; he would think of nothing that was not painful, odious, horrible. He thought about the torture which had just been inflicted on him and of the monstrous injustice of which he was a victim. He thought of the millions who had been and were still being slaughtered in the war; he thought of their pain, all the countless separate pains of them; pain incommunicable, individual, beyond the reach of sympathy; infinities of pain pent within frail finite bodies; pain without sense or object, bringing with it no hope and no redemption, futile, unnecessary, stupid. In one supreme apocalyptic moment he saw, he felt the universe in all its horror.

They forcibly fed him again the following morning and again on the day after. On the fourth day pneumonia, the result of shock, complicated by acute inflammation of the throat and pleura, set in. The fever and pain gained ground. Dick had not the strength to resist their ravages, and his condition grew hourly worse. His mind, however, continued to work clearly—too clearly. It occurred to him that he might very likely die. He asked for pencil and paper to be brought him, and putting forth all the little strength he had left, he began to make his testament.

"I am perfectly sane," he wrote at the top of the page, and underlined the words three times. "I am confined here by the most intol. injust." As soon as he began, he realised how little time and strength were left him; it was a waste to finish the long words. "They are killing me for my opins. I regard this war and all wars as utter bad. Capitalists' war. The devils will be smashed sooner later. Wish I could help. But it won't make any difference," he added on a new line and as though by an afterthought. "World will always be hell. Cap. or Lab., Engl. or Germ.—all beasts. One in a mill. is Good. I wasn't. Selfish intellect. Perhaps Pearl Bellairs better. If die, send corp. to hosp. for anatomy. Useful for once in my life!"

Quite suddenly, he lapsed into delirium. The clear lucidity of his mind became troubled. The real world disappeared from before his eyes, and in its place he saw a succession of bright, unsteady visions created by his sick fantasy. Scenes from his childhood, long forgotten, bubbled up and disappeared. Unknown, hideous faces crowded in upon him; old friends revisited him. He was living in a bewildering mixture of the familiar and the strange. And all the while, across this changing unsubstantial world, there hurried a continual, interminable procession of dromedaries—countless high-domed beasts, with gargoyle faces and stiff legs and necks that bobbed as though on springs. Do what he could, he was unable to drive them away. He lost his temper with the brutes at last, struck at them, shouted; but in vain. The room rang with his cries of, "Get away, you beasts. Bloody humps. None of your nonconformist faces here." And while he was yelling and gesticulating (with his left hand only), his right hand was still busily engaged in writing. The words were clear and legible; the sentences consecutive and eminently sane. Dick might rave, but Pearl Bellairs remained calm and in full possession of her deplorable faculties. And what was Pearl doing with her busy pencil, while Dick, like a frenzied Betsy Trotwood, shouted at the trespassing camels? The first thing she did was to scratch out all that poor Dick had said about the war. Underneath it she wrote:

"We shall not sheathe the sword, which we have not lightly . . ." And then, evidently finding that memorable sentence too long, particularly so since the addition of Poland and Czecho-Slovakia to the list of Allies, she began again.

"We are fighting for honour and the defence of Small Nationalities. Plucky little Belgium! We went into the war with clean hands."

A little of Pearl's thought seemed at this moment to have slopped over into Dick's mind; for he suddenly stopped abusing his dromedaries and began to cry out in the most pitiable fashion, "Clean hands, clean hands! I can't get mine clean. I can't, I can't, I can't. I contaminate everything." And he kept rubbing his left hand against the bedclothes and putting his fingers to his nose, only to exclaim, "Ugh, they still stink of goat!" and then to start rubbing again.

The right hand wrote on unperturbed. "No peace with the Hun until he is crushed and humiliated. Self-respecting Britons will refuse to shake a Hunnish hand for many a long year after the war. No more German waiters. Intern the Forty-Seven Thousand Hidden Hands in High Places!"

At this point, Pearl seemed to have been struck by a new idea. She took a clean page and began:

"To the Girls of England. I am a woman and proud of the fact. But, girls, I blushed for my sex to-day when I read in the papers that there had been cases of English girls talking to Hun prisoners, and not only talking to them, but allowing themselves to be kissed by them. Imagine! Clean, healthy British girls allowing themselves to be kissed by the swinish and blood-stained lips of the unspeakable Hun! Do you wonder that I blush for my sex? Stands England where she did? No, em-phatically no, if these stories are true, and true—sadly and with a heavy bleeding heart do I admit it—true they are."

"Clean hands, clean hands," Dick was still muttering, and applying his fingers to his nose once more, "Christ," he cried, "how they stink! Goats, dung . . ."

"Is there any excuse for such conduct?" the pencil continued. "The most that can be said in palliation of the offence is that girls are thoughtless, that they do not consider the full signifi-cance of their actions. But listen to me, girls of all ages, classes and creeds, from the blue-eyed, light-hearted flapper of sixteen to the stern-faced, hard-headed business woman—listen to me. There is a girlish charm about thoughtlessness, but there is a point beyond which thoughtlessness becomes criminal. A flapper may kiss a Hun without thinking what she is doing, merely for the fun of the thing; perhaps, even, out of misguided pity. Will she repeat the offence if she realises, as she must realise if she will only think, that this thoughtless fun, this mawkish and hysterical pity, is nothing less than Treason? Treason—it is a sinister word, but . . ."

The pencil stopped writing; even Pearl was beginning to grow tired. Dick's shouting had died away to a hoarse, faint whisper. Suddenly her attention was caught by the last words that Dick had written—the injunction to send his body, if he died, to a hospital for an anatomy. She put forth a great effort.

"NO. NO," she wrote in huge capitals. "Bury me in a little country churchyard, with lovely marble angels like the ones in St. George's at Windsor, over Princess Charlotte's tomb. Not anatomy. Too horrible, too disgus . . ."

The coma which had blotted out Dick's mind fell now upon hers as well. Two hours later Dick Greenow was dead; the fingers of his right hand still grasped a pencil. The scribbled papers were thrown away as being merely the written ravings of a madman; they were accustomed to that sort of thing at the asylum.

THE BOOKSHOP

IT seemed indeed an unlikely place to find a bookshop. All the other commercial enterprises of the street aimed at purveying the barest necessities to the busy squalor of the quarter. In this, the main arterial street, there was a specious glitter and life produced by the swift passage of the traffic. It was almost airy, almost gay. But all around great tracts of slum pullulated dankly. The inhabitants did their shopping in the grand street; they passed, holding gobbets of meat that showed glutinous even through the wrappings of paper; they cheapened linoleum at upholstery doors; women, black-bonneted and black-shawled, went shuffling to their marketing with dilapidated bags of straw plait. How should these, I wondered, buy books? And yet there it was, a tiny shop; and the windows were fitted with shelves, and there were the brown backs of books. To the right a large emporium overflowed into the street with its fabulously cheap furniture; to the left the curtained, discreet windows of an eating-house announced in chipped white letters the merits of sixpenny dinners. Between, so narrow as scarcely to prevent the junction of food and furniture, was the little shop. A door and four feet of dark window, that was the full extent of frontage. One saw here that literature was a luxury; it took its proportionable room here in this place of necessity. Still, the comfort was that it survived, definitely survived.

The owner of the shop was standing in the doorway, a little man, grizzle-bearded and with eyes very active round the corners of the spectacles that bridged his long, sharp nose.

"Trade is good?" I inquired.

"Better in my grandfather's day," he told me, shaking his head sadly.

"We grow progressively more Philistine," I suggested.

"It is our cheap press. The ephemeral overwhelms the permanent, the classical."

474

"This journalism," I agreed, "or call it rather this piddling quotidianism, is the curse of our age."

"Fit only for——" He gesticulated clutchingly with his hands as though seeking the word.

"For the fire."

The old man was triumphantly emphatic with his, "No: for the sewer."

I laughed sympathetically at his passion. "We are delightfully at one in our views," I told him. "May I look about me a little among your treasures?"

Within the shop was a brown twilight, redolent with old leather and the smell of that fine subtle dust that clings to the pages of forgotten books, as though preservative of their secrets —like the dry sand of Asian deserts beneath which, still incredibly intact, lie the treasures and the rubbish of a thousand years ago. I opened the first volume that came to my hand. It was a book of fashion-plates, tinted elaborately by hand in magenta and purple, maroon and solferino and puce and those melting shades of green that a yet earlier generation had called "the sorrows of Werther." Beauties in crinolines swam with the amplitude of pavilioned ships across the pages. Their feet were represented as thin and flat and black, like tea-leaves shyly protruding from under their petticoats. Their faces were egg-shaped, sleeked round with hair of glossy black, and expressive of an immaculate purity. I thought of our modern fashion figures, with their heels and their arch of instep, their flattened faces and smile of pouting invitation. It was difficult not to be a deteriorationist. I am easily moved by symbols; there is something of a Quarles in my nature. Lacking the philosophic mind, I prefer to see my abstractions concretely imaged. And it occurred to me then that if I wanted an emblem to picture the sacredness of marriage and the influence of the home I could not do better than choose two little black feet like tea-leaves peeping out decorously from under the hem of wide, disguising petticoats. While heels and thoroughbred insteps should figure—oh well, the reverse.

The current of my thoughts was turned aside by the old man's voice. "I expect you are musical," he said.

Oh yes, I was a little; and he held out to me a bulky folio.

"Did you ever hear this?" he asked.

Robert the Devil: no, I never had. I did not doubt that it was a gap in my musical education.

The old man took the book and drew up a chair from the dim *penetralia* of the shop. It was then that I noticed a surprising fact: what I had, at a careless glance, taken to be a common counter I perceived now to be a piano of a square, unfamiliar shape. The old man sat down before it. "You must forgive any defects in its tone," he said, turning to me. "An early Broadwood, Georgian, you know, and has seen a deal of service in a hundred years."

He opened the lid, and the yellow keys grinned at me in the darkness like the teeth of an ancient horse.

The old man rustled pages till he found a desired place. "The ballet music," he said: "it's fine. Listen to this."

His bony, rather tremulous hands began suddenly to move with an astonishing nimbleness, and there rose up, faint and tinkling against the roar of the traffic, a gay pirouetting music. The instrument rattled considerably and the volume of sound was thin as the trickle of a drought-shrunken stream: but, still, it kept tune and the melody was there, filmy, aerial.

"And now for the drinking-song," cried the old man, warming excitedly to his work. He played a series of chords that mounted modulating upwards towards a breaking-point; so supremely operatic as positively to be a parody of that moment of tautening suspense, when the singers are bracing themselves for a burst of passion. And then it came, the drinking chorus. One pictured to oneself cloaked men, wildly jovial over the emptiness of cardboard flagons.

> "Versiam' a tazza piena
> Il generoso umor . . ."

The old man's voice was cracked and shrill, but his enthusiasm made up for any defects in execution. I had never seen anyone so wholeheartedly a reveller.

He turned over a few more pages. "Ah, the 'Valse Infernale,'" he said. "That's good." There was a little melancholy prelude and then the tune, not so infernal perhaps as one might have been led to expect, but still pleasant enough. I looked over his shoulder at the words and sang to his accompaniment.

> "Demoni fatali
> Fantasmi d'orror,
> Dei regni infernali
> Plaudite al signor."

A great steam-driven brewer's lorry roared past with its annihilating thunder and utterly blotted out the last line. The old man's hands still moved over the yellow keys, my mouth opened and shut; but there was no sound of words or music. It was as though the fatal demons, the phantasms of horror, had made a sudden irruption into this peaceful, abstracted place.

I looked out through the narrow door. The traffic ceaselessly passed; men and women hurried along with set faces. Phantasms of horror, all of them: infernal realms wherein they dwelt. Outside, men lived under the tyranny of things. Their every action was determined by the orders of mere matter, by money, and the tools of their trade and the unthinking laws of habit and convention. But here I seemed to be safe from things, living at a remove from actuality; here where a bearded old man, improbable survival from some other time, indomitably played the music of romance, despite the fact that the phantasms of horror might occasionally drown the sound of it with their clamour.

"So: will you take it?" The voice of the old man broke across my thoughts. "I will let you have it for five shillings." He was holding out the thick, dilapidated volume towards me. His face wore a look of strained anxiety. I could see how eager he was to get my five shillings, how necessary, poor man! for him. He has been, I thought with an unreasonable bitterness—he has been simply performing for my benefit, like a trained dog. His aloofness, his culture—all a business trick. I felt aggrieved. He was just one of the common phantasms of horror masquerading as the angel of this somewhat comic paradise of contemplation. I gave him a couple of half-crowns and he began wrapping the book in paper.

"I tell you," he said, "I'm sorry to part with it. I get attached to my books, you know; but they always have to go."

He sighed with such an obvious genuineness of feeling that I repented of the judgment I had passed upon him. He was a reluctant inhabitant of the infernal realms, even as was I myself.

Outside they were beginning to cry the evening papers: a ship sunk, trenches captured, somebody's new stirring speech. We looked at one another—the old bookseller and I—in silence. We understood one another without speech. Here were we in particular, and here was the whole of humanity in general, all faced by the hideous triumph of things. In this continued massacre of men, in this old man's enforced sacrifice, matter equally triumphed. And walking homeward through Regent's Park, I too found matter triumphing over me. My book was unconscionably heavy, and I wondered what in the world I should do with a piano score of *Robert the Devil* when I had got it home. It would only be another thing to weigh me down and hinder me; and at the moment it was very, oh, abominably, heavy. I leaned over the railings that ring round the ornamental water, and as unostentatiously as I could, I let the book fall into the bushes.

I often think it would be best not to attempt the solution of the problem of life. Living is hard enough without complicating the process by thinking about it. The wisest thing, perhaps, is to take for granted the "wearisome condition of humanity, born under one law, to another bound," and to leave the matter at that, without an attempt to reconcile the incompatibles. Oh, the absurd difficulty of it all! And I have, moreover, wasted five shillings, which is serious, you know, in these thin times.

THE DEATH OF LULLY

THE sea lay in a breathing calm, and the galley, bosomed in its transparent water, stirred rhythmically to the slow pulse of its sleeping life. Down below there, fathoms away through the crystal-clear Mediterranean, the shadow of the ship lazily swung, moving, a long dark patch, very slowly back and forth across the white sand of the sea-bottom—very slowly, a scarcely perceptible advance and recession of the green darkness. Fishes sometimes passed, now hanging poised with idly tremulous fins, now darting onwards, effortless and incredibly swift; and always, as it seemed, utterly aimless, whether they rested or whether they moved; as the life of angels their life seemed mysterious and unknowable.

All was silence on board the ship. In their fetid cage below decks the rowers slept where they sat, chained, on their narrow benches. On deck the sailors lay sleeping or sat in little groups playing at dice. The fore-part of the deck was reserved, it seemed, for passengers of distinction. Two figures, a man and a woman, were reclining there on couches, their faces and half-bared limbs flushed in the coloured shadow that was thrown by the great red awning stretched above them.

It was a nobleman, the sailors had heard, and his mistress that they had on board. They had taken their passage at Scanderoon, and were homeward bound for Spain. Proud as sin these Spaniards were; the man treated them like slaves or dogs. As for the woman, she was well enough, but they could find as good a face and pair of breasts in their native Genoa. If any one so much as looked at her from half the ship's length away it sent her possessor into a rage. He had struck one man for smiling at her. Damned Catalonian, as jealous as a stag; they wished him the stag's horns as well as its temper.

It was intensely hot even under the awning. The man woke from his uneasy sleep and reached out to where on a little table beside him stood a deep silver cup of mixed wine and water. He drank a gulp of it; it was as warm as blood and hardly cooled his throat. He turned over and, leaning on his elbow, looked at his companion. She on her back, quietly breathing through parted lips, still asleep. He leaned across and pinched her on the breast, so that she woke up with a sudden start and cry of pain.

"Why did you wake me?" she asked.

He laughed and shrugged his shoulders. He had, indeed, had no reason for doing so, except that he did not like it that she should be comfortably asleep, while he was awake and unpleasantly conscious of the heat.

"It is hotter than ever," he said, with a kind of gloomy satisfaction at the thought that she would now have to suffer the same discomforts as himself. "The wine scorches instead of cooling; the sun seems no lower down the sky."

The woman pouted. "You pinched me cruelly," she said. "And I still do not know why you wanted to wake me."

He smiled again, this time with a good-humoured lasciviousness. "I wanted to kiss you," he said. He passed his hand over her body possessively, as a man might caress a dog.

Suddenly the quiet of the afternoon was shattered. A great clamour rose up, ragged and uneven, on the air. Shrill yells pierced the dull rumbling growl of bass voices, pierced the sound of beaten drums and hammered metal.

"What are they doing in the town?" asked the woman anxiously of her lover.

"God knows," he answered. "Perhaps the heathen hounds are making some trouble with our men."

He got up and walked to the rail of the ship. A quarter of a mile away, across the smooth water of the bay, stood the little African town at which they had stopped to call. The sunlight showed everything with a hard and merciless definition. Sky, palms, white houses, domes, and towers seemed as though made from some hard enamelled metal. A ridge of low red hills rolled away to right and left. The sunshine gave to everything in the scene the same clarity of detail, so that to the eye of the onlooker there was no impression of distance. The whole thing seemed to be painted in flat upon a single plane.

The young man returned to his couch under the awning and lay down. It was hotter than ever, or seemed so, at least, since he had made the exertion of getting up. He thought of high cool pastures in the hills, with the pleasant sound of streams, far down and out of sight in their deep channels. He thought of winds that were fresh and scented—winds that were not mere breaths of dust and fire. He thought of the shade of cypresses, a narrow opaque strip of darkness; and he thought too of the green coolness, more diffused and fluid and transparent, of chestnut groves. And he thought of the people he remembered sitting under the trees—young people, gay and brightly dressed, whose life was all gaiety and deliciousness. There were the songs that they sang —he recalled the voices and the dancing of the strings. And there were perfumes and, when one drew closer, the faint intoxicating fragrance of a woman's body. He thought of the stories they told; one in particular came to his mind, a capital tale of a sorcerer who offered to change a peasant's wife into a mare, and how he gulled the husband and enjoyed the woman before his eyes, and the delightful excuses he made when she failed to change her shape. He smiled to himself at the thought of it, and stretching out a hand touched his mistress. Her bosom was soft to his fingers and damp with sweat; he had an unpleasant notion that she was melting in the heat.

"Why do you touch me?" she asked.

He made no reply, but turned away from her. He wondered how it would come to pass that people would rise again in the body. It seemed curious, considering the manifest activities of worms. And suppose one rose in the body that one possessed in age. He shuddered, picturing to himself what this woman would be like when she was sixty, seventy. She would be beyond words repulsive. Old men too were horrible. They stank, and their eyes were rheumy and rosiny, like the eyes of deer. He decided that he would kill himself before he grew old. He was eight-and-twenty now. He would give himself twelve years more. Then he would end it. His thoughts dimmed and faded away into sleep.

The woman looked at him as he slept. He was a good man, she thought, though sometimes cruel. He was different from all the other men she had known. Once, when she was sixteen and a beginner in the business of love, she had thought that all men were always drunk when they made love. They were all dirty and like beasts; she had felt herself superior to them. But this man was a nobleman. She could not understand him; his thoughts were always obscure. She felt herself infinitely inferior to him. She was afraid of him and his occasional cruelty; but still he was a good man, and he might do what he liked with her.

From far off came the sound of oars, a rhythmical splash and creak. Somebody shouted, and from startlingly close at hand one of the sailors hallooed back.

The young man woke up with a start.

"What is it?" he asked, turning with an angry look to the girl, as though he held her to be responsible for this breaking in upon his slumbers.

"The boat, I think," she said. "It must be coming back from the shore."

The boat's crew came up over the side, and all the stagnant life of the ship flowed excitedly round them. They were the centre of a vortex towards which all were drawn. Even the young Catalonian, for all his hatred of these stinking Genoese shipmen, was sucked into the eddy. Everybody was talking at once, and in the general hubbub of question and answer there was nothing coherent to be made out. Piercingly distinct above all the noise came the voice of the little cabin-boy, who had been to shore with the boat's crew. He was running round to every one in turn repeating: "I hit one of them. You know. I hit one. With a stone on the forehead. Didn't he bleed, ooh! didn't he just!" And he would dance with uncontrollable excitement.

The captain held up his hand and shouted for silence. "One at a time, there," he ordered, and when order had a little been restored, added grumblingly, "Like a pack of dogs on a bone. You talk, boatswain."

"I hit one of them," said the boy. Somebody cuffed him over the head, and he relapsed into silence.

When the boatswain's story had rambled through labyrinths of digression, over countless obstacles of interruptions and emendations, to its conclusion, the Spaniard went back to join his companion under the awning. He had assumed again his habitual indifference.

"Nearly butchered," he said languidly, in response to her eager questions. "They"—he jerked a hand in the direction of the town—"they were pelting an old fellow who had come there preaching the Faith. Left him dead on the beach. Our men had to run for it."

She could get no more out of him; he turned over and pretended to go to sleep.

Towards evening they received a visit from the captain. He was a large, handsome man, with gold ear-rings glinting from among a bush of black hair.

"Divine Providence," he remarked sententiously, after the usual courtesies had passed, "has called upon us to perform a very notable work."

"Indeed?" said the young man.

"No less a work," continued the captain, "than to save from the clutches of the infidels and heathen the precious remains of a holy martyr."

The captain let fall his pompous manner. It was evident that he had carefully prepared these pious sentences, they rolled so roundly off his tongue. But he was eager now to get on with his story, and it was in a homelier style that he went on: "If you knew these seas as well as I—and it's near twenty years now that I've been sailing them—you'd have some knowledge of this same holy man that—God rot their souls for it!—these cursed Arabs have done to death here. I've heard of him more than once in my time, and not always well spoken of; for, to tell the honest truth, he does more harm with his preachments to good Christian traders than ever he did good to black-hearted heathen dogs. Leave the bees alone, I say, and if you can get a little honey out of them quietly, so much the better; but he goes about among the beehives with a pole, stirring up trouble for himself and others too. Leave them alone to their damnation, is what I say, and get what you can from them this side of hell. But, still, he has died a holy martyr's death. God rest his soul! A martyr is a wonderful thing, you know, and it's not for the likes of us to understand what they mean by it all.

"They do say, too, that he could make gold. And, to my mind, it would have been a thing more pleasing to God and man if he had stopped at home minting money for poor folks and dealing it round, so that there'd be no need to work any more and break oneself for a morsel of bread. Yes, he was great at gold-making and at the books too. They tell me he was called the Illuminated Doctor. But I know him still as plain Lully. I used to hear of him from my father, plain Lully, and no better once than he should have been.

"My father was a shipwright in Minorca in those days—how long since? Fifty, sixty years perhaps. He knew him then; he has often told me the tale. And a raffish young dog he was. Drinking, drabbing, and dicing he outdid them all, and between the bouts wrote poems, they say, which was more than the rest could do. But he gave it all up on the sudden. Gave away his lands, quitted his former companions, and turned hermit up in the hills, living alone like a fox in his burrow, high up above the vines. And all because of a woman and his own qualmish stomach."

The shipmaster paused and helped himself to a little wine. "And what did this woman do?" the girl asked curiously.

"Ah, it's not what she did but what she didn't do," the captain answered, with a leer and wink. "She kept him at his distance—all but once, all but once; and that was what put him on the road to being a martyr. But there, I'm outrunning myself. I must go more soberly.

"There was a lady of some consequence in the island—one

of the Castellos, I think she was; her first name has quite slipped my memory—Anastasia, or something of the kind. Lully conceives a passion for her, and sighs and importunes her through I know not how many months and years. But her virtue stands steady as the judgment seat. Well, in the end, what happens was this. The story leaked out after it was all over, and he was turned hermit in the mountains. What happened, I say, was this. She tells him at last that he may come and see her, fixing some solitary twilight place and time, her own room at nightfall. You can guess how he washes and curls and scents himself, shaves his chin, chews anises, musks over whatever of the goat may cling about the body. Off he goes, dreaming swoons and ecstasies, foretasting inconceivable sweets. Arrived, he finds the lady a little melancholy—her settled humour, but a man might expect a smile at such a time. Still, nothing abashed, he falls at her feet and pours out his piteous case, telling her he has sighed through seven years, not closed an eye for above a hundred nights, is forepined to a shadow, and, in a word, will perish unless she show some mercy. She, still melancholy—her settled humour, mark you—makes answer that she is ready to yield, and that her body is entirely his. With that, she lets herself be done with as he pleases, but always sorrowfully. 'You are all mine,' says he— 'all mine'—and unlaces her gorgeret to prove the same. But he was wrong. Another lover was already in her bosom, and his kisses had been passionate—oh, burning passionate, for he had kissed away half her left breast. From the nipple down it had all been gnawed away by a cancer.

"Bah, a man may see as bad as that any day in the street or at church-doors where beggars most congregate. I grant you that it is a nasty sight, worm-eaten flesh, but still—not enough, you will agree, to make yourself a hermit over. But there, I told you he had a queasiness of the stomach. But doubtless it was all in God's plan to make a holy martyr of him. But for that same queasiness of his, he would still be living there, a superannuated rake; or else have died in very foul odour, instead of passing, all embalmed with sanctity, to Paradise Gate.

"I know not what happened to him between his hermit-hood and his quest for martyrdom. I saw him first a dozen years ago, down Tunis way. They were always clapping him into prison or pulling out his beard for preaching. This time, it seems, they have made a holy martyr of him, done the business thoroughly with no bungling. Well, may he pray for our souls at the throne of God. I go in secretly to-night to steal his body. It lies on the shore there beyond the jetty. It will be a notable work, I tell you, to bring back so precious a corpse to Christendom. A most notable work. . . ."

The captain rubbed his hands.

It was after midnight, but there was still a bustle of activity on board the galley. At any moment they were expecting the arrival of the boat with the corpse of the martyr. A couch, neatly draped in black, with at its head and foot candles burning two by two, had been set out on the poop for the reception of the body. The captain called the young Spaniard and his mistress to come and see the bier.

"That's a good bit of work for you," he said, with justifiable pride. "I defy any one to make a more decent resting-place for a martyr than that is. It could hardly have been done better on shore, with every appliance at hand. But we sailors, you know, can make anything out of nothing. A truckle-bed, a strip of tarred canvas, and four tallow dips from the cabin lanterns— there you are, a bier for a king."

He hurried away, and a little later the young man and the girl could hear him giving orders and cursing somewhere down below. The candles burned almost without a tremor in the windless air, and the reflections of the stars were long, thin tracks of fire along the utterly calm water.

"Were there but perfumed flowers and the sound of a lute," said the young Spaniard, "the night would tremble into passion of its own accord. Love should come unsought on such a night as this, among these black waters and the stars that sleep so peacefully on their bosom."

He put his arm round the girl and bent his head to kiss her. But she averted her face. He could feel a shudder run her through the body.

"Not to-night," she whispered. "I think of the poor dead man. I would rather pray."

"No, no," he cried. "Forget him. Remember only that we are alive, and that we have but little time and none to waste."

He drew her into the shadow under the bulwark, and, sitting down on a coil of rope, crushed her body to his own and began kissing her with fury. She lay, at first, limp in his arms, but gradually she kindled to his passion.

A plash of oars announced the approach of the boat. The captain hallooed into the darkness: "Did you find him?"

"Yes, we have him here," came back the answer.

"Good. Bring him alongside and we'll hoist him up. We have the bier in readiness. He shall lie in state to-night."

"But he's not dead," shouted back the voice from the night.

"Not dead?" repeated the captain, thunderstruck. "But what about the bier, then?"

A thin, feeble voice came back. "Your work will not be wasted, my friend. It will be but a short time before I need your bier."

The captain, a little abashed, answered in a gentler tone, "We thought, holy father, that the heathens had done their worst and that Almighty God had already given you the martyr's crown."

By this time the boat had emerged from the darkness. In the stern sheets an old man was lying, his white hair and beard stained with blood, his Dominican's robe torn and fouled with dust. At the sight of him, the captain pulled off his cap and dropped upon his knees.

"Give us your blessing, holy father," he begged.

The old man raised his hand and wished him peace.

They lifted him on board and, at his own desire, laid him upon the bier which had been prepared for his dead body. "It would be a waste of trouble," he said, "to put me anywhere else, seeing I shall in any case be lying there so soon."

So there he lay, very still under the four candles. One might have taken him for dead already, but that his eyes, when he opened them, shone so brightly.

He dismissed from the poop every one except the young Spaniard. "We are countrymen," he said, "and of noble blood, both of us. I would rather have you near me than any one else."

The sailors knelt for a blessing and disappeared; soon they could be heard weighing the anchor; it was safest to be off before day. Like mourners at either side of the lighted bier crouched the Spaniard and his mistress. The body of the old man, who was not yet dead, lay quiet under the candles. The martyr was silent for some time, but at last he opened his eyes and looked at the young man and the woman.

"I too," he said, "was in love, once. In this year falls the jubilee of my last earthly passion; fifty years have run since last I longed after the flesh—fifty years since God opened my eyes to the hideousness of the corruption that man has brought upon himself.

"You are young, and your bodies are clean and straight, with no blotch or ulcer or leprous taint to mar their much-desired beauty; but because of your outward pride, your souls, it may be, fester inwardly the more.

"And yet God made all perfect; it is but accident and the evil of will that causes defaults. All metals should be gold, were it not that their elements willed evilly in their desire to combine. And so with men: the burning sulphur of passion, the salt of wisdom, the nimble mercurial soul should come together to make a golden being, incorruptible and rustless. But the elements mingle jarringly, not in a pure harmony of love, and gold is rare, while lead and iron and poisonous brass that leaves a taste as of remorse behind it are everywhere common.

"God opened my eyes to it before my youth had too utterly wasted itself to rottenness. It was half a hundred years ago, but I see her still, my Ambrosia, with her white, sad face and her naked body and that monstrous ill eating away at her breast.

"I have lived since then trying to amend the evil, trying to

restore, as far as my poor powers would go, some measure of
original perfection to the corrupted world. I have striven to give
to all metals their true nature, to make true gold from the false,
the unreal, the accidental metals, lead and copper and tin and
iron. And I have essayed that more difficult alchemy, the transformation of men. I die now in my effort to purge away that
most foul dross of misbelief from the souls of these heathen men.
Have I achieved anything? I know not."

The galley was moving now, its head turned seaward. The
candles shivered in the wind of its speed, casting uncertain,
changing shadows upon his face. There was a long silence on
the poop. The oars creaked and splashed. Sometimes a shout
would come up from below, orders given by the overseer of the
slaves, a curse, the sound of a blow. The old man spoke again,
more weakly now, as though to himself.

"I have had eighty years of it," he said—"eighty years in the
midst of this corroding sea of hatred and strife. A man has need
to keep pure and unalloyed his core of gold, that little centre of
perfection with which all, even in this declination of time, are
born. All other metal, though it be as tough as steel, as shining-
hard as brass, will melt before the devouring bitterness of life.
Hatred, lust, anger—the vile passions will corrode your will of
iron, the warlike pomp of your front of brass. It needs the golden
perfection of pure love and pure knowledge to withstand them.

"God has willed that I should be the stone—weak, indeed, in
virtue—that has touched and transformed at least a little of baser
metal into the gold that is above corruption. But it is hard work
—thankless work. Man has made a hell of his world, and has set
up gods of pain to rule it. Goatish gods, that revel and feast on
the agony of it all, poring over the tortured world, like those
hateful lovers, whose lust burns darkly into cruelty.

"Fever goads us through life in a delirium of madness.
Thirsting for the swamps of evil whence the fever came, thirsting
for the mirages of his own delirium, man rushes headlong he
knows not whither. And all the time a devouring cancer gnaws
at his entrails. It will kill him in the end, when even the ghastly

inspiration of fever will not be enough to whip him on. He will lie there, cumbering the earth, a heap of rottenness and pain, until at last the cleansing fire comes to sweep the horror away.

"Fever and cancer; acids that burn and corrode. . . . I have had eighty years of it. Thank God, it is the end."

It was already dawn; the candles were hardly visible now in the light, faded to nothing, like souls in prosperity. In a little while the old man was asleep.

The captain tiptoed up on to the poop and drew the young Spaniard aside for a confidential talk.

"Do you think he will die to-day?" he asked.

The young man nodded.

"God rest his soul," said the captain piously. "But do you think it would be best to take his body to Minorca or to Genoa? At Minorca they would give much to have their own patron martyr. At the same time it would add to the glory of Genoa to possess so holy a relic, though he is in no way connected with the place. It's there is my difficulty. Suppose, you see, that my people of Genoa did not want the body, he being from Minorca and not one of them. I should look a fool then, bringing it in in state. Oh, it's hard, it's hard. There's so much to think about. I am not sure but what I hadn't better put in at Minorca first. What do you think?"

The Spaniard shrugged his shoulders. "I have no advice to offer."

"Lord," said the captain as he bustled away, "life is a tangled knot to unravel."

SIR HERCULES

"THE infant who was destined to become the fourth baronet of the name of Lapith was born in the year 1740. He was a very small baby, weighing not more than three pounds at birth, but from the first he was sturdy and healthy. In honour of his maternal grandfather, Sir Hercules Occam of Bishop's Occam, he was christened Hercules. His mother, like many other mothers, kept a notebook, in which his progress from month to month was recorded. He walked at ten months, and before his second year was out he had learnt to speak a number of words. At three years he weighed but twenty-four pounds, and at six, though he could read and write perfectly and showed a remarkable aptitude for music, he was no larger and heavier than a well-grown child of two. Meanwhile, his mother had borne two other children, a boy and a girl, one of whom died of croup during infancy, while the other was carried off by smallpox before it reached the age of five. Hercules remained the only surviving child.

' On his twelfth birthday Hercules was still only three feet and two inches in height. His head, which was very handsome and nobly shaped, was too big for his body, but otherwise he was exquisitely proportioned and, for his size, of great strength and agility. His parents, in the hope of making him grow, consulted all the most eminent physicians of the time. Their various prescriptions were followed to the letter, but in vain. One ordered a very plentiful meat diet; another exercise; a third constructed a little rack, modelled on those employed by the Holy Inquisition, on which young Hercules was stretched, with excruciating torments, for half an hour every morning and evening. In the course of the next three years Hercules gained perhaps two inches. After that his growth stopped completely, and he remained for the rest of his life a pigmy of three feet and four inches. His father, who had built the most extravagant hopes upon his son,

491

planning for him in his imagination a military career equal to that of Marlborough, found himself a disappointed man. 'I have brought an abortion into the world,' he would say, and he took so violent a dislike to his son that the boy dared scarcely come into his presence. His temper, which had been serene, was turned by disappointment to moroseness and savagery. He avoided all company (being, as he said, ashamed to show himself, the father of a *lusus naturæ*, among normal, healthy human beings), and took to solitary drinking, which carried him very rapidly to his grave; for the year before Hercules came of age his father was taken off by an apoplexy. His mother, whose love for him had increased with the growth of his father's unkindness, did not long survive, but little more than a year after her husband's death succumbed, after eating two dozen of oysters, to an attack of typhoid fever.

"Hercules thus found himself at the age of twenty-one alone in the world, and master of a considerable fortune, including the estate and mansion of Crome. The beauty and intelligence of his childhood had survived into his manly age, and, but for his dwarfish stature, he would have taken his place among the handsomest and most accomplished young men of his time. He was well read in the Greek and Latin authors, as well as in all the moderns of any merit who had written in English, French, or Italian. He had a good ear for music, and was no indifferent performer on the violin, which he used to play like a bass viol, seated on a chair with the instrument between his legs. To the music of the harpsichord and clavichord he was extremely partial, but the smallness of his hands made it impossible for him ever to perform upon these instruments. He had a small ivory flute made for him, on which, whenever he was melancholy, he used to play a simple country air or jig, affirming that this rustic music had more power to clear and raise the spirits than the most artificial productions of the masters. From an early age he practised the composition of poetry, but, though conscious of his great powers in this art, he would never publish any specimen of his writing. 'My stature,' he would say, 'is reflected in my verses; if the public were to read them it would not be because I am a poet, but because I am a dwarf.' Several MS. books of Sir Hercules's poems survive. A single specimen will suffice to illustrate his qualities as a poet.

"In ancient days, while yet the world was young,
  Ere Abram fed his flocks or Homer sung;
When blacksmith Tubal tamed creative fire,
  And Jabal dwelt in tents and Jubal struck the lyre;
Flesh grown corrupt brought forth a monstrous birth
And obscene giants trod the shrinking earth,
Till God, impatient of their sinful brood,
Gave rein to wrath and drown'd them in the Flood.
Teeming again, repeopled Tellus bore
The lubber Hero and the Man of War;
Huge towers of Brawn, topp'd with an empty Skull,
Witlessly bold, heroically dull.
Long ages pass'd and Man grown more refin'd,
Slighter in muscle but of vaster Mind,
Smiled at his grandsire's broadsword, bow and bill,
And learn'd to wield the Pencil and the Quill.
The glowing canvas and the written page
Immortaliz'd his name from age to age,
His name emblazon'd on Fame's temple wall;
For Art grew great as Humankind grew small.
Thus man's long progress step by step we trace;
The Giant dies, the hero takes his place;
The Giant vile, the dull heroic Block:
At one we shudder and at one we mock.
Man last appears. In him the Soul's pure flame
Burns brightlier in a not inord'nate frame.
Of old when Heroes fought and Giants swarmed,
Men were huge mounds of matter scarce inform'd;
Wearied by leavening so vast a mass,
The spirit slept and all the mind was crass.
The smaller carcase of these later days
Is soon inform'd; the Soul unwearied plays
And like a Pharos darts abroad her mental rays.
But can we think that Providence will stay
Man's footsteps here upon the upward way?
Mankind in understanding and in grace
Advanc'd so far beyond the Giants' race?

Hence impious thought! Still led by GOD's own Hand,
Mankind proceeds towards the Promised Land.
A time will come (prophetic, I descry
Remoter dawns along the gloomy sky),
When happy mortals of a Golden Age
Will backward turn the dark historic page,
And in our vaunted race of Men behold
A form as gross, a Mind as dead and cold,
As we in Giants see, in warriors of old.
A time will come, wherein the soul shall be
From all superfluous matter wholly free:
When the light body, agile as a fawn's,
Shall sport with grace along the velvet lawns.
Nature's most delicate and final birth,
Mankind perfected shall possess the earth.
But ah, not yet! For still the Giants' race,
Huge, though diminish'd, tramps the Earth's fair face;
Gross and repulsive, yet perversely proud,
Men of their imperfections boast aloud.
Vain of their bulk, of all they still retain
Of giant ugliness absurdly vain;
At all that's small they point their stupid scorn
And, monsters, think themselves divinely born.
Sad is the Fate of those, ah, sad indeed,
The rare precursors of the nobler breed!
Who come man's golden glory to foretell,
But pointing Heav'nwards live themselves in Hell.

"As soon as he came into the estate, Sir Hercules set about remodelling his household. For though by no means ashamed of his deformity—indeed, if we may judge from the poem quoted above, he regarded himself as being in many ways superior to the ordinary race of man—he found the presence of full-grown men and women embarrassing. Realising, too, that he must abandon all ambitions in the great world, he determined to retire absolutely from it and to create, as it were, at Crome a private world of his own, in which all should be proportionable to himself. Accordingly, he discharged all the old servants of the house and replaced them gradually, as he was able to find suitable successors, by others of dwarfish stature. In the course of a few years he had assembled about himself a numerous household, no member of which was above four feet high and the smallest among them scarcely two feet and six inches. His father's dogs, such as setters, mastiffs, greyhounds, and a pack of beagles, he sold or gave away as too large and too boisterous for his house, replacing them by pugs and King Charles spaniels and whatever other breeds of dog were the smallest. His father's stable was also sold. For his own use, whether riding or driving, he had six black Shetland ponies, with four very choice piebald animals of New Forest breed.

"Having thus settled his household entirely to his own satisfaction, it only remained for him to find some suitable companion with whom to share this paradise. Sir Hercules had a susceptible heart, and had more than once, between the ages of sixteen and twenty, felt what it was to love. But here his deformity had been a source of the most bitter humiliation, for, having once dared to declare himself to a young lady of his choice, he had been received with laughter. On his persisting, she had picked him up and shaken him like an importunate child, telling him to run away and plague her no more. The story soon got about—indeed, the young lady herself used to tell it as a particularly pleasant anecdote—and the taunts and mockery it occasioned were a source of the most acute distress to Hercules. From the poems written at this period we gather that he meditated taking his own life. In course of time, however, he lived down this humiliation; but never again, though he often fell in love, and that very passionately, did he dare to make any advances to those in whom he was interested. After coming to the estate and finding that he was in a position to create his own world as he desired it, he saw that, if he was to have a wife—which he very much desired, being of an affectionate and, indeed, amorous temper—he must choose her as he had chosen his servants—from among the race of dwarfs. But to find a suitable wife was, he found, a matter of some difficulty; for he would marry none who was not distinguished by beauty and gentle birth. The dwarfish daughter of Lord Bemboro he refused on the ground that besides being a pigmy she was hunchbacked;

while another young lady, an orphan belonging to a very good family in Hampshire, was rejected by him because her face, like that of so many dwarfs, was wizened and repulsive. Finally, when he was almost despairing of success, he heard from a reliable source that Count Titimalo, a Venetian nobleman, possessed a daughter of exquisite beauty and great accomplishments, who was but three feet in height. Setting out at once for Venice, he went immediately on his arrival to pay his respects to the count, whom he found living with his wife and five children in a very mean apartment in one of the poorer quarters of the town. Indeed, the count was so far reduced in his circumstances that he was even then negotiating (so it was rumoured) with a travelling company of clowns and acrobats, who had had the misfortune to lose their performing dwarf, for the sale of his diminutive daughter Filomena. Sir Hercules arrived in time to save her from this untoward fate, for he was so much charmed by Filomena's grace and beauty, that at the end of three days' courtship he made her a formal offer of marriage, which was accepted by her no less joyfully than by her father, who perceived in an English son-in-law a rich and unfailing source of revenue. After an unostentatious marriage, at which the English ambassador acted as one of the witnesses, Sir Hercules and his bride returned by sea to England, where they settled down, as it proved, to a life of uneventful happiness.

"Crome and its household of dwarfs delighted Filomena, who felt herself now for the first time to be a free woman living among her equals in a friendly world. She had many tastes in common with her husband, especially that of music. She had a beautiful voice, of a power surprising in one so small, and could touch A in alt without effort. Accompanied by her husband on his fine Cremona fiddle, which he played, as we have noted before, as one plays a bass viol, she would sing all the liveliest and tenderest airs from the operas and cantatas of her native country. Seated together at the harpsichord, they found that they could with their four hands play all the music written for two hands of ordinary size, a circumstance which gave Sir Hercules unfailing pleasure.

"When they were not making music or reading together, which they often did, both in English and Italian, they spent their time in healthful outdoor exercises, sometimes rowing in a little boat on the lake, but more often riding or driving, occupations in which, because they were entirely new to her, Filomena especially delighted. When she had become a perfectly proficient rider, Filomena and her husband used often to go hunting in the park, at that time very much more extensive than it is now. They hunted not foxes nor hares, but rabbits, using a pack of about thirty black and fawn-coloured pugs, a kind of dog which, when not overfed, can course a rabbit as well as any of the smaller breeds. Four dwarf grooms, dressed in scarlet liveries and mounted on white Exmoor ponies, hunted the pack, while their master and mistress, in green habits, followed either on the black Shetlands or on the piebald New Forest ponies. A picture of the whole hunt—dogs, horses, grooms, and masters—was painted by William Stubbs, whose work Sir Hercules admired so much that he invited him, though a man of ordinary stature, to come and stay at the mansion for the purpose of executing this picture. Stubbs likewise painted a portrait of Sir Hercules and his lady driving in their green enamelled calash drawn by four black Shetlands. Sir Hercules wears a plum-coloured velvet coat and white breeches; Filomena is dressed in flowered muslin and a very large hat with pink feathers. The two figures in their gay carriage stand out sharply against a dark background of trees; but to the left of the picture the trees fall away and disappear, so that the four black ponies are seen against a pale and strangely lurid sky that has the golden-brown colour of thunder-clouds lighted up by the sun.

"In this way four years passed happily by. At the end of that time Filomena found herself great with child. Sir Hercules was overjoyed. 'If God is good,' he wrote in his day-book, 'the name of Lapith will be preserved and our rarer and more delicate race transmitted through the generations until in the fullness of time the world shall recognise the superiority of those beings whom now it uses to make mock of.' On his wife's being brought to bed of a son he wrote a poem to the same effect. The child was christened Ferdinando in memory of the builder of the house.

"With the passage of the months a certain sense of disquiet began to invade the minds of Sir Hercules and his lady. For the child was growing with an extraordinary rapidity. At a year he weighed as much as Hercules had weighed when he was three. 'Ferdinando goes *crescendo*,' wrote Filomena in her diary. 'It seems not natural.' At eighteen months the baby was almost as tall as their smallest jockey, who was a man of thirty-six. Could it be that Ferdinando was destined to become a man of the normal, gigantic dimensions? It was a thought to which neither of his parents dared yet give open utterance, but in the secrecy of their respective diaries they brooded over it in terror and dismay.

"On his third birthday Ferdinando was taller than his mother and not more than a couple of inches short of his father's height. 'To-day for the first time,' wrote Sir Hercules, 'we discussed the situation. The hideous truth can be concealed no longer: Ferdinando is not one of us. On this, his third birthday, a day when we should have been rejoicing at the health, the strength, and beauty of our child, we wept together over the ruin of our happiness. God give us strength to bear this cross.'

"At the age of eight Ferdinando was so large and so exuberantly healthy that his parents decided, though reluctantly, to send him to school. He was packed off to Eton at the beginning of the next half. A profound peace settled upon the house. Ferdinando returned for the summer holidays larger and stronger than ever. One day he knocked down the butler and broke his arm. 'He is rough, inconsiderate, unamenable to persuasion,' wrote his father. 'The only thing that will teach him manners is corporal chastisement.' Ferdinando, who at this age was already seventeen inches taller than his father, received no corporal chastisement.

"One summer holidays about three years later Ferdinando returned to Crome accompanied by a very large mastiff dog. He had bought it from an old man at Windsor who found the beast too expensive to feed. It was a savage, unreliable animal; hardly had it entered the house when it attacked one of Sir Hercules's favourite pugs, seizing the creature in its jaws and shaking it till it was nearly dead. Extremely put out by this occurrence, Sir Hercules ordered that the beast should be chained up in the stable-yard. Ferdinando sullenly answered that the dog was his, and he would keep it where he pleased. His father, growing angry, bade him take the animal out of the house at once, on pain of his utmost displeasure. Ferdinando refused to move. His mother at this moment coming into the room, the dog flew at her, knocked her down, and in a twinkling had very severely mauled her arm and shoulder; in another instant it must infallibly have had her by the throat, had not Sir Hercules drawn his sword and stabbed the animal to the heart. Turning on his son, he ordered him to leave the room immediately, as being unfit to remain in the same place with the mother whom he had nearly murdered. So awe-inspiring was the spectacle of Sir Hercules standing with one foot on the carcase of the gigantic dog, his sword drawn and still bloody, so commanding were his voice, his gestures, and the expression of his face, that Ferdinando slunk out of the room in terror and behaved himself for all the rest of the vacation in an entirely exemplary fashion. His mother soon recovered from the bites of the mastiff, but the effect on her mind of this adventure was ineradicable; from that time forth she lived always among imaginary terrors.

"The two years which Ferdinando spent on the Continent, making the Grand Tour, were a period of happy repose for his parents. But even now the thought of the future haunted them; nor were they able to solace themselves with all the diversions of their younger days. The Lady Filomena had lost her voice and Sir Hercules was grown too rheumatical to play the violin. He, it is true, still rode after his pugs, but his wife felt herself too old and, since the episode of the mastiff, too nervous for such sports. At most, to please her husband, she would follow the hunt at a distance in a little gig drawn by the safest and oldest of the Shetlands.

"The day fixed for Ferdinando's return came round. Filomena, sick with vague dreads and presentiments, retired to her chamber and her bed. Sir Hercules received his son alone. A giant in a brown travelling-suit entered the room. 'Welcome home, my son,' said Sir Hercules in a voice that trembled a little.

"'I hope I see you well, sir.' Ferdinando bent down to shake hands, then straightened himself up again. The top of his father's head reached to the level of his hip.

"Ferdinando had not come alone. Two friends of his own age accompanied him, and each of the young men had brought a servant. Not for thirty years had Crome been desecrated by the presence of so many members of the common race of men. Sir Hercules was appalled and indignant, but the laws of hospitality had to be obeyed. He received the young gentlemen with grave politeness and sent the servants to the kitchen, with orders that they should be well cared for.

"The old family dining-table was dragged out into the light and dusted (Sir Hercules and his lady were accustomed to dine at a small table twenty inches high). Simon, the aged butler, who could only just look over the edge of the big table, was helped at supper by the three servants brought by Ferdinando and his guests.

"Sir Hercules presided, and with his usual grace supported a conversation on the pleasures of foreign travel, the beauties of art and nature to be met with abroad, the opera at Venice, the singing of the orphans in the churches of the same city, and on other topics of a similar nature. The young men were not particularly attentive to his discourses; they were occupied in watching the efforts of the butler to change the plates and replenish the glasses. They covered their laughter by violent and repeated fits of coughing or choking. Sir Hercules affected not to notice, but changed the subject of the conversation to sport. Upon this one of the young men asked whether it was true, as he had heard, that he used to hunt the rabbit with a pack of pug dogs. Sir Hercules replied that it was, and proceeded to describe the chase in some detail. The young men roared with laughter.

"When supper was over, Sir Hercules climbed down from his chair and, giving as his excuse that he must see how his lady did, bade them good-night. The sound of laughter followed him up the stairs. Filomena was not asleep; she had been lying on her bed listening to the sound of enormous laughter and the tread of strangely heavy feet on the stairs and along the corridors. Sir Hercules drew a chair to her bedside and sat there for a long time in silence, holding his wife's hand and sometimes gently squeezing it. At about ten o'clock they were startled by a violent noise. There was a breaking of glass, a stamping of feet, with an outburst of shouts and laughter. The uproar continuing for several minutes, Sir Hercules rose to his feet and, in spite of his wife's entreaties, prepared to go and see what was happening. There was no light on the staircase, and Sir Hercules groped his way down cautiously, lowering himself from stair to stair and standing for a moment on each tread before adventuring on a new step. The noise was louder here; the shouting articulated itself into recognisable words and phrases. A line of light was visible under the dining-room door. Sir Hercules tiptoed across the hall towards it. Just as he approached the door there was another terrific crash of breaking glass and jangled metal. What could they be doing? Standing on tiptoe he managed to look through the keyhole. In the middle of the ravaged table old Simon, the butler, so primed with drink that he could scarcely keep his balance, was dancing a jig. His feet crunched and tinkled among the broken glass, and his shoes were wet with spilt wine. The three young men sat round, thumping the table with their hands or with the empty wine bottles, shouting and laughing encouragement. The three servants leaning against the wall laughed too. Ferdinando suddenly threw a handful of walnuts at the dancer's head, which so dazed and surprised the little man that he staggered and fell down on his back, upsetting a decanter and several glasses. They raised him up, gave him some brandy to drink, thumped him on the back. The old man smiled and hiccoughed. 'To-morrow,' said Ferdinando, 'we'll have a concerted ballet of the whole household.' 'With father Hercules wearing his club and lion-skin,' added one of his companions, and all three roared with laughter.

"Sir Hercules would look and listen no further. He crossed the hall once more and began to climb the stairs, lifting his knees painfully high at each degree. This was the end; there was no place for him now in the world, no place for him and Ferdinando together.

"His wife was still awake; to her questioning glance he answered, 'They are making mock of old Simon. To-morrow it will be our turn.' They were silent for a time.

"At last Filomena said, 'I do not want to see to-morrow.'

" 'It is better not,' said Sir Hercules. Going into his closet he wrote in his day-book a full and particular account of all the events of the evening. While he was still engaged in this task he rang for a servant and ordered hot water and a bath to be made ready for him at eleven o'clock. When he had finished writing he went into his wife's room, and preparing a dose of opium twenty times as strong as that which she was accustomed to take when she could not sleep, he brought it to her, saying, 'Here is your sleeping-draught.'

"Filomena took the glass and lay for a little time, but did not drink immediately. The tears came into her eyes. 'Do you remember the songs we used to sing, sitting out there *sulla terrazza* in summer-time?' She began singing softly in her ghost of a cracked voice a few bars from Stradella's '*Amor, amor, non dormir piu.*' 'And you playing on the violin. It seems such a short time ago, and yet so long, long, long. *Addio, amore. A rivederti.*' She drank off the draught and, lying back on the pillow, closed her eyes. Sir Hercules kissed her hand and tiptoed away, as though he were afraid of waking her. He returned to his closet, and having recorded his wife's last words to him, he poured into his bath the water that had been brought up in accordance with his orders. The water being too hot for him to get into the bath at once, he took down from the shelf his copy of Suetonius. He wished to read how Seneca had died. He opened the book at random. 'But dwarfs,' he read, 'he held in abhorrence as being *lusus naturæ* and of evil omen.' He winced as though he had been struck. This same Augustus, he remembered, had exhibited in the amphitheatre a young man called Lucius, of good family, who was not quite two feet in height and weighed seventeen pounds, but had a stentorian voice. He turned over the pages. Tiberius, Caligula, Claudius, Nero: it was a tale of growing horror. 'Seneca his preceptor, he forced to kill himself.' And there was Petronius, who had called his friends about him at the last, bidding them talk to him, not of the consolations of philosophy, but of love and gallantry, while the life was ebbing away through his opened veins. Dipping his pen once more in the ink he wrote on the last page of his diary: 'He died a Roman death.' Then, putting the toes of one foot into the water and finding that it was not too hot, he threw off his dressing-gown and, taking a razor in his hand, sat down in the bath. With one deep cut he severed the artery in his left wrist, then lay back and composed his mind to meditation. The blood oozed out, floating through the water in dissolving wreaths and spirals. In a little while the whole bath was tinged with pink. The colour deepened; Sir Hercules felt himself mastered by an invincible drowsiness; he was sinking from vague dream to dream. Soon he was sound asleep. There was not much blood in his small body."